THE HUNTER'S GAMBIT

The Archanium Codex: Book One

NICHOLAS MCINTIRE

Published by Black Dove Press, 1504 Clover Lane, Fort Worth, TX 76107
For information about bulk purchases, either in print or eBook form please contact Black Dove Press at 817 320 2886.
Manufactured in the United States of America.

A First Edition

ISBN 13: 978-1-7338491-2-8
ISBN 10: 1-7338491-2-8
Ebook ISBN 13: 978-1-7338491-0-4
Ebook ISBN 10: 1-7338491-0-4

Map and Interior Illustrations by Erin Lameroux
Interior book design (print and ebook) Nicholas McIntire
Cover created by The Cover Collection

10 9 8 7 6 5 4 3 2 1

For my father, Michael.

Thank you for always believing in me, even when I couldn't find a way to

believe in myself.

I love you.

<u>The Archanium Codex</u>

The Hunter's Gambit

A Wicked Wind (Coming 2020)

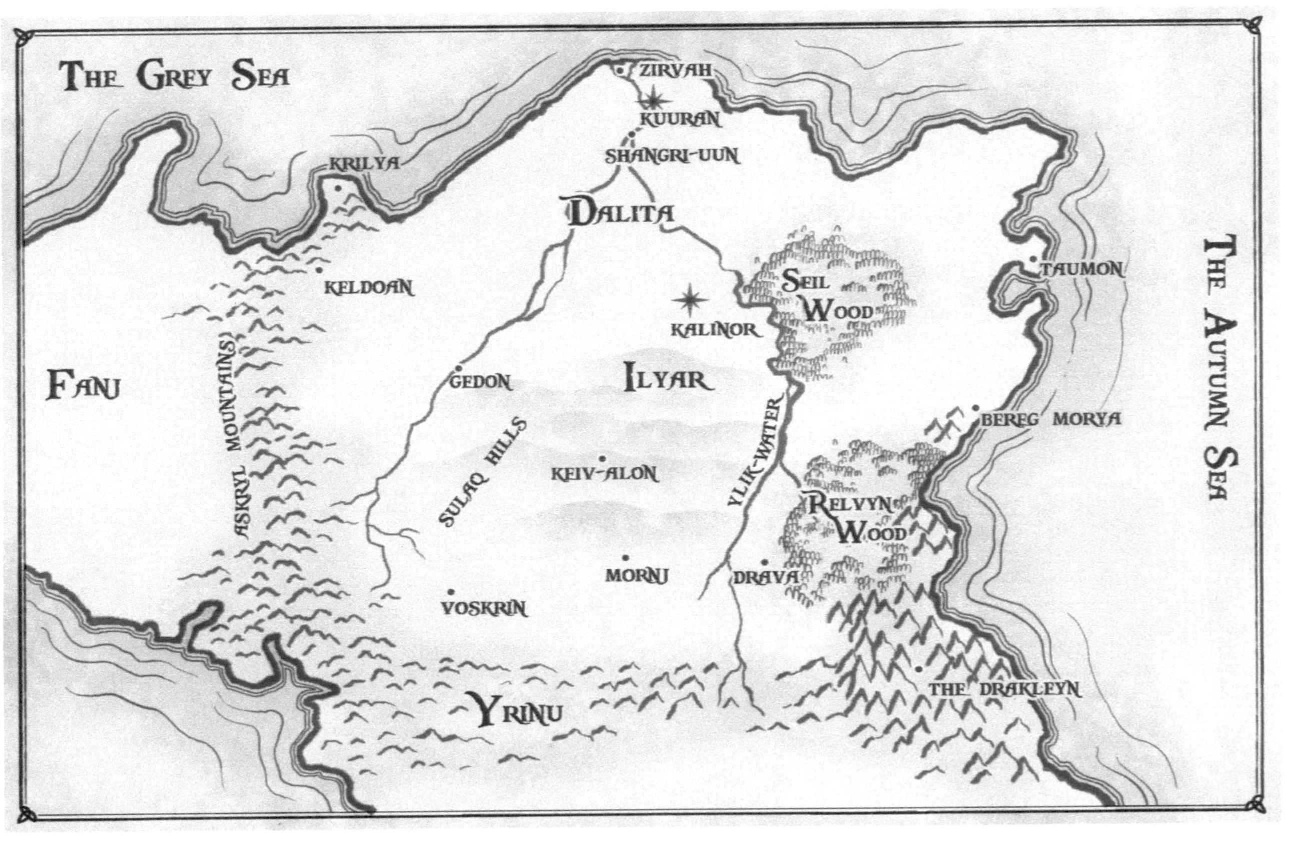

THE GREY SEA
THE AUTUMN SEA
ZIRVAH
KUURAN
SHANGRI-UUN
KRILYA
DALITA
TAUMON
KELDOAN
SEIL WOOD
KALINOR
FANU
GEDON
ILYAR
BEREG MORYA
ASKRYL MOUNTAINS
SULAQ HILLS
YLIK-WATER
KEIV-ALON
RELVYN WOOD
MORNU
DRAVA
VOSKRIN
YRINU
THE DRAKLEYN

PROLOGUE

ONE LAST SCAR

"IT'S NOT GOING to work."

"Calm yourself, you're making me nervous. I make mistakes when I'm nervous." Cassian said flatly, his fingers tracing the incessantly shifting lines of chartreuse light and black flame that hovered before him.

Richter scowled, running a hand through his flaxen hair. As though he didn't know that. As though he didn't know Cassian better than any man or woman in the Oborin Order. Or in the world, for that matter.

"More can go wrong here than right. You should have studied those meridians till you went blind."

Cassian nodded absently, his attention fixed on an axis point that kept tumbling from his fingertips, "If you're so particular about my equations, why didn't *you* shape them?"

"Because I'm not stupid." Richter snapped. Cassian heard a long slow exhalation behind him and fought a smile.

Richter was terrified, though he'd never admit it. Gods, *he* was terrified, but Richter was a very different sort of man. For Richter, anger buried any emotion that didn't lead to laughter, whiskey, or sex; and even then it wasn't always a sure bet.

"I'd just prefer to keep my mind intact, thank you." Richter grumbled after a sullen silence. "I *hate* constructs. Too many bloody variables."

Cassian let the other man wander and talk through his nerves, offering Richter his attention sparingly, allowing himself a smile when Richter spouted that cocky bravado Cassian found so endearing.

He heard Richter cease his aimless pacing, felt Richter's thick fingers press against his back, just where his heart hammered against his ribs.

"Too many variables." Richter hissed. His hiss became a growl, "As you're about to prove."

Cassian blushed, trying to force the other man from his mind and failing. "Why are you *here?*" he demanded instead.

Richter's face darkened, bravado casually abandoned. "Because I might have to kill you."

Cassian jumped, angry at himself for reacting to the statement, even though he knew it was coming. Even though it had to be said. Even though it had to be *Richter*.

"We don't know what's going to happen, Cass. But if you're wrong...."

Cassian swallowed, "I know."

The sound of Richter's sword clearing the scabbard ran ragged across Cassian's nerves.

"Well, at least you'll have the best run-through of your life." Richter purred.

Lover and executioner. With Richter, those two were suddenly hard to separate.

"It's going to work." Cassian murmured.

"When you've banished the Kholod and we can get on with our bloody lives, let me know." Richter grunted. "Now either get to it or unravel the damn thing. Much longer and it'll just implode in your face." He stepped closer and brushed his hand across Cassian's cheek, "And I'd hate to see that ruined."

Cassian ignored his Hunter and closed his eyes, allowing the construct to wrap around him.

They stood in the center of the Voralla. From this place, the Magi of old had tapped into the Apsis, where the Great Sphere of the Archanium came into direct contact with the realm of the living.

From this place, Cassian sired their salvation or destruction.

The world shifted as Cassian's vision washed with the familiar swirling morass of the Archanium.

An endless combination of color, sound, and emotion tumbled around him. Every twisting ribbon represented a singular spell, those spells making up the vast and disparate regions of the Great Sphere. Cassian sifted through them until he found a small eddy of orange and fuchsia.

It coiled around him, danger and joy inextricably intertwined.

It was haunting.

Cassian quivered as he pulled the colors into their world, sending it into the constructed magic before him. The spell ignited, pushing the air from the room with a hollow boom that lifted Cassian off his feet. He floated in a fraction of time, gasping for breath, finding nothing.

He glanced at Richter.

The Hunter raised his blade towards Cassian's heart in silent response. Ebony tendrils of the Hunter's Mantle wound around the blade's edge, licking at the air as they reached the point, flashing crimson to their root, burning sinuously up Richter's powerful arms.

Cassian floated for that impossibly long moment, staring into Richter's feral coyote eyes.

The world imploded, thrusting Cassian through a pinhole of reality and into the vast expanse of oblivion. There was no light, no sound.

But gods, there was *pain*.

Time lost meaning in the darkness, yet he felt the immediacy of his own annihilation.

A second implosion thundered through his skull.

Cassian smashed into earth. Thirsty, unyielding earth. He rolled to his side, choking on dust, gasping to fill the void in his lungs. He retched violently, blood fountaining from his mouth. The desiccated soil drank him in eagerly.

Cassian rolled onto his back, running a hand across his mouth and greedily gulping air. He slowly became aware of the Other sky, intermittently green, yellow, and black; colors mirroring his construct. His *brilliant* construct. How many times had Richter warned him of the dangers?

And now it seemed Richter was right.

He winced, knowing that in the mortal world there was a very sharp sword pointed at his heart. Richter was prepared to end his life should the construct become unstable, and with good reason. Such a spell could hand victory to the Kholod in an instant if Cassian made a single misstep. Anything short of perfection allowed for the possibility of failure, and the stakes were simply too high.

His people had been enslaved by the Kholodym Dominion for over a thousand years. Using occult magics, the Kholod had bound themselves to the Archanium, manipulating the Magi like grotesque puppets. And this at the cost of the Magi's freedom, their *humanity*.

Lives possessed limited value to their Kholod masters.

Cassian had escaped that cruelty, freed by a savage Magus with wild, golden eyes. Few had been so fortunate. Richter had no sooner freed him than enlisted him in the war, and Cassian had been all too eager to fight back.

Yet after years of warring with the Kholod, and with so little to show for it, a unique weapon seemed the only remaining path to victory. Something *created*, something unexpected. Something new that would sweep the Kholod from their world and into another.

Into *this* hell.

And then they instructed *him* to build it.

Cassian pushed himself to his feet, stumbling. He spat blood as he tried to gain some measure of his bearings. The air alone was so different in this place. Breathable, but far thinner. He tried to walk, but each step fell heavier than the last.

After a few moments to determine this Other world suitable, Cassian reached for the Archanium; to complete the construct and return to his own world as quickly as possible. To Richter and the world he wanted back, even if it had never wanted him.

The Archanium flashed brilliantly across his vision for a

heartbeat before flickering out.

Cassian whimpered, reaching out again.

He gasped at the shock of failure. Every nerve in his body howled.

We are intrigued.

"Who's there?" he called uncertainly.

Very intrigued.

And then he felt it. A presence unlike anything he'd ever encountered. A presence as twisted as the world it inhabited.

"I'm sorry if I've angered you." he shouted, growing desperate. "I came here by mistake. I was just leaving."

No.

Cassian was flat on his back, though he couldn't recall falling. A bright, coppery film of fresh blood filled his mouth, but he felt nothing. No injury, no pain.

The air took on a disquieting drone.

Cassian felt something drool down his face. He touched his cheek and felt the blood flowing from his ears and nose.

"Please!" he begged. "*Please*, just let me go. I never meant to come here, I promise!"

But We are pleased with your ingress. We are lonely. We are bored. We have been hungry. You will bring Us satisfaction.

The buzzing increased to an unbearable intensity and Cassian screamed as his eardrums burst.

So delicate. So soft. We like it.

"Stop!" he sobbed, tears and blood mingling as they dripped from his eyes. His vision was fading into a rapidly reddening haze. "Gods, stop!"

Gods? We don't let them in here. This world is Ours. But We think We like yours. We want more.

Cassian's mind leapt at their mention of his world, "Yes! More! I'll give you more. More, just make it *stop!*"

The drone deepened and Cassian felt several explosions within his skull. What was left of his vision swam as nausea flushed through him. His mouth was so thick with blood that he could hardly form words.

We like it. We hunger. We want to feed.

The words echoed in his mind even as his last thread of sanity threatened to snap, his screams reduced to a long crimson gurgle.

And suddenly he understood the nature of the voice.

It was a presence.

A Demonic Presence.

Richter kept his blade trained on Cassian as his Magus floundered in an unseen current.

The midnight shadows and yellow-green light of the construct had burrowed into Cassian's core, piercing his body as his mind traversed the vast distance between worlds. Richter focused on the man before him. A man he'd saved a lifetime ago. A man stupid enough to be brave. A man he was stupid enough to love.

The Mantle itched.

Cassian jerked, vomiting blood across the polished marble floor. Richter stepped forward a pace and halted the point of his sword a handspan from Cassian's chest, growling, resisting the urge to drop the blade and pull the other man's body from the construct. In the same moment he reached into the Archanium and wrapped a shield around Cassian.

The Mantle roiled and writhed.

His shield snapped into their world and Cassian's body jerked.

Richter's heart pounded in his ears. For all his arrogance, these experiments troubled something elemental within him. Something primal. It felt unnatural to be toying with the Archanium like this, whatever the potential gain.

Cassian's head snapped back as his body convulsed. The tip of Richter's sword hovered a breath from Cassian's heart.

And just as suddenly as the construct had swept Cassian up, the yellow-green light and swirling black evaporated. Richter's blade clattered across the floor as he caught Cassian's limp form, ignoring the puddle of congealing blood that soaked his trousers as he knelt, Cassian's head cradled in the crook of his arm.

There was no pulse.

A wave of panic crashed over him. He pressed his ear to Cassian's chest for confirmation, heard the steady flush of air into the other man's lungs. Richter's heart seized in his chest at the emptiness in

Cassian's.

He sent the Mantle into the Magus, but the black halted at his wrists, refusing him. Tears flooded Richter's vision even as he dove into the Archanium, searching.

Desperate.

Cassian's eyes snapped open and Richter froze. The Archanium washed from his vision as he stared disbelieving into the other Magus' eyes, blinking panicked tears from his own.

Yellow-green light flashed in the depths of Cassian's gaze, but it was gone an instant later. Richter pulled Cassian closer to him, cradling the smaller man's form delicately, as though he might shatter at any second.

"Are...are you *alright?*" Richter managed, fighting the unnatural feeling of having Cassian pressed against him without the familiar rhythm of his love's heart.

A rough rumble resonated through Cassian, a pitiful half-cough, half-laugh.

"I'm alive, apparently." Cassian managed.

Richter's concern deepened. Cassian's voice was still his, yet so different from the nervous young man who had invoked the construct moments before. Rather, he sounded like a man who had just been screaming for hours on end.

He pressed Cassian tightly to him for another long moment before Richter finally allowed Cassian to lean back. The smile that lit Cassian's face melted much of the doubt, the fear in Richter. There was something undeniably different about the man who had come back to him, but the gods only knew what Cassian had seen, had experienced, while in the portal of the construct.

"Alive." Richter repeated, deciding that this was not the moment to belabor the silence in Cassian's heart, or the dread in his own.

"Alive," Cassian rasped, his exhausted smile widening, "and *hungry.*"

❧

NINE YEARS LATER

"I suppose one can't fault his bravery, even if he brought this on himself."

Elise shot her husband a glare, "*Charity.* You would have him become the very monster we're fighting. And I'll remind you that his *humanity* has kept him fighting at all, derision and pronouncements of guilt aside."

Makar turned to his wife and offered a long-suffering smile, "I'm humbled by your example."

He embraced her, his silver wings wrapping around her thin frame protectively. She allowed the embrace to last only a moment, a moment she savored, before turning back to the most recent report; one amongst hundreds scattered across her desk like drifts of snow.

The Angelus sighed, "So what's the word?"

"My Magi have completed their spellforms and are standing by." she muttered as she read. "Your scouts have confirmed his position within three leagues, and Richter is guarding the Apsis, waiting to spring the trap."

Makar grimaced, "You think him heroic, don't you? Your feral pup and his abominations."

"He's done *everything* asked of him and more."

"And your affection for him will only get you killed." Makar countered brusquely. "He's *bait*, Elise. That's the only value he has now. He's a lamb brought to the killing floor. His survival is of little importance. Ours is essential."

Elise stepped away from her husband, stamping out the emotions warring within her. She loved Makar dearly. When other angels had turned away her requests for aid, protecting a fragile truce with the Kholodym Dominion rather than follow their One-God's edicts to aid those in suffering and slavery, Makar had led his people by his own example.

Angelic hypocrisy was hardly new to her, yet she required their strength, and their magic, if anyone were to have a chance at survival. He had come to her aid, and in time became instrumental in her people's greatest victories. She'd placed hard-won faith in him, and in turn he'd placed his, and his Host's, faith in her. In her intelligence and her abilities.

Gods, but she had never needed that faith more than now.

The winter plagues had made their way through the mortals swiftly enough, decimating their numbers in a handful of weeks. Her Magi were faring only marginally better.

The world was decaying before their very eyes, their food rotting, their homes consumed in inexplicable fires or drowned in torrents of scalding floodwater, locusts swarming through any crops that didn't burn or boil.

The locusts had spread the plague, and with the plague came the madness. The mad sought the flame and flood, and their burned husks and bloated corpses only hatched more locusts. So much destruction in less than a year, ever since he, since *it*, had returned from the far North.

She had received no word from her people in the South for months, and while Elise worried for them, she had neither the time nor the resources to spare. Gods, she hardly had a *thought* to spare any longer. Kholod overlords moving in from the South and West, and the Demon wrecking havoc from whatever warren he'd sought out.

Yet, even with the world crashing around her, even with the pestilence and famine, the angels would have been content to remain secluded in their grand Basilica, its great golden doors sealed to the crushing mobs of mortals begging for the mercy and sanctuary promised to them by their faith.

Except for the grace of their Angelus.

As much as Elise hated to admit it, the Demon's time tormenting the angels had allowed her own people precious time to breathe, time to regroup and push the Kholod west. Time to finish the Dominion War for good. Or so they'd hoped. Even now scouts brought her word that Askryl's Wall had been breached.

They were coming. The Kholod were coming.

If her trap was sprung prematurely, if the Demon escaped this time, she and everyone she held dear would be crushed between Demon and Dominion. Spread too thin to fend off one, much less prevail against two.

Unless Richter played his part perfectly. Unless Makar was able to perform his own part in her scheme and spring the trap at the right moment. Too soon and Cassian might escape. Too late, and not only would Richter be forfeit, but the very world itself.

No, they *all* had to be perfect.

The *Seraphima* had to be perfect.

Makar caught her mood, silvery wings drooping behind him, "I'm sorry, darling." The words drifted out in a broken whisper, "I know you fear for him." Elise allowed him to embrace her once more, but refused to betray the pain stabbing through her heart.

His mouth hovered an inch from her ear, "Richter has already lost what he loved most. He has no illusions now." His voice trembled, "But in this last moment, I want only to hold you and pretend my wings are bright armor and not weak feathered flesh."

Elise nodded against his shoulder, words beyond her command.

A knock sounded at the door and he lifted her mouth to meet his for the most finite of moments before gently breaking away.

"And now, darling Elise," Makar said, voice strong once more, his azure eyes clear as a summer sky, "see to Richter."

⁘

"Are you absolutely sure you're up to this?"

Richter sat in a tight crouch, staring blankly ahead, his golden eyes focusing on nothing and everything at once.

This was the room.

A white room filled with black memories. Once again he found himself in the center of the Voralla, the Apsis so close he could feel the tapestry of the Archanium brush against the rough golden hairs of his beard.

The Magus standing above him tapped her foot impatiently. Richter ignored her. He might address her pointless question when he was ready, but he would not be rushed into something this important. Not now, not after all they'd suffered. All *he'd* suffered. After everything Cassian had done to his own people.

To Richter.

Elise's presence above him grew increasingly oppressive and in deliberate defiance he recalled the memories he'd failed to bury one last time. Watching Cassian decay had been agonizing, standing helpless as the man he loved slowly crumbled before him. And Richter had seen it from its genesis.

He had to acknowledge *that* much to himself now, if never to another soul.

But Richter always had a solution. Always a salve or spell, anything to push back the poison. They'd all paid dearly for his hubris.

It had been years before the Oborin Order began to question him; years for Cassian's behavior to slowly, insidiously become ever more erratic, for his twisting judgement to lead them to stunning victories, but only ever at greater cost. And yet, ever the stalwart soldier, the clever Hunter, Richter had explained away every misdirection, every misdeed.

Each new perversion.

Until now.

Now, at long last, bereft of tricks or tales to spin, he was here, at the very place he and Cassian first let in the bane. *Here*, under the solemn shadow of countless lives lost, the world they had both fought to create rotting at his feet. Like Cassian, cracking and flaking away into tatters until all that remained was cancerous corruption gnawing at the scraps. And an incessant buzz in his ears.

Cassian had let the Demonic Presence into this world, into his soul. And yet, as Richter had admitted far too late, it had twisted their love to pierce his own heart just as keenly.

He had offered to bear the full weight of responsibility. To pay for his offenses with the only thing of worth he still possessed. To atone for what he and Cassian had done. Their intentions had been pure, but that mattered little in the aftermath.

Elise knelt next to him and laid her arm gently across his shoulders. The Mantle lifted from his bare skin, its talons caressing her delicate wrist. "Richter, darling," she said in that voice that always recalled his mother, for good or ill, "we *have* to begin. Your children are growing restless, and he could Fade at any moment. We can't lose him, Richter."

He came to his feet in a liquid motion, offering a hand to the woman who now knelt before him. She hesitantly accepted it, her gray eyes studying him, searching his face. He could smell her uncertainty, her fear. He wondered if she saw pity reflected in his eyes.

Richter turned to the Apsis, to the sprawling mass of creatures that watched him patiently. Many stood stiff and stoic, though a fair number twitched in the torment of displacement, that caustic conflict that pitted their innate desire for the shade of the Seil Wood against their deep and determined obedience.

Obedience to Richter. Obedience to the Hunter.

The sight of them threatened to tug a sad smile from his stony facade. His children, as she had called them. He doubted the Wood would disagree with such an assessment.

Any trace of happiness withered. The spirits and beasts of his Wood were here for *him*. And in return, he was consigning them to the fate he alone had earned.

But there was no other way.

Cassian was close enough for the plan to work. For the snare to be set with the most appropriate bait. As much as he pushed the idea from his head, it still hurt that Richter's presence alone wasn't enough to draw Cassian out into the open. But his Cassian was gone. He had to be.

"He won't leave." Richter said with more confidence than he felt, "He'll be too intrigued by the crumbs I laid out. He'll be hungry for something more substantial."

Elise turned from her own evaluation of his devoted army and managed an encouraging smile. Impossibly, Richter thought she was actually attempting sincerity. "It will work, Richter. We've worked out every parameter, every axis, every bloody *Song*."

Richter recalled hearing a similar sentiment years, a lifetime, ago. A brand burned against his heart with each flash of memory.

He took a deep breath, reaching for a barrier, a buffer against the pressing need of his reality and the ramifications it would have for him; for his world.

For whatever was left of Cassian.

Richter placed a hand firmly on her shoulder and gave a gentle squeeze. "I'm ready, Elise." It was a lie, but perhaps it comforted her. "Just make sure your flying rats are prepared for what's coming."

She pursed her lips, "Makar is waiting for my signal. Once Cassian has entered the chamber, it will be over." She rested her fingers over his own, "And your debt will have been paid."

Richter grunted, dropping his hand as he turned back to his little demons. "We both know the truth of that." He reached into the Archanium, beyond any region he'd accessed in the past, into a region of pure magical creativity. Into the last realm Cassian had touched before they'd let the bane in.

Feeling him embrace the Archanium, Elise retreated from the room, shutting the heavy iron-bound oak door behind her. He allowed himself a sardonic smile. Doors would protect no one, not from what was coming. *Nothing* would protect them, whatever Elise and her angels claimed.

Still, this had to happen. This moment, this final meeting. It was his debt, and one he embraced. A debt he would atone for.

That had been enough to satisfy the Order and the angels both. And yet atonement was ultimately a minor consideration in the tumble of thoughts and emotions that stormed through him.

No, if this was to be their final meeting, he would look into Cassian's eyes one last time. He would verify with every remaining shred of his humanity that Cassian was wholly gone from this world or any other.

Thus one more volley, one last charge into the van; at least one last chance to say good-bye.

The spellform snapped into existence and Richter opened himself to the Apsis, to the strength it afforded him.

The watchfire had been lit.

If they wanted the Demon to sniff him out, he would draw a blood meridian across the Great Sphere that could not be ignored.

Plunging ever deeper into the Archanium, Richter reached out and wrapped the key elements of his spellform around his children.

The spell set its hooks into each of them, into the very demonic nature of each being. So different from the demon Cassian had unleashed, but just similar enough to serve Richter's need.

Across his back, the Mantle writhed as it was drawn towards the net he cast, but Richter held it back, keeping it bound tight to himself with promises of greater feasts to come.

He completed the final axis connections, binding his demons inescapably to the spellform and shushing the Mantle across his shoulders back into its endless black. He hadn't tendered empty promises of the feasting to come, but neither had he provided the buck tied for slaughter.

The spellform warped, taking on the twilight colors of the Aftershadow, deep and almost imperceptible shades of gray, green, and aubergine.

Richter pulled in a hasty breath before reaching across the Great Sphere and summoning a swirl from a region that was all too elementary, practically reaching to a far-distant pole for this single spell. It was a spell they taught children just reaching for the Sphere, and it was the spell that would make his trap irresistible to the Demon.

The simple thread warped and whorled around his construct, infusing the shadow-colors with an otherworldly vitality, the shadows gaining new depth and sinking into a pitch black that rivaled the Mantle's hypnotizing, inky darkness.

From the roiling gloom erupted piercing sheets of burning green and yellow. A deep vibration built in the center of his chest as he directed a child's base illusion spell around the core of his construct, altering its scent, its ripples across the surface of the Great Sphere.

The Demon was powerful and clever, though lacking any of Cassian's artful subtlety. It would be hunting for something dramatic, something to rival its ability, its connection to this world through Cassian's corpse. But that connection could be contained, perhaps even severed. Not by any magic Richter could summon, and certainly not with the combined essence of his demonic children of the Wood, but rather by summoning something that didn't even properly exist.

At least not yet.

The Voralla shuddered and convulsed. Richter readied himself, knowing that there was no way to truly prepare for what he was about to face. He poured yet more of himself into the construct and felt its binding fibers split and weather under the vast energy he was attempting to contain.

It was a fool's errand.

Any Magus would have known better, but Richter already had a reputation for being foolhardy.

A shadow began to take shape across the room, the surrounding air shimmering and distorting. Richter poured everything into the blazing, roiling whorl of light before him. He was so *close*. Richter could *smell* him, the stink of rotten flesh, and worse by far, the unmistakable putrescence of the Demonic Presence forcing itself into his world.

The shape refined into the physical representation of the Demon in Richter's world. Into what had once been a man. Into Cassian.

Richter.

The voice shook the Voralla.

Not Cassian's soft treble, but the harsh buzz of the Presence. Every step Cassian took vibrated painfully in Richter's chest. He held onto the Archanium, wrapping the final threads around his construct.

We want it, Richter. Give in to Us, Richter.

The Demon reached him and thrust its hand into the core of Richter's construct, the full force of its power pouring corruption into the magic Richter had summoned, its claws grasping for Richter.

Just before the Demon had him, Richter cut his connection to the Apsis, rolling to the side as the resulting release of so much unspent energy exploded, catching Cassian in its center.

Richter was on his feet a moment later, rushing the stunned form of the Demon. He passed the remains of his construct, a small bubble of shadow, binding his children and shielding them from what was about to happen.

Cassian was already rising from the floor, but it no longer mattered. Richter was close enough. He *would* be satisfied.

The Demon regained his feet the moment Richter's hand reached him. The Mantle exploded from his wrist, diving into the Demon and pulling, *drinking* life. Humanity.

Richter screamed.

The Mantle whipped away, bands of golden light rippling across the black, slithering into Richter's flesh and searing every nerve in his body. He dropped to his knees, the Mantle writhing around him and flailing without focus as it retreated up his nerveless fingers.

And then Cassian was standing over him, staring down with those same, soft brown eyes. "Richter."

It was Cassian's voice. Richter felt the tears well up even as he fought them back. He knew it was an illusion. He had his answer. But the lie still carried comfort and pain in equal portion.

"We *want* it, Richter."

Richter felt something tear inside him. He felt Cassian's hand brush his shoulder, and with that touch came indescribable pain. He knew his life was over, but he never broke from Cassian's brown-eyed gaze.

His muscles gave out under the constant torment and he collapsed to his side, the burning, *burrowing* pain only intensifying as the edges of his vision began to cloud with a sickly, sulfurous fog.

He heard the door burst apart. He heard screams, even felt some muster the Archanium before their howls terminated sharply. He lay in a world devoid of noise, excepting the Demon's singular sound. Except for that inescapable *droning*.

The world jolted and Richter realized he was hearing a new scream. One he had not heard in so very long. Not since the day he'd pulled a frightened youth from the slave pens on a fool's errand.

Pristine blue-white light battled the chartreuse miasma for command of his vision. Somehow, the intense cold of the light burned through him keener than Cassian's touch.

He felt something heavy crash to the ground only inches from his face and something soft come to rest against his cheek. He blinked, even as the Demon's fires roared to a new intensity. It was suddenly important that he know what had fallen against him.

His vision, what wasn't lost to the yellow-green fog of the Presence, came into rough focus.

Cassian lay only a handspan away, his eyes fixed on Richter. The same soft brown despite the desiccated flesh of his face. His hand brokenly extended, fingers long-since rotten gently grasping at Richter's cheek.

The light of the Seraphima built around them, the air regaining the same searing cold, a counter to the Demon's fire that threatened to overtake him at any moment. Cold that burned deep enough to remind him that he was still alive, if only for just a moment longer.

"Richter." Cassian's voice rattled as a piercing wail filled the air, nearly banishing the name from Cassian's lips.

A tear finally slipped free, burning its way down Richter's face. He could smell his flesh sear as it dragged across his cheek before finally dripping from the edge of his jaw. One last scar; one he would never begrudge.

His heart seized in his chest, a staggered beat, but Richter never broke from Cassian's gaze. Demon fire be damned, this would be the last thing he saw, that voice whispering his name the last thing he heard.

The wail suddenly shifted into song. A beautiful, aching song of healing. Peace. Even in death.

Cassian's fingers brushed his bearded cheek one last time. Those beautiful brown eyes blinked. Cassian fought to open his mouth as the light became blinding, as the yellow-green fog blighted Cassian from his sight forever.

Just before fog and fire consumed him entirely, he heard Cassian's final whisper.

"We want to *feed*."

CHAPTER 1

VISIONS AND VOICES

"GRANNY JORNA?"

"Is that my Bael?"

The crone giggled like a girl of fifteen summers. Bael found it charming. Magical. A haven from the hell of his own life.

"You sent for me?" Bael asked, carefully closing the tent flap to guard her near-blind eyes from the sunlight. He reached to the roof and untied the hide, venting the heavy pinion smoke.

Jorna had sat in her hide tent as long as Bael could recall, always shrouded in her smoke; always knowing exactly where he was, or where he *ought* to be. She had never been endeared to his siblings, but Bael was different. Bael was her entire world.

And she was his ray of sunlight, despite the gloom that surrounded her.

"Know what I just saw?" she asked, staring into empty space as she adjusted the coals, "Oh, it was the most wonderful thing, dearie! *You! I saw you!*"

Bael hid a smile at her over-exaggeration. She always spoke to him as though he were the most important person in the room. It made him feel special.

Magical.

But he wasn't special, nor particularly magical. Not like his siblings. Nothing like Azarael or Darielle, though to Bael that was a blessing.

His sister had her own sort of madness, and no one dared go near her unless they wished to share in it. She was beautiful, there was no doubt. But violent and volcanic with molten copper hair and a penchant for telling the darkest truths about one's own soul. And she was always right.

He hadn't seen his sister in a year, and for that he was profoundly grateful. When Darielle deigned to appear again, he would do anything to stay out of her way. It was usually safe enough by the toad pond; even safer in the Seil Wood.

But not in Granny Jorna's tent. *Never* in her tent. His haven was the one place Darielle was sure to visit.

Darielle did not adore Jorna, but they had a powerful relationship. The two women shared a variety of talents, and thus from a young age Darielle had frequented Jorna's tent nearly as often as Bael.

"And what did I do in this vision?" he asked, pushing the specter of his sister away. "Something heroic, I hope?"

Jorna offered a toothless grin, "Tut-tut, dearie. I can't spoil the secret. You know better than that." She gazed sightlessly around the room, then leaned in close, "But it will change everything!"

Bael sat back on his heels, maintaining a smile he knew she couldn't see, feeling the familiar clutch at his heart.

Prophecy wove every living being into its weft and weave, and when the vision was of significant importance, the key players were kept in the dark to avoid corruption. Corruption could render the prophecy invalid, and an unscrupulous prophet could wreck havoc of untold magnitude.

While his grandmother's vision might contain untold good for him, he knew that couldn't be the case.

Good things simply didn't happen to him.

"Oh, what's that?" Jorna crowed suddenly, cupping a wrinkled hand to her ear.

"I don't hear anything, Granny." Bael sighed, glancing over his shoulder.

"Oh, Bael," Jorna whispered, leaning close again, "I do believe your sister has just arrived."

As though summoned.

Bael shuddered.

Two unspeakably bad things in one day.

He politely excused himself from the tent before Darielle could arrive to reveal a third.

It was better to be the toad boy, to hop about and fetch this and that while the learned men considered the mysteries of the Dark God. Anything to avoid drawing attention to himself.

Bael's usual defense was hiding from it all; from Darielle and her imperious appearances; from his father and his faith; from his brother Azarael and his obsession with twisting the living form. But he could always seek out his mother.

He found her in the tent of his Lord Father and Master Rafael. She was besieged by another one of her crippling headaches, but Bael climbed onto the narrow cot with her.

"Don't worry, Mama." he whispered. He needed her, her guidance and her grace, and when her headaches took over he had no one else to defend him from his father's rages.

Bael placed his hand on his mother's face and opened himself to his faith. He prayed as hard as he dared, beseeching the Dark God to grant him rare but sometimes-permissible mercy. His mother cried out all the more and began sobbing.

"Sorry! Sorry, Mama!" Bael whimpered. "I was trying to heal! I swear on the Book of Volos!"

His mother gave an uncharacteristic chuckle, though he could hear her pain through it all, "Bael, dear, you know I love your father, but you needn't prattle on with that dreck while he isn't here."

Bael opened his mouth, shocked. The pain made her mad at times, but he'd never heard such blasphemy from her lips. Mother was always at devotional to the Dark God alongside Father and himself. With Azarael and Darielle both having abandoned the

Commune in the past year, he was left alone to perform the sacraments and prove his devotion to his father's god.

Azarael had been lucky to escape with his life, but his abomination hadn't lived through the night. Bael hadn't seen his brother since. Darielle had been far more subtle in her escape, vanishing into thin air during devotional a month later.

Bael's mother had been in a constant state of concern ever since. Darielle and Marra had never seen eye-to-eye, and Darielle's arrival today spelled greater trouble to come. She would be seeking counsel with Jorna; only then come to rub salt in her mother's emotional wounds.

His sister was, after all, a proper prophet. An impossible prophet, in his mind. Such people were supposed to be blind old crones with a sight of the futures to come. Prophets were supposed to be like Jorna.

Yet Darielle's beauty didn't make her any less a prophet, or any less dangerous. Bael recalled eavesdropping on her when Jorna predicted a cataclysmic war that would eradicate the Cult of Volos. The blow delivered by an angry and ancient god possessed by demons. He had been less than four summers at the time and the thought gave him night terrors still. At a mere five summers, Darielle had just seemed bored.

She never seemed interested in what should happen, occupied instead by events she felt she ought to have a hand in. She obviously wanted to control certain matters, while others couldn't possibly interest her.

His sister was largely a mystery to him. Sometimes sweeter than even Jorna, other times inexplicably cruel, often in the same conversation. And if someone else meddled with her prophecies, she became violent.

Deadly.

So what was she doing here *now*?

Bael weighed his options, but given what Jorna had told him that morning, he knew he couldn't risk letting Darielle speak with her, especially since her vision was about him. Jorna couldn't tell him what the prophecy contained, but Darielle was another matter entirely.

His mother was snoring softly as he stepped out of her tent. He tried not to make his urgency too obvious to others in the Commune, and by the time he reached Jorna's tent, the front flap was already knotted tight. He bit back a curse, offering an immediate plea for forgiveness instead.

He circled back through the village to an old gable that rested on Jorna's tent. He used his usual grips and climbed the gable, allowing the nearby mulberry tree to support his weight over the hide vent. He knew it was a risk to spy on the two women, but the more he thought about it, the greater his determination grew.

Darielle wasn't here to really confer with Granny Jorna and have a chat with their mother. She was after something far larger. She always was. And he couldn't believe there was a coincidence between Jorna having a vision about him and Darielle's sudden return.

No one had visions about toad boy. *Ever.*

"Did you see it?" Darielle asked calmly, handing Jorna a cup of tea. Bael could barely make out her thin, fragile shape through the smoky haze.

"Child," Granny Jorna prattled, "I see a great many things—"

Crack. Granny Jorna crumpled to the floor with a shriek. Bael could just see the blood pouring from her right leg.

Darielle rose smoothly and sniffed her tea cup. "Mint? Are we peasants now? How sad." The cup shattered in the embers of the fire.

Darielle stepped towards the old, blind woman and gripped her hair with such force that Bael gasped in shock. He immediately winced at his mistake. He was doomed.

She glanced up, her eyes piercing into his own. She crooked a finger and he could feel himself falling into the tent, his body halting just above the hissing flames.

Whenever she ushered him forth it was always massively uncomfortable, but unerringly effective.

"Hello, Toady. So nice of you to drop by." Darielle cooed, pulling his face close to her own. His clothes were beginning to smoke, but the flames refused to set him alight.

The Dark God be praised, did his sister command the very fire itself? Such a revelation would hardly have shocked him just then, as his tattered jerkin began to singe and spark.

"What are you doing here?" Bael screamed back. "Why'd you hurt Granny?"

Darielle shoved her finger against his chest. He could feel his heart beat, feel the blood pumping up his neck and through his temples. The constant *lub-dub* of his pulse.

For the first time in his life, Bael conjured the Archanium against his sister. He willed the darkest things he could imagine into being.

And then he felt his prayer somehow *twist*. He could feel the energy he'd summoned pouring into Darielle's spell, enhancing her power, and that power flowing back into him ten-fold.

He flung himself at her, abandoning magic for the fury of his fists. His bastard father always said he was the progeny of some various royal bloodlines, that he might prove useful someday. It was a warning, to stay out of trouble. To stay alive.

Bael no longer cared. He hated how she effortlessly made all of his horrors real. Just like Father. He *had* to stop her.

It took him several seconds to realize that he was still frozen in the same position, still hovering before his sister, her finger now pressed deeply into his chest, his heart hammering painfully in his ears, his jerkin now flaming around his thin, pasty torso, yet failing to burn his flesh.

"So *violent*." she chortled. It was gratingly similar to the sound Granny had made earlier. Now the old woman was sobbing instead.

"I like that." Darielle breathed, drawing her mouth next to his ear and speaking in a whisper so soft he could hardly perceive it himself. "It shows *potential*."

Bael tried to snarl, but his mouth wouldn't move.

Darielle stepped back and considered Bael the way a spider might contemplate a fly. She tapped her chin thoughtfully, "I think you might *just* be ready. But you're far too ignorant."

"I'm not stupid." Bael spat, surprised by how hoarse he'd become. The heat of the fire was suffocating. His jerkin had long since burned to cinders, as had his breeches. He hung above the flame naked, white and sickly, like the toad he was. And yet his flesh refused to burn.

Darielle turned away, leaving him suspended, "I didn't say 'stupid', Toady. I said 'ignorant'. You haven't seen what I have."

She gave a contemptuous glance to her sobbing grandmother

before setting her emerald eyes back on him, "Let's change that, shall we?"

As her finger bored into his temple and images exploded across his vision, he could hear Granny pleading, begging Darielle to stop, to release him.

He was only dimly aware of the begging when it ended abruptly. And then her hell consumed him.

THE SOUTHERN PLAIN

Swing. Aleksei ignored the protest from his muscles. *Cut.* He lost himself in the rhythm. *Swing.* His body twisted to the right. *Cut.* He pulled the blade back, dropping a thousand defiant stalks.

Aleksei.

He nearly dropped his scythe. A moment later, Aleksei Drago stood straight and planted the butt of the snath in the red soil. He looked up and caught sight of his father working only ten paces away.

"Did you say something, Da?"

Henry Drago stopped his cutting and frowned, "Can't say I did. You aren't getting too hot, are you, Son?"

Aleksei shook his head, returning to his work rather than attempt to explain. It was unlikely he could have explained it at any rate.

"Just the wind playing tricks." he muttered as he stepped forward and dropped another wave of wheat to the side.

They had been cutting the south field for the better part of the day. Aleksei was pleased with his progress, but he couldn't help wish he was at Redman's Pub, rather than cutting wheat in the blazing Harvest sun.

The sun bit deeper into the horizon, and Aleksei felt the sweat dribbling down his back begin to cool. He paused to wipe the wet and grit from his face. After hours in the field, the dust had a habit of turning sweat to mud.

"Ten more paces and we'll quit for the day." Henry called.

Aleksei gave a gruff nod, hefting his scythe and falling back into the rhythmic swing of Harvest. His hands burned from grasping the rough wood of the snath and grip for so many hours. He could already feel the blisters bubbling up under his roughly callused palms.

Still, when Aleksei turned to regard his progress, he felt the familiar surge of pride that came with a solid day's work at its end. The fruits of his labor lay behind him in neat rows, waiting to be bundled and stored. Once they were sorted and tied, he could eat and collapse into bed for a decent rest.

Of course, the next day would bring more of the same. There were six more acres of wheat to cut, and then the west field besides before he could hang up his scythe for the season.

As he cut, Aleksei stared tomorrow cautiously in the face. The second day of cutting was always worse than the first, the third worse than the second. Aleksei imagined his hands would be bleeding by the end of the third day, calluses or no.

As Aleksei emerged from his thoughts, he realized that he was standing at the field's edge, his scythe hanging impotently from his hand. He shook himself out of his musings and followed his father back toward the barn. The faster he got the grain bundled, the faster he could wash up in the pond and get something to eat. And then sweet, merciful sleep.

He might get to bed before the moon rose, but dawn would still break too early.

Aleksei.

He jumped, turning quickly to identify the source of the voice.

The south field was empty. His father was already in the barn. Aleksei spared a few more moments to search the farmstead, then jogged back to the barn. It was childish to be frightened of shades and spirits, but Aleksei decided it was better not to take any chances.

He found his father cleaning his scythe. Aleksei grabbed an oiled rag and followed suit, all the while pretending he'd walked in casually from the field. He'd consistently earned his reputation as a competent and trustworthy son. He wasn't about to let a simple flight of fancy put that in jeopardy.

Aleksei hung his scythe against the barn wall and snatched up a ball of twine. He set back for the field, drawing his knife and preparing for the monotonous work of bundling.

I have need of you, Aleksei.

He dropped his knife.

With a whispered curse, Aleksei bent to fetch the blade. When he straightened he found his father regarding him curiously.

"Are you *sure* you're alright, Son?"

Aleksei nodded forcefully, "Sure thing, Da. Why?"

Henry shrugged, "I don't know. You just seem a little out of sorts, that's all." He considered a moment longer before adding, "Why don't you get cleaned up? We can clear the rest of this tomorrow."

"Yes, sir." Aleksei said readily, sheathing his knife and grabbing a length of gray toweling off the barn door. He was at once relieved and surprised by his father's easy dismissal. He couldn't remember the last time either of them had called an early night, much less his father volunteering the idea.

As he walked towards the small pond that punctured the otherwise flat land behind the farmhouse, Aleksei searched through the events of that afternoon in his head. Had he been acting all that strangely? Was it that obvious he was unsettled?

Perhaps that's it. he thought to himself. Perhaps he was just tired. A little food and some sleep would set him right, and then he could tackle the next day's work with the fearsome abandon he'd mustered during the long summer.

Aleksei stripped out of his breeches and sank into the cool, forgiving water of the pond, resolving to put the strangeness from his mind. The deeper he sank, the more confident he became in the restorative power of rest. His hands might even heal enough during the night that they wouldn't start bleeding till next week.

"Keep dreaming." he grunted to himself, resting his back against the warm rocks bordering the pond.

This far into Harvest, the water was still cool enough to provide hot, tired muscles a welcome respite from the brutal ravages of the sun.

Aleksei relished the comfort of the water as long as he dared, but mere moments later he struggled out into the tepid air and dried off. It wouldn't do to dawdle when he was supposed to be getting to bed.

Dinner amounted to two apples and a heel of hard bread. Aleksei knew he should eat more than that, but somehow he hadn't worked up much of an appetite.

And then he was mounting the stairs and falling into his narrow bed. Despite the thin comfort afforded by his threadbare straw mattress, his exhaustion was more than sufficient to drag him down into sleep before he'd even registered the pillow beneath his face.

A heartbeat later Aleksei opened his eyes, and found himself surrounded in a faint golden fog. There was no movement in the air, no scent, nothing.

North, Aleksei.

He started at the sudden intrusion of a man's voice.

"What?"

I have need of you.

"Who are you?" Aleksei demanded.

North, Aleksei. North.

As he dissolved back into oblivious slumber, Aleksei caught the unshakable image of fierce, seeking emerald eyes.

Chapter 2

Wheat and Chaff

"Boy."

Bael struggled to open his eyes, but it was just too hard.

"Boy!"

His father's unmistakable rumble penetrated his fog of sleep, but he still couldn't rise from the miasma of light and sound. Darielle's visions haunted his every thought, every image a fiery brand searing his mind over and over again.

"*Toad!*"

The word cut into his oblivion, igniting rage at the insult in its wake, whipping up a conflagration so intense even his sister's wicked trick could scarcely survive.

Bael opened his eyes to find his Lord Father Rafael glaring down at him with seething eyes, so black that he couldn't differentiate the iris from the pupil without concentrating. Bael just stared back. He'd always avoided his father's gaze, but now he just stared back, studying the man. He, like his sister, had been so very fortunate to inherit the intense emerald eyes of their mother.

At least that was one *thing you couldn't control about me.* Bael thought bitterly as he stared into those mad, black eyes.

Rafael took a step back, and Bael could see the beginnings of discomfort in his face. "*Woman!*" he barked, turning away from Bael and marching away. "He's alive and awake. Tend to him. My flock and my God await."

His father left the tent the same way he left every space, in a flurry of rage and black sackcloth. Bael found himself pitying the man for the first time in his life. Rafael was a servant of the Dark God, but he seemed to have found so little joy in his devotion.

The thought brought Bael up short.

Where had it come from? Had anyone heard it? Would he be whipped for his blasphemy? Were they listening to his thoughts? *Could* they really listen? Could his Lord Father? *Was* he listening? Would Bael be banished? Might it have been better if Darielle had killed him as she had surely killed Granny?

But, then again, wasn't he *right?*

Marra drifted into view with a damp cloth and sat beside him, gently wiping his forehead. Bael wasn't sure what purpose the action served, but he found comfort in the sentiment, if not the cool river water running down his face.

Where had that come from? Such thoughts were....

Bael closed his eyes tight, yet it was still too bright. The thoughts kept pouring into his mind, the aberrant, dirty thoughts. Selfish thoughts. Thoughts he'd never have dared to conjure, much less admit to before his sister's arrival the day before. Or days. He really wasn't sure how long he'd been unconscious.

Bael realized that his mother had stopped wiping his forehead and he forced his eyes open.

"Darling, am I hurting you?" she asked, her voiced barely a whisper.

He managed a crooked smile, "I'm sorry, Mama. No, it was nice. Thank you."

Marra gave a sigh and her entire body relaxed. "That's good." she managed.

While she resumed wiping his forehead, Bael studied her face. Her beautiful, sad face. Her cheekbones were high and well-positioned. Her nose petite and pretty without being too small. Her eyes the same shocking green of his own. Of her entire family, or so he'd been told. Green or blue, it seemed. Like the river, Jorna had told him as a boy. Granny Jorna with her milky white eyes that had once been as black as his father's. And as common.

Not his mother's; not his. And never royal.

"Is Granny..." he began, feeling a sudden sob well up in his chest.

Marra shook her head, "She'll live. The healers are, of course, not what they were in the city, but they believe the worst of her injuries can be contained until her body responds. Of course, given her age it's difficult to say. I've been praying with her. Your Lord Father has been occupied with...other matters of late, so I've been tending to her."

"How long was I asleep?" Bael asked softly, placing a hand over hers. He could see the pain through the clarity of her eyes, as though she were suffering just by being awake.

"Days, dear. Many days. Perhaps a week? I've lost count, tending you and your granny. The womenfolk have had their hands full since your sister's visit."

Visit. Marra always made everything sound so pleasant. But then, of course, she'd been raised that way. She was a queen in her own right, though that had been long ago. And she had given it up to be with her true love, his Lord Father.

What a wretched mistake. Bael thought.

That thought. Where had it come from? Had anyone heard it? Was his Lord Father still listening? Had he been listening from the beginning? Whether or not anyone was scrying his thoughts, did that make him any less *right*?

Bael felt a growing irritation at his own cowardice. He forced himself to relax, but kept his eyes open this time to spare his mother her worry. If any of his Lord Father's scryers *had* been listening to him, they would already have been in to arrest him, to stake him to the ground outside until his fate could be determined.

Heretics were not permitted in the Commune, and the scryers

enforced piety with deadly dedication.

Bael himself had praised their efforts on the times he had been caught with impure thoughts about his own lot in life. He had praised them all the more when they'd whipped him time and time again in front of the others. Those scars never faded, but rather reflected his faith all the more. He had endured, the others be damned.

The others. The others who had laughed. The others who called him 'Toad'. Who'd kicked him in the mud when he was a boy, and now whenever he didn't hop and fetch fast enough for their liking.

But that time is limited. Before long, their knees will bend. And then they will tremble.

Those thoughts...Bael's irritation blossomed into anger. The Dark God be praised, but Bael wondered if Darielle's true intent had been to drive him unquestionably mad. If so, she had apparently succeeded.

And if the scryers hadn't picked up on his unintentional blasphemy yet, it would only be a matter of time. Especially if these thoughts kept returning to him unbidden. Especially if he kept *agreeing.*

Let them come. Bael thought defiantly.

His encounter with Darielle had been more enlightening than she might have known. Yes, she'd twisted his spell back at him, but Bael had never held that much of the Archanium before. Nowhere *near* that much power. He found the possibilities such power could afford him deeply exciting.

"I need to see Granny." he said finally, assured that he'd collected sufficient control of his thoughts and feelings. He knew who he was; he knew what he believed. He *believed* what he believed.

Didn't he?

His mother's expression fell, "Darling, I'm not sure she's even awake. She was so badly used by your sister. After you were knocked down, I hear things carried on for some time."

Bael pushed himself up on the bed. He felt as strong and capable as ever, if a little disoriented. "No." he said, keeping his voice calm for the sake of his mother's fragile nerves. "No, Mama, I need to see her now. I need to understand what happened. It's important." He turned to look her in the eye, "Mama, believe me, it's *very* important."

Marra's face went ashen. She dropped the cloth and stood up, taking a step back. "Are you sure you're strong enough?" she managed.

Bael gave a curt nod.

She gave a laugh that Bael first misunderstood as a choking sound. "Gods, but you look like my sister." was all she said before he left the tent.

As he stalked across the grounds to his grandmother's tent, Bael tried to put the pieces together. Why was his mother acting so strangely around him? What secrets was she keeping? Whatever it was, she'd kept it deeply buried for nearly two decades and never let it slip once.

And yet now she was losing her composure, speaking blasphemy out loud, *certainly* having unclean thoughts. The scryers hadn't picked up on her either.

Bael expected them to notice the Toad. The Lord and Master's wife, on the other hand, might be a different matter for them. Perhaps they were protecting her. The idea comforted him in a world devoid of such a luxury.

Bael clung to his illusion.

Dark God be praised, if only I could provide her protection. he thought to himself.

He did not stop to wonder at the thought. He did not concern himself with the scryers or his father. If they heard, they heard. And he was happy to handle the consequences, whatever they might be.

His rising anger shielded him from the natural fear he knew he ought to feel. But his mother and Jorna were the center of his world. If he couldn't protect them, what was the point of living?

The sight of Granny Jorna's ruined tent drew him up short.

It was a shambles, little more than a smoking hide piled with dying embers and ash.

Darielle had clearly been unhappy when she left.

He was crawling through the ash, wondering *how* he had intended to protect Granny Jorna, when he felt a hard grip on his shoulder.

"And what are we doing here?"

A scryer.

"I'm looking for my grandmother." Bael muttered.

"What was that?" the scryer asked, tightening his grip.

One of the Darielle's visions flashed across his sight. He fought the impulse, but lost immediately. The floodgates holding back his mounting rage burst.

"I said," Bael growled, embracing his faith and filling himself with a prayer to the Dark God, "that," the grip loosened, "I'm looking," he heard the scryer choking as he crumpled the man's windpipe, "for my grandmother."

Bael stood and turned to face a suffocating man. The man was one of his father's favorites. His face was turning a fascinating dusky blue.

"You look cold." Bael whispered. "I can fix that."

The scryer burst into flames. Bael released his control of the man's breath just to hear him scream.

Bael stood still and watched as the fire of his faith burned the man to white ash. And then he stomped through the remains, scattering the scryer to the wind. In his wake he left the ruined tent and a dozen faces frozen in confusion, anger. *Fear*.

Word reached the medic tent before he did. Of course it had. He had just executed a high-ranking scryer without obvious cause or authority. Yet with unmistakable ability.

That apparently allowed him special access that would have normally been denied him. He wondered what would have happened if they'd told him he couldn't see Granny Jorna.

The thoughts that passed through his mind were disturbingly similar to the visions Darielle had placed there just a handful of days past. He hadn't anticipated putting truth to her visions quite so soon. He hadn't anticipated the *rage*.

But these people were mostly safe. As long as Jorna and Marra weren't threatened or harmed, no one need suffer that bastard scryer's fate. That one had gone too far, had had too little sympathy and too much suspicion. Bael felt no remorse over his passing, only insulted at the dead man's presumption.

Where had that come from? The question was now only a dim echo in the chaotic thunder of his thoughts, scattered in the gale of his mind before it was even fully recognized.

The sight that greeted him in the medic tent was another matter.

The woman was broken.

Bones obviously shattered and jutting from her papery skin. Blood caked and cracked around her eyes and fingernails. Several of her toes were missing, leaving only burned stumps and fractured fragments of white and brown seared bone.

And her eyes. Her eyes were the worst.

Rather than the milky whiteness of age, there was simply nothing. No bloody sockets, no bandaging, literally *nothing*. Empty pools of darkness that drooled smoke down the sides of her face. The droplets of shadow dissipated before they reached the floor, bursting and twisting out of existence.

"Good gods." he whispered before he even realized what he'd said.

But despite his obvious blasphemy, the healers in the room quietly filed out without meeting his gaze.

"Bael, dearie? Is that you?" Jorna whimpered, the darkness in her empty sockets intensifying into a full rush of oily smoke.

Bael rushed to her side, "Granny, it's me! I'm here to be with you. What can I do?"

"Well for the love of the Dark God, don't try to heal anything. Those bastard charlatans have no claim to the title, and if it's time for another 'treatment', just kill me now."

Bael was stunned to hear her spouting blasphemy with as much abandon as his mother. Would they all be executed for heresy? He countered his fear with anger. He was here to see her. She was alive. That was what mattered.

A small piece of paper fell from Jorna's humble coverings, flitting to the floor.

Bael caught it, his eyes catching his sister's handwriting, *A gift*. Whatever that meant.

"You killed a scryer." Jorna said, smirking.

"You...how did you know?" he stammered, tucking the paper into his breeches and snapping back to the moment at hand.

Jorna chuckled. Her laughter brought on a coughing fit that lasted several minutes. Some of her coughs brought up blood. Bael resisted the urge to heal her. He knew he was limited at best in that area.

Limited like all of his father's acolytes. Their path, the Path of Volos, took them too far to the edge of the Great Sphere to reach the healing magics they so desperately needed right now. His father's acolytes were not trained to be healers.

They were trained to be weapons.

When her coughing finally settled, Jorna allowed herself a chuckle, "You're asking how I know things that happen, that *may* happen? I never pegged you for a stupid boy from the toad pond. You're smarter than that. Your sister told you as much before she muddied up your mind."

"But what about you? Why would she do this to you?" Bael demanded.

Jorna gave a tired shrug, "Let me tell you what. Your sister is... different. She does as she does. If she'd wanted me dead, I'd be dead. I'm not, not yet, so I guess it's not my time by her clock. You're not either, so obviously she still wants something with the two of us. Darielle isn't a good girl, but you can't say she doesn't have direction."

"She tried to kill both of us." Bael snarled.

Jorna sniggered, "She didn't, did she? But she *did* share something with you. Something she shouldn't have?"

Bael groaned inwardly. "She showed me the prophecy you had about me. But she put it in my head, the way *she* saw it. It...it was horrific." That last word was barely a whisper.

Jorna cackled. "She showed you *that?*"

Bael raised his head, "What did you expect?"

Jorna was overtaken by another coughing fit. She shook and sputtered for a handful of minutes before she finally regained control of herself.

She wiped blood from her mouth and fixed him with that terrifying, empty gaze, "I expected that she might give you your options, but it sounds like she only gave you *her* version of events."

Bael sank to his knees and leaned close to his grandmother, "I'm so confused." Recent turmoil aside, he still wasn't brave enough to cry.

She patted his head with her good hand, "Of course you are, dearie. Of course you are. But here's the sun through the smoke: what

Darielle saw was only one path the Dark God has in store. If she wins, all those horrid things will come true. I can't deny her accuracy. But there's another way."

Bael looked down, preparing himself for visions that could possibly rival Darielle's. Instead, he heard Jorna giggle.

"What? What is it?" he asked, suddenly angry that she hadn't shared her vision.

Jorna's smile widened, her nightmare eyes widening in comedic fashion, "You just have to find the *boy*."

The next morning Aleksei woke feeling barely rested. He stumbled out of bed and dressed quickly. As he headed downstairs, he paused before their small shrine to the Great Mother Mokosh, Goddess of earth and fertility.

"Let these phantoms be taken from me." he whispered, touching the limewood statue with reverence. Aleksei wasn't sure if it would do much good, but he was quickly becoming desperate, and the Great Mother had always seemed to look favorably upon him.

From the clatter of the skillet on the stove, he knew his father was already up and moving about their small kitchen, assembling breakfast.

"Morning, Son." Henry called cheerfully when Aleksei descended into view.

Aleksei nodded his greeting, then glanced out the window into the black morning. The sun wouldn't be up for another few hours now, but they'd be out in the field well before, finishing the bundling that should have been done the night before.

His father placed two bowls of steaming porridge on the heavy kitchen table. Aleksei restrained a sigh as he turned and sat on his worn stool, pulling his breakfast closer and taking a few cursory bites. The food was bland but filling.

Aleksei had long grown used to it, though he couldn't help but remember the now-mythic meals of his old home. His mouth watered recalling the piles of roasted venison and fresh fruit that had been nearly omnipresent fixtures of every meal.

He had been a boy when they left the Ri-Vhan, yet the memories of his mother's people and their village in the trees of Seil Wood still surfaced in his dreams.

Aleksei recalled his dream from the night before and shivered. Instead he turned his thoughts back to the tasks ahead of him. Nothing good could come of dwelling on such dreams. They were better best forgotten.

"How are you feeling?" Henry asked softly.

"Better." Aleksei lied.

"Truly? Well, I'm glad to hear it."

Aleksei heard what his father was trying to say. Henry was concerned. He didn't like seeing his son upset, but if Aleksei wanted to talk about it he would be there to listen.

"Shouldn't we head out to the field?" Aleksei asked after a pregnant pause. "The crows'll be getting up soon."

Henry shook his head, "I finished the bundling last night."

Aleksei stared at his father. That must have taken half the night!

"The rest of the field, then? Did you want to cut it this morning?"

Henry nodded, "In good time. We're weeks ahead of the first frost, Son. At the pace we've been setting, we'll be done and stuck in for the season Market Day from next. Now, I don't fancy breaking my back for a fistful of days just to sit around from here till Solstice."

Aleksei gave up. He knew better than to play these little games with his father, as amusing as the older man found them. "Well fine. Then what did you have in mind?"

Henry glanced at his son with a twinkle in his pale brown eyes, "I thought we might go into town."

Once more Aleksei found himself regarding his father as though the man had gone mad.

"*Town?*"

"Aye." Henry said definitely. "Tomorrow's Market Day, you know? I thought we could take some of our bushels up to Goodman Miller's. I reckon everyone's just about out of summer barley flour, and from what I've been hearing from Mother Margareta, we have the first ripe crop of the season."

Aleksei was speechless.

"Unless, of course," his father said with a smile, "you'd like to stay and finish cutting the south field."

"*No!*" Aleksei blurted. "No, I think you're right, Da. Besides, we're nearly out of flour ourselves."

"Is that so? Well, all the more reason to hop on the road. Why don't you get Dash up and ready?"

Aleksei grinned and hurried from the farmhouse, out into the predawn darkness. The path to the barn was obscured in shadow, but Aleksei followed it with the precision born from a lifetime of memory.

He pushed the doors open and pulled their small cart out of the corner, busying himself with the tack and harness before realizing that he'd forgotten to get Dash in his excitement.

Aleksei hurried past the pens holding their handful of sheep and pulled open the stall door at the far end of the barn. While he couldn't see, Aleksei knew where he was as surely as he'd found the path from the house.

"Dash?" he whispered into the darkness.

A warm nicker greeted him from the depths of the stall and Aleksei smiled, stepping forward and reaching out into the darkness. He felt the draft horse's soft nose nuzzle his hand.

"Come on, boy. We're going to town."

Dash snorted and trotted past Aleksei. He followed the horse to the front of the stable, where Dash waited patiently to be harnessed to the cart. As Aleksei worked, he realized how profoundly grateful he was to have the old draft horse. A younger horse would either have stayed in its stall until it could see better, or might have bolted and broken a leg.

But Dash never moved in a hurry when he didn't have to, never rushed anything or moved recklessly. He knew what was expected of him and performed his tasks with a steady determination that was prized in his breed.

Aleksei finished fitting the harness and turned to the bushels of wheat his father had stacked against the east wall.

As he loaded the cart, Aleksei became aware that he could actually *see* what he was doing. He glanced over his shoulder and found his father standing in the doorway, holding a lantern.

"Thought you might have a bit more luck with some light." Henry said with a wry smile.

Aleksei nodded his appreciation as he loaded the last bushel,

"Thanks, Da."

Henry's smile faded into a frown, "You've never had much trouble getting around in the dark, have you?"

Aleksei shrugged, "I don't know. I guess I'm just used to the way things are set up around here."

Henry nodded, but he clearly wasn't convinced.

"We'd better get moving. At this rate it'll be near dusk by the time we reach Voskrin."

Aleksei smiled at his father's exaggeration, but nodded dutifully and led Dash out of the barn. They walked down the path that led to the road and turned north towards the village, both men confined to their thoughts.

Morning crept lazily across the sky, rendering the landscape in undulating shades of aureate, ocher and emerald. Aleksei kept his eyes fixated on the cloudscapes transforming before them. Indigo and violet shaded the pink until the sun burst over the horizon and bathed the world in its ruddy gold.

They walked in the comfortable silence of familiarity. Aleksei imagined his father's head was filled with the concerns of every farmer this time of year. Would it rain before they finished their work? Should they have remained at home and finished the Harvest? What if the crop was ruined in their absence?

Aleksei was content to leave Henry to such thoughts. He had plenty of worries of his own.

The voice had returned with the sun.

It was softer now, but Aleksei recognized it nonetheless. It was no trick of the wind or the heat. It was the green-eyed man's voice from the dream.

Midmorning had come and gone by the time Voskrin came into view. Despite the darkness of his thoughts, Aleksei couldn't help but smile. The village meant so many warm things to him.

Still, he had to help his father unload the cart before he would be let loose to find his friends. He led Dash into the village square and past the homes of the thatchers and coopers and smiths. They walked clear through to the other side of the village and turned right past the Tanners' pungent workshop, finally pulling up short of the mill.

And then Aleksei was lifting bushels of wheat while dodging

requests from Goody Miller to come inside and try her vinegar pie, fresh from the oven.

It was nearing mid-afternoon by the time Aleksei managed to politely excuse himself from her table and stagger out into the rest of the village. He wandered into the middle of the square and was just about to head for Redman's Pub when a familiar voice sounded from behind him.

"Well, aren't you a sight?"

He turned and found a grinning Katherine Bondar standing a pace away, looking enormously pleased with herself.

"How's that for quiet?" his friend asked triumphantly.

It had been a childhood game of theirs to try and sneak up on the other one. Thus far Katherine had not been successful.

Aleksei never lost.

"It doesn't count if we're in the village." Aleksei explained patiently, wiping the sweat from his brow "We have to be in the woods *outside* of town. That's what makes it hard."

Katherine made a face, "I don't know about that. Seems like it's not that hard for you."

Aleksei smiled, "That's because I'm better at it."

Katherine was about to counter when the color suddenly drained from her face, "Gods, here he comes."

Aleksei frowned, "Katherine, don't swear. It's common."

Katherine shook her head gravely, "It's Pyotr Krovel. And he's going to show up and drag you off to the pub, isn't he?"

As Pyotr stepped into earshot Katherine stopped talking, offering a polite smile to the lanky young man while glaring daggers at Aleksei.

"Aleksei Drago," Pyotr laughed, clapping Aleksei roughly across the back, "it's been an age since I've seen you."

Aleksei offered up a half-hearted smile, "It's nice to see you, Pyotr."

"'Nice', Aleksei?" Pyotr pouted, turning to Katherine, "Well how's that for a friendly hello? Gods, Aleksei, you only get up to Voskrin, what, twice a season? What're you doing up here anyhow?"

"Da and I brought up our first cut of wheat."

"And you're done already? What are you two up to now?"

Aleksei tried to keep a scowl from surfacing. He'd been hoping to get to see Katherine without Pyotr's intrusion. They had all grown up together, but over the past few years Pyotr had grown increasingly absent, either apprenticing at the smithy or drowning himself in drink at the pub.

Katherine was far more likely to want to go hiking in the small wood north of town. On occasion, they'd hunt for squirrels, though the little yew bows her brothers used were ill-suited to the task.

"We were about to head up to the glade for a little walk." Katherine interjected, saving Aleksei from having to craft an excuse.

Pyotr looked startled for a moment before realizing that Aleksei had remained silent, that he hadn't suggested grabbing a pint with Pyotr and leaving Katherine behind.

"Well," Pyotr said after a long pause, "how about that? You sure you wouldn't rather go grab a drink and relax for a spell? I'm sure you've more than earned it by now."

Aleksei was trapped. If he refused Pyotr, he could spend the afternoon squirrel hunting with Katherine, while Pyotr would be back at the pub telling the other lads tales that Aleksei would spend the rest of the winter putting to bed.

If he turned Katherine down, she'd rightly think him a coward for not telling Pyotr off like he wanted to, but she would be much easier to mollify in the end.

While he wanted nothing more than to spend time with his friend, he simply couldn't risk having his name dragged through the mud simply on account of Pyotr's wounded feelings.

Aleksei knew his decision had already been made for him. "You know, Petya, a drink actually sounds pretty good right now." He forced a smile he didn't feel, glancing apologetically to Katherine as Pyotr dragged him towards the pub. As he walked away he mouthed an apology, his eyes pleading with her for understanding, if not forgiveness.

Her big brown eyes narrowed, and then she shrugged, turning her back on him and walking briskly towards the village green. Aleksei winced at the look of pure disappointment, the hurt she had leveled at him, at her *dismissal*, staring at her retreating form and feeling every bit the coward and the cad.

Even as they passed through the pub door and he was greeted by a roar from the other lads, his mind couldn't have been further away.

He wanted to be with Katherine, not in this dank pub that stank of sour mead and the stale sweat of men who'd been toiling at their trades since well before dawn. As he sat amidst the other village boys, a big, powerful hand landed on his shoulder. Aleksei looked up into the face of Kiriel Bondar. He did not look happy. Kiriel's brother Ruslan stood a pace behind him, his face a match to his twin brother's obvious anger.

"I just saw my sister walk away from you *crying*. Why don't you come outside with us, maybe explain why Katherine was so upset, what'dya say?"

Aleksei swallowed hard. "I'm so sorry, Kiriel. I really had no idea she was so upset, but I'm sure it's all my fault. Let me find a way to make it up to her?"

Ruslan stepped in and gripped a handful of Aleksei's shirt. "No need to trouble yourself, farm boy." Katherine's two strapping brothers hoisted him to his feet. "We've got the perfect solution for you."

As the two men half carried him toward the pub's backdoor, Aleksei spared a quick glance at the other lads. Some were staring intently into their pints, as though the bottoms of their empty steins had become suddenly fascinating. Others, like Pyotr, offered him furtive, apologetic shrugs. None rose to follow the three men, or to offer Aleksei their support.

Right as they reached the backdoor, just as Aleksei was running through every strategy he could possibly conjure through his panic, he heard Pyotr sigh heavily. "Well boys, I guess that's what you get for blowing off a prize like Katherine Bondar for a pint with your mates. *Idiot*."

Aleksei felt his face flush with anger as he was pushed out into the small alley behind the pub.

Chapter 3

Shadows in the Storm

Sweat rolled down the hard angles of Aleksei's face, dripping from his nose and chin as he worked. Lift, throw, lift, throw. The motion was methodical and soothing, and it was exactly what Aleksei needed at the moment.

He stepped back to survey his progress and managed a grin. In a single morning he'd shifted half of the hay from the west field into the barn. Perhaps tomorrow he and his father could finish carting it up to the loft. And then there would be little to do until it was time to plant next spring.

Aleksei restrained another surge of hope. It had been at least a week since he'd last dreamt of the strange voice, and those terrifying green eyes. It was near a Market Day since the last voice had echoed through his mind. His prayers had finally put an end to this... *disorientation* altogether.

It was now well into Harvest, and the work on their tiny farm was practically complete. And once it was, he and his father could spend their days relaxing by the fire. Maybe he would spend the last few weeks before the first snow chopping firewood. They could never have too much—

Aleksei.

He froze, back stiff as he glanced around the barn and then out into the field. No one. At least no one he could see.

Aleksei, I have need of you.

Aleksei shuddered, running a hand across his forehead and turning his eyes towards the farmhouse.

He was alone.

North, Aleksei, north.

He closed his eyes and the golden mist rushed back to him.

It was always the same, the voice, the golden mist, and those brilliant emerald eyes that spoke far more power than any simple farmer could fathom in a thousand lifetimes.

North, Aleksei. I have need of you.

"Who are you?" he whispered, but that never changed either.

The voice never responded, never even seemed to notice that Aleksei was speaking. It simply repeated itself. *North. I have need of you.*

What need? Aleksei was more than a little apprehensive about the voice. What need could anyone have with *him*? Surely whatever was needed could be found somewhere else. In some*one* else. Why him?

Fate made that decision long ago, Aleksei Drago.

His eyes snapped open and his pulse quickened, fear tumbling rampantly through his veins. This was the first time the voice had deviated. Before, everything had been composed of the same series of phrases. But now...now something was very different indeed.

Fate will make you come to me, Aleksei. Do not fight it. Do not run. It will find you. I will find you.

Aleksei wanted to weep with frustration. Even if he were mad enough to consider following the voice, 'North' was hardly enough to go on.

"Aleksei?"

He jumped at his father's call and turned, trying to bury the emotions sweeping across his face. Fear, panic, despair. What was he supposed to do?

"Come on boy, it's supper time." his father said with a bright smile. "This can wait until tomorrow and then we'll do it together. Finish in half the time."

Aleksei nodded, "Alright, Da. I was coming in anyhow."

His father's brow creased, "Something troubling you, Son?"

Aleksei tried to banish the uncertainty from his face, "Troubling? Nah, I was just thinking that the sun was getting to me."

His father's face lightened and his smile returned, his pale brown eyes twinkling knowingly, "That sun can play mighty tricks on you if you don't mind it. Especially during Harvest. Trickiest thing in the world, that old sun."

Aleksei relaxed and nodded his agreement, fetching his shirt from the hook inside the barn where he'd left it. As Aleksei snapped the buttons into place, he was keenly aware of his father watching him. He knew Henry was concerned, but the last thing he wanted to do was trouble his father with his flights of fancy. How could he explain something he didn't understand himself? At best, Henry might just think he was addled in the head.

Would the voices ever leave him alone? Would the man with the green eyes finally decide he wasn't worth the trouble and move on to someone else? Someone more willing? Gods, but he hoped so.

And even as the thought entered his mind, he knew it would not, *could* not be. He was trapped. Trapped by...what had the man said?

Fate.

He rolled the word over in his mind, trying to comprehend what it was about that word that carried such a strong feeling of bitterness. Why did he shy away from it so? Something tugged at his thoughts, just on the edges of consciousness, but he found no answers in the silence. Some part of him rebelled against the word. Something inside of him *hated* it.

"Fate." he whispered.

"What?"

Aleksei realized he'd spoken the word aloud and looked to his father's questioning face, "Da, do you believe in Fate?"

Henry frowned, "Fate, Son? Can't say I do. I've lived too long and seen too much that Fate just can't explain. If there was Fate, then everything would have to have a reason. And I just can't see the reason in some things."

Aleksei knew what his father meant. The memory of his mother haunted his father day and night, as it haunted him.

Why were some things just so...so *senseless*?

Nothing is senseless, Aleksei. But sometimes we are too blind to the world to understand the 'whys', and sometimes we don't receive answers. Sometimes we do, but they aren't the answers we want.

Aleksei felt a sudden surge of anger at the voice's intrusion. Was it reading his thoughts now? Would he ever have a moment of peace, when some stranger was not listening inside his head?

You've never truly been alone, Aleksei. Privacy is an illusion crafted for the powerless. And now your anger stems from the knowledge you have gained. I know that is not the answer you wanted, but that does not keep it from being true.

Damn you, Aleksei thought angrily, *let me be!*

He waited for a response, but was greeted by silence. It was only several hours later that Aleksei realized his wish had been granted.

Henry spent the rest of the day watching his son closely. Something was undeniably troubling him, but until Aleksei decided to open up to him there was nothing he could do.

"He'll tell you in his own time, Henry." he muttered under his breath.

So he waited. Every now and then he would engage his son in conversation, but every time he thought Aleksei might be on the brink of telling him something, the conversation fled to some superficial topic. Did he think it would rain by Market Day? Who did he think would bring the biggest pig to the Harvest Festival? Did he think Mother Margareta would come to bless their fields before the first frost?

Henry answered each question as though it was the direction he meant to steer the conversation, and refused to allow his frustration to surface. But by the end of the evening, he was no closer to understanding his son's troubles than he'd been that morning.

Finally Aleksei rose from his seat before the fire, put his book away, and went to bed. Henry watched him go, more troubled than ever. The boy had never gone to bed without a word before. He always had some last comment to make, even if it was just to wonder at the next day's activities.

Henry sat before the dying embers of the fire well into the night, thinking. He didn't remember falling asleep, so when the voice woke him his eyes started open.

Hello, Henry.

He looked around, trying to get his bearings.

Gone was the heat of the hearth, the comfort of his chair. Instead he stood in an enveloping fog of shimmering gold.

He could see no one.

"Where am I?" Henry demanded.

A dream, Henry. This is merely an illusion. I apologize that I cannot offer you more comfortable surroundings at the moment.

"Who are you?" Henry called, feeling a touch foolish, shouting at phantoms.

His question went unanswered.

Henry, I've come to ask a favor.

"Who are you?" Henry repeated flatly.

There was a moment of hesitation before the voice responded. *A man much like yourself, Henry Drago. One who only wants what's best for your son.*

"Speak then."

When the favor was uttered, Henry blinked in confusion. A thousand questions bubbled to the surface, yet he found that he only possessed the strength to ask one.

"Why?" he choked, surprised by the weakness in his own voice.

The air before his face shimmered and distorted, as though he were looking through intense heat. Slowly, images formed. Images of Aleksei. An Aleksei he didn't recognize.

"Why are you showing me this?" Henry managed.

Because I want you to see what your son could become. The man he could be, if you'd only let him. If you just do as I say.

"I don't trust you." Henry barked back. "I can't even see your face."

Another image shimmered into being. A man, though Henry saw

nothing remarkable about him. The man leaned forward and whispered in his ear, and Henry heard the unmistakable ring of truth.

In that moment he thought he might have preferred a dagger to the heart. It would have been far less painful to simply die at the end of a highwayman's blade than to agree to *this*. Either way, he would lose the most precious thing he had.

"Bargain struck." Henry whispered bitterly, a tear winding its way down his cheek.

You're doing your son a great service, Henry Drago.

The voice even sounded earnest.

Henry started to say something, but even as he opened his mouth, darkness swirled around him. He slipped back into the empty chasms of sleep.

✦

He sat back, a frown fixed firmly to his face. It had taken months, but they'd finally managed to locate the one he'd been searching for. And yet just as he made contact, he could feel it; another set of claws already sinking into the man.

He glanced at the woman sitting across from him, emerald eyes gauging her reaction in the dim firelight. "Well?"

She looked back at him, the golden flecks in her own peridot irises glimmering, "I...I don't know what to make of it. Honestly, I don't. But we aren't the only ones who've taken an interest."

He chuckled, but the laugh lacked humor. "He was supposed to be forming a bond with *me*. Even across the distance, I thought that's what you saw in your vision."

She averted her eyes to the low-burning hearth, "It was. It *is*. But it's possible my vision didn't show me everything."

"Like what?" His voice was low and dangerous. "Like the presence of another? Another after the very same prize? How likely is that? And yet here we are." His face contorted with rage. He slammed his fists on the desk before him, slopping wine from his goblet across the cuffs of his crimson silk coat.

"*How?*" he bellowed.

She shook her head, her heart pounding in her ears, "As I said, I don't know. But whoever is reaching out to him has also formed a bond with him. At the moment, however, this new player's claim seems no stronger than your own."

"But that's supposed to be impossible." he growled. "You said these bonds were only formed between two people. Only *ever* between two people."

She paused, still staring into the flames, before meeting his green-eyed gaze, "There is an exception, but it doesn't make much sense in this context."

He sat back, lacing his fingers together in front of his stormy expression, "Explain."

She swallowed again, "A bifurcated bond has been formed before, but never invoked. Bonds can sometimes form through instinct, or need, or love. But a bifurcated bond is only ever formed for one reason.

"Someone has invoked a Primary prophecy."

He inhaled sharply. "How?"

She shook her head, "I can't say. But this boy is an eye in the storm; this prophecy has been invoked in his name. You and the other player, whoever it is, are now the two ends of the fork, each of you a terminal destination. Whatever he ultimately decides will alter the direction of the Primary prophecy irrevocably."

"And we have no control over the boy?"

She shrugged, "We have the ability to influence events, as you have seen tonight. But this is a delicate business, make no mistake. Being too heavy-handed can be just as dangerous as lacking any presence at all. It's a matter of the utmost delicacy." Her eyes shimmered again in the gush of sparks from the hearth, "Not exactly your strong suit."

He ignored her jibe. "And which Primary prophecy would you be referencing? At least that should shed a little light on what to expect."

"That's just it," she whispered, her attention riveted now on the fickle, flickering flames in the hearth, "there *is* no Primary prophecy that meets these criteria. Several share similar elements, but of all the books in the Voralla, none depict an invocation quite like this. We're wandering in the dark."

Feeling his frustration mounting, she hurried on, "But if we're operating in shadows and smoke, then so is the other player. The

Voralla has one of the oldest libraries on prophecy in the known world. Every Primary ever recorded is in the vaults somewhere. The chance of this...other player having the same access as you is highly unlikely."

He paused, taking in her words, then burst out into a mirthless laugh, "Do you hear yourself? Really, do you realize what you've just implied?"

She frowned, "If you want to get angry about this, that's your business, not mine. I'm not trying to offend you, just put things in perspective."

"And what a fine job you've done of it." he snorted. "Now, not only do we have competition for a boy, nay a man, who may be an eye in the storm, but we may have competition from *outside* the Voralla?"

The weight of the implication finally registered on her face. "So then...you believe the rumors? You believe there are other Magi out there? Other schools that the Voralla knows nothing about? I can hardly imagine how such a thing could be possible."

A knock sounded at the door.

"Come." he snapped.

A servant slowly opened the door, "Highness, the Queen has sent for you."

He sighed, "Tell her I'll be along in due time." The servant lingered. "Leave us." The door snapped shut just as the servant stepped back.

He returned his fierce emerald gaze to his companion, still intensely studying the dying flames. As though her life depended on the survival of those weakening, flickering flames.

He supposed in many ways the comparison was apt enough, for both of them.

"Yes," he said finally, his voice keen as a razor, "there are *others*."

⚘

Morning greeted Aleksei gently, rousing him from a dreamless oblivion. It had taken him hours to finally find some rest, and his relief was immeasurable when he woke without encountering the specter of the green-eyed man. His wish had been granted. The man was gone.

He made his way down the narrow stairway and walked into the kitchen, frowning at what greeted him. Their rough wooden table was laid out with provisions for what Aleksei could only guess was a journey.

But a journey where? His father hadn't said anything about travel. There was still wood to chop and hay to store. The first snow might be weeks away, but there was no telling when the winds would usher in the chill of Northern air. Working outside in the cold was not something he, nor any farmer, relished.

"I see you're up." Henry said from behind. Aleksei jumped.

He turned, "Da, where are we going? I thought we were going to finish the hay this morning."

His father shook his head and smiled, though Aleksei caught the deep sadness in Henry's eyes. "*We* aren't going anywhere, Son. *You* are."

Aleksei frowned, "Me? But I thought—"

His father tried to hold the smile, but it was forced, "You're needed, Son. In the North."

Aleksei thought his heart should stop. He forgot to breathe. He could hardly process what his father had just said.

You know the truth he speaks, Aleksei.

Aleksei fought back a sob of frustration. He thought he'd freed himself of the damned voice, but now he knew the truth. He would *never* be free from it. It would hound him until the end of his days, or until it drove him mad, whichever came first.

Or until you simply do as I ask.

"Why?" he finally managed.

His father looked out the kitchen window, and Aleksei followed his gaze. Dash waited patiently outside, a saddle fitted snugly about his muscular frame.

"Because you're needed, Son. It's the only answer I can give you."

"I'm not needed *here*, Da? Don't *you* need me?"

Henry bit back the pain in his voice, "You are more of a help than I can say, Aleksei, and I love you dearly. But no, I don't *need* you. Not like this. If you stayed here, you'd be wasting something... extraordinary. And honestly, I think you'd know it too. They need you in the North, Son. And their need is much more important than mine."

Aleksei stood there, stunned by what his father was saying to him. And then the questions came pouring forth. What did Henry mean by 'extraordinary'? What had his father learned? What was still being kept from him?

"And I'm sorry I can't give you the answers you want, Son. But I think you know who can. *Find* him."

"But how can I...." Aleksei began, fighting back the tears springing into his eyes.

"You're strong, Aleksei. You've always been strong. That won't fail you now."

Henry swallowed back his own tears and tried to smile again, "Now you'd better get on the road. The sooner you get beyond the Southern Plain, the better. You don't want to be riding under the Harvest Sun too long if you can help it."

"But where am I *going*?" Aleksei cried, his voice breaking. It was happening too fast. His life was slipping through his fingers moment by moment and there was nothing he could do about it.

"North, Son. North. You'll know where you're headed as you get closer. That's all I know to tell you."

Aleksei looked into his father's eyes and saw the sadness, the regret that burned within him. His father wanted to know just as badly as he, to know just what sort of place he was so blindly sending his son.

Finally, after a long silence, Aleksei nodded. "Alright, Da. If you want me to go, then I'll go."

"I'll never want you to go, Son." Henry whispered, his face contorting with pain. He had already lost his wife, and now he was losing his son, too. Aleksei would still be alive, but he would be so far away.

"But promise me something, Aleksei."

Aleksei nodded, "Anything, Da."

"If you find this place and if it's not what *you* want, what *you* need, promise me you'll come back. Even if this isn't what you want either, at least we can figure that out together."

Aleksei finally allowed a tear to wind its way down his cheek, "I promise, Da."

Henry stepped forward and wrapped his arms tightly around his son, hugging him as close as he could, as though any moment Aleksei might turn to mist and vanish forever. Henry stepped back and managed a sardonic smile. Aleksei might remain solid as stone, but surely enough he was about to vanish.

Henry didn't watch his son ride away. In truth, he couldn't bear it. As long as he'd never seen Aleksei leave he could always pretend the boy was out in the barn, or by the pond he'd swum in as a child. It was a good hour before Henry allowed himself to sit down in his chair and sob.

CHAPTER 4

A SHIFT IN SAVAGERY

ALEKSEI RODE NORTH, his face disconsolate as the familiar farmland passed and faded away behind him. A tangible fear wormed its way through his heart. What was he *doing*? For the first time in his life, Aleksei didn't know where he was headed. There was no structure to this, no one to tell him what needed to be done or where he was supposed to go.

He had a single direction; that was all.

By mid-afternoon Aleksei was passing the last farms before Voskrin. He allowed himself to relax a little. He was still in familiar territory. But once past the village, he would be the furthest he'd ever been from home since they'd left the Seil Wood.

Aleksei smiled softly as the memories drifted back through his mind. He remembered little about the Wood, mostly faded images, but they always made him smile. He'd been happy there, *truly* happy.

He'd fit in. He'd felt at peace. And while he loved the Southern Plain, he also knew it for what it was.

His father's attempt at escape.

His mother had been Ri-Vhan, the forest people who inhabited the trees of Seil Wood, and when she died Henry had come to resent everything that brought back her memory.

Except him.

He knew his father was pained by how much Aleksei resembled his mother, although he rarely let it show. Occasionally, Aleksei caught those moments of hurt when Henry lowered his guard, but he loved his father all the more for the attempt.

As he rode into Voskrin, he was spotted almost immediately. Aleksei considered kicking Dash into a gallop as Katherine came towards him, but ultimately decided better of it. He couldn't just leave without saying good-bye. At the same time, he had no desire to attract the ire of her brothers.

He slipped out of the saddle just as his friend reached him, and smiled at her youthful, buoyant expression.

"Aleksei? I didn't expect to see you until Solstice! Did your Da send you into town for something? My father just bought new bows off a peddler. He claims they're red-hearted rowan, but *I* said...."

Aleksei shook his head, "I'm sorry, but I'm afraid I don't have the time. I'm heading out."

Katherine frowned, "Heading out? Aleksei, I don't catch your meaning."

Aleksei tried to keep a smile on his face, "Thought I might travel around a bit, see the realm. You know, like we always said we'd do?"

Katherine started laughing.

Aleksei sighed.

She thought he was joking. They'd spent many a summer night talking about one day riding out of Voskrin forever, to become heroes in a great city. But they had long ago given up such dreams as the impossible fantasies of children.

When she realized Aleksei wasn't laughing, Katherine stopped. "You're serious, aren't you? Have you gone completely *mad?*"

"Who's gone mad?"

Both turned towards Pyotr, who seemed to have appeared from

thin air.

"Aleksei's leaving." Katherine said softly.

He stared at Aleksei in confusion, "Leaving for where?"

"I can't say. Da said I needed to head north. He said I'd only be wasting my time if I stayed here."

Pyotr looked angry, "Wasting your time? What, you have something bigger or *better* to do? Did you become a knight since the last time I saw you?"

"I am the same man today that I was yesterday." Aleksei growled.

He paused, glancing around the village, looking at the faces of his friends. Katherine's luminous brown eyes, the look of utter confusion written across her fine features. And Pyotr. Simple, slow-witted Pyotr. Of course Pyotr couldn't understand what was happening. Katherine, on the other hand, seemed to understand the situation perfectly. He was abandoning her, but he saw no anger, no hatred in her eyes, only endless bewilderment.

"But where will you go?" she managed, fighting back tears.

Aleksei shrugged, "I don't know yet. I suppose I'll find my way."

"But surely there must be some other way!" she demanded, her anger suddenly surfacing. "You can't just leave like this! Have your Da talk to the Elder. He'll understand! He'll fix things."

Aleksei reached out and gently took hold of Katherine's arm, "I don't *want* him to fix things."

And for the first time since he'd left the farm, Aleksei heard the conviction in his voice. He didn't want to turn around and go home. Something inside of him needed to follow the voice, to discover the truth behind the dreams. To understand why someone had chosen *him*.

He stepped back and looked around Voskrin one last time. It broke his heart to leave, but right then it was clear to him. He didn't want this. He didn't want this life. He looked at Katherine and Pyotr. He didn't want their lives, and he couldn't have them.

It had never occurred to him that he might be so different from his friends, certainly not in the way his life was set, but now he knew beyond a doubt that it was true. He wasn't meant for this life.

"Good-bye." he said with a sad smile, giving Katherine a heart-felt hug. He shook Pyotr's hand, trying to ignore the other boy's stunned silence. And then he climbed onto Dash's back and rode out of town.

He tried to keep them from seeing the tears running down his face. Aleksei rode, looking straight ahead. This was not his first time leaving a home he loved.

He rode, turning his eyes from the things that inevitably recalled fond memories. He never wanted those to haunt his last thoughts of home. He wanted to remember his father, sitting at that rough table, telling him to go, while also achingly begging him to return.

He wanted to remember his friends as they were now, not as they had been all those years ago. The gods only knew when he'd see any of them again.

And suddenly Aleksei was passing the fair grounds, where he'd spent so many enchanted days, clutching his father's hand as they moved from booth to booth, watching fools' skits put on by the locals. He was leaving it all behind, and something deep inside told him that it would never be the same. He might return to this place, but he would never belong again. He passed the grounds and found himself in unfamiliar territory.

What was the rest of Ilyar like? Were the people the same? He pushed the thoughts aside as best he could. He knew that no answers awaited him. Not here, only down the road.

Whatever purpose this voice, this green-eyed man had for him, Aleksei still had to reach him before he could find answers. And in order to get there he had to survive the journey.

Would there be brigands on the road? He knew that the Legions kept way-stations on the major roads, but they couldn't patrol all day and night. What would he do if someone tried to rob him?

The life of a farmer did not lend itself to combat. True, he was a competent archer, but he had only ever shot at squirrels and rabbits. His belt knife would likewise do him little good against experienced thieves.

As the shadows lengthened, his worries and doubts grew. He began to jump at nothing, the whisper of the wind, the flight of a bird. His mind twisted reality into possibility and illusion. Yet by the time night fell completely and he pulled a few paces off the road, he had encountered nothing but the local fauna.

Aleksei sighed in relief as he built his campfire and began to rummage through the pack his father had prepared for him. Some hours ago it had occurred to him that he hadn't eaten breakfast before leaving, and his worries and fears had so consumed him on his ride north that he'd hardly thought of food.

Now he was starving, and as he sorted through the various provisions his father had packed, he was relieved to see there was plenty of food to last at least two or three days. After that...well, he would figure that out when he got there.

He was just biting into an apple when the crunch of dry leaves and twigs sounded from behind him.

Aleksei hurried to his feet and spun around, his heart racing when saw two gleaming swords casting the firelight across the clearing. It was a pair of Legionnaires.

"Well, what have we here?"

Aleksei frowned. The uniforms were correct, as were the swords, but their scent told him these weren't the straitlaced soldiers he'd heard about in tales. Something about them smelled...wrong.

"Just a farmer making his way north." Aleksei said amicably, slowly reaching for his belt knife.

"Aye," said one of the men, eyeing Dash. "Making his way north on a very handsome horse. How'd you come by it?"

Aleksei straightened to his full height, "My father gave him to me."

The two men shared a glance. He was bigger than either of them, but that counted for little against their blades. It didn't take a lot of training to cut down a farm boy. "Your father, eh? And where's he?"

"Back at home, waiting on me." Aleksei said cautiously. Something was definitely wrong.

One of the men grinned. It was not a nice expression. "Well, won't it be a shame that you'll be walking all that way?"

The other nodded his agreement, "That is, unless you give us trouble. Then you might not make it back at all."

Aleksei tried to reconcile their words with the idea of Legionnaires he'd grown up with. "What're you saying?"

"I don't know, Gus, what are we saying?"

"I don't know, Jack, I think we're saying that if the farm boy puts up a fight, he's likely to end up on the point of my sword."

Jack nodded, "That's what I *thought* we were saying."

Aleksei tried desperately to make sense of it all. These men were just going to *take* Dash?

Something primal stirred within him.

A strange feeling descended on him as he watched the motions of each man, studying the way they stood, their individual balances. In the back of his mind, Aleksei was aware of each observation, yet he didn't feel like *he* was the one making them.

"You can't have my horse." he said calmly. When had he become *calm*?

"Can't we?" Jack asked, genuinely surprised. "Well, what a shame. You hear that, Gus? We can't take his horse."

Gus chuckled, "Too bad for us." He took a step forward.

"I'm warning you." Aleksei growled, his voice still impossibly cool and collected, "You *cannot* take my horse."

He was warning them? Of *what*? Aleksei's mind raced. Where were these words coming from? He had little doubt that his threat would be ignored or even mocked. But they were going to take Dash. And what was to stop them from killing him all the same?

But even as he struggled to understand everything that was happening, he felt no panic.

"Well, when you put it that way...." Gus chuckled, taking another step forward.

The feeling grew. Aleksei's vision clouded at the edges.

And then something *shifted*.

He hurled the half-eaten apple into Jack's face. A heartbeat later his hand shot out and caught Gus in the stomach. As the man doubled over, Aleksei brought his knee hard into the Gus' face.

The man collapsed, but even as he fell Aleksei caught the sword that dropped from his nerveless fingers and pivoted to face Jack, kicking out with his foot and catching the man high in the throat.

Aleksei froze, realizing that he had Jack pinned to a tree, his foot cutting off the man's air supply. In his right hand he held Gus' sword, pointed towards the man's prone form on the ground.

His vision cleared.

"Get out of here." Aleksei managed. He let his foot down and glared coolly at Jack, "Take your friend and get out of here. And if I see you again, I'll kill you."

The two men scrambled to get out of the clearing as fast as they could. It was only when they were gone that Aleksei slumped to the ground.

What had he *done?* He didn't know how to fight. He'd never wielded a sword in his life, yet here he was. Aleksei suddenly realized that his right hand still clutched the Legionnaire blade. More worrisome still was the comfort he felt with the sword in his grip. The understanding that it *belonged* there.

The strange feeling evaporated as quickly as it had appeared, and a sense of absolute disgust overwhelmed him. Aleksei rolled to the side and retched violently into the underbrush, his body heaving painfully. A part of him had *enjoyed* the violence, and that very thought made him sick.

Exhaustion overwhelmed him. He slumped against his pack, fighting to keep his eyes open. As he fell into a fitful sleep, the voice echoed in his head.

Aleksei thought he heard it laughing.

⟡

Bael sat back on his heels, staring into the smoking embers of Jorna's pinion fire.

Her tent had been reconstructed without a word from his Lord Father. The remains of the scryer Bael had incinerated had been cleared with the rest of the debris from Darielle's visit, and a new hide tent erected in its place.

In a shocking revelation that rocked their small congregation, his Lord Father Rafael revealed that the scryer Bael had murdered was under the influence of the Lord of Lies and Light, Dazhbog.

Bael, though a mere pawn in the Dark God's embracing shadow, had acted as a vessel of purity, and had removed the filth of betrayal from their sacred congregation.

Bael was as stunned as the rest to hear the words escape his father's cracked lips. In truth, it sounded as though Volos himself was dragging each word out of Rafael with white-hot pincers. But preach them he did, and his word was law.

Bael became something of a hero overnight, rather than the

murdering toad boy he knew he was. There was nothing *just* in killing that man.

Bael had felt a flash of anger and irritation and had thought nothing more of it. He'd felt no divine hand guiding his actions, only the mad visions of an insane woman poisoning his mind towards a darker path.

But no longer.

Not after what he'd just witnessed in the smoke of Granny Jorna's fire.

The 'boy', as she'd originally called him, was so much more than that. He was something unlike anything Bael had ever beheld. Simple, powerful; unsullied by the wickedness that his father always claimed gripped the world beyond their cloistered Commune.

And yet, despite the weeks Bael had been watching the other man toil away in his fields, pray to his false gods in the night, or weep with confusion at Bael's consistent intrusion into his thoughts, it had come as a complete shock when Aleksei Drago had packed his belongings and headed north.

Away from a father who loved him.

That alone left Bael shaken.

But not so shaken as watching through Aleksei's eyes as the two men approached his campfire and were immediately defeated. Defeated by a peasant boy who seemed to possess less ferocity than the wild squirrels Bael trapped in the woods.

And now Aleksei Drago was heading north. North, towards Bael. Towards the voice that had dogged his dreams for days and weeks now. It was nearly too much for Bael to comprehend.

He wasn't sure whether he ought to be more surprised by Aleksei's actions, or by the fact that he could now feel some small connection between himself and the farm boy. He said as much to his grandmother.

Jorna gave a low cackle, dribbles of black smoke falling from her empty eyes and mingling with the fog of her tent, "You've been diligent enough. I would be quite surprised if the boy wasn't forming *some* connection with you. It might even be stronger still if there were not another to interfere."

Bael frowned at her through the haze, "But how is that possible?

Your vision said nothing of another seeking the same prize."

She nodded slowly, her gaze somehow penetrating him to the core, "And Darielle's vision? Did you see nothing of this other seeker? For if this other is successful, I fear that your sister will prove herself to be right yet again."

Bael suppressed a shiver.

Darielle's vision promised him only darkness and death. A life he could hardly imagine, much less desire. But no, through the flashes of black flame and the screaming, Bael saw no other seeker. He didn't even really see Aleksei, though Jorna promised that the farm boy played heavily into her own prophecy.

"I'm doing everything I can." he finally allowed, brokenly. "I've done everything you've told me to. And there is *another?*"

"Tut-tut, young one. You'll get nowhere if you drown yourself before you can truly swim. The presence of the other seeker means one very important thing that you've missed." Jorna leaned forward, "This is not a simple piece of spellwork, Bael. If there is another seeker, one who can reach our boy, then we are playing a very different game than I first imagined."

Bael felt rage swirl up in him as he leapt to his feet. "It's not a bloody *game!*" he screamed.

The fire roared in response to his rage, a column of green and gold fire blasting through the top of the tent and showering him in tiny flecks of sparking ash.

Bael stood in the acrid snow for a moment before lowering his head in shame.

"I'm sorry. That was horrid of me, especially with what Darielle's put you through. I just...I just *can't....*" The rest of his words dissolved into unintelligible murmurs that escaped around his sobs of frustration.

From across the firepit, Jorna watched him cautiously.

"Careful with that temper, dearie." she said in a choking whisper. "Or it will get you burned."

❧

Jonas Belgi stood before his aunt, his face cool and collected.

"This is a mistake. One with dangerous consequences if you don't play your hand *very* carefully."

Andariana regarded her nephew with a mixture of surprise and concern. Jonas was not one to get worked up over minor political machinations.

"There's nothing I can do, Jonas. You must understand that."

"You're the *Queen*." he said softly, his tone never hinting at his true emotions. Somehow, that just made it cut all the deeper. "If *you* can't do something about it, then what good are you?"

"Don't be petulant." she snapped, instantly regretting the flash of irritation she had betrayed. "You knew from the beginning that this was a possibility. Don't take your anger out on me because of your miscalculations."

"I will *not* marry the girl."

"You were the one who saw the urgent need to have Bertrand Perron as Chancellor, were you not?" she asked pointedly.

Jonas' emerald glare matched her own like flint on steel.

"This alliance is hardly ideal." Andariana continued lightly.

She lifted a trinket from her ornate desk and began to absently pass it through her fingers. Anything to provide distraction from her nephew's intrusive intensity.

"But just because you marry Eleina Perron doesn't mean you have to love her. Or even like her. You never have to be within a hundred leagues of the trollop, but you *will* have to marry her to uphold our end of the alliance."

Jonas ran a hand through his thick, chestnut hair. In her own youth, Andariana would have broken something of incalculable value or gulped down a bottle of Dalitian firebrandy to numb her frustration. She had been increasingly tempted to follow the latter plan in the past few months.

Whatever it took to feel something besides the entitled rage that gripped the both of them. She deeply disliked feeling this way, and her nephew was no different. Jonas was hardly one to sacrifice his freedom, even for political gain.

But she had made Bertrand Perron the Chancellor of Parliament based on Jonas' advice, both believing the noble to be strongly on their side. Thus far, that much had proven true and she was grateful for Jonas' guidance. The gods knew she needed her nephew's wits more than ever of late.

However, only days ago Perron had pushed a motion through Parliament that was so egregiously opposed to everything Jonas held sacred, it was hard to comprehend.

Andariana studied him for a moment, suddenly divining the source of his frustration. "This isn't about the betrothal, is it?"

Jonas scowled, "I did not champion Lord Perron to have my own agenda tossed aside. After his outburst this morning, the 'betrothal' is salt in an open wound."

Andariana dropped the trinket on the desk and placed her face in her hands. She allowed herself a deep breath. This had been brewing from the moment Perron had proclaimed his first official motion of censure, but only now did she understand the true source of Jonas' ire.

The gods be damned, was it *her* fault an Archanium Magus had been caught breaking the law? She allowed herself a sardonic smile at the thought. Of course it was. Because Jonas said so.

In truth, Andariana thought the matter was as preposterous as Jonas. A Magus, a girl in truth, had been caught using her magic to summon fire, to ward off the chill from the northern winds that ran ragged through Kalinor this late into Harvest.

But the use of the Archanium for anything that could be deigned a weapon had been outlawed since the war. Worse, the girl had been turned in by another Magus, one of Sammul's most promising acolytes.

The girl was being severely reprimanded for her actions, and there were even rumblings of imprisoning her. Fear was running rampant in the chambers of Parliament, and so Andariana had done the only thing that seemed sensible at the time.

She had turned the matter over to High Magus Sammul. Over to the man whose duty it was to train and instruct the Magi of Ilyar. She had thought him to be lenient on the matter, that he would protect his own, or at least handle the matter quietly and fairly within the confines of the Voralla.

She had been mistaken.

And that mistake had ignited Jonas' ire. Sammul had been in Parliament that very morning, pushing for the girl's imprisonment. Andariana was left wondering how long it would be before talk of banishment, even execution, began to circulate.

"I fail to see how this directly affects you, Jonas." she said finally, fighting the tone of desperation creeping into her voice. "*You* aren't a Magus. *You* haven't trained in the Voralla. Only a handful of people even *know* that you can touch the Archanium."

Jonas took an aggressive step forward, "It affects me greatly, Andariana. Who do you think has been bringing me the books I need to educate myself? Who do you think showed me how to access the Archanium in the first place?"

Andariana slumped back in her chair. This was much worse than she'd originally feared.

Jonas rested his knuckles on her desk and leaned forward, "Why do you think Sammul has been so venomous about the whole affair?"

The gods knew she'd been wondering the very same thing before her nephew had stormed into her chambers. "You think he's punishing Ilyana for helping you?"

"Sammul is afraid of me." Jonas insisted. "He doesn't have control over me, and that terrifies him."

"Sammul doesn't know that you can touch the Archanium."

Jonas snorted, "He can *feel* it. Just because we haven't officially told him doesn't mean he's ignorant. Worse, I think he can feel my talents getting stronger. That could only mean that I'm getting help from someone in the Voralla. He had to be enraged when he discovered who it was.

"And now he's capitalizing on the fear Parliament holds for us, of the Archanium, to get his revenge. When the chance presented itself, he pounced."

Andariana sighed as she considered his words, doing her best to ignore his eyes on her. She knew she looked worn, tired. Vulnerable.

"You can't let fear rule your realm for you." he growled softly. "Marra tried that, if you'll recall, and it led to civil war. A war that is now the very reason these laws *exist*. If she hadn't allowed that zealot into her court, the nobility would never have had cause to fear us. She caused this mess with that religious maniac and left you to mop it up."

"Jonas, it's out of my hands." Andariana said, half-pleading with her nephew. He understood how politics worked, damn it! She shouldn't have to defend herself to him like this.

"It's *not*, Andariana. And if you allow this to go unchecked, what next? I can't imagine Sammul keeping quiet about my talents, not if he ever gets public proof. Will they accuse *me* of something equally 'threatening'? If you're going to be a puppet like your sister, you might as well declare it publicly!"

Andariana shot to her feet, "You forget yourself!"

In the next moment she was in her chair once more, her head spinning. She had felt the air solidify around her, had felt the firm pressure push her back into the satin seat of her chair. He hadn't hurt her, but the point was made. Her heart fluttered in her chest as she looked up into his eyes.

"I think it's you who's forgetting." Jonas snapped.

When she acknowledged her understanding, Jonas released his hold over her. She allowed herself a tiny trickle of fear. She'd agreed to raise her sister's son as heir apparent to her own daughter, but she had never bargained for *this*. Not that she'd had much choice in the matter, but how Jonas had discovered such secrets and shadows was beyond her understanding.

Andariana put up the mask of a queen, one she had used in the decades since her coronation to move the conversation along without divulging how unsuited she felt for her station in life.

Jonas continued, calmer now. "If Sammul makes a move against me, *then* Andariana, I promise you it will *become* your problem. But then it will be too late for Ilyana. Possibly for all of us."

"It is already too late for Ilyana." a new voice intoned from the door.

Jonas turned and regarded Sammul. The man commanded more than three hundred Archanium Magi in the Voralla, but he most certainly did not command Jonas.

The Prince lifted a chestnut eyebrow, "We'll see, Sammul. Nothing has been decided. And while you are in command of an... investigation, you are not in control of the final verdict."

Andariana marveled at her nephew. She had asked Sammul to investigate, but at the time she had assumed that he would also pass judgment on the matter. Matters of the Voralla usually fell under the jurisdiction of the High Magus. But Sammul had taken the matter out of the Voralla, and in that moment he had made it a concern for the entire realm. *Her* realm.

Jonas had just effectively handed the decision back to her.

Her face remained impassive, but she couldn't help but feel a mild surge of irritation. For someone who claimed to have no desire to rule, her nephew could certainly be commanding when he saw fit.

Jonas glared at Sammul and then turned to his aunt, his face shifting into a smile. She felt like a mouse being stared down by a serpent. "I will leave you with the High Magus, Majesty. No doubt the two of you have many things of great import to discuss."

She returned his smile with equal sincerity and warmth, "*Thank you, Nephew.*"

He turned on his heel, nodded impassively at Sammul, and walked briskly from the room.

CHAPTER 5

DISCOVERIES

BY MIDDAY ALEKSEI started to notice the trees. At first there were thin shrubs that blended in with what he supposed must be the lower Sulaq Hills, but as midday became late afternoon, oaks and poplars began to dominate the landscape.

Aleksei frowned.

He thought he was in the Sulaq Hills, which wasn't unreasonable. The Sulaq Hills ran for almost two hundred leagues north to south. But the only forested area in the Hills was just outside the city of Keiv-Alon, and that was a six-day ride. A *long* six-day ride. With a shrug, Aleksei patted Dash's thick golden neck.

"Guess you're faster than I gave you credit for, old boy." he chuckled. It was an uneasy sound.

As he crested a hill, Aleksei gasped. Below him stretched a verdant river valley full of massive trees that reminded him painfully of the Seil Wood. And nestled amongst the trees, almost as though it was a patch of new growth, stood Keiv-Alon.

It was impossible.

Aleksei closed his eyes and wondered if this wasn't another dream. Would he wake to find himself still working his way through the southern Hills, only dreaming of the city? Yet his eyes opened onto the same scene as before, and he shook his head in wonder.

You're getting closer.

Aleksei jumped.

Can you feel it, Aleksei? Don't you realize what's happening?

Aleksei was suddenly very afraid.

There was something else going on, and he didn't understand what. The farther north he went the stranger things became, but until this moment he had just thought it was an illusion. He'd written it off as simple paranoia, and explained away the oddities as a series of unrelated events.

And there was the voice, putting the lie to all his hopes, his prayers.

The Legionnaires were but a stepping stone.

"What do you mean?" Aleksei demanded, growing angry.

A stepping stone? He'd nearly killed two men, yet the voice acted as though they were trivial and unimportant.

They are trivial and unimportant, Aleksei. You are the only one who's important right now. You are the only one who matters. If you had killed those Legionnaires, it would have made no difference. They are inconsequential.

"You're talking about people's lives!" Aleksei shouted.

Some lives are worth less than others.

Aleksei shook his head, refusing to listen anymore. Wanting the voice to go away. Would he not be there soon enough?

If you arrived in the next heartbeat, you would not be here soon enough.

Aleksei's shoulders slumped forward in defeat. He couldn't win. Was it not enough that he'd left his home, his *father*, to follow the whisperings of some disembodied voice in his head? Gods, there were madmen who had better reasons for action than this.

"I'll get there," Aleksei growled, knowing he still had no idea where 'there' was, "soon enough. But until then, can you not leave me in peace?"

Silence.

Aleksei breathed a sigh, glad that he had at least bought some respite. He urged Dash forward, descending into the valley and hoping against hope that he'd heard the last of the voice for a time. On his way down the rocky terrain, he prayed to every god he could think of that all of this...abnormality could be left behind as easily.

He reached the walls of the city just before nightfall. The guards gave him little more than a cursory glance as he passed through the gates. A simple peasant, not a threat. They returned to watching the approaching darkness.

Aleksei rode through the broad cobblestone streets of the city, trying not to gawk. He'd never seen a building with three stories before. The lights and smells and noises were all new to him. He did his best to keep his wits about him. Cutpurses and thieves lived in cities too, and he had to be watchful. He had little money as it was; he could hardly afford to lose it.

Aleksei finally found an inn that looked to be within his means and a feeling of apprehension stole over him.

The sign that hung above the doorway was faded, but it appeared there had once been a horse or a stag painted in white. Underneath were faded lines and curves in red, which Aleksei assumed had once been letters.

It would have to do.

He walked Dash around the side of the inn, searching for the stable. Instead he found a post where two mangy ponies were tied.

Aleksei winced.

"Sorry, boy. I guess this'll have to do for tonight."

Dash twitched his ears in what Aleksei supposed could only be irritation, but he allowed Aleksei to lead him to the post and secure his reins. Aleksei used the complex hunting knots his father had taught him, praying to the gods no one would come in the night and simply cut Dash loose. He did not relish losing his one source of transportation and companionship.

Once he was satisfied that Dash was secure, Aleksei made his way to the front of the inn and stepped into the common room.

The moment the door closed behind him, he wondered if it would not be safer to risk brigands on the road. The room was hot and stuffy, filled with the stink of sour mead and unwashed flesh packed too tightly together in such a small space. At the far end of the room stood a makeshift bar tended by an enormous man in a greasy apron, his one remaining hand scratching irritably at the coarse black beard that hung halfway down his thick chest.

Aleksei took a deep breath and immediately regretted it. He half-choked as he made his way past a sea of boisterous, drunken men. Several times he was nearly bowled over by a bustling servant girl, rushing between tables, enduring the pinches and leers of the patrons with careless smiles and murderous eyes.

When he finally reached the desk, the innkeeper looked at him as though he'd stepped in from another world. "Long way from home, aren't you, son?"

Aleksei affected an expression that he hoped would pass for nonchalance, "How much for a room?"

The innkeeper considered, turning his head to spit a glob of black saliva into a pot on the desk, "Piece of silver."

Aleksei fought to keep his face passive, "That's robbery! This place isn't worth more than five coppers at the *best*."

The man loomed over him, "The price ain't negotiable. It's a piece of silver or get out."

Aleksei was about to resign himself to it and pay the man when he felt that same disconcerting *shift* shudder through him.

"I'll give you ten coppers. More than anyone in their right mind would ever pay, and that includes dinner. Unless, of course, you'd like the Guard in here asking questions."

What did *that* mean? Aleksei wished he knew where those words, that confidence, came from.

Whatever it meant, understanding flared in the man's eyes. "Aye, ten coppers then."

Aleksei slapped the coin on the bar, deciding not to come any closer to the other man than he had to.

"Top of the stair, third door on your left."

Aleksei nodded and tried not to bolt up the stairs as fast as he could. He found the room and stepped quickly inside, turning to lock it tight.

There was no lock. Not only was there no lock, there was no

suggestion that there had ever *been* a lock.

He sat down on the straw mattress, fighting back tears of frustration.

Gods, why had he ever left his farm? If he'd simply ignored the voices he could be at home right now, sitting in front of the fire and enjoying a hot meal with his father.

Instead he was in a strange city, all alone in a tiny room that stank of sweat and vomit, wondering whether some thief would slip in during the night and slit his throat.

There was a knock at the door and Aleksei leapt to his feet, his hand instantly going to his side. To what? His heart sank with realization. To where his sword should be. Where his sword *belonged*.

He took a deep breath and opened the door, wondering just who would be waiting on the other side.

It was a servant girl.

"Dinner, sir." she said flatly.

Aleksei looked down and saw the earthen bowl of thick yellow stew she held in her hands. He took it gently from her and reached into his purse, pulling out a copper and handing it to her.

Her face lit up, "Thank you, sir."

He smiled, then looked down at the stew, "So what is this?"

She rolled her eyes and leaned forward conspiratorially, "Whatever the cook found in the gutter. This ain't the cleanest establishment around these parts."

He chuckled dryly, "I'm beginning to see that."

She cocked her head to one side, "You ain't from 'round 'ere?"

Aleksei shook his head, "I'm from down in the Southern Plain."

She nodded, "My mum's from down there. Pretty place, she says."

He smiled, "Yes, it is."

"So why come up here?"

"I've been asking myself that same question. I guess I just got the feeling I wasn't headed in the right direction."

She studied him slowly. "I like you." she said after a long pause, "I'd like to help you out."

He frowned, "What do you mean?"

Aleksei had to fight to keep from grimacing at her gap-toothed smile. "Bert, he's the one that runs the place, I think he's planning some mischief for you down there. Says he don't like your attitude."

Aleksei's eyes widened. The news wasn't all that surprising, but the logistics were a different matter. He still had Gus' sword in his pack, and he might be able to wave it around and scare off one man, maybe even two. But if the innkeeper was able to convince his patrons that there might be some profit in jumping a country boy on his own....

"Don't you fret, dear." the girl said with a harsh laugh. "Go down to the room at the end of the hall. Door's got a lock on it alright. No one's staying in this shithole anyhow. I'll tell 'em I saw you slipping out the back. They won't know the difference."

Aleksei thought a moment, then nodded. "Alright. I guess that'll have to work then. Thank you very much."

Her smile brightened, "Not often I get paid extra by a gentleman, sir."

And with that she was gone, vanishing down the stairs into the din below.

Aleksei looked at the now-cold bowl of stew in his hands. He walked inside and set it on the floor in disgust. The rats could have their fill of that, but after hearing what the girl had to say, he wasn't about to touch it.

He quickly gathered up his pack and stepped out of the room, closing the door behind him tightly. Aleksei hurried down the hall, half-fearing they were already on their way up the stairs.

The room at the end of the hall had a lock on it, though Aleksei couldn't tell how well it would hold. He had the feeling that if someone really wanted to get in, it wouldn't provide much warning. But at the very least it might wake him before they were on him, and that could be the difference between life and death.

Aleksei grimaced as despair washed over him. How had things changed so quickly? Two days ago his only concern had been pitching hay into the barn, and now he was hoping to survive the night?

He shook his head, trying to shed the overwhelming doubt and fear that gripped him. It would do him little good.

Instead he reached into his pack and drew out the Legionnaire blade. Again the same sense of comfort and peace stole over him...and this time Aleksei didn't fight it. That feeling had saved his life once already. It seemed silly to push it away at a moment like this.

Rather, he reveled in the solace, allowing his muscles to relax. He walked past the bed and crouched in the corner of the far wall, holding the sword at the ready before him. It was easily the most defensible position in the room. If they were to come at him, they would only be able to attack him from the front.

As soon as the thought entered his mind, he recoiled. How did he know that? Was it common sense? Patterns and forms began to take shape in his mind, and he tried to make sense of them. What did they mean? Were they important, or merely his exhaustion playing tricks on him?

Sometime during the night Aleksei fell asleep, his muscles locked into position, the sword still held ready in his hands. But no mob came to his door.

He dreamed again.

Again he stood in the vast expanse of golden mist, but this time a figure stood before him. A man. He bowed slightly to Aleksei, and Aleksei realized that he could see *through* the man.

"It's easier for me to reach you now. You're closer." the man said pleasantly.

Aleksei shuddered. Would he ever get used to having someone else read his thoughts?

"Is this going to be another speech about what you need? If it is, I really should be getting some rest. I'm on my way. Isn't that enough?"

The man suddenly looked concerned, "Do you hate me, Aleksei?"

Aleksei frowned. Hate him? The man wanted to know if Aleksei *hated* him? Why should he care?

"Because if you do," the man said softly, "it will have serious consequences."

Consequences? Aleksei ran a hand through his short blond hair, wishing he could ask the man questions.

"Actually, that's why I called you here tonight. I realize that you have been told painfully little. The fact of the matter is, some of what

I've kept from you has simply been because I don't know myself."

"What do you mean?" Aleksei paused a moment as the words came out, surprised to hear his own voice reverberate across the dreamscape.

"There are certain things," the man said finally, "that have become clear to me. Things that I know are important. Like you. I know that you are important, but I don't know why. What *is* clear is that I will know the answer by the time you reach me."

"And where are you?" Aleksei asked.

The man sighed.

Aleksei thought he actually looked upset by the question. "I still can't tell you. I only hope that the reason will become clear as you make your way here. But you *will* find your way here. However, there are some things that must happen first, things you haven't faced yet that must come to pass before you reach me."

"Such as?" Aleksei didn't know how much the man knew, but some things were still very definitely being kept from him.

"Even if I knew, I couldn't tell you. You must react to everything through instinct, and if you knew what to expect, you might hesitate. Please believe me when I say that neither of us can afford that."

Aleksei nodded. He thought he was beginning to make some sense of it all. Yet in the last few days he had come to realize just how little of the world he truly understood.

"I have also come to you tonight," the man continued, "because I will not be able to visit you again until you reach me. Circumstances are...changing here. I am being watched, and even using my talents to reach out to you is treated with intense suspicion."

Aleksei sighed. There was still so much that he didn't understand, and yet he realized he felt a swell of sympathy for the man. It was beginning to sound like he was just as much a pawn in all this as Aleksei himself.

"Fate." Aleksei muttered.

The man chuckled, "Ah yes, Fate. The truth, Aleksei, is that Fate has only as much power as we allow it. No invisible hand will swoop down to carry you here and no force will magically move to stand in your way. The decision is yours. It will always be yours. Fate is merely a tool that others use to justify their wants and needs.

"I believe that you will be of great use here, and so I used Fate to that end. But you're in Keiv-Alon because *you* climbed on your horse and rode there; not because Fate pushed you."

Aleksei opened his mouth to protest, but suddenly realized the man was right. No one had actually forced him to do anything. They had suggested and goaded certainly, but in the end it had been his decision, his own decisive action that led him to where he was. He couldn't blame anyone but himself for his decisions.

"All I can ask, Aleksei, is that for the moment you believe in my intentions. I have faith in what I'm telling you, and I believe you'll find something here that you've never dreamed of. I just ask that you see what I have to offer you."

Aleksei nodded after a long moment of consideration. "I can accept that."

The man smiled and Aleksei realized that it was the first time he'd seen him do that. It was a strikingly pleasant look.

"I know I'm asking so much from you, Aleksei. Should you choose to find me, I will ask even more. But I would not if I didn't believe that you're the only one who can help me."

Aleksei managed a nod. His mind was reeling with the things the man had said, and he found that he had no words of his own.

The man sighed, "And now I must go. As must you. Wake up, Aleksei. Dawn is here."

Aleksei gasped and opened his eyes.

He breathed a sigh of relief. The room was just as he'd left it. He wondered what would have happened to him if they'd broken in while he was in the dream. Would he have waked?

Hurrying to his feet, Aleksei grabbed his pack from the bed and started for the door.

He froze.

What if Bert was waiting for him at the bottom of the stairs? Aleksei didn't relish the idea of having to deal with the man.

His eyes darted to the small window cut into the eastern wall. He pulled back the moth-eaten cheesecloth stretched across as a makeshift screen and peered down at the ground. It wasn't that far a drop, and Aleksei was relieved to see Dash still tied to the post where he'd left him.

It seemed fortune was on his side for the moment.

Aleksei put his sword back in the pack and gently dropped it from the window. A moment later he followed, being careful to brace his landing. It hurt considerably less than he'd anticipated.

Dash whinnied softly and rolled his great brown eyes when Aleksei approached. He couldn't help but grin at the horse's excitement to see him. He untied the knots and led his horse from the inn.

It wasn't until he was several blocks away that he allowed himself to breathe easier.

Aleksei followed the main street past the hawkers and apple carts that lined the central walkway. He craned his neck every now and then, attempting to see past the line of wagons and horses. He wasn't exactly sure what part of the city he'd ended up in, but if he could gain his bearings he might be able to find the north gate.

As he moved through the street, Aleksei became inexplicably aware that he was being followed. He had no indication of who was behind him or what their intentions were, only that they were there.

His mind raced as he moved through the crowds. In his current state of paranoia, it was difficult for Aleksei to believe that this new follower meant him anything but harm.

Best to deal with it out of sight.

That last thought struck him as strange. Deal with it? How? He groaned inwardly as he felt the strange *shift* from deep within.

An image of Jack and Gus formed in his mind, one man lying on the ground, clutching his broken, bleeding nose, the other gasping for breath as Aleksei's boot pressed harder against his throat.

No! Aleksei snarled in his mind. *I will* not *do that again.*

But even as he thought the words, he found himself leading Dash towards an empty alley. The shapes and patterns from the night before readily snapped back into his mind, showing him the quickest motions needed to draw his sword from the pack, how to position his feet before his pursuer was on him.

Aleksei entered the alley and walked until he was a good twenty paces from the main street. Hopefully no one would pay any attention to what happened here.

A cloaked form turned into the alley and Aleksei slipped his hand inside the pack, gripping the leather handle of his sword tightly. His pursuer drew closer and Aleksei caught a glint of steel under the black cloak. A dagger. He frowned at that. He'd only seen a flash of the sun on metal. He wasn't even sure it was a blade.

But instinctively, he *knew* it was, even as his hand eased away from the sword. He couldn't explain it, but he knew that he had to trust his instincts. They had saved him before, and he could only pray they would save him now.

"Don't want no trouble with you, boy. Just hand over your coin and be on your way."

Aleksei could think of nothing to say, so he remained silent.

Watching. Waiting.

The man stepped closer and his left hand slipped from the confines of the cloak, revealing a long, curved dagger. "You don't want to make me use this, do you?"

"You can walk away. You still have that option." Aleksei said coolly.

He had become weary of people trying to take what was rightfully and honestly his. Did everyone in this gods-forsaken world want something for nothing? Hadn't any of these people ever heard of hard work?

The man continued to advance.

Obviously not.

Aleksei waited until the man was a bare pace away before he moved.

His hand darted out and caught the man's wrist, twisting it back, hard. The man cried out as the bone popped out of socket. The dagger fell from his fingers.

"Return to the street, sir. Please." Aleksei knew that he was not pleading with the man, merely offering advice.

The thief snarled and launched himself at Aleksei. Aleksei waited this time until his attacker was mere inches from him before he clutched the man's left arm, twisting it around and using the man's momentum to his advantage. The man's snarl became a gasp as he hurled past Aleksei and landed hard on the rough cobbles of the alley.

"*You!*" came a shout from behind Aleksei. He turned to see three

Legionnaires rushing towards him. "Stop right there!"

His confidence evaporated and Aleksei vaulted onto Dash, fear suppressing his natural self-disgust as he dug his heels into the horse's flanks. Dash leapt forward, over the thief and out into the street. Aleksei's heart thumped painfully in his chest as he steered Dash forward. He didn't know where he was headed, but he had to get away from the Legionnaires.

As he rode, cutting through side streets and narrow alleyways, checking over his shoulder every now and again. Nothing so far.... He passed through a small residential community, dodging children and wash lines. Although he was fairly sure that the Legionnaires were somewhere far behind him, he didn't doubt that they would sound the alarm.

Yet when Aleksei finally found his way back to the main road, he felt strangely calm once again. As he rode towards what he finally realized was the north gate, Aleksei understood the return of his collected confidence.

Even if the Legionnaires had sounded an alarm, they would be looking for a man in a hurry. A man running away from something. And as long as one of those three original men didn't see him, there would be no way to tell him from anyone else making their way through the city. He doubted that in a city of this size too much effort would be wasted on any crime short of major theft or murder, and he was guilty of neither.

At least, not yet. he thought bleakly.

A few minutes later, he made his way through the gate and back out onto the road. The walled prominence of Keiv-Alon vanished behind him.

Chapter 6

Blood that Binds

"Gods," Jonas muttered, rubbing his temples, "what am I *doing*?"

The prince sank back in his chair, breathing heavily. He was exhausted, yet the feelings of shame and foolishness far outweighed his petty physical needs.

Had he told Aleksei the truth even *once* or was he just making it all up?

It was easy to be cryptic and mysterious, yet he was feeding the man a load of prognostications that were absolutely baseless. Were it not for the dreams and the voice, there was little reason for Aleksei to give his words any more credence than a beggar on the street.

Jonas felt fortunate that his petty tricks were enough to impress the farm boy. He felt more fortunate still to have been allowed windows where he could observe Aleksei's actions and thoughts through the Archanium, though they were difficult to glimpse.

Especially with *another* watching at the same time.

But trying to explain the meaning of it all as though Jonas understood what was happening was taking its toll. He was beginning to feel responsible for the poor man, blindly making his way through the realm with only dreams and voices to guide him.

And not all that well.

Jonas stifled a yawn. It was so inconvenient to be human. He was hardly one of the most adept Archanium users in Ilyar, and such exercises were especially draining for him. The Archanium touched every living thing, but the closer an object was, the easier it was to control or manipulate.

And Aleksei was by no means close.

The connection they shared was heavily taxed by the distance between them, to say nothing of the inconsistencies in Jonas' training.

Jonas had only a general idea of what he was doing. When he needed to do something specific, he researched and experimented until he made it work.

Dreamspeak was one of the simpler tricks he'd tried successfully, but that was a far cry from casting an image of himself in the dream. That most recent experiment had nearly taxed him beyond capacity.

Truthfully, Jonas wasn't sure if even Sammul could project himself into a dream all the way to the Southern Plain. Keiv-Alon had been hard enough, and even then he had not been solid. The ancient masters could not only project themselves, they could control their environments with precision, heal or destroy minds across vast distances with apparent ease.

It might have been simpler to ride down in person, to speak with Aleksei face to face. But then again, there was another player to deal with. And as Jonas knew next to nothing about the other Magus' ability, it would hardly be wise to risk any sort of confrontation. Besides, Aya had warned often enough against being too heavy-handed.

No, it made far more sense for Aleksei to come to him.

As dangerous as it was to attempt this, Jonas firmly believed that the eventual gain would outweigh the risks.

At any rate, he was being monitored. Someone, and he had mounting suspicions, was watching him, sensing the way he used the Archanium. Though if it was Sammul or the other player, Jonas was still unsure. Sammul could make all the accusations he wanted, but he'd have to convince others first, and Jonas could handle whatever political games the High Magus wanted to play.

But when word of his abilities finally escaped, he knew he'd be met with considerable resentment among the Archanium Magi. That was the one game Sammul would win handily.

Sammul's flock were innately distrustful of any Magus not trained in the Voralla. Jonas hadn't been trained by anyone, and that would leave a lot of questions unanswered for his enemies.

He wondered how enraged Sammul would be at the idea of an untrained Magus trying to bond a man tied to an unknown Primary prophecy. Especially a Magus he did not control.

Sammul was already bristling at the uncertainty Jonas presented.

Unfortunately, it was an uncertainty that Jonas shared. There were moments when he reached for the Archanium and fell flat, and yet others still where he managed feats beyond any Magus in the Voralla.

He had been enormously lucky thus far, but Jonas was well aware that such luck was no substitute for a solid theoretical and practical foundation. But whatever his personal failings, to Sammul, Jonas was an enigma. His abilities were likely the subject of much speculation, and Jonas intended to keep it that way, whether such illusions were grounded or not.

A soft knock at the door shook him from his thoughts. Gods, who would be wanting him at this hour?

"Come." he called wearily.

The door opened and a tall, thin man stepped in. His gaunt face was wrapped in uncertainty; his wiry red hair oily and disheveled. He looked as exhausted as Jonas felt.

"Hade." Jonas said, rising from his chair.

Hade managed a weak smile, "Evening, Jonas. How...how are you faring?"

Jonas returned the smile, hoping it masked his own weariness. "Well enough. What can I do for you?"

Hade was one of the few Archanium Magi aware of Jonas' abilities, yet he was far from distrustful. If anything, Jonas thought Hade placed too *much* faith in him.

Jonas had always liked the young Magus, though he could be overanxious and timid in the face of authority. The gods may have given Hade the ability to touch the Archanium, but they had certainly never seen fit to hand him bravery in the same turn.

The Magus sat on the edge of a tufted ottoman across from Jonas. "It's about Ilyana."

That explained the exhaustion and the worried lines creasing the man's face. Hade was in love with Ilyana; that was no secret. But this level of concern was uncharacteristic of the man.

Brave or no, Jonas knew him to be a good deal more confident than *this*.

"What do you mean?" Jonas asked, leaning forward.

"They...they won't let me see her." Hade said, looking down at the floor. "I haven't seen her since they caught her...well you know. No one is allowed past the guards."

Jonas pushed his exhaustion to the back of his mind and stood, "Then why don't we go pay her a visit? I hadn't realized she was being shut away from society for her 'crime'. She's probably starved for company."

Hade frowned, "But they're not letting anyone in! I just said—"

Jonas fixed Hade in his green-eyed gaze, "Somehow, I think they'll make an exception for us."

Hade licked his lips nervously and nodded, following Jonas from the room. Jonas sighed. It had taken him a while, but he now realized what it was that was worrying Hade.

Ilyana had technically broken a law, but she had done nothing that every other Magus in Ilyar was not also capable of.

Her harmless use of the Archanium, and the actions being taken against her, brought many frightening questions to the fore, especially for the other Magi. Where was the line Ilyana had crossed? How would they know if they too crossed that line? Would it be when they were summoned before a court and convicted?

A ring of guards stood around the door to Ilyana's chambers, barring anyone from entering or exiting. Armed guards for a girl who'd dared summon fire. The very idea fueled the fears growing in Jonas' heart.

When the guards saw them approach they stiffened, holding their pikes straight and shields high.

Jonas strode casually up to the commanding officer, "Excuse me, Sergeant. I'd like to speak with the Magus Ilyana."

The sergeant looked uncertain, "Our orders are to allow no one entry, Highness."

Jonas' eyes narrowed, "And who issued those orders, Sergeant?"

"The High Magus Sammul, Highness."

"Sammul commands the Voralla. Since when does his authority outweigh mine in the *Palace*, Sergeant?"

The sergeant swallowed, glancing around the hall nervously, "Begging your pardon, Highness."

Jonas nodded, his eyes hard, "I'll forgive it this time. Now, no one else is to be allowed in besides us. Not even Sammul. Do I make myself clear?"

The sergeant saluted, "Yes, Highness."

The guards hurried out of his way as Jonas walked past the man, Hade close behind him.

Ilyana's 'cell' was actually one of the nicer apartments in the lower east wing of Kalinor Palace. It was lavishly decorated in salmon pink and sky blue velvet, the walls painted with elaborate seascapes. Two great gilded windows looked out onto the East Lawn.

And the Voralla.

Jonas thought it cruel.

The infamous Ilyana was sitting on a divan before the window, fine golden hair hanging about her shoulders in myriad thin braids. At the moment, her watery blue eyes were lit with both hope and despair, the emotions warring for dominance of her innocent features.

Jonas smiled as the door closed behind him, "Good evening, Ilyana. I hope we're not disturbing you."

Her face lit up, "Hade! Jonas! Gods no, not at all, I assure you. I've been so lonely. It's been *horrible*. Right now a friendly face is more than welcome. What have you heard?"

He smiled at her desperate torrent of words, and at her question. Sentimental and fragile she may be, but Ilyana certainly possessed a pragmatic streak that exhibited itself from time to time.

"They mean to make an example of you." he said softly. "To warn the others from acting foolishly."

She opened her mouth to speak, but he forestalled her with a hand, "Ilyana, I'm not condoning their thoughts or their actions. I'm just stating fact. As for what we do next, well, that's another matter entirely."

"You've spoken with the Queen?" she asked hopefully.

Jonas nodded, "I have, and she agrees with me. But getting Parliament to see eye to eye with us might be a little more difficult."

Her face paled, "*How* difficult?"

Jonas took a deep breath. "Ilyana, what you have to understand about Parliament is that they're not actually angry at *you*. You're merely the whipping boy. They're pouring their fear and loathing, all the things they resent about us, all of the things that make them uncertain, into this whole farce. If not you, it would have been Hade, or Aya, or anyone who happened to be in the wrong place at the wrong time.

"Parliament has no idea what we're capable of. They fear what they don't understand, and they've never understood *us*.

"They think that if they can frighten the other Magi sufficiently with a fate similar to yours, then maybe they can rest a little easier at night, knowing that we aren't going to rise up and seize the realm."

Ilyana gasped, "How could they think that? Jonas, how can they *possibly* believe that any of us could be like that? Our magic doesn't even work that way. I just don't understand what they're afraid of!"

Tears of frustration poured down her cheeks. Hade hurried to her side, and she buried her face in his shoulder.

"Ilyana, these men didn't walk around the Voralla and see the gardens and the courtyards where you meditate, and decide you were a threat. They're acting based on the simple fact that you have power, no matter its intended purpose. You have power they do not control, and that makes you dangerous."

"And what about *you*?" she asked softly.

He frowned, "How do you mean?"

"You said that they thought *I* was dangerous. But you didn't include yourself. Why not?"

Jonas winced, wishing he'd been thinking clearer. He needed sleep more than he'd thought.

"Even if Sammul has told them that I can use the Archanium, I'm the Prince of Ilyar, and I've received no formal training, in accordance with constitutional law. Therefore, I can't possibly be a threat to them because I am both part of the social machine they believe they control, *and* because I haven't been trained the way you and Hade and the others have."

"But—"

"What you know," Jonas said quietly, his voice dangerous, "you know because of your abilities. Because of your connection to the Archanium. They have no such ability, and so they have no reason to think of me as anything more than a prince who is neither next in line for succession, nor necessarily that powerful.

"Even if I can touch the Archanium, members of the royal family are expressly forbidden from enrolling in the Voralla. And I'm hardly the first to fit that description, as you well know."

Ilyana swallowed hard and nodded.

Jonas glanced around the room, his frown deepening. "Ilyana, where is Marrik?"

She started to answer, but couldn't speak past the sobs that assailed her once again.

Marrik was Ilyana's Knight. Every Magus in the Voralla had a Knight. Bound together by the magic of the Archanium to work as a team, the Knights ensured that nothing physical harmed the Magi while they conjured their spells.

But if Ilyana was imprisoned here in the apartments, it was only because of her status as one of the elite. Magi were afforded such deference. Archanium Knights were another matter.

Jonas didn't say a word. Instead he came to his feet and walked back to the door. The guards outside were still alert and cautious. He pulled one from the neat arc they'd formed.

"Highness?" the young man asked uncertainly.

"Go to the dungeon and fetch the Archanium Knight Marrik. Bring him here. If anyone questions you, you are acting under my orders. Is that clear?"

The guard nodded, his eyes wide.

Jonas turned his glare to the sergeant, silently daring the man to contradict him. The sergeant nodded solemnly, "As you command, Highness."

Jonas stepped back into Ilyana's rooms. "They're bringing Marrik now."

Her face regained some of its former brilliance, "*Thank* you, Jonas."

Jonas nodded absently, lost in his own thoughts. Why hadn't he seen it sooner? It seemed so obvious now.

If every Magus was feared because they controlled magic that the Lords of Parliament neither commanded nor understood, then they were doubly feared because each Magus was bound to a Knight.

There were over three hundred Magi in the Voralla, and therefore over three hundred Knights, each part of an efficient military unit, trained to work as a team.

The Magi of the Voralla might have very few destructive abilities, but swords were swords. And Archanium Knights were no mere foot soldiers. After all, the bond between Knight and Magus worked both ways.

Did the nobles fear the Knights more than the Magi? Andariana had a small, but highly trained army literally camped on her lawn. It mattered little how many soldiers each lord contributed to the Legion, if the lords themselves were surrounded day and night by three hundred Archanium Magi and their Knights.

"Idiots." he muttered.

Ilyana frowned and started to say something when the door opened and a man stumbled into the room.

His face was haggard, rough with a week's growth of beard. His eyes were sallow and tired, but there was a fire that still burned within them, that seemed all the brighter for it.

"Marrik!" she gasped, leaping from her seat next to Hade.

The Knight embraced her, wincing when she squeezed too tight.

Jonas glanced at Hade and wasn't surprised to see traces of an age-old jealousy. Magi and their Knights held certain affections for one another, and that closeness was unavoidable.

Outsiders who fell in love with Magi were often unable to maintain any real romantic relationship. It simply wasn't reasonable when someone was so intimately bound to another. The emotional requirements were too high, the price unimaginable.

Instead, it was far more common that Magi and their Knights formed an intense and interpersonal emotional bond.

While they weren't always romantic in nature, the bond

inevitably formed the primary relationship in both their lives.

After all, when the life of one depended solely upon the life of the other, it was difficult to care about people beyond the bond with the same level of ferocity. Loving your Bonded was not too far from loving yourself.

Hade might love Ilyana, but nothing would ever come of it.

Yet as Aleksei comes north, I'm sharing his bond with another Magus. A Magus I know nothing about, except that he lusts after the same thing I do. Jonas couldn't help but sympathize with Hade in his murk of jealousy.

Jonas stood to the side, watching Ilyana and Marrik. He suddenly recalled yet another reason Parliament had no need to fear him. He had no Knight. He was untrained, and lacking an Archanium Knight.

And for the first time since he'd reached out to Aleksei, Jonas realized what else had been nagging at him.

A growing sense of desperation.

Aleksei stood at the fork of the mighty Ylik Water, a frown etched across his face. Several leagues in the distance he could make out the shadowed prominence of the Seil Wood, its trees towering into the sky, some scraping at the clouds.

He had left Keiv-Alon but three hours ago.

By all rights, Aleksei ought to have another seven, perhaps eight days of travel before he reached the Wood. But at this distance, he guessed he would reach it by dusk.

Something very strange was going on, and he wished to the gods he knew what it was.

Aleksei pressed his knees into Dash's sides and rode apprehensively towards the Wood. True, it had once been his home. He had lived in the trees with his parents, and had been content. But that had also been a long, long time ago. Would he be welcome among the Ri-Vhan? Would they remember him? Would they care?

There was only one way to find out.

The sun was setting by the time he reached the tree-line, but Aleksei didn't fear the darkness.

Though he remembered little of his time amongst the Ri-Vhan, some things still leapt unbidden into his consciousness. And so he spent the last few moments of dusk searching along the banks of the river for the lembak trees, and more importantly for the mushrooms that grew in the hollows of their roots.

Just as the light was fading from the canopy above, Aleksei caught sight of the circular lembak leaves.

He looped Dash's reins around a low branch and crouched near the bank of the river, reaching down into the space between the thick, rope-like roots of the tree, rising a moment later, his prize clutched triumphantly in his fist.

After a few sure strokes of his belt knife, Aleksei paused to admire his torch. The fungus began to glow a brilliant blue, casting a circle of light around him. Aleksei smiled.

The darkness was still too heavy to ride under, so he walked Dash deeper into the Wood, keeping a careful eye on the unkempt path for badger holes and stones.

Few people dared tread this deep into the Wood, and with good reason. The Seil Wood was a magical place, and nowhere was that magic more concentrated than in the heart of the forest. Many of the paths in the deep Wood could only be navigated by the Ri-Vhan. He hoped his half-blood would be enough.

It was painstakingly slow progress, but Aleksei was determined. It was, after all, extremely inadvisable to camp on the forest floor this deep. Fey creatures lived in this part of the Wood, and while they wouldn't necessarily harm him, he wasn't sure they'd leave him unmolested either.

He didn't worry for Dash. Animals were generally left alone. Men were another matter.

His heart fluttered with relief when he finally spotted the stunted old willow.

It was one of the few willows that grew in the Wood, existing in a small pool of moonlight, where a break in the canopy made its survival possible.

But if that memory served Aleksei correctly, the survival of this particular tree was no accident of nature.

He circled the tree, his brilliant torch cast aside now that he could see in the clear white moonlight. He knew it was somewhere, but his memories were so hazy. He had been so young....

There. Aleksei stepped confidently to a branch that curved curiously away from the trunk of the tree, almost level with his waist. In the moonlight, the branch looked almost like the mouth of a horn.

It *had* to be the same tree.

Aleksei knelt next to the branch and pressed his lips against the hollowed end, blowing as hard as he could through the branch and into the tree.

Gods, he hoped this worked.

"Are you trying to wake the whole bloody *village?*" a gruff voice demanded from behind him.

Aleksei jumped to his feet so suddenly, he struck his head on one of the willow's upper branches and nearly fell to the forest floor.

He took a moment to regain his footing, then looked at the speaker who had startled him.

"I was trying to call the Ri-Vhan."

The tall blond man nodded, "Aye, and you've succeeded. Who are you? And how do you know how to use the Hunter's Horn? Or to carry one of *those?*" he indicated the phosphorescent fungus lying just outside the pool of moonlight.

"My name is Aleksei Drago. I used to live among the Ri-Vhan."

"I remember the name." the man said slowly. "So why are you here now?"

"I'm looking for Roux Devaan." Aleksei said, trying to sound confident.

It had been almost a decade since he'd thought of his cousin. Too many painful memories, too many memories of his mother.

The man frowned for a long moment, as if trying to recall something, then nodded. "Aye, I can take you to him."

Aleksei's pulse thrilled, "You can? Thank the gods! I didn't know if...."

The man chuckled, "If what? If you'd be remembered? The Ri-Vhan have long memories, Aleksei Drago, especially for our own."

Aleksei smiled . "It would appear so."

The man offered his hand, "I'm called Gaël. It's a pleasure to welcome back one of our lost."

Aleksei's smile didn't change, but he wondered at the term.

"Thank you." he said instead.

"Your horse will be fine down here on the floor for the time being. In the morning I'll come down and check on him, free him of that saddle for a while."

Aleksei relaxed a little bit, "I'd appreciate that, thank you."

"No thanks needed. You're Roux's cousin, lest I'm mistaken."

Aleksei frowned, "I am."

Gaël shrugged, "That's good enough for me."

Aleksei thought about that for a moment before finally deciding that the man must be friends with Roux. Why else would he so willingly offer aid to a complete stranger?

"Anyhow, if you'll take hold of my hand we can return to the village."

Aleksei shuddered. He'd forgotten.

He clutched Gaël's hand and closed his eyes as the world gave a sickening lurch around him. He felt like he was swimming in honey, and he knew that if he opened his eyes he would see nothing but smoky gray and white forms, moving far too fast to make out with any accuracy, yet unquestionably disconcerting.

And then everything snapped back into place and Aleksei opened his eyes.

He stood on one of the great central platforms, the heavy wooden beams under his feet supported by thousands of years of ancient vine and interwoven branch. And beneath that, the incredible drop to the forest floor far, far below.

He had returned to the Ri-Vhan.

Gaël was watching him curiously, "Darting not sit well with you?"

"Pardon?"

Gaël shrugged, "You seemed to have a hard time Darting up here."

Aleksei closed his eyes as he remembered.

His mother was gone. It had been so sudden, so unexpected, yet no one was truly surprised. He didn't understand. And then his father had gathered him up in his arms and carried him out of their small home, out onto the great platform.

A man, Aleksei's uncle, had placed a hand on his shoulder and then everything changed. The world moved around him as Aleksei and his father were taken down to the forest floor. Taken down for the last time.

"I don't have too many fond memories of it." Aleksei said after a long pause.

Gaël laughed ruefully, "Not many do. No, sir. Mostly just the young."

Aleksei nodded mechanically and Gaël seemed to catch his apprehension. "Well, anyhow, I need to be taking you to Roux's place."

Aleksei allowed himself to be led through the sleeping village proper, his eyes drinking in the familiar landscape, his ears reveling in the once-loved sounds of the night.

He could hear the forest breathing. It was in the sigh of the cicadas and the hooting of the great horned owls, the wind cresting and crashing above him, as though he was under an ocean of leaves.

Aleksei walked down familiar lanes, past identical huts, each constructed in the same organic style, heavy vines growing up and around their supports until the circular walls took shape, the roofs thatched in river reeds and long-stemmed fern. They looked so alien after his fifteen years in the farmhouse, yet he remembered when he'd been comfortable here.

As they passed the huts, Aleksei realized that they were approaching the only home in the entire village that could be called a house. It was grown out of the front of one of the giant oaks that towered so unnaturally high, great branches leafing out to form the roof of the house before the trunk ascended higher still and dissolved into the confusion of the canopy. The walls were branches fused together by hundreds of thousands of tiny flowering creeper vines, the door woven from reeds and dead wood. It was the home of the leader of the Ri-Vhan.

The House of the Ri-Hnon.

The reed door opened to reveal a man, only a few summers older than Aleksei. His face was vibrant and alive, his golden eyes wild and excited. His hair was a mess of tangles and curls that reflected so much of the forest undergrowth.

Gaël bowed low, "Ri-Hnon, this man has asked to see you."

Aleksei was speechless. He could only stare at the man before him in wide-eyed wonder. Stare at the leader of his people.

At this fey, feral child of the Wood.

When he finally managed to find words, they seemed hopelessly inadequate. "Hello, Roux."

CHAPTER 7

MARKED

ALEKSEI BREATHED A heavy sigh of relief when his cousin broke into a grin and stepped forward, hugging him tightly. "*Gods*, but it's been a long time!"

Aleksei managed a nod, hardly able to draw a breath, wrapped as he was in Roux's oaken embrace, "Fifteen years, if I'm not mistaken."

Roux stepped back and shook his head in wonder, "And yet *look* at you! You were a boy when you left, barely more than a babe in your father's arms and *now*...."

Aleksei grinned at that. It was all well and good for Roux to call him a boy, but Aleksei didn't remember his cousin as being very many summers his senior.

"I was wondering if I could stay with you for a night or two." Aleksei said, now somewhat hesitant.

Roux's smile brightened, "I was going to insist on it. But if you're a willing victim then you are welcome to remain as long as you like. Whatever claims of ownership those plains dwellers might have, *we* are your people and *I* am your kin."

Aleksei relaxed, "I was hoping you'd say something like that. I haven't had an easy time getting this far."

Roux's face darkened, "What do you mean?"

Aleksei glanced back at Gaël, who was waiting stiffly a few paces behind him. "Maybe we should go inside and let this goodman get back to his bed?"

"So we should. Gaël, thank you for bringing my cousin to me, but I'd hate to draw your wife's ire by keeping you any longer."

Gaël visibly relaxed, "Many thanks, Ri-Hnon."

Roux chuckled as he ushered Aleksei inside.

"So," Aleksei said as the woven door was latched behind him, "the Ri-*Hnon*? How did you stumble into *that* misfortune?"

Roux laughed harshly and stepped into a warm, circular room with a fireplace burning merrily in the center. "Well, for whatever reason the Wood saw fit, I received the Calling when Hughel vanished three seasons ago."

Aleksei shook his head in wonder. The Calling was what denoted the leader of the Ri-Vhan. It was one of the most treasured blessings the Wood could bestow.

The Ri-Hnon listened to the Wood and the creatures within, interpreting their pleas and messages so as to better lead their people. There seemed to be no rhyme or reason to the succession, either. Roux was of no blood relation to Hughel, nor did any of the previous Ri-Hnon have any obvious connection. The Wood simply Called the one best fit for the job.

"I can't say I'm surprised." Aleksei said finally, "It suits you well."

Roux nodded absently, "I'm still not used to this, though." He indicated the soft gold of his eyes, the mark of the Wood's benediction.

Aleksei tried to imagine what he would have done if his eyes suddenly shifted into another color and the wind in the trees began speaking into his mind. He suppressed a shudder as he realized that something not too far from that had happened to him of late.

"So how did you manage to wander so far from home?" Roux asked, golden eyes twinkling.

Aleksei shrugged, not wanting to bring up the voice or the dreams at the moment. "I just felt like I wasn't all that needed on the farm and thought I might travel north again. Maybe see some part of Ilyar that wasn't so cultivated."

Roux laughed, knowing his cousin wasn't telling him everything, but willing humor him for the moment. "Then you've certainly come to the right place." Roux picked the kettle off the coals and poured Aleksei a cup of strong tea. "You said you didn't have an easy time getting here. How do you mean?"

Aleksei winced. Rather than answer, he took a sip of tea. It burned his tongue, but bought him time. Gods, but this would require him to tell Roux several things he would rather just forget.

"Roux," he said after a long moment, "I'm not sure what's happening to me. The day I left the farm, I ran into two Legionnaires. They came into my camp and wanted to take my horse."

Roux's eyes widened, "But clearly they failed."

Aleksei nodded, then reached into his pack and withdrew the Legionnaire sword, "I took this from one of them. I don't know how I did it."

"There were two of them, Roux. They *both* had swords. And one minute they were coming at me, and the next one of them was on the ground and the other..." Aleksei grimaced at the memory, "the other I had pinned against a tree."

Roux frowned. "How was this possible?"

"That's not all. I left the Southern Plain three *days* ago."

Roux started to say something, but Aleksei held up his hand, "I know what you're going to say. I'm not mad, Roux. I'm *not*! I don't know why I'm here and not halfway to Keiv-Alon right now, or how I could have left there this morning and stand before you now. It doesn't make any *sense*."

"Roux?" a voice came from the doorway, and Aleksei turned to see a man in his middle years standing there, his face a combination of familiar and alien features.

"Father," Roux said with a smile, "we have an unexpected guest."

Roux's father walked into the room, his eyes focusing on Aleksei's face. "But..." he managed, "*surely* not. A...Aleksei?" He said the word as though his mouth had difficulty remembering its pronunciation.

"Good evening, Uncle Theo."

"Good evening *indeed*, Nephew. What brings you all this way north? Surely your father didn't send you away willingly."

Aleksei had to chuckle at that, "He wanted me to see the world,

Uncle. He said I wasn't really needed on the farm, and that I should go to seek my fortune in the North."

"Ha," Theo laughed, "so you came *here*? I regret to inform you, Nephew, that there is very little 'fortune' among the Ri-Vhan. You'd have better luck in Kalinor."

Aleksei started.

Kalinor.

The word just sounded inexplicably right to him, and Aleksei grew suddenly afraid. If the dream man was in Kalinor, then he had somehow managed to end up right on its doorstep. How was that possible? How had he wandered north with no more idea of where to go than a cryptic whisper in his head and ended up mere leagues from his destination?

It was too close to coincidence for his liking.

"I'm not sure I'd know what to do in Kalinor, Uncle. I'm afraid it might swallow me whole." Aleksei managed.

Theo laughed, "Too true, Aleksei. I'm not sure that farm boys should be allowed in such big cities, not at your age. Too many temptations."

Aleksei nodded, but his heart was thumping in anticipation and fear. He had a destination. He now knew where he was headed for the first time since this maddening debacle began. The only challenge remaining was to find the dream man in the largest city in Ilyar.

Why did it have to be the Capital? He wondered.

His own experiences in Keiv-Alon had not filled him with confidence in his abilities to survive among city folk, and if the stories were true, Kalinor was ten times the size of Keiv-Alon.

Theo's hand on his shoulder jolted Aleksei from his thoughts, "You look tired, son. Best get you to bed before you fall asleep standing up."

Aleksei smiled, realizing that he'd not had a proper night's rest since leaving home. He opened his mouth to agree but only managed a gaping yawn.

Theo winked at Roux and led Aleksei back into the recesses of the house, throwing aside one of the heavy drapes the Ri-Vhan used for doors within their homes and nodding to the hammock stretched before them.

"You get some sleep, and we can all talk more in the morning." he said, giving Aleksei's shoulder a fatherly pat. "But right now sleep's the best thing. For all of us."

Aleksei nodded, needing no encouragement. He practically stumbled into the room, dropping his pack to the floor and pulling his shirt over his head. He didn't even get his boots off before collapsing into the hammock. He was asleep before his head hit the pillow.

✦

Roux Devaan stared deep into the dying embers of the fire, his mind a turbulent storm of unrest.

A *half*-blood?

While Aleksei had been recalling his strange journey, Roux had listened through the ears of the Wood. But the trees insisted that his cousin spoke every word true. At least every word Aleksei *believed* to be true.

His cousin was either telling the truth, or had completely and utterly lost his mind. Yet Roux could hardly credit the latter. Aleksei seemed as sound of mind as any other man. But then how was it possible? There was more. There *had* to be something Aleksei wasn't telling him. Perhaps when he heard the rest, the pieces would fit together into something that resembled sense.

Roux recalled the blade Aleksei had shown him. It was a Legionnaire blade, but how had Aleksei taken it from an armed man? He remembered Henry Drago well enough, and it seemed highly unlikely that in the last fifteen years Aleksei had become an adept in anything beyond baling hay and plowing fields.

He shuddered at that. The entire concept of agriculture made Roux nervous. The idea of forcing the land to yield to the desires of men went against every part of life he understood. Life was meant to be lived in harmony with all that surrounded you, not forcing those surroundings to conform to your will. More than that, the Ri-Vhan were not farmers; they were *hunters*.

That thought cast light on a greater problem, that some of the things Aleksei had said might be attributed to something else. It was a troubling thought, but if it were true.... Roux banished the idea. Aleksei was a half-blood, and no half-blood had *ever* been born...it simply wasn't *possible.*

His thoughts scattered as his eyes came to rest on the darkness of hearth, the last embers extinguishing and giving up ghosts. Again he found no answers, only smoke and shadow.

That night Aleksei dreamed. But it was not the now-familiar golden mist or the green-eyed man.

It was unlike anything Aleksei had ever experienced.

He was running through the Wood, stripped to the waist and barefoot. It seemed his feet should be screaming in protest as they coursed over broken twigs and jagged stone, but he felt no discomfort.

Thump.

He could feel a heartbeat pulse in the air, though it was not his own.

Thump.

Aleksei changed course suddenly, darting to the right. He felt his prey move the same way a moment later, still unaware of the man silently stalking it.

Thump.

Aleksei closed the gap between them, his right hand readying the bow he held clenched in his fist. In his left he held a single arrow. Only one? Surely....

His prey darted out before him and Aleksei notched his arrow, his feet still flying swift and sure over the tangled undergrowth of the Wood. The boar squealed in terror as it caught sight of its hunter, darting back to the left and vanishing into a cluster of heavy thorn bushes.

Aleksei ignored the maneuver, dashing up a low rock formation instead and leaping into the air, twisting. The boar bounded into view, scrambling through the tangles of the thorn bushes, trapped as it desperately tried to break free. Aleksei released his arrow, feeling it glide gently on the wind as it flew towards its mark.

Even before his feet touched the forest floor, Aleksei knew the arrow hadn't missed. He could feel the impact, the sudden stillness of his prey. The pulse had stopped.

He knelt down next to the still form of the boar, dipping his fingers in the blood that ran down the animal's side and dragging them across his bare chest.

You are Marked.

He leapt to his feet, searching for the speaker.

You are my Hunter, Aleksei Drago. Be true.

Before Aleksei could even think to ask a question, to wonder at the voice, he slipped back into deep and dreamless sleep.

CHAPTER 8

BEST LAID PLANS

SHADOWS CAST LAZY patterns amidst the sunlight, creating a shifting mosaic across Tamara's bright blue velvet bedspread. She moved slowly about, pausing before each of the brilliantly lacquered cabinets in her chambers. She selected a few items from each and placed them on her bed, frowning as she tried to recall anything she might be forgetting.

"Leaving?" Jonas asked from the doorway.

Tamara turned, her face brightening into a luminescent smile, "I'm wintering in the South."

Jonas frowned, "You're wintering at Igraan?"

Tamara rolled her eyes. "Mother doesn't want me up here in the cold. She says I should be down in the South with the birds instead."

Jonas tried to keep his frown from deepening. It could simply be that Andariana didn't want Tamara to catch a chill this year, and perhaps she *would* have a better time in the South. But Jonas knew his aunt very well, and he couldn't escape the feeling that there was a much more calculated reason to have Tamara five hundred leagues distant.

His mind raced as he watched her move around the room, her powder-pink gown catching stray wisps of sunlight and shimmering jubilantly. She looked like a butterfly flitting from flower to flower.

Andariana was obviously worried about something. Why move the heir to a southern estate unless you were concerned that something might happen to her in the Capital?

Parliament? Jonas banished the thought before it was even fully formed. The nobles might be power-hungry, but they weren't stupid. Removing Tamara from the line of succession would make Jonas heir, and surely Parliament would be wary of anything that might put Jonas on the throne.

They did not fear his skills in the Archanium, but it took no skill to know that Jonas was a dangerous politician. He had grown up surrounded by, and at times embroiled in, Kalinori power struggles and intrigues. Tamara at least might be directed by her heart, but never Jonas.

No, Jonas would prove too powerful a monarch for Parliament.

But if not the Lords of Parliament, then who? Andariana had made no comment or complaint about her neighboring rulers that might explain her uneasiness.

"What's troubling you, Cousin?" Tamara demanded playfully, her hands on her hips.

Jonas broke away from his reverie and smiled, "I apologize. I'm dwelling on some very unpleasant thoughts."

She crossed her arms, "You know that's terribly bad for your humor? And without humor, what's the point in living?"

Jonas couldn't help but laugh at that. If only the rest of the world saw things through Tamara's eyes, life would certainly be a more innocent affair.

She crossed the space between them, taking his hands in hers, "Come with me! Surely there can't be much here to engage your attention. You must be *incredibly* bored! Come with me to Igraan."

He smiled at the excitement in her face, "It's very tempting. But alas, I must remain."

She sighed, "Well if you *must* remain, try to sound less like some poor piece of noble trash. They're *all* talking like that these days, you know."

"*Who's* talking like that?" Jonas demanded, pleased by this respite from his darker thoughts.

She smiled, "All the lords who've decided they need to marry me."

Jonas arched an eyebrow, "Have they? Do they hope to win your heart with the power of such poorly chosen words?"

She walked over to one of the gilded mirrors that lined the north wall and glanced down at her figure, "I'm not entirely sure it's my *heart* they're after."

He chuckled, but his mirth soon faded as his mind set back to its calculations.

"What sort of escort is she sending with you?"

Tamara rolled her eyes, "Two Magi and their Knights."

Jonas frowned, "Only two Magi? That's *all?*"

Her mouth quirked into a frown of her own, "*And* their Knights. We're not at war, Jonas. And two Magi should be more than enough to frighten away any brigands.

"Besides, Mother is sending me down there in utmost secrecy. No one knows a thing about it. Anyone who asks will be told that I'm going to visit Lady Selvyn in Keldoan." She giggled, "I think it's all rather fun, really. The secrets and all. Like a game!"

Jonas smiled, but it did not reach his eyes. Exactly. A game. And Jonas would be much more at ease if he could see the board. His eyes settled back on Tamara, and he grimaced as another thought raced through his mind.

At least he knew who the pawns were.

He had to speak with Andariana, and soon. He hated not knowing.

"Well, I'm afraid I must leave you to your preparations, Cousin."

"Undoubtedly one of those dreadful things you *must* attend to."

His smile returned, "One of my many machinations that needn't trouble you. Have a pleasant journey."

She kissed his cheek, "If you get too bored with all these pressing palace intrigues, come and stay a few weeks. I would love the company."

He embraced the princess tightly, "Kalinor will be all the poorer without you."

Jonas left her to her innocent thoughts and fancies about the southern countryside, heading swiftly down the hall towards his aunt's formal audience chamber.

He had not gone fifteen paces when a silvery voice called to him. "Highness?"

Jonas halted stiffly and turned to face Eleina Perron.

His future wife.

Eleina walked gracefully towards him, her ruby lips parted in an affectionate smile. "I thought it was you. You're always so reclusive that I feel honored just to catch you out of your chambers."

Jonas bowed formally, just a hair higher than he should have. "I didn't expect to find you in the Palace this early in the day, Your Grace."

She laughed lightly, "Highness, the ladies of the court do not all rise at noon, as some would have you believe. I myself have been up since dawn."

Jonas managed a bored smile. "Well, Lady Perron, as charming as it always is to see you, I must be heading off. I have pressing business with the Queen."

Her perfect porcelain face soured, "Yes, I always forget how easy it is for you to gain an audience. The rest of us must wait about like commoners."

"How tiresome." Jonas managed. "Forgive me."

He made another brief bow and turned on his heel. He swore he could feel her calculating eyes watching him walk away.

Andariana held full court three days out of the week, but today she would be meeting with trade merchants and the guild masters of Kalinor City itself. Jonas knew the importance of keeping both merchants and masters happy, but at the moment he was willing to risk their displeasure.

As he entered the room, he was surprised to find Andariana alone, sitting on the edge of the massive table that dominated the chamber, her flowing auburn curls cascading down her back in a girlish manner.

The image struck him as extremely unlike her. Gone was the mask of iron-forged will and cold determination. All that remained was Andariana, a woman more than a queen.

She looked up from the folded piece of paper she'd been studying, her green eyes wildly indignant that someone had entered without knocking. He knew she would hate to think that anyone might see her in a moment of vulnerability.

Her face softened when she saw him.

"Hello, Jonas. Have you just come for an idle chat or was there something particular on your mind?"

Jonas noticed that as he approached she tucked the piece of paper away in one of the folds of her gown.

"Something particular, I'm afraid." he said softly.

"Oh?" she said, standing and smoothing the front of her crimson silk gown.

"Why are you sending Tamara south for the winter?"

Her face quickly shifted into a gentle smile. "Well, I thought that things in Kalinor can get so stuffy during the colder months, and since we have that wonderful manor we might as well put it to...."

Jonas held her gaze, but let the silence linger.

Her smile wilted.

"I am growing unsure of some particular nobles." she admitted. "I thought it was better not to have the monarch, the heir to the throne, *and* the Prince of Ilyar in the same place at the same time. Just in case they decided to take precipitous action."

Jonas nodded, "That makes sense. Why such a small escort then?"

The smile returned, now coy and self-congratulatory, "Jonas, if I sent her south with a hundred Legionnaires, I would be announcing to the world that I fear for her safety within my own realm, that I fear some sort of organized attack. But if instead there are five people traveling south under the cloak of secrecy, isn't that much more effective?"

"It would depend on the strength of the secret." he said softly. "If the wrong person were to hear it...." He didn't have to finish.

"It's a risk." she sighed. "But right now, I feel as though inaction would be worse."

Jonas nodded, "You may be right. And Tamara is the only one who can be moved at the moment."

Andariana looked sharply at her nephew, "What do you mean?"

Jonas winced, realizing a moment too late that he'd said more than he'd intended. "I have matters of my own to attend to, Aunt. You know that."

She studied him for a long moment before finally nodding.

He restrained a sigh of relief.

And then she surprised him, "We have our pleasant little fiction, Jonas, and I'd be a fool to believe that you don't have your own secrets and shades, the same as the rest of us." He stared at her in surprise when she leaned forward and gave him a soft, motherly embrace.

"Just don't get too lost in yours." she whispered.

Jonas was so startled he had no words to return the sentiment. Instead he hugged her to him. She was the closest thing he'd ever had to a mother, and for all their posturing and scheming, he knew she was only looking out for him. He fought back tears as the realization struck. It was quite possible that she was the only person in the world who had ever truly cared for him like this, who had *protected* him.

As they parted, both slipped into a comfortable silence, returning to their own thoughts and intrigues, the moment broken. Neither noticed the shadowed form in the far corner of the room smiling in satisfaction.

⚜

"There now, don't you look like a proper prince?"

Bael stared at his mother, then back to his reflection in the faded silver mirror. It was one of the few possessions she'd been allowed by his father, though he cursed her vanity often enough. Rafael had ultimately allowed it as an indulgence, wicked but necessary, to remind her that only true devotion to the Dark God could erase the sins of her past.

Bael saw nothing of the sort in his dull reflection. Rather, he saw a man in a fine sapphire silk coat and white wool breeches staring back, his burnished golden hair falling into an intricate braid draped across his shoulder. He saw himself reflected back, and again the jarring images Darielle had forced into his head roared to the fore.

For just a moment, the toad boy was gone, replaced by someone of worth, of *power*. Yet Bael was also keenly aware of how quickly it would dissipate. He had to be incredibly careful, pay attention, listen without speaking, keep control of his emotions *and* his abilities.

These were considerations that would have seemed mad mere weeks ago. Mere weeks ago he'd been the Toad. And then his dear sister had decided to pay a visit, and it seemed like he'd been paying for it ever since.

Except Darielle had miscalculated.

Rather than be cowed or frightened by her fury, Bael had only become stronger. More confident, more powerful. His innate ability in the Great Sphere had manifested itself again and again. It had always been there, but he'd been afraid to touch it, afraid to make a mistake, to anger the Dark God or worse, his Lord Father. But once the Archanium had woken inside him, he'd seen something in his Lord Father's eyes he'd never beheld before.

A burgeoning glimmer of respect.

It was for that very reason that he had been summoned to his Lord Father's tent this day. It was for that reason that his mother had opened her meager chest of belongings and pulled forth the coat and breeches, relics from his grandfather, she claimed. The clothes of a king. The king he was born to be.

Of course such thoughts were heresy, but since Bael had burned that scryer to ash, it seemed as though there were suddenly more dangerous heretics deserving of punishment. Especially now that his Lord Father had declared Bael a vessel of the Dark God's justice.

But as surprising as this sudden change of station felt, Bael couldn't shake the feeling that his Lord Father had been preparing for it for some time. He saw it in the way the man suddenly spoke to Bael of secret matters regarding the Commune, confessions of his own conversations with the Dark God, and invitations to important meetings.

Bael found himself trying to understand exactly what it was Aleksei Drago had left behind. He suddenly found himself with a father. Not a loving father like Henry Drago, but a father still, rather than just a judge.

And he found himself to be a son, rather than a disappointment.

Yet while his life in the Commune continued to improve, his

connection to Aleksei Drago had all but vanished. He could still feel the man, shockingly close now, but when he tried to cast his voice into the boy's head he received only a painful echo and a powerful headache.

Granny Jorna had been particularly useless, claiming it had something to do with forest spirits and powers that were beyond her. Bael was quickly coming to suspect that Granny Jorna was not the paragon of magical authority he'd once imagined.

He was also beginning to wonder if she didn't prefer him to be her sweet little toad boy, who would comfort a crone like her when no one else paid heed to her penny prophecies. Perhaps she was trying to sabotage his efforts to gain acceptance, to claim his rightful place.

Or perhaps he had finally seen her reach the limits of her abilities. Perhaps he needed to align with greater powers now that he was being noticed.

That was why this meeting was so important.

His Lord Father was meeting with one of his most loyal acolytes. A man with considerable power, political and magical alike. Bael imagined he might learn a good deal from such a man, given the chance. Such a man might even be able to help him best this other player. Or, at the very least, help Bael decipher who the other player could be. Even that much would be a boon.

His mother brought out a tarnished silver brush and began to sweep the dust from the sapphire silk. He stood there, jostled from his thoughts of potential power, wondering if this was how lords felt every day, having underlings tend to their needs and appearance. Somehow he couldn't imagine it, and yet he knew it was part of his birthright.

And besides, while many lords woke up with this sort of thing, how many had a *queen* prepare them? He wondered if this was a first, a fallen queen preparing her son for a meeting in a hide tent, serving him rather than the other way around.

He found the whole experience surprisingly to his liking.

"There we are." Marra said softly, replacing the brush in her chest with great care and snapping it shut. "You look the proper prince indeed. As you should."

He turned away from the mirror and flashed her a proud smile,

"Thank you, Mother. I would never have been able to appear in the Dark God's temple in anything less, saving as a supplicant. You have made me feel a proper lord, a man worthy of the Dark God's notice and honor."

He hugged her close and she gave a rare laugh. "I try to do you justice, Son. The justice you are *due*." she whispered. "I am here for you. Always."

Bael felt tears well up in his eyes, and did his best to banish them with limited success. His mother so rarely spoke of her feelings that when she did, he often found it so shocking that she was long out of sight before he had a chance to react. But with all this recent activity and attention, there was no toad pond to crawl back to, no slime to cry into. Now his tears dripped onto the carefully preserved silk.

"The Dark God preserve us," he muttered, "I've ruined your coat."

She shushed him gently, kissing his cheek and pulling a cloth from her chest, "Hardly ruined dear, just a trifle damp. I shed my fair share of tears back in my day as a princess, *certainly* as Queen. But my maids were brilliant at hiding it. No reason you can't benefit from their experience."

Bael vacillated between smoldering and grateful as his mother cleaned first his coat, and then his face, of any telltale tears. On the one hand, he appreciated her aid and compassion. On the other, he feared that she would make him appear weak in face of his Lord Father. He would hate to bash it all to pieces on the appearance of a silly coat just as he'd gained Rafael's favor.

"Thank you, again." he managed before stepping out of her tent. He heard her say something, but the sudden bustle of the Commune drowned it out. If it was important, he'd hear it later.

But he had more pressing concerns.

Bael walked with a confidence he *believed* in, rather than felt, all the way to his father's cathedral. In truth it was just a larger hide tent, the skins uncured and stinking. Smoking herbs inside masked some of the smell, but by no means all. Bael had wondered time and time again why the Dark God's children were at once the ones chosen and the ones to suffer.

Shouldn't someone of his station be seated in luxury, judging those less pious than himself? Yet his Lord Father discouraged anything that could be construed as luxury or vice, claiming that the Dark God demanded they be supplicants to His rule. Bael was beginning to see the cracks in that fractured logic.

The moment he entered the Cathedral of Volos, he heard a conversation stop short. A man was kneeling before his Lord Father. The man had golden hair like his own, just a bit darker and cut short. He was older, possibly in his fiftieth summer. And he looked at Bael's father as though the man were the Dark God himself.

"Bael." his Lord Father intoned as he entered the room.

The kneeling man turned and gasped.

The sound had hardly escaped the man's lips when a whiplash flickered through the Archanium, throwing the man to the ground, "You will show *respect* in the presence of your betters." Rafael snarled.

The sandy-haired man righted himself, wiping the blood from the split in his lip, "My apologies, Master. I will seek penance with the Dark God for my transgression. I was merely struck by the... family resemblance."

Another crack, and the sandy-haired man landed flat on his back a good twenty paces from Rafael. "I don't give twelve damns *where* you serve the Dark God. If you bring blasphemy like that into my house again, I will abide by His rule and crush you into oblivion. *My* blood flows through that boy's veins. That is the *only* blood of import in this congregation." The sandy-haired man cried out. "Do you understand?"

"*Yes!*" the man screamed.

Bael cringed. The sandy-haired man had excited his Lord Father's temper. That, and the vanity of Bael's coat and breeches, the mere *suggestion* of the House of Belgi, seemed to have put Rafael on edge. Bael wanted to tell the sandy-haired man to stop talking, lest he wake a slumbering Salamander.

Finally, Rafael relaxed his grip on his faith and the sandy-haired man was allowed to breathe for a moment.

"Bael," Rafael said offhandedly, almost as though he'd forgotten Bael was even there, "this is Sammul. He is *refuse*, but he serves the Dark God."

Bael stepped forward, "You said I bore a family resemblance. Tell me what you meant. What family?"

Sammul appeared mystified by the question. He glanced at Rafael, but the man nodded reluctantly. Sammul bowed his head to Bael, "Master Bael, I only meant that I noticed some resemblance to your cousins, Jonas Belgi, Prince of Ilyar, and Princess Tamara, Crown Princess and Heir to the Ilyari throne. I meant no disrespect. Only that you favor the Belgi line." He cleared his throat, "Your mother's line."

Feeling his father's hard black eyes on him, Bael took a deep breath and looked down at the man, "What were you saying before I interrupted?"

Sammul glanced to Bael's Lord Father. Receiving another nod, he went on at some length about the schedule and the plan. That for the last three decades he'd done everything in his power to render Ilyar's prized Archanium Magi little more than sad puppets without any real talent or efficacy.

The previous generations of Magi had either fled, or had met sudden but unfortunate ends while in the Voralla. It was all at once shockingly clandestine and painfully obvious. Yet thus far, the plan had proceeded unopposed and unnoticed.

In the end, it didn't seem as though it had been difficult to dismantle an age-old era of magic practitioners, so long as they were denied certain texts and were led by someone who refused to teach them anything of value. Sammul had played an instrumental role since he'd been a boy, and all at Rafael's behest.

This had been generations in the making, and *that* was why Bael was supposed to be at the meeting. Should anything happen to Rafael, Bael was to carry on the flame of fanaticism and keep the plan in motion.

"What about the older Magi?" Bael asked after a moment of silence.

Rafael frowned, "What do you mean? The *heretics*?"

Bael nodded, "Sammul, what happened to the Magi who lived in the Voralla before you became High Magus? The ones who would have put holes through your methods and lies to your words? Where are *they* now?"

Sammul shrugged, "We were able kill many of them, though by no means all. Some scattered to the winds, but by the time we took over training things had fallen into such disrepair that it no longer seemed to matter.

"We introduced an adapted curriculum and no one challenged it. Those who might have objected had long since gone from the Voralla, so it was simple enough.

"My acolytes, begging your pardon Master Bael, *our* acolytes ensure that strict rules are always enforced for the smallest infractions, in accordance with Master Rafael's teachings." He coughed, wiping blood once more from his mouth. "None of the old guard has returned since those early days, Master Bael. And the new accept the new rule. *My* rule. My personal acolytes ensure that the discipline is meted out...*appropriately.*"

Bael narrowed his eyes, "So there is no one currently in the Voralla who can send dreams? No prophets? Nothing of that sort?"

Sammul froze. Rafael frowned, looking into the face of his creature. And then a look of understanding crawled across his face.

"Sammul, what aren't you telling me?" Rafael asked. No, *commanded.*

"There is one Magus in the Voralla who has a limited talent for prophecy." Sammul allowed.

"And why have you left it alive?" Rafael demanded. "The ramblings of a heathen can only serve to muddy the words of the Dark God."

"Because she could be useful." Sammul snapped back. "You have a prophet for a daughter. How useful is *she* to you? Have *her* words served the Dark God? Why have you left *her* alive?"

Bael expected to see Sammul burn hot and fast. Instead his father took a step back and hung his head in a rare display of personal shame, "I suppose you have a point, whelk. What other transgressions have you obscured from the sight of your God?"

"The Prince." Sammul said grudgingly.

"Jonas?" Rafael asked, leaning forward. "What of him?"

Sammul managed a shrug, "I don't know what to say, Master. He has access to the Great Sphere, but I don't know where his talents lie. I keep trying to scry it out of him, but something is protecting him.

Almost as though he has the protection of a powerful Bonded, though I know that to be false."

Bael felt a flush of fear. He was establishing a bond with the same man, wasn't he? *Jonas* was the crack in the ice that Sammul couldn't predict. At the same time, the Prince was in close proximity to a Magus the talent for prophecy. It made the worst kind of sense.

Bael felt a now-familiar rage boil up within him, but he forced it down. He could hardly cause a scene right now, certainly not *here*. But if this other Magus was the Prince of Ilyar, if this other Magus was Jonas bloody *Belgi*, then Bael had a new enemy.

No, rather, a very *old* enemy indeed.

His own cousin, a man he'd never met. A man who already had everything. A prince who was trying to steal everything Bael had ever dreamed of right out from under him.

A prince who just might succeed.

Jonas sighed, running his hands through his chestnut hair and glancing at the woman sitting across from him. She was watching his face intently, her pale green eyes, flecked delicately in gold, lit by concern in the firelight of his study.

"Well?" she asked.

"I feel like a fool."

Aya smiled sympathetically, "You're doing the best you can."

Jonas arched an eyebrow, "Really? My *best* is apparently a string of barely coherent riddles. I'm manipulating this poor man, and I can't even tell him *why*. And then half the time he's talking to someone *else*. Answering someone else's questions."

"I've explained this to you before, Jonas. You can't give him too much information or he might make a mistake. You can't risk that."

"I know. But I'm starting to feel something. Something... *unusual*."

Aya pursed her lips, "It's called compassion."

Jonas ignored her. "He's forming a bond with me, but there's something else happening that I understand even less."

"The other player?"

Jonas stared at her, "He's getting stronger. I thought you were the one in command of all the answers. *You're* the prophet, *I'm* just trying to understand which end is up."

Aya sighed, "You're right, it's just that forming a bond based purely on proximity is rare, to say nothing of a *bifurcated* bond. And at any rate, you still have to invoke it. Assuming, that is, that your young man has any interest in staying here. Or that he even *arrives*."

"As I said before, you're the prophet. And he's not *my* 'young man', not yet. But stranger still is the way these bonds are manifesting."

Aya frowned. Each Magus and Knight pair shared a bond, forged through the Magus' link to the Archanium. From the Knight the Magus received the strength and endurance to access the Archanium for extended periods. As to what the Knight received, that varied depending on the power and nature of the Magus.

Most Magi could only enhance their Knight's present abilities. Aya knew that Ilyana's Marrik possessed the strength of a handful of men. Her own Raefan was gifted with stamina. He could train, or if needed fight, for days without tiring. Yet both of these were fairly common gifts for an Archanium Knight. Of the Magi in the Voralla, only Hade's Knight, Vadim, benefited in an unusual way and no one, not even Sammul, had been able to understand why.

Hade was not a powerful Magus, and yet for some reason that defied explanation, Vadim had developed an immunity to fire. It was the most extreme example of a benefit transmuted through the bond any of them had ever seen.

At least, until now.

"*Time*." Jonas said quietly. "It's becoming more pronounced the closer he gets. I'm not really sure how it works. I know *he* doesn't understand it. But in any event, he's managed to get from the Southern Plain to Seil Wood in three days. I don't know how, but he seems to be drawing from my connection to the Archanium."

"And that of the other player." Aya reminded him. "If there is another Magus forming a bond with the boy, there's no telling what kind of power he's able to access, even if he doesn't understand it." She paused a moment, tapping her lip. "Do you think it will last?"

He frowned, "Gods, how should *I* know? I don't see how it can. I imagine it takes an enormous amount of energy to draw like this. You said yourself that once the bond becomes permanent, it will change.

If he chooses to bond me or the 'other player', as you call him, doesn't it *have* to change?"

Aya nodded, both confirming Jonas' supposition while wondering what that change would be. It was rare that a Magus and a Knight formed a bond through instinct, and even when they did it usually happened very quickly. Two bonds forming simultaneously between three people who'd never met was bordering on the impossible.

Yet for that bond to be of such a peculiar nature spoke not only of both Magus' raw power, but also of the sort of man Aleksei Drago seemed to be. Whoever this boy was, there was obviously more to him than Jonas had divined.

"When will he arrive in Kalinor?" she asked.

"*If* he arrives in Kalinor? I don't know, why don't you tell me? *You're* the prophet."

Aya's hand absently ran through the streak of white in her hair. Her path through the Archanium had taken a slightly different turn than the rest of Sammul's flock, and as a result she had developed a rare talent for prophecy. It was weak, true, but so far Jonas had found many of her revelations to be quite helpful.

"Now you know," she reminded him gently, "that if it relates to you directly I won't be able to help you."

He nodded his understanding. Prophecy was based in a tenuous region of the Archanium, and prophets guarded their knowledge of the future zealously. It was quite a chore to be a prophet, as Aya's discretion was at times ultimately important in ensuring key events occurred at the appropriate times. And often such events were doomed to fail if the primary players were aware how things were supposed to unfold.

She closed her eyes, letting herself slip into the swirl of color and emotion that was the Archanium, searching for the spell she needed. It took several minutes to sift through the river of wards and enchantments that clouded her vision, but she finally caught sight of the clear blue slipstream of prophecy.

Images tumbled through her mind, and as she caught each one she examined it, taking note for future reference before moving on to the next. She wasn't sure how long she sat there, but eventually she opened her eyes to find Jonas still across from her, his eyes excited.

"You've found something?"

She nodded, "But I don't know how much good it will do you."

"Anything you can tell me is more than I knew before."

"There's a decision he has to make. The fork is fast approaching. If he chooses you, he'll enter through the East Gate. From the Wood. He'll be lost. He's not used to cities, and he'll need a sign."

Jonas smirked. "That sounds like Aleksei."

"Does that help?"

"Only if he chooses to come to Kalinor, but yes, I suppose it does help somewhat. With what you've just told me, I can probably find him before he gets to Market Street. Once he gets there it'll be much more difficult to pick him out of the crowd, so I'd like to find him before then."

She smiled, "Well, I wish you luck."

"Did you get any sense of time from the visions?"

She shook her head, "A few days at the most, but nothing more specific than that. I would imagine he'll arrive by tomorrow or the day after, but that's purely conjecture."

"Thank you for that."

"Glad to be of service, Highness." she chuckled.

He shuddered, "Please, not you too. I only accept that title from my enemies and my inferiors, and you are neither."

Aya watched him as he walked her to the door. He was obviously deep in thought, his face troubled.

She wondered what was going through his head. The man was more than a little secretive when it came to specifics, especially when it meant revealing his own strengths and limits.

And though he might tell her the nature of a thing, even something as personal as the bond he was forming with his potential Knight, it would be unlike him to go into any detail on the matter.

Another idea struck her. What if Aleksei Drago didn't *want* to be Jonas' Knight? What if he chose the other path? The deeper echoes along that timeline were clothed in shadows and smoke as far as she could tell. What if he reached Kalinor and decided he didn't *want* this life?

Being an Archanium Knight wasn't too difficult these days, not since the civil war, but something told her that being Jonas' Knight would be *very* different indeed, if for no other reason than because he had a habit of throwing himself into power struggles. That, and the Prince's penchant for making powerful enemies.

Aya was fairly certain that if Jonas had not taken up Ilyana's cause, her friend would have been banished to Dalita or Yrinu already. His willingness to fight for his beliefs was one of the qualities that made Jonas a good prince, and a good friend. But she imagined it would also make life as his Bonded an extremely long exercise in frustration.

She wondered if Aleksei Drago was up to the task.

CHAPTER 9

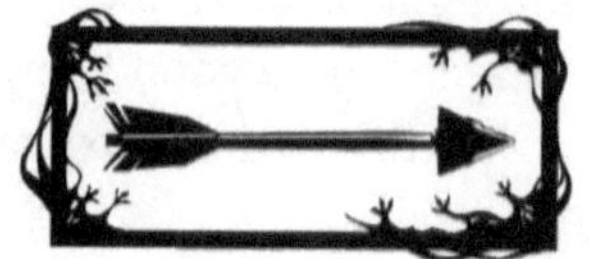

HALF-BLOOD, HUNTER

ALEKSEI ROSE WITH the sun, feeling remarkably refreshed. He wondered if it was the comfort of being in a place he'd once called home, or merely a product of true rest following extreme exhaustion.

The specter of the dream hung in faded tatters at the edge of his consciousness, though he could hardly recall it as he lay in the hammock, staring up at the sunlit leaves that formed the ceiling.

Today he would be amongst the Ri-Vhan for the first time in fifteen years, and he felt sick with worry. How many things would he see that might stir memories he'd shuttered? How many places would bring back his mother's face, her smile? He shivered and squeezed his eyes shut, pushing the images from his mind.

Seeing the village in the darkness had been one thing. The homes had all looked the same, the lines of distinction blurred to the point of obscurity. Nothing leapt out to make him remember.

But something told him today would not be as blissfully vacant.

He rolled out of his hammock and had to search for a moment before he located his shirt, lying in a pile on the floor near the doorway. As he pulled it over his head, Aleksei wondered if Roux might have some clothes he could borrow. His badly needed washing, and he had no intention of meeting the man from the dream smelling like a barn.

Aleksei retraced his steps, walking back into the circular room where he and Roux had spoken the night before. He found his cousin seated near the fire, eating his breakfast.

"You're up early." Roux noted as Aleksei joined him.

"Am I?"

Roux nodded, "I remember you sleeping till noon. Now you rise with the sun?"

Aleksei shrugged, "Habit from the farm. It's cooler in the morning and I get more work done."

Roux considered for a long moment, chewing the warm, flat bread that was the staple of the Ri-Vhan diet. "What will you do today?"

Aleksei frowned as a thought leapt into his mind. "I don't know. I thought I might go hunting, if there's a party going out. I've been on a horse for three days. I need to stretch my legs a bit."

Roux smiled, "There is indeed a hunting party going out today. And I have no doubt they'd be happy to accommodate you."

"What are you boys doing up so *early*?" Theo muttered from the doorway, "It's not healthy to rise before midmorning, didn't you know?"

Aleksei chuckled. It didn't matter if Roux was the Ri-Hnon, no more than if he'd been the King of Ilyar, he was still a 'boy' to Theo.

"Father," Roux said lightly, "if I spent as much time as you trying to be 'healthy' I'd sleep half my life away."

"Perhaps the respite would calm that flippant tongue of yours." Theo grunted, walking off towards the kitchen muttering under his breath.

Aleksei glanced at his cousin, "Is he always like that in the morning?"

Roux laughed, "He's gotten worse the last few years. Ever since his joints started aching, he's become an irascible old man. Not that I can really blame him. If I was stuck in the village all the time, I'd complain too."

Aleksei nodded. He'd always had the freedom to move about as he willed, though he'd never thought of it as a luxury. Even if he *had* spent the last fifteen years on a farm, the option had always been there to walk as far as he cared in any direction.

But the village had definite boundaries, and for those poor souls whose bodies had given out on them, or who simply lacked the talent for Darting, the village could quickly become a very confining place.

Roux rose and dusted the crumbs of his breakfast into the hearth. "Well, enough of this idleness. The hunters will be leaving soon, and I wouldn't want you to miss it and be trapped up here as well."

Aleksei stood, "Do you have a bow I can borrow? Da and I only had one between us, and I decided he'd need it more than I would."

"Of course." Roux's mouth suddenly quirked into a smile, "You mean you don't want to hunt with your pretty Legionnaire blade? I can't *imagine* why not."

Aleksei chuckled, following his cousin into a small storeroom. Roux rummaged through stack after stack of bundled hides, furs, and packages of root flour. After a few moments he emerged victorious, holding a short bow and quiver aloft as he stepped back out of the maze he had created.

"The party will supply you with arrows. This string is fresh so you shouldn't need any spares, but if you do the other hunters ought to have plenty."

Aleksei smiled, inexplicably thrilled to hold the bow. Was it simply because, unlike the sword, he knew how to use this weapon? Or that he would be hunting deer today, not men?

"Thank you." he said, almost overwhelmed with emotion. It was a bloody *bow*! What was wrong with him?

A flash of dream shot through his mind, standing over a dead boar, his arrow protruding from its breast by only a hand-span, its blood streaked across his naked torso.

Aleksei blinked and the image vanished in a swirl of color.

"Come on," Roux grunted, "if we stand around forever, we'll end up like Father."

Roux stepped out of the storeroom, waiting for Aleksei to follow before heading to the front door. "We'll be back later." he called into the recesses of the house.

There was no response.

"He's sulking." Roux muttered, walking out into the daylight.

Aleksei followed and stopped in his tracks, his suspicions

confirmed. The village in sunlight was a very different place.

It was still early, but here and there Ri-Vhan bustled about their daily chores, carrying soiled clothes, piles of flat bread, or strings of wriggling fish. Roux led him down into the village center, where a small group of men had already congregated.

Upon seeing Roux, the men dropped to their knees, heads bowed. Aleksei glanced at his cousin, who just rolled his eyes.

"Gentlemen," Roux called, "this is Aleksei Drago. He is my cousin, visiting from the Southern Plain. He would like to help you with your hunt, if you have no objections." As Roux said the last part, he made it clear that there had *better* not be any objections.

The men of the hunt glanced at each other before a bright-eyed man with thick black hair looked up, "We would be honored to have his company, Ri-Hnon."

Roux smiled, "Excellent. I'll leave him to you, then. Try not to mistake him for a stag."

The men chuckled and rose to their feet as Roux gave Aleksei a friendly pat on the shoulder and walked away. A twinge of anxiety blossomed in Aleksei's gut.

The black-haired man who had spoken stepped forward and offered his hand, "Aleksei, was it? I'm Luc, Hunt Master of the Ri-Vhan." His face fell slightly, "It's only an honorary."

Aleksei smiled and shook Luc's hand warmly, "I'm sure it's well deserved."

The other men guffawed. They knew all to well how much difference a true Hunter would have made amongst their ranks and all of them, Luc especially, felt a bit silly parading around calling themselves a hunting party when traditionally it had been made up of the Hunter alone, followed by six men who gathered the kills.

Aleksei introduced himself to the rest of the party and set about helping them secure their gear. Of the eight gathered, only five, six with Aleksei, actually hunted. The other two carried great rucksacks strapped to their shoulders. They followed the party, gathering the kills.

Luc explained that, though they usually set out for deer, more often than not they had to substitute rabbits and other small game.

"The deer of the Wood are extremely agile." he said ruefully,

"And generally there's only enough light in the day to shoot down one, two if we're fortunate."

Aleksei nodded, "How many do you set out for?"

Luc shrugged, "Three or four is what we'd like to bring home, but I don't think I've lived a day when the hunting party brought down more than two." He hefted his quiver, bristling with arrows fletched in green feathers. "How many arrows did you say you needed?"

Aleksei suppressed a shudder. He felt the now-familiar *shift* settle around him.

"You want four deer?" he asked softly.

Luc frowned, "In a dream life? I'd say four."

"Then I'll need four arrows."

Luc regarded him with surprise, and the men who'd heard Aleksei looked cross. He suppressed a wince. He knew he looked indescribably arrogant at the moment. He certainly *felt* that way. But Aleksei couldn't deny that something inside of him knew he needed four arrows for four kills.

The image of the dead boar flashed again through his mind, and Aleksei thought he might be sick.

Luc handed him four arrows, the warmth gone from his eyes. "Good luck." he said woodenly.

Aleksei managed a smile, "Thanks."

"Luc?" one of the men asked. "Are we ready?"

Luc nodded, still holding Aleksei's gaze, "Aye, we are lads. Let's hope that our added company will get us that second deer today."

The other men chuckled, comforted in the new spin on an old joke. They seemed just a bit uneasy, and slightly more insulted by the farm boy. Aleksei didn't blame them, but how could he explain his unexpected arrogance away?

A hand clapped across his shoulder and the world melted around him in a blink.

⚜

Roux studied his cousin, even as he was taken down to the forest floor. His suspicions were growing, but he had no real evidence yet, only a thought tickling the back of his mind.

"A *half*-blood." Roux muttered in wonder. Gods, how many times had those words tumbled through his mind since Aleksei's sudden appearance at his door the night before? How many nightmares had wrestled him in the darkness?

A light gust of wind from the south mingled with the sunlit pools surrounding him, and in that he heard the voice of the Wood. *I am well pleased, Ri-Hnon. He is true.*

Roux suppressed a shudder.

There were two types of people born into Ri-Vhan society. By far the most prominent were Treedarters, men and women who used the Archanium to move from place to place in flash of blinding speed.

The only problem was that on occasion, a Treedarter would release the Archanium too quickly. When that happened, there was nothing to save them from the long fall to the forest floor. Such deaths were a fact of life among the Ri-Vhan.

It was how Aleksei's mother died.

And then there were Hunters, so few and far between that to have more than one in a generation was unheard of. They tracked their prey through pulse and feel, and once their target was in sight, they never missed.

At the same time, they were infused with a deep sense of balance. A Hunter could look at a doe and know instinctively that her fawn would not survive if he shot her down. In such cases the Hunter would move on to prey that was less important to the balance of the Wood.

Hunters were so highly prized that it offended Roux to think that his cousin might be one of the chosen few.

Aleksei's blood was only half Ri-Vhan, his father having come from a village on the eastern ranges of the Wood. It was an affront to have the Wood select an outsider and a half-blood as Her Hunter.

And it made him sick to hear how pleased the Wood was at having found Aleksei.

⚜

Aleksei screwed his eyes shut as he passed through the strange world of light and shadows, then back into the Wood with a sickening lurch. Was it his imagination, or had that jump not been quite so painful?

The forest floor was quiet and the men fanned silently outward, bows at the ready. Aleksei took a look around and breathed in deeply.

Images tumbled through his mind faster than he could make sense of them. A pond surrounded by brilliant tiger lilies, a drop-off where the soil was too loose, one of thousands of myriad paths through the Wood, this one with a badger hole just off the road and sixteen paces to the east.

He exhaled and opened his eyes.

The men were gone, having left him in the center of the clearing. He smiled.

So much the better.

What? So much the *better*? What if he got lost? What if they didn't come find him? Would he wander around all day with only *four* arrows and nothing to shoot?

His next breath cleared his worries away, and he found himself pulling his boots off. They suddenly felt...cumbersome. Aleksei sighed, wishing he understood himself better of late.

Something moved behind him and he turned slowly.

It was a doe.

Her face was white, her eyes serene. He caught her scent and understood. She was past her prime, though not yet old. She had no fawns to care for, and no bucks clashed in the Wood for a chance to mate with her.

A gift, Hunter.

Aleksei jumped. A voice, but this sounded nothing like the dream man's insistent tone. Instead, it spoke with all the serenity and compassion of a very old woman. A mother. He knew immediately that it was the voice of the Wood.

But a gift? What, the *doe*? Even now as she watched him, Aleksei felt a pang of sympathy for her. He understood. She was a sacrifice. And she knew this, yet it did not terrify her.

Visions again filled his mind. He saw a young fawn vanish into the brush. A piercing cry rang through his mind and he cried out as well. The fawn did not return, and Aleksei realized that he was seeing through *her* eyes. Something had taken her fawn, and it was no Hunter's arrow.

She did not want to be taken like that.

She was content to be offered a swift end. A *kinder* end.

Tears filled Aleksei's vision, clouding his sight before spilling down his cheeks. He reached over his shoulder and drew a single arrow.

The doe stepped forward and raised her head proudly, exposing her breast. Yes, best to aim for the heart. It would be the fastest way.

Aleksei drew the arrow back, closing his eyes so he didn't have to watch.

He released.

Even before the arrow had left the string, he knew where it would strike. The sounds that immediately followed were less surprise than confirmation. Confirmation he didn't need. He heard it strike the doe's breast, felt it slide between the powerful muscles of her chest until it struck her gently beating heart.

Aleksei opened his eyes, his own heart pounding painfully in his ears as he gazed down at the still form of the doe. Her eyes were already glassy with the embrace of death.

He knelt down next to her still form, pulling his shirt open and dipping his fingers in her blood. With his left hand he streaked the blood across his bare chest, leaving four lines of livid crimson brilliantly outlined against the light tan of his skin.

"Thank you for your sacrifice, friend doe." he whispered, tears trickling down his cheeks and dripping from his chin.

"*Aleksei?*" It was Luc's voice.

He sounded afraid.

Aleksei rose to his feet and turned to face the Hunt Master, his face vacant of the emotions that coursed through him. "I have taken down a doe for you. Honor her sacrifice and return her bones to the Wood when you have taken what you need."

Luc nodded, speechless, eyes darting from the deep gold of Aleksei's eyes to the four lines of blood streaked across the Hunter's chest.

Aleksei held his gaze for a long moment, then turned and vanished into the Wood.

Luc waited until he could no longer see Aleksei, then knelt down next to the fallen doe, staring at the single arrow that protruded from her breast. It was perfect. As though she had offered her life to him.

When the other men of the hunt returned, they found him sitting next to the doe, his eyes rimmed red. "Go find Aleksei." he said softly. "Our Hunter will tell you where the three other deer lay."

Roux sat high in a yew tree, watching the hunting party drag a fourth deer into the clearing. Like the others, a single arrow protruded from its hide. Like the others, the shot was flawless.

A gift. For my Hunter. The voice of the Wood rustled through his mind.

Roux shuddered. He had certainly harbored suspicions, but the truth of the matter was beyond disconcerting.

The Wood was *pleased.*

He had spent only three seasons listening to Her voice, but in that time She had never sounded anything but calm, serene, and passive. Now he detected a hint of emotion in those deep, aeon-rich tones.

For *Aleksei.* Not for Roux, the Chosen, the Ri-Hnon. No, for an arrogant half-blood who had happened into the Wood on accident. And now *he* received the favor of the forest while Roux could only absorb praise meant for another.

He took a deep breath. Jealousy at his cousin's fortune would not help him now; Aleksei would be gone soon enough. And then Roux would once more be the undisputed leader of his people, the Hunter just a fading memory of an age-old legend.

On a whim, Roux Darted to the forest floor, surprising the men busily gathering the deer carcasses.

"Ri-Hnon!" Luc said, falling to his knees.

Roux raised a hand to forestall the others, "Continue with your work."

The men returned to cautiously lifting the deer and making their jumps to the village.

"Hunt Master, may I speak with you?" Roux said softly.

Luc nodded and stepped a few paces away from the rest of the party, pausing under the shade of the yew. "Ri-Hnon?"

"How is it, Hunt Master, that we've been blessed with *four* deer today when the best any party has ever managed before was two? Surely it had to be more than a desire to show off for my cousin."

"I don't really know how to explain it myself, Ri-Hnon, except by what I saw. When you left us in the village center, I offered Aleksei as many arrows as he would take from my quiver. He asked me how many deer I wanted and took only as many arrows. I just thought he was brash, so the men and I spread out to hunt, leaving him on his own.

"I started tracking a rabbit, but I found myself regretting my decision to leave him in the clearing, so I doubled back to see if he might like some company after all." Luc took a deep breath and Roux frowned. Obviously the experience had been more revealing than he'd first thought.

"Ri-Hnon, I returned to find Aleksei a pace from where I'd left him, bent over the body of a doe. As I approached, he dipped his fingers in the doe's blood and drew them across his chest."

"He marked himself?" Roux whispered.

Luc indicated the arrow stem still protruding from one of the deer, "These shots are impossibly clean, Ri-Hnon. As if the deer offered him the best position possible. I can imagine no other way that he could have brought down four deer in only a few hours."

Roux thought a moment before speaking again, "And what do you make of it all, Hunt Master?"

Luc shook his head, "I've never seen the like of it, but I know what I saw. Ri-Hnon, there is no doubt in my mind that your cousin is the first Hunter our people have seen in decades, perhaps in well over a century. Certainly in my lifetime."

"Unfortunate, then, that they'll never know."

Luc looked up sharply, "*What?* You can't mean to keep it from them! Ri-Hnon, the people *deserve* to know. Hunters give the Ri-Vhan hope. To deny them that...."

"What hope is there," Roux demanded, "in a *half*-blood Hunter, who will be gone by midday tomorrow? A Hunter who might never return? Is *that* the savior our people want?"

Luc squared his shoulders, "Better to treat them honestly than leave them praying for a future they'll never see. You know as well as I that there's never been more than one Hunter at a time. Not for centuries. Why leave your people praying for a Hunter to appear when he already walks the world, even if he may not live among us?"

Roux frowned, "What do you have to gain, Luc, from the Ri-

Vhan knowing what Aleksei is? You would lose stature. The people would have a new hero, one you could never *hope* to equal."

Luc's eyes flared, "Begging your pardon, Ri-Hnon, but people respect me because I put food on their tables, not because I pretend to be something I'm not. Aleksei's birthright as our Hunter does nothing to lessen *me*. Just as it does nothing to lessen you. No Ri-Vhan resents you for not being a Hunter, so what are you afraid of?"

Roux suddenly realized that the tables had been turned. Somewhere during the conversation he had lost control of the situation. *Damn* Aleksei Drago for making him falter before his Hunt Master.

He took a deep breath, "Where is he now?"

Luc frowned, "I'm not sure as I know. Jaq found him and learned where the other kills were, but then he came back to get us. I admit we forgot about Aleksei, what with bringing in the meat."

Roux nodded, "Thank you. You may return to the village." Luc turned to go, but Roux reached out and caught his arm, "Luc, tell the people what you want. No doubt your men are already spreading the story. Give them their hope, and we shall see whether it's misplaced."

Luc managed a stiff nod, then vanished.

Roux glanced around the clearing before closing his eyes. *Where is he?*

There was a faint breeze through the canopy, and a frond of yew leaves fell, brushing against a dead limb covered in green and yellow lichen. *Eastern edge, near the tigerlily pool.*

Roux took a step forward and the Wood melted around him, shifting into the writhing shades that inhabited the world between. And then he stood just outside a circle of larch trees, his eyes searching for his cousin.

He caught movement on the opposite edge of the pool and stepped out into the sunlight where Aleksei could see him.

Roux wasn't entirely sure what sort of abilities might have awakened in his cousin, but he wanted Aleksei to know that he came peacefully, whatever his emotions may be at the moment.

"Roux."

Roux jumped at the sound of Aleksei's voice behind him, cursing himself for showing weakness. He turned to face his cousin and had to clench his jaw to keep it from dropping in shock.

The Aleksei he had left in the village center that morning had been a simple farm boy clutching nervously at his borrowed bow, excited for the chance to stretch his legs a bit, even though he might not contribute anything to the cause.

That boy was gone.

It was still Aleksei, of that there was no question. His golden eyes still shone with a deep-seated goodness that experience could damage, but never erase. Likewise, there was still a definite innocence about him.

But in his face, Roux saw a hardness that had never existed before. He was shirtless, his muscular chest streaked with overlapping lines of thick, dried blood.

The Hunter's Mark.

His breeches were tattered and torn at the cuffs, and he was barefoot.

He looked wild. Feral.

"I see you've come into your heritage." Roux said gently.

Aleksei strode forward and Roux noticed that as he moved, he made no sound. "The Wood has shown a small amount to me, yes."

"And you recognize the significance of this?"

"I know how rare it is," Aleksei's brilliant eyes darkened, "especially as a *half*-blood."

Roux winced. Gods, had the Wood told Aleksei of his conversation with Luc, too? "Aleksei—"

"Don't worry, Roux." A bitter edge had crept into his cousin's voice, "I won't be here much longer to steal your glory. I'm leaving within the hour."

Roux started to say something, then thought better of it. Certainly the same man, but harder. Much harder.

"Won't you say good-bye to your people before you leave?" he asked finally.

Aleksei's face softened, "I won't deny them the chance to acknowledge me."

Roux stepped forward and tentatively placed his hand on Aleksei's shoulder, "May I take you back to the village?"

His cousin nodded.

The world around them faded for a heartbeat, then straightened back into the familiar form of the village center. Men and women were crowded around them in a circle, children clinging to their mother's skirts, eyes wide in wonder.

Roux glanced to his cousin's face, but Aleksei merely smiled.

A man stepped forward and bowed deeply, "Greetings, Hunter."

Behind him the crowd surged forth, each one bowing low and repeating the words. Aleksei spoke with each man and woman, listening to their fears, their hopes, their dreams.

Roux marveled at the man's easy way with people, and their willingness to confide in him things they would never have told Roux. Even the children came forward from behind their parents to just stare, or ask a question.

Aleksei remained in the village center until the Ri-Vhan were satisfied that they indeed had a Hunter, that he was a man they could place their hope in and not be disappointed.

Roux had to fight to quash his own burning jealousy. Even when he'd been revealed as Ri-Hnon there had not been this sort of reaction. The Ri-Hnon was a fact of life. A Hunter was a figure stepping out of myth and into the daylight.

As the last group of Ri-Vhan drifted away, Aleksei glanced at him and Roux realized that sympathy shone in his cousin's eyes. Aleksei understood what Roux was going through, and he empathized.

"I'm sorry. I know this has to be trying."

"How magnanimous of you." Roux whispered.

Aleksei smiled, either ignoring Roux's sarcasm or not having heard it, and walked away.

Chapter 10

A Shattered Seal

ALEKSEI WANDERED AWAY from the Ri-Vhan, from the lives of a people he at once claimed as his, yet hardly knew. They were a part of him, certainly, but he could never be one of them. The gulf had grown too wide, and now he recognized the feeling for what it was. He was a guest amongst them. No matter how they might beg him to remain, he could never be their hero. That position belonged to someone else.

If only he would take it.

Aleksei let his mind drift away. He had come back for a very specific purpose, but only now did he truly understand it. He had come to say good-bye. Not to people or places, but to memories. Good-bye to a life he had yearned for, without ever asking *why*.

He stood at the edge of the great platform that suspended the village, staring out over the vast expanses of canopy that stretched before him, a hundred leagues of Wood in every direction. It was a marvelous place, and one he hated to leave. He would miss its beauty. And its serenity.

But the Ri-Vhan were not his people.

"Remembering?" Roux asked from behind him.

Aleksei nodded, not bothering to turn.

"Don't go." Roux said softly.

Aleksei smiled, "I don't belong here. Your people want a hero. But they don't understand that they already have one."

❦

Roux felt his jaw tighten. He wanted to hate Aleksei, to hate him for possessing the gift Roux coveted above all else. For the fact that the Ri-Vhan, *his* people, adored this man more than they'd ever cared for him. And for no other reason than the title they could ascribe him.

Instead he stepped forward and embraced his cousin, letting his hurt flood away. Aleksei hugged him tightly, and as Roux stepped back he saw that Aleksei's face was once again as it had been the night before; save for the brilliant gold of his eyes, now the uncanny mirror to Roux's own.

Aleksei offered a shy smile, "I don't suppose you have a shirt I could borrow?"

Roux laughed at that, leading Aleksei back towards his house. Gods, but it felt like years, rather than hours, since there'd been anything to laugh about.

Aleksei was quick about retrieving his pack and bidding his uncle good-bye.

"You're leaving already?" Theo wailed. "Dash it all, and here I'd been dreaming of conversation that didn't center around hunting and the huckleberry harvest."

Aleksei smiled, "Another time, Uncle."

Theo nodded. It was a pleasant fiction nonetheless.

When he was finally ready, Roux took Aleksei to the forest floor. There, by the Hunter's Horn where Aleksei had left him, stood Dash. The draft horse had been brushed and the tack well oiled.

"Gaël was true to his word." Aleksei said with a grin.

Roux smiled at his cousin, "Don't forget about us, Aleksei. If you ever find yourself in need, know that we will come to your aid."

Aleksei slid onto Dash's back and nodded, "Thank you, though I hope I'm allowed a friendly visit now and then."

Roux chuckled, "Perhaps. Ride well, Aleksei Drago."

The Hunter spared his cousin one last glance, then turned Dash to the west. In a matter of seconds he was out of sight and Roux allowed himself a deep sigh, "Keep him safe, Mother Wood. I pray his heart remains ever true."

❧

"Did you see it?"

Bael scowled at his grandmother, "Of *course* I saw it. What does it *mean*? Four streaks of blood? Is that important?"

She muttered something unintelligible under her breath and reached for another handful of herbs. She cast them into the embers, releasing a burst of heady smoke.

"He's been marked," she said finally, "as a Ri-Vhan Hunter. They don't come along too often, but from what I heard as a girl, they can be *formidable*."

Bael glanced at her, suddenly more interested in her knowledge than he had been in recent days, "What do you know of them?"

Jorna shrugged, "They have different senses, different abilities than normal men. Can hunt by feel, pulse, and scent. Can track in the dark, and never miss a shot they commit to. They can meld with the shadows and cannot be harmed by mortal men. Rare, rare. *Very* rare."

"Are you sure about all of that?" Bael asked.

Jorna shrugged her shoulders, "Some of it might be flights of fancy, dearie, but stories exist for a reason. There has not been a Ri-Vhan Hunter that I know of since long before I was born, but my people still feared them all the same. You don't get stories told about you unless there's something very real behind all of it. Something *dangerous*."

Bael felt a giddy rush thrill through him, "And he's coming to me?"

"*Might* be coming to you." Jorna corrected sharply. "He's in the Seil Wood, and the Wood's magic prevents my talents from seeing much of anything. You have that fledgling bond, child. *You* should know better than I."

"I might know more if I was the only one." Bael grumbled.

Ever since he'd suspected that another Magus, possibly his own cousin, was trying to lure Aleksei away from him, Bael had become increasingly irascible. And increasingly desperate.

Aleksei was his salvation, his one chance to avoid the horrors that Darielle had revealed to him during her last visit. Darielle's visions still haunted him. And the closer Aleksei came to him, the more vivid the visions became. Specters reminding him of his urgent need for Aleksei Drago to appear and save him from the path to prophetic infamy.

But a Ri-Vhan Hunter? This was quickly becoming even better than anything Bael could have imagined. This was no longer a simple farm boy, but a man who commanded unique abilities of his own. A man to be *feared*.

Bael had limited dealings with the Ri-Vhan, only daring into the Seil Wood on occasion when food around the Commune had proved too thin. Every now and then a hunting party would encounter the tree people, but their only real communication came in the form of warnings. Warnings to stay on the outskirts of the Wood and not venture too deep.

His father claimed the Ri-Vhan were demons in the skins of men and needed to be purged from the sacred Wood they blighted, that they were actually attempting to destroy the greater forest and thus must be punished.

A few of his acolytes had even tried to track down the elusive Ri-Vhan village, but not a single one returned. This only further convinced Rafael that the Ri-Vhan were a godless tribe of malevolent sprites. Still, with Aleksei being one of them, perhaps he could convince his father to sue for peace.

Bael sighed. He had a better chance of convincing squirrels to sing. His father was not a man bent towards any task his god didn't command of him. Any stranger arriving from the Wood would be met with open hostility at best. If he were to convince Aleksei to side with him, Bael knew he would have to leave the Commune behind.

But if his choices were between that and fulfilling his sister's dark predictions, he would gladly abandon his home. It wasn't much of a home to begin with. True, they no longer called him Toad to his face. That was the greatest accomplishment he'd made in the last five years among his people.

Bael was more than ready to leave these small people behind, to become someone of value, of *merit*. He would never find that among his father's people. For that, for true worth, for *greatness*, he would need Aleksei Drago's strength and courage.

Bael's magic was strong, but he often lacked the conviction to bring it forth. This fault had made him a target early on. As a child, he'd been bullied for his unwillingness to fight the other children.

Children in the Commune learned to wield the Archanium as a weapon from the time they could walk. Weakness in the face of an open challenge usually singled out those who would not survive past their twelfth or thirteenth summer. Bael had survived because he was pitied, and because no one dared kill the child of the Master, his Lord Father.

But that fact alone could not buy him friends or fondness. Instead, he'd endured only cruelty, the same cruelty his faith demanded.

I'm not weak now. He thought triumphantly. *I'm stronger than they thought. I just needed a push. My sweet sister provided that well enough, and now he's coming here. And once he's here, they'll see why it was a mistake to cross me. He'll show them that I can be a hero. And they'll finally understand that underestimating me was the last mistake any of them will ever make.*

The entrance to Granny Jorna's tent swept open and one of his father's acolytes poked her head in, "Master Bael? Your Lord Father has requested your presence in his tent immediately."

Bael sighed, letting his flights of fantasy dissipate with the rest of the drugged smoke, "I'm coming."

As he rose to leave, Granny Jorna suddenly grasped his arm. He looked down into her wrinkled face to demand an explanation when he caught her eyes. Black mist gushed from both her sockets, filling the tent with a darkness unlike anything he'd witnessed before.

"He is coming. The paths will converge. The fork approaches faster than the blink of an eye, but only fire remains. Only fire."

Bael stared at her as she shook herself free of her trance. The smoke trickled off, slowing to the occasional droplets of midnight mist he had become accustomed to.

"Is that all?" he asked sharply.

She stared up at him, her wrinkled brow creased in confusion, "Is *what* all?"

Bael scowled and stormed from the tent, shutting the old woman back in her smoke-filled coffin. She was starting to severely nettle him. At times, he thought he understood Darielle's hatred for her, why his sister might have wanted to wound the creature, if not kill her.

Much as he'd been as a boy, it seemed Jorna was now pitied rather than feared, only allowed to live because of who, rather than what, she was. By Rafael's own logic, she was a living embodiment of blasphemy. The irony was almost too much to bear: a woman who now exemplified the very thing she'd long ago trained her son to deride and stamp out.

He followed his father's acolyte, taking in the Commune. He was finally noticing how humble his surroundings were, now that he was determined to leave it all behind. He saw the same hovels and hide tents as before, but what had once been his entire world was suddenly rendered as rude, too poor to ever suit him.

He didn't belong to this world. He was a prince, and it was his due, his *right,* to be treated as such. Sitting in smoky tents that stank of boar fat and boiled frogs was no place for a prince.

It was only a matter of time, though. Aleksei was on his way.

He entered his Lord Father's tent, surprised to find the man alone. The stern expression on Rafael's face was less of a shock, excepting that the older man's anger didn't seem to be directed at Bael.

"I have an errand for you."

"Yes, Father." Bael said solemnly, "What would you have me do, Father?"

Rafael studied Bael for a long moment. "I've decided it's time long overdue that we struck a blow to your mother's traitorous family. One of your cousins is making her way south. Sammul just sent word that she's leaving under utmost secrecy, which means she'll be lightly guarded."

"And you would like me to deal with her?" Bael guessed.

Rafael barked a harsh laugh, "*You?* Hardly, Toad."

Bael tried to keep the hurt from showing on his face. He'd thought they were past all that, but it wasn't realistic to think that his father would be become a different person in the matter of a few days. If anything, it served as a reminder that no matter how far Bael might have risen in the estimation of the Commune, to Rafael he would always be the same, lowly Toad. The only thing that had changed was that Bael was now slightly more useful.

"No," his father droned, "you will carry a message to the man who *will* carry out the attack. He will be waiting for you on the western edge of the Seil Wood. Tell him to arrange his archers at this location."

Rafael handed Bael a slip of paper sealed in blood-red wax, crested with a crow's foot. "This will tell him where to place his men. You need merely give him the message."

Bael took the message and tucked it into the pocket of his homespun trousers, placing his hand over it protectively to ensure he didn't accidentally lose it. This was an important mission, even if little was required of him.

Still, he was being trusted to Fade to the western edge of the Seil Wood and meet with an assassin. That was hardly a simple task.

Never mind that his own father had just called him Toad.

It would soon be over.

Rafael sat back at his desk and began scrawling something onto a piece of tree bark. When Bael didn't leave, the Master looked up angrily, "What are you still doing here? *Go!*"

"Is that all you want, Father? For me to deliver the message? Nothing else?" Bael asked, trying to keep the unwanted eagerness from his voice.

Rafael didn't even look up, "What more would I want with *you*, Toad?"

Bael turned on his heel and left the tent without a sound. He had done his best not to get too far ahead of himself. Had done his best not to expect too much of a father who treated him as an irritant at best. He hadn't, however, expected this level of indifference after the progress they had made. Perhaps it had all been in his head.

Bael ducked off the path and stepped into the woods. When he reached the toad pond he crouched down and pulled the letter from his pocket. He snapped the wax seal with his thumbnail and tossed the cracked red wax into the water.

His eyes poured over the missive, memorizing its details. He liked some of the ideas, but others he found a bit too gentle for his own taste. With a thought the scrap of paper went up in smoke.

Bael blew the drifting ash over the pond, watching with distant fascination as it was enveloped by the slime and murk. He sat back on his heels and thought for a solid hour, trying to come up with a better solution to his father's 'problem'.

And then it came to him.

There was a princess, one who would be exposed to attack. There was an assassin, poised to remove her guards and take her prisoner. And there was a prince who was meddling in his affairs and trying to pull Aleksei away from him. A prince who would be next in line to become King of Ilyar if the princess was killed in an ambush. A prince who had already been discovered by Sammul to be a Magus.

The pieces clicked together faster and faster in Bael's mind.

By the time he reached his own small hovel, Bael was well ahead of his father's plan. He scrawled his own orders on a piece of tree bark, dribbling a bit of tallow across the opening. He focused his faith on the melted fat and it reshaped itself into a red glob, imprinted with a crow's foot.

Or near enough.

Aleksei rode at a brisk canter, guiding Dash along paths he'd never known existed. The Wood seemed a different place from the one he'd entered the day before. What had been a series of faded images in his mind's eye had been replaced by a knowledge so intimate it seemed innate as breathing.

Even though he'd never seen this part of the Wood, Aleksei knew exactly where he was. It was the first time he'd actually been conscious of moving so fast. Seeing the trees outside of Keiv-Alon, or the dusky prominence of Seil Wood far before time should have permitted was one thing, but the complete and perfect realization that for every step Dash took, he moved twelve was a decidedly different experience.

At this pace, Aleksei would be at the Wood's edge in a few hours. From there it would take mere minutes for him to reach Kalinor.

Aleksei felt his pulse quicken at the thought. His destination was finally within reach. And the dream man would be waiting.

"For *what?*" he muttered to himself.

For you, my Hunter. The voice of the Wood was gentle and sweet, though Aleksei thought he detected a hint of possession in Her ancient tones.

"But why?"

To make you whole.

He sighed and let himself drift amidst his thoughts, wondering how the Harvest was going, how his father was doing without him. Was it true he didn't need Aleksei's help? Or was Henry merely being the stoic man Aleksei had always suspected was hiding under that warm exterior? He wished he knew.

He fares well.

Aleksei jumped, not expecting the Wood to have listened, much less care. How did She know? He silently hoped the Wood would explain Herself, but She apparently decided to leave that much a mystery. Aleksei shrugged. The Wood had little reason to lie to him. He wasn't even sure if She was *capable* of lying.

Gods, Aleksei, he thought, *now you're conversing with trees and wondering at the nuances of their conversation?*

He ran a confused hand through his hair. Maybe he *was* going mad. He had never actually ruled out the possibility. Could this just be one more clue in a long series of obvious indicators?

Dash turned at a bend in the path and Aleksei drew him to a halt, his eyebrows drawn down in confusion.

A gift, Hunter. To ease your doubts.

Not fifty paces from where Dash stood the Wood terminated, opening out into several leagues of farmland before the brilliant white walls of Kalinor rose majestically towards the sky.

"But how...." he began.

Hunter! Aleksei gasped instinctively as he heard the tone of fear in Her voice. *Hunter, there are men near. Their words serve a darker purpose. Make haste!*

Aleksei's head jerked to the side, where he could suddenly feel the presence of two figures several hundred paces distant.

Where he could hear two thundering heartbeats.

He slipped off Dash's back, patting the horse's flank. "Stay."

The draft horse bowed his head, and Aleksei spared a brief moment to realize Dash had *understood*. Then he was jogging lightly through the Wood, his feet ghosting over dead leaves and fragile twigs. When he was twenty paces away, Aleksei realized that he clutched his sword in his right hand, the point dragging in the air just behind him. Ready to spring forward should he require its protection.

"–should be an easy job. We're in position already. Target should arrive in a day, two at the most."

"Perfect. And you're sure she won't escape?"

"You said there were only five, right? And if we take down the two unarmored ones first, the Knights drop too?"

"Immediately. They can't sustain the death of their Bonded."

"So three shots for four archers. Not very good odds for the target, eh?"

"The odds matter less than the result. I want a courier here in a week proclaiming her unfortunate ambush and murder by brigands. And I want it to be traced. You know where."

"Aye, sir, I know where. Shouldn't be too difficult to set up. Only one with a motive and all that."

"Very well. Here's half your pay. You'll receive the other half when the job is completed."

Aleksei heard the sound of money jangling in a purse, then risked a look around the tree he hid behind.

He couldn't see either man's face, though the one nearest him wore the uniform of a Legionnaire. The other man was too obscured by the shadows to clearly make out. The shadowed man tensed, "You said you came *alone*."

"What? What are you talking about?"

Aleksei silently cursed.

"Tell your man to show himself."

The Legionnaire turned, his rough-shaven face a mask of confusion, "Dammit, I didn't *bring* another man."

"A spy?" the shadowed man breathed. "Perhaps from the Palace?"

Aleksei looked around wildly for a place to hide. He didn't know what would happen if they found him, but he had no intention of finding out.

The Legionnaire did not concern him. He'd dealt with their kind before. But the shadowed man seemed...different. Smelled different. Aleksei couldn't nail down exactly what it was. He only knew the man was inherently dangerous.

Run, Hunter. They shall not catch you.

Aleksei spared no time for thought. He turned and ran as fast as he could.

Behind him, he heard one of the men break out into a curse, immediately followed by the same inexplicable feeling of danger. On instinct, Aleksei threw himself to the left. A bolt of fire burned through the air where he'd been a moment before, splashing across an oak trunk.

He kept moving, running as fast as his legs could carry him until he reached Dash. Aleksei vaulted onto the horse's back, digging his heels into Dash's sides. The horse took off at a gallop towards the city, heedless of anything but the need to move faster.

As they raced away from the Wood, Aleksei turned to see the Legionnaire emerge, sword at the ready. There was no sign of the shadowed man.

Aleksei sighed. He was safe.

He allowed Dash to gallop for another league, slowing him to a canter when he felt they were sufficiently far away. No man on foot would be able to catch up to him now.

He rode the rest of the way to the city gates deep in thought, turning over the conversation he'd just heard. What had those men been discussing? He could feel the...*wrongness* of their intent. They meant somebody great harm, that much was clear. But who? That had never been mentioned.

Aleksei felt suddenly helpless. Surely he should tell someone, but what would he say? He'd heard nothing that could be directly incriminating.

Maybe he would tell the dream man, when he found him. Surely *he* would know what to do. If he didn't, Aleksei would be out of ideas.

A moment later all thought of the men and the Wood vanished from his mind. He stood before a great gate, stunning white walls spreading like wings to either side, embracing the city into the distance. Something shifted deep inside of him, and he knew its

meaning as clearly as he'd known anything in his life.
He was home.

CHAPTER 11

MYSTERIES UNMASKED

WITHIN THE PRISTINE majesty of its walls, Kalinor was madness. Aleksei was jostled from either side as he led Dash down one endlessly confusing street towards another that seemed exactly the same, save that it was possibly larger. Not even Keiv-Alon was this massive, this overwhelming.

He caught himself gawking, even though he knew it made him an easy target for cutpurses and thieves.

He no longer feared them as he once had. If they came at him, he would have to deal with them. And that inevitably brought the Guard, who would have questions.

Even as that thought struck him, Aleksei realized that his eyes were flicking to alleys and balconies, searching for viable points of escape or attack. He was so busy mapping the layout of the street that he didn't even notice the man who had stopped just ahead of him.

Before he could pull himself to a halt, Aleksei stumbled into the man and they both fell to the street.

Aleksei was instantly on his feet again, offering his hand to the other man along with his sincere apologies. The man smiled and took Aleksei's hand, coming to his feet and dusting himself off.

"Sorry." Aleksei said, scratching the back of his head in embarrassment.

The man laughed and righted the crimson scarf he wore across his shoulders, "My fault entirely."

Aleksei froze. He was staring at a very handsome man, gripped by a pair of piercing emerald eyes.

"I...I'm not sure how you could tell in this madness." Aleksei managed, trying to understand the sudden warmth in his chest.

"It can be a little overwhelming at first, I suppose. But you'll be surprised how quickly you become accustomed to it."

A cart had come up behind Dash, and the driver was shouting angrily. The spell that bound Aleksei snapped, and he turned away from the man, apologizing to the driver. He took Dash's reins and moved on down the street.

The dream man walked next to him.

"How did you find me?" Aleksei asked after a long silence.

"I can speak into your thoughts and dreams from hundreds of leagues away. Why would you be surprised that I could find you in *Kalinor?*"

Aleksei mulled this over for a few moments before he realized that the man was leading him.

"Where are we going?"

The man nodded to the west, towards another set of shimmering white walls.

"The Palace."

Aleksei started, "I can't go to the Palace!"

The man seemed bemused, "Why not?"

Aleksei stared at him incredulously, "I'm a peasant."

The man arched a chestnut eyebrow, "*Are* you?"

Aleksei shook his head and walked beside the man, deeper into the maze-like mire of the capital.

Even in the chaos of aromas and odors Kalinor exuded, Aleksei realized that he could pick out the other man's scent. He smelled like cedar, pepper, and roses in an intoxicating combination that Aleksei understood as being distinctly *his.*

Aleksei wondered if he reeked of deer blood and sweat by comparison. Gods, he hadn't even washed away the blood he'd streaked across his chest. It hadn't seemed important at the time, but as they walked through the crowded city he grew increasingly concerned about smelling like a savage. When the man looked away, Aleksei took a self-conscious glance down his shirt.

There was no blood caked across his chest.

More perplexing still, there was no hint that there ever *had* been. And rather than the stinking of rancid deer blood muddied by sweat, he detected something profoundly different.

The sweat was still firmly present, but he was also cannily aware of other notes complicating his scent. Cinnamon and leather and wood smoke filled his nostrils. Beyond his dreams in the Wood, or the deer that had offered themselves to him, it was the most keenly aware Aleksei had been that he had *changed* since the dawning of the day.

He walked next to the other man, but time lost meaning. The man remained quiet and he did the same. His mind was far too entangled in the changes he was picking up. The world was quickly becoming a different place, and before he'd had a chance to adapt to one development, another made itself bluntly apparent.

The air around him thrummed with millions of heartbeats, all set to individual paces, none of them his own. He noted the scent of every creature that passed him, man or beast, whether he wanted to or not. Other odors made themselves brusquely apparent.

They passed a midden heap and Aleksei had to fight to keep from staggering away. Gods, was this a blessing or a curse? How many new revelations would he encounter before he had a grasp on being a Hunter?

He began to deeply regret leaving the Ri-Vhan so hastily. Shouldn't he have stayed? Learned about his heritage, whatever it entailed, before riding off to Kalinor? *You're hardly a realm away.* Aleksei thought, shaking his head, *Whatever this man holds in store for you, it's only a short ride to the Wood. The Ri-Vhan will welcome their Hunter, even if you* are *a half-blood.*

"I know you worry because you care." the dream man said softly. Aleksei was startled to realize that he could hear the other man over the din of the city. "But you can put your mind to rest, at least as long as we're together. We're both seeking answers, Aleksei, but we need to understand each other before either of us can begin to unpack our secrets."

"So you still talk in riddles, even in the flesh." Aleksei grunted.

"Well," the man chuckled, "*I* do. I can't speak for the other one."

Aleksei frowned, "The *other* one?"

"Almost there." the man said absently, nodding down the road.

The Palace walls were much closer now. Aleksei looked away, battling the building anxiety. He turned his attention to the structures he was passing.

The avenue had widened, and they walked between two great cathedrals, one dedicated to Volos, God of Death and the Aftershadow. The other had been built in honor of the God of Storm and Sky, Stribog. Aleksei stopped to stare at the structures, each ornately decorated in carvings and friezes.

"Are you coming?"

Aleksei realized that the man in the scarlet scarf hadn't stopped when he had. He hurried after the man, catching up to him at the Palace's massive East Gate.

"So are you ever going to tell me who you are?" Aleksei growled. "I've put up with a *lot* so far. Far more than any man in his right mind ought to. You can answer me a simple question."

The man smiled gently and bowed, "My apologies. My name is Jonas Belgi. Welcome to Kalinor, Aleksei Drago."

Aleksei frowned at the name. *Belgi?*

"You're the *Prince?*" Aleksei stammered, feeling his face flush.

"Yes." Jonas said, looking for all the world as though the title were more burden than honor. "But I prefer Jonas."

Aleksei thought he should drop to a knee or bow or *something*. But hadn't Jonas just bowed to *him?* What was all that dream nonsense about toads, then? Was that the "other one" Jonas had mentioned? None of it was adding up as much as he'd hoped.

He kept returning to the memory of knocking Jonas into the street. To those emerald eyes. To the perplexing fog that filled his mind every time he picked up Jonas' scent.

"So what do you want with me?" he asked, bewildered.

He'd expected the dream man, or *men* apparently, to be, well... enigmatic, but not *royal*. He'd expected someone powerful, but not as confusing as the dreams and whispers he'd spent the past few days chasing. Given the speed of his travel, he'd expected to find someone of incredible power, but not a bloody *prince*!

Jonas smiled. It was a handsome smile, without guile or malice, and Aleksei felt confident that he would have known the difference. Jonas was presenting himself openly and honestly; Aleksei felt he ought to respect that.

"Why don't you come with me into the Palace?" Jonas suggested, his smile never wavering, "It's a bit more comfortable there, and we can talk without the," he waved towards the packed street a few paces away, "*charm* of the city."

Aleksei considered a moment, then nodded. The dream man. Or at least *a* dream man. The knowledge that there was another troubled Aleksei more and more as he ran it through his mind. But still, *this* man had goaded, pushed and pulled him until he now stood at the threshold of Kalinor Palace itself. Whatever else may be said about Jonas Belgi, he was without a doubt the most perplexing man Aleksei had ever met.

They reached the East Gate and the guards stiffened and bowed deeply as Jonas passed. Aleksei swallowed hard. He searched for a moment when he'd felt more uncomfortable and came up empty-handed.

The reality of Kalinor Palace was instantly apparent. Aleksei stopped in his tracks, combing his fingers through Dash's mane as he stared at the majesty that surrounded him.

They stood on a broad road, paved in the same white stone as the walls. The Palace sprawled before them, a hundred ivory spires, each tipped in golden tile reaching towards the clouds, nestled amongst the undulating walls of the structure.

It was breathtaking.

On either side of the Palace were a series of smaller buildings, all built in the same style save one. Set across a vast lawn, Aleksei noticed an enormous structure that rivaled the Palace in scale. At first he'd merely assumed the two were connected, but now he realized how different this other edifice was. It was built from the same white stone, but the carvings along its straight, rigid walls were so intricate that they were scarcely to be believed.

Jonas followed his eyes and smiled, "The Voralla."

Aleksei shook his head. The Voralla was a place of myth and magic, one deeply steeped in the Archanium. He'd never thought to actually set eyes on it. Until now, he hadn't even been sure it *existed*.

"Are you...one of *them*?" he asked quietly.

"A Magus?" Jonas laughed. "Not in the literal sense. I've certainly never been trained at the Voralla. Members of the Royal Family are never trained, even in spite of our gifts."

Aleksei was surprised by the bitterness edging Jonas' voice.

"So why did you bring me here?" Aleksei asked after an awkward pause.

Jonas smiled, "Eager?"

Aleksei scowled. If he hadn't known better, he would have thought Jonas was as nervous as he was. The man *smelled* nervous. "I hope you'll understand if I want to get to the point after riding five hundred leagues."

"Ah, but they felt more like *one* hundred, didn't they?" Jonas asked archly, concealing his anxiety as easily as changing the topic of conversation. His scent remained the same.

"I guess you can explain that to me as well?"

"To a degree. I don't understand it completely myself." Jonas took a deep breath, "Aleksei, I called you here because I need your help. Every Magus has a Knight, bonded to them during their training at the Voralla. But since I never trained there..."

"You don't have a Knight." Aleksei finished.

Jonas nodded, "Correct. I have no proper training. For me the Archanium is largely a mystery, but one that has allowed me some measure of insight. However, I've learned from extensive study that I can only accomplish so much on my own. Every Magus needs an Archanium Knight.

"So I began a search. I thought I'd find one in the Legions or the Palace Guard. But instead I found myself looking farther and farther south. I can't explain *why*, really. All I know is that something in you called out to me. There's something inside of you that felt intensely compelling."

"You're saying *I* found *you*?"

"I'm saying there was resonance." Aleksei thought he saw a flash of irritation flash across the Prince's face. "That we called to each *other*. As the one directly connected to the Archanium, it was my responsibility to interpret that call, and to make sure that you and I had a chance to meet."

"So how does that explain me traveling five hundred leagues in four days?"

Jonas sighed, "That's one mystery I can't explain yet. Whenever a Magus forms a bond, the Knight receives a sort of...*blessing* from the Archanium. In the past, Knights have been granted an increase in strength, or inhuman endurance. A friend of mine became impervious to flame. That was the rarest gift I'd ever witnessed. Until you."

Aleksei tried to maintain his skepticism, but found himself grudgingly fascinated.

"Aleksei, for whatever reason, the gift you have been bestowed is *time*. And as I'm sure you've figured out by now, I'm not the only one who has been searching for you. I don't know how it works, or how it will change when or *if* you and I become Bonded.

"Someone far more knowledgeable has explained bifurcated bonds to me. We'll speak more on that later. For the moment, just understand that bonds never stay the same.

"Your ability to move across the country as you have will vanish, or at least change, when and if you bond to me. Or the other player in this farce. Either way, in place of what you have experienced...well, as I said, I can only guess. There isn't exactly a lot of precedent in this arena."

Aleksei sighed, trying to make sense of it all. Everything Jonas said seemed more and more farfetched to him, yet at the same time he felt the Prince was telling him the truth.

"But *time*?" Aleksei asked. "What does that *mean*? How am I supposed to control it?"

"I can't help you with that." Jonas admitted. "I just pray that you'll find your own answers, as I'm finding mine. But, if you're willing, I'd like to explore these questions together."

Aleksei frowned, "You said you were never trained in the Voralla, but I don't know what that means. You can obviously use the Archanium. You've walked through my dreams and spoken into my mind. That doesn't make you a Magus?"

"I never received a formal education, but that is a far cry from saying I have no talent in the Archanium. My talents are simply... different."

"Different how?"

Aleksei felt Jonas' irritation flare in his chest, and in his mind. He felt a touch of sympathy for the other man. How was Jonas supposed to explain something as complex as the Archanium to someone who had never touched it? And if Aleksei decided to leave him and go to the other player, explaining his abilities would leave Jonas at a considerable disadvantage.

At the same time, *not* being open and honest with Aleksei would just as swiftly send him running in the opposite direction. It was an impossible situation. Aleksei marveled as Jonas' thoughts tumbled through his head. Could he now hear Jonas' thoughts as easily as the Prince heard his?

He opened his mouth to ask, but Jonas forestalled him with a shake of his head. "I've been training myself for years, Aleksei. There are myriad different meridians running along, *through* the Archanium, and as I studied them I found myself on a path very different from the others in the Voralla. Not even in the same region, actually. I can do things the others can't. I have access to regions they can only dream of."

"Does that make you more powerful?"

"Possibly." Jonas conceded. "But their training has lent them a consistency that I have yet to master. All the power in the realm doesn't matter much if you can't muster a spark."

Aleksei sighed, trying to take in Jonas' words even though he didn't understand much of what the Prince was saying. Meridians? Regions? And besides, Jonas had said the others couldn't do what he could, but he never said *he* wasn't capable of matching *their* talents. How much power did the man command? And what of the other player who had been calling him? Where was *he*? Why wasn't he here too, battling Jonas Belgi for Aleksei's....what? Allegiance? Affection?

"That's probably enough." Jonas said, "For the moment, at least."

"Alright, so what do you want from *me*? To become an Archanium Knight? *Your* Knight? What does that mean?"

"It means that your life will become intertwined with mine. Completely. If I die, so will you."

Aleksei's eyes widened. "Why would *anyone* agree to that?"

Jonas smiled, "The idea is that by becoming Bonded, we become two halves of a whole."

Aleksei started as the voice of the Seil Wood flickered through his mind. *To make you whole.* She had whispered that when he'd been thinking about Jonas. But what did that *mean?*

"It is much harder to defeat either one of us because we are Bonded." Jonas continued, oblivious to the phantoms in Aleksei's head. "You would protect me from physical harm, just as I'd protect you from all things magical. But I can't guard you every moment, as you must guard me. It's for that reason that the bonding spell grants you a gift. It's meant to lend you an edge in any confrontation."

Aleksei's head was spinning. He still hadn't fully recovered from the first revelations of the day, much less *this.* "How long do I have to think about this?"

Jonas shrugged, "As long as you want. In the meantime, you can stay here in the Palace. Or you're free to return home, if you wish. I don't want you rush to judgment on a matter as important as this." Jonas paused. "You can even seek out the other player, if you want."

Aleksei could see the pain in Jonas' face as he said the words. "Alright. I'll stay the night here, I suppose." The very idea of sleeping in Kalinor Palace was at once welcome and terrifying. "Is there somewhere to stable Dash for the night?"

Jonas' smile returned, and Aleksei could feel the man's relief. "Of course. The stables are on the West Lawn. I will wait for you in my chambers."

Aleksei frowned, "Your chambers?"

"Just ask a servant and you'll be given directions. I've prepared them for your arrival."

Aleksei nodded, more confused than ever by this man. "Thank you."

Jonas looked up into his eyes. For the first time since they'd met, Aleksei saw something beyond the intense intelligence that burned in the Prince. This was a man who was willingly exposing his vulnerabilities, a man who was being honest, and earnest, in a way that was clearly uncomfortable. But as uncomfortable as it may be, Jonas seemed to understand that it was also *necessary.*

"Thank *you*, Aleksei Drago. If for nothing else than exerting the sheer effort of coming this far to entertain a voice and a dream."

Aleksei wasn't quite sure how to respond to that, but Jonas saved him the trouble by walking away. Aleksei watched the man vanish into the entrance of the Palace before he allowed himself a sigh.

He had spent the last few days alternately dreading and yearning for this moment, only to have it to end so abruptly. The dream man was unmasked, his purpose made clear. The only mysteries that remained were matters of magic that Aleksei wasn't even close to understanding, and yet somehow that comforted him.

With a grunt, both confused and contented, Aleksei led Dash towards the West Lawn.

"Staying for a while, sir?" the groom asked as he led Dash into the spacious whitestone stable.

Aleksei paused, "I'm not sure."

The groom nodded, "Very good, sir."

He took Dash's reins and led the draft horse back into the cool recesses of the building, leaving Aleksei standing in the doorway.

He was unaccustomed to people doing his work for him. The idea of servants rushing around to do his bidding filled him with a sense of horror bred by years of hard work. Aleksei turned and made his way into the Palace, trying to ignore the curious glances he received. He supposed he *did* look odd, dressed in the clothes of a peasant, smelling of dust and sweat.

Aleksei walked for a while, just taking in the sweeping beauty of the Palace. He didn't want to hurry where Jonas had directed him, to seem too eager. He needed time to think about what he'd heard, and what it could mean. Was being bonded to Jonas any different than living with the Ri-Vhan as their Hunter? Would he be happier in the Wood? Would he be happy in *either* place, or did he need to leave this palace and this city and hurry home as fast as he could?

No voices invaded his thoughts, much to his relief. He was allowed the freedom to ponder and question in silence, wandering through hallways, some quiet, others bustling with people.

He ignored everything as he walked. The cool stone of the Palace felt good after the heat of the city streets, and he realized how relaxed he felt in the Palace. Despite the glances and glares from people dressed much finer than he, Aleksei realized that something about the Palace felt...right.

After an hour or so of wandering, Aleksei decided it was time to find Jonas. He stopped a passing maid, "Where might I find Jonas Belgi's chambers?"

The woman seemed startled, but nevertheless gave him directions. He thanked her and marched towards the west wing.

He was walking down yet another enormous corridor when a voice sounded behind him, "I trust you enjoyed your walk?"

Aleksei nodded, "It's beautiful. The people could stand to be friendlier, though."

Jonas chuckled. "The disadvantage of looking like a farmer, I suppose."

"Why did you say it like that? That I *look* like a farmer? What do *you* think I am?"

Jonas regarded him seriously as they stepped into his chambers, "I believe I know you for what you are, Aleksei Drago, and for what you may become."

Aleksei rolled his eyes, "More riddles?"

"There is more to you than your homespun clothing and the dirt beneath your fingernails. Something that I cannot yet put into place. But you are no mere farmer, Aleksei."

Aleksei sighed, "Well, I guess you do have me there."

Jonas' eyes narrowed. "Do I? So what else are you?"

Aleksei straightened his back and looked directly into Jonas' eyes. "I'm the Hunter."

Jonas smiled, "Very good. A hunter. That's a promising start."

Aleksei laughed. Jonas was so stunned by the reaction that he could only stare at the farm boy before him in utter confusion.

Aleksei shook his head. "You misunderstand. I meant to say that I'm the *Ri-Vhan* Hunter."

If his laughter had startled Jonas, this new revelation left the Prince speechless.

"How is that possible? You're from the Southern Plain."

"My mother was Ri-Vhan." he said softly. "We only left for the

Southern Plain after she died."

Aleksei could tell that Jonas was still trying to wrangle with the idea of Aleksei Drago being a Hunter. But the Prince pulled himself together with remarkable speed.

"Then, as I said, there is a great deal more to you than meets the eye. You're a Hunter. That in itself is enough to make you a lord among men."

"So why should I accept your offer?" Aleksei asked sharply, deciding to press his advantage while he possessed some modicum of control. "Why not return to the Ri-Vhan and become their exalted hero? Or to my farm where I could work the rest of my days in peace?"

Jonas hardly seemed perturbed by the question, "Because you would be miserable anywhere else. You would either grow to hate the Ri-Vhan for their timidity, or your farm for its boundaries. The Ri-Vhan have their leader. They would be undoubtedly overjoyed to have you among them, but they don't *need* you.

"As for your father, he seems like he can manage quite well on his own. And if he tires of the hard work, he is more than welcome to come to the Palace and live out the rest of his days in comfort."

That brought Aleksei up short. He hadn't realized that accepting Jonas' offer would have such lofty ramifications. "My father could retire to the Palace? You would honestly allow a peasant to live here?"

"Why not? You're a peasant, yet I'm offering you one of the most coveted titles in Ilyar."

Aleksei scowled, "Coveted?"

"You would be bound to the Prince of Ilyar. You would therefore share in all the comforts that come with my position. It's one of the only ways to attain nobility in this realm without being born into it."

He waved his hand towards the window, "There are a thousand farmers who would *leap* at the chance to be my Bonded and enjoy a life of luxury. A thousand more who would do it for the potential danger and adventure of being bound to the Prince of Ilyar."

"Then why don't you ask one of *them?*" Aleksei snapped.

Jonas smiled patiently. "Because I don't *want* any of them, Aleksei. I want *you. You* are the one who called out to me. *You* are, as far as I'm concerned, the only one who really matters. *You* are an eye in the storm. *You* are the only one who is necessary."

"Necessary for *what*?" Aleksei demanded.

"I'm not sure yet." Jonas admitted. "That much hasn't been made clear to me. All I know is that our bond is important. The bond I formed with you, that this other player, this other Magus has formed, signals something important. If I were not convinced that we were meant to be Bonded, then I would have been content with a Legionnaire and let you go off to find this other player."

There was a finality in Jonas' tone that Aleksei found unsettling. He was so confident, so certain. But about what? Aleksei wished to the gods he knew.

"It's a pity you didn't come a few days earlier. My cousin Tamara just left for our estate at Igraan, or I'd introduce you to her. She makes a charming dinner companion to say the least." He chuckled and placed a comforting hand on Aleksei's shoulder, "But I suppose you need rest in any event.

"Take your time, Aleksei. This isn't something you want to rush into without a great deal of thought. All I ask is that you consider what I've told you. There are answers out there, Aleksei, for *both* of us. Will you help me find them?"

Aleksei smiled, "I'll think on it. Now if it's alright, I'll, uh, I'll take my leave?"

Jonas led Aleksei out into the corridor, nodding a few doors down, "I've already had the maids make up the room. The kitchens are three flights down. If you get hungry this evening, fell free to help yourself."

Aleksei nodded, grateful for Jonas' hospitality if nothing else. "I guess I'll see you in the morning."

Jonas smiled, "I look forward to it. Sleep well, Aleksei Drago." And then he turned and stepped back into his chambers, shutting the door gently behind him.

Aleksei frowned as he turned away from Jonas' rooms. Something the Prince had said stirred his memory, but he couldn't place it. Not yet. Gods, but he wished he knew what it was.

His feet now dragging with exhaustion, Aleksei stumbled through the door of the chamber Jonas had indicated and kicked off his boots before collapsing onto the large bed. He drifted into sleep, comfortable for the first time in days, oddly at home with his surroundings.

CHAPTER 12

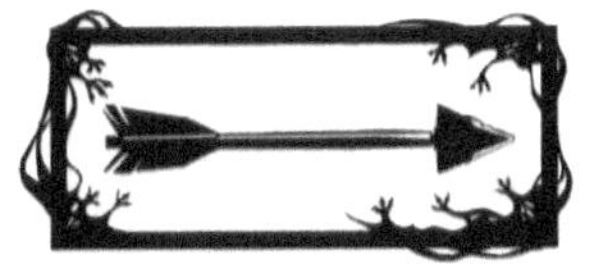

CATCHING ARROWS

BAEL RETCHED VIOLENTLY into the ditch. His stomach was on fire from the pain and confusion, the sheer terror that radiated across the fragile bond he'd forged with Aleksei Drago. With every increasingly dry heave, another knot of fire punched him in the gut.

He had been *so* close, and in his fear he had ruined everything. He had sensed someone spying on him, and his first instinct had been to lash out, to attack. Only now did he realize that the reason he'd even *felt* the other man was because of their bond.

And now Aleksei was well within the walls of Kalinor.

Bael wondered if his rival had already tracked down the young Hunter. Even now, Jonas Belgi was probably sinking his entitled claws into Aleksei's heart. Even now Jonas Belgi was stealing away Bael's only chance at salvation.

He made his way into the Commune, ignoring the frightened and furtive glances of his father's faithful. They were nothing to him, not any longer.

The flap to Jorna's tent flew open as Bael collapsed into a huddled wreck before her fire.

"*Troubled*, dearie?" she croaked.

Bael glared up at her, "I tried to kill him. It was *him*, in the Wood.

It was Aleksei. I felt him there. I felt the bond. But...but I didn't know what it was. I thought I...." Bael coughed several times, trying to push the tears from his eyes before dissolving into wracking sobs.

"I *warned* you, Bael. I *told* you to watch your temper. It seems you got burned this time, sweetling."

Bael glared at her, "Are you *insane?* My future hangs on this, and I just drove the one person who could fix it into Jonas Belgi's hands."

Jorna leaned forward, smoke drooling from her empty sockets, "*Our* future *depended* on this, and now you've made a properly royal mess of everything."

"How dare you?" Bael demanded, standing and gripping the Archanium.

His connection to the magic snuffed out just as suddenly as it had appeared.

"Sit." Jorna grunted.

Bael slammed to the ground. He was certain he'd felt a bone break. He stared into her empty eyes, fighting back a wave of nausea, transfixed by the embers of hatred he found burning within.

"I *tried*, sweetling." Jorna hissed. "You were my frog prince. You were lovely. And then you *changed*. Just like Azarael, just like Darielle. Just like YOU. The children your father made are a sick stock, but I held my tongue. No more. YOU will not be like the others. YOU will *obey*. YOU will *mind*. YOU will do as I say, or I will burn you from this cursed world. Am I clear?"

Bael felt an impossible chill sweep through him even as the air was pulled from his lungs in a ghostly fog. He had no breath. He could feel his lungs screaming for air as ice crystals spidered their way up his face.

"Yes." he mouthed.

Jorna cackled, "That's a good little Toady. *Good* Toady." Her voice became a coo, "Now listen to me, little Toady. You've grown way above your britches. If you were younger I'd just switch you, but we're past that, aren't we, Toady?"

His head felt about to burst, yet no matter how he tried, Bael couldn't muster the faintest glimmer of faith, of magic. She was in complete control. The Dark God be damned, but he had never felt such power radiate from the woman.

A spike of agony shot through his entire body, forcing his muscles to contract in abject pain. A scream rose within him that he could not possibly give voice to.

"Now, dearie," Granny Jorna purred, smoke pouring from her eyes, "we're going to fix this *mess*. And if we don't, you're going to cry blood until you're *sorry* for what you've put your Granny through."

⟊⟊

Aleksei's eyes snapped open and he sat up, searching the darkness. The night had been free of Jonas' voice, but that was a far cry from saying he hadn't dreamt. He'd spent what few hours of sleep he'd managed being plagued by attacks from all sides, though he could see none of his attackers.

Now he sat in the darkness, his eyes searching the room but finding it empty. He was safe.

Aleksei rolled out of bed.

Whatever clinging threads of exhaustion had plagued him earlier were gone for the moment, and he needed to stretch his legs. He felt claustrophobic in the dark. Maybe a little exercise would clear his head.

He shut the door quietly behind him, deciding that he needed to eat something.

For a heartbeat he considered waking Jonas and asking the Prince to accompany him, but swiftly abandoned the idea. Undoubtedly Jonas would think him foolish for being frightened by a nightmare. Aleksei was determined not to show weakness in the Prince's presence.

He moved silently down the hall, following Jonas' directions towards the kitchen. Food would help clear his head. He might even be able to sleep again before dawn came. That would be a welcome change, and he decided he might even allow himself the luxury of sleeping *past* dawn.

Aleksei turned a corner and paused. Several doors down he noticed a light. Someone else was awake, even at this hour.

Trying to be as quiet as possible, Aleksei crept past the doorway. It would not be good for an unknown peasant to be caught roaming the halls of the Palace at this hour.

"—will be gone soon. And then we only have the Prince to deal with."

Aleksei stopped. The words were faint but he could make out the basic syllables.

"She's moving south. They're waiting in the Sulaq Hills. It should be the work of moments."

Pieces of an intricate puzzle began to spin in Aleksei's head. He closed his eyes and focused his attention entirely upon the sounds emanating from the chamber.

"And you're sure the evidence will lead back to the Prince, Master?"

"Certain."

And the pieces finally clicked.

Aleksei remembered Jonas' mention of the Princess Tamara.

She was headed to her lands in the South. He remembered the men in the Wood. They had spoken of a target, a 'she'. And now these two men were conversing in the small hours of the morning.

He froze, realizing with a start that the voice of the one being called 'Master' belonged to the same man who'd thrown fire at him in the Wood. And they were going to assassinate the Princess in hopes of framing Jonas for the entire debacle?

What should he do? Should he run to Jonas and tell him what he'd heard? Would the Prince *believe* him? Would he even be able to do anything about it? Aleksei recalled what Jonas had said. His strange ability to cross great distances would vanish if he bonded either man. But it still remained.

If he could get to the Princess in time.... *What?* Aleksei battled his uncertainties as they stacked up, each one more convincingly dismal than the last. He was riding into obvious danger and, much worse, a danger that was completely unknown to him. But he knew where Igraan was. It wasn't more than fifty leagues from Voskrin. He knew which roads she would be on.

It was a risk to say the least, but Aleksei felt compelled. He turned on his heel and bolted in the other direction, ghosting through the halls of the Palace towards the entrance hall.

Aleksei slipped out into the chill of the night and dashed through the dew-slicked lawn, his feet bare but oblivious to the cold and the wet. He had only one purpose in mind, and it would take an act of the gods to stop him now.

He found the stables much as he'd left them, with the notable absence of the groom. Dash was in a stall near the entrance. Apparently the groom hadn't been all that confident that Aleksei would be staying for any length of time.

Aleksei didn't waste time saddling the horse, vaulting onto his back and digging his bare heels into the horse's flanks.

Dash leapt forward, out of the stable and into the night.

Aleksei wasn't questioned at the gate, and as he passed rapidly through the streets of Kalinor, he marveled at the ease with which Dash navigated the city. Less than a day before, they'd both been lost to their wits' end in this twisting labyrinth of alleys and streets, yet now the draft horse shot through them as though he'd been born traveling their twists and turns.

For his part, Aleksei clung to Dash's mane and kept watch for Guardsmen who might mistake them for criminals. And then they were rushing past the South Gate, as yet unscathed, unnoticed. Aleksei shook his head in amazement as Dash roared down the road, south towards the Sulaq Hills.

His eyes moved to the horizon, where the sun was yet several hours away. Aleksei fervently hoped it would be enough time. The distance he needed to travel was vast, and the clock ticking in his head made it all the more terrifying, yet Aleksei's mind was consumed with the vision of a girl screaming as her horse was shot out from under her.

Aleksei watched in horror as she tried to run, only to be pierced through with arrows herself. He tried to close his eyes, the image too terrible to bear, but it would not leave him. He was forced to stare into her pale blue eyes as her life faded into her blood-soaked gown.

He urged Dash on to greater speed, racing the dawn and the inevitable doom lurking in the Hills.

Farms and towns flashed past by him so fast, Aleksei hardly even realized they were there before they vanished. He didn't care. If it was a gift to move this swiftly, he would make the best use of it possible.

Dawn broke over the horizon, but Aleksei paid it no mind. Any sense of fatigue had been burned away by adrenaline as Dash rushed him forward to meet his fate.

⁂

The Sulaq Hills passed by and Tamara smiled in delight. She loved the Hills in the autumn, their wildflowers bursting with color and vibrancy. This year the rains had been especially heavy, and the flowers resonated thanks in vibrant hues.

Before and behind her, the Magi rode in silence, their Knights surveying the ridges for signs of movement. Tamara wasn't worried, but after having spent a few days traveling in open country, she was starting to feel thankful to have her honor guard.

It wasn't that she felt vulnerable. No one could have a thing to gain from her kidnap or death except Jonas, and the idea of her cousin as a threat was laughable. Nevertheless, her escort would not be accused of being lazy, and she was glad for it.

A life constructed within the limits of palace walls and hunting lodges had left Tamara with a deep sense of uncertainty when confronted by the vastness of the open sky, the boundless nature of hills rolling to meet the horizon. To her mind there was no boundary to what threat or blessing could be born of that horizon.

Tamara sighed, her mind returning to the flowers and summers long past.

She and Jonas had played in these hills many times, when they'd made similar trips south with her mother. They would stop in Keiv-Alon, and there would always be a nursemaid to take them into the Hills so they could run amongst the flowers.

It had been on one of those outings that Jonas had touched the Archanium for the first time.

The memory jolted her, but Tamara didn't force it away. She liked remembering. It was *important* to remember.

She had been running a bit farther away than Jonas, and he'd chased after her. They couldn't have been more than five or six summers old. Even then Jonas had that sense of duty and responsibility about him. She remembered little of him as a carefree child.

Tamara's foot had struck a stone and as she fell, she heard Jonas cry out in surprise. She'd turned just as a snake rose from behind the stone to strike her, its mouth yawning wide.

She'd hardly had time to recognize the danger, much less attempt an escape, before it sprang. Tamara had screwed her eyes shut, tensing for the bite. But it never came.

A moment later Jonas was shaking her shoulder, tears streaming down his face.

"Are you alright, Tamara?"

She'd looked around for the snake, but couldn't see it anywhere. But she could smell something burning.

"Yes." she'd managed weakly.

He'd hugged her tightly and she started to cry. The nursemaid found them clutching each other, each drying the other's tears. The woman had been frantic, saying it was probably the lightning that scared the children, and thank the gods it hadn't started a fire.

That was when Tamara realized that Jonas had saved her. She hadn't been able to explain it at the time, but she'd known somehow.

"Princess!" Dava shouted behind her.

Tamara turned in her saddle to look at the Magus. Her blood froze.

A large man was galloping towards them on a massive horse. His blond hair was wild, his eyes murderous.

Dava's Knight turned and drew his sword to meet the would-be attacker.   And then the world went mad.

Dava and Uriah cried out at the same moment. Tamara gasped as thick, black-shafted arrows seemed to sprout from their throats. Their Knights began to vomit blood.

Tamara screamed.

Aleksei urged Dash on, wincing as he saw the first volley fired into the two Magi. Beside them their Knights began to convulse. Aleksei shuddered as he desperately tried to reach the Princess in time.

He passed a Knight as the man doubled over, blood fountaining from his mouth. Aleksei could see her, the girl who could only be Tamara. She was screaming in panic, staring wildly around at the death that had simply materialized around her.

And then he was next to her.

Time slowed. Aleksei could feel the arrows leave the archers' bows. He lunged forward from Dash's back and wrapped one arm around the Princess, twisting his body and lifting her clear of the first arrow's path.

A heartbeat later, his free hand shot into the air just above her head and caught the second arrow.

Time regained its speed with a jolt and Dash surged forward, leaving the bodies of the Magi and their Knights behind as the distance between them multiplied. It was only after a league or so that Aleksei realized that Tamara had stopped screaming and had begun to bite his arm.

"Hey!" he roared, twisting her around so she sat in front of him on Dash's back.

"Let me *go!*" she screamed. "What do you *want?* Money? I don't *have* any!"

She was sobbing now, and Aleksei realized that she thought he was part of the attack.

"I'm not *robbing* you." he shouted over the thunder of Dash's hooves.

"So you're just going to *kill* me? Is that it? Why couldn't you just let me *die* back there with the others?" she cried.

Aleksei looked skyward. Was there anything he could say that would make her understand?

"I was sent by Jonas." he lied. "He sent me to protect you."

She stilled, her attacks subdued, though her body was still wracked with sobs. Gods, he wished he could see her face. "Jonas?" she managed.

"He realized what was going to happen, and he told me to get to you as fast as I could."

"So why don't you take me *back* to him?" she demanded.

Aleksei pulled Dash to a halt and took a moment to look around. He was stunned to realize how much ground they'd covered. He recognized their location and it was as far as could be from the Sulaq Hills.

"We're in the Southern Plain." he whispered. "Gods, of *course* we are. What was I thinking riding *south?*"

"What?" she whimpered, bewildered.

Aleksei shook his head. There was no way to explain it to her, not in a way she would understand. *He* hardly understood how it was possible.

"We need to stop, at least for a moment. I have to rest, and so does my horse. We won't get far if we're both about to drop." Aleksei said absently, his eyes scouting for a place to camp.

There. The Southern Plain was dotted by tiny wooded glades like the one he'd camped in his first night away from home. Now he rode towards the nearest one, exhaustion already creeping up on him. Aleksei had only slept a few precious hours the night before, and since the small hours of the morning Dash had been racing towards the Sulaq Hills.

Tamara was silent and sullen as Aleksei rode into the glade and slid off Dash's back. He offered his hand to her and after a brief pause, she allowed him to help her down.

"I'm sorry for how sudden all this is." Aleksei said gently. "But please, just trust me for right now. I'll take you to Jonas, don't worry. But first we have to go a bit farther south to get supplies. Otherwise, we won't make it back to Kalinor."

Tamara sat on the ground and stared straight ahead. She no longer seemed to acknowledge that he was present or speaking.

"I'm sorry about your friends." Aleksei said softly, placing a comforting hand on her shoulder. Tamara flinched at first, but then relaxed. She finally nodded, her tears trickling in a stream down her cheeks, the pain dripping from her chin into her folded hands.

CHAPTER 13

A NOBLE PEASANT

BAEL PACED ACROSS the pale blue and gold carpets. His mind was racing, full of anticipation and dread. It would be a small feat for his father's men to Fade to the Southern Plain and return with news of their victory. He prayed to the Dark God that his own plans had come to fruition without incident.

There was a flicker across the Archanium, and a new figure stood in the center of the room. When his blue eyes caught sight of Bael, they widened with surprise.

"Master Bael! I...I hadn't anticipated..." Sammul fell to the floor in a shocked cry of pain.

Bael stepped forward and towered over the other Magus, "I want answers and information, Sammul, not apologies."

"Master Bael?" Sammul whimpered, suddenly uncertain.

There was another flicker across the Archanium, and Sammul

screamed until he began to cough blood. In truth, Bael wasn't even sure if the spell would *work*, but he'd seen his father attempt the same thing before with limited success. He was more than pleased with his own results.

"I *said* I want *answers*." Bael growled, placing his boot on Sammul's neck, "Now, can *you* provide them? Or shall I move on to one of your little sycophants?"

"I'll tell you whatever you want!" Sammul bellowed.

"I want the *truth*. What happened down there?"

"They failed!"

Bael stood stock still, barely controlling his tightly wound rage. Once his grandmother had given him permission to release the years of repression and torment, he'd found it increasingly difficult to master his emotions. This was no exception.

"*Who* failed? *How*?"

"I don't *know*." Sammul sobbed. "One moment we were about to eliminate Tamara, and the next someone flew out of the ether, grabbed her from her horse, and just...disappeared. My archers were at a loss even as I executed them."

Bael eased his heel from Sammul's neck. The other Magus trembled as he regained his feet, rubbing the sore spot. "What I *can't* understand is how anyone even knew we were going to be down there. The Princess was traveling in utmost secrecy."

"It was Aleksei." Bael muttered faintly.

"I beg your pardon?" Sammul asked, perplexed.

Bael waved a hand dismissively, "You wouldn't understand. But I do. I made a huge mistake." An idea took root in Bael's mind. He rounded on Sammul, stepping very close to the Magus even as he embraced the Archanium, "But *you*. If you breathe a *word* of this to my father, I will cut you like a fish. Do you understand?"

Sammul's face turned defiant. Bael could feel him reaching for the Archanium, could feel him grasp and flounder. Sammul's steel blue eyes watered with the strain. Finally Sammul's gaze sank to the floor, "Yes."

"Yes *what*?" Bael snarled, gripping the Archanium tighter still.

Sammul crumpled to the floor without a sound, blood drooling from his eyes and ears. His gaze turned slowly upward, back to Bael's sparkling emerald eyes.

"Yes, Master."

Tamara blinked at Aleksei.

She was just beginning to come out of her fugue and recognize where she was, what was happening. For a time there, she was quite sure she'd gone mad. All she could hear were the sounds, the wet throb of the crossbow bolts striking flesh, the screams, the splatter of blood and vomit as men, good men, her *friends* died.

Some time in the late afternoon, her mind became alert once more. Her lifetime of training in the art of leadership, the very thing that was supposed to make her an excellent queen when her time came, and the grace to handle difficult situations without losing her composure had resurfaced. Gradually she had pulled herself back to sanity, though the road had certainly been treacherous.

Since that epiphany, she had been studying the only thing of interest.

Aleksei.

Despite everything that had just happened, happened in the span of a *moment*, she had found comfort in his warm tone and patient voice. She allowed herself to believe that he truly was what he claimed. Surely Jonas would only send someone he trusted to protect her?

But questions remained unasked and unanswered. Why had Jonas not come himself? That troubled her. If Jonas had known about the threat, surely he would have done everything in his power to save all of them. *All* of them. This man obviously meant her no harm, yet she could not bring herself trust him completely. Not yet.

But here he was, slowly sitting up and rubbing the sleep from his eyes. Patiently watching her after having left her unattended through the night. Surely her kidnapper would remain awake until his compatriots were near enough to keep an eye on her.

Whatever the truth, there was something decidedly odd about him. He wasn't like any other man she'd met. He was neither too harsh nor too soft. He radiated patience and calm, yet she remembered how quickly he had acted when he saved her. She knew without a doubt that if he had not appeared, she would be dead.

Tamara made up her mind. Whether he meant her good or ill, she would wait for him to make his intentions clear. It would do her no good to run off if he was a savior, and even if he weren't, what would she do? She had no food or supplies. He was right. Without provisions, they couldn't make the journey back to Kalinor.

She glanced around, wishing to the gods she had a better idea of where she was. The impossibility of their position was still held with a degree of skepticism in the back of her mind, despite the countryside and its obvious support of his claim.

He believed they were in the Southern Plain, but that was an enormous province, one of the largest in the realm. They could be practically anywhere in southwestern Ilyar. But perhaps he knew where they were better than she.

Actually, from this angle she found him to be quite an attractive man, which surprised her. Surprised her mind could conceptualize such a thing of beauty after being exposed so suddenly to the intense ugliness of the day.

He was much larger than the nobles, and even the Archanium Knights, she was used to seeing, rising to nearly three paces in height. His square jaw and bold brow lent him a commanding air she wouldn't have expected of such a young commoner. And there was an intelligence in his preternatural golden eyes that matched the obvious power of his body.

A truly odd man. Just the sort that would fascinate Jonas. Strangely, that realization comforted her.

"You're still here." he muttered, seeming surprised in the twilight.

She shrugged, "Where would I go? For the moment I'm safer with you. At least I know *you* don't want me dead. That's more than I can say for anyone else out there."

"Well, I'm glad you're speaking again. Are you hungry?" he asked, coming to his feet.

"*Famished.*"

He smiled, "I'm going to go find us some food. Any chance you could gather some wood?"

She paused, then nodded.

"I'll be back in a few minutes." he said before vanishing into the gathering darkness.

Tamara rose and began to look around the campsite. Wood? She was to gather *wood*? She laughed quietly to herself as she began to collect twigs. She, the Princess of Ilyar, heir to the throne, was gathering wood for a fire like any common kitchen maid.

It was exhilarating.

True to his word, Aleksei returned a few minutes later. He cradled three dead rabbits. Tamara gasped, dropping her twigs.

"Excuse me." she muttered, gathering her sticks. "I'm unaccustomed to seeing such things." Tamara cursed herself for sounding so naïve, but her irritation warred heavily with her need to be far away from Aleksei when he gutted the poor creatures.

Even the thought was enough to turn her face green.

"You might want to gather more wood on the *other* side of that tree." he said pointedly.

She hurried out of the campsite.

Aleksei sighed irritably, and set about skinning and cleaning the rabbits. Fortunately there had been no impulse to mark himself this time. He wondered what Tamara would have done if she'd returned to find him half-naked, rabbit blood drooling down his chest.

It had been uncannily easy to trap and kill the rabbits, and though Aleksei was not usually bothered by hunting animals, he found himself strangely affected by the experience.

They were so gentle and calm. It *hurt* to kill them. But he needed their meat, and he had the feeling they had offered themselves.

"Is this my curse?" he muttered to himself. "I can hunt any animal in Ilyar, but only as long as I can feel its pain?" He would almost rather return to the cold combination of precision and luck afforded by his bow at home.

"Have you found enough wood?" he called softly into the near-dark.

For a moment, fear lanced through his heart. What if she'd been taken while he cleaned the rabbits? What would he do? Would he be able to track her? What if the assassins had caught up to them? The moment passed and Tamara stepped around the tree, her arms full of twigs and small branches.

Aleksei fought back a laugh as she deposited the wood on top of her previous collection. The image of a princess gathering firewood was more than a little amusing to a him. It was hardly something he'd ever expected to see.

"Thank you." he said instead, gathering the smaller twigs along with a handful of dried leaves he'd collected while hunting the rabbits.

He cleared a small area of undergrowth, building his fire with the speed born from long years of experience. In a matter of minutes, he had a small blaze. He spitted the rabbits and balanced them against two stones over the fire. As he worked, Aleksei was keenly aware of Tamara's eyes on him, watching him with apparent fascination.

"How long will they take to cook?" she asked, her voice barely above a whisper. He could hear the eagerness in her voice; the desperation.

Aleksei turned the spits and shrugged, "Longer than you'd think. I have to be sure they're cooked through, 'else their meat could make you sick. And neither of us can afford that at the moment."

Tamara's face contorted in frustration. Aleksei empathized. If she was hungry, he was starving. He hadn't eaten since leaving the Ri-Vhan. It had taken the remainder of his fraying will to stop himself from sinking his teeth into the rabbits raw. Something deep within him, something primal *hungered* for the fresh kill while it still bled. He resisted, but only just.

Tamara quietly studied the ease with which he worked. She'd never seen anyone start a fire with sticks before. Normally servants would enter a chamber with a brazier of hot coals and rags soaked in sweet-smelling oil. This man had simply conjured the fire from thin air.

The smell of roasting rabbits made her mouth water. She hadn't eaten since dawn, and her hunger was nearly overpowering.

Aleksei noticed her eager glance at the fire.

"They'll be ready in a few minutes." he promised.

She sighed, working hard to maintain her mood and composure. How could he sit there and be so calm? Was he not the least bit nervous? What if the men who had tried to kill her earlier followed them? What if brigands noticed their fire and tried to rob them?

What would he do?

"Are you going to stand the entire day? Or would you like to sit down?" he asked, his voice cutting through her fears.

Tamara realized how silly she must look and quickly took a graceful seat on the stony ground.

"Where are we?" she asked finally, attempting some small effort at conversation.

Aleksei glanced around, frowning, "Oh, twenty or thirty leagues north of Voskrin."

She frowned. *Voskrin?* "That's a tiny little hamlet in the deep Southern Plain, lest I'm mistaken. Not too far from Igraan."

Aleksei nodded, "That's right."

Tamara shook her head in wonder. There was such conviction in his voice that she was actually starting to believe him. But if he was telling the truth, that meant they'd reached this place in little over an hour from the Sulaq Hills. The *northern* Sulaq Hills.

She was supposed to believe that this common man and his big draft horse had transported her three hundred leagues in a matter of *hours?* And *after* he'd saved her from an ambush that had killed two Archanium Magi *and* their Knights...by catching arrows out of the air.

And yet, in the span of a few hours, that seemed to be exactly what she'd personally experienced. Perhaps she'd lost her mind after all.

"Who *are* you?" she asked, trying to muster what was left of her dignity.

"My name is Aleksei Drago. I'm a farmer."

Tamara laughed. Surely he must realize how absurd he sounded? A *farmer?*

"Do you honestly expect me to believe that?" she demanded, her uncertainties warring with his convictions. "Are there many farmers such as yourself in the Southern Plain? If so, then I must say the Legions are sorely missing out on all your talents." She snickered sardonically.

Aleksei's face darkened at her laughter, "I thought people in your station had better manners. Or is that just us common folk?"

She was stunned by his retort, and at the same time amazed at how...comfortable he was around her. He displayed no awareness of his inferiority, or the feigned awe that she'd become accustomed to in Kalinor. He treated her much as she imagined he'd treat *anyone*. Tamara wasn't used to being treated like a commoner, yet she wasn't offended.

"How did you know I was in danger?" she asked softly.

"I heard men planning to ambush and murder a girl heading south. It matched with something I'd heard earlier that day, and something Jonas said."

"So you *do* know Jonas?"

Aleksei nodded, "Oh yes, I know him. Not well, of course, but I met him in Kalinor yesterday."

Tamara shook her head. The man had been in Kalinor *yesterday?* No, this man was no simple farmer. Of course, the fact that *Jonas* had been speaking with him proved that beyond all doubt.

"And what did my cousin want with you?"

Aleksei frowned, "What do you mean?"

"I *know* Jonas Belgi. He doesn't simply summon farmers up from the Southern Plain for his own amusement. If he summons someone to him, it's usually for something important. Though in your case," she added, looking him up and down, "I can't *imagine* what that could be."

Aleksei sighed deeply. "For the last several weeks, Jonas has been speaking into my dreams."

Tamara sat up in surprise.

"He kept telling me to come to him. At first I didn't know where that was. I reached Keiv-Alon in two days, which should have been impossible, and the Seil Wood a day later. When I got to Kalinor, Jonas told me that it was because of a bond we shared."

"Bond? How is that possible?"

Aleksei continued, apparently ignoring her question. "He said he wanted me for his Knight. That the bond growing between us was the reason I was moving so fast. He said I was linked to *time*."

"And how did you respond?" Tamara demanded, surprised by the fact that Jonas had concealed this from her, but also that Aleksei had not apparently accepted.

"I said I'd have to think about it."

She shook her head in amazement, "You turned down the Prince of Ilyar? *You*? A *peasant*?"

"It's *my* life, Princess." Aleksei snapped. "That doesn't belong to the royal family yet, now *does* it?"

She was shocked by his directness, but slipped back into silence. This man was no common farmer. In fact, there was nothing *common* about him.

And something else, something strange about his air she couldn't quite place. *Gods*, but she wished she knew what it was. Tamara hated dealing with people when she didn't know the tricks they had hidden up their sleeves.

"I told him I would have to think about it. And I have."

"And what have you decided?" she pressed.

"That's between me and him." Aleksei said softly, returning his attention to the fire and turning the rabbits over.

Tamara sighed heavily. She wouldn't get any more out of him for the moment. Yet what he had told her was interesting in and of itself. Jonas had asked this man to be his *Knight*? That was intriguing indeed. Her cousin undoubtedly knew much more about Aleksei than he was willing to divulge. Not unlike him, really. He had always treasured his secrets.

She watched Aleksei as he tended to their meal. Once he was Jonas' Bonded, he would become nobility, even *royalty* after a fashion. She had a hard time envisioning this man, whatever he really was, as an Archanium Knight. She wondered how he would fit into Ilyari society. *Could* he ever fit in?

He would be Jonas' Knight. She thought to herself. *It wouldn't matter.*

The more Tamara thought the idea over, the more pleased she became. Hours of entertainment would be created just by watching Parliament attempt to swallow their self-importance in the presence of such a man.

No one would question the Prince's Knight.

And then she remembered. No one would *know*. Unless something forced his hand, Jonas would never publicly acknowledge having a Knight, or using the Archanium for that matter. She wondered how he planned to keep it a secret. Such luxuries were difficult to come by in Kalinor, especially for someone of his station.

And when the secret got out? How would the other Knights react? Until now, there had been a definite gulf between Sammul's Magi and Jonas, and the Knights were a very tangible symbol of that difference.

Jonas was untrained, and therefore just an adept lacking proper knowledge. If Jonas bonded Aleksei, that gulf would narrow. Would the other Magi feel threatened? How would Sammul react?

No matter how much the decision bothered the Magi in the Voralla, their irritation and discomfort wouldn't matter one whit to Jonas. Once he set his sights on something he wanted, it was his.

And Volos take anyone who gets in his way. she thought wryly.

Aleksei pulled the rabbits from the fire, and Tamara's attention immediately returned to her surroundings. *Gods*, but she was hungry!

He laid the spit across two stones away from the fire, looking up into her disappointed face.

"They have to cool a bit." he explained patiently. "Otherwise you'd burn your hands."

She stared at him, trying to look as pitiful as possible, but Aleksei held her gaze sternly until she finally looked away. She was accustomed to far superior fare, not three measly rabbits on a stick. But right then those rabbits looked better than anything served at the impossible number of banquets and feasts she'd ever attended.

Incredibly, Aleksei appeared to be ignoring her.

"Won't the smell of the rabbits draw wolves? Or *bears*?"

Aleksei looked up at her and frowned, "Well, there *aren't* any bears this far south. They prefer heavily forested areas like the Seil Wood or the central Sulaq Hills. And the wolves won't come near the fire. It frightens them."

"But if they were starving...." she began.

"A pack of wolves doesn't usually starve at the end of Harvest, Princess. A lone wolf might, but I could deal with one wolf, no matter *how* hungry."

There was an edge to his voice that startled Tamara. That was no idle claim, yet she couldn't imagine how even Aleksei, big as he was, could manage to kill a wolf with his bare hands.

There was an uncomfortable silence. Aleksei looked back to her, his eyes curious, "Do you just invent things to be frightened of?"

Tamara glared at him, "I beg your pardon? After yesterday, can you *blame* me?"

He had the decency to look ashamed of himself.

Who was *he* to accuse her of flights of fancy?

After what seemed like hours, Aleksei lifted the spit and slid one of the cooked rabbits off the end, offering it to her.

She took the rabbit greedily and began to pull it apart, ignoring the drops of grease that splattered on her silk riding dress. Aleksei wrinkled his nose in distaste, eating his own rabbit quickly and methodically.

When Tamara had finished her rabbit, she looked ravenously at the last one, still cooling on the spit. Aleksei wiped his hands on his breeches, then followed her eyes to the third rabbit.

"Take it." he said emotionlessly.

She started to reach for it, then paused. "Are you *sure* you don't want it?" she asked, wincing.

He shook his head, "You need it more than me. Finish it and try to get some sleep."

She grabbed the spit, then frowned when he stood. "Wait! Where are you going?"

"I'm going to scout around to make sure we're alone in the glade. You'll be safe, don't worry. Get some sleep. We have a ways to go before we can truly rest."

Tamara nodded uncertainly, looking around herself in bewilderment, "But what am I to sleep on?"

Aleksei regarded her with a combination of confusion and not a little irritation, "The ground, Princess. If it's good enough for me and the beasts of the field, it's plenty good for you."

And then he was gone, leaving her only with shock and a sudden resurgence of tears.

CHAPTER 14

AFFIRMATION

ANDARIANA SAT IN her study, her eyes swollen and red-rimmed.

Carrier pigeons had arrived from Keiv-Alon. Tamara's guard had been discovered dead in the road, and the Princess was nowhere to be found. Yet there was no message with the bodies, no demand of a ransom.

Jonas stood near the fire, his green eyes hard. First Aleksei had vanished, and now the news of Tamara. His mood was rapidly deteriorating. But at least he knew where *Aleksei* was.

On the Southern Plain, impossibly enough.

He was *very* interested to know just how the man had accomplished such a feat in less than a day. Even with the bifurcated bond fueling him, Jonas hadn't thought Aleksei capable of that sort of power.

But Tamara remained a mystery to him. And Jonas *hated* mysteries.

Yet as much as he knew, Andariana needed to grieve or fret for her daughter, and as much as Jonas wanted to speak to Aleksei and divine his decision, they both had something far more pressing at the moment.

Sammul stood in the center of the room, his face impassive. He had come bearing a letter from Parliament.

"So Parliament has made its decision?" Andariana asked tightly, her voice remarkably controlled.

The question was rhetorical. She held the deliberation in her hand.

"Majesty," Sammul said, bowing his head, "I brought word as soon as it reached me."

Her emerald eyes flared, "And is Parliament sending you as an *emissary* now, Sammul? I hadn't realized that you had stooped to the level of errand boy."

Sammul opened his mouth to speak, but Andariana forestalled him with a hand. "*Banishment?* They have found Ilyana *guilty?* Of *what?* Using the power the gods saw fit to grant her? Surely you can see the dangers inherent in this argument, Sammul. If we limit the Magi from doing anything but pretty tricks, what good are they?"

"But Majesty, if fire were to be used as a weapon—"

"If fire were to be used as a weapon, High Magus, then I presume it would be used against our enemies. Now, the fact that we *have* no enemies at present hardly seems reason to banish a girl for an error in judgment, don't you agree?"

Sammul's jaw tightened, "I do, Majesty."

"This is my decision, High Magus, and you may take it to the Lords of Parliament as you so faithfully brought me their message in the first place. Tell them that I value their counsel in the matter but my decision is as follows.

"The Magus Ilyana is to be released with her Knight Marrik. They are to return to their regular duties as defenders of Ilyar. She will be reprimanded on the potential dangers of using the Archanium as weapon, and then the issue will be dropped.

"The Lords of Parliament are free to question my decision as long as they understand that *despite* their dissatisfaction, it *stands*. I am the Queen, and I have spoken on this matter. Do I make myself clear, High Magus?"

"Perfectly, Majesty." Sammul said tightly.

"Thank you. You are dismissed."

The Magus turned and stormed from the room, retaining only enough self-control to keep from slamming the door as he left.

Jonas masked his satisfaction, "It won't be a popular decision."

Andariana sighed, "Important decisions rarely are. But it's as you said. If I allow this to go uncontested, there's no telling where we'll find ourselves a year from now. I will *not* be likened to the Kholodym Dominion."

Jonas sighed, glad that his aunt was as conscious of the comparison as he. The Dominion Wars had all but faded from the memories of the Ilyari, but they never ceased to haunt the Magi. He absently twisted the silver ring on his first finger, the constant reminder of the Magi's victory a thousand years ago. He would do everything in his power to keep the horrors of that age from *ever* revisiting their realm.

"I appreciate your resolution in the matter." Jonas said finally, allowing himself a small smile. "Now if I may be excused?"

She frowned, "Where are you going?"

He considered how much he could tell her. He didn't want to provide her false hope, but rather allow a glimmer of possibility.

"I might have a way to find Tamara." he said evenly.

"How?"

"There is a Ri-Vhan Hunter." he said, deciding to leave out Aleksei's full identity for the moment. "He's currently in the Southern Plain, and I believe he may be able to track her. If he can take me to where she is being held...." Jonas let the silence carry the terrible implication.

"I've already sent pigeons to Keiv-Alon. By tomorrow morning, every Legionnaire within thirty leagues will be sweeping through the Sulaq Hills. It will take you days to get there by horseback! Even a Hunter would be hard pressed to—"

"I have another way."

Andariana studied her nephew. "Go." she said, closing her eyes.

Jonas leaned down and kissed his aunt's cheek before hurrying from the room. Aleksei was on the Southern Plain, but Jonas wasn't sure how much longer that would hold true. Had his farm boy abandoned him? If he hadn't, why was he so far away? *How* was he so far away?

Whatever the answer, Jonas could move swiftly himself. He had yet to uncover the long-lost magic that would allow him to Fade instantly from place to place, but he had found other means.

He marched down the hall, trying to resist the urge to break out into a dead run. If he could get to Aleksei, would the Hunter be able to track her? Would he even *want* to? How long would it take him? Jonas wished to the gods he understood Hunters. Or Aleksei.

Jonas reached his chambers and slipped inside, hurrying to his bedchamber and shedding his courtly clothes. He changed quickly into warm, functional Ilyari wool.

Jonas flung the windows open to the crisp Harvest night. He closed his eyes and breathed deeply. It was not first time he'd attempted something like this, but he would have to sustain it for far longer than he was accustomed.

He didn't feel fear so much as logical concern. Jonas had no real guide in his understanding of the Archanium, and there was no way to measure the lasting impact of his attempts at proper spellcraft. Ilyana and Aya had helped him with basic details, but he was certain that his own experiments far outreached anything either woman had experienced.

He could only hope that his instincts wouldn't mislead him.

The image of a falcon appeared in his mind, and Jonas tried to recall every feature from memory. Each individual feather, the curve of the beak, the rise of the crest. As he pictured the bird, Jonas reached into the Archanium.

The first time he reached out and found nothing. It took several agonizing attempts before Jonas actually reached forward and fell into the Great Sphere, centered exactly between the two hemispheres of the Archanium, the Archanae; the raging storm that was the Nagavor above him, and the strong, deep ocean of the Akhrana beneath.

The vast field of swirling colors and emotion flooded his vision. He glanced across the churning sea of energy, searching for the spell he required.

There.

Reaching out, Jonas touched the whorl of color and wrapped it around the image of the falcon.

He could feel himself change, could feel his fingers elongate as his legs shortened and his hair flared out into the feathers that spilled across his body. Each second dragged on in excruciating detail, each image cutting deeply and filling him with the exquisite pain of the shift. The transformation took mere moments, but to Jonas it seemed hours.

He stepped onto the window ledge, flexing his wings and stretching his neck. He hoped to the gods that this form would be fast enough to reach Aleksei before the man moved somewhere else.

With an experimental flap of his wings, Jonas launched himself into the air over Kalinor, circling higher and higher on a thermal until he was gliding hundreds of paces above the Palace. Then, with a single-minded determination, he turned south.

Aleksei caught their scent in the small hours of the morning. The wind was blowing to the southeast, and while his nose pricked at the unusual smells, they weren't completely unfamiliar.

Traders from Fanj had come through Voskrin with all manner of culinary exoticism and cutlery when he was a boy. He recalled their spice carts, and the bright and vibrant scents they carried. He also recalled tales of Fanja slaver tribes disguised as peddlers to lure the unwary and alone.

By the time he could hear the carts on the wind, he had already woken Dash. Tamara, however, was proving to be a very different sort of problem.

"We have to leave now." Aleksei whispered, shaking her shoulder. "There are people coming, but I think we can get to my farm by dawn."

"Your *farm?*" she grumbled, rubbing her eyes in the darkness.

Aleksei sat back on his haunches. He suddenly realized he'd never told her where they were headed. "It's south of Voskrin," he said softly, "and the safest place I can think of right now. We both need proper rest and a hot meal more than anything. *Especially* you.

"There are people heading this way." he said pointedly when he saw her frown. "They could be harmless peddlers, but they could also be much worse. It's my job to make sure no harm comes to you. Right now, getting you out of the open is more important than *anything* else."

"Your *job?*" she asked softly.

Aleksei blushed, glad that the darkness hid his embarrassment. Who did he think he was? He was talking like some hero from the storybooks when he was actually more concerned about their possible capture. He could fight off a few brigands, but a slaver party was something else entirely. "There's no point in catching arrows if you end up in a slaver's cart." he whispered.

Aleksei ran his fingers through Dash's shaggy mane, brushing out the worst of the tangles and grit and ignoring her frown. He cursed himself for not grabbing Dash's tack. But even without a saddle or supplies, at least he was used to riding bareback. He doubted Tamara would find it a pleasant experience in her silk riding gown.

He lifted her easily onto the horse's back, climbing up behind her. Aleksei guided Dash gently onto the road, careful to avoid any badger holes that had been dug into the glade paths. Once on the road, Aleksei set the horse at a trot to the south. At that pace, they would reach Voskrin in an hour or two, and the farm perhaps an hour after that. That was assuming, of course, nothing *peculiar* happened.

Aleksei wondered if they would suddenly find themselves in an Yrini mist maze by mistake, but the landscape passed just as he expected. The sun was just beginning to peek over the horizon when Dash pulled onto the lane that led to the barn.

He smiled at seeing the farm again. Only a few days ago it had felt as though he would never return, and now here he was. His heart swelled at the familiar slope of the barn, the rough angles of his father's house, so wildly disparate from the pristine glory of Kalinor.

But it wasn't the same.

Aleksei had wondered if he could ever become that simple farm boy again, and as he rode down the lane the truth sank in. This was not his life, not any longer. This world belonged to a boy who only half-recalled the land beyond the fairground, whose idea of adventure was hunting squirrels and rabbits in the glades with Katherine Bondar. This was not the life of a Hunter. Or an Archanium Knight.

And it never could be.

Dash slowed to a walk as they approached the barn, and Aleksei slid off the horse's back, leading him into the cool darkness. He helped Tamara down, then stabled the horse and turned towards the farmhouse.

Gods, but his father was going to be surprised when he walked through the door. He grinned at the thought of Henry's face when he walked into the kitchen, the Princess of Ilyar right behind him. Would his father believe him?

Tamara caught up to him and looked apprehensively at the house, "He won't be angry if we wake him, will he?"

Aleksei chuckled, "I doubt it. I *am* worried he won't believe who you are, though."

Tamara seemed shocked by the idea.

Aleksei practically ran the last few paces to the door. He opened it softly, not wanting to frighten his father if he was still asleep, and stepped into the house. The hearth was burning low, but the house was filled with the warm scent of smoking pine. He smiled fondly and walked into the kitchen.

Henry sat at the table, his simple breakfast of apples and bread laid out before him. Aleksei noticed that the bread knife lay close at hand, just in case of trouble.

"Is that you, Mother Margareta? Surely you aren't so lonely *this* early in the morning."

"Da?"

Henry turned sharply, his eyes widening.

"*Aleksei?*" he whispered, coming to his feet and rushing forward to embrace his son. "*Gods*, but it's good to see you."

He held Aleksei at arms length, "How are you? Where have you been? Why are you back so *soon?*"

Aleksei laughed under the barrage of questions. "I'm fine, Da. But the rest might take a bit of explaining."

Henry nodded slowly, looking beyond his son and noticing Tamara for the first time.

"Da," Aleksei said, "this is Tamara."

He thought it best of leave out her title until he had a chance to explain.

Henry gave his son a curious look and bowed in a surprisingly courtly fashion, "Henry Drago, Miss."

"Well met, Master Drago." Tamara said politely.

"Da, perhaps we should sit down. We need to talk about the last few days."

Henry nodded, returning to his seat and folding his hands patiently.

Aleksei thought for a long moment, wondering how to best explain the last five days to his father. He finally settled on the most direct approach he could think of. "Da, the night before last I left Kalinor."

Henry stared at him. Aleksei didn't wait for the obvious questions. "I reached Keiv-Alon the day after I left the farm, and Seil Wood the day after. I spent some time with the Ri-Vhan."

He saw pain lance through Henry's eyes, "Roux Devaan is the Ri-Hnon, Da." Henry sat forward, interest apparently overcoming both his skepticism and the pain of his past.

Aleksei quickly related everything that had happened since he'd reached the Ri-Vhan, glossing over most of the things Jonas had told him. Telling Henry that he was the Hunter was enough shock for one day as it was.

"We've been riding since the dark hours of the morning." Aleksei finished, nodding to Tamara.

⟁

Henry stared at his son, then glanced at the Princess. Her identity didn't really surprise him more than anything else he'd heard that morning. His son was the Hunter? And possibly Archanium Knight to the *Prince*? Yet even those revelations were minor perplexities in a storm of confusion. How had Aleksei traveled so far so *fast*? How was that even possible? Part of him wanted to deny the truth of what Aleksei said, but he knew his son. Aleksei was never one to make up tall tales.

And there was something else about his son, something he hadn't been able to place until now.

The boy had grown up.

A man sat across from him now, his coyote eyes burning with experience, with knowledge that Henry found unnerving. Aleksei had grown into a man in a handful of *days*, and a dangerous man at that. And Henry would weep for the sweet boy he'd sent away, weep for what the world had done to his son in such a short time, and for what might still lie in wait.

Still, he found himself rejoicing for the man his son had become. His heart swelled with pride at the thought of Aleksei putting the pieces together, of his son riding knowingly into danger and rescuing Tamara from assassins. While the circumstances were strange, the unmistakable mark of courage was evident.

He recalled the dream he'd had the night before he'd sent his son away. He recalled the visions the man had shown him, and while many had yet to come to pass, he knew deep in his heart that he had made the right decision. It was both affirming and heartbreaking. Gods, what trials awaited this boy?

"You must be exhausted!" he said, forcing himself from his thoughts and recalling his manners. "Highness, I regret that I can only offer you the humble accommodations of a peasant, but you are free to partake in whatever comfort you can find."

She smiled, "Thank you, Master Drago. I must confess that even a rough pallet would be a vast improvement from sleeping on the ground."

"I think we can manage a sight better than a pallet, Highness." Henry said with a laugh, "If you'll allow me to lead the way?"

She followed Henry from the room, offering Aleksei a demure smile. Aleksei followed as Henry did his level best to extol the virtues of the farmhouse, all the while apologizing for the lack of palace comforts. At the top of the narrow staircase he directed Tamara to his room.

"I'll sleep downstairs tonight." he said with a polite nod over her objections. Henry could see her desperation at the sight of a proper bed, even one as lackluster as his own. "I can keep watch in case anyone has tracked you down here."

Aleksei nodded and Henry had to fight to keep his emotions in check. Aleksei had never been so confident, but Henry knew he was glimpsing the future in his son's simple gesture. There was a presence there. New, yes, but *fierce*. Commanding. Resolute. Words he would never have ascribed to his son one week past. Pride and concern battled for control, even as he wished Tamara pleasant dreams and closed the door.

Aleksei stood only a pace away, his hand lightly resting on the statue of the Goddess Mokosh. Aleksei glanced up, his golden eyes catching Henry's. For a moment, those eyes gripped Henry's heart in his chest. The piercing glare of a predator.

And then Henry saw the glimmer of tears in the morning sun. The spell shattered as he stepped forward and swept his son into his arms, feeling Aleksei's body convulse in silent sobs, tears seeping into his shirt as he held his son. He held Aleksei tightly, wondering how long this might last before his son was swept away yet again.

His throat tightened, but Henry pushed away his tears. There would be time for that later, but after everything Aleksei had endured, his son had more than earned the chance to cry on his father's shoulder.

His sweet boy was still in there.

And rather than be overjoyed, Henry recognized the terrible truth. The Aleksei he'd raised hadn't been crushed by the influence of nature, or magic, or fear. He had endured every challenge, had faced dangers that *no* man should have to confront. Aleksei had learned so much about life beyond the simple world Henry had created for him, and in such a short time.

And he had done it without gambling his humanity. Whether Aleksei was the Ri-Vhan Hunter or the Prince's bloody Bonded, or even just a big lad from a small farm, his tears told Henry unequivocally that he was still the same boy Henry raised. A boy, a *man*, he was deeply proud of.

Henry held his son until Aleksei gathered himself. The boy stood back, shoulders broad as an ox, and wiped his eyes on a dusty shirtsleeve. "I'm sorry, Da. I'm exhausted. I'm starving, but I can hardly stay standing. I've just been so *scared*."

Henry saw the tears welling up again. He offered his son a smile, lest he break himself, and gripped the boy's shoulder tightly. "There's no shame in being afraid." he said gently. "But *courage*, Son, is feeling that fear, letting it hammer your guts to ribbons, and still doing what's right. *That's* the measure of a hero. And *that's* what you've shown yourself to be."

He pulled Aleksei close again, pressing a kiss into the boy's filthy flaxen hair. "But even heroes need rest." he whispered. "Even heroes need to feel *safe* now and then."

Aleksei hugged him so tightly Henry thought his ribs might shatter. And then the boy let go and stepped into his cabinet of a room, collapsing onto his cramped, hay-stuffed mattress. Henry stood in the doorway as the sun climbed the sky, watching his son's sleeping form and finally allowing himself the luxury of tears.

"Sleep well, Son." he whispered finally. "You're safe now."

That I could keep you safe forever.

⚜

Jonas soared over the myriad farms and villages of the Southern Plain. He thanked the gods he could sense Aleksei through their tentative bond; he would never have found the man on his own.

With every flap of his wings he grew that much closer. And the faster he reached Aleksei, the faster they could find Tamara. *If she's still alive.* he thought bitterly. Fast though he was, it had still taken several days to reach the Southern Plain.

His sense of Aleksei suddenly shifted, and Jonas dropped into a dive, catching sight of the tiny farmstead only moments before he landed with a flutter on the grass. He hopped towards the farmhouse before briefly touching the Archanium, returning to his human form.

Jonas walked up to the farmhouse and paused, not sure if he should walk in or knock. The door swung open, and Henry Drago stood before him, the man's face both pleased and confused at once.

"Highness." he said, inclining his head.

"Master Drago." Jonas said pleasantly. "I was hoping to speak to your son."

"He's in the barn right now. Won't you come in? I'm sure he'll be finished in a few minutes."

Jonas put on a smile, "I'm afraid it's a matter of some urgency."

"*Jonas?*"

His eyes jerked past Henry's sizable form and settled on the bedraggled form of his cousin.

"*Tamara?*"

He pushed past Henry and rushed forward to embrace her, hugging her tightly to him.

"I feared the worst when we found the others." he breathed.

"It was *horrible*, Jonas! And so *sudden*. One moment we were riding along peacefully, and the next..." She shuddered with memory, and he saw something new in her face. She had seen things, experienced things, for which she had no preparation. There was a deep sadness that had been absent days before.

"What happened? *How...*" he couldn't finish, but they both knew what he'd almost said. How had she *survived?*

"Aleksei rode out of nowhere and pulled me from my horse. The arrows...missed us. I think he *caught* one. And then we were on the Southern Plain." Her voice was as mystified as her face.

Jonas shook his head. Aleksei *saved* her? How? How had he gotten to her so *fast?* How had he *known?* Even if he'd left Kalinor in the dead of night, he shouldn't have been able to reach the Sulaq Hills in time for the attack.

"I need to speak with him." he said to himself.

As he started away, Tamara halted him. "He said he's made up his mind."

Jonas felt panic surge through him, "He said that? Did he tell you his decision?"

She shook her head, "He said it was between the two of you. He's been through *so* much, Jonas. Please be kind to him?"

Jonas sighed, offering every assurance he could think of. He knew Henry was listening to every word he said, but there was only so much he would allow either of them. He had found quite a bit to say in his flight across Ilyar, but they were not his intended audience.

Tamara offered him a gentle kiss on the cheek. "He's in the barn."

Jonas turned and started back out the door. He swallowed hard, resisting the urge to wipe the sweat from his forehead. He stepped cautiously towards the barn, his mind racing as he walked, cursing the Harvest sun for the sweat that slicked his chestnut hair black and soaked his shirt. He'd wondered if Aleksei had left to think, or perhaps as a way of giving his answer.

More than fearing abandonment, Jonas had worried that Aleksei had decided to seek out the other player, that this mysterious Magus would offer Aleksei something Jonas could not. He hated mystery, and the other player certainly possessed that in spades.

But now he realized it had actually been something quite

different. Part of him was angry with Aleksei for not alerting him to the danger Tamara was in, but he also wondered if he would have gotten there any faster for it. After the toll his flight had taken, the *time*, he knew the answer. From Tamara's own account, Aleksei had barely made it in time as it was.

Jonas reached the entrance to the barn. Aleksei sat amidst an untidy pile of hay, methodically binding armfuls into neat bales. He didn't even look up when Jonas' shadow fell across him.

"I wondered how long it would take you to follow me." Aleksei said calmly.

"Well, I was actually going to ask if you could help me track Tamara. But you seem to have accomplished that without my help."

Aleksei glanced up at the Magus, "I'm sorry I didn't have a chance to tell you. I was terrified that if I waited a moment longer, I'd be too late. I almost *was*."

Jonas smiled, "So I've heard. And I don't know how to thank you. Kalinor is frantic with worry, wondering what manner of villains have kidnapped or killed the Princess. No one suspected that someone had actually *saved* her."

Aleksei shook his head, "It's a marvel that I did, let me tell you." He explained about the men in the Wood, and then the voices he'd heard in Kalinor. Jonas' face darkened.

"Men in *Kalinor* plotted this?"

Aleksei nodded gravely, "They did. And one of the men in the Palace was the same man who tried to kill me in the Wood. A Magus. A Magus very interested in seeing *you* blamed for Tamara's death."

Jonas closed his eyes, trying to imagine a Magus stupid enough to plot something like that. Not even *Sammul* would stoop to murdering Tamara, if only because that would make Jonas heir to the throne. But if it wasn't one of the Magi in the Voralla, then who?

He sighed. It would have to wait until later. Tamara was safe. And he had something more important to take care of.

"Tamara said you'd made up your mind."

Aleksei grunted as he tightened the heavy cord around another bale. "I have."

"And?" Jonas asked, holding his breath.

Aleksei looked up, his golden eyes piercing Jonas to the core.

"Why do you want me for your Knight?"

"What do you mean?"

"You said in Kalinor that you didn't want anyone but me for your Knight. But you didn't tell me *why*."

Jonas' mind raced. How could he explain this in terms Aleksei would understand? How did he say that he just *knew*? That was obviously not going to be satisfactory. He frowned, lost in thought. *Why?*

"Because of all the men I've encountered, Aleksei Drago," he said finally, "*you* possess the purest heart. Because from the moment I touched your mind, I knew that I could trust you with my life. Because I know that I have been born for a purpose, just as I know that if anyone else stands at my side, I will fail. Because I *choose* you, Aleksei Drago."

Jonas thrust out his hand, "Will you choose me?"

Aleksei studied him silently, but Jonas could hear his thoughts like a clarion blast.

Aleksei reached up and grasped Jonas' hand.

"Yes."

CHAPTER 15

THE BLACK BOX

BAEL FADED INTO the dim afterglow, his essence and matter straggling along the final threads of gloam. Fading in the noonday sun took a matter of moments, but with the light waning so severely, it took nearly every second left in the day for Bael to finally take a solid step onto the homespun rug of his tent.

Not that it mattered. Not that *any* of it mattered. It was over.

As infuriating, and disheartening, as it had been to learn of his plan's failure, and from *Sammul* of all people, there had still been a thread of hope. Small, but still lingering, like a strand of spider silk.

That had been stolen when his tentative bond with Aleksei Drago snapped. The once-palpable closeness to another being had suddenly been sundered, leaving Bael with a deep, gnawing emptiness. He wasn't sure it would ever leave him.

He took another step, not because he wanted to, but because he was *supposed* to. Farm boy or no, he had a destiny to fulfill. He stared the new horizon down, through the darkness and into the face of dawn.

He had used every trick, every manipulation, every twist of truth to win the future he wanted. A future of hope. A future he *deserved*.

But the Dark God was fickle in His benedictions. Bael's father claimed to be in the Dark God's graces. His followers were loyal, and his family's piety had kept their congregation safe from the Voralla and its pagan lies for nearly a century. So why were Rafael's children cursed? Why was *Bael* doomed for being his father's son?

"You've been meddling."

Rafael's voice was hardly an intrusion into his thoughts. He had known his father was waiting for him from the moment he first began Fading into the tent. Of *course* his father was waiting for him.

It was *his* turn, after all.

It was so clear now. He'd followed his brother and sister, dwelling on the false hope that his father's Dark God would be just, if certainly not kind. As the son of the Lord and Master, as an *heir*, Bael had foolishly believed that he might one day prove to be worthy.

Instead, he was relentlessly confronted with the opposite. He was not worthy. He was the Toad. But he was the Toad *because* of who his father was, rather than in spite of it. He was part of a congregation that followed the Dark God above all else. Above pagan ideals of love or compassion. Among the Dark God's faithful, such lies were merely weakness under a blinding cloak.

So why would *he* be special? He hadn't earned anything on his own merit. He'd only managed to garner respect by murdering an even crueler man in a fit of rage.

In the beginning, that development had perplexed Bael. But it was clearer now. The Dark God had seen fit to grant him some measure of sanity in his fog of regret.

Perhaps it was a kindness of sorts.

"And *you* haven't been paying attention." Bael told his father calmly. It was a novel feeling, but one he'd slowly grown to understand.

Like Azarael, like Darielle, he knew this was *his* time to be tested.

Rafael stepped forward angrily, "You forget yourself!"

The striking hand was so obvious that Bael marveled in the predictability of the entire charade. Had it always been like this? He had never thought himself terribly simple, but he was beginning to reevaluate.

He didn't bother to raise a hand to defend himself. Not anymore. It wasn't necessary. His father's hand stopped a good pace from him, frozen in the air, quivering.

"What devilry is this?" Rafael snarled.

Bael's despair melted like fog in sunshine. It was a light of focused anger, and it readily consumed his self-pity and remorse. It burned the brighter for it.

"I have a better question." Bael said calmly, staring deep into his father's black eyes, "How long ago did you forsake the Dark God?"

Rafael's eyes widened. His shock seemed only matched by his rage at being trapped by Bael's faith. Faith his father may have suspected, but had never seen leveled against himself.

Bael decided he wasn't much interested in the response, so he shoved a gag of air into his father's mouth to silence the spluttering. The knot of air vibrated angrily, shattering Rafael's teeth like clattering crystal. But at least it kept the screams tightly contained.

"I'm fairly certain *no* one wants to hear what you have to say any longer, old man." Bael chuckled, suddenly amused by the sad puppet he'd made of his Lord Father. "Not ever again. At least, not once you're revealed as a heretic."

He searched Rafael's eyes for any glimmer of recognition. He wanted his father to understand what he was about to do. His father, as had been his custom of late, turned out to be prodigiously disappointing.

Bael clucked his tongue, much in the way his Granny Jorna clucked hers when she found someone particularly lacking. He supposed it was a charming trait they shared, and that thought only filled him with greater joy.

He was *from* these people, from the cringing, enraged man before him, from the crone with eyes of smoke and a streak of cruelty he'd very honestly inherited.

Bael couldn't claim to be sorry. Not now, not any longer. He was done with that. He was done with apologizing for *being*. And he was done with being the *Toad*.

He was Bael Belgi.

Not a pauper but a prince, not a maggot but a Magus. The Magi of old had commanded tremendous power, not through fear and fidelity, but because they *could*.

Bael had a far better reason than that. He had nearly been freed from this existence, but that freedom had been snatched away. He had nearly held the heart of a true hero, and yet just as the boy became a man, that heart had been stolen from his grasp by a usurper.

If he'd harbored any doubts about Jonas Belgi's powers, they were gone. Jonas Belgi had stolen *everything* from him. He'd never even had the *chance* to tempt Aleksei Drago to his cause, his side. The plans he'd set in motion should have worked, should have driven Aleksei away from Jonas and straight to him.

But he couldn't dwell on what *hadn't* happened, he could only seek to embrace whatever place Fate had in store for him. However, that made one thing painfully obvious; he would find no more answers in this dim little hamlet. Well, no more answers beyond the one.

Bael crooked a finger, much as he'd seen Jorna do a thousand times, and marveled as his father's struggling body dragged across the ground towards him. Rafael's feet clawed at the rugs and the dirt, but Bael was in control. For the first time in his life, he was truly and completely in control of another individual.

Perhaps Sammul had been good for something after all.

"How do you open the black box, Father?" Bael snarled.

Rafael was openly crying now, and Bael could see that his father was starting to choke on the blood pooling in his mouth.

With a sigh, Bael allowed the knot of air to slip, frowning as a fountain of bright blood sprayed across his tent. He gripped his father's jaw and sent every healing spell he knew into the man's ruined mouth. For a moment he thought Rafael might collapse.

But then again, he had never been taught how to heal with faith, with magic. Only how to *hurt*.

He turned Rafael's face sharply and stared into the man's eyes. "This was only the first of your lessons, Father. I *told* you I'd been paying attention to every single one. I suppose all I can do as a dutiful son is *show* you."

Rafael's eyes slowly returned to their natural glare of hatred. "The black box is *never* to be opened." he managed, before Bael shattered his jaw.

This time he didn't bother to clog his father's mouth. Instead, he roped air around Rafael's neck and tightened it. When he was satisfied that his father wouldn't choke to death, Bael started walking.

The moment they were out of his tent, he set the entire place alight. The flames screamed into the sky, yellow and hungry.

Rafael struggled at his invisible leash, trying to pull himself to his feet. But with the shock of losing his teeth and the shattering of his jaw, the man looked more wretch than leader.

As Bael dragged his father into the square, the faithful began to emerge from their tents, drawn by the hideous screams that usually accompanied the much-awaited execution of a heretic or deserter.

They were stunned into submission when they saw Bael dragging his father, their Lord and Master, to the center stage.

The Oracle, chief among scryers, forced his way through the crowd, his eyes wild with shock at the sight of Rafael. Bael was amused to see that the man even tried to collect his faith in a convincingly display of power.

Bael stood still, holding his father by a leash of air, his face calm, "Berius, lovely day, isn't it?"

The Oracle paused a moment in confusion. In that moment, Bael touched a jagged fragment that tore across the maelstrom of the Nagavor. He had no idea what it was supposed to do, but he understood the general idea as it careened through him.

The rest of the crowd was treated to the unexpected vision of Berius, Oracle and Master of Scryers, being briefly hefted in a sudden gust of wind before he was shredded into a viscous pulp that splattered across the gathered masses.

Bael noted with some small satisfaction that a number of onlookers still had their mouths open as their Oracle met the Dark God.

He continued his march up the dais, pulling his father into the air and suspending the man before the shocked Commune. Part of him considered it a special privilege to be able to horrify such brutal people.

And they hadn't even seen the real show yet.

"BAEL!"

Bael turned and waited patiently as Jorna staggered from her tent. He had wondered how long it would take the crone to understand what was happening. He smiled broadly and gave the blind woman a wave, "Granny Jorna, join me!"

The crone paused, her smoking eyes growing darker as she scried the future. Whatever she saw, it seemed to be enough for her to hobble forward on her stick and make her way to the dais.

"Now *sweetling*," she panted heatedly as she approached him, "I know we've had our differences recently. I know I've been hard on you, but it's only because you're my *favorite*. You *know* how I watch out for you. How I *love* you."

The tar-black tears drooling from her sockets left soot stains across the pine planks of the dais...and across Bael's fine boots. He glanced into her smoking eyes, and then bent forward and covered her mouth with his.

Her eyes went wide as he inhaled sharply.

The smoke from her eyes trickled away to tiny ringlets, before evaporating entirely. Bael continued inhaling without pause, drawing deeper on the Archanium as he accepted what he now realized was his sister's gift to him.

When the crone was finally empty, he let her desiccated corpse collapse to the dais with a dry *crack*. Her head split open like a moldy pumpkin on impact.

Bael exhaled and felt his head clear further. The path was so *plain* to him now. It was almost as though the Dark God...No, as if *he* was in control of his own fate.

"Thank you, Darielle." he mused as he turned back to the suspended form of his father. He thought Rafael might be suffocating, so he allowed the man crash to the dais beside his mother's corpse.

When Rafael looked into his eyes, Bael felt a twinge of satisfaction. The man was *finally* starting to understand. "A touching family reunion, wouldn't you say?" Bael growled.

"You—" Rafael choked.

Bael cut him off with a kick, ignoring his cry as he slammed against the husk of his mother. Rafael had never been a proponent of sentimentality, and Bael didn't see why any of that nonsense needed to start now.

"Ladies and gentlemen of our beloved Commune," he began, smiling into the bewildered faces of his father's filthy zealots, "I have been visited by the Dark God Himself in a vision. A vision of profound prophecy."

Whispers surged amongst the rabble. Bael felt nothing but contempt.

"This man," he declared angrily, "has been selling you false promises! He has promised the vengeance of the Dark God Volos, the master we all serve, but he has committed the greatest heresy of all in his conquest for power!"

The whispers quieted, but Bael was so wrapped in the Archanium that he could have heard a mouse choke a hundred leagues away. He could certainly decipher the rising expectancy among a group of simpletons.

"I am a more *benevolent* master. I do not want to stray from the path of the Dark God. Rather, I want to bring *light* to something my father has been hiding. Something I've only just discovered myself." He waited, allowing the anticipation to grow.

His brother Azarael had attempted something similar a year before, but Azarael had the unfortunate condition of being irredeemably mad. He had unveiled a four year old girl that he had fused with a newt as his proof that the Dark God spoke through him.

Azarael had been lucky to escape with his life. The newt-girl had been flayed and then burned, still alive, just to be certain of the Dark God's pleasure.

And Bael had learned his lesson well. He would make no such mistakes or missteps.

He waited, knowing that at any moment his deliverer would arrive. The theater of it was almost more than he could bear.

And then she appeared.

"Mother." he sighed.

Marra stared at the scene transpiring on the dais in a fugue of shock and sympathy. "Bael, *please*. Please don't kill him."

"Bring me the black box." he snapped.

Marra paused a moment, then straightened her shoulders, "No. You will release my husband, you will atone for what you have done, and you will forget all this *nonsense*. *Now!*"

Bael watched the rage roil across her face, and even as he felt a part of his humanity slip away, he managed a laugh. "Do you think *anyone* cares what you have to say now?" he demanded. "You have birthed three monsters to a man who treats you like human waste. Why would anyone listen to *you*? You are no queen, not any longer. You are a shadow of a woman. You are sadness. You are despair. You are failure in every form.

"You are the perfect consort to Death, because you are a pale imitation of life. And you would have *me* become the same?" Bael's hand moved to hover over his father's silent form. He clenched his fist and Rafael jerked to his feet with a jagged scream, clutching his chest. "I fear that my father's heart can't take much more strain from his heavy burden as Master of our beloved congregation. In fact, I'd daresay he will succumb completely in a matter of minutes. Unless I get what I want."

Bael snapped and Rafael dropped to the dais, twitching but no longer screaming. "Now go fetch the *box*."

Marra stared at her son for a breathless moment. Her heart felt like it was tearing itself in two. Her *baby*, the only one of her children who had given her any hope, had inexplicably turned into the monster that she so feared.

He had turned into his father.

"You know where the box is. *Fetch* it." Bael snarled.

She looked at him, then at the twitching form of her husband, bloody, bruised and broken on the dais. Marra realized then that she felt no pity for Rafael. No pity for his mother, the cracked husk that had contained Jorna's particular sort of wickedness.

Her gaze returned to Bael's emerald glare. "What will you do with it?" she asked calmly.

Bael stiffened. She knew he was perplexed by her question. Her words were now her only defense against her son's madness. Her wits were all she had to protect what was left of her family, of her *soul*.

"I will fulfill my destiny." Bael said flatly. "I will take the Third Key and I will open the Cathedral of Dazhbog."

Marra felt like fainting on the spot. Her vision swam.

"You would *release* the Dark God?" she quavered.

"I will. And my people, *our* people, will finally bask in His glory as He remolds this broken world in His image."

Marra straightened, studying her son, trying her best to understand this sudden lunacy, this power that possessed him. She sought the answer in his beautiful, terrible eyes. But the fog of his madness revealed nothing.

Sammul stepped onto the dais and bowed to Bael, "Master Bael, there are tomes in the Voralla that speak of the keys and the trials that await the Pilgrim. If you truly mean to take on this responsibility, it would be my pleasure to assist you in any way possible."

Bael smiled, "Thank you, Sammul. Your aid will be invaluable. Bring me everything you can find. In the meantime, *Mother*, fetch the box."

Marra stared at Sammul in dismay. He had been their secret weapon for decades, and her husband had done everything in his power to see that Sammul succeeded in his role at the Voralla. At times, Marra had been unsure if Rafael loved Sammul as the son that Bael had never been, never *could* be.

Until now.

It struck her as suddenly funny that in rising to meet his destiny, Bael had taken out his rage and demonstrated his true power not under his father's tutelage, but *against* Rafael and Jorna. The horror of what Bael was doing faded from her mind.

He was taking responsibility, fulfilling his birthright, *exactly* the way Rafael had always wanted. She stifled a laugh as she wondered whether her husband had pictured himself in his current state when Bael finally came into his true talents.

"Very well." she said finally. "I will fetch the box. But *you* will come with me. If you're going to pursue this madness, you might as well be prepared for the challenges to come."

With that she turned on her heel and marched towards the cathedral. Behind her, she heard a startled cry of agony. A woman screamed. Her smile emerged as the screams intensified.

She didn't even pause to acknowledge her husband's abrupt execution. It was no longer important. *He* was no longer important.

Now it was only Bael. Another terrible horror of a son. But the only son who made her *proud*. Even as a monster, she accepted that he was the least of three evils. She had birthed three demons, each extremely talented, yet unimaginably cruel.

Still, they were *her* children, *her* monsters. And if this one would become the greatest devil of all, she supposed she had no choice but to welcome his success. If she was to survive her children, she had no option but to invest in their success.

Even though it meant ending the world, *her* world, Marra realized that she didn't particularly care. Her world had only offered disappointment and sadness. A husband who had given her more pain than any woman should ever endure. A realm that had turned its back on her, despite her best intentions. Children who could break the world. Or worse.

She would not miss this world, she decided. She would quite like to see what this Dark God would do to those who had hurt her, used and abused her. *That* sounded far more interesting than playing house in the shithole that was the Commune.

Marra reached the hide doors of Rafael's cathedral. They opened for her on a burst of air, and she glanced over her shoulder to find Bael and Sammul only paces behind her. The congregation followed at a distance, curious to see what their new Master would do, if he was telling the truth about their former leader. If he was telling the truth about the cathedral.

And the Third Key.

Marra had no such questions or qualms. She knew her son spoke the truth. She had done everything she could to keep her children from learning of their father's terrible secret, and their horrid inheritance. She had hoped that the Third Key would never be found, never be glimpsed, or even remembered. It seemed that Sammul and Darielle had other plans.

She swept through the cathedral, walking confidently to the third sept and stopped beneath a primitive frieze slathered on the hide wall of the massive tent. A small brazier crudely fashioned from brittle pig iron sat beneath the frieze, permanently unlit as a reminder of the encroaching darkness, and of the world's inherent impurity. She placed her hand on the brazier's side, her finger finding the proper groove in the coarse metal. She slid the hidden panel aside.

Marra reached into the darkness and withdrew the black box.

The key rattled inside. Bael snatched it from her hands greedily, tearing off the lid and grasping the Third Key as though it were the rarest of treasures.

The tiny copper bird glimmered in the weak firelight. She had always thought it such a pretty trinket to possess such a repulsive purpose. The Third Key. With it her son could unlock the first door to the Cathedral of Dazhbog. And with Sammul's help, it was possible he would find each subsequent key, and unleash the Dark God on the world.

Bael handed the key to Sammul, "Let us go tell the people of their new destiny. Let them rejoice in the shadow of the Dark God, for soon He shall be free once more."

Sammul bowed before him and left the sept, the Third Key clutched tightly in his hand.

"There's more." she said softly.

Bael turned to her, "What?"

Marra reached into the hole and withdrew a rolled parchment. "Instructions, Son. This is a map to the Cathedral of Dazhbog. It's been hidden for an Age, but your grandfather spent the better part of his life searching for it. And finally, he believed, he found the Cathedral's entrance. But this is a sacred site. It will be heavily guarded. You will have to be very careful if you want to make it to the entrance."

Bael chuckled, "We'll see how these 'guards' handle the people of our congregation. We are weapons, Mother. *Terrible* weapons. Our swords will cut down our enemies, and they will weep."

"I only want you to be careful." Marra allowed.

"I will take care," Bael said with a sad smile. "I want *you* to take care as well, Mother. Embrace the Dark God, and find peace in his Aftershadow."

Marra opened her mouth to protest, but Bael was faster. She felt his hand on her forehead and the spark of the Archanium that exploded in her brain.

Dying was so much more painful than she'd ever imagined.

CHAPTER 16

BONDED

Shift. Aleksei darted back, bringing his practice sword around to counter the blow. *Shift*. Vadim came barreling towards him like an arrow through water.

Aleksei lashed out with his boot and caught the Knight's knee. Vadim cried out and twisted away as his feet flew out from under him.

In that instant, Aleksei returned his attention to the first attacker, striking three blows in rapid succession and relieving the man of his weapon.

He spun back towards Vadim and thrust his sword against the man's throat. Time slammed back into place with a sickening lurch and, for a moment, Aleksei nearly lost his balance.

He stood in the center of the ring, his practice sword leveled at Vadim's neck while the other Knight lay on his side, clutching his wrist.

"Match." shouted the mediator, and the benches around the ring erupted with both cheers and jeers of staggering intensity.

Aleksei stood there, panting heavily, trying to catch his bearings before his stomach rebelled completely. He glanced down at the defeated Knights, at their murderous eyes.

"Well met." he offered pathetically.

Vadim rushed to his feet, "Beginner's luck, farm boy."

Tamrix stood, ignoring Aleksei's proffered hand and rubbing his wrist. "We don't usually train quite so *hard*." he growled.

Aleksei's face flushed, "Sorry. I was just trying to keep up with the both of you."

Tamrix glared at him, and Aleksei weathered it with tired acceptance. Since he had arrived in Kalinor, his honesty was rarely met with anything but open hostility.

Yet despite the values he clung to, something within him had changed. It was akin to the shifts in time that he was slowly beginning to master, though not *nearly* as confusing.

This was something deeper, something *powerful*.

Hade and Toma rushed to their Knights, but as Aleksei scanned the benches he saw no sign of Jonas.

A moment later, he looked upwards and saw the Magus regarding him critically from a high window. He waved cheerily and Jonas nodded. He could feel the other man's pride beaming across their bond.

An impressive first day. Jonas' voice echoed in his mind.

Aleksei grabbed a length of toweling and wiped the sweat from his face. His body ached from the blows he'd sustained during the training bouts. And while the practice swords were merely bundles of reeds, their sting was enough to leave a welt at the least.

Marrik walked up to Aleksei and clapped him on the back. Aleksei winced as a wave of pain shot through him. Marrik's gift from the Archanium was strength, and the man seemed to forget that from time to time.

"Impressive, farm boy. Very impressive indeed. I don't know that I've ever seen anyone win a match on his first day. *Certainly* not against Vadim."

Aleksei managed a tired smile, "Like he said, it was just beginner's luck."

Marrik snorted, "Don't sell yourself short, boy. That was an impressive feat for even the most trained Knights. You have limited experience with a blade, which only makes it that much more amazing. Honestly, if we just get you a touch more training, I'd bet you'll be nigh unbeatable."

Aleksei laughed at the idea, trying his best to cover how deeply uncomfortable Marrik's praise made him. He'd never been so lauded in his life, and to suddenly have such adulation heaped upon him by someone as lofty as a seasoned Archanium Knight made him deeply uneasy.

"Too bad there's not a war on." Aleksei said with a shrug.

Marrik's face darkened, "It's *never* a sad thing to be without enemies, Aleksei. Count every day of peace a blessing. Every solider, no matter how lowly, hates war above all other things."

Aleksei felt foolish for the second time that day, though this stung more. Foremost among the Knights, he found himself seeking Marrik's approval, but thus far it was an elusive benediction.

A hand clapped on Aleksei's shoulder. "Well, boy, that was *quite* the sight to see."

Aleksei turned, arching an eyebrow as he took in the sight of the portly, mustachioed man speaking to him.

"Thank you, Sir." he said mildly, bowing his head.

Behind him, Marrik performed a much more formal salute. "Lord Captain Lenox, it's a pleasure as always."

Aleksei stiffened. The *Lord Captain*?

The paunchy man before him broke out into a large grin, his cheeks flushed, "You haven't been too hard on one of my boys, have you Marrik? Wouldn't want to start bad blood between the Guard and the Voralla!"

Marrik shrugged, "We've treated Aleksei fair enough, Lord Captain. It's kind of you to let him train with us."

Of all the Archanium Knights, only Marrik and Aya's Raefan knew that Aleksei was bound to Jonas. The rest simply thought he was a captain in the Guard. A man favored by the royal family for a great service he'd provided, though no one knew the particulars.

Announcing that Aleksei had rescued Tamara from assassins would lead to questions, especially as often as he spent time with

Jonas. The danger of someone figuring out that they were Bonded, and thus that Jonas was a Magus in his own right, was too great.

Lord Captain Lenox snorted, "I can hardly reject a request from the Prince, now can I?"

Aleksei repressed a sigh, now very uncomfortable with the whole situation.

It was bad enough that the two men were talking about him like he wasn't there. That one of the men was the commander of *all* military forces in Ilyar somehow made it worse.

"Well," Lenox continued, finally turning to him, "when you tire of this bunch, head over to the barracks. Doesn't look like these boys can teach you much about swordplay."

Aleksei returned the smile, "Thank you, Sir. I'll be over later today."

"I hope to see you. Have a pleasant afternoon, gentlemen."

Aleksei stared at the Lord Captain as he walked away.

"Not *bad*." Marrik muttered. "He's a ridiculous man, to say the least, but you clearly impressed him."

Aleksei shook his head. He had read stories about the Lord Captain of the Legions, but they had usually been stories of cunning, skill, of brilliant tacticians outwitting their foes. Somehow Lord Captain Lenox did not strike him as the sort to be outwitting anyone any time soon.

After a few more moments in silence, Aleksei excused himself. "I believe Jonas is expecting me for the midday meal."

Marrik seemed surprised, "It's custom for the newest Knight in the Voralla to eat with the rest of us in the mess hall. It gives us all a chance to get to become better acquainted."

Aleksei smiled, "To be fair, Marrik, I'm *not* a Knight in the Voralla. I'm a captain in the Guard. If nothing else, it would make people ask questions."

Marrik shrugged, "I suppose you're right." As Aleksei turned to go, the Knight put a hand on his arm. "But such distinctions shouldn't preclude you from being my friend."

Aleksei's smile widened, "Of course not. Thank you."

Marrik nodded, apparently pleased not to be turned away.

Aleksei made his way out of the practice yard and into the Palace, awkwardly fielding bobs and curtsies from passing staff. Never in his *life* had anyone bowed and scraped before him, yet now he was made perpetually aware of his station, often as a superior to those around him.

The only real refuge from this sort of behavior was to be found in either Jonas' apartments or his chamber in the barracks. At present Jonas' rooms made him uncomfortable. He wasn't used to being surrounded by so much finery.

Aleksei rounded the last corner and ran straight into the Queen, almost knocking her over.

"Majesty!" he exclaimed, jumping back to avoid a collision.

Andariana quirked a smile, "*Really*, Captain Drago, am I so frightful to you?"

Aleksei missed her playful tone, "No, Majesty, not at all. I'm sorry if I've upset you."

"I appreciate your...*sensitivity*, Captain." she said dryly, "Are you headed to see my nephew?"

It took him a moment to register the change of topic, "Yes, Majesty. I've just finished my training period."

Her rosy lips curved into a smile, "I can *see* that."

Aleksei realized his shirt was soaked with sweat, practically transparent and plastered against his skin, his hair a mess. He felt her eyes trace down his torso and his face flushed.

"Enjoy your luncheon, Captain Drago. I hope to see you at dinner." She nodded her head to him and continued on her way down the hall.

Aleksei took a moment to gather his thoughts. That was certainly not how he'd imagined a chance encounter with the Queen.

"Aleksei?"

He looked up and found Jonas regarding him curiously.

"Is everything alright? You look a little flustered."

Aleksei sighed, "I just ran into the Queen. Almost knocked her on the bloody *ground*, actually."

"Well, I doubt she would mind too much. She's quite taken with you."

Aleksei shrugged uneasily, "I'm beginning to get that impression."

Jonas chuckled. For some reason, the prince received enormous pleasure from seeing Aleksei so easily unsettled by his various admirers throughout the Palace.

"Do you want to clean yourself up first? Or are you ready for lunch?"

Aleksei frowned, surprised that he'd been given the option.

"I should wash up. I don't want to sully your fine furniture."

Jonas shrugged, "It's up to you. You can wash up in my apartments, if you like. I have a few of your uniforms in a wardrobe."

Aleksei was surprised by the suggestion, but he nodded and headed off towards Jonas' rooms. Jonas followed, lingering by the doorway. His face colored as Aleksei stripped down. Aleksei washed the sweat away, aware of Jonas' eyes on his body and perplexed by the prince's sheepishness.

He turned, towel in hand, "You said my uniforms are where again?"

Jonas looked away, his face turning a deeper scarlet. "In the maple wardrobe."

Aleksei chuckled. "Catch." he said playfully as he passed, tossing Jonas his towel. Jonas barely caught the wet towel in time, and Aleksei resisted a grin at Jonas' intense confusion. It reverberated through their bond, and he marveled at the complexity of the emotions he could feel emanating from the other man.

The more time he spent with Jonas, the more he liked the man. He had found a friend in the Prince, and Aleksei realized that they were actually very well matched. Where Jonas was stubborn, Aleksei was accommodating within the bounds of good sense. Where Jonas was spoiled and petulant, Aleksei was grateful and patient.

Still, every now and then Aleksei reminded the Prince that, just as he was having to accommodate the Kalinori lifestyle, he came with his *own* culture, and that was something Jonas would also have to grow accustomed to.

He doubted princes paraded around in the buff very often, but on his farm, nudity had hardly been cause for shame. There was no real privacy on such a small property, and he couldn't count how many summers he'd spent swimming at the watering hole with Pyotr and the Bondar brothers after a day of cutting wheat. They swam naked because wearing trousers meant laundry, and the idea of *adding* work during Planting or Harvest was laughable.

Jonas and his very private, immaculately groomed existence had no room for such basic freedoms.

"So, is lunch prepared?" Aleksei asked as he buttoned up his shirt.

The prince nodded, attempting to his regain his composure. "It is. In fact, we'd better get to it before the partridge cools."

They made their way into Jonas' dining chamber and sat on either side of an ebony table, inlaid with ivory in a pattern of inverted Dalitian holy symbols.

Aleksei studied the symbols, "These look familiar."

Jonas frowned, "You've seen these before?"

"I've seen a book that contained a few of them." Aleksei paused as he attempted to recollect the why and how of it. His eyes lit with memory, "This is Angelic Symbology."

Jonas arched an eyebrow, "Very good. Would it be rude to ask *how* you came across such a book?"

"My father was raised up around here, on the other side of the Seil Wood. His mother was from Dalita, and one of the books she brought with her had some of these on the binding. I used to try to make sense of them when I was a boy."

"My father was Dalitian. An angel, actually, so I suppose there's something about that aspect of my heritage I like to keep close." Jonas paused. "These symbols are inverted."

Aleksei blinked. "Does that mean something?"

"It makes them demonic, according to Angelic faith. I just find it rather amusing."

Aleksei nodded, though he couldn't be more confused. What would an Ilyari prince want with a demonic table? But then he recalled Jonas' preoccupation with other religions and their own uses of the Archanium. Perhaps this was merely some conceit the man allowed himself, though how his Angelic heritage played into it mystified Aleksei.

"Pardon me for asking, but if your father was an angel, why don't you have wings?"

It was an innocent-enough question, but Aleksei couldn't miss the pall that fell across Jonas. The Prince was silent for a long moment before finally answering, "I *had* wings, at least I was born with them. But I didn't keep them long. Sometime remind me to show you my scars."

Aleksei had the sharp realization that he'd strayed into dangerous territory. Gods, but was it possible to have a casual conversation with this man? As they began to eat, Aleksei watched Jonas. The prince had impeccable manners, and Aleksei did his best of emulate them. But after so much mimicry, he finally decided to break with decorum and simply speak.

"Sorry if I seem rude, but can we *talk* during a meal?"

Jonas laughed boisterously. Aleksei found it a most pleasing sound, even if Jonas might be making fun of him.

"Honestly, Aleksei, there's no need to stand on such formality when we're alone. State dinners require specific manners, rules of behavior that you will be versed in well ahead of time. But you can treat informal moments as just that."

Aleksei felt his face flush. He hated revealing his ignorance, even though there was really no way to avoid it as he acclimated to his new life.

"So come then, what would you like to talk about?"

Aleksei sat back from his meal, taking a sip of wine to clear his throat. "I've been meaning to ask you about your ring."

Jonas raised his eyebrows, swallowing his last bite and relaxing back into his chair. "Which ring would that be?"

Jonas had worn the same two rings every day that Aleksei had known him; an impressive emerald on his left middle finger, rich in its intensity, and brilliantly clear, like a mirror of the prince's own eyes. Golden ram's horns encircled the stone, a nod to the Belgi sigil echoed in pennants and livery found throughout the palace.

The second ring, gracing Jonas' right forefinger, was an unassuming affair, simple silver, dull even in the sun. Yet it was this ring that drew Aleksei's attention far more than the emerald.

"The one you play with constantly. On your right hand. When I started paying attention I noticed how...unusual it was."

Jonas looked down at his right hand. At the simple silver band on his first finger. A second band wrapped around the first, stylized to resemble soft, overlapping feathers.

"It's a symbol." Jonas said simply. "Every Archanium Magus wears one, though the individual creates the outer band based on their personal character."

"I've noticed. Ilyana's is some sort of flower."

"Violets." Jonas said absently. "Beautiful, but fragile."

"So why wear them? They obviously aren't a mark of training."

Jonas chuckled at the look Aleksei leveled in his direction. "Certainly not, or else I wouldn't have one. No, these are crafted when any Magus, no matter their talent level, reaches adulthood. It's a reminder of a different time."

"The Dominion Wars?" Aleksei guessed.

Jonas shrugged, "What else? The Kholodym wore rings very similar to these. They were the counterparts to the chains the Magi were forced to wear. When the ancient Magi rose up against the Kholodym Dominion, they started wearing the rings from their defeated masters as a sign that they were free Magi, no longer enslaved. As time passed, the rings ceased to be prizes taken from the Kholod dead and became more symbolic."

"And wearing one doesn't make anyone suspicious about your actual abilities?"

Jonas shrugged, "I think it just makes people think I'm arrogant, or that I'm trying to display some sort of perceived power. As you well know, I've never used the Archanium in public.

"Besides, I prefer people to think I'm a little bit silly, a little naive. Someone who makes easy mistakes, someone given to flights of fancy. It makes it easier to...influence others when they don't believe you're capable of manipulation in the first place."

Aleksei nodded, suddenly a little more aware of the sort of man he had bonded.

"Now," Jonas said, dabbing his mouth and resting his elbows on the table, "if you have no objection, there are some matters I'd like to discuss with you. I think I've discovered the reason for the unusual abilities you displayed before you became my Bonded."

Aleksei leaned in, "Which is?"

"When a bond forms the way ours did, you gained a rare gift. But because the bond wasn't finalized, that gift was unstable. Until you agreed to become my Bonded, I didn't understand it myself. Your uncanny speed was a *sure* sign of instability, because the kind of power required for you to move across space that swiftly is enormous, and ultimately, unsustainable. When you consider that another Magus was bonding with you at the same time, the amount of power at your disposal was unprecedented during that preliminary period."

Aleksei nodded, "You mentioned this the day we met."

Jonas smiled. "But what I found more confusing were the moments when you fought back and *won*, when you knew the right things to say at the proper moments. Feats you should never have been capable of, moments of clarity that your life had never prepared you for."

Aleksei shivered as he recalled that eerie *shifting* as it had manifested in the first days of his journey north.

"Aleksei, you are bound to time. Our connection is one that flows through the very *fabric* of time. I think that you were unintentionally calling on a future self to protect you when you felt threatened."

Aleksei stared at Jonas in silence.

Jonas continued, "I didn't say it would make the most sense, and it *is* only a theory. But as you agreed to be my Knight, I can only assume that you'll receive great amounts of training in war, as well as in life.

"If you were subconsciously pulling that into the present, it wouldn't surprise me. Any prophet can tell you how unstable the future is. Given the tenuous nature of our bond, it makes even more sense to me."

"Well that makes one of us."

There was still so much Aleksei didn't understand about the power that bound him to Jonas, and the sheer volumes of history that accompanied such knowledge, yet he was wary enough to only seek a small amount at a time. He was trying to work his way through the things Jonas had told him, but he understood so *little*.

It will come to you with time. Jonas' voice whispered in his mind.

It will get easier.

CHAPTER 17

A PLACE CALLED HOME

"I'M MISERABLE."

Andariana watched her nephew sink into a deeply padded sofa, attempting to conjure words of comfort. None came to mind.

"Wedding preparations have been underway since you made that idiotic contract with Chancellor Perron. Surely it wouldn't surprise you that an occasion of such importance has the entire palace in an uproar?"

"And I *told* you I refused to marry Perron's daughter. Did you think my mind had changed in the past month? Or did you think me so distracted that I wouldn't notice everything being arranged behind my back?"

Andariana's face colored. "You cannot shy away from your agreements, Jonas. My sister tried to do just that, and it ended in a brutal civil war. If you anger Perron now, now that you have placed him in a position of such power, the consequences could be dire."

"*Damn* the consequences!" Jonas snapped. "I'm *not* doing it."

Andariana considered her nephew carefully.

She recognized so much of his mother in his determination, in his dog-headed stubbornness. She had lost two sisters to that war. It pained her to think that her nephew might now be on the brink of ruining the realm she had fought so hard to rebuild.

Perhaps a change in tactics was in order.

"I'm not completely without sympathy, Jonas. I can certainly understand how much harder this must be for you, now that Captain Drago is here."

Jonas sat up sharply, glaring at her with those fierce emerald eyes. "I beg your pardon?"

Andariana suppressed a smile. "Don't play coy, Jonas. I'm not a child, and I can read your emotions better than you'd care to believe. I'm not sure *why* you thought that bonding a Knight would void your contract with Perron, but as long as you are operating in secrecy, it won't make a whit of difference."

Jonas eyed her cautiously, "You want me to publicly announce my abilities?"

"That would only raise more questions, which *you're* not prepared to answer. But whether you've been trained or not, Sammul knows. He's made enough insinuations to suggest that he thinks he might be the only one, but he's searching for information. And now that he knows, your secret can only serve to harm you.

"Now, there are ways to approach this that are not nearly so brash, nor quite so embarrassing, as simply announcing your abilities. Any public statement would only suggest that we knew what we were hiding all along, and that you made promises to Perron under false pretenses. That gains us nothing. Besides, such a tactic would be wasted on a power-hungry pig like Perron.

"Jonas, even if the entire *realm* were to know of Captain Drago's association with you, you would still have to marry the girl. This is not a matter of emotions. This isn't about *love*. It is purely political. I've told you before, she can spend her entire year in Taumon by the sea for all you'll care. It's a simple contract, nothing more. But your command of the Archanium, sanctioned by the Voralla or not, won't stand in Perron's way of marrying into the Belgi line."

Jonas clenched his jaw. Ever since Aleksei had arrived, his

anxiety had been climbing, his nerves unceasingly on edge.

"Then what are you suggesting I do, Andariana? Just marry her and then send her away? Whatever you have to say about the political implications of such an arranged marriage, there are still *expectations*. Expectations I have no interest in meeting. I can't just send her away to live as a spinster by the sea with her handmaids."

Andariana sighed, "There are other means, Nephew. *Believe* me, women of noble standing and peasant birth both have been employing them since time began to escape an unsuitable match.

"We simply have to find a way to turn the tables on Perron. But it will take time, and *delicacy*, if we're to achieve such a thing without sending the entire realm into chaos. I'm not saying it cannot be done, only that you might have to meet some less...*pleasant* expectations of a bridegroom before we're able to put an end to this sordid mess."

He glared at her, rising and walking to the door. "I was hoping you'd be a bit more understanding. I see my hope was misplaced. Small wonder you ended up trying to please all parties to the satisfaction of none. I imagine your tactics will work about as well as they did for Marra twenty years ago."

She sat there as he wrenched the door open, then vanished through doorframe. The door slammed behind him.

Andariana Belgi dabbed at her eyes as tears finally formed. *So much like his mother. So much like Rhiannon. And so much chaos would follow.*

She reached into the tiny, secret pocket of her gown and withdrew the letter. The single piece of her beloved that she still retained.

And once again, she devoured the words on page. Words that gave her solace in her darkest moments. The last words her husband had written her.

Yours in love and devotion, Seryn.

⁂

The mess hall was a crowded chaotic sea of activity, and Aleksei felt fortunate to manage a plate of food and a seat. It would be easy to go to Jonas' rooms and enjoy a small banquet, but Aleksei wanted to spend some time with the men of the Guard.

After all, Aleksei was unsure what sort of officer could command respect when he wouldn't even fraternize with his men.

The fact that he was an *officer* was still wearing new, and Aleksei wanted his men to believe that they had someone capable in command, someone who cared about their lives. About their dreams.

I need to speak with you.

Aleksei jumped at the sudden intrusion into his thoughts.

He considered abandoning his meal and heading for Jonas' quarters. But Jonas would have said something more urgent if he needed Aleksei immediately.

Aleksei took a seat amongst the men of the Fist he commanded, determined to spend at least a few minutes with them before rushing off. They smiled at first, but then eyed the ranking on his epaulet.

"Evening, men." Aleksei said with a smile and nod.

The longer he sat there, the more uncomfortable he felt. Wasn't *he* supposed to be one in charge?

But he could smell their fear, their distrust.

"So," Aleksei said, sitting back, "how are you all this evening?"

They looked at one another, searching for a response.

"Ready for battle." proclaimed a younger man, barely out of boyhood from the looks of him.

"Solider, what's your name?" Aleksei asked.

"Hollings, Sir!"

"Hollings, *why* are you ready for battle? We aren't at war. If we were, yes, I'd expect you to be ready for the first thing that came at us. But we're eating dinner right now. So tell me, Hollings, how are you?"

Hollings stared at Aleksei for a long moment before responding, "I...I guess I'm doing well, Captain. I miss my girl at home."

"Aye? Where's your girl?"

"Keiv-Alon, Sir."

Aleksei broke into a smile, "Thank you, Hollings. Nyland, what about you?"

"Well, Sir," Nyland began.

Bang!

Aleksei jumped to his feet as two men on the far side of the hall dropped their plates and pulled their belt knives.

Shift. Time slowed as Aleksei slid across the room and stepped in between the two Legionnaires. As one drove forward with his blade,

Aleksei grabbed his wrist and twisted it around, back towards the soldier's face. The man cried out in shock and dropped his blade.

Time slammed back into place, and both men gasped at the sudden change.

"What's going on here?" Aleksei roared.

"He was insulting in the extreme, Captain!" snapped the soldier he'd disarmed.

Aleksei glared at the speaker, then turned to the other man, who still fingered the handle of his knife. "What did you say to him?"

The man mumbled something so low Aleksei had to strain.

"*What?*" he managed, barely keeping his temper.

This was all over a childish comment? And one disparaging the Southern Plain? What sort of fools *were* these men?

The soldier looked up sharply, "You *heard* that?"

Aleksei released the man he'd disarmed, turning to the man still holding his blade. "Let me *explain*, Private, that just because some of us come from the Southern Plain does not mean that we are simple, nor inept. Now report to your commanding officer and tell him what happened here. And in the future, keep a civil tongue in your head and your blade in its sheath."

Aleksei dismissed him and turned to the second soldier, who was gingerly massaging his wrist. "Why did his words offend you, soldier?"

The man looked at Aleksei in terror. "You...You're not going to kill me, are you?"

Aleksei frowned, "Gods, what has gotten *into* you? This is Her Majesty's Legion. Nothing here is done without a trial." Aleksei's brow drew down. "Tell me why you felt the need to fight a fellow Guardsman, solider."

"Begging your pardon, Captain. He was making disparaging comments about your birthplace, Sir. I felt I should set him right."

The mood broke, and Aleksei fought to keep his laughter from surging forth. "I appreciate your allegiance. But every man here is in service of Her Majesty, from the Southern Plain or from the northern most reaches of Keldoan, we're all Ilyari. Never, I repeat *never* is there a need for hostility amongst your fellow men. Do I make myself clear?"

The man stared at the floor, but his response was hearty. "Yes, Sir!"

Aleksei nodded in satisfaction, then turned on his heel and headed towards Jonas' apartments. *Gods*, but he hoped the man wasn't in one of his moods again.

❧

Jonas drummed his fingers against the arm of his chair. A book laid open in his lap, but he had hardly glanced at its pages. Damn that man, where *was* he?

It had been half an hour since he'd summoned his Knight, and still nothing.

The relationship between Knight and Magus was one of fundamental trust. Jonas needed to *know* that he could trust Aleksei with his life without question. Because in many ways, he was about to put all of that to the test.

The entire ordeal with Andariana, the wedding, *all* of it was flaying his senses more than he cared to admit. And the hell he'd created for himself was about to come to a swift and brutal end, one way or another. He *needed* his Knight. He needed someone he could be *trust*, no matter what happened in the days to come.

The door swung open and Aleksei stepped in, attempting a smile.

"What did you need?"

"I sent for you half an *hour* ago."

Aleksei frowned, "I was in the mess hall."

"When I summon you, I expect you to be here." Jonas snapped.

"You said that you wanted to *talk*. It hardly sounded urgent." Aleksei growled. "A fight broke out as I was talking to my men. I stopped it before someone got hurt. They were drawing knives."

"You put me at risk for some common *soldiers*?"

Aleksei crossed the room in four easy steps and glared down at the prince, his golden Hunter's eyes glittering. "I am *not* your servant, Jonas Belgi. We are *equals* or we are *nothing*. Am I clear?"

"You have a duty to *protect* me." Jonas barked.

"Are you in danger?"

Or are you just wasting my time because you can?

The words crashed through Jonas' mind like a thunderclap. Before the Prince could open his mouth to respond, Aleksei turned and stormed from the room. When Aleksei slammed the outer door, the wood splintered.

Jonas sat back in his chair, his thoughts tangled in confusion. He could feel Aleksei's rage radiating across their bond, could feel the man growing farther and farther away. He was still in shock from the way Aleksei had spoken to him.

But at the same time, Aleksei's Hunter nature was manifesting in a way he'd never anticipated. The man was becoming more feral by the day, and his patience for pleasantries seemed to be wearing thin.

More disturbing was Aleksei's *grasp* of their bond. Jonas wasn't entirely sure if other Knights could speak into their Magi's thoughts directly. That was supposed to be an ability the Magus wielded alone.

Jonas' eyes widened as Aleksei's voice filled his mind again. He could hardly believe the invective the man used, and yet it certainly served to remind Jonas that Aleksei was not alone in *his* thoughts. There was a ferocity emerging, and Jonas feared he was quickly losing his leash on his Knight.

Leash? You should be *so lucky*. Aleksei snarled.

I'm sorry. Jonas thought back, his concern melting into desperation.

You don't know how *to be sorry, Jonas Belgi*.

Jonas tried to respond in kind, but incredibly, found himself unable to reach out to Aleksei's mind. The man's anger seemed to block his voice.

He tried again, exerting more force.

Nothing.

He relaxed his grip on the bond. And then he buried his face in his hands. "You're a damned *fool*, Jonas Belgi." he groaned, keeping his tears at bay. Why was he so *angry*? Why was he taking his frustration out on Aleksei? Gods, why was he *shaking*?

Aleksei had become his best friend, his *only* friend, and yet he was suddenly treating the man like a subordinate?

No. No, he was trying to control a man he really wanted to spoil. He viewed Aleksei's rough-and-tumble upbringing as a life deprived of access, of convenience. And Aleksei refused to let him.

It had been the work of moments to ensure bowls of fresh apples were delivered outside Aleksei's room each morning. Not delivered *to* his room, just left outside. Yet Aleksei considered even *that* an extravagance.

Much as he hated to admit it, Jonas had actually been hurt that Aleksei wouldn't allow him to do more, that he rebuffed Jonas' attempts to provide him even the smallest of luxuries.

It had never occurred to him that Aleksei might view such overtures as a means for Jonas to exercise his own perceived superiority. As a means for Jonas to exercise *control* over his Knight. After all, it stood to reason that if Jonas could offer something, he could also take it away.

Gods, what sort of man did Aleksei think he *was*? The confusions trickling back through the bond signaled that Aleksei was as uncertain at the moment as he was himself.

Jonas came to his feet and rushed from his chambers. The corridor was empty, but he could feel Aleksei moving back towards the barracks. There had to be a way to head him off.

Jonas ran down the hallway in the opposite direction, past surprised servants and curious nobles as he worked his way through the labyrinth of the palace. He had grown up in the place; he ought to know a faster route than his bloody farmer of a Knight.

Still, he found himself at the man's bedchamber a good five minutes after his Knight had bolted the door. He was going to have to do *something* about the proximity of their chambers. He couldn't have Aleksei so far away. And then he suddenly realized that he didn't *want* Aleksei to be so far from him. Ever.

"Aleksei?" he murmured. He knew his Hunter could hear him. He wanted to hear Aleksei's voice more than anything in that moment. It was a part of him that could no longer be concealed.

There was no reply.

Jonas wanted to slink back to his chambers and wait for Aleksei to calm down. Gods, but the man had a temper to match his own. That alone should be worrying. He had angered Aleksei, but only out of petulance and panic. That was clearly unacceptable.

The anger radiating from the other side of the door was palpable.

The anger, and the *hurt*.

Jonas resolved that he wasn't moving until he could speak to his

Knight. He still felt guilty enough for dragging Aleksei across the entire realm for his convenience. That journey had been incredibly difficult for an uninitiated boy from a tiny nothing of a village.

And now Jonas stood there, attacking the very man he'd begged to help him. The very man who had given up his entire former life based on a vow Jonas had made. A vow he'd just tarnished.

"I've obviously made a mistake." he muttered under his breath. "I'm not used to standing on equal footing. With *anyone*. I understand that this is new to you, but it's new to *me* too. Surely that has to make *some* sense." His voice cracked as that last sentence tumbled out.

There was silence from Aleksei's room for a long moment. And then the door unlatched and the Knight pulled it open. Jonas stepped back when he saw the look in the other man's eyes.

"You can come in if you wish." Aleksei said stiffly.

Jonas stepped into Aleksei's small room, noticing for the first time how spartanly the space was furnished. In the last several weeks he'd never once bothered to visit Aleksei in the barracks.

"Now listen to me *very* closely." Aleksei growled, shutting the door firmly and pulling Jonas back into the moment. "I'm not quite sure what you had in mind when you asked me to be your Knight, but I'll be *damned* if I'm going to spend the rest of my life being treated like one of your lackeys. I don't give a *damn* what your title is. That's not the measure of a man. I care how you treat people, me most of all. Do I make myself *clear*, Jonas Belgi?"

Jonas stared at his Knight, hardly knowing what to say.

"I truly *am* sorry, Aleksei." he breathed brokenly. "I thought I understood our bond, what we were to each other. I suppose we were both wrong about that."

A moment later Aleksei's face was a half-inch from his own. "I don't care *what* the Magi in the Voralla do with their Knights. You've made me aware time and again what you think of their kind. You're not like them, but neither am *I*. So stop trying to act like I'm playing by their rules.

"You're making this up as you go, Jonas. I'm not a fool. I understand that. But don't be surprised when you can't always write the rules the way you want them."

Jonas just stared up into Aleksei's eyes. He had never met a man who was not in the least bit impressed with his authority, with his title. Aleksei Drago was the rare man who saw right past all of Jonas' pretense, all of his posturing. Which was exactly why Aleksei was such a perfect match for him.

Jonas looked down. "I'm so sorry, Aleksei. I just..."

Aleksei lifted Jonas' face in his hand. Jonas felt a shiver rush down his back.

And then Aleksei's mouth was against his.

Jonas' eyes widened before he relaxed into Aleksei's arms.

The kiss lasted only seconds.

And then Aleksei pulled away, casting his gaze into the far corner of the room.

"I'm sorry. I had no right to do that."

"*No,*" Jonas began. "Aleksei, I...."

"And now," Aleksei said hurriedly, "if you'll pardon me, I need to be alone for a while."

Jonas nodded, fighting to steady himself. He wasn't sure how long his legs would continue support him.

"I understand. When you're ready, I'll be in my chambers."

He was surprised to have managed even *that*. Jonas stepped quickly from the room and shut the door soundly behind him.

Gods, what had just *happened*? His heart was pounding in his chest, his forehead covered in sweat.

One thing resonated clearly in his mind. He was no longer in control of this relationship. He was no longer in control of *anything*.

Jonas walked slowly back to his chambers. His head was swimming. He could hardly think except to guide himself.

"Your Highness?"

Jonas winced as Eleina Perron whispered up behind him.

"Your Highness, are you quite well? I noticed you walking down the corridor in a most confused manner."

Jonas turned his head to stare into her large liquid eyes. "What do you want?"

She laughed lightly, "Prince Jonas, you are always so *brusque* with me. If I did not know passionate men better, I should take offense!"

"I'm not passionate," Jonas responded woodenly, "I merely mean to know your intentions."

Eleina arched an eyebrow, "Well, one must wonder when her betrothed is constantly seen entertaining gutter trash."

Jonas' face froze, "I beg your pardon?"

She rolled her eyes, "Highness, the court can hardly stop talking about you...*consorting* with that peasant. 'Captain' Drago, is it?"

Boom!

Jonas felt his jaw clench so tightly he thought his teeth might shatter. His eyes were narrowed to emerald slits as he stared up at Eleina Perron.

Up.

Jonas suddenly came back to himself. He stood in the middle of the hallway, his hand outstretched. Eleina hovered a pace above him, her fragile body pressed against the wall.

And then Jonas realized that he was holding the Archanium in a vice grip. He released it immediately, and Eleina slid to the floor with a shriek.

She rose cautiously and fixed him with a glare that radiated such hatred and fear that Jonas immediately felt horrible for what he'd just done. He looked around and saw the many terrified stares of both servants and nobles alike.

Whether or not he liked it, his secret was now surely out. The only consolation he felt was that he hadn't accidentally killed the poor girl. Still, his rage at her insolence quickly overwhelmed his horror at lashing out at her.

"You will *never* refer to Captain Drago as 'gutter trash'." His own words surprised him as he glared daggers at Eleina, "If I *ever* hear such words from your mouth again, I will burn you from this world. Am I *clear?*"

She stared at him, her fear now far exceeding her anger. And then she vanished down the corridor in a swirl of silk and tears. Jonas slumped to the floor, feeling entirely drained.

What had *happened* to him? Had he completely lost his mind? And yet, part of him felt more than justified in his actions. He couldn't rationalize such an assault, yet in the back of his mind he wanted more. He wanted *blood* for the insult she had leveled against

Aleksei.

Don't hurt someone for a petty insult. Not for me.

The thought burst like a tempest in Jonas' mind. He wanted to bury himself in his chambers, never to be found again. He wanted to vanish into the sea. *Anything* rather than invite Aleksei's displeasure.

That thought struck him as strange. When had this change come about? A mere half-hour ago he'd been ready to remind the man exactly who Jonas Belgi was. And now his knees felt weak at the very thought of Aleksei Drago.

Ultimately, Jonas did the only thing he could think of. He hurried to his rooms, closed as many doors as he could, forgiving the one that Aleksei had shattered, and hid himself under the covers of his bed with a bottle of Dalitian firebrandy.

It was only moments before he heard the outer door groan open. He lay beneath a heap of quilts, desperately trying to pull his thoughts together as he felt Aleksei drawing closer and closer.

The door to his bedchamber creaked open and his entire body tensed. He heard the door close. The quilts were pulled away, and he had no choice but to face his Knight.

But Aleksei wasn't there to berate him. Instead he reached down and took the firebrandy from Jonas' grip. The Knight took a long pull before climbing into the bed next to Jonas. Aleksei lay there for a long moment, just staring at him. Even through the bond, Jonas couldn't read the other man's emotions.

Aleksei reached out a hand and laid it on Jonas' arm. His eyes piercingly, ravenously gold, fixed Jonas' own. "What is this?" Aleksei asked softly.

Jonas swallowed. "I'm not sure I know, exactly." he admitted.

Aleksei's face broke into an unexpected smile, "Well then, that makes two of us."

Jonas kept staring into Aleksei's eyes, transfixed by the man's face, by the connection he now felt burning across their bond. He was being studied by a predator, and he was the prey.

Aleksei leaned forward and kissed him, gently this time. Softly. Jonas was just glad he was already lying down. He was certain his legs wouldn't have supported him this time.

His Knight finally broke away, running his hand down the length of Jonas' face. "I guess we'll just have to figure this out. Together."

Jonas nodded, unable to form the words he needed. Instead he just moved closer and wrapped his arms around Aleksei's thick chest, resting his head in the crux of the man's arm.

Aleksei's arms wrapped around him, cradling him in strength and security. It was the first time Jonas had felt protected in ages. Not since his mother had held him as a small boy had he felt this *safe*, this contented.

He realized that he was crying. "Good gods," he murmured, "what's *wrong* with me?"

Aleksei planted a soft kiss in his chestnut hair. "You're home."

Jonas suppressed a sob. For the first time in his life, he understood what it was to truly *belong* somewhere, and to some*one*. And he never wanted to leave.

CHAPTER 18

DESPERATE MEASURES

"MAJESTY, AT THE very least, you must admit this is shocking!"

Andariana frowned, "Sammul, as I understand it, *you've* been well-aware of my nephew's talents for some time. You should hardly be surprised."

Sammul rose up indignantly, "I entertained *suspicions*, but I never thought the Prince would attack an innocent *girl*."

Andariana sighed, "While his actions are unfortunate, it changes nothing. Often enough, Magi discover their abilities due to a sudden onset of powerful emotion. I have heard something akin to those very words come out of *your* mouth. Thus, I see no reason that Jonas should be treated differently than any other accidental adept."

"Parliament will not be happy. Chancellor Perron least of all."

Andariana clenched her jaw. "Last I was aware, High Magus, Parliament did not command *me*. Quite the opposite, actually. They will receive my edicts, and that will be that."

Sammul stiffened, "What are you suggesting, Majesty?"

Andariana smiled, "It's simple, really. Jonas is to be acknowledged as an adept in the Archanium. I will make no motions to have him trained in the Voralla, but I *will* ask that you send a trusted Magus to aid him in his understanding, simply to make sure he doesn't accidentally harm anyone else, of course."

"Of course." Sammul managed. "And of his supposed Knight, Majesty? The bonding spell is not something most 'accidental adepts' can access, much less invoke."

"Yes." Andariana said thoughtfully. "I suppose with Jonas now revealed we might as well drop the pretense surrounding Captain Drago. I'll have his position formally acknowledged, and his rooms moved to the west wing where he can be close to the Prince. Who knows, perhaps some good will come of this?"

Sammul's face sank into a glower, "As you say, Majesty."

Andariana smiled.

"Thank you for coming to me with your concerns, Sammul. Though we sometimes have different viewpoints, your counsel is always appreciated."

Sammul forced a smile, "Happy to be of assistance, Majesty."

He bowed quickly, turned and exited the chamber. Gods, but he *hated* that woman!

By the time he reached his chambers in the Voralla, he was seething. She casually trespassed on *his* territory without a second thought. She had *commanded* a Magus be sent to the Prince? Who was she to command *anything* within the Voralla?

He slammed the door and gripped the Archanium, locking the door and warding the room from eavesdropping. He felt like screaming.

"Good afternoon, Sammul."

He froze.

"Master Bael."

Bael stepped out of the shadows and smiled. His emerald eyes shot right through the High Magus. His madness had taken him to new heights, in both power and cruelty.

The Master took a seat across from Sammul, his face expectant.

Sammul sat back into a chair, doing his best to affect comfort and ease while his insides were twisting in knots.

"You seem agitated." Bael observed.

"It's a minor annoyance. Hardly important." Better to change the subject. "Have you had any luck finding a suitable...*replacement*?" he asked, masking his interest as best he could.

The Master sat across him, and from his posture it was difficult to remember that these were Sammul's quarters, rather than his.

"I haven't located him yet. He's become very difficult to track these last few years. But I'll find him soon enough. There's really no need to rush, Sammul. I want the gears well-oiled when we put everything into motion. No sense going to all this trouble if it's simply going to fall apart in the end."

Sammul nodded, "I forget how patient you are."

Bael laughed harshly, "I'm not my father, Sammul. He and I differed in many ways. He was only willing to go so far to bring his vision into reality. I have no such limitations."

Sammul fought a grimace. Bael had grown into a challenging man. And very, *very* dangerous.

"How goes your other...endeavor?" Sammul ventured.

Bael sighed, "Not well. The Angelus worked dutifully to hide every little piece away, and Dalita is not very charitable towards our kind."

"Perhaps there is another way, Master. Perhaps...."

Bael raised a cautionary hand. Sammul dropped his gaze immediately.

"Forgive me. I meant only to further your interests to the best of my ability."

"I appreciate your concern. But for the moment I have things well in hand. Now then," the Master said, fixing Sammul with his frigid gaze, "what news of the Prince?"

Sammul swallowed hard. "I've just come from the Queen's chambers. It would seem that Jonas has assaulted a noblewoman in the Palace. With the *Archanium*."

Bael's mouth crooked into a smirk. "So, the little whelp has found his wings. I'm not altogether surprised, but I must say, I didn't expect him to be a *violent* man. Certainly not against a helpless woman."

Sammul nodded, "The Prince has...a bit of a temper. I don't

believe the girl was aware of his abilities. Either way, it serves our ends nicely."

The Master nodded, "I am curious, though. If Jonas could lash out with so little training, that speaks to his power. And his path."

Sammul groaned inwardly.

Each Magus traveled a different meridian through the Archanium. It was often easy enough to guess at the abilities one may possess from the meridian they trod. But Jonas had hardly wielded the Archanium long enough for such things to be apparent.

Still, his future actions would speak to his direction whether he liked it or not.

"But it isn't important right now. Watch him. We have bigger problems to deal with."

"Master Bael, if I may–"

A knock at the door cut Sammul off.

Bael rose. Sammul felt the other man fill himself with the Archanium.

"Answer it." Bael commanded.

Bertrand Perron stalked through the halls of the Voralla, edging past startled Magi and their Knights. The Knights watched him casually enough, though their hands strayed to hilts as he passed.

Perron ignored them as he moved through the maze-like fortress, heading upwards towards Sammul's chambers.

He was on the verge of outrage, but his pragmatism still held sway. He needed advice, and at the moment there was only one man he could think of who might offer more than sycophantic drivel.

The Prince's attack on his daughter still sent shockwaves through him, and yet it also created a great many questions. Yes, it was outrageous that the man had attacked Eleina. Worse still, it revealed the Prince as an Archanium Magus. The last thing Perron wanted was to ally his line with *anyone* connected to the Archanium.

The stigma among the higher houses of nobility would be unbearable.

But with the union came power. Power that would be impossible to deny, as long as the Belgi line held the throne.

That thought struck him as unusual even as it passed through his mind. Of course there were *other* roads to power, but he'd never entertained notions of deposing his monarch. Such things were messy at best, and the instigators rarely remained in power long.

He arrived at Sammul's door and knocked tentatively. He was as unsure of Sammul as any noble, yet the man seemed to think in a surprisingly similar fashion.

The door swung open.

Sammul smiled. "Chancellor Perron. What can I do for you?"

Perron stood as tall as he could, "High Magus, I have some matters of grave importance to discuss with you. Are you free at the moment?"

Sammul bowed, stepping away from the door and inviting Perron in. This was going very well so far.

Sammul took a seat in a large chair that had seen better days. Perron frowned. It seemed unusual for a man in Sammul's position to have anything in his rooms that was less than opulent.

"Can I offer you some brandy?" Sammul asked dryly.

Perron shook his head vigorously, "Thank you, no. I need a clear head for this."

Sammul sat back into his chair, "You're here about the Prince's little incident."

Perron stiffened. "I am indeed. Though I'm a bit surprised the news reached you so swiftly."

Sammul snorted, "Chancellor Perron, the news has already swept the Palace. Surely you know that it would have reached the Voralla just as quickly. In fact, I've just returned from an audience with the Queen."

Perron nodded coolly, "And what did she say?"

Sammul quirked a smile. "Her Majesty was very quick to condemn the Prince's actions."

Perron leaned forward.

"She has accepted that everyone now knows the nature of Jonas' abilities. As such, she has declared his behavior as that of any adept put to the test during a passionate situation. That is a common way of discovering a connection to the Archanium, though usually not in a man of Jonas' age. She is also going to allow his Knight quarters near the Prince."

Perron froze. "*Knight?* What are you talking about?"

"There is a certain captain in our Legion, one who was most auspiciously promoted, Chancellor. He performed a great service for the Crown. A service that was beyond the realms of human capacity."

"But not of an Archanium Knight." Perron muttered.

Sammul smirked. "A peasant by the name of Drago, I believe. Allegedly the rank was bestowed because of his bravery on behalf of the Crown. He saved the Princess from a very untimely death. An *orchestrated* death."

Perron's eyes flashed with shock.

"Orchestrated? But how do *you* know.... Good *gods*, Sammul. Surely *you* were't involved in something so...fiendish." Perron's alarm was rising higher and higher the longer he stayed in the chamber. What manner of man had he placed his confidence in?

A new voice broke like the tide across Perron's ears, "He was, but *I* am more to blame than my little puppet."

Perron spun as another man fluctuated in and out of the shadows.

A short man with flaming gold hair and eerily familiar emerald eyes stepped forward. He was wearing a heavy black cloak, but his movement belied that of an assassin.

He moved with a sense of purpose. A sense of danger.

"You are Chancellor Perron?"

Perron could only nod under the power of that gaze.

"I am Bael."

Perron realized that he was clenching his jaw.

"I know who you are." he managed. "You favor your mother more than your father."

Bael laughed, "Aren't you perceptive, Chancellor? But I'm afraid my father is no longer with us. His death has provided me with a new opportunity to, shall we say, change the rules a bit?"

"I'd sooner be pecked apart by crows than ally with the likes of *you*." Perron snapped.

Bael arched an eyebrow. "*Really?* Let's test that, shall we?"

Darkness surrounded Perron. He opened his mouth to scream, but he heard only laughter.

⚶

Jonas reclined in his study, pouring over a book on the different social interpretations of the Archanium. It was a challenge to truly understand, having only recently learned to embrace the Archanium like a Magus.

The Ri-Vhan also used the Archanium, but in a very different way, the angels of Dalita another still, and the Ul'Brek in Fanj yet another. It was all very confusing, and in many ways much more complicated than Jonas was capable of understanding.

At least, for the moment.

Aleksei sat not a pace away, his eyes studying a volume of military history.

Jonas had been surprised enough that his Knight was literate. The rural folk so often prized labor over education.

But Aleksei's tenacious drive to learn was more shocking still. Upon hearing of Jonas' extensive personal library, Aleksei seemed to find endless pleasure in seeking out the histories and tales that made up the library, devouring one after another.

Jonas could not have been more pleased with the man.

At the moment, his Knight was engrossed in the history of the first Archanium Magi who freed themselves from the Kholodym Dominion. Jonas glanced at the title and smiled.

Richter. One of the greatest heroes in history. The first Hunter. A Magus. A *saint*.

Born in a time when there had been no need of Knights. A time when the Magi themselves had been such terrible weapons with both sword and Archanium that the world trembled in their wake.

Fitting enough. Jonas thought.

There was much in Aleksei that Jonas did not understand, but more that filled him with pride. The man was *his* Knight.

Jonas had met with a certain amount of jealousy when Aleksei was acknowledged as his Bonded. The other Magi were surprised enough to discover their prince's true abilities. To find his Knight to be such a jewel in the brambles was another shock altogether.

There was a knock at the door.

Jonas glanced at Aleksei, but the Knight was engrossed in his book.

"Enter." he called.

A maid hurried in and made a deep curtsey. "Begging your pardon, Highness. But Chancellor Perron requests–"

Perron stormed past her, shoving the girl to the side. She caught herself against the wall, staring up at the Chancellor in fright.

"Jonas Belgi, you will declare your intentions here and now!" Perron barked.

Before Jonas could open his mouth, Aleksei moved like liquid from his languid position. He was suddenly standing an inch from the Chancellor's face. Jonas felt his heart skip a beat.

The man moved so *fast*.

"You are in the chambers of the Prince," Aleksei growled, "and you *will* act accordingly."

Perron's face reddened. "What...what is this nonsense?"

Jonas realized that the Chancellor was addressing him.

"Chancellor Perron," Jonas said icily, "I believe Captain Drago just made his point very clear. You will treat my servants with the utmost respect. I take any affront to them as an affront to myself."

Perron's face reddened but he silenced himself.

"Aleksei, let him enter."

The Knight glanced at his prince before turning to the servant girl. She was weeping as he led her from the room. Jonas could hear the Knight whispering to her all the way.

"What do you want, Bertrand?" Jonas demanded the moment they were alone.

Perron bristled, "I want you to honor your half of the contract, *Highness.*"

The man practically spat the title.

"I have an Archanium Knight, as you are no doubt aware, Perron. Yet you still wish me to pursue a marriage to your daughter? A woman I *assaulted?*"

"That is beside the point." Perron insisted.

"*Is* it?"

"Highness," Perron growled, "we both made a contract. And since I have fulfilled *my* end..."

"Fulfilled *your* end?" Jonas demanded. "You have done precious little to aid the Belgi line. You have demonized the Magi for possessing the same powers you would seek out in a time of war. You have directly opposed the Queen in every move she has made. Tell me, Lord Perron, what has 'your end' of the contract netted *me*?"

Perron breathed heavily. "I took a very important stand on Magi and the use of fire."

A bright flame ignited between them.

"And how does that benefit me?" Jonas snarled.

Perron gasped.

Jonas stared past the tiny flame, and into Perron's wide brown eyes. "I used the Archanium against your own child. As a *weapon*. Where is *my* trial? Where is the outrage you displayed against the Magus Ilyana for conjuring such a simple spark? Hardly the same as my own display. And yet, here you are demanding I *marry* your daughter?

"You *know* what I am, and what I may become, Chancellor. People like me, like Ilyana, have a responsibility to protect this realm. But I would be lying if I failed to mention our shared concern. Archanium Magi were enslaved for a thousand years, doing the work of evil men for no greater crime than the unlucky happenstance of our birth. I believe I speak for every Archanium Magus, trained or not, when I say that we *all* have a vested interest ensuring that such things never happen again.

"I'm not saying this to threaten you. But I want to be absolutely clear when I tell you that I will *not* tolerate further persecution of Magi in Ilyar."

Jonas snapped and the flame vanished. "Our contract was one of mutual benefit. You have yet to aid my political designs. I, on the other hand, have worked very hard to place you in a position of power. You have abused that power. As far as I am concerned, our contract is now void."

Perron opened his mouth, but Jonas raised a hand. "The situation has been turned to your advantage, Chancellor. I would strongly urge you to welcome that, and let things be."

Before the Chancellor had a chance to renew his protests, Aleksei's hand landed firmly on his shoulder.

"Lord Perron, I think it's best if you leave now."

⌘

Perron was in a whirlwind of confusion. He had completely lost control of the situation, yet he was still trying to retrace his steps, to discover where it had all gone of wrong.

And then he was standing in the corridor, staring at the intricately carved door to the Prince's chambers. It hung at a slight angle from the cracked wood of the frame. The detail was immediately lost in the storm of his thoughts.

He wandered to his chambers in a disoriented fog. His plans seemed to be crashing around him, and yet he felt powerless to even lift a finger in dissent.

He shut the door behind himself and walked to the hearth, bracing himself against it as his mind raced.

"Don't be *too* unhappy, Chancellor."

Perron tensed when he heard Bael's voice behind him. He turned angrily on the Magus. "You said this would be a victory. *You* said–"

Bael raised a hand, and Perron's mouth snapped shut with an audible *click*.

"Chancellor, I said that this confrontation would serve to benefit you. And it has. You now know your true allies, and those who are false have been revealed. You stand at an important crossroad. Do you continue to toil under the yolk of a monarch who distrusts you? A woman who has thrown your every edict and judgment aside to suit her own personal lust for power?"

Perron eyed the Magus suspiciously, "What are you proposing?"

Bael shrugged his shoulders, "At the moment you are at a severe disadvantage. You command no Magi, you have no ability to barter with the Voralla. And whatever Sammul says, his Magi are more tied to their queen than to him.

"But imagine, for a moment, that you had Magi of your own to command. Powerful Magi. Men and women more weapon than human. Would that level the playing field?"

Perron's eyebrows shot up, "You know of such Magi?"

Bael laughed, "Chancellor, the Voralla is hardly the only place Ilyari adepts find training, merely the largest, the most prestigious.

"But not every adept can travel to Kalinor. In the years since the war, quite a few groups have appeared here or there. None with a tenth of the Voralla's numbers, of course. But we do exist.

"Imagine, Chancellor, the bargaining power we could lend you."

Perron frowned, "But you said their numbers don't come close to equaling the Magi under Andariana's command."

Bael leaned forward and smiled, "Some pieces are worth more than pawns, Chancellor. The abilities of those in the Voralla are practically without value. The power of *my* Magi far exceeds the Queen's pawns. We are the wheat, they the chaff.

"And what if I told you there was something else? Something even greater? Something that could stand up to every Magus in Ilyar, and still emerge victorious?"

"You have knowledge of this?" Perron whispered.

"Soon enough, Lord Perron, I will *command* it. But for now, we must be patient. Everything due to men like us will come, but only at the appropriate time."

Chapter 19

A Feast for Volos

Lord Simon Declan gazed out the carriage window, his thoughts deeply troubled. Beside him, Lord Arred Bazin was muttering to himself. Declan caught a phrase here and there, but his own worries dominated his mind at the moment.

Chancellor Perron had summoned both of them to his private townhouse in the city. That in itself was not terribly unusual. The Chancellor often requested certain nobles to attend him at his residence, whether to discuss trade negotiations between individual holdings, or to discuss politics in general.

But as they rode past the Palace gate, Declan noticed at least three other carriages, each bearing the coat-of-arms of another major House. More curiously, each major House he'd seen represented lands that directly bordered either Perron's own, or those of his closest allies.

Bazin's frown proved the other man was more troubled by this than he, but Declan had to admit that inviting so many nobles, each a Head of House, on the same night spoke of either stupidity or arrogance.

There was a gentle rap on the glass, and Declan realized that the carriage had pulled to a halt. He straightened and glanced at Bazin.

The man was composing his face into a calm, stony mask.

Declan was worried for his friend. Unlike many of the members of Parliament, Arred Bazin did not wear the mantle of nobility easily. He had far too much heart, and too little sense, for the rigors of life in Kalinor.

The door opened slowly, and Declan stepped out into the crisp autumn air. Night was falling on the city, bringing with it an undeniable chill. Declan was determined to ignore it as he made his way to the well-lit threshold of Perron's townhouse.

The House of Declan was not nearly as wealthy or powerful as many of the Houses gathered here, but what he lacked in resources he made up for in sharpness of both thought and speech.

He paused at the door only long enough to allow Bazin to catch up to him. The two men had long been friends, but more than that, they were well-known allies. At the moment, Declan wanted to remind some of the more powerful Houses that he was not without his own alliances.

They were announced at the door and shown into a small study. The room was mostly full when the two men entered, and Declan had to fight to keep his face impassive.

There were indeed a great many Heads of House in the room. But some were conspicuous in their absence. The more faces Declan studied, the more he realized that the men and women in the room had one thing strikingly in common.

Their lands occupied the southern regions of the realm. In most cases, hundreds of leagues south of Kalinor. It was unusual enough that Declan knew there was no accident in it.

Perron stood before the hearth, a glass of brandy swirling in his palm. He looked at once smug and uncertain. It made for an odd mixture on the man's face.

"Gentlemen," Perron began once Declan and Bazin had taken their seats. It pained Declan to know that they were the last to arrive. "I presume many of you are curious to know why I've asked you here tonight."

There were murmurs from some of the gathered nobility, Bazin included. Declan maintained his silence.

"As you are well aware," Perron continued, "these last few years have been an interesting test of our mettle. The Queen has continually pushed against us and, by and large, we have allowed it. We issue edicts in the interest of the realm, and she regards them as mere suggestions. To call this humiliating would hardly scratch the surface.

"*We* must decide how we are to move forward. If we do nothing, we will eventually cease to exist altogether. I fear we have but one final opportunity to take a stand before Andariana Belgi attempts to have us abolished completely."

Declan could hardly credit his hearing. Was the man absolutely *mad?*

But from the sounds of the others in the room, Declan realized that he was much in the minority.

"Lord Perron," he said, standing slowly, "forgive an old man his misunderstanding. What *exactly* are you proposing here? I agree that Andariana has become more involved with everyday matters in the last year or two, but that is a far cry from saying that Parliament has a foot in the grave.

"Andariana knows very well *why* Parliament was established. She would never dispense with the legitimacy we give her throne."

Perron smiled, "Well said, Simon. However, being relegated to an advisory council is hardly different than having the whole bloody business dissolved. We would certainly have the same authority either way."

"Aye." came a new voice.

Declan turned his head to see a large man with a ruddy face struggle to his feet.

Hugo Malak, Lord of Relvyn, boyhood friend of Bertrand Perron. Declan rolled his eyes.

"And besides," Malak continued, "if we have no authority, how can we guarantee our safety?"

Declan's eyebrows drew down. "Malak, what are you on about? We're in the heart of Kalinor itself. The Voralla is less than a league from this very house. What danger could you possibly fear?"

The moment the words had passed his lips, Declan wanted them back.

Malak laughed, "The *Voralla*, Simon? You trust Andariana's witches with your safety?"

"I hardly think the Magi follow the Queen's orders above those of the High Magus, Hugo." Declan snapped back. "The Magi have always been free of Ilyari judicial restrictions. They have their own courts, their own system of governance. I fail to see what Andariana has to do with *them*."

"I, too, once held much the same opinion."

Everyone's mouth dropped open as a figure stepped out of the shadows beside Perron.

"*Sammul?*" Bazin whispered to Declan's left.

"High Magus," Declan said quickly, "what light would you shed on all this?"

Sammul smiled, and Declan's heart sank. Until the man had spoken, Declan had held hope that Perron and Malak were merely trying to bully the rest of the Southern nobility. It would not be a unique occurrence.

But Sammul's presence changed everything.

"I'm afraid that Lord Malak's intimations are true. If the Magi in the Voralla received instructions from Andariana, they would follow them. Even against my orders."

The nobles erupted into shouts of alarm and panic.

"Quiet." Sammul said calmly.

The room quieted instantly.

Declan jumped, realizing that the man had just used the Archanium. As much as he admired the Magi for their dedication and their abilities, he was unnerved to know that everyone in the room, himself included, had just been touched by Sammul's power.

"You must understand, gentlemen, that Andariana is now in a very unusual position among monarchs. She has gained the Voralla's trust. Until now, we have kept a friendly truce with the Ilyari people. One based on mutual respect and assistance. But ever since it was revealed that the Prince is one of us...well you can imagine the eagerness of some Magi to strengthen that truce. To trust that Andariana has their interest at heart."

Declan searched the faces in the room. They were all fixated on Sammul, their eyes wide and fearful. He felt the same fear, but it was grounded by a strong sense of reason. He had never seen a Magus use the Archanium for anything but the good of others.

And he had a logical caution regarding the Archanium Knights, certainly. But those men served only to protect the lives of their Magi. They held no military rank outside of the Voralla.

"Sammul," Perron's voice pulled Declan back into the moment, "how can we restore things to the way they *should* be? Surely you're no happier about this situation than we are."

"Indeed I'm not, Chancellor. But as long as Andariana holds the throne, the Magi are unlikely to be swayed."

A thread of ice ran through Declan's heart.

"But if she *didn't*," Malak barked eagerly, faithfully picking up the bone at his feet, "then the Magi would return to your flock?"

Sammul shrugged, "I believe that to be the case, Lord Malak. They admire Andariana, and her apparent devotion to them. But such allegiance wouldn't necessarily transfer to another monarch. Providing, of course, that it wasn't Jonas or Tamara."

Another eruption in the room, far more vitriolic than before.

"Wait just a moment!" Declan shouted.

The room reluctantly calmed.

"Ladies, gentlemen, while I have a hard time following much of your logic, one thing remains to be explained." His eyes swept across the room as the other nobles glared at him. "If, as you say, the Magi are under the thrall of the Queen, then won't they resist any attempt to remove her from the throne? Their interests are being met better now than with another monarch to contend with."

Sammul smiled. "Very well put, Lord Declan. I've had much the same thought myself. And it is for that very reason that I've brought someone *else* here this evening."

Murmurs of confusion became shouts of surprise when another man twisted into view in front of the hearth.

He was short and cloaked in black. His face was calm, but his eyes carried an understood threat.

"Good evening, my Lords and Ladies." he said gently. "I apologize for my abrupt entrance, but Sammul was concerned you would be put off by an outsider amongst you."

"And who are you, sir?" Declan demanded.

The man bowed swiftly, "I am Bael. I have come here tonight at the special invitation of Chancellor Perron to offer you my services."

"Your...services?" Declan managed.

Bael smiled. Declan wanted to run for the door. "Indeed, Lord Declan. I understand that the Lords of Parliament find themselves in an untenable position. Sammul has asked me to assist you, should you need help leveling the game board."

"*You* are powerful enough to stand up to the entirety of the Voralla?" Malak asked in awe.

Bael laughed and Declan cringed. "Hardly, Lord Malak. But between myself and my congregation, I believe we can provide you the weight needed to bargain. No Magus wants to harm another. Our presence would simply ensure that everything is handled as peacefully as possible."

Despite his objections, Declan found himself being swayed by the man's words. He didn't know how trustworthy either Magus was at the moment, but at least the rest of the nobles in the room were hearing the same message.

"And once we work out our differences," Declan pressed, "what will you and your followers do then?"

Bael bowed his head, "We will ask to be allowed to study at the Voralla, Lord Declan. My father left the Voralla, as so many do, as a young man because he disagreed with their methods. As his successor, it is my hope to bring our flock back into the fold. When Sammul approached me, I thought this might be the best way to bring that about."

"What of the Queen?" Malak asked, leaning forward. "Have we resolved a position on what is to be done with her?"

Declan straightened, "Hugo, we have already allowed that having Andariana abdicate in favor of either Tamara or Jonas is unacceptable. Who else would you suggest? Every Head of House in Ilyar would be jockeying for the crown. It would throw the realm into a civil war far worse than the last. I hardly think anyone in this room is ready to go to those lengths merely because they feel uneasy."

"There is one man with a strong claim." Perron allowed.

Declan arched an eyebrow. "Who then, Bertrand?"

"Emelian Krasik."

The room fell silent. Nobles looked at one another, at a loss for words.

"The man has been dead for twenty years." Declan stammered.

"I thought much the same, Simon." Perron responded, his smirk condescending, "Until Magus Bael alerted me to the fact that the man is very much alive. Mad, but nevertheless alive."

Declan fought to keep his knees from buckling.

Emelian Krasik.

The man had plunged Ilyar into a civil war. It had resulted in the disappearance of Queen Marra, and Krasik's own madness. That inexplicable boon had brought the war to a sudden halt. Without Krasik as a figurehead to marshal around, his army collapsed.

The man had been spotted here and there months after the war, roaming the countryside and picking at the dead. Yet no one had ever been able to track him down. By the time reports reached a Legion camp, the man had vanished once again.

He was hardly more than a phantom now, lingering only in children's stories as the Old Crow, who would get you if you misbehaved.

Hardly a candidate for the crown.

"That would plunge the realm into a war bloodier than the first." Declan sputtered at last. "Our lands would be decimated. To even *suggest* it is madness."

Perron nodded amicably, "No one is suggesting we rush into war, Simon. But I, for one, feel better knowing that we have means to bargain with. Granted, hardly an optimal situation. But something to think about."

Declan shook his head. His mind was quickly filling with a great too many specters, and all of them made him want to hide in bed for a month.

"I'm afraid I must leave you all to this." he stammered, turning and walking to the door. "I've been up far too long today as it is. I must find my bed now. Good evening."

He walked swiftly into the hallway and headed for the door.

Bootstrikes sounded behind him, but he didn't bother to turn. He had to get out of that house as quickly as his elderly legs would carry him.

He hurried down the stone steps and climbed into his carriage. He shut the door firmly, only to have it spring open a heartbeat later as Lord Bazin climbed in across from him.

The carriage lurched forward, and for a long moment the two men only stared at one another. Declan fought the urge to burst into tears of frustration. Bazin's face was florid. The man looked as though he were about to burst.

"Never...." Bazin puffed, "in all my days did I imagine I would hear such talk. It was all I could do to hold my tongue in that room."

"I'm glad you did." Declan cut in. "Arred, a very dangerous hour just passed. And what we heard, what we witnessed, would have been for naught if you'd angered either of those Magi."

Bazin nodded curtly. "I know that, Simon. But the moment we arrive at the Palace, I'm going to Lord Captain Lenox. He *must* be made aware of this meeting immediately."

Declan's gray brows drew down. "You *cannot* do that! Don't prepare a feast for Volos so casually."

Bazin's eyes flashed. "There is nothing 'casual' in this, Simon. This is of grave importance. Such things can't be combated if the Legion is kept in the dark. The Lord Captain must know whom to watch. The sooner spies can be set on them, the better."

"Please, Arred, *sleep* on what you've heard. Your blood is high right now. Let a few hours pass before you make your judgments."

Bazin shook his head violently. "I will not allow this insanity to continue unpunished, Simon! I'm going to the Lord Captain. He will know what to do."

Bazin slapped the roof of the carriage as they passed the Palace gate. The carriage drew to a stop, and the lord was out hurrying towards the Palace before Declan could utter another word.

Simon sighed heavily.

The specters in his mind roared to the forefront. He would hardly sleep a wink that night.

⁂

Perron sat alone in his study. The sun was warming the sky but still out of sight. His eyes were bleary from lack of sleep, though he dared not rest until Bael returned.

The very thought of the man made his heart quake.

The gods had forsaken him. Forsaken him, and left him in the thrall of a man touched by an affliction unlike anything Perron had ever seen.

The air in front of the fire twisted, and Perron felt a stammer in his chest.

"Not as much trouble as I expected." Bael said crisply, pulling back his hood.

A tiny spark of hope flashed through the Chancellor. "Really? Well, that's encouraging news, isn't it?"

Bael raised a golden eyebrow, thrusting out his right arm and pulling the cloak away.

Two corpses landed heavily on Perron's floor.

The first frozen face was hardly a surprise. Arred Bazin had been a risky choice, but the man had been very passionate in life. His leanings could have gone either way.

The second was not expected.

Perron stared into the glassy eyes of Lord Captain Lenox. That last spark of hope extinguished.

"What's wrong, Chancellor? You seem displeased."

Perron restrained himself. "Magus Bael, I must admit surprise at the second casualty. Is it not a bit arrogant to murder the Lord Captain of the Legion?"

Bael snorted, "The man hardly put up a fight. He went down much easier than Lord Bazin. And whoever she puts in his place will die just as fast if he gets any fool ideas of glory."

Bael stepped away from the bodies and turned to leave.

"Wait!" Perron barked, his dread growing. "Where are you going? What about the bodies?"

Bael sighed, "I have been much too generous with my time, Perron. I cannot hang around Kalinor while you worry yourself into an early grave. I am far too close to unlocking the Presence of the Dark God. And when I do, more than Ilyar will tremble before us.

"I assume you are clever enough to clean this up. It will look like an accident. Lord Bazin tripped. The good Lord Captain had too rich a dinner. See, now I've even done you one last favor.

"Good evening, Chancellor Perron."

And then the Magus was gone, leaving Perron to stare down at the empty faces of two men he'd once called friends.

Aleksei sat stiffly in his military dress uniform, his eyes fixed on the priest walking in circles around the body of Lord Captain Lenox. Every third rotation, the priest would call out the same incantation.

A group of acolytes surrounding him repeated it back, and the process would begin again.

It was the strangest funeral Aleksei had ever witnessed.

They sat in the cavernous Cathedral of Volos. Black marble columns striped in midnight blue rose ominously towards the vaulted ceiling. Deep blue flames burned in hanging iron braziers lining the pews to either side.

Their muted glow provided the only light, as befitted a structure dedicated to the God of Death and the Aftershadow. The extreme wealth on display, from the gilded longhorn skulls mounted around the central altar, to the intricate bone inlays that comprised the floor surrounding the ceremonial spaces, left little doubt that Volos was also the God of Cattle and Coin.

Aleksei wanted to run out of there as swiftly as possible.

On the Southern Plain, funerals were a simple affair. The body was returned to the soil in a short service dedicating the dead to the care of Mokosh. Mother Margareta would say a few words for the family, light a candle, and that was that.

But in Kalinor, the dead were passed from the world of the living to the Aftershadow, and into the care of Volos. Immolated as part of the service, their sins were burned away, leaving only their spirits to transcend to the next world, untethered by earthly fetters.

It made Aleksei's skin crawl.

He glanced at Jonas and was surprised to find the Prince's face transfixed by the body of the Lord Captain. Aleksei watched him for a few moments, but Jonas' eyes never wavered.

Aleksei frowned. *What are you looking at?*

There's something wrong with this. Jonas' voice rumbled through his mind.

Where do you want to begin? *This is macabre at best. I've never seen people act this way.*

Jonas grunted. *Don't be obtuse. I mean there's something wrong with Lord Captain* Lenox.

Aleksei gritted his teeth. *The man's dead, Jonas. I don't think he has much to worry about.*

Never mind. Jonas snapped. *I'll explain after the service.*

After another hour of droning in a dead language Aleksei couldn't understand, the priest raised his hands to the people in the pews. Everyone except Aleksei raised their hands in response, and uttered a word he'd never heard before.

And then it was over.

Aleksei looked around, bewildered. Fortunately, the rest of the congregation had already come to their feet and were heading for the great double doors, back into the daylight.

Except for Jonas.

Aleksei followed his Magus down a series of steps, to the center of the cathedral. The High Priest of Volos was still muttering incantations as Jonas approached. Acolytes cleared away books and candles, glancing at the two men curiously.

"Excuse me, Cleric." Jonas said politely.

The priest stopped his prayer in surprise. "Highness?"

"I need to examine the Lord Captain before you finish the ritual. It's a matter of great importance."

The Cleric appeared surprised by Jonas' request, but nodded his acceptance.

Jonas stepped past the priest and ran his hand through the air above the Lord Captain's body.

Aleksei shivered as he felt Jonas open himself to the Archanium. He couldn't tell what the Magus was doing, but the fact that Jonas was touching the Archanium at *all* surprised him.

Jonas straightened.

"Thank you for the indulgence, Father." he said quickly, bowing and turning on his heel.

Aleksei hurried after him, but neither spoke until they were back in the blinding sunlight.

"What's going on?" Aleksei demanded.

Jonas' green eyes were grave. "Lord Captain Lenox was murdered with the Archanium."

Aleksei frowned, "Are you sure?"

"I have no doubt. There were...echoes of some very dangerous magic all around him."

"Why would a *Magus* want to kill the Lord Captain?" Aleksei asked. "And which of the Magi could even manage such a thing?"

"I'm not sure exactly how it was done, so it's difficult to say. I need to take a look at his office. Can you go to the Voralla and find Aya? Between the two of us, we should be able to figure this out."

"I'll be there as quickly as I can." Aleksei promised, hurrying off towards the East Lawn.

Jonas sighed deeply. The loss of the Lord Captain was a serious blow to Ilyar, yet it had seemed an innocent enough affair. The man had been complaining of chest pains for some time now. His early death was not entirely shocking.

The death of Arred Bazin, however, was something else. Two men of such import in the same night was more than enough to pique Jonas' curiosity. But until now, there had been nothing to go on.

Yet from the moment he laid eyes on Lenox's body, Jonas had seen something peculiar. Actually *finding* the Archanium echoes had taken him most of the funeral service.

But once he tested his theory, the echoes blossomed into view.

Whoever murdered Lenox knew what they were doing. And they certainly didn't want anyone poking around in their wake, nor the Lord Captain's for that matter.

By the time he reached the Lord Captain's office, Jonas' mind was buzzing with possibilities. The magic that had killed Lenox was located in a very specific region of the Great Sphere, summoned from deep within the storm that was the Nagavor, the destructive, chaotic hemisphere of the Archanium.

But the Magi in the Voralla followed very different meridians altogether, diving down into the steady, placid seas of the Akhrana. Different enough that none of them could possibly reach that far across the Sphere.

So that left Magi outside of the Voralla, which only confused matters all the more. There were hundreds of Magi scattered throughout Ilyar, but every single Magus in Kalinor lived in the Voralla.

Additionally, the Lord Captain hadn't left the city in months. Only a Magus in the Voralla would have knowledge of his activities. It was simultaneously unlikely that an outside Magus would have a substantial enough motive to kill the man.

Excepting the one that tried to kill Aleksei in the Wood...

Jonas opened the door to the office and staggered.

The room was a blinding mass of Archanium echoes. Worse, the clear intent that ran through them was so anarchic, so *dark* that Jonas fought to keep from retching.

He swallowed the bile rising in his throat and burst into a fit of violent coughing.

"Jonas?"

He heard Aleksei's voice, but it sounded so far away.

He slowly realized he was on the floor, gazing up at his Knight.

"What happened?" he wheezed.

A smile broke across Aleksei's face. He gathered Jonas into a tight embrace, kissing his forehead. "Gods, for a moment I wasn't sure if you were going to come around."

Jonas managed a weak smile. Aleksei's arms felt like a crushing vice.

"Did you go into Lenox's office?" the Prince managed.

Aleksei's grip relaxed. "For a split second, long enough to pull you out. I was more concerned about you than anything in there."

Jonas pushed himself his feet, steadying himself against the wall. "I'm fine. I just had a reaction to something in the room."

"Jonas."

He turned when he heard Aya's voice.

"That was no *reaction.*" the prophet said solemnly as she drew closer. "Whoever killed the Lord Captain also left a trap for the unfortunate Magus who decided to go sniffing around. You're incredibly lucky that Aleksei pulled you out when he did. I don't completely understand the spellforms myself, but I'd wager he just saved both your lives."

Jonas walked to the doorway of the office and peered in.

The Archanium echoes were as strong as ever, but he no longer felt ill in their presence.

This had already become far more complicated than Jonas had

first imagined.

"Aya, what do you see?" he asked.

Aya frowned, "What do you mean? I see an office."

Jonas blinked. "The Archanium echoes. What do they look like?"

Aya's eyes narrowed, "I don't *see* any Archanium echoes. I can tell that it was used in this room recently, but I don't see any actual spell residue."

"You can't see *anything*? This room looks like it's on fire to me."

Aya's eyes widened. "Sometimes, if your path is at an opposite extreme of the magic used, you can't see the actual echo. These were very dangerous spells, so it's not surprising that I can't see them. I doubt *any*one in the Voralla could. But that also begs another question."

"Why can *I*?"

Aya shrugged, "You're generally self-trained, Jonas. That's taken you along a very different meridian. I believe you know what that may be."

Jonas nodded again. He knew. But this was not the time to go into a philosophical discussion about the ramifications of his path through the Archanium.

"I need to speak to Andariana." he said, turning and heading towards the Queen's chambers.

"She's holding Court today." Aya offered. "She's announcing her choice to replace Captain Lenox."

"Then I need to hurry."

Jonas broke into an unsteady run. His lungs ached from coughing and he still felt weak, but it was *imperative* that he reach his aunt before she announced the promotion.

The moment he'd seen the Lord Captain's office, he'd known what had to be done. It would not be a popular decision, but it was the only one that could work. He hated even thinking it. He hated the entire notion to the core.

But he had no choice.

By the time he reached the throne room, he was gasping for air. Aleksei was right behind him the entire way, and he could feel concern burning through their bond.

Jonas pushed his way into the throne room.

Andariana was in the middle of her speech, but she stopped the moment she saw him.

"Gentlemen," she said quickly, stepping down from the throne, "I apologize, but we will now take a five minute recess."

There was a murmur amongst the men, who were watching both Jonas and Aleksei with considerable confusion and interest.

Jonas stepped back into the hallway. Andariana waited until Aleksei pulled the doors shut before she rounded on her nephew.

"What *is* it? It had better be important."

"More important than you can imagine." Jonas panted. He glanced at Aleksei, "Can you keep the corridor clear?"

Aleksei nodded and took off at a trot down the hallway.

Jonas explained the last half hour to her, leaving nothing out. Andariana's skepticism quickly shifted to shock.

"This is incredible." she whispered. "But we still have no idea *why* the Lord Captain was murdered?"

Jonas shook his head, "But I imagine we'll find much the same on Lord Bazin. Neither of those men died by accident, Andariana. Someone had a vested interest in killing them. And anyone else who got too curious."

The Queen shivered. "So what am I to do?"

Jonas sighed. "The only thing you *can* do."

Minutes later, Andariana stepped calmly into the throne room and walked crisply to the dais. She turned, sitting straight-backed in the heavily carved throne, surveying the gathered generals and lesser officers.

"Gentlemen, I apologize for making you wait. Understand that it could not be avoided.

"Some very unsettling news has just reached me. It seems that the late Lord Captain was in fact *murdered*."

This sent shockwaves of outrage and excited whisperings through the assembly. Andariana seemed to brace herself for what was to come.

"He was murdered with the Archanium."

The room exploded into angry shouts and oaths. She raised her hands for silence, but the officers were too enraged to notice.

A thunderclap resounded through the room, bringing them all to a terrified silence.

"Gentlemen, your *queen* is speaking." Jonas said.

They glared at him, but maintained their silence.

"As I have yet to understand the motive for the Lord Captain's murder," Andariana continued, "I can only assume that the next man I appoint will face the same danger."

Another wave of murmurs rippled through the assembly. Jonas raised a hand, and they died out immediately.

"*Therefore*," Andariana continued, her face betraying nothing, "I regret that I cannot possibly name *any* of the esteemed generals gathered here today to the post of Lord Captain.

"No normal man could possibly survive against a Magus wielding such dangerous magic. The *only* men who might stand a chance are among the Archanium Knights."

There was silence. This was clearly the last thing they expected to hear.

"However," she said quickly, before any assembled could gather their wits, "I do not command the Voralla. The Magi and their Knights are subject to their own laws and hierarchies. It is not my place to name one of their kind to our military ranks."

The assembly took a collective breath.

"Therefore, I am forced to select the *only* man who meets my criteria. A man from among your own ranks, with the skills necessary to survive the post. I'd like you all to stand for your new Lord Captain. Captain Aleksei Drago."

⋞⊛⊱

All eyes turned to Aleksei.

He had been watching the doors in case of trouble. As he slowly turned his head, he found the eyes of all his superior officers fixed on him. His face reddened as he took in the glares of seasoned generals, watching as a brash young *boy* was named to the most coveted military position in the realm.

And then the weight of it struck him.

He now *commanded* these men. Every single one.

As a group they saluted.

Aleksei gulped silently, then crisply returned the salute.

He felt about ready to faint.

"*Hail*, Lord Captain Drago."

The call resounded through the throne room.

He had not a single clue what to do next. Fortunately, they dropped their salutes and he followed suit.

And then it was over. The men began to talk amongst themselves. He watched their faces carefully, but by and large, the senior officers looked relieved. He doubted any of them wanted to follow a man murdered with the Archanium. Especially since there seemed to be no motive.

Aleksei had been assigned to the most powerful military role in Ilyar, but also the most dangerous. There were few who envied him.

"Lord Captain?"

He turned to find Jonas standing there with a slight smirk.

Aleksei scowled, "Did you *plan* this?"

The Prince shrugged, "I wanted to warn you, but I was afraid you might refuse the role. This really is the *only* solution, and I couldn't allow your humility to get in the way."

"I don't like being manipulated, Jonas."

Jonas laughed, "You are now *the* authority in Ilyar. The Lord Captain, who must be obeyed. In the last five minutes you've gone from being a Knight and the Prince's Bonded to being on almost equal political footing with *me*. A simple 'thank you' might be in order."

Despite his shock and his fading anger, Aleksei allowed himself a laugh. The idea struck him as absolutely ludicrous, but the reverence that the title carried was growing on him.

"Lord Captain?"

He turned and smiled as a man only a few years his senior saluted. He returned the salute, "What's your name, solider?"

"Colonel Charles Ander, Sir."

"Colonel Ander, it's a pleasure."

Ander seemed unsure of what to say next. "Lord Captain, I...I mean no disrespect. But I appreciate the suddenness of Her Majesty's proclamation, and your previous rank as a Guard Captain hardly gave you time to prepare...to understand certain... complexities. Would you permit me to take you through some of the finer details of Her Majesty's Legion?"

Aleksei offered the Colonel a broad smile, though in all truth he wanted the hug the man in thanks. "I think that would do me a great deal of good, Colonel. I imagine I'll be richer for the experience."

Ander relaxed visibly. "Thank you, Lord Captain. I was afraid that I spoke beyond my bounds."

Aleksei shook his head, "Colonel, we both know the reason I was promoted. I can survive in this position better than anyone else in this room. That does *not* make me a military expert. Not yet, at least. I only hope that with your guidance, and with the assistance of the other officers present, I might learn the particulars of commanding Her Majesty's Legion to the best of my ability."

Ander saluted again, "Thank you, Sir. I'll speak with you tomorrow, then, at your earliest convenience."

Aleksei returned the salute. "Perhaps after the midday meal, Colonel?"

Ander saluted one last time, excusing himself.

Jonas walked over from a group of generals. Aleksei had noticed how stormy they looked when they approached the Prince, but they seemed in much better spirits as they headed from the room.

"What did you tell them?" Aleksei asked quietly.

"I simply reminded them of the manner in which Lord Captain Lenox died. A few extra details ensured that they were more than glad to see you named to the position than any of them."

"I just *pray* you made the right decision." Aleksei muttered.

Jonas smiled sardonically, "I know what I'm doing."

But Aleksei recognized the moment for what it was.

The moment Jonas might have signed both their lives away.

CHAPTER 20

THE LOST RETURNED

THE OCEAN CRASHED beneath the platform, showering the party in spray. In the moonlight it seemed as though clouds were sweeping across them.

Bael ignored the irritant. He had eyes only for the cliff face.

For the mammoth gate it housed.

Within the cliff stirred a rich and ancient power. A power imprisoned, writhing with the promise of release.

A man stood before him, dripping with sea spray and shivering in terror.

"Open it, Raim." Bael said softly, pressing the tiny copper bird into the other Magus' hand.

"As...as you command." Raim stuttered.

Bael stepped back. The Magi behind him were only too eager to follow his lead.

No one knew what lurked behind the gate. But fortunately for them, Raim had been selected to find out.

Extremely dangerous magic was being practiced this night, but to be on the receiving end of aeon-rich spellcraft was not conducive to survival amongst Bael's followers.

Raim hurried to the gate, pressing the bird into the center of the Angelic Crest.

For a moment nothing happened. Raim held the Archanium, apparently ready for whatever the long dead Magi of old might have prepared.

With a great grinding of gears and the rending of ancient wards, the gate fell apart like rotten cloth in a stiff breeze.

Bael coughed and waved smoke from his eyes as his followers cleared the platform of sparks and debris. Raim stood exactly where he had a moment before, seemingly unscathed.

Bael smiled.

The platform rumbled. Bael had to clutch at the cliff face to maintain his footing on the slippery stone.

A terrible wail poured forth from the mouth of the mountain. Bael covered his ears lest he go deaf. The men and women behind him followed suit.

Raim stood still, transfixed by whatever he saw within the cavern.

And then the cliff erupted, vomiting a titanic deluge of midnight into the shattering storm. Bael turned his face from the sudden heat, trying not to breathe in the stench that issued forth.

When he looked back, Raim was lying battered and broken at the edge of the platform. At Bael's gesture, a Magus hurried over to the prone form, spending only a second to confirm the man's impending death.

"He won't live more than a few minutes." the man called.

Bael nodded and quickly turned into the cavern.

The moment he entered, the room lit with an incandescent glow. He ran his hands over the intricate carvings that covered the walls and pillars of the space.

The Third Transept.

The runes and pictograms told the story of the Magus Cassian. A man who had lived a *thousand* years before Bael. A man who had possessed the same power Bael now sought, at least for a time. A man who had wreaked havoc for nearly a decade.

It was a cautionary tale, meant to dissuade the overly curious or foolish.

Bael was neither. He knew *exactly* what he was seeking. He knew what it would do to him, and what it could do to his world. None of it mattered in the least. He would possess it, and then all that was due to him would be *his*.

He would serve his father's memory, if not exactly in the way Rafael had envisioned.

And he would show Jonas Belgi what it was to be powerless. What it was to hurt.

What it was to be *alone*.

Bael strode to the Second Gate and smiled.

"Stephen." he called.

A young copper-haired man stepped tentatively forward. "Master?"

Bael held up a second small statue before the young Magus. "Are you prepared?"

Stephen nodded earnestly, "I am, Master."

"What happened to Raim was unfortunate. These chambers hold warnings and traps the likes of which we cannot comprehend, crafted in a bygone and forgotten era. But if you believe in our cause, if you believe in our teachings, the Dark God will favor you."

Stephen bowed his head, whispering a prayer as Bael pressed the small token into his shaking hands. "As you command, Master Bael."

Bael stepped away from the gate, ignoring the excited chatter of his followers. His attention was riveted on Stephen, to the small greenstone statue of a rusalka he clutched uncertainly.

It had taken Bael's father decades to find the Third Key. Sammul had recovered the Second Key from the Voralla mere *weeks* ago. It was a risky gamble to open the first two gates now, when he had not one single idea of what waited on the other side. It was riskier to open them without the true treasure, the Prime Key. But until it could be located, Bael would possess any piece of his birthright he could claim.

And besides, the time had come. Jonas Belgi was growing stronger seemingly by the day, and all of Bael's plans were moving along too swiftly to delay any longer.

No, it *had* to be tonight.

Stephen embraced the Archanium and pressed the small statue to the Angelic Crest, just as Raim had before him.

This time, Bael could see the wards rip apart and hear the gears turn. But rather than rip itself apart, the gate simply vanished.

Bael breathed an inward sigh of relief.

Stephen tensed for a pregnant pause. But this time, there was no fury to rip apart his fragile flesh. Even the Grey Sea itself seemed to be holding its breath.

Nothing came.

Bael waited until it was clear that Stephen would survive, at least another few moments.

"Stephen and I will continue alone." he called to his congregation.

There was no telling what awaited them in the Second Transept.

He walked up to his Magus and clapped the man roughly on the back. "After you, my dear boy."

Stephen nodded shakily, stumbling into the Second Transept.

Bael followed at a leisurely pace, taking in this new space as his eyes scoured the stone.

It was not nearly so beautiful as the Third Transept. If anything, it looked like a more primitive attempt at the same story.

Upon closer inspection, Bael realized that what had once been incredibly articulate carvings had *melted* over time. Apparently, what lay beyond was such a corrupting influence that it had eroded even the stone.

And then he saw it.

Before the Prime Gate floated a man-sized silhouette. It looked very much like a shadow, except it was frozen in midair, a patch of darkness suspended a pace off the ground.

"A construct." he whispered.

Stephen frowned, "After this long? Master, by now even the most powerful construct would have unraveled."

"No, great care was taken here." He studied it intently, viewing it from all angles; noting the way the Archanium had bent itself to accommodate the Magus who created it.

It was a breathtaking piece of magic.

"Consume it."

"Master?"

Bael whipped around and glared at Stephen, "*Consume* it!"

Stephen's knees shook as he walked towards the shadow construct. He reached tentatively forward and opened himself to the Archanium.

Before he could touch it, the construct leapt at him, writhing around his body. When he opened his mouth to scream, the construct leapt up into his mouth.

Stephen's eyes went wide as the construct forced itself down his throat, burrowing into his being.

He collapsed in a nerveless heap.

Bael waited for him to move, but the Magus remained motionless.

With a sigh, Bael walked over to Stephen and kicked him roughly. The man's eyes flashed open and he sat up like a man possessed. He breathed in heavily and stared at Bael.

"You are still *lacking*, Pilgrim." he shouted. "You are *lacking!*"

He collapsed again. Bael was about ready to burn the man from existence when Stephen finally stood, breathing evenly and looking around in confusion.

"What...what was that?" he whispered.

"A very old warning." Bael said dismissively. "But no one would leave a construct like that for a simple message. I lack the key to open the Prime Gate, that much is clear. I had hoped that there was some sort of test in here, some means of attaining it. That seems to be a fiction.

"But tell me, Stephen, do you feel...unusual?"

The other Magus frowned, keeping his silence for a moment. And then he smiled.

"Where's *Raim?*"

Bael led him back to the distended body of the fallen Magus.

Stephen reached into the Archanium, into a forbidden region. A spellform settled onto Raim's shivering husk.

Everyone stared as the dying Magus' body convulsed. And transformed.

Bael smiled.

"Get ready, Jonas Belgi. I'm coming for you."

❧

Aleksei sat up sharply.

He panted in the darkness, sweat dripping down his back. Images flashed through his mind, some so terrible he had to force back tears.

Jonas stirred beside him, tossing in Aleksei's reflected anguish. The deep scars tracing down his back, an eternal reminder of where his wings had been, shone pale pink in the ghostly moonlight.

Aleksei pulled the sheets away and stepped into the light pouring in from an open window, allowing the autumn air to breathe across his naked chest.

I hurt. The Wood's voice burst through his mind.

Over the past year he had made many trips into the Seil Wood, to assure Her he was being a dutiful Hunter. She always welcomed him, but never *warmly.*

He'd wondered if his bond with Jonas affected his connection to the Wood. He wondered if She was jealous. If She was even *capable* of jealousy.

It had been months since he'd heard Her voice in his mind. But tonight something was very different.

Mother Wood, are you alright? He tried of focus his thoughts. The day had taken its toll, but he was Her Hunter, and he had a deep and intrinsic duty to protect the Wood.

The Lost, they have returned, *Hunter. So many!*

Aleksei frowned. *You sound glad, Mother.*

I am fond of them. They have returned. *But Hunter, their return speaks of a darker fate.*

Tell me. Aleksei thought quickly.

As the dream faded, terror was rapidly overtaking exhaustion.

Gaze on this, Hunter.

Visions filled his mind.

A giant form born in flame rose and crushed a group of screaming people. When it moved on, nothing remained but ash.

A man cloaked in the Archanium struggled against a giant wyrm, each trading blows before the man was rent in two. A behemoth of whitestone smashed Kalinor Palace to splinters.

One after another, images flooded through his mind. Aleksei felt tears flow from his eyes as the Wood showed him the carnage that was to come.

These are images of what once occurred, and what may again if the Pilgrim is not stopped. The return of the Lost speaks of much that I had hoped forgotten. You are in danger, *Hunter. As long as the Pilgrim walks, you are in danger.*

What would you have me do, Mother? Aleksei thought anxiously.

He wanted to change those visions, to save the dying. He felt helpless.

When the time is right, I will call on you. You must *answer, Hunter. Protect your Chosen. He knows what must happen, though it terrifies him. Protect* him. *Give him your strength. He will need much in what is to come.*

Beware *the Pilgrim.*

Fear *the Demonic Presence.*

"Eaten?"

Aleksei stared at the pages spread across his desk. "That's what it says, Colonel. Seven men found in the Seil Wood, just west of a village called Timurus. All were dead. Some were partially eaten. Others were riddled with bite marks." Aleksei glanced up at the man sitting across from him. "The commander of the outpost was unable to identify the animal responsible."

Colonel Charles Ander stiffened at the last remark. "Forgive me, Sir, but I don't understand. Wolves or bears, either leaves easily distinguishable patterns."

"The commander doesn't believe that these men were killed by either, Colonel."

"Well, there are any number of unusual creatures within the Seil Wood, Lord Captain. Surely that comes as no surprise."

Aleksei shook his head, "Such creatures never venture much beyond the Wood's Heart, Colonel. And certainly never to the Wood's edge. She keeps them close for their own safety."

Before Ander could ask another question, Aleksei held up a second report. "This is from the village of Drava, just west of the Relvyn Wood. A very similar report, but with some decidedly different elements.

"Dead men here, too. Bitten and clawed to death, but without identifiable markings. Then something even stranger. They claim that their men walk into the Relvyn Wood and reemerge as beasts from the Aftershadow, beasts 'of horn and bone, with razor claws and the faces from a nightmare'."

Ander stared at Aleksei blankly. "I beg your pardon, Sir? Couldn't that be mere peasant superstition?"

Aleksei frowned.

It was possible, but then again, he'd never known his own peasant neighbors to be anywhere near that inventive with their superstitions. He glanced at the report again.

"This is from the outpost in Drava. The commander is claiming to have seen these beasts, and he assures me that this is no flight of fancy or trick of the mind. These 'beasts' have attacked the villagers. The outpost commander in Drava has lost five men to the creatures so far."

Ander breathed in sharply. "That sounds like madness."

"I agree, Colonel. But there's something else that confuses me. It's odd enough that villages near both the Seil and the Relvyn Woods should have identical reports. It will be easy for me to discover the truth surrounding the deaths in the Seil Wood. As for the beasts in Drava, that's another matter."

"So what should we do, Sir?"

Aleksei sat back in his chair, "I'll deal with the report from Timurus. As I said, that should be simple enough to sort out. In the meantime, I'd like you to read over the papers from Drava. See if we've missed anything."

Ander saluted as Aleksei came to his feet.

"I'll be back in a few hours." Aleksei said as he reached the door and pulled on his coat.

Ander saluted again and Aleksei sighed, pulling the door open and stepping out into the corridor. It had been a year since the Queen had named him Lord Captain, and the other officers were still unsure how deferential they ought to be.

Many were still trying to work out what *actual* power he now wielded. When Andariana had named him, the speech had been more concerned with his ability to survive in the position rather than his military prowess and, with it being peacetime, many of his decisions were purely organizational. He still had yet to be tested in war, and the idea filled him with more than a little terror.

Aleksei wove his way through the hallways, avoiding the larger thoroughfares. He had no interest in wading through a sea of salutes and pleasantries.

It took him only a few minutes to reach the West Lawn and the stables.

"Lord Captain Drago!" the stable master said, snapping to attention.

Aleksei smiled, "Master Gearing, can you saddle Agriphon?"

The man had hardly made a bow before he started barking orders at the stable hands.

Aleksei stood by the doors, watching boys not much younger than himself hurry around with tackle, strapping gear to the great black warhorse. Aleksei had found him tied in front of the stables the morning after his promotion.

A gift from Jonas.

The Magus had explained that a man of his rank required a horse to match. And while he still rode Dash whenever he could, he understood that the old draft horse was not the ideal battle mount.

Agriphon danced forward, halting crisply before Aleksei. The beast was tall and powerful. He was every farm boy's fantasy come to life.

Aleksei swung himself into the saddle and, with a light tap, the warhorse surged beneath him. He'd only had scattered chances to ride the stallion, and after a lifetime riding plodding draft horses, he still wasn't accustomed to Agriphon's sheer power.

It took longer than he would have liked to get out of the city. The streets were clogged with merchant traffic, and Agriphon's size only served to slow his movement between ox carts and peddler wagons.

But once he cleared the East Gate, Agriphon broke into a heady gallop. Aleksei laughed as the air rushed past him, taking in the rich autumn air.

The air in Kalinor held none of the rich complexities of the wild. In the city, his senses always felt dulled by the never-ending noise and the smell of too many people pressed too tightly together. Tracking amongst all the chaos was a nightmare.

But out in the open, his nose was picking up all the details that were drowned out in Kalinor, his ears finding the gentle rhythm of the earth and the air. The Seil Wood rose up above him before he'd even had a chance to truly acclimate to the change in environment, and he rode gratefully beneath Her branches.

Mother Wood, he called, *I come with questions.*

Welcome, Hunter.

Mother, men have died beneath Your branches in the last few days. I need to know what killed them.

The Lost, Hunter. The Lost are hungry.

Aleksei frowned. *The Lost? You spoke of them the other night, but you didn't tell me much about them. Are they the dead come back to life?*

The Lost are the children he took from me, Hunter. Long ago.

And they were a warning?

When the Demonic Presence was sealed from this world, he *took the Lost. The leshii, the rusalka, the vodnoia. They took my* demons *from me. My* precious little demons.

Aleksei stiffened. *Aren't demons inherently evil, Mother?*

In their way, Hunter. But they balance the good that lives within Me. Together, life turns without interruption. The people beyond My branches have forgotten the Lost, and they must learn to fear them again. Then the balance will be restored.

Aleksei frowned, *But you only speak of demons.*

My demons help maintain the balance of the Wood; they return the darkness that was stripped from me. I am complete with my Lost and my Children.

Aleksei sighed, *I understand, Mother. I have one more question.*

I keep nothing from My Hunter.

Have you ever beheld a beast made of horn and bone, with razor claws and the face of a nightmare?

Wind tore through the trees above him, but Aleksei heard nothing from the Wood. After a long silence, he felt something moving through the forest ahead of him. A blast of frigid air erupted from the underbrush, filling his mind with a tiny, terrified chattering as it whipped past him.

The Pilgrim is closer than I feared. The power of Her voice nearly knocked Aleksei from his saddle. As he regained his bearings, Aleksei reached up and felt a trickle of blood drip from his ear.

Beware the Pilgrim.

Fear *the Demonic Presence, Hunter*.
When the voice quieted again, Aleksei realized he was shivering.
He glanced down at his coat sleeves.
They were covered with frost.

CHAPTER 21

RIDDLES IN THE DARK

JONAS STARED AT the page, trying to force the runes to make sense. Before him lay a jumble of strange characters, only some of which he understood. Most were alien.

With a curse, he slammed the book shut and tossed it onto a side table. While he might be able to impress Aleksei with his knowledge of Angelic Symbology, he was more than lacking when it came to vocabulary.

The book completely eluded him.

There was a gentle knock. Before the sound completely registered, Aleksei slid into the room, locking the door behind himself.

"I didn't expect to see you this late." Jonas said, smiling.

"I just left your aunt's sitting room." Aleksei growled.

Jonas arched an eyebrow, "And?"

"*And* I've just ordered four hundred men to Drava." He paused and glanced at his Magus, "And twenty Magi."

Jonas frowned, "Drava? That's no bigger than Voskrin. And you're sending *Magi*? Will the Voralla even honor your request? And why so many Legionnaires?"

Aleksei stared into the fire, "Something down there is taking the men who enter the Wood and...changing them."

"Changing them *how?*"

Aleksei sighed, "Into some sort of beast. The commander described a creature covered in bone and horn, something with claws."

Jonas fixed his gaze on Aleksei. "You *can't* be serious."

The glimmer in Aleksei's golden eyes confirmed the report.

"Gods," the Prince whispered, "what does it mean?"

"I'm not sure, but I spent this afternoon in the Seil Wood. There have been some deaths on the fringes, so I went to find out why.

"She said it was a warning. But when I mentioned the beasts in Relvyn, She...had a reaction. I think it was something like a fit. She said the same words She used when the Lost reappeared. When I suggested that the Lost were causing the trouble in Drava, She sounded...*offended.* She said it was a spell, but had nothing to do with 'Her little demons'."

Jonas' eyes widened, "Did She threaten you?"

Aleksei shook his head, dropping into a seat on the floor, resting his back against the settee Jonas had occupied for the better part of the evening. "Nothing like that. She sounded afraid. Honestly, She sounded *terrified.*"

"So what did you do?" Jonas asked, leaning forward.

Aleksei laid his head against the settee and groaned, "I went to see Roux. The Ri-Vhan have documents that talk about the Lost. He promised he would send Treedarters to warn the villagers in Timurus, to instruct them in proper behavior, and to recognize warning signs.

"Something similar will have to be done in the Relvyn Wood, but that will take time. Time and understanding of exactly what we're dealing with down there."

"But you said the appearance of the Lost is a cause for greater concern."

Aleksei nodded, "She told me that they are some lesser form of demon. Not dangerous unless you're a fool, really. But deadly. And worse, their return is a warning.

"As are the beasts in the south. Or at least the spell that created them."

"A warning?" Jonas muttered. "That someone is trying to find this Demonic Presence?"

Aleksei sighed, "Have you heard of it?"

Jonas frowned, absently running his fingers through Aleksei's hair. "It sounds familiar. I've been looking through every book I can get my hands on in the Voralla, and I've only seen it referenced a time or two. But the Vault is enormous, and I have access to only the most basic texts. I would need a high-ranking Magus to get access to the hidden and encrypted texts. Certainly any texts that date back to the Kholod Wars."

"Whatever you have to do, Jonas, we *need* to know more about this. I asked Roux about it, and he promised to look through the Ri-Vhan collection. But those books span the last thousand years. It's no small feat."

"Well, I highly doubt Sammul will grant me access to the restricted areas." He paused. "But I might have another way."

Aleksei sat straighter, twisting. "What do you mean?"

Jonas shrugged, "The Ilyari are hardly the only nation with ancient texts. The angels of Dalita are just as likely to have books from the Kholod Wars. And I doubt anyone will turn me away there."

Aleksei arched an eyebrow, "I know your father was an angel, but is that enough to get access to their most prized secrets?"

Jonas looked away from Aleksei, "In a manner of speaking."

"*Why?*"

The Magus returned Aleksei's gaze. His emerald eyes wavered.

"Because my father was also a prince."

⌘

Kevara Avlon, Angelus to the Host and Empress of all Dalita, was drunk.

She lay in her aerie, golden wings framing her tiny form as she stared listlessly at the ceiling.

Above her, delicate birds swirled about in the sky around depictions of various miracles of the One-God. All of it was rendered in the finest detail by the most talented artisans of her empire, and yet she hardly saw the murals anymore.

Her world was ending.

Beside her, a half-empty bottle of firebrandy lay near a pile of golden paper. Those papers reported the most intriguing and worthy information from Ilyar in the past month. Such messages often contained economic news, intelligence of trade negotiations and the like.

That pattern had come to a choking halt.

The Ilyari Queen was sending Archanium Magi *and* Legionnaires to the south upon suspicion of unexplained attacks.

And something else. A description of a beast. Of a *revenant*.

"Grandmother?"

Kevara Avlon raised her head from the velvet cushions that surrounded her and smiled weakly. "*Leigha*, darling, will you join an old woman in her misery?"

The young angel glided down to her grandmother and frowned at the bottle she saw lying to the side.

"Grandmother, what's wrong with you? The entire Basilica is in an uproar. Evening services were held by *Malachai*, and suddenly the entire Host is convinced you've taken ill. As it stands, I'm afraid I'd rather lie than tell them you're just drunk."

Surprisingly, the Angelus laughed, "It's *so* easy for you to judge me, Leigha dear. But tarry a moment. Come here."

The angel paused for a long moment before floating gracefully forward. Irritated though she may be, Kevara knew Leigha was curious to know what might have caused such a drastic reaction from a woman so prim and self-possessed.

"Read this." Kevara Avlon whispered, handing Leigha a single sheaf of paper.

Her granddaughter looked down and scanned the words. The paper fell from her hand as she reached for the bottle and took a long pull.

The Angelus laughed again, "Very good, child. You *understand* then?"

Leigha wiped her mouth and nodded, closing her eyes.

"The Second Transept has been opened." she whispered. "Dear God, Grandmother, what can be *done?*"

Kevara Avlon shook her head, "Who knows? It all depends on the

Prime Key, doesn't it?"

Leigha frowned, "But surely it's in the Reliquary. Why would we allow such a thing out of our sight?"

The Angelus shrugged, "Darling, it's been one *thousand* years. And unfortunately, not all of my predecessors were as...*conscientious* as I am. Many sought to build our empire, rather than protect the past. And sometimes the latter was sacrificed in the name of the former."

Leigha blinked, "Are you telling me we *traded* the Keys for political *favor?*"

Kevara Avlon shrugged, "It's *one* of the theories I've come up with over the years. Not *all* of them, you understand. But definitely the Prime Key."

"But *why?*" Leigha cried out angrily.

Her grandmother smiled, "Well tell me, dear, why worry about the Prime Key if you simply take care to protect the Third? If they cannot open the Third Gate, why worry over the other two."

"But the Third Key was stolen *centuries* ago." Leigha groaned.

"Yes well, it's a bit late to fret about that now, isn't it?" Kevara slurred, "By the time the Third was stolen, the Prime Key was long gone. God only knows *where.*"

Leigha took another pull from the bottle. "Shouldn't we send word to Ilyar?"

Kevara Avlon considered for a long moment. "No." she said finally. "No, the scriptures are *quite* clear on this. We must wait and watch. They might come across something on their own. If we tell them everything now, it *could* make them short-sighted."

Leigha nodded her understanding, "As you say, Angelus."

The Angelus smiled.

"That's a good girl."

⚜

Aleksei walked softly across the South Lawn, his mind roiling with the developments of the day. He had long since learned that the Lord Captain carried enormous responsibility, but he doubted Captain Lenox ever dealt with cryptic warnings from the Wood or strange beasts in the South.

While he did his best not to think ill of the man, he couldn't help but wish he had his old life back. Being a mere captain in the Guard was something to be proud of. Being the Lord Captain of Her Majesty's Legion was something to be *feared*.

Feared by others, not by the bearer of the title. But with the danger of holding the title, and being so *young*, Aleksei knew he had a target on his back. It was why he'd been granted the role to begin with.

Andariana should have just called him what he was. Bait. A year had impossibly passed, and gods he was weary of being afraid.

He wandered towards the single structure that dominated the South Lawn.

The Cathedral of Mokosh.

Aleksei pushed open one of the giant doors that led into the sanctuary. It was empty at this hour, save for the small flame that burned before the altar.

His footsteps cast echoes through the massive chamber as he contemplated what he'd just done.

Strange creatures were rising up around them, and he'd just ordered four hundred men to what could very well be their deaths. He had *no* idea what they were up against. Perhaps the Magi could sort something out.

Perhaps they couldn't.

Aleksei stopped several pews from the front of the altar and knelt, resting his head in his hands.

His entire life on the farm had been dictated by the whims of the Goddess, and he felt She had always favored him and his father. It was difficult to keep such a small farm going, yet each season they had enjoyed good fortune.

But now it was not respite from the winter's chill, or early rain that he required. He needed solace. From the time he was little, Aleksei had felt a certain bond with Her, a comforting, motherly connection.

And right then he needed *hope*.

Hope for a future that grew dimmer by the day.

Heavy footfalls jerked Aleksei out of his contemplation. He looked sharply around the sanctuary, trying to place the source of the sound.

A flicker of movement caught his eye and he stood.

A man was walking towards him, on the other side of the massive marble columns that supported the vaulted ceiling.

He was cloaked in heavy black wool.

"Hello?" Aleksei called.

The man said nothing; he simply kept approaching.

"Who are you?" Aleksei demanded.

No response.

A scent filled Aleksei's nostrils. He coughed as the heavy, acrid stink swirled in his mind. He felt a deafening echo surround him. It pulsed without pounding.

The man's heart.

He fingered the sword at his hip.

The doors of the Cathedral burst open, and Aleksei turned to see a small sparrow flit through the doorway, melting into the shape of a man.

He turned back to the black figure, but it was gone.

"Aleksei!"

He turned to Jonas, "What is it?"

"Where *is* he?" Jonas panted.

"Who?"

"The *Magus*. I came as soon as I felt him."

Aleksei turned back to where the man had been. "He... *disappeared*. I didn't see where he came from, and he didn't say anything. He just kept walking towards me."

Jonas frowned, "And then he just vanished?"

Aleksei nodded, "When you came through the door."

"Did you see his face?"

Aleksei shook his head, "I have his pulse. I have his scent. He... reeks of death."

"That sounds about right."

Jonas started towards the vestry, but Aleksei stepped in front of him, "What aren't you telling me?"

Jonas clenched his jaw a moment before relaxing, "He's the one, Aleksei. He killed Lord Captain Lenox and Lord Bazin. He almost killed *me*. When I find him...."

Aleksei gripped Jonas' shoulders, "*What?* What will you do? Do you have a *plan?*"

Jonas paused, "No."

Aleksei looked deep into Jonas' eyes, "*Never* attack another Magus, never attack *anyone*, without a plan. It might fall apart in a moment, but you *can't* just give them the upper hand like that."

The Magus stared right back at Aleksei, but at least he had the sense to look chagrinned.

"Let's see if he's still hanging around." Aleksei finally allowed. "Did he embrace the Archanium here?"

Jonas paused, "No. Not here."

The Prince ran towards the altar. Aleksei followed closely, drawing his sword. He was shaken enough to have encountered the man who killed his predecessor, and while he hadn't recognized the Magus, he had the man's scent. He could hear the man's heart.

He followed Jonas down into the vestry, and deeper still into the catacombs that lay beneath the Cathedral.

Labyrinthine though they were, Jonas seemed to have no difficulty finding his way. Aleksei stalked behind him, desperately trying to remember which way they'd come.

Jonas vanished into a hole that appeared burned through the catacomb wall.

Aleksei followed, and dropped into the sewer below.

"*Stop.*" Jonas called.

Aleksei dug in his heels and turned to make sure they were alone. The stench of waste and decay pervaded the air, but he couldn't find a trace of anything new. The freshest scent was from the strange Magus.

But there was something else.

"Something's down there." Aleksei whispered.

Jonas turned, frowning, "What?"

Aleksei moved past the prince and reached a hand down into the murk.

A body bobbed to the surface, bloated and rotting.

A Guardsman.

Aleksei's blood boiled.

Jonas studied the man's corpse in confusion. More boy than man, the soldier stared at the sewer ceiling in frozen surprise.

After a few moments of watching the body bob up and down on the low current, he crouched down and ran his hands through the air over the body. Reaching into the Archanium, Jonas searched the body for a cause of death.

"Any ideas?" he asked after a moment.

The Knight crouched next to him, "His scent is...strange. There's no disease in his blood, nothing out of the ordinary beyond the beginning signs of decay. Did you detect any broken bones?"

Jonas shook his head, "Near as I can tell, this man should be perfectly fine. It's as if his heart just...stopped beating."

Aleksei cursed and stood, studying the walls of the tunnel that fed into the Ylik Water to the east.

"What about echoes? Can you see anything?"

Jonas stood and stared at the stones, searching for Archanium echoes clinging to the stone like moss.

And then they flashed before his eyes.

"Who is capable of reaching this far into the Nagavor?" Jonas wondered aloud.

The Akhrana embodied the firmament of the Great Sphere, a tranquil sky held aloft on pillars of growth and order. Serving to balance these magics, the Nagavor was a churning nether born of ruin and mayhem.

Sammul's Magi were limited in their power, restricted to the outermost meridians of the Akhrana. *None* of the Magi in the Voralla could touch magic like this.

"And you're sure this was a *Magus*?" Aleksei asked.

Jonas nodded, "It had to be. Dalitian angels, Yrini warlocks, the Fanja Ul'Brek; they all use the Archanium, but in completely different ways. These echoes could *only* have been produced by a Magus. One who walks a far meridian of the Nagavor."

Aleksei frowned, "I don't understand. Why would a Magus with this sort of power want to sneak into Kalinor? He could just as easily walk up to the front gates and ask to be let in. None of the Voralla Magi would be able to sense a Magus that far from their own path."

"But they would still feel the general presence of the Archanium around him. And if anyone had seen his echoes before...."

"Then we might recognize him." Aleksei finished. "So why come up through the Cathedral? How was he to know that someone wouldn't be worshiping, or keeping a vigil? Someone who could just as easily sound the alarm?"

"He couldn't. If he could, he would have realized that you were in there. Or perhaps he didn't care. This Magus is certainly powerful enough to destroy a mere acolyte or priest."

"Or a Lord Captain." Aleksei noted bitterly. "But he doesn't seem confident enough to confront another Magus. He certainly wasn't frightened by me, but once *you* showed up, he vanished."

"And what a pretty trick *that* was." Jonas muttered, his eyes narrowing.

There were a good many things Jonas wanted to know about this Magus. The whole event raised a number of suspicions in his mind, but he couldn't put it together just yet. What would a Magus of this power want in the *Voralla*?

The Voralla was filled with ancient magic, but so many secrets, so many treasures had been lost since the Kholod War. Anything truly valuable was locked up in the Vault, and even *he* couldn't get in there. The harder Jonas reached into the Archanium for answers, the more they eluded him.

He touched the wall again and frowned. "I don't suppose there's any chance *you* can track this echo?"

Aleksei shook his head, "It doesn't work like that. If I had a fresh scent, a drop of blood, anything tangible I'd be fine. But I can't follow an Archanium echo. And his scent is fading too fast down here. It matches the rest of this filth too closely."

Jonas nodded. He'd figured as much, but with Aleksei it was always best to ask. He'd seen the man perform too many impossibilities in the year they'd spent bonded.

"But what would he *want*?" Aleksei asked finally. "I mean, why tromp through a sewer? Why risk detection?"

Jonas shrugged, "There are countless reasons in the Voralla alone. It's over a millennium old, Aleksei. There is lore in that palace that is both misunderstood *and* underused, mainly because it's all ancient. We've lost *so* much knowledge since the Kholod Wars. Perhaps this Magus knows how to use one of the artifacts from the War, or perhaps he needs one of the books in the Vault."

Aleksei frowned, "That Magus didn't kill Lord Captain Lenox for sport. He *knew* something."

Jonas considered for a moment. "Quite possibly. We don't know *why* Lenox was killed. Or Bazin, for that matter."

"Yes, but there was a Magus involved. And he used the Nagavor."

"But it's more than that." Jonas muttered. "Aleksei, the more time I have to study these echoes, the more they feel like...like they came from *me*."

Aleksei arched an eyebrow, *"You?"*

Jonas nodded, "As though I *created* them, except that I don't use the Archanium like this. There's no subtlety in it. This Magus uses the Archanium like a battering ram. Even if I *could* touch the Nagavor at this depth, I wouldn't use so much blunt power. My connection to the Archanium works differently, It requires some measure of balance. Not this one."

"Jonas?"

The Prince saw his Knight's eyes widen, fear flashing across their bond. He turned sharply.

His blood ran cold.

The corpse of the Guardsman had changed. In place of the boy's body, a beast of horn and bone rose from the water, and Jonas found himself staring into the face of a nightmare.

Water poured from the hard, boney projections that erupted from where the mouth should be, and dripped from its clawed hands. It looked at the two men with eyes that glowed with a faint, sickly yellow light, as though trying to discern what they were. Then it lurched forward unsteadily.

Aleksei reacted instantly, lifting his sword in one smooth motion and darting forward, thrusting his blade to the hilt in the creature's belly.

It didn't even flinch.

The Knight kicked up with his boot and broke the creature's neck, but that only halted it for a moment. It looked at Aleksei with those murky, soulless eyes and lunged for his arm.

Jonas brushed past Aleksei and grasped the hilt of the sword, protruding impotently from the monster's stomach. He clutched the

Archanium tightly and took half a second to search the malevolent echoes saturating the tunnel for the spell he wanted. He gripped the whorl of vermillion and fear he required.

Jonas was hurled away from the creature with the force of the explosion. He landed on his back in the muck, looking up in time to see the corpse shiver in the air before bursting into a cloud of quicksilver.

A moment later it vanished, seeping into the walls of the tunnel.

Aleksei helped Jonas to his feet and retrieved his sword, "I think it's time we left."

CHAPTER 22

THE UNSEEN HAND

ILYANA OPENED HER red-rimmed eyes and stared at the door.

"Ilyana?"

It was Hade.

"Ilyana? Are you in there?"

She clutched tighter to Marrik, hiding her face against his powerful chest. She didn't want to see Hade. She didn't want to see *anyone*. Why couldn't they understand that? Why couldn't they just leave her *alone*?

"Ilyana, I need to talk to you."

Marrik gently slid his Magus from his lap and stood. She raised a hand beseechingly, trying to halt him, but she didn't have the strength to voice it.

The massive Knight reached the door and pulled it open silently. He slipped from the room, and for a moment she could hear him speak in that low, dangerous tone he reserved for the most dire occasions.

She had only heard him talk like that once before, months ago. It had landed him in the dungeon for a week.

Outside her window, she could hear the sounds of children being called back to their homes. Life in Drava, with few exceptions, seemed to be continuing unabated. But the laughter of those children sent a flood of memories rushing through her once again.

It had taken weeks to travel down to the little wooding village. Weeks for the beasts to feed on the villagers, despite men from the garrison in Mornj arriving to keep the beasts at bay.

She had spent those weeks of travel wondering what they would encounter when they finally arrived. But nothing had prepared her for *this*.

His hand had been so fragile, so thin. The blood in his hair had been so thick that the source of the wound was impossible to distinguish from the rest of his tattered scalp. And yet, through all of it, he held onto his smile. For *her*. She had asked him to smile for her, and he had.

Until the end.

The sobbing overcame her again, and then Marrik was there, gathering her up in his arms and whispering empty platitudes that somehow made things seem a little better.

"He was so young." she whimpered against his chest. "Six summers, Marrik. *Six! What* could do *that* to an innocent little boy?"

It seemed Marrik had discovered no answers in the few minutes he had left her side, but that didn't stop her from voicing the question again. It was simply one of the many things she could not understand, and for which someone, *anyone* owed her an explanation.

If the gods were so powerful, then how could They allow this sort of thing to happen? That had become one of her favorites in the last hour or so.

"You can't heal *everyone*, Ilyana." Hade had said at the time, apparently trying to console her.

"But we *should*." she had whispered back, and she believed that now more than ever. What good was having power if she couldn't do anything *with* it.

In the end, the most she was able to do for these people was to take their pain and make their journey into the Aftershadow as smooth as possible.

Before the burning.

"Stupid tradition." she muttered to herself. "Silly, *stupid* tradition."

Marrik nodded gravely, having discovered hours before what she meant.

The people of Drava were a superstitious lot, and the bite of a beast was believed to be infectious. After all, if these *were* the village woodcutters returned as nightmares, what was to say that those they attacked wouldn't transform into abominations as well?

Though there was no proof that the dead would actually rise twisted and changed, the citizens of Drava were taking no chances. Every body was burned within an hour of death.

And so the boy, like so many others, had been pulled from Ilyana's helpless arms and dragged to the bonfires to join the other hapless or foolish townsfolk who had been caught outside on the cusp of day.

"But we'll get our revenge, *won't* we Marrik?" she whispered.

"Of course." he said, stroking her hair. She could feel his conviction through their bond, and it brought her a small measure of comfort.

Many changes had come over Ilyana in the year since her imprisonment, and Marrik had had trouble adjusting to the woman she had become. She knew he was having difficulty reconciling the idea of Ilyana the healer and Ilyana the fighter.

There was another knock at the door, and she heard Marrik growl in irritation.

"Ilyana?"

She sat up in surprise. Rather than Hade's pleading whine, as she had expected, the Magus Daro stood on the other end of the door, sounding more desperate than anything.

Marrik looked at her questioningly, but Ilyana nodded, "Open the door, Marrik. Something must be troubling him or he wouldn't be here. I can't turn my back on the others, even if they've turned from *me.*"

Marrik's jaw clenched, but he opened the door.

Behind Daro, Ilyana was surprised to see the Magi Rada and Bel.

"May we come in?" Daro asked uncertainly.

Ilyana nodded, "Please."

The three Magi stepped into the room, glancing cautiously at Marrik. Judging by the look he was directing at them, Ilyana wasn't entirely surprised.

"What can I do for you?"

Daro looked back at the other two before clearing his throat. He seemed on the verge of tears. "Vadim is leading a charge tonight. The Lord Captain sent him with strict orders about engaging the creatures, but Vadim wants to take the fight to them. We've never had to do *anything* like this before."

"So what does that have to do with me?"

Daro glanced at the other two Magi nervously before bowing his head. "*Please*, Ilyana, teach us fire."

❧

Byron leaned heavily against his pike, staring out into the darkness of the Relvyn Wood. It was well past midnight, yet so far there had been no sign of the creatures.

According to the townsfolk, there should have been at least *one* sighted around sunset, yet there had been nothing so much as a glimmer of movement behind the tree line. Several Legionnaires had abandoned their vigil, and sat grouped around the campfire, their attention riveted to the game of Stone Tower being played out between a sentry and Lieutenant Michals.

He sighed, wanting very badly to join his friends by the fire. He glanced back to the forest.

"L...Lieutenant Michals?" he said uncertainly, realizing a moment later that he had merely whispered. "*Michals!*" he barked, turning his head sharply in the direction of the fire.

But the men weren't looking at him. Their faces were instead focused on the figures moving haltingly through the trees. In the firelight, their faces became pale and frightened mockeries of the men he knew.

Michals was the first to break free of the trance that had ensnared them. "Sound the alarm!" he roared. Byron turned on his heel and dashed to the post that suspended the great brass signal bell.

At the frantic ringing, lights appeared in the windows of the homes and the inn. Byron could see figures bustling about in front of the windows, some peering out fearfully, others dashing to dress and rush outside.

"Form up, men!" Michals shouted, grasping a pike and staring into the night.

Byron followed his gaze and felt his blood turn to ice. The creatures had not advanced much yet, but the sheer volume of them terrified Byron. He had imagined there would be fifteen or twenty at the most. Yet now more than fifty lurching forms moved towards them. His grip tightened on his pike and he set his jaw.

There was a rush of air next to him, and he turned to see the Archanium Knight Vadim ride up on his impressive roan stallion.

"How long have they been advancing, soldier?" the Knight called down.

"I only just saw them a few minutes ago, Sir."

Vadim nodded, narrowing his eyes at the approaching wave. He turned and began barking orders. "Legionnaires, form up into lancet position around the Magi. Knights, to the vanguard. Magi, hold back until I give the signal."

Byron hurried alongside the rest of the men to form up in a lancet, holding his pike outward in a defensive position and glancing nervously around.

The Magi sat atop their horses, conversing quietly and appearing oblivious to the approaching wave of the bizarre beasts. The Knights had already grouped ahead of the Legionnaires, and even now they began their charge.

Byron watched in horrified fascination as several of the Knights' mounts were immediately pulled down by the beasts. He watched the creatures reach up and wrap their claws around the necks of the horses with horrifying speed.

The Knights hacked at horn-armored arms, but the moment the creatures gripped the horses, they began to bite, to *scrape*. Byron caught sight of one of the creatures, its face and chest smeared with blood and bits of fur before it was trampled with a horrifically loud *crunch*.

Yet for every beast crushed or hacked apart by the Knights, ten more swelled in replacement, claws and mouths eager for both horse and man alike. One of the Knights was pulled from his horse and immediately set upon by the creatures. Several of the others had turned to help free their fallen comrade when Byron heard an ear-splitting scream from behind him. He turned to see one of the Magi fall limply from her mount and strike the earth with a sickening *thud*, blood drooling from her mouth.

He felt a hand on his shoulder and jumped, turning to see another Magus standing behind him. Her clear blue eyes blazed, "Let me through."

Though he had been given strict orders to guard the Magi, Byron wasn't so much of a fool as to bar the path of a Magus. He stepped aside hastily, watching in confusion as she marched unarmed towards the melee.

Ilyana gritted her teeth to keep from screaming. The panic within her had welled up far beyond her capacity to cope, but she could not lose control now.

To give in was to die.

"Gods be with me." she murmured under her breath, reaching into the Archanium and gripping the swirl of dark color that passed before her vision.

A blossom of fire leapt from her hand and consumed the beast that was grappling with Marrik. Her Knight jumped backwards in surprise as his opponent burst into flame. He looked around wildly before spotting her a few paces away.

With a new look of determination, Marrik swung his bastard sword and cut the flaming creature in two before leaping over the burning remains and rushing to her side.

"What are you *doing* out here?" he demanded angrily.

"My *part*." Ilyana snapped back, turning and sending forth another blossom of fire.

This time the creature turned from Vadim and began lurching towards the Legionnaires.

"You shouldn't risk yourself like this!" Marrik said angrily.

"So I should be like *Rada*, then? I don't fancy dropping dead in my saddle, thank you."

Marrik turned as the flaming monster neared them. He stepped forward and swung his sword. But a moment before the sword should have cleared the beast's head from its shoulders, it leapt back. Marrik was caught off balance by the failure to make contact, and in that moment the beast darted in, grasping the Knight's shoulder and sinking an impossibly sharp claw into him.

Marrik grunted in pain and groped for his belt knife.

Ilyana screamed as the flames burning the body of the beast caught Marrik's half cloak and began to travel menacingly up his back. She could barely think to reach into the Archanium and extinguish the flames from both her Knight and the monster.

Marrik kicked the creature back and swung his sword again, aiming lower this time. The blade removed the creature's top half and it fell to the ground, still trying to pull itself feebly towards them.

Marrik grunted in disgust and brought his boot down on the monster's head, crushing it, and forcing the body to still.

"Come on, I've got to get you back to the...." Marrik began, but as he looked up his voice trailed away.

Ilyana turned swiftly and felt her heart stagger. The neat formation had shattered. Here and there, men in ragged groups tried to fend off the creatures, without much success.

Of the remaining Magi, she noted that another body had now joined Rada's on the ground. Bel and Daro were trying to assist the Legionnaires, though their attempts at fire were not having much effect. Only Hade hung back uncertainly, his eyes wide and fearful as he observed the battle unraveling before him.

She turned back to Marrik to find him engaged with two more of the beasts. Her eyes widened as she saw the true extent of the damage to his shoulder. She could feel his exhaustion through their bond, and a cold weight settled in her stomach. He couldn't last much longer. And if he fell....

"Fall back!" she shouted to him. "Marrik, fall back!"

If he heard her, Marrik didn't respond. He kept swinging his sword one-armed, each swipe forcing the beasts to take one step back before they advanced another three.

It was becoming harder and harder to lift his sword, and she knew that in a matter of minutes they would be on him, claws and fangs biting into him until he was torn apart.

In a surge of desperation, Ilyana reached into the Archanium and threw the most powerful shield she knew around Marrik. When he lashed out again, his sword clattered harmlessly off the invisible boundary of the spell and fell from his hand.

"Ilyana!" he roared, but she seized the opportunity to dart forward and grab his good arm. With all her strength, she dragged him back towards the village.

It was only when they reached the nearest wall of the inn that Ilyana looked out onto the clearing between the town and the forest. The beasts were reluctantly retreating towards the trees.

She wondered whether they could feel victory, or if something entirely different was calling them back. Her eyes returned to the field, and her breath caught in her throat. Of the command, only a handful of Magi, including Vadim himself, remained. Hade was helping his Knight gather the bodies of the dead and pile them in the center of the field.

Ilyana regarded it all dispassionately. Later, she would weep for the men and women who had given their lives, who had fought so bravely for the people of Drava.

For now, she could hardly summon the energy her tears demanded. She clutched her bleeding Knight, helping him towards the inn, ignoring the gruesome work taking place behind her.

Vadim had lost those lives, no one else. Let the blood be on *his* hands.

✦

Aya's fingers dug into the soft arms of the chair. Her eyes were screwed shut, as though she could block the images flashing before them. Thin trails of tears traced crooked paths down her cheeks. Every now and then she would let out a pathetic whimper.

Jonas imagined it closer to a scream she couldn't articulate.

He sat back in his own chair, ignoring the scathing glare he was receiving from Aya's Knight, Raefan. Archanium Knights disliked seeing their Magi in pain as a rule, and Raefan disliked Jonas even more for causing it. Even if he was only indirectly responsible.

But for the information Aya could give him, Jonas was more than willing to risk Raefan's ire.

Behind him, Aleksei leaned casually against a bookshelf, his eyes averted from the agony being visited upon Aya. Instead, he tried to focus on something outside the window, which was difficult enough in the darkness, even without the whimpering coming from the woman in the chair.

"*No!*" she screamed, "No, get *off* of him!"

She sat up and her eyes flew open, green-gold irises glowing brilliantly for a moment. Aya gasped and slumped back in the chair, free from her vision. Tears poured from her eyes as she stared past Jonas in shock.

He hated asking Aya to scry the present. It was painful to watch, excruciating to experience. He would just as soon have missed this meeting if he weren't terrified of losing some small piece of information that might prove vital.

Jonas waited a long moment in silence, allowing Aya a chance to steady herself. Though he was impatient, he also knew that a few minutes would not tip the balance one way or another. In the long run, he would rather receive answers from Aya when she was composed and clear of mind.

"They're gone." she whispered finally.

"Who?" Jonas asked patiently.

"The Legionnaires. To a man. They were routed, and then they were killed."

"And the Magi?"

"Five remain."

Jonas nodded to himself. He honestly hadn't known *what* to expect. Nevertheless, the numbers told him everything he needed to know.

"What about Drava?" Aleksei asked after a moment.

"Drava stands. But it could topple with the mere suggestion of attack."

Jonas and Aleksei shared a look of concern.

"We could send another message to the men in Mornj," Jonas said, "have them march into Drava, evacuate the town...."

"*No.*" Aleksei said sharply. "Sending more men will only add to the death count. I don't want to risk losing half of our forces down there."

"Then what do you propose?"

Aleksei took a deep breath. "I think *we* need to visit Drava."

It took the prince a moment to understand what Aleksei was saying. When the realization sunk in, he was less surprised than curious.

"Why?"

Aleksei glanced at Raefan and Aya before responding. "Because *we* can deal with this. More than that, we might be able to figure out why this is happening in the first place."

Raefan glanced at the two men in confusion, "And what's to say that you won't be butchered just like the others? I trained with Jeran and Benjamin for years. They were good Knights. Perhaps not as talented as you are, Aleksei, but I doubt you would do much better in the end."

"Jeran and Benjamin were good men, Raefan, and I mourn their loss. They were *all* good men, and I can't promise that I won't fall as easily as they. But I have to at *least* investigate. Jonas can do things that the other Magi cannot. And, as it is, we have very little to work with."

Raefan clenched his jaw, but finally nodded.

"You are too important to risk, Raefan." Jonas said softly, "I'm sorry, but Ilyar cannot afford to lose both you and Aya so easily."

"But we can risk losing *you*, the Prince of Ilyar, and *Aleksei*? My apologies, but I don't follow your logic."

Jonas winced. He wished they didn't have to lead the other man on like this, but he couldn't risk telling them exactly why he and Aleksei would succeed where the others had failed.

As of yet, no one was aware of the extent Jonas could draw on the Archanium, or of Aleksei's ability to tap his connection to time. And both Jonas and his Knight were still too unsure of their talents to make any claims.

"Fortunately," Jonas said quietly from his chair, "you don't have to understand your orders to follow them."

Raefan opened his mouth angrily to speak, then thought better of it. "Of course, Highness."

Jonas looked away from the Knight and smiled reassuringly at Aya, "Is that all you saw in your vision?"

She considered for a moment before answering, "Vadim is angry. Enraged. He feels like...like Aleksei set him up to fail. I could feel resentment building within him."

Aleksei frowned, "He practically *begged* me for that command."

"How is Hade reacting to this?" Jonas asked.

"That wasn't clear. But knowing Hade and his penchant for mindless agreement, I'd say he's probably harboring similar feelings."

Jonas nodded, "Very well. Thank you for doing this, Aya."

She rose, recognizing her dismissal, "I'm glad I could be of aid. Good night."

When they had left Jonas' rooms, the Magus stood and walked to the window. "Well?"

"When do you want to leave?" Aleksei asked, taking a seat in the chair Aya had just vacated.

Jonas considered, "I think you need to leave as soon as possible. I'll wait until no one's paying attention and join you in a few days. I don't want to take any chances in case that strange Magus has people watching us. And I'll be able to travel faster anyway."

Aleksei stood to go, "I'm going to pack then. I'll draw less attention if I leave now."

"Wait."

Aleksei stopped. "What is it?"

Jonas regarded his Knight curiously, "Is everything alright?"

"You mean *besides* losing a lot of good men for nothing?"

"That's not what I mean. You haven't been sleeping well."

"I've got a lot on my mind."

"There's something else." Jonas insisted.

Aleksei took a deep breath, "There's been something...*off* in the Wood recently."

Jonas sat and studied his Knight, "Since the Lost appeared?"

"I suppose. Their return must be throwing the animals into confusion."

"And this is keeping you awake?"

Aleksei sighed, "Sometimes. She keeps telling me that the spirits are restless, but I'm not exactly sure what She means."

Jonas nodded, now deep in contemplation. "I just wanted to make sure you were alright. I worry about you."

Aleksei flashed that handsome smile that Jonas realized had been missing of late. "I just want all this sorted out. It's not wearing on me very well."

"Be careful."

Aleksei leaned down and gave Jonas a gentle kiss, "Come down as fast as you can. I have a feeling you're going to be more effective than me."

When Aleksei was gone, Jonas continued to stare out onto the empty Lawn, threads of despair tickling at his heart. That nagging feeling had once again returned to him. The answer seemed somehow closer; to make more sense.

Beasts in Drava. Unrest in the Wood. Unexplained Magi in the Palace. Each element pulled at the corners of his mind, but he couldn't understand *why*. Jonas chased them into the waiting arms of sleep.

❧

The door opened silently, and Sammul looked up at the sudden draft. The door shut and two figures materialized. The first was a heavyset man, his face white. The second was one of Sammul's most loyal servants.

"Thank you, Delira." he said calmly.

The woman nodded, spared the pale man one last contemptuous glance, then vanished. When the door had shut again, Sammul beckoned the man closer.

"Come here, Bertrand. I'm not going to bite you."

Perron regarded Sammul cautiously before shuffling forward. "You...you summoned me?"

Sammul held back a laugh, "Indeed I did, Bertrand. Have a seat." He paused, considering the best way to deliver his news to the noble. "Now then, I assume you've heard the reports from Drava?"

Perron jumped at that last word. "Yes, Sammul, I've heard."

"To a *man*, Perron."

"A few Magi survived." the lord muttered.

"Indeed they did. And this should prove to you that although our plan has a good possibility of succeeding, it is not impervious."

Again Perron flinched.

Sammul imagined it had been much harder to regard the Queen

as his enemy than Perron could have guessed. Harder still to consciously unleash terror and death upon his own people. But it was too late now, no matter which way he turned it. His path was set.

"What of Krasik, then?" Perron asked.

"Krasik is where he was, where he should be, and at the moment is being prepared to launch his attack on our good queen. But don't look so *distressed*, Chancellor! This is what you *wanted*, isn't it?"

"Oh, of course." Perron stammered. "Of *course*, Sammul. It's just that...."

"*What*, Perron? Are you losing your resolve? Because if you *are*, I'm sure Lord Malak will be more than happy to take some of your responsibilities until you are more...*sure* of our cause."

"*No!*" Perron blurted, "No, I know what must be done."

"For the sake of *Ilyar*, Perron."

The man nodded, looking down at the floor, "Aye, for the sake of Ilyar."

"Now then," Sammul continued briskly, "as commander of the forces in the South, it is your job to make sure that any call for aid is not answered with undue haste.

"Drava can be rebuilt. The troubles in Drava will not strangle Ilyar. But they *will* send a very clear message to the people of this realm that change is the only course of action. And then there is the matter of revealing yourselves as the resistance."

Perron looked nervous at that, "And when will that be?"

Sammul waved a dismissive hand, "You must make your case to the public first. Thus, the sacrifice of Drava. If the Ilyari see Andariana's incompetence at dealing with the situation in the South, they will begin to lose faith in their monarch.

"If your men are doing as instructed then the Legions should not be overly surprised to hear the rumors come to life. The people of Ilyar will demand an answer. And Parliament will be ready to provide them one."

"Andariana will not abdicate willingly, Sammul. You know that better than I. And the Palace Guard will hardly allow us to march into Kalinor and seize the throne. Their loyalty is to Lord Captain Drago. *Everyone* knows that. I've also heard that more than a few Magi are influenced by Prince Belgi; perhaps even more than *yourself.*"

Sammul kept his face impassive, but rage burned in his eyes.

"The unfortunates who follow the Prince are of no consequence." Sammul snarled. "*I* command the Voralla, Perron, and *I* alone. *I* command the Magi of Ilyar. If a few dissidents prefer to delude themselves into thinking that they're safer following Jonas, they are free to throw their lives away. But the majority of the Magi will come when *I* call them."

"As you say, Sammul, as you say." Perron muttered hastily.

Sammul took a deep breath, calming himself only with the greatest effort. It would be pointless to lose his temper now, when everything was still so fragile. No, he would have to be patient.

"What about reports on the Prince and the Lord Captain?" Sammul asked after a long moment.

Perron shrugged, "There's not much to say, is there? The Lord Captain spends most of the day in his office or inspecting the Guard. The Prince emerges from his chambers around noon to eat with Princess Tamara. He generally pays a visit to the Lord Captain after the midday meal, and then he retreats to his chambers again. The Lord Captain spends most nights with the Prince."

"And *what*, dare I ask, is the Prince doing sequestered in his chambers for so many hours?"

Perron let out a tired sigh, "I'd like to tell you, Sammul, but I'm afraid no one really knows. I can't pay off his servants, and every time I've tried to have someone listen in, they've come away with such a headache that they remain bedridden for days afterwards...You don't think he *suspects* anything, do you?"

Sammul waved the suggestion away, "Impossible to say with Jonas. He could suspect you, or me, but what he *knows* is anyone's guess. Does he spend much time with the Queen?"

Perron shook his head, "Rarely. Their relationship seems casual, if friendly. I believe he only makes an effort to see her when he wants something."

Sammul snorted, "This is your report? That the two act exactly as one would expect given their positions?"

Perron's brow lowered, "I can't make them give away their thoughts. Their actions are easy enough to monitor, outside of the

Prince's chambers, of course."

"They're easier to ward." Sammul grunted. "Jonas is smart enough to keep any delicate information to himself.

"Where are they right now?"

"Last I heard, Drago and the Prince were holed up in the Prince's rooms with another Magus."

Sammul glanced at Perron sharply, "*Who?*"

"Aya. And her Knight, I think."

Sammul breathed out evenly. Aya. Unsurprising, but vexing nonetheless.

"Very well. Have your eyes and ears listen for any mention of what took place in the Prince's chambers tonight. Perhaps her Knight will get drunk and let something slip; they're usually the easiest to squeeze for information."

"As you command, Sammul." Perron said, trying to mime supplication.

The door swung open silently.

"Good evening, Perron. So nice to see you again." Sammul said softly, turning away as Delira's cloak enveloped the Chancellor.

CHAPTER 23

INTO THE WOOD

MOONLIGHT BATHED THE sleeping city as Aleksei guided Dash onto the road. No one would notice the old draft horse missing, and with Agriphon still safely stabled, it might buy them a few days before anyone realized that Aleksei had left Kalinor.

At the moment, secrecy was critical.

Hunter.

Aleksei pulled Dash up short and turned his head to the east.

Mother Wood? he thought, *What is it?*

I have need of you, Hunter. It is of great urgency.

Aleksei breathed in deeply and turned Dash towards the East Gate. He couldn't imagine what the Wood could need. He first thought was that the beasts had been discovered beneath Her branches. Her tone *had* changed in the past few days.

Hurry, *Hunter.*

The voice struck him like a hammer. This wasn't like anything he'd heard from her before.

She sounded *terrified*.

It took Aleksei half an hour to clear the East Gate. His mind raced the entire time, trying to determine what might scare an entity like the Wood. He had difficulty imagining such a thing.

The uneasiness he'd felt earlier grew as he raced towards the Wood. By the time the tree line came into view, it was bordering on painful.

What's wrong, Mother?

I have been poisoned, Hunter.

Aleksei rode into the Wood, and the pain in his chest lifted.

You have come to Me, Hunter. I thank you.

Aleksei frowned, realizing that the unrest he'd felt had been the Wood urging him to Her.

What's wrong, Mother? he repeated.

My Lost, Hunter. Their presence has waked a poison that slept within me.

Aleksei's mind was filled with the visions from the nights before. People consumed in fire. The forest in flames. A great white behemoth stalking through the embers of Ilyar.

They brought it into the Heart, Hunter. When they chased My Children.

Aleksei took a deep breath. *Who, Mother?*

The Kholodym. They sought to destroy My Children. To destroy Me.

Aleksei's eyes widened. What could possibly destroy the Wood Herself?

They were cast out of this land before the poison could mature. It withered, but did not die. And now it stirs once more. If it is not destroyed, it will grow and consume, until I am no more, Hunter. Until My Children are gone from this world.

"What am I to do, Mother?" he asked aloud.

You are my Hunter, my Protector.

Aleksei nodded in assent. "Take me to it, Mother Wood, and I will do my best."

Leave your animal to my care. He will only serve to hinder you.

Aleksei slid off Dash's back and stroked the horse's neck soothingly. "I'll be right back, old boy. Try to stay out of trouble."

The horse pawed at the path in irritation. Aleksei smiled, "I'm sorry, but you can't come with me right now. I'll be back to get you in a little while."

He patted the horse once more, then looked up into the dense canopy. The moonlight was dim, and soon he'd be plunged into complete darkness.

"Mother Wood, if I can't see, how will I know my enemy?"

The darkness will protect you, Hunter. Your eyes will serve you better in the dark.

Aleksei sighed. Gods, but he hoped She was right.

He walked down the trail, noting that as he moved the trees blurred and twisted around him. She was taking him to another part of the Wood. He continued walking, and suddenly the trees were much closer together, much larger. The air grew warmer, thicker. Aleksei realized that he was moving into the Wood's primeval Heart.

The texture of the trail changed. The hard-packed earth gave way to distended stones and fragments of what appeared to be some sort of shell.

Stop.

Aleksei froze in mid-step, watching, *listening.* The last of the moon's light vanished from the trees, and darkness descended in the Wood. Aleksei breathed slowly, evenly, and listened.

Hunt.

He dropped into a crouch, instinctively lifting a piece of the odd shell he had seen in the path. He pressed it against his nose and took in its scent, breathing in sulfur and char. It sent a cascade of images through his mind, most of which he couldn't understand. Finally, a singular vision clarified itself in his head.

Robed figures were standing around a hole in the earth. It appeared to be a well, but rather than water, it was filled with molten fire. The figures drew alien runes around the well. Some moved in an odd rhythm, though Aleksei could hear no beat or pulse to follow.

From the fire rose a shape. At first Aleksei thought it was a being of some sort, but as the robed figures manipulated it, he recognized it as a filmy egg. Something was writhing within, pushing against the soft barrier that imprisoned it. Something was being *conceived.*

The vision evaporated, and Aleksei was left with the distinct impression of something long, something serpentine.

A low growl built at the back of his throat. He sniffed at the air and instantly caught the creature's sharp, sulfurous scent. It was off to the east, motionless, possibly scenting him as well.

Aleksei drew his sword, moving off the path and through the dense underbrush. It knew he was approaching. It could *feel* him. And Aleksei could smell something else in the air.

Anger.

Every time he had tracked something in the past, he had smelled its fear. This creature did not seem to possess such an emotion. It only desired to destroy him so it could continue fulfilling its purpose.

His feet whispered across the ground, his mind endowed with such an intimate knowledge of the Wood that he didn't need his eyes to know where the dry twigs and leaves lay, or where the ground dipped and rose.

The wind shifted and Aleksei realized that the creature had shifted as well. It was no longer before him as it had been a moment ago. Now, it was....

Aleksei threw himself to the side as the air lit with brilliant green fire. He rolled hard across a broken tree limb and gashed his face against a rock.

He leapt to his feet in the next instant and, rather than running away from the creature, ran straight for it.

The move was so unexpected that, for a moment, the creature hesitated. In that moment Aleksei threw one arm around its neck and swung up onto its back.

It was a mistake.

Even as he attempted to drag his sword across the creature's throat, the blade bounced off its scales, harder than steel. A moment later, the creature rolled and hurled him to the forest floor, crushing him with its incredible weight.

The air was knocked from his lungs, and Aleksei desperately tried to draw breath. With the creature pressing down against him, it was impossible. He began to panic, his lungs screaming for air, his head throbbing.

The creature, a giant serpent of some sort, suddenly twisted away and Aleksei rolled to his feet, darting towards his sword. A heavy column of fire followed behind him, but only struck the tree he swung behind at the last moment.

His hand shot down into a bush, and he caught the sword by the blade. The sound of the serpent's scales on the underbrush rustled behind him.

He twisted and hurled the sword towards the sound.

There was a high-pitched scream, and then silence.

Aleksei dropped to the ground, panting. The blood rushing from the deep cut to his face was making him dizzy. From the sharp pains in his chest, he knew that several of his ribs had broken when the snake threw him; his hand ached and bled from grasping the razor-edge of his blade.

He pulled himself to his feet and stumbled to where his instincts told him a lembak tree grew. He reached down among its roots and grasped one of the mushrooms that grew there. With a few sure strokes of his knife, he lifted the now-glowing rella fungus.

The eerie blue light cast the forest into a world of sharp light and jagged shadow. Several paces from where Aleksei stood, he found the serpent. His breath caught in his throat at the sight of it. He wondered if he would have *ever* been able to fight it, had he seen it in the daylight.

It was huge, at least twelve paces in length. Its eyes were the size of dinner plates, and the same milky white as its scales. It was frozen in place, mouth stretched wide, either to strike or to breathe another blast of fire; Aleksei could only guess. And there, in the back of its mouth, sprouted the hilt of Aleksei's sword, pinning its head to the tree.

He walked purposefully forward and put a foot on the serpent's jaw, reaching in and gripping the sword. He jerked the blade out of the tree, sliding it contemptuously from the serpent's brain.

On instinct, Aleksei reached back into the creature's mouth, dipping his fingers in the black blood that drooled down its cavernous throat.

He opened his shirt with his free hand and ran his bloodied fingers diagonally across his chest.

I thank you, Hunter. The voice of the Wood had regained much of Her joy and vivacity. The tones of pain and fear were gone. *You are indeed true.*

Aleksei frowned at that. He had heard the Wood use that word before, but only once. Then it had been a command. *Be true.*

But now?

You travel to my Brother Wood, Hunter?

"I travel to the village of Drava, on the edge of the Relvyn Wood."

He is in pain, Hunter. He has no Children to tend Him, no Hunter to protect Him. He is in need. Go to Him.

"I go as swiftly as I can." he said wearily.

Your beast carries you well, but you must move swiftly if you are to be in time.

Aleksei sighed in irritation. What did She want him to *do?* How was reminding him of his inadequacies going to aid him?

Dash was suddenly beside him, and Aleksei hugged the horse as tightly as he dared. His ribs throbbed.

Ride west, Hunter. Your beast will bear you well.

Aleksei frowned. He needed to go southeast. Going west would just take him to other side of Ylik Water. He needed to be on the Water's eastern side, so why would She want him to head west?

Ride west, Hunter. She whispered.

Aleksei gave up trying to understand the Wood. As he rode Dash back onto the path and to the west, it struck him that he was questioning the logical abilities of a forest.

"Perhaps I hit my head harder than I thought." he muttered, lifting the glowing stump higher so Dash could see where he was going. They rode deeper into the Heart of the Wood.

Night swallowed them.

Dawn splashed rosy light across the small garden, but Ilyana's eyes were dead to such beauty. The color of morning only served to remind her of the washbasin after she'd scrubbed her hands of the blood.

So much blood.

Healing was difficult for her, even though she was one of the most talented of the Magi in the Voralla. It took a great deal out of her to reach that deeply, to witness so much pain.

She knelt beside a wilted rose, sick and dry from lack of water. At her touch, the flower stiffened and the color rushed back into its petals. The rose opened in all its dewy brilliance.

Ilyana stifled a tear.

How could she restore beauty so effortlessly, yet be utterly unable to help the people in the inn, the ones with large pieces of flesh ripped from their legs and shoulders, the ones who woke screaming in the night for fear that something was gnawing at them? It seemed a cruel joke of the gods.

Why give her the power, but withhold the ability to do anything *useful* with it?

Ilyana came to her feet and wandered out of the garden, tears flowing freely down her cheeks. The sight of the village was almost enough to crumple the tatters of her fragile spirit.

She stopped and found herself standing on the battlefield. Her eyes moved to the tree-line, where she had first seen those creatures, those beasts of horn and bone lurching out of the shadows. There was a flicker of movement in the darkness.

Her breath caught in her throat.

It's just trick of the light, she told herself. Her mind was toying with her. Ilyana looked away, shaking her head in disgust. It was the light and shifting shadows warming to the new day, that was all.

But when she looked back to the trees, her eyes widened.

A figure had appeared at the forest's edge. For a split second she was sure it was one of the creatures. She prepared to summon her blossoms of fire and blight the creature from the world.

Then she stopped. The figure led a horse. He was watching her, trying to gauge whether or not she could see him. Finally he stepped out from the shadows. The closer he got, the more familiar he seemed. Ilyana gasped.

"Where...where did *you* come from?"

"Hello to you, too." Aleksei grunted.

It was only then that Ilyana realized that his face was covered in blood and his right hand was holding his left arm protectively across his chest.

"Aleksei," she stammered, "gods, what's *happened* to you?"

He cast her an angry glare, "Can we save the questions until I've had a pint and a chance to clean myself up?"

Her face went scarlet. "Of course. I apologize."

His face softened, "I'm sorry, it's not your fault. I had a rough time getting here."

From the looks of him, Ilyana knew that to be a dramatic understatement. But still, it was difficult to keep the questions from bubbling up inside. How had he *possibly* come down here so fast? And what had he been doing in the Relvyn Wood? Perhaps that was why he looked so ragged. Perhaps he had just barely escaped the beasts lurking in the Wood.

"Well, come along and we'll get you set up at the inn." she said, trying to lighten her voice. "You can have your pick of rooms. They're been mostly empty since...." She couldn't bring herself to finish the sentence.

He rested a comforting hand on her shoulder, "Aya told us what happened. I'm *sorry*, Ilyana."

She nodded silently, a tear winding its way down her cheek. "It's been hard."

They walked the rest of the way to the inn in silence. A stable boy took Dash's reins, after gawking at the sight of Aleksei; his sword hilt and face covered in black blood, some his own, some alien in the way it drank the dawn.

When the door of the inn opened, every face turned to see the newcomer. Ilyana was surprised by how everyone in the room stared at him, some with hope brimming in their eyes, others with awe. She looked up at him. To her he just looked *tired*.

"Come on, I'll take you to your room and you can get yourself cleaned up." she said softly.

He nodded, glancing at the sallow faces that followed his every movement. At that moment, Aleksei had no interest in meeting whatever expectations these people had of him. As he walked wearily upstairs, Ilyana instructed the innkeeper to have a bowl of last night's stew and a pint of dark ale brought up as soon as possible.

When she reached his room a few moments later, she found him sitting on the bed, head in his hands. She could hardly tell if he was breathing.

He looked up at her. "I'm going to eat something and then go to sleep. Wake me if there's a problem, but otherwise I am not to be disturbed."

Ilyana felt her heart hammer in her chest. She had never been given proper orders, certainly never from Aleksei Drago.

For the first time since she had arrived in Drava, she felt as though someone was *leading* them. She had the distinct impression that if she did exactly as he said, everything would be alright. She need only do as she was bid. He would deal with the rest as necessary.

Ilyana felt an enormous weight lift from her chest. She hadn't realized until that moment how anxious she'd felt without someone to lead them. She'd thought that was Vadim's job, as it was his command.

She remembered when she had been sympathetic to Vadim for having been supplanted by a farm boy who'd never held a sword. That sympathy was now gone forever, and from its ashes rose a deep respect for Aleksei Drago.

"Your...dinner is on its way up." she said, a touch of reverence suddenly in her voice.

He smiled, "Thank you, Ilyana."

When she left, Aleksei allowed himself to close his eyes again. It seemed an age since he'd last slept. If those creatures attacked now, he'd almost rather they tear him apart, rather than summon the strength to fight.

Ilyana returned a moment later, bearing a tray with a washbasin and a pitcher of steaming water. "Here you go. There's a maid with your dinner right behind me."

"I appreciate your kindness more than I can say."

Ilyana blushed, "Get cleaned up. You're no good to anyone bloody and exhausted."

The maid bustled in with a tray laden with a large bowl of stew and a dark earthenware pint. "Eat up and get your strength back, Lord Captain." she said gravely.

Aleksei smiled at her as she set the tray on the table next to the bed. She blushed, offered him a deep curtsy, and hurried out.

"What's going on here?" he asked Ilyana as she turned to leave.

"Lord Captain?" Ilyana asked, perplexed.

Aleksei indicated the door the maid had just vanished through, "Everyone I've seen in this town has stared at me like they don't think I'm real. I would have expected that maid to be at least a little put out with having to bring a tray to me, rather than have me eat down in the common room like everyone else. Instead she tells me to get my strength back. This entire town feels like it's waiting to *breathe*. Why?"

Ilyana opened her mouth several times to speak before she was finally able to articulate the words, "We've only been here three days, Aleksei. But it's been *ages* since these people have had anyone to lead them."

He frowned as she bid him good morning and shut the door behind herself. What could she possibly mean by *that*? He stood and walked over to the table where Ilyana had left the basin and the pitcher.

It took several minutes to scrub the dried blood from his face and identify exactly where the true injury lay. The cut itself was only about a finger-length long, but the beginnings of a bruise from striking the stone scored the right half of his face. Gods, even *blinking* was painful.

Aleksei's sword hand appeared much the same. Between his face, his ribs, and his hand, he doubted he would get any sleep at all.

He ate as quickly as he could, relishing the warmth of the stew and the cool ale before pushing the table away and pulling off his boots. If he could fall asleep before the next person came in, perhaps they would be unable to wake him up.

Aleksei pulled off his shirt and froze. The blood of the great serpent was no longer striped across his chest.

Instead, strange designs marked his shoulders and upper arms. At first glance, they looked like tattoos. On closer inspection, Aleksei realized that they were the same color as the serpent's blood, the same light-drinking ebony. But where the blood should have become dried and crusted by now, this had melted into his skin.

Aleksei studied the design. It seemed largely made up of undulating interconnected crescents.

Scythes. He thought, his confusion warring with his curiosity.

More disconcerting still, as the design curved around the hard muscles of his chest, Aleksei noticed what appeared to be grasping paws, three-fingered, each finger terminating in a wickedly sharp talon. They seemed to reach from the darkness and claw towards his heart.

Hard as he tried, Aleksei couldn't decipher what the pattern was supposed to represent, or how such a thing had even *happened*. He supposed it was either a result defeating the serpent, or from traveling between one Wood and the other. Either way, he was sure the Wood would have an explanation for it. He no longer possessed the energy to speculate.

He collapsed onto the bed, asleep the moment he closed his eyes.

Chapter 24

Before the Scythe

Aleksei was laughing, though he couldn't remember why. Jonas had just finished saying something, and he couldn't stop laughing either.

Not far away, Aleksei's father was telling Tamara about the time he saved a newborn colt from the burning barn. Her clear blue eyes were wide with excitement and wonder at his masterful, if somewhat exaggerated, telling of the story.

Andariana wasn't far away, languishing under the shade of an enormous oak with a golden-haired woman Aleksei didn't recognize. The Queen's hair had been braided with summer roses and wildflowers, her face lit with a youthful laugh.

He felt an overwhelming sense of peace, an easiness of being he had become unaccustomed to. Jonas gave him an impish smile and leaned forward conspiratorially, "Lord Captain?"

Aleksei frowned. That didn't sound at *all* like Jonas.

"Lord Captain!"

Aleksei sat up with a jolt, opening his eyes into the fiery dusklight filtering through the windows of his small room. He looked blearily at the man standing next to his bed.

Marrik.

"Lord Captain, they're *coming*."

Aleksei blinked and rolled out of bed, groping for his sword belt. The fog of sleep still hung heavy, but Aleksei tried his best to ignore it. His body would have to make due with whatever rest it had scavenged.

He looked down at his shirt and decided to go on without it. Putting it back on would take time he didn't have, and it would provide him with little protection as it was. He buckled his sword belt and started out the door.

"How many of them are there? When were they first sighted?" he barked as he hurried down the stairs.

"Perhaps a score. Only a few minutes ago. No one has initiated combat yet."

Aleksei wiped a hand over his face. "Alright. Gather the Magi. I need them to keep the creatures contained with whatever they've got. Use fire if they have to. *Anything*, just so they can't surround us. I only want a few to be able to get through at a time."

"And us?" Marrik asked, his eyes flickering from Aleksei's face to the shifting black lines on his shoulders.

"You're going to flank me on either side, but hang back a bit. If one of them gets through me, I'm relying on the five of you to take it down."

Marrik nodded uncertainly, apprehension creased into his forehead. "Sir, if I may, these creatures are relentless. They won't stop for anything."

Aleksei managed a smile, "Worry about dealing with the ones who escape me. Worry about *yourself*, Marrik. Those are things you can control."

Marrik nodded again, his uncertainty little diminished, "Yes, Lord Captain."

Aleksei took a deep breath before pushing his way out into the cooling dusk. The other Knights were waiting for him, their faces stony. Ilyana and Hade stood with the other Magi off to the left, discussing something very intensely.

Marrik made his way over to the Magi and began giving them Aleksei's orders. Aleksei headed for the Knights, "I want you to keep back, not *too* far behind me, but a safe distance. Form a wedge around me. When one of them gets through, it'll be your job to take it down."

Vadim seemed confused, but nodded, "As you say, Lord Captain."

Aleksei smiled. Vadim probably thought he was committing suicide. *Well then*, he thought, *won't* this *be an interesting lesson for him?* But even as the thought passed through his head, he recognized the frailty of his bravado.

Ilyana and Hade stepped up to him.

"Can you do it?" he asked, glancing between the Magi, noting their obvious discomfort.

Hade glanced at Ilyana nervously, but she nodded, "I believe so, yes." She considered for a moment, "So you want us to...funnel them towards you?"

"Exactly. Can you use the Archanium like that? Create barriers to guide them to us?"

Ilyana smiled, "This sort of magic is closer to where our gifts lie."

"Good. Remember, the main objective is to keep them from overwhelming us. If only two or three can get through at any given moment, it won't matter how many there are."

"We'll do our best." Hade said meekly.

"That's all I can ask."

Aleksei turned away from the Magi, glancing at the mass of lurching beasts. Dealing with one in the sewer had been disturbing, but standing there, watching a mob of the creatures lunging towards them...Aleksei felt as though he'd stepped into the depths of the damned.

"Mother Wood, may your Hunter prove true this day." he whispered, drawing his sword.

He felt the markings across his shoulders warm, as though in response. He glanced back at the Knights, "Remember, stay as far back as you dare."

They looked perplexed, but no one questioned the order.

Aleksei returned his attention to the advancing horde. They were getting closer. He stepped forward to meet them, glancing at the sides of the mob to see when they would hit the Magi's wards. A moment later, the first of them was on him.

He cut into it, working with great difficulty to avoid consideration for who this had been before. It was painful knowing that each nightmarish face had once belonged to a man or woman, knowing that they had families, children, who could be watching at this moment from nearby buildings. Families they would tear apart if given the chance.

But the terrible truth was that those people were no longer among the living; only their twisted, mutated bodies remained.

Aleksei struck without inhibition or caution. He attacked strategically, his cuts designed to inflict the most bodily damage. The first beast lost its head in a swipe that ended in a cross slash, bisecting the second. As more and more pressed in upon him, he cut faster.

A chop to the neck, backslash across the middle, an upswing cutting from left hip to right shoulder. Each one fell before him, and as they began to pile up, so too did the press of the beasts behind them stumble upon their fallen companions.

Still, the sheer weight of numbers threatened to overwhelm him. He began to cut just an arm or leg away before shoving the revenants back towards the other Knights. The Magi barriers were working, but with the relentless nature of the beasts, it was difficult to maintain the same level of brutal efficiency. He swept off another head, following it with a jagged uppercut that split the next creature nearly in twain.

Yet for every one he cut down, three took its place. Aleksei realized he was losing ground. His sword quickened, driven by his ferocious need for survival. He cut into them with a renewed savagery, keeping his sword high, and cutting through necks and shoulders with brutal speed. Still they came.

He swung hard to the left and split one in half. In that moment, two creatures from the right lunged for him.

Time slowed.

Shift. Aleksei twisted, allowing the momentum of his swing to carry him in a near circle. He brought his sword high in a spinning arc that cut both beasts down in the same swipe. Another creature lunged from the center, and Aleksei changed the course of the swing to clip half of the monster's head clear off.

Bits of bone and brain showered him, covering his exposed torso with gore. He fought on, oblivious to the growing burn of the markings on his shoulders.

Behind him, the Knights had stopped fighting. Not a single creature had made it past Aleksei for the last five minutes.

Instead they stood there, staring in disbelief as their Lord Captain fought, moving with a speed that should have been impossible. The strange markings across his shoulders and upper arms, black when the battle began, were now glowing an intense crimson. No one knew what to make of such a strange occurrence, but neither did they question it.

Aleksei suddenly faltered, crying out in pain and falling to a knee. Vadim rushed forward and speared the foremost creature on his sword, kicking it back into the horde. It was quickly trampled and crushed beneath the relentless churning of the onslaught. At the same, time Marrik moved in and grasped Aleksei's arms, pulling him out of the path of the oncoming mass.

"There's too *many* of them!" Vadim shouted as he swung again and again, taking down another beast each time, yet hardly depleting their numbers.

Aleksei rose unsteadily to his feet and looked at Marrik, whose arm reached out to help steady him, "Go help the others. Split the oncoming between the five of you. I'll be right back."

He turned and started away from the field.

"What are you going to do?" Marrik shouted.

"*Harvest.*" Aleksei called back.

Aleksei worked his way away from the battlefield. He noted Vadim's snarled disdain, and a few of the Magi moved to prevent him from leaving the field of combat with their horses, but Ilyana reigned them in with a sharp word and they obeyed. He offered her a nod of thanks as he moved away from the killing field, his stride strengthening with each step.

He knew what he needed. He knew how to stop the bloody beasts, but he needed a weapon that was his *own*. His Legionnaire blade slipped from his bloody fingers as he finally found himself standing in the heart of a barn, hauling a rusty scythe with a clean, razor-sharp edge from its perch and hefting it over his shoulder.

Aleksei could hear the sounds of sword on flesh, the curses of men as they battled back an enemy that knew neither pain nor fear.

That so many had died at the claws of these creatures invigorated him with a rage unlike anything he'd ever known. He was bleeding from multiple wounds, but those would heal. The dead, on the other hand, could rise at the pleasure of whatever madman was crafting this lunacy.

He circled behind the majority of the horde, taking only a moment to study the flimsy barriers the Magi had erected to channel the revenants towards his Knights. He glanced towards the Relvyn Wood and shuddered at the sheer number of lurching forms moving towards the five unwitting Archanium Knights he'd left behind.

Aleksei hefted his scythe and strode out into the pasture, watching the encroaching horde. As he stopped stock-still in the center of the grass, some of the revenants pressing in on his men took notice and turned, sighting fresh meat.

Aleksei felt a familiar thrill run through him. The first revenant stumbled within range.

Swing. Aleksei ignored the protest from his muscles as the scythe cut through muscle and horn. *Cut.* He lost himself in the rhythm, each offending limb severed, each offered opportunity taken. *Swing.* His body twisted to the right, reaping over-ripened flesh. *Cut.* He pulled the blade back, ripping another soul asunder.

Swing.

Marrik stared at the oncoming tide of horn and bone. Between the five of them, they kept the beasts back without losing too much ground. As he fought, he wondered how the Magi were holding up. While he knew this was far more in the realm of their talents than fire, or even healing, he wasn't sure if they were up to this level of intensity. And if those wards failed, things would become very dire indeed.

The tide of creatures suddenly slowed. They still came with the same unrelenting lurch, but there weren't as many of them. Finally, there were only a handful between the Knights.

"What happened?" Marrik shouted. "Where'd they go?"

He cut down the last one coming towards him and searched for Aleksei. What he saw made his heart stagger a beat.

Aleksei stood in the field beyond the Magi's boundaries, holding a gory scythe. The field around the Knight was thick with the corpses of the creatures. Each had been sundered horribly, spilling gore and long-stilled blood across the field.

Aleksei advanced towards them, his bare torso covered in blood, one arm protectively covering his chest, the other holding the blood-soaked scythe. As he came closer, he discarded the scythe with disgust.

"Are you alright?" he asked.

Marrik winced at the exhaustion that weakened his voice. "Yes, yes we're all fine." He was still trying to overcome the image of Aleksei carrying that dripping scythe.

For just a moment, with those blazing markings across his arms and shoulders, he had looked like Volos Himself.

"What about the Magi?" Aleksei asked.

Marrik realized that he hadn't seen them since the battle was joined. He turned and scanned the field. He moaned when he finally saw them, lying crumpled on the ground.

Vadim was already trying to bring Hade back around when Aleksei reached them.

"They're exhausted." Vadim said, though there was no trace of bitterness in his voice. "They used everything they had."

Aleksei studied each Magus carefully. Jonas had told him that Magi had died from overexerting themselves. "Keep them there." he said finally. "Hold their heads back so they don't choke on their tongues. I'll be right back."

Marrik looked up at the Knight in confusion, "Where are you going?"

Aleksei didn't answer. He simply kept walking until he was swallowed by the deepening shadows of the Relvyn Wood. Aleksei had spent his entire life either in the Wood or on a farm. In that time he had learned a good deal about the healing properties of certain plants.

But becoming a Hunter had heightened his awareness of the various balances in the Wood beyond anything he had learned through experience alone; the poisons and antidotes, the plants that could heal and those that could stop a heart. It took him mere minutes to find what he sought, the fuzzy yellow leaves of the meramie plant.

He emerged from the trees to find the other Knights frantic with worry. They stared at him in confusion as he knelt next to two of the unconscious Magi. Taking the meramie leaves into his mouth, Aleksei quickly crushed them with his teeth. He spat out the residual liquid and pulled the sticky amber paste from his mouth, dividing it swiftly it into five pieces. He placed a piece under each Magus' lower lip.

"What is *that*?" Vadim asked.

"Meramie." Aleksei said quickly, moving between the five remaining Magi. "It's a plant that's usually given to mothers during childbirth, to give them added strength. It stimulates the heart and mind, but if used too frequently it can cause arrest or brain fever."

The Knights exchanged worried glances with one another.

"How long does it take to work?" Daro's Knight Telkun asked.

"A few minutes. The sap from the leaves has to enter the bloodstream and reach the heart. It'll take just a few more minutes to kick in. Just make sure you take it out when they wake. You *don't* want them to swallow it."

Ilyana's eyes snapped open and she inhaled sharply. Marrik pulled back her lower lip and withdrew the amber paste, discarding it behind him. The others sat up a moment later. Hade shook his head and spat the leaves out in disgust.

"Dear gods, what was *that*?" he moaned, spitting at the ground.

"Something that just saved your lives." Marrik said gravely.

"Is it over?" Ilyana asked, staring at the carnage that surrounded her.

Aleksei nodded, "At least for the moment. I harbor no illusions that we've dealt with all of them."

"We can't keep this up." Vadim grunted. "Sooner or later we're going to be overrun, and *then* what?"

"I intend to deal with it before that has a chance to happen." Aleksei said simply.

"How?" Hade asked, rubbing his head.

"I'm not sure yet. I'll have to wait and hear what Jonas has to say when he arrives. But I agree, we can't continue to fight them this way."

"When will Jonas arrive?"

Aleksei shrugged, "Can't say. I expect it will be in the next day or two."

"And what if they attack before then?" Ilyana asked nervously.

Aleksei looked into her eyes, and she gasped at the depth of dread and worry radiating from him, "Pray they don't."

A soft rap sounded at the door, and Jonas looked up from his book.

"Enter."

Aya stepped in, Raefan hovering just behind her. Jonas allowed himself a smile.

"What did you want to see me about?" she asked.

Jonas lifted his book, its title gleaming in the firelight.

The Demon Cassian.

"Jonas, what *is* that?"

He stood and handed her the book. "The answer to a great many questions."

From his grim expression, Aya knew it wasn't the answer Jonas had wished for.

"What do you need me to do?"

Jonas turned to the large window that dominated the southern wall of his library. "I need you to read this. When you've finished, give it to Andariana. It's imperative that she understand the contents of this book, and *quickly*."

"And you?" she asked softly.

"I'm leaving for Drava. Aleksei will need me there as swiftly as possible, but I need *you* to close the window for me after I've gone. I don't want anyone to know I left from my chambers."

Aya nodded stoically, "As you say."

He drew her into an embrace, then stepped to the casement and stepped onto the ledge. In a heartbeat he'd melted into a small falcon.

Jonas leapt from the ledge and allowed his wings to stretch, to catch the current and bear him higher and higher into the night.

The night's revelations had been sobering. He knew what they were up against, and for the first time in his life, it filled him with utter despair. He had never wanted to be so mistaken in his entire life.

But this time he *knew* he was right. The pieces fit too perfectly.

He stared out across the horizon, taken by the beauty of his realm. The way the woods slowly gave ground to rolling hills. In the moonlight, the entire countryside was bathed in ghostly white, giving the land the illusion of absolute purity. It felt like he was dreaming.

Every now and then, the tranquility was punctured by a campfire, but on the whole it seemed Ilyar was sleeping peacefully.

A profound sadness fell over him.

Gods, that it could stay like this forever.

CHAPTER 25

SPECTRES AND SHADES

ALEKSEI PACED THE now-familiar length of his room, staring down at the small bedside table covered with both a detailed map of the region and the congealing remains of his dinner. Red pins flagged various points on the map, indicating the areas where the creatures had been seen across the region. They were spreading.

He sat down on the bed, head in his hands. They had yet to attack Drava again after the battle the day before, but that meant nothing. Perhaps they would simply move on to another village. And *then* what?

There was a tapping at the window, but Aleksei ignored it. His head was full of scenarios, complex renderings of battle plans that couldn't possibly be executed until reinforcements arrived from Mornj. *When* they arrived. He had sent two pigeons and a mounted man since his arrival, but the garrison had yet to respond.

The tapping against the window resumed. Aleksei stood out of irritation, throwing it open and staring out into the night.

A bird shot past him.

Relief washed across his irritation. He shut the window and rushed to the bed where the bird had landed.

"It's about time you got here." he growled.

The falcon shivered, suddenly elongating into Jonas. The Magus smiled, "Miss me?"

Aleksei shook his head, "I don't even know where to begin."

"Well it can't have been *that* bad, can it? I mean, not until you reached Drava."

Aleksei arched an eyebrow. He pulled his shirt over his head, revealing the writhing markings that dominated his upper arms and shoulders, the claws that reached beseechingly for his heart and pawed at his throat. They had cooled to their burning black, but otherwise remained unchanged.

"Dear *gods*." Jonas whispered, standing and tentatively touching Aleksei's left shoulder, following one of the designs with a finger. He jerked his hand away when the swirl of black began to spiral up his fingertip.

"Do you know what it means?" Aleksei asked, though he wasn't entirely sure he *wanted* to know.

"In a way. I think this...this is the *Mantle*. From what I've read about Ri-Vhan Hunters, from what there is *to* read, only one was ever gifted the Hunter's Mantle."

"Gifted?" Aleksei said doubtfully, "This is a *gift*?"

"In theory. The Hunter has to prove himself worthy to bear the Mantle. But to even be given the *chance* is an incredible honor. You'd have to perform a great service to the Wood."

Jonas' eyes lit with understanding, "What did you *do*?"

The Knight sighed deeply, "I killed something. A giant serpent."

Jonas frowned, "Giant serpent? There *aren't* any giant serpents in Ilyar."

"Not anymore." Aleksei muttered, glancing out the window.

"*No,*" Jonas said forcefully, "during the Dominion Wars, the Kholodym unleashed several kinds of 'serpent' against the Magi. These were so difficult to kill that after the war there was a massive purge of the realm for the eggs. They were called Salamanders. The Magi could only truly drive the Kholod away by ridding Ilyar of

Kholod *magic*. The Salamanders were extensions of that magic, so they had to be destroyed as well. But I don't understand how one survived this *long*."

"It was in the Heart of the Wood." Aleksei said, shrugging. "She said they put it there to poison Her, but when they were driven out, it went to sleep."

Jonas considered for a long moment, then the realization stuck him, "You're telling me *you* killed a bloody *Salamander*?"

Aleksei scowled, "I'm telling you I killed a giant serpent with white scales, white eyes, and the charming habit of breathing green fire."

Jonas stared at him, "You killed a Salamander." It was not quite a statement of disbelief. Not quite.

Aleksei nodded, "And as you know, I mark myself with the blood of my kill. It's part of my bond with the Wood. It's confirmation of my victory."

Jonas frowned, "So?"

"*So*," Aleksei said irritably, "when I got here a few days ago I took off my shirt to go to sleep, and instead of finding streaks of dried snake blood across my chest, I found *this*."

The Magus frowned, "You've been here for *days*?"

Aleksei chuckled, "Ah, I forgot that part. The Wood told me to ride west into the Heart, because I would go too slowly otherwise. I didn't want to because I didn't want to waste any more time than was absolutely necessary. But I did as She said, and when I exited the Wood I was just outside Drava."

"How is that possible?"

"The Woods are connected. The Seil Wood called Relvyn Her 'brother'. She said that since the Relvyn Wood had no Hunter to protect Him, I was being sent for a while."

"Did She say anything else?" Jonas asked, leaning forward.

Aleksei considered for a long moment, "Well, after I killed the Salamander, She told me I was 'true', but I'm not exactly sure what that means."

Jonas nodded, "That was it, then."

"What? What do you mean?"

"That was when She placed the Mantle on you. You proved

yourself a true Hunter, and so you were rewarded."

"But what does that *mean?*" Aleksei demanded. "How does this *reward* me? You said *I* had to prove worthy of *it.*"

Jonas raised his hands defenselessly, "I said I'd read what I could find on the subject, but I am far from an expert on this. When She said you were 'true', She meant a true *protector.* Other Hunters might have only used their skills to hunt the animals of the Wood and the like, but you came when called and used the gifts She gave you to protect Her.

"From what I understand, the Mantle is an extension of trust. It is the Wood's blessing on Her Hunter, wherever he goes."

Aleksei shrugged, "I suppose that makes sense. It started to feel hot when I fought yesterday, and it changed from black to red, but I didn't really feel any appreciable difference. I was still just as tired, I was still moving just as fast."

"Well, you don't appear to have to done *too* poorly for yourself." Jonas remarked dryly.

"What do you mean?"

Jonas shrugged, his voice somber, "Of all the men sent down here, you've sustained few notable injuries. And yet you were in the most danger. You arrived alone, and led the remains of Vadim's failed command against the same assault, yet you have only a scratch on your face and a bruise."

"That's from the Wood."

In spite of the circumstances, Jonas couldn't help but laugh, "Well, there you have it."

"I think some of my ribs are broken, too." Aleksei put in after a moment.

Jonas' mirth evaporated, "That Salamander beat you up pretty badly, didn't it?"

Aleksei nodded, "I tried to cut its throat."

The Magus winced.

Aleksei managed a chuckle. It was amazing that something like the Salamander, which had been such an ordeal yesterday, could now be reduced to a laughing matter.

Jonas placed his hand gently on Aleksei's chest, and Aleksei felt the warmth of healing flow through him.

"So how *did* you finally kill it?" Jonas asked after a moment of silence. He had finished with Aleksei's ribs and slashed palm, cupping the Knight's face in his hand, sending the Archanium into the soft flesh, righting what had been damaged, mending the broken blood vessels with the same ease a seamstress would mend a tear.

"Blind luck." Aleksei muttered. "It threw me, so I ran for my sword. I couldn't see anything; it was too dark. But I think that also meant it couldn't see me very well. Anyhow, I found my sword and just...*threw* it. Out of desperation more than anything else. And then I didn't hear it anymore, so I figured it must be dead. I got one of the rella mushrooms that grow around lembak trees, the ones I told you about that glow when you cut them?"

Jonas nodded.

"The Salamander had been rearing. I think it was about to strike. The sword went through its head, out the back of its mouth."

The Magus stared at his Knight in amazement. "If you had *any* idea how much trouble Salamanders caused in the Dominion Wars... how much difficulty the ancient Magi had in discovering their weaknesses...." He took his hand away from the Knight's face, leaning in and giving Aleksei a gentle kiss. "There you are, all better."

Aleksei grinned, running his hand over the area where the bruise had been, "Thank you."

"Aleksei," Jonas said with no small amount of trepidation, "there's something I need to speak with you about."

The Knight frowned, "I can't say I like your tone."

Jonas chuckled humorlessly. "As I was leaving Kalinor, I began to think about some of the...more unusual things that have been happening recently."

"Such as?"

"Such as the sudden appearance of the beasts down here."

Aleksei caught his Magus' mood, "There's something more to this, isn't there?"

Jonas closed his eyes, and after a moment Aleksei realized the man was praying. When he opened his eyes again, the Knight thought he detected tears. "Someone is seeking the Prime Key."

"Prime Key?"

Jonas sat back on the bed and cradled his face in his hands. After a moment, he looked up. "Have you ever heard of the Magus Cassian?"

"You mean the *Demon* Cassian?"

Jonas sighed, "They're the same man, in essence. Cassian was merely a pawn of a powerful demonic force. But he only *unleashed* the demons in an attempt to sweep the Kholod from this world."

"So why didn't the demons simply come here themselves? Why possess Cassian?"

Jonas shrugged, "The demons lack the magic to enter our world. When Cassian entered theirs, they were able to use him as a vessel. But they were unable to create a corporeal form, and thus were trapped within him."

"The story I was told was very primitive, but it never mentioned anything about a key or possession. Only that the Demon was eventually defeated by the angels."

Jonas snorted contemptuously, "The Magi of the time felt that the Kholod were a larger threat. So when Cassian grew too destructive, the angels created a tangential power called the Seraphima. By summoning this magic, the Angelus battled Cassian, and trapped his spirit in a statue. That statue was then sealed away within the Cathedral of Dazhbog."

Aleksei was becoming rapidly more confused, "Jonas, there *is* no Cathedral of Dazhbog. The daylight is His Cathedral."

Jonas waved Aleksei's words away, "A myth created to hide the truth. If no such place existed, no one would search for it."

"So where *is* it?"

"Carved into the northern cliffs of Dalita, near a village called Krilya."

Aleksei actually laughed at that, "The *angels* built a cathedral to *our* God of Light? I thought they called us heathens."

"Precisely. Cassian was a follower of the gods, not of the angels' One-God. The hope was that by calling upon one of our gods, incidentally the one most similar to their One-God, the site would be blessed and rendered immune from the corruption of the Presence within. It was superstition in its highest form, but it appeased the angels."

"Where are you heading with this?"

Jonas tried to keep his patience. It was very difficult to give someone an entire history lesson on a subject he had no knowledge of, to say the least. But he needed Aleksei to do more than just remember the things he was told. Jonas needed him to *understand* them.

"The angels created gates to seal away the Demonic Presence. These were efforts of both Magi and angels, so neither side could use the Archanium to undermine the other. When the gates were constructed, certain entities were sealed behind each of them.

"Part of the reason was to seal away the horrors that Cassian had brought into the world. But others were placed there as a warning."

"Hence the return of the Lost?" Aleksei guessed.

Jonas nodded, "The Wood told you that the Lost were lesser demons. They were trapped behind the third gate. Their sudden reappearance was supposed to warn us that someone was seeking the Demonic Presence."

Jonas' face took on a darker cast. "Behind the second gate, the angels sealed away a constructed magic, something created of the Archanium, but which exists *outside* of it. The Mantle on your shoulders is just one such example, though *it's* conjured from Wood magic."

Aleksei reflexively reached up and brushed the markings. They thrashed at his touch, one taloned paw lifting from his skin and caressing the length of his hand.

"It has been rumored that the constructed magic they sealed away behind the second gate allowed Cassian to feed the souls of his victims to the Demonic Presence. The remaining husks were transformed into mindless beasts. Creatures called *revenants*."

"Dear gods." Aleksei whispered. "And there's only one gate remaining?"

Jonas nodded grimly.

Aleksei's head was spinning with the possible implications, "What happens if the Prime Gate is opened?"

Jonas shrugged, "Whoever opens the Prime Gate receives the same power that Cassian once commanded. But the key to the Gate has been hidden for a millenium."

"Do you know where it is?"

Jonas shook his head, "That's what I'm saying. The Prime Key hasn't been seen in a thousand years. Even reports *describing* it are apocryphal at best."

Aleksei stared at Jonas. "What? Why wasn't it hidden away?"

"After a few hundred years, artifacts like the Prime Key become a traded commodity, used more to garner political favor than anything. What's more, some very clever grifters realized that, as there was no real way to test whether the key was real or not without access to the Prime Gate, it was next to impossible to spot a fake. There's no way of telling what it looked like, or where it ended up."

Aleksei lapsed into silence, trying to reconcile this new information with the things he'd seen in Drava. If the revenants were being commanded by a Magus seeking such power.... A chill swept through him.

"So," Jonas asked after a moment, "you fought off the revenants with two broken ribs and a gash in your sword hand?"

Aleksei nodded, jerked from his thoughts, "It wasn't as bad as it sounds. I mean, I've broken ribs before. I got kicked in the chest by a colt when I was a boy, and then I still had to do all of my chores. *That* hurt. This wasn't nearly so bad. As for my hand...I don't know, once we engaged the revenants, it burned, but it was far from my primary concern."

Jonas marveled. He had been curious upon learning that his Knight was from a small farm. What could a farmer *possibly* know that could aid him in a world of magic and political intrigue? It had only taken Aleksei moments to clear any delusions Jonas had about his competency.

There was a knock at the door, and Aleksei rolled his eyes. "Gods, what do you people *want*?" he roared.

Jonas stood as Aleksei went to the door, trying to make himself look as composed and regal as he could. Only a very select handful of people had ever seen Jonas at complete ease, and of them only Aleksei was in Drava.

The door opened and Ilyana stood on the other side, her face creased with worry.

"Are you alright?" she asked.

Aleksei frowned, "Of course I am. Why, what's wrong?"

She shook her head, "I just thought I felt something...different in here and I–" She froze, her eyes focused on his face.

"What is it?"

"Your face is *better*." she said softly. "How could you possibly...." Her eyes moved past him and she gasped when she caught sight of Jonas. "Great gods, when did *you* get here?"

Jonas sighed inwardly. He would have liked to remain unannounced at least a little longer, at least long enough to bed his Hunter for one night. "Only moments ago. It's good to see you again, Ilyana."

She rushed past Aleksei and threw her arms around the prince, "Gods, Jonas, you have no *idea* what it's been like here!" She stepped back, suddenly self-conscious that she had hugged the Prince of Ilyar. "We aren't skilled enough to *do* this!"

He frowned, "Do what?"

She shook her head, her fine blond hair shaking out around her shoulders in a tangled cascade, "*Any* of it. The fighting, the healing. The shields we created the other evening were at least *useful,* but even *that* pushed us past exhaustion."

Jonas glanced at Aleksei, but the Knight indicated that he would explain later. He looked back to Ilyana, who was now on the precipice of tears. "We *can't* survive another attack, Jonas. We *can't!* I still don't know how we managed *last* time."

Jonas tried to smile warmly, "Have faith. Aleksei's not going to let anything happen to you, and neither am I. Not if we can help it."

She smiled at him, her ocean eyes glittering with unshed tears, "*Thank* you, Jonas."

He nodded and pulled her into one more gentle hug, "We're going to get to the bottom of this, Ilyana. I promise. Give us a few days, and we'll work it out."

She nodded and hugged him back, then turned away, "I'm going to bed. I just wanted to make sure you didn't need anything, Lord Captain."

Aleksei smiled gently, "Get some rest."

She bowed her head, "Thank you. Good night Highness, Lord Captain."

When the door shut behind her, Jonas glanced at Aleksei, "What did she mean?"

"About the battle?"

The Magus nodded, and Aleksei briefly laid out the tactics he'd used in the last fight.

Jonas arched an eyebrow at the end of the account, "I'm impressed. I would never have thought to use the Magi like that."

Aleksei chuckled, "If we'd let our sheep just roam wherever they pleased, any number of things could happen to them. If they were in the pen, we could control them, keep them safe, and keep them accounted for.

"I wasn't about to let those things get on the other side of me. I couldn't let them surround us, but there were few enough that I felt they could be corralled with the Archanium. After that it just became a simple slaughter job, except they were lunging for our throats."

Jonas shook his head in amazement yet again. Aleksei's combination of open-faced honesty and forthright directness led many to believe that he was simple, a puppet to those more devious and intelligent than himself.

Jonas, on the other hand, knew exactly what his Knight's behavior meant; only that as he ran his sword through your gut, he would tell you *exactly* why you deserved it.

"So, what were you planning for tomorrow?" Jonas asked after a long silence.

Aleksei walked over to the small table and pointed to his map, "The Relvyn Wood was a stronghold during the Dominion Wars, right?"

Jonas nodded, "The Wood for the Magi's side, yes, and the mountains beyond it for the Kholodym. There was a fortress in the mountains called the Drakleyn; it was one of their last and most powerful strongholds, until about five years before the end of the War."

"What happened?"

Jonas chuckled despite the severity of their situation, "A Magus named Elise dropped a mountain on it. She discovered a way to use sound to crack the foundation of the mountain overshadowing the Drakleyn, and it crushed the fortress. Along with everyone inside."

Aleksei frowned, "Well apparently there's something left of the structure. The woodsmen here all told me stories about seeing towers and walls high in the mountains. They claim it's haunted or some such nonsense. But if you say the Drakleyn was crushed during the Dominion Wars...."

Jonas shrugged, "That's the *story*. The reality of the situation might be very different. At the time, all that was important was that the Kholod inside were dead, and that the magic of the place no longer functioned."

"I don't understand. How can a *structure* have magic?"

"The Voralla has magic. Why not any *other* structure?"

"But the Voralla has magic because it exists in the same place as the Apsis, where the Archanium touches our world." Aleksei said, clearly confused. "Was the Drakleyn a similar such place?"

Jonas shook his head, "The Kholodym didn't use the Archanium. I've never actually seen a reference to what the source of their magic was, but it obviously held some sort of sway over the Archanium.

"They used some of it to enslave the Magi, to touch the Archanium *through* us. Much of their architecture was designed to convey their magic in various ways. There are very few examples of Kholod architecture left, but each structure served a purpose. The Drakleyn was one of their strongholds because it was built as a *weapon*. When its magic was operational, there were any number of horrors it could inflict on the surrounding area. That's why it was so hard to attack; no one could get close enough to launch an assault before they were destroyed."

"Well according to the locals, some part of it still exists," Aleksei said, looking back to his map. "The mountains form a ring, and the ruins are at the back of the valley. It's a highly defensible position, because those mountains are all but impossible to climb. The only real way into the valley is through the pass in the Wood. If anyone wanted to have a place to consolidate their power, this would be it."

Jonas considered for a long moment. He agreed with Aleksei's assessment of the situation, but he worried about who might be hiding back there. They knew it had to be a Magus tied to the Nagavor, the destructive hemisphere of the Great Sphere, *that* much had already been made clear.

But Jonas could only guess at what sort of powers such a person would possess. Or how his own talents would respond if he were confronted by such a Magus. The prospect did not fill him with an enormous amount of hope.

"Alright," he said finally, "here's what we're going to do."

CHAPTER 26

OLD CROW, LITTLE SPARROW

HADE STEPPED AWAY from the window, admiring his work. It had taken over an hour, but the final window of the inn had finally been boarded up.

"*Here* you are."

He turned his head and smiled as Vadim approached. His Knight had been in a strange mood of late. He seemed *changed*. Hade remembered how angry Vadim had been before Aleksei's arrival.

He had ranted for hours about how this was all part of the Lord Captain's design, that he had been sent to ruin himself. But since Aleksei's victory in the field, Vadim had been silent. His rage seemed cooled, the obsessive fire quenched.

Hade wondered if it wasn't the relief of having someone else in command.

"What are you up to?"

Hade nodded at the inn, "Finishing up. And waiting."

"Waiting?"

Hade turned away from the inn, towards the trees. Vadim

followed Hade's eyes to the tree-line, then to the figure standing in the field before the Wood.

Aleksei.

"He's a surprising man." Vadim said after a long moment.

Hade glanced at his Knight, searching for any trace of animosity in his Bonded's voice. He could find none.

"Indeed. I would not have expected it of a farmer."

Vadim chuckled harshly, "Nor I. What is he *doing* out there at this time of day?"

Hade shook his head, "I can't tell. At first, I thought he might be going out for sword practice, but he has yet to draw a weapon. He's stood there for nearly an hour now."

Vadim frowned. It was curious to say the least, but then again *many* of the things Aleksei did made little sense to him. He had made the mistake of taking such actions as expressions of ignorance.

The price had been his pride.

"You've heard of Jonas' arrival?" Hade asked after a pregnant pause.

Vadim nodded, "Though I must admit I am amazed that they could arrive so swiftly. We traveled at a good pace, and it took us weeks. They would have had to leave only days behind us, and Jonas claims to have been in Kalinor as recently as the night before last, Aleksei only slightly longer ago than that."

"Do you doubt them?" Hade asked.

The Knight shook his head, "They would have nothing to gain from lying, would they? But I do find it peculiar."

Peculiar. It seemed a most fitting word for the Prince and his Knight.

A shadow passed over them, and Hade glanced up. It was a sparrow, flying towards the Wood. He frowned. Why did that strike him as odd? Surely there was nothing remarkable about seeing a bird. And yet, it tugged at his memory.

"Did you see that, Hade?" Vadim asked quietly.

"The bird?"

"That's the first bird I've seen since we arrived. I'd never realized it before, but that's what makes this place so deathly silent. No birds, no deer rushing through the Wood. Just *silence.*"

Hade nodded. Whatever it was in the Relvyn Wood that was controlling the revenants, as Jonas had called them, it had frightened off the fauna from the area. So why would a bird be flying *into* the Wood?

"Perhaps whatever it is that's been sending those things at us has left." Hade said optimistically.

Vadim regarded him with skepticism, "Doubtful."

Hade sighed. He returned his attention to the field and Aleksei. The Knight was just as he had been, standing straight, his focus on the Wood before him. One hand rested on the hilt of his sword, the other hung loosely at his side. Peculiar *indeed*.

Aleksei suddenly turned and walked directly towards them. As he drew closer, Hade jumped at the look in the man's eyes. They seemed to take command of him, to clutch at his heart. Before the Lord Captain had even opened his mouth, Hade knew that he would obey without question.

Aleksei reached them and nodded his greeting. His usual smile was absent, leaving grim determination in its place.

"They're coming." he said calmly. "They will be here in an hour, two at the most. Do *not* engage them. Don't go *near* them, even armed. Get everyone in the town inside. Board up the doors; barricade them, whatever you have to do. Arm the townspeople, but under no circumstances is anyone to go outside as long as the revenants are in the open. Those who are willing are to be evacuated to Mornj. All others *must* agree to remain indoors."

Vadim frowned, "Wait, where are you going?"

"I have something I must see to in the Wood. I'm leaving *you* in command. The nature of this attack is different from the previous ones. I'm not exactly sure how yet, but I know that you cannot take them on. This village must look as though it's deserted. Do you understand?"

Aleksei's golden eyes were so commanding that Vadim didn't dare say anything besides, "Yes, Sir."

"Good. Now get to work, you don't have much time."

Vadim searched for words, but finally only managed a weak, "As you command, Lord Captain."

Aleksei nodded to them once more, then turned and ran towards the Wood. He was swallowed by the shadows in moments.

Jonas shot over the trees. He could feel Aleksei behind him, not yet in the Relvyn Wood. Good.

He had begged Aleksei to remain in Drava with the others, though not because he didn't trust his Knight's prowess in battle. In his sparrow form, Jonas was much faster than Aleksei, even given Aleksei's ability to move rapidly through the forest.

He wanted to get to the back of the mountain pass as swiftly and safely as possible, and one small animal was a much harder target to strike than two grown men.

As he flew over the deeper sections of the Wood, Jonas began to feel a twinge of anxiety. Perhaps it was simply because of his size at the moment.

Perhaps it was because he was flying into an unknown danger and, unlike Aleksei, he'd never really been tested in a fight. Whoever was creating and controlling the revenants was clearly a powerful Magus, and one steeped in the Nagavor. Could he stand up to such a destructive creature? Would he even have a *chance?*

The mountains rose up around him, their jagged peaks capped with snow. He shivered at the sight of them. The ruins of the Drakleyn would be nestled somewhere in the back of the range, half-buried in rubble. He did *not* relish seeking them out.

Jonas was now well into the Wood, where the great ring of mountains broke to allow a thin river of trees into the wide bowl created by the walls of the peaks standing opposite. As he flew over the valley, his sense of foreboding grew.

Is that a remnant of Kholod magic? He wondered, *Or is that me jumping at phantoms?*

When he was a league or so out from the edge of the mountains, he descended to the forest floor. Whoever controlled the revenants would feel Jonas coming. Jonas didn't want to present such an easy target.

He fluttered down into the underbrush and shifted once again, this time into an animal he had never seen in the flesh. The coyote was small and golden, similar to a wolf but not quite so broad in construction. They were native to southwestern Ilyar and various sections of Fanj, yet well suited for travel through the forest. Small enough to escape notice, but large enough that nothing short of a bear would bother him. Aleksei had given him the idea, knowing the animal intimately.

It took the better part of an hour to work his way through the rough country, steadily progressing upwards. He noticed that the soil was becoming rockier, the vegetation sparser. By late afternoon he spotted the edge of the Wood and dropped into a lope.

The mountains towered above the trees, casting the entire valley into deep shadow. Jonas trotted out past the tree-line and began his search for a path. While he was not nearly as adept as Aleksei at reading the land, and certainly not proficient enough to cut a path of his own, he had learned much in the last year. Aleksei had taken him into the Seil Wood on several occasions to teach him what he could about tracking and traveling cross-country.

Now he put those skills to use, searching the rocks the way he had been taught until, at last, his efforts were rewarded. Jonas trotted to where the pattern of the rock shifted, and found a winding trail that vanished up into the mountains.

"Well, *you're* a long way from home, aren't you boy?"

Jonas started, turning to find an elderly man standing behind him. How had he not felt the man's presence?

"Oh, didn't mean to *spook* you there, boy." the man said kindly. His white hair waved wildly in the wind, his eyes such pale blue that they were almost colorless. There was something disturbingly familiar about him. "My, my. I've not seen one like *you* in twenty years, no sir."

Jonas stared into the man's eyes. Despite his wavy white hair and the wear of unkind years, there were some indelible traits that were unchanged.

With a horrifying recognition, Jonas realized who was addressing him.

It was Emelian Krasik. The Old Crow.

"Don't see much of anything up here, really. Not since *Bael* showed up, anyhow."

Jonas frowned. *Bael?* Was that the Magus responsible for the murders of Lord Bazin and the former Lord Captain? And if so, what would he be doing around the likes of Emelian *Krasik?*

"I always told my Zarina, coyotes were the smartest dogs in the woods. She never much cared for them, but *I* did. So loyal. *Noble,* too."

Hearing the old man mention his wife sent chills through Jonas. He had met Zarina Krasik only once, and even then he'd been too young to really remember her very well. But that had been before the war. They said she'd gone mad eventually, after the death of her son, Seryn. They said she'd died of a broken heart.

Looking at this man, standing amidst the broken bones of a dead mountain, Jonas suddenly understood how that might be possible. Before him stood the man who'd started a civil war that had raged for much of Jonas' early life. A man who had commanded the death of his own sons. That he was still alive was shocking.

A presence suddenly materialized behind Jonas, and the Prince had to fight to keep himself from darting for the tree-line.

"Ah, *here* you are, Krasik."

The old man looked up and smiled blankly, "Hello, Bael. I was just chatting with my friend here."

The man called Bael stepped into view, and Jonas felt his heart clutch in his chest. The man was short, his blond hair hanging lankly about his squared face. His deep green eyes glittered.

Jonas could feel the strength of the man's connection to the Archanium, the dark corruption that pumped thickly through his veins. It matched the echoes he'd felt in Kalinor.

Here was the Magus he sought.

"Where did *you* come from?" Bael asked, squinting at Jonas. He looked back at Krasik, "Odd that he's just standing there, don't you think? I've never seen a wolf do that before."

Krasik smiled at Bael as though patronizing a slow child, "He's not a *wolf*, Bael. He's a coyote. They're from the west, around Fanj. I don't know *what* he's doing here, but in any event, he's not likely to be intimidated by *us*."

Bael grinned at Jonas. It was not a nice smile, "Perhaps I should give him a reason to be."

"No." Emelian said mildly, and Bael dropped to his knees with a cry, clutching his head. "You will leave this creature be. Do you understand?"

"*Yes!*" Bael screamed. Krasik nodded and the Magus gasped for breath, rubbing his temples and slowly regaining his footing, "Begging your pardon, Zra-Uul. I spoke out of ignorance."

Jonas made note of the word. Where had he heard it before? Had he seen it in a book? Gods, what *was* it?

Krasik took a step towards him, and he took an involuntary step back.

"Look, you've *frightened* him." Emelian admonished. It was as though the exchange of a moment ago had never happened. What had he done to the Magus? And why wasn't Bael retaliating?

From what Jonas could sense, Bael should have the power to destroy Krasik with a thought. Yet he acted the supplicant. Something *very* strange was happening.

"It's *alright*, boy. Don't be alarmed."

"I don't like this." Bael grumbled.

Emelian regarded the Magus with confusion, "What?"

"You said these...dogs are from the west. What would one be doing in the Relvyn Mountains? And *alone?*"

Krasik shrugged, "Some men in the east use them as hunting dogs. It could be that this one was used in such a fashion, and simply broke free. With all the chaos you've been causing, it would hardly be surprising."

"Perhaps." Bael growled.

Why isn't he touching the Archanium? Jonas thought.

A simple touch would be all he needed to know that Jonas was not what he seemed. He glanced up at Krasik. Perhaps that was one of the things that would anger the old man.

"Zra-Uul, we *really* must be getting back. It will be dark soon, and you wouldn't want to be caught out here in the dark."

Krasik laughed harshly, "These woods are hardly a danger to me."

"If you slip off the trail, you will fall like any other man. You are too important to risk so casually."

Emelian sighed, "Very well, Master Bael. Let us go. I must say, your friends had better be right about this whole mess, or I will be *most* put out."

"Have no fear," Bael said with a smile, "everything has been planned with the utmost care."

"Oh, undoubtedly. But that was what your *father* told me the last time. I assume you're aware of how *that* little charade played out?"

Bael nodded, "Many unforeseen things occurred, Zra-Uul. This time will be different."

"Oh, of course. It always *is*, isn't it?" Emelian muttered as he disappeared up the path. "*Coming* Bael?"

"In a moment." the Magus responded. "I want to make sure no one is following us."

"Yes, yes, very well. But do not tarry too long." There was a pause, and then, "And *Bael*, if I think you've done *anything* to that beast, I will *not* be pleased with you."

"Of *course*, your Grace." Bael said through gritted teeth.

There was a long silence, and then the Magus turned back to Jonas. He glared at the dog he saw, squinting again as though trying to see through him. "What manner of creature are you?" he muttered to himself. "Count yourself lucky, dog. If you stay around here, the old man might not be able to protect you next time. And then we'll have a good time, you and I."

Jonas growled at the man, curling his lips back to reveal his sharp white teeth.

Bael glared at him a bit longer with those cruel green eyes, eyes that were startlingly familiar, before turning back up the path.

Jonas waited several heartbeats after the man had vanished to dart back into the Wood. His heart raced as he ran through the forest, leaping over fallen tree trunks and ignoring the scattering of the smaller animals in his path.

The depth of Bael's power, the sheer *magnitude* of it, was terrifying. Jonas wasn't sure what he had been expecting, but *that* wasn't it. There was also the bizarre chance of finding Emelian bloody *Krasik*.

Zra-Uul. That name kept nagging at his memory, but he couldn't recall the context. Gods, what *was* it? Whatever it was, it seemed to grant Krasik a certain level of power. The way he had struck out at Bael, and that Bael had not responded in kind, told Jonas that it was more than a simple honorary.

He judged that he was far enough away from Bael to shift again, and transformed into a falcon. He needed to get back to Drava as soon as possible.

As he flapped his great wings and ascended above the canopy, Jonas wracked his brain for some solution to their most pressing problem. He had hoped to confront the Magus, to perhaps either incapacitate or, if necessary, kill him.

But from what he had felt of Bael's power, it was doubtful that striking the man down was feasible. And if he was the same Magus who sought the Demonic Presence…. Jonas shivered at such a possibility.

As much as he might think of his own talents, Jonas had never put them to such a test. He did not relish the idea of taking on such a powerful opponent on his first attempt.

He was flying over the pass, deep in thought. His wings were stretched wide, carrying him effortlessly through the air one moment, and the next he was spiraling down at an incredible speed. Pain unlike anything he'd ever experienced blazed through his left wing, but he couldn't turn his head to inspect it. He could hardly watch the ground as it spun closer and closer towards him.

Jonas struck the trees hard, his wings catching and tearing on the sharp branches as he tumbled through the canopy to the forest floor below.

Striking the ground, he thought he might lose consciousness from the pain. Any mortal man would have in an instant, but he could feel Aleksei's strength pour into him. His Knight, his Hunter, his *love* had incredible reserves Jonas had never anticipated. Was his Bonded a bloody *god*?

"Well, it seems I was right after all." Bael said coldly, walking towards him. "You didn't really think you *fooled* me, did you? I've seen Shifters before, you know. It is an uncommon gift, I'll grant you, but it is by no means difficult to detect. Krasik might have been taken in by your disguise, but you couldn't possibly believe you would fool another Magus with that, now could you, *Jonas*?"

Jonas touched the Archanium only lightly enough to shift back into his human form. There was no point in retaining his shape. He might as well face this Magus as a man.

He tried to push himself into a sitting position, only to find that his left arm wouldn't respond. He looked down at the barbed shaft protruding from his bicep. A hot wave of nausea washed over him, and for a moment he thought he might be sick.

"Pity, though. I'd hoped the fall might kill you, and I could be done with it. Still, I think I may find pleasure in taking your life myself, *Highness*." Bael spat at title.

"I must say, your Knight made a mess of my earlier plans. It's such a pity that he'll die with you. I really could have used a man with his...intriguing qualities."

Even though the haze of pain and nausea, a realization dawned on Jonas. "It was *you*." he snarled. "*You* were the other player, the other Magus trying to bond Aleksei."

Bael shrugged, "I'll admit I was...disappointed by his decision. He would have been a useful asset."

"He would sooner cut your heart out." Jonas growled, pushing away the pain. The agony of his arm was secondary to the knowledge that he was about to die. That with his death, Aleksei would die as well. As that understanding tore through him, all other concerns became practically negligible.

A man stepped out from behind a tree, a crossbow in hand. "You want me to finish it, Master?"

Bael waved the man away, "No, thank you Stephen. Though I must commend you on your accuracy."

Jonas noted with some surprise that *both* men were Magi, both strongly steeped in the Nagavor.

"No, I'd much rather use him for one of our little *pets*. Can you do it?"

The other Magus scratched his head, "He'll have to be a step away from death. He's too strong otherwise."

Jonas hid his confusion. *Stephen* commanded the revenants? Surely a Magus of Bael's strength wouldn't entrust a magic like the Demonic Presence to an *underling*.

Bael nodded, "Not surprising, given his parentage." That cruel smile returned, and he aimed a kick at Jonas' side. "*Well*, Prince Belgi? Would you like to be one of my charming pets? Imagine your friends' surprise when they see you staggering from the Wood with the rest of my children, the same hunger, the same fever in your blood. How do you think that will make *Aleksei* feel? The others might not recognize you, of course, but I have a feeling he might.

"Bring him along, Stephen. And make sure he's shielded. I don't want him trying to escape." Bael regarded the Prince and chuckled, "Not that he's in much condition to be doing much of anything at the moment."

Bael turned to go, then paused. "Stephen?"

He turned and was unable to stop the gasp that escaped him. The other Magus was staring at Bael in shock. A moment later he fell forward. His body struck the ground with a sickening *thud*. His head kept rolling for another three or four paces.

"How...." Bael demanded. His words were cut off as three feet of red steel burst from his chest.

Aleksei stepped out of the shadows, his eyes dripping with rage. "Crawl back to your master, you little worm. Crawl back, and let him know that I'm coming for him."

He wrenched the sword from the Magus.

Bael collapsed like a limp doll. Aleksei gave him a contemptuous kick to the head and wiped his sword on the back of Bael's fine blue coat, then rushed to Jonas' side. "Can you stand?"

Jonas tried to summon the strength to lift himself, but only succeeded in sending another wave of hot pain and nausea through himself.

"*Shh.*" Aleksei whispered, gathering his Magus in his arms and lifting him gently from the forest floor. "Don't worry, I'll get us out of here. Save your strength."

Jonas tried to nod, but found himself incapable of even *that* minute effort.

Aleksei kissed his forehead gently, "Save your strength. Rest now, darlin'."

The Magus managed a smile and closed his eyes, knowing suddenly and unequivocally that he was safe.

Despite the pain, he managed to slip into an uneasy oblivion.

CHAPTER 27

DUTY AND DIVERGENCE

JONAS AWOKE IN alien surroundings.

He was comfortable and warm, but he didn't recognize the room. It was oddly constructed, organic in the way it followed natural lines and curves. A fire burned merrily not two paces from where he lay.

"*Ah*, you're wake at last."

He twisted in his bed and immediately regretted it. His left arm throbbed horribly, and he had to close his eyes and breathe evenly for a few moments to regain his bearings.

"Try not to move too much." the man said as he came into view.

Jonas' eyes widened. Before him stood an unusual man. A man he had come to think of as a friend in the last year.

"My most sincere greetings to you, Ri-Hnon." he mumbled, disturbed by how weak his voice sounded.

The Ri-Hnon smiled, "And to *you*, Son of Ilyar. Aleksei asked me to watch over you while he attended to something in the Wood."

Jonas frowned, "How did I come to be in the *Seil Wood*? I thought...."

Roux shook his head with a helpless smile, "Save your strength, Jonas. I will explain later, when your head is clear."

Jonas began to protest, but Roux held up a hand, forestalling him. "Aleksei has given you several herbs, one of which numbs your pain. It also numbs your mind. I will explain the particulars to you later, when your senses have sharpened. For the moment just know that you are extremely fortunate to have a man like my cousin for your Knight. He's a berry in the brambles, that one."

The Magus managed a weak smile, "Yes he is. You've seen the Mantle, then?"

A light seemed to flash behind the gold of Roux's eyes. He nodded, his smile gone, "Indeed I have. And it is a very serious matter indeed."

Jonas' brow drew down, "I don't understand."

Roux raised a hand, "We'll talk about this later. Right now you need to rest."

Jonas sighed. It would do no good arguing with the man. He was as obstinate as Aleksei.

The door, not much more than a wicker panel, swung to the side and Aleksei stepped into the room, one hand cradling a small cloth bundle. Jonas was shocked at the sight of him. For just a fleeting moment, his Knight looked as wild as Roux.

He wore no shirt, instead displaying the black Mantle for all to see. Jonas supposed, amongst the Ri-Vhan such a display would be important. Four streaks of dried blood streaked diagonally across the hard muscles and light golden fur of his chest. He handed the bundled cloth to Roux and muttered something under his breath.

The Ri-Hnon nodded solemnly, then stepped out of the room. Aleksei turned to Jonas and smiled broadly, "He lives!"

Jonas returned the smile to the best of his ability, "What's going on? How are we in the Seil Wood? How long have I been out?"

The Knight leaned down and kissed him gently before he considered a moment, "Perhaps half a day? You slept the night through, and then most of the morning. I love you *too*, by the way."

Jonas tried to laugh, but only ended up coughing violently. "And this?" he asked, indicating the room about him.

"The home of the Ri-Hnon." Aleksei said, as though such an answer should be obvious. He realized the deeper question Jonas was asking and smiled, "The Relvyn Wood is as ancient as the Seil. I told

Him of my need, and He showed me the path back here. I had to get you somewhere with healers, and begging your pardon, but I wasn't about to entrust your life to the Magi in Drava."

Jonas chuckled at that. He instantly regretted it, as sharp stabs of pain shot through him.

"How did you know where I was?" he slurred when he regained his breath.

Aleksei's face took on sudden gravity, "The Wood spoke with me. I asked Him about the creatures moving beneath his branches. He told me about the Magi steeped in the Nagavor who had come and gone under His shade, and I was concerned. So I asked Him to take me to them. I was on my way when He told me that you'd been shot down."

"But how did you get to me that fast? How did you get to the pass so quickly?"

Aleksei tapped his shoulder, and the black markings rippled at his touch, "I told the Wood that I needed to get to you, so He took me there."

Jonas nodded, closing his eyes, "I wish you'd killed Bael."

Aleksei frowned, "Who?"

"The Magus you ran through. He killed Lord Captain Lenox and Bazin. He was the one in the Cathedral of Mokosh. He was the other Magus that tried to bond you."

As he said the words, Jonas understood the deeper implications. They had wondered why a Magus of such dark power would be skulking around the Voralla. At the time, Jonas had suggested a thousand reasons that might exist in the Voralla alone. But suddenly only one made absolute sense.

The Prime Key.

Aleksei frowned, "I tried to keep that thrust from being fatal, but unless one of his Magi found him before nightfall he couldn't have possibly survived. Between that and the kick to the head, I might very *well* have killed him. I'd much prefer that he fear me, and that he spread that fear to his master."

Jonas held back a sigh. "Aleksei, I think Bael is seeking the Demonic Presence."

"But I heard them talking. He acted as though the other Magus,

Stephen, was summoning the revenants. You said yourself that such power lay behind the second gate. That's why I made a special effort to kill the man."

Jonas tried to nod and immediately regretted it. "I have a feeling Bael is more cautious than I gave him credit for."

"How do you mean?"

Jonas managed a small smile, "If you opened one gate and found a sea of lesser demons, what would you expect to find behind the second?"

"Something worse?"

Jonas nodded, "I don't think Bael was stupid enough to risk facing something he couldn't handle."

Aleksei grunted. If such was the case, they might just have bought themselves a little time.

"So what's our next move?" Jonas asked softly.

Aleksei sighed, "Well, for the moment, *you* regain your strength. Now that you're conscious, the Ri-Vhan Healers can tend you. It's not as perfect as your healing, but it's a far cry better than those misguided fools in the Voralla.

"Once that's taken care of, we'll head back to Kalinor. You're going to need a bit longer to recover, I think, and we need to figure out what our next move is going to be."

Jonas sank back into the rough cushions, "Alright. What are you going to do about Drava?"

His Knight suddenly looked very tired. He ran a hand across his face and breathed deeply before answering, "I left Vadim in charge before I went into the Wood. If nothing else, we've given them time to fortify things. I might have to go to Mornj *myself* and get some troops out into the Relvyn region. Those villages need to be protected. Yrinu hasn't shown any signs of aggression in decades, so I think we can spare the men."

Jonas nodded again. It was about all he could do at the moment. Why was he suddenly so tired? Surely he couldn't be *this* weak.

Aleksei smiled gently, "You look about ready for the crows. Go back to sleep, Jonas. I'll wake you in an hour or so for your medicine."

"Medicine?" Jonas asked in dread.

Aleksei winked, "Don't worry. It'll make you forget your own name, much less that your arm's broken and your right leg's in shambles."

Jonas chuckled softly as he drifted back into his dark, dreamless sleep.

When Jonas woke again, Aleksei was sitting not far away, deep in conversation with Roux. The two men were speaking in low tones, but Jonas suspected that even had they been talking at a normal volume he wouldn't have been able to understand them.

Whatever Aleksei had given him was muddling his head, and it was all he could do to keep his eyes open. The room swam in blurry swirls and warm blankets of light, but Jonas wasn't bothered by the experience. Rather, it simply seemed the way of things at the moment.

He realized as he lay there that nothing about his situation seemed to affect him. He could remember Aleksei telling him that his arm was broken, and while he understood what that meant, it didn't bother him.

He recalled his encounter with Emelian Krasik and the Magus Bael with the same intensity as he remembered the color of Tamara's dress the last time he'd seen her. No one thought or concern took precedence over any other.

"Ah, he's awake."

Jonas tried to focus on the face floating a few paces away. He recognized Aleksei's voice and tried to manage a smile.

"Is he aware?" Roux asked.

"Mostly. I've given him quite a bit yuselk, so he's not feeling any pain at the moment."

Roux frowned, "Where did you find *yuselk*? I didn't realize it grew in the Wood this time of year."

Aleksei shrugged, "There was a patch along the southern border. I'm not really sure *how* it's growing this late in the year myself, now that you mention it, but I asked the Wood where I might find some, and that's where She took me."

Roux shook his head in wonder, "She's taken quite a shine to you, hasn't She?"

Aleksei chuckled, "Apparently so. I think She's been lonely

without a Hunter to protect Her for so long."

Roux nodded, "Understandable. I mean, I can *interpret* Her messages, but not as directly as you can. I suppose our dealings with Her depend upon the different services we provide?"

Aleksei shrugged again. It wasn't something he spent a lot of effort thinking about, but he could understand Roux's desire to grasp it. He remembered how hard it had been for his cousin to accept Aleksei being named Hunter.

He looked at Jonas, and an expression of sympathetic misery broke across his face. The Magus looked terrible, lying there on the bed Aleksei had built, covered in blankets and watching them, his normally brilliant green eyes dulled by the drugs in his blood, and the pain his body refused to acknowledge.

"How are you feeling?" he asked.

Jonas smiled weakly, "I'm *not*."

"Good. The Healers will be here after a bit, and then you'll be in better condition. We'll be able to go to Kalinor in a day or two."

Jonas didn't waste the energy trying to nod. Instead he closed his eyes and attempted to slip back into sleep, hoping to conserve what little strength he possessed.

Aleksei turned back to Roux, satisfied that Jonas was resting peacefully, "So you were saying? About *this*?" He indicated the markings of the Mantle.

Roux nodded, "Right, well, as I said before, no one has seen a Hunter marked by the Wood before, not in living memory. We have accounts of such a thing happening, but the last Hunter described as having markings like yours died during the Dominion Wars."

"And none of these accounts mention what the Mantle *does*?"

Roux shook his head, "Aleksei, when I say that the last Hunter to possess the Mantle died during the Dominion Wars, I'm speaking of the *first* Hunter.

"I'm talking about *Richter*."

Aleksei felt a chill sweep through him.

Richter was a legend. Aleksei wasn't even convinced such a man had ever even *existed*. He idolized the man, if the tales were even half true, and yet to be the first to possess the same magic as a Magus who lived a thousand years ago was unthinkable. He had killed a hatchling Salamander. Had it been so long since She had bestowed this magic that that was all it took any longer? Or was he missing something?

"However," Roux continued, "there's a good deal of language that refers to balance and restoration. It's apocryphal at best, and nearly impossible to put into the context of the time."

Aleksei cursed under his breath.

It was enormously vexing to be gifted with something, and yet know so little of its nature. And the last bearer had been *Richter*? He tried to ask the Wood, but Her response was always the same, and offered no solutions.

A gift, for my Hunter.

He sighed and walked over to the fire, staring into the flames as he mulled over Roux's words. Hunters were rare enough, but for none to be so marked since the Dominion Wars was confusing. What purpose would the Wood have in holding back the Mantle, and why would She choose to grant it *now*?

Perhaps it was nothing more than an odd series of coincidences, but Aleksei found that somehow unlikely. He needed to understand the *reason*.

His thoughts were interrupted by the sound of voices in the front room. He heard his Uncle Theo's deep voice speaking in grave tones, and a moment later his uncle appeared in the doorway, followed by a woman who looked to be several years younger than Aleksei, and a man who had to be Theo's age, if not older.

"Aleksei," Theo said, smiling warmly, "this is Gaitan and Sorein. They're here to help Jonas."

Aleksei nodded soberly, then crouched next to his Magus and touched his right arm. Jonas stirred, then opened one bleary eye.

"Jonas, you need to wake up. The Healers are here." he said softly.

Jonas smiled and attempted to crane his neck to see what manner of people had arrived to heal him, only to remember that he'd torn practically every muscle in his neck during his fall.

The woman called Sorein knelt at his side and smoothed her hand across his face, "There there, dear, try not to move."

Jonas glanced at Aleksei, and the Knight's mind was suddenly filled with words.

Who is this woman, and why does she think I'm six summers old?

Aleksei bit back a laugh and tried to scowl at his Magus. Jonas' levity was a good sign. It would help him heal faster.

Aleksei's attention was diverted by the sound of clinking glass. He turned his head to see Gaitan reach into a hard leather case and withdraw a series of small glass jars, each filled with a different colored liquid. Aleksei watched the man intently, noting which potions he withdrew and which he left in the case.

The Ri-Vhan art of healing had long held great fascination for Aleksei.

Sorein reached into one of the pockets of her loose-fitting dress and withdrew a slender wooden tool, which Aleksei thought looked rather like a paintbrush. Gaitan produced a similar tool and turned to Sorein, his face inquisitive.

"What are the afflicted areas, then?"

Aleksei opened his mouth to answer, but Sorein answered instead, touching Jonas' forehead and speaking in voice devoid of emotion.

"Broken left arm, torn muscles throughout the neck and back, the right leg's completely shattered. The injuries seem...*off*, though. I don't know how to describe it."

Sorein was at a loss for words. Aleksei sighed. Of *course* the injuries wouldn't seem right.

"When he sustained the injuries," Aleksei said wearily, "he was a bird."

The two Healers looked at him as though he'd gone mad.

"I beg your pardon?" Gaitan said, his brow drawing down.

"Jonas. He was a bird when he was shot through the left wing and fell to the forest floor. It was only *after* that he shifted back into the form of a man, and therefore the injuries would seem odd in placement, because they were originally caused in the body of a bird."

"Then we must heal him as a bird." Sorein proclaimed. "He can change back, can't he?"

Aleksei turned to Jonas, who was regarding them all with irritation born of being treated as though he weren't in the room.

"Is your head clear enough to shift?"

Jonas considered a moment, then nodded, "I think so. If not, nothing bad will happen, I simply won't be able to change."

Aleksei nodded, "Alright then, we need you to shift into whatever bird you were when you were shot out of the air."

"You make it sound so graceful." Jonas muttered as he reached into the Archanium.

It wasn't the same experience he was used to, certainly. His connection to the swirling mass of color, emotion and sound was more tenuous than usual, almost *slippery*. It took more attempts than Jonas cared to admit before he'd even managed to get any sort of hold on the Archanium. Several minutes more passed before he touched the spell he needed and slid into the shape of the falcon.

"Remarkable." Gaitan breathed.

"I've never worked on an animal before." Sorein said suddenly, drawing her eyebrows down in consternation.

"He's *not* an animal," Aleksei said patiently, "he's a man in the *shape* of an animal."

Both Healers regarded him skeptically, then resumed practicing their art.

Aleksei scowled, walking over to where his Uncle Theo stood with Roux. These people were there to heal Jonas, not to get into a metaphysical argument about the nature of the Archanium.

"Don't worry yourself too much, my boy." Theo said confidently, "He'll be strong as an oak soon enough."

Aleksei nodded, feigning optimism.

He had a great many things weighing on his mind at the moment. He'd hoped that the Ri-Vhan would have answers for him, some simple explanation for the bizarre markings that now covered his shoulders, only to learn that such markings had not been seen in a thousand years.

To add tender to the flame, Jonas was still deeply concerned about something he had heard during his encounter with Emelian Krasik and the Magus Bael. He'd indicated it could be very serious indeed, but he wouldn't know until he looked at some of the books in the Voralla.

And then there were the reinforcements, or lack there of. It was becoming clear to Aleksei that he was going to have to go to Mornj himself and figure out exactly who, or what, was keeping his orders from being followed. The people of Drava could not be protected by a handful of Magi and their Knights. Perhaps he would go while Jonas was searching for information on this...Zra-Uul.

Sorein cried out suddenly, and Aleksei's head snapped to where the Healers were tending Jonas.

"He *snapped* at me!" she exclaimed. She looked at Aleksei accusatorially, "I thought you said he was still a man!"

The falcon that was Jonas narrowed his eyes, "I *am* still a man. You seem to have forgotten that while you were torturing my wing."

Sorein returned to ministering to his wing, touching it much more delicately this time. Aleksei winced in empathy. If Jonas hurt with that much yuselk in his blood, Sorein must have been rough indeed.

He spent the next several minutes watching over her shoulder to ensure Jonas' comfort, and after a while Aleksei's fascination overcame his annoyance at her carelessness.

The Healer dipped her brush-like tool into a pot of bright yellow potion, wiping it gently on the edge of the jar before painting intricate patterns across the length of Jonas' wing. The potion shimmered briefly, then sank into his wing, sending a faint wisp of golden steam into the air. He saw Jonas shiver as the potion set into his bones, encouraging them to knit back together.

He knew that had it not been for the yuselk, the man would be in a great deal of pain just about now. Ri-Vhan Healers were gifted in their art, and their methods were effective. They were not, however, *pleasant*. It was extremely painful for a body to grow bone and knit tissue at such an accelerated rate.

Gaitan finished drawing his pattern across Jonas' leg in the crimson formula he'd been working with, then nodded in satisfaction.

"That ought to do it. He'll need plenty of meat for the next few days, to replenish the resources his body is using to heal, and he'll be weak for a little while, but there shouldn't be any permanent effects."

Aleksei smiled his appreciation, "Thank you."

The Healers glanced at each other before Gaitan responded, "You bring meat to our table and safety to the Wood, Master Hunter.

It is the very *least* we can do for you."

Aleksei stared at them, not quite sure how to respond. He was saved a moment later when Uncle Theo and Roux began chatting with them, gently ushering them out of the room. Aleksei turned back to Jonas, who had returned to his human form.

"Are you alright?"

The Magus shrugged one shoulder, "I'm not sure. I think I can move easier than before, but I'm still so numb from that...*what* did you call it again?"

"Yuselk. It's a root that grows in the late spring."

Jonas nodded, "Right, yuselk. Well it's doing its job *spectacularly*, so I'm not really sure how effective all that was."

Aleksei smiled, "You're fortunate. I've been told it's almost worth waiting for your body to heal on its own, rather than be healed with their potions. They say the healing hurts more than receiving the actual injury."

Jonas frowned, "Why don't they just give people some yuselk? It seemed to work pretty well for me."

"Probably because it's very hard to find when it's in season, and even then it's only potent when it's fresh, so it can't be dried. It's extremely temperamental, so they can't cultivate it, but even if they could, the Ri-Vhan are terrible farmers so they wouldn't."

He noticed that Jonas was studying him.

"*What?*"

Jonas chuckled, "That was more of an explanation than I was expecting."

"I was trained from a very young age in this sort of thing. It was going to be my livelihood, until somewhat recently."

Jonas laughed, relieved that doing so didn't send spears of agony shooting through his chest. "Fair enough."

"Oh, and Roux said he'd never heard of anyone being marked with the Mantle, and the last time it was recorded was during the Dominion Wars. The last man to bear it was *Richter*."

The Magus' eyes widened, "The Wood hasn't bestowed the Mantle since *Richter* died? That's a little unusual, wouldn't you say?"

Aleksei nodded irritably, "Very. I'd rather it was a common occurrence that someone could *explain* to me."

"You said that the Wood called it a gift? I don't think She would grant you something like this if She didn't think it would be beneficial to you.

"I'll research any mention of it in the Voralla. Some of the books in the vault date to the Dominion Wars, and even if I can't get to them, *Aya* can."

Aleksei nodded, absently touching the Mantle and shivering as it pulsed against his fingers. Touching it made him feel wild, feral.

Hungry.

He pulled his hand away, shaking his head to chase the feeling away. As a rule, he avoided anything that made him feel out of control, and the feelings aroused by the Mantle were too primal for comfort.

"I think I may have to go to Mornj." he said, switching to yet another troubling subject.

Jonas nodded calmly, "You could travel through the Wood to Drava. It would be a shorter ride from there."

"That's what I was planning. I don't mean to spend too long there, in any event. I need to get those troops mobilized to Relvyn, both to protect the people, and to make sure the lumber is making it up to Bereg Morya. If that lumber stops moving, it will make life a lot more difficult for *all* of Ilyar."

Jonas smiled, "Now you're thinking like a noble."

Aleksei's face darkened, "No, a *noble* would think only of the lumber, but not of the people producing it. A farmer realizes that without the well-being of the woodsmen, there *is* no lumber to protect."

Jonas scowled, but he knew Aleksei was right.

He was about to say something else when his vision suddenly blurred. He tried to shake his head, to ward off the dizziness that was creeping over on him, but it bit deeper. His head struck the pillow.

Aleksei leaned forward and pulled Jonas' blankets closer around his neck. Jonas was only barely conscious now. Not surprising, given what his body had just been commanded to do. Aleksei had been wondering how long it would take for the full effects to kick in.

Jonas regarded Aleksei with heavily lidded eyes, "Thank you, love."

"Rest now." Aleksei whispered, placing a kiss on the Prince's forehead.

Jonas was already asleep.

Chapter 28

Erstwhile Enmities

Sammul cowered before Bael's dreamform, wishing to the gods that he brought better news, "They're gone."

"I know they're *gone*, idiot." Bael spat. His voice was choked, and Sammul's dream shivered.

"But I don't know *where*, Master."

"They were in the Relvyn Wood. Surely they cannot have vanished completely." Bael demanded.

Sammul swallowed. "My sources in the region confirm that the Lord Captain vanished into the Wood, and neither he nor the Prince have been seen since."

Bael growled, "Surely they would have sought refuge in the village, or one nearby."

"They have not been seen, Master."

He tensed, expecting the usual punishment that resulted from speaking out of turn. Nothing happened. He opened his eyes and glanced up at the towering shadow of the Master.

"And the revenants, Master?"

"Destroyed. We sent them into the villages to...recruit, but something went wrong. Someone anticipated our actions. Of course, it's all useless now."

Sammul nodded his agreement. Losing Stephen had been a serious blow, though he would never say as much to the Bael. He valued his life too much.

"It is of little importance." Bael whispered finally. "We have the Prime Key. It is only a matter of time before the moon rises again."

Sammul nodded furiously. He had been a good servant. The Master had the Prime Key. He was a good servant. The Master had been pleased. Bael had transformed so much from the toad boy that Sammul could hardly recall his former life. Now he only thought of Bael as his Master. Anything less would result in punishment.

"Aleksei Drago," Bael said after a long moment, "tell me what you know about him."

Sammul searched his mind for anything he could say, any scrap he could offer.

"He was a farmer, Master. From the Southern Plain."

"And?"

"His mother was Ri-Vhan." he said hopefully. "I do not believe there is anything unique about him."

Bael chuckled harshly, "You underestimate him, Sammul. The Lord Captain is a most surprising man."

"As you say, Master."

"Where is his farm, exactly?"

"I know only the region, Master. I have never inquired further."

Bael was silent for a moment. "But his family still lives there?"

"Only his father, Master."

Bael's dreamform nodded, "He is close to his father?"

"I...do not know, Master."

"I want to know as much as I can about the good Lord Captain. Bring me what I want the next time we meet."

"As you command."

The dream flickered as it was swallowed by shadows.

※

Vadim checked around the corner, searching for any signs that the revenants were out.

Nothing.

He darted around the inn and to the door, pounding the signal he and Hade had agreed upon. He could hear the heavy bar sliding away, and the door swung open.

Vadim hurried into the common room and shut the door, sliding the crossbar into place as he did so. There had been no revenants spotted for days, but there was no sense taking chances.

He walked over to the large table that served as their base of operations in Drava, and spilled the contents of the rucksack on his shoulders across the field map Aleksei had left behind.

Hade hefted a heavy sack of flour, relief washing across his face, "I was afraid they'd taken everything."

"Almost." Vadim said darkly. "The larder's going to be low on supplies until the villagers return with the Legionnaires."

Hade scooped up an arm full of goods, heading back into the kitchen. Vadim watched him go and sighed. He supposed he shouldn't be unhappy.

Everything Aleksei had said had come true.

They had done as instructed, alerting the townsfolk to the impending attack, helping them board up their doors and windows. By the time they were finished, Drava looked like a ghost town.

And then the revenants appeared, lurching through the narrow streets, searching for fresh meat, finding nothing. Some had stopped in the middle of town, congregating in the square, waiting for signs of life.

So it had remained for nearly an hour, almost until sunset. Vadim had watched the creatures anxiously, wondering what they would do if they ran out of food. Surely he would have to engage the creatures at *some* point.

But as the sun descended, the oddest thing happened.

One moment the revenants were standing in the square, some searching the boarded windows hungrily, and the next they simply collapsed. As though invisible strings above their heads had been cut.

But his optimism had faded later that evening, when neither Aleksei nor Jonas appeared. *Surely* they should have returned by now.

Vadim glanced out the boarded window of the inn, squinting into the tree-line. Every moment he wasn't foraging for food, he was watching those trees, praying to the gods he would see them emerge. More than once he had wanted to go into the Wood to search for them, but Aleksei had expressly forbidden such a move, and Vadim obeyed his orders.

He had to have faith in his commander; it was the little hope he still possessed.

Hade returned from the kitchen and joined Vadim at the window, "Any sign?"

Vadim shook his head, "Not yet." He chuckled mirthlessly, "You know, there was a time I considered Aleksei Drago a farmer with lots of luck, but no brains. I figured he just did whatever Jonas told him to. I hated him for being a lapdog, for being faster, for being young, for gaining power so quickly."

Hade stared at his Knight in shock. He'd never heard Vadim say such things before. Of course, he'd known of the man's jealousy of Aleksei; that was hardly something to be remarked upon. Yet to hear his friend speak so candidly was surprising.

"But he proved me wrong." the Knight finished after a long silence. "He offered me the chance to prove that I had action to back up my words. And I failed him."

"Vadim–" Hade began, but the Knight forestalled him with a hand.

"I *failed* him, Hade. And all of the men whose lives he entrusted to me. By all rights, he should have sent me back to Kalinor to clean the Prince's chamber pot for the rest of my life." He paused for a moment, "But he *didn't*. He gave me another chance. He believed in me, Hade, and I *refuse* to let him down again."

Hade nodded his agreement, not exactly sure what else he could do. It wasn't like Vadim to speak so openly, certainly not about such a sensitive and personal issue. It did, however, explain a great deal about the way his Knight had been behaving of late.

Vadim suddenly turned from the window and snatched his sword belt from the table.

Hade frowned, "Where are you going?"

The Knight looked at his Magus with fervor in his eyes, "I'm going to find them, Hade. I know they're in there, and they could be injured. I *have* to know."

Hade followed him to the door, reminding him that Aleksei had *ordered* them to stay in Drava.

Ilyana and Marrik were taking the villagers who were willing to leave to Mornj, until the troops that Aleksei requested arrived to protect them. The rest were in the inn, depending upon Vadim for protection.

If something happened to him, what would the villagers do? Hade left unspoken that if something happened to Vadim, it would happen to him as well. He had seen his friends vomit blood and drop dead in their saddles. It was certainly not the end he wished for himself.

Vadim reached the door and threw the bolt aside, blocking out Hade's words as he pulled the door open.

Aleksei stood there, his golden eyes calm, his face collected. He was bare-chested, and the bizarre black markings across his shoulders and arms throbbed faintly in the fading light.

In the dusk they looked the color of old blood.

"I need a shirt and my horse." Aleksei said gently.

Vadim stood speechless, trying to understand what he had just heard. Aleksei watched him a moment, then calmly pushed past him and made his way upstairs.

As he descended the stairs, pack in hand, a crisp linen shirt now covering the markings of the Hunter's Mantle, Vadim finally found words.

"Where have you *been*? Are you alright? Where's Jonas? Where are you going? What happened in the Wood?"

Aleksei stared as the questions came flowing out of the Knight. When Vadim was finished, Aleksei spoke.

"There is a Magus called Bael deep in the Relvyn Mountains. He is with Emelian Krasik. I killed another Magus called Stephen, who I believe was the one responsible for summoning the revenants."

Vadim nodded.

"Jonas was injured trying to get back here. I took him to the Ri-Vhan for healing. He is in Kalinor now, and I'm headed to Mornj to figure out exactly *why* the last five orders I sent for troops have been ignored and unanswered."

The other Knight stared at Aleksei as though he'd just spoken in another language. "You went to the Seil Wood? How did you have time to...I don't understand."

Aleksei tapped his shoulders, "It's complicated. Just understand that I have a connection to the Wood, and we'll leave it at that."

Vadim nodded slowly, trying to absorb everything he was hearing.

"Is there anything you need?" Vadim asked finally.

Aleksei shook his head, "Only for you to hold things here as you have. Watch for the revenants, but I don't expect more to appear any time soon. I think we dealt our enemies a bigger blow than we realized. For the moment, try to maintain the fiction that Drava is deserted, until reinforcements arrive."

"Will you return with them?" Vadim asked hopefully.

"I can't say right now." Aleksei said gravely. "You will be in charge of the men. I want the woodcutters to return to work as soon as they can. Have the Legionnaires provide guard detail for the woodsmen, and for the shipments. We can't let the lumberyards in Bereg Morya dry up."

Vadim blinked in surprise at that. It was possibly the last thing he'd expected the Lord Captain to say.

"Can you do that?" Aleksei asked, snapping Vadim back into the moment.

The Knight nodded, "As you command, Lord Captain."

Aleksei smiled and shook Vadim's hand firmly, "Thank you. May the gods be with you."

"And you, Sir."

Aleksei waved his farewell to Hade, then hurried out the door and around the side of the inn to the stable. The doors were shut and tightly nailed, but Aleksei had little difficulty pulling the boards away.

Dash was inside, prancing with the excitement of seeing Aleksei again.

"Hey there, boy," Aleksei said with a warm smile, "sorry to leave you like that. Something...unexpected came up. What do you say we go for a ride?"

The horse quivered in excitement as Aleksei brushed him down and strapped on his tack. He slid onto the horse's back, then turned Dash on the road west, toward Mornj. And answers.

Tamara sat in her chambers, one hand cradling her head as she stared listlessly out onto the Palace Lawn. Life was such a bore in the Palace without Jonas to lunch with, or Lord Captain Drago to watch at sword practice.

She hated it when her cousin had to leave on business, mostly because she was certain he was off having grand adventures and doing dangerous, daring things while she sat at home in the Palace, and listened to her tutors bore her with economics and history.

Why it mattered that the Yrini warlocks had assaulted Fanj fifty years ago over some prince's thoughtless remark, some prince who had undoubtedly been dead for years, was beyond her. How was *that* going to aid Tamara in ruling the realm when the time came?

Anyone with common sense knew it was a bad idea to insult an Yrini warlock. Anyone who didn't realize such an obvious truth deserved whatever they got.

There was a sudden flutter of color outside the window. A tiny sparrow lighted on her windowsill, and Tamara smiled. It hopped about, pecking at invisible crumbs and looking inside in the most curious manner. After a moment, it tapped tentatively on the glass. A moment later, it tapped firmly.

Tamara frowned, startled by the bird's peculiar actions. She'd never seen a bird behave like that. She went to the window and opened one side of it, stepping back in wonder as the bird flitted into her room and perched at the top of the chair she'd occupied not a moment before.

"How delightful!" she laughed to herself, clapping her hands.

The bird began to sing, and for a moment Tamara was perplexed. It was the same song her nursemaid had sung to her so often as a child! But the only other person who would ever have heard that tune was....

"Jonas!" she laughed. "Jonas, darling, you've returned!"

The bird shivered and then elongated, filling the chair until it was her cousin sitting before her, his handsome smile stretched wide.

Tamara flung herself into his arms, kissing his cheeks and hugging him fiercely. "I can hardly believe it!" she said, "I was just thinking to myself how much a bore life is here, without your wit to make it bearable."

Jonas chuckled and hugged his cousin lightly, "I wish I could say the great wide world was much better, but it also becomes boring in its own way after a while."

She struck him playfully on the arm, "You're joking, surely!"

The Prince winced at the strike, "Oh, would that I was, Cousin. Believe me. I've not had an easy time of it these last few days."

She frowned, "How so?"

Quickly Jonas related some of the less gruesome details of his absence. By the end of his story, her face was wide with shock, "But how is this possible? I understand that the Archanium is vast and mysterious, but for such things to occur! And to *you* of all people!"

"Indeed," Jonas muttered, "so do not envy me too deeply, Cousin. I doubt you'd appreciate the quality of adventure if you'd taken a crossbow bolt."

"I almost did." she reminded him archly. "Perhaps *you* shouldn't travel in such a vain manner. Mother would have you strung up by your thumbs, and never hear of you leaving again if she knew."

Jonas' face darkened, "Which is why we can't tell her."

"If she had her way, you'd never leave the Palace *again*, much less on such a rash errand. And in such a form!"

Jonas arched an eyebrow. "Yet she is content for Aleksei to risk his life, even though in so doing he risks *mine* as well? Surely she hasn't thought this through."

"Well, she has had a great deal on her mind of late."

"What do you mean?"

The princess glanced at the door warily, but Jonas waved his hand casually. "It's warded."

She nodded, "It's Parliament. They've been breathing down her neck in the most ferocious manner over the incident in Relvyn. They're questioning her wisdom in sending such a small force, and then criticizing her for sending Magi down there when they are not officially part of the military. They bicker about the way things ought to be run, and say Grandfather would never have allowed such attacks to continue for so long.

"Worse, now the Legion generals are siding with Parliament. They've brought up several accounts of military folly that they claim are her fault. It's been *vicious*, Jonas. It truly has."

Jonas sighed, "I wish I was surprised by any of this. Anyone we ought to be particularly concerned with?"

"Who would you guess? It's always the same ones, isn't it? Perron and Malak are the worst, of course. I swear sometimes I can see Malak foaming at the mouth. He's turning into quite the ideologue."

"I don't know that I'd be *too* worried, were I you. Your mother is a brilliant woman, and a very capable ruler. She will deal with Parliament as only she can, and that will be that."

Tamara's face darkened, "Do you *really* think so? I'm afraid I can't share in your confidence. Remember, Cousin, I've been in Kalinor while you've been out fluttering hither and thither. There have been a great many changes that you might not have been privy to."

The Magus sighed, "Well that doesn't sound encouraging, especially coming from *you*."

Tamara frowned, "I'm not sure where I earned this reputation of being foolish and empty-headed, Cousin, but whatever truth may surround such rumors, I am certainly not *blind*."

Jonas smiled, "No one is accusing you of anything, Tamara. It's just that you have a habit of believing the best of people, even when such an opinion doesn't seem merited. So when *you* are troubled by such things, it speaks to me of a greater severity."

Tamara's face lightened a touch, "Well, I am not the cynic you are. Though I hardly find fault in that."

There was a knock at the door, and Jonas quickly dissolved the ward.

"Enter." Tamara called.

The door swung open to reveal a petite maid, "Your Highness... es," she said, her large brown eyes widening in surprise and horror as she realized Jonas was in the room, "I present Her Majesty, the Queen."

Andariana swept into the room, her sapphire silk gown whispering across the polished marble floor. She nodded a dismissal to the maid, who made a deep curtsy and rushed from the room, closing the door as she left.

Andariana's surprise upon catching sight of Jonas was quickly swallowed back into her mask of regal forbearance.

"What news of the front, Nephew?"

Jonas smiled slightly. At least she didn't ask where he'd been.

"Last I knew, the revenants had been greatly depleted in number. In fact, we might have set their plans temporarily awry."

"*We*, Jonas?"

"Aleksei and myself." He paused, throwing another ward of silence around the room.

She sighed, "I might have guessed. I'd feared him off on some other mission. His warhorse was left in the Palace stables, so I assumed it was a mission of a personal nature."

Jonas shook his head, "Aleksei's the reason the numbers of revenants are so greatly reduced. He's also the reason there might not be any more for some time."

She arched an eyebrow, "Really? Why is that?"

"Because he killed a Magus named Stephen, who I believe was the one responsible for summoning the creatures."

Andariana took this in stride, nodding slowly, "And where did you encounter this Magus?"

"In the Relvyn Wood, shortly after they attacked me."

Andariana's eyes widened, "I see." She was still unaware of Jonas' ability to shift into other forms, and he meant to keep it that way. Undoubtedly, the thought of him flying would terrify her. Such fears would seem all the more justified now. "And yet you appear no worse for it."

"Aleksei took me to the Ri-Vhan. Their Healers tended to me." Jonas said matter-of-factly.

The Queen sighed, "Very well. I am willing to accept all of this, Jonas, but would you kindly explain to me *how* it is that you and the Lord Captain are capable of such movement through the realm? Last I was aware, the Seil Wood was in no way close to Relvyn."

Jonas paused for a moment, trying to decide how much he should tell his aunt. After all, the less she actually knew, the less she could let slip to someone who might not be trustworthy, and at the moment that list was ever-growing.

"I'm not sure I understand it all myself. I believe it has something to do with Aleksei's talents as a Ri-Vhan Hunter. The Wood seems to be able to usher him between the Seil and the Relvyn Woods."

Andariana's eyes widened, "The...*Wood* does this? You speak as though the Wood was a being."

Jonas considered how to best respond, "She is, Aunt. The Wood is an ancient being of incredible magic. She predates even the Kholodym, and therefore it is impossible to say *exactly* how old She is. However, She is most certainly a creature in Her own regard. One capable of thought and speech, after a fashion."

The Queen shook her head in wonder, "I'm sure you'll forgive me if I have difficulty fathoming such a thing."

Jonas spread his hands before himself in a conciliatory gesture, "Then take my words at face value, and understand that I speak of matters related to powerful magic that is beyond my own comprehension."

Andariana collapsed unceremoniously into an armchair and sighed, "Very well, Nephew. Forgive the interrogation. I'm afraid I've spent all my time of late discussing logistics with politicians. You'll understand if I am unused to dealing with people's words at face value."

Jonas chuckled, "Of course, Aunt." He paused there, considering how to approach the next item he needed to bring to her attention. "Now, before I was wounded, I was returning from a rather unsettling encounter in the Relvyn Mountains. There are ruins of an ancient structure there called the Drakleyn. It dates back to the time of the Kholodym. It is at present, I believe, being used as a base of operations."

Andariana sat straighter, "For what?"

Jonas sighed, "I'm not precisely sure. There was a Magus there called Bael, who I didn't recognize. He was deeply steeped in the Nagavor. The other man I encountered was Emelian Krasik."

Andariana leapt from her seat as though scalded. Her eyes were wide and suddenly fearful. "Krasik? Are you *sure*?"

Jonas nodded, "Certain. But it doesn't stop here. Bael called Krasik the '*Zra-Uul*'. Do you know that name?"

Andariana considered a long moment, "I recall the name being mentioned several times during the last war." She paused, and Jonas could tell she was choosing her words very carefully. "I was barely twenty at the time, so you must understand that I was quite sheltered then. Whenever I heard it uttered, there was the understanding that it meant something terrible, but my sister never told me what. *Why?*"

Jonas frowned, "Because I think I've seen it referenced before, in one of the books in the Voralla. I was going to go down to the Vaults later today and search for it, but I was hoping it would sound familiar to you."

The Queen sighed, "Could it simply be some sort of honorary? The Krasik line is rife with...interesting ancestry, some *very* questionable."

"I hoped the same thing, but I regret to tell you that it appears to be something more. As I said, I don't really grasp the nature of how it works, but whatever it was, it dropped Bael to the ground in a heartbeat. And the Magus was obviously wary enough not to retaliate."

The Queen watched her nephew closely. "Jonas, what are you *not* telling me?"

The Magus cursed silently. Gods, how did she always *know?* "Did you read the book I gave to Aya?"

Andariana nodded cautiously, "I found it a bit confusing, but yes. Why?"

"I believe Bael is seeking to open the Cathedral of Dazhbog."

Andariana's hand went to her mouth, "You not serious! Is there any chance of his success?"

"Yes. He's already entered the Second Transept. It's possible he has the Prime Key already."

Andariana retreated behind her iron façade. "Very well. We will get this sorted out. *All* of it."

Jonas doubted his own ability to deal with Bael, much less that of Sammul's useless Magi. Combine that with whatever abilities Krasik might possess, and Jonas thought there was a great deal more to fear than Andariana was willing to admit.

He glanced over at Tamara and winced at the combination of anger and horror that battled for command of her face. "But what of

Lord Captain Drago? Why didn't he return with you?"

Jonas' expression soured, "Aleksei has gone to Mornj. He sent several requests for reinforcements while in Drava, but received no response. He believes there is something. or possibly some*one* in Mornj who is countermanding his orders. He's...investigating."

Andariana frowned, "Why didn't he simply have me write to them?"

Jonas shrugged, "You know how Aleksei is. He is much more satisfied if he deals with something like this in person. He's never been one to rely on letters or words above actions."

She sighed, "I just hope he's careful. Mornj can be a rather... rough place. That's one of the reasons we built a garrison there."

Jonas smiled, "I have a feeling that he'll do rather well for himself, then."

Chapter 29

Debt Collection

Aleksei sat astride Dash, irritably watching the cart before him. Half an hour has passed since they'd been stopped at the gates of the city, and the guards were *still* quibbling with the driver over some document or another.

Every now and then he considered revealing who he was simply so that he might get into the city faster, but he knew that announcing his presence would only make his job harder. He needed information, and in his experience, it was best gathered when the target was caught off guard. When he made his presence known, he wanted it to be as much a surprise as possible.

The cart was finally waved through, and Aleksei urged Dash forward. He kept his own face hidden in the hood of his cloak. The light rain gave him ready excuse to keep his face obscured.

"State your business." the guard said in a bored voice.

"Collecting on a debt." Aleksei said gruffly.

The guard glanced behind him at the gatehouse, where his

friends were visibly drinking ale and throwing dice. The man snorted. "Good luck with that. Off you go."

Aleksei nodded his thanks and rode through the massive gates, into the city of Mornj.

Dash navigated the crowded streets with a comfort that struck Aleksei as deeply amusing. He couldn't help but recall his first visit to Kalinor.

Aleksei remembered how wide-eyed he'd been in the city. *Gods*, but that seemed a lifetime ago.

Now he moved through the flow of people and carts, one hand always floating near his knife. Cities were not kind to the unwary, as Aleksei had learned the hard way. Still, that encounter had not gone the way the thief intended.

Aleksei turned down High Street, and searched the brightly painted hanging signs. After wading through a sea of hawkers and tradesmen, he finally spotted an inn and made his way steadily towards it.

The sign was of a woman holding a tray. The words below identified it as The Silver Tankard. Aleksei slid off of Dash's back and led him around to the small stable behind the structure.

A stable boy came forward and opened his hands for the reins. Aleksei handed them over, along with a silver mark. "Take good care of him, and there'll be another one for you when I come back."

The boy's eyes widened, and he nodded dumbly as Aleksei walked into the inn. The innkeeper, a large woman bearing a vague resemblance to the woman on the sign, was wiping the bar with a greasy rag when he walked up.

"How much for a night?" he asked in a low tone.

She looked him up and down, then leaned forward, "Silver mark. That's with dinner and a pint."

Aleksei slid across ten coppers, "Just the room, then."

She eyed the coppers, then nodded, "As you like. Fifth door on the right upstairs."

Aleksei thanked her and went to his room, throwing his pack on the bed and pulling off his travel clothes. If he was going to throw his weight around at the garrison, he'd better look the part. He dressed quickly, hiding his uniform beneath his cloak and pulling his hood up the moment he stepped out of the inn.

He melted into the throng of people, moving like molasses through the streets of Mornj, slowly making his way towards the gray prominence of the garrison in the distance.

With the rain slowing traffic to a near crawl, it took Aleksei the better part of an hour to reach the garrison. As he stepped under the broad awning that welcomed the coaches and mounts of arriving officers, a guard stepped up to him.

"Your business, sir?"

Aleksei pushed back his hood and looked the man in the eyes, "I'm here to see Colonel Balwick."

The man seemed surprised at the directness in Aleksei's voice. "And your name, sir?"

"Aleksei Drago."

The guard coughed in surprise, then looked Aleksei up and down. The Lord Captain frowned impatiently.

"Um, of course, Sir. Begging your pardon, Sir. F...Follow me."

Aleksei nodded and gestured for the man to lead the way. He followed the guard through the poorly lit corridors, noting the disheveled state of the soldiers in the halls. It was a far cry from the order of Kalinor, and the smell of sour ale and sweat was almost enough to make him sick.

After walking what seemed like leagues of hallways, the guard stopped before a heavy iron-bound door. "Here we are, Sir. Would you like me to announce you?"

Aleksei smiled, "No, I can introduce myself. Thank you, soldier."

The guard saluted reverently, then vanished into the maze of corridors. Aleksei sighed, wondering if he'd be able to find his way out. He turned his mind back to the matter at hand, and knocked on the door once before pushing it open.

Inside, the office was brightly lit. A fire blazed furiously in the hearth against the far wall, and tallow candles burned in sconces on the walls to either side. A large oak desk dominated the center of the room. An imposing, well-built man was seated behind it, bald head bent as he studied a sheaf of paper.

He looked up in surprise as the door shut firmly.

"What do you want?" he demanded gruffly.

"Colonel Balwick?" Aleksei asked calmly.

"Yes, I'm Balwick. Who are you?"

"I'm your Lord Captain."

The Colonel stared at him for a moment, then burst out laughing. "Oh, that's rich. Might as well say you're the Prince of bloody Ilyar."

Aleksei sighed and walked forward, sweeping off his cloak and folding it over one of the wooden chairs that sat before the desk. His epaulets clearly marked his rank in gold. "You are in charge of the forces in Mornj, are you not?"

Balwick frowned, "Listen, I don't know what sort of *game* this is, but I'm a busy man."

Aleksei arched an eyebrow, "I should say you are. *So* busy that you can't follow orders from your commanding officer."

Balwick's face darkened.

Aleksei leaned forward across the desk, "I've sent *five* sets of orders to this garrison. Four pigeons and one man. I have been met with silence each time. Tell me *why*."

The Colonel stood in what Aleksei assumed was an attempt to intimidate him by size.

Aleksei straightened.

The man's voice dropped to a dangerous pitch. Aleksei felt the Mantle begin to tingle. "You're asking some very dangerous questions, *Lord Captain*. If you aren't careful, you're gonna upset some *very* dangerous people, *understand*?"

Aleksei watched the man as he slowly advanced around the desk and towards him. "I'd stop where you are."

The man smirked in response. He kept advancing.

Aleksei's arm shot out and caught the officer by the throat. Balwick tried to surge forward, to press his obvious size advantage, but he couldn't move.

Aleksei looked him in the eye, "I'd order you to answer my questions, but my orders don't seem to have much effect, *do* they?"

He slammed his knee into Balwick's crotch, stepping to the side as the man doubled over and bringing his elbow down on the back of the man's head.

The Colonel collapsed onto the floor, and Aleksei placed his boot against Balwick's neck. "Why weren't my orders followed?"

"Was...told not to." Balwick wheezed.

Aleksei pressed harder, *"By?"*

"Can't...say."

The Knight dropped into a crouch next to the big man and drew his knife, "Really? Ain't that a funny thing, because if you *don't* tell me, *I'm* going to cut out your tongue. And then you won't be able to say anything at all, now will you? Should I prove how capable I am?"

"N...no!" Balwick shouted.

Aleksei smiled, "Good lad. I'm glad you see the logic here. *Who* told you not to obey my orders?"

"M...Malak." Balwick spat.

Aleksei frowned, "Hugo Malak? Lord of Relvyn?"

"Y...yeah." the man gasped.

Aleksei stood and regarded the Colonel with disgust, "Get up."

The man pulled himself to his feet, his eyes scared. Aleksei thought that, for the first time, Balwick actually recognized who he was.

"You wouldn't really have done it, would you, Sir?" Balwick asked, rubbing his throat.

Aleksei frowned as he sheathed his knife, "What?"

"Cut out my tongue?"

Aleksei shrugged dismissively, "Well, that depended entirely on you, didn't it? You told me the truth, so I didn't have to resort to more...*primitive* means of persuasion. I expect when even the lowest people are given the choice, they'll opt for the truth."

The Colonel nodded emphatically, as though to imply that he had been planning on telling Aleksei all along.

"Now then," the Lord Captain said calmly, "I'll give you an hour before I send the guards after you. If they catch you, you'll face a court marshal and hanging for attempted assault on your commanding officer, among other things. If I were you, *I'd* get going."

It took a moment for Aleksei's words to sink in. Balwick's eyes widened, "But Sir,"

"Your hour has begun. I recommend you make the most of it."

The big man stared at him a moment longer, then turned and hurried out the door.

Aleksei sighed.

He'd ridden hard to get here in a timely manner, and now he found there was much to be done before the garrison was in any condition to deploy troops. The sudden lack of a commanding officer made it all the more difficult.

Aleksei opened the door of the office and stepped out into the hall. A young Legionnaire was hurrying by, trying to avoid notice.

"Soldier, I would speak with you." Aleksei said kindly.

The young man straightened and saluted Aleksei awkwardly, "Yes, Sir."

Aleksei watched the soldier as he stepped back into the office. The young man looked ill-trained, his actions mimicked rather than learned. Aleksei made a mental note to look into the training schedule. No doubt it required a bit of adjustment.

"At ease, soldier." Aleksei said, sitting behind the massive desk and folding his hands, "Colonel Balwick has just been discharged. Tell me, who was his second-in-command?"

The young man looked confused, unsure how to answer the question. When he finally ventured forth an answer, it was tentative.

"I believe Major Rysun was the second-in-command, Sir. But he hasn't been in the garrison for several months now."

Aleksei nodded, "Very well. Does anyone know where he is at the moment?"

The soldier looked increasingly uncomfortable, "Aye, Sir. The Major spends his days at The Black Adder, on Market Street."

Aleksei frowned, "This place is an inn?"

"A tavern, Sir."

The Knight considered for a moment before sighing to himself. "Alright, bring me the Master of Arms and the Master of Stables. Tell them that Lord Captain Drago would have a word with them."

The young man's eyes widened, "T...The Master of Arms, Sir?"

"And the Master of Stables. I want them both in this office in half an hour."

"Yes, Sir."

"Well, off you go then." Aleksei said, waving towards the door.

The young man stood there for a moment, then rushed from the room.

Aleksei buried his face in his hands, closing his eyes against what he knew was brewing into a fearsome headache.

While part of him wanted to ride for Kalinor as fast as he could and deal with Malak, his more pragmatic side said that this garrison had to be cleaned up, and its soldiers brought up to task, or there would be no point in sending them *any*where.

He busied himself with the papers scattered across the desk, arranging them and trying to gain a sense of the state of the garrison. From the reports people had been sending Balwick, it became clear that there were capable people down here, they were simply being ill-used or ignored.

Aleksei took out a pen, slowly creating a list of names on a piece of parchment. As he read through the reports, he noted the placement of each man and the nature of the report. Some of them were downright rubbish, but others were quite valuable.

Worthwhile or not, though, the name went onto his list. He needed to know the men he had at his disposal, and which of them he could count on.

After what seemed only moments, there was a knock at the door. He looked up from his reports expectantly, "Come."

The door opened and the soldier hurried in, saluting again, "Lord Captain, the Master of Arms and the Master of Stables are here to see you."

Aleksei nodded, "Show them in, soldier."

The man stepped aside to allow two older men into the room. They each studied Aleksei warily.

He looked at the Legionnaire, "Thank you, that will be all for the moment."

The young man saluted again, then hurried out.

"Gentlemen," Aleksei said, rising from his chair, "thank you for answering my summons on such short notice. I apologize if I distracted you from your duties, but I thought it best to inform you that there's been a change in the leadership of this garrison."

One of the men raised a snowy eyebrow, "Where is Colonel Balwick, Sir?"

Aleksei smiled pleasantly, "Colonel Balwick has been relieved of his post, Master...?"

"Apologies, Sir." The man said hastily, "My name is Stewart."

Aleksei nodded, "Master Stewart, the Colonel has been discharged, and will not be returning. *I* am in command of this garrison until such a time as I deem it in accordance with my standards, and appoint a commander. I was hoping you and Master...?"

The other man seemed surprised that he was being addressed, "Walsing, Lord Captain."

"That you and Master Walsing would help me with this garrison. This post has been run with leniency and neglect. Let me make it clear that I will change both of those practices, starting now. But I need *your* help to do that. Are you up to it? Or do I need to appoint new officers to your posts?"

The men shared an alarmed glance, then shook their heads.

"My Lord Captain, both of us are more than willing to aid you in whatever way you see fit." Stewart said earnestly.

Aleksei smiled, "Good. Master Stewart, if you could draw up a training schedule for the men, and bring it to me by this time tomorrow? Master Walsing, a list of the animals that occupy your stables and their exercise rotations. And I'll need lists of inventory and any pieces of equipment in need of repair or replacement from both of you. Are there any questions?"

The two men shook their heads.

"Very well, you're dismissed."

They saluted smartly. As they left, Aleksei thought he noticed both men walking a touch straighter than when they'd arrived. He smiled, encouraged by the response he'd received.

Aleksei stood and snatched his cloak from the chair. Now that Walsing and Stewart were busy with his logistics, he had something urgent to take care of.

The rain had picked up since he'd been outside last, and Aleksei pulled his hood up against the warm wet of the autumn storm. He stopped at the edge of the large awning, turning to one of the guards.

"Do you know the direction of Market Street?"

The guard nodded, "It's up that ways a bit. Follow Tin Street for a few blocks, and you'll run right into it."

Aleksei smiled his thanks and hurried out into the rain.

The throng of people had thinned in the past hour, and now the streets were clogged with traders and farmers trying to get out of the city before dark. Aleksei caught himself feeling a touch homesick as he spotted an old farmer and his wife sitting on their ramshackle cart.

That life seemed so far away from him now, as though it had been lived by someone else completely. Despite the privilege his position now afforded him, he found himself missing that simplicity, that surety.

He found Tin Street and turned left, walking smoothly through the thoroughfare of kiosk shops and fruit carts. As he walked, he had the vague sense that he was being watched. But when he stopped to examine one of the carts, he could see no one tracking him through the thinning crowds.

You're just being paranoid. He chastised himself. *No one even knows you're here.*

Aleksei resumed walking, finding Market Street, and a moment later spotting the sign for The Black Adder. It reminded Aleksei of the inn he had stayed in on his first trip to Keiv-Alon.

He pushed his way into the common room, and found it so full of smoke he could hardly see. The sound of raucous laughter, along with the stink of burned mutton and stale beer, provided a fog of their own. Aleksei regarded the room with disdain. *This* was the preferred haunt of the man he sought? It did not bode well.

The man at the bar was thin and wiry. He reminded Aleksei of a weasel.

"I'm searching for an officer of the Legion." Aleksei said, pushing a silver mark across the bar. "A Major Rysun?"

The innkeeper nodded, "Aye, he's in the corner."

Aleksei followed the man's gaze to a table where a solitary man sat with a flagon of ale. The man was watching him.

He made his way to where the Major sat, smiling with as much sincerity as he could muster. "You're Rysun?"

The man nodded, running a hand through his rough black hair, "I am. Who wants to know?"

Aleksei pulled a chair to the table and sat, "My name is Aleksei Drago. I'm searching for the Major Rysun who was second-in-command to Colonel Balwick."

Rysun's lip curled contemptuously, "That would be me, then. So what's the charge gonna be? Desertion? Insubordination? Do I get a trial, or are you just going to string me up?"

Aleksei regarded the man calmly, "Let me ask you something. You've heard of me, yes?"

The other man nodded cautiously, "You have a certain reputation."

"Does my reputation mark me as an unfair man? Unjust?"

Rysun looked away from Aleksei's gaze, "No, Sir."

Aleksei spread his hands on the table, "Then why would you immediately assume that you were going to be treated unfairly?"

The Major turned suddenly defiant, "Because that seems to be the way of things in Mornj at the moment, what with *Balwick* running things and all. Justice doesn't figure much into his vocabulary."

The Lord Captain quirked a smile, "That's why I dismissed the man. If he's smart, he's halfway to Keiv-Alon by now, and watching over his shoulder to make sure I don't change my mind, and decide to hang him after all."

Rysun's eyes widened, "Balwick's not in command?"

Aleksei leaned forward, "I don't appreciate it when my subordinate officers attack me. I tend to kill people when they try. Balwick got off easy.

"But *you*, you are still an officer of the Legion, unless you've decided you'd like to formally *desert*. If such is the case, then I will of course have to take you through the tribunals for processing.

"*If*, however, you felt persecuted or abused by your commanding officer, and thought that by hiding out here," Aleksei indicated the raucous room around them, "you might avoid future mistreatment, then I think we can come to some sort of understanding."

Rysun regarded him suspiciously, "Meaning?"

Aleksei shrugged, "I understand the motives for your actions. But just because I *understand* them doesn't mean I'll *ignore* them. It was wrong of you to run from your duty as a Major in Her Majesty's Legion. You abandoned your men to the mercy of an unfit officer. I'd prefer that you'd written me and made your case. I can hardly make sensible decisions if my information is faulty."

"But why are you even *bothering* with me?" Rysun demanded.

"Because this garrison needs a commander, and *I* don't have the time to correct all the problems in this place. But if I determine that you're a good man, an honorable man, it will save the trouble of training someone else to do the job *you* should be doing in the first place.

"The Legion needs every good man it can get, but we gain nothing if we throw away every one who makes a mistake. No one is perfect, and I don't hold people to such expectations. I *do*, however, expect that you will be answerable to your men for leaving them to the mercy of a brigand while you drowned your sorrows in ale."

Rysun sighed, "I understand, Sir. May I ask what my punishment is to be, then?"

"It will be *far* more difficult for you to regain the respect of your men than to deal with any punishment I could dream up. Let that be your penance for your desertion, and we'll leave it at that."

The Major stared at him.

"I'll give you a day to gather yourself. At sunset tomorrow, I expect you back in the barracks. You will be shaven, washed, and look as an officer of the Legion is required to. Failure to appear at the directed time will result in *me* coming after you. I assure you that you *don't* want that. Do you understand?"

Rysun paused for a moment, then nodded, "Yes, Sir."

Aleksei smiled, "Good. Then I'll see you tomorrow. Good day, Major."

He stood and quietly left the inn, pulling his hood back up as he stepped out into the street.

The moment he began walking, Aleksei became aware of the person following him. The man was perhaps fifteen paces behind, but Aleksei could feel him there, tracking him.

The Mantle tingled with anticipation.

He sniffed at the air and caught the man's scent, heavy tones of mildew and smoke, mixed sour sweat. There was something else there, too.

Determination.

Aleksei weighed his options. He could confront the man, which would likely lead to a fight. Yet there was a great deal he was unable to tell about his pursuer from this distance. Too many unknowns. He would have to lose him instead.

Aleksei ducked into a narrow alley and searched for anyone who might be watching.

No one.

He took a deep breath and looked upwards, where the two buildings were connected by a small plank walkway. If he could get up there, he would be back at the inn by the time his tracker realized he'd lost his target.

Aleksei inhaled deeply. He was going to have to concentrate, what with Jonas being so far away. The farther they were from one another, the more effort it took for Aleksei to draw on his bond with the Magus.

His nose told him the man was drawing closer. If he was going to get out of there, he had better act fast.

Aleksei pressed himself against the west wall of the alley, then leapt forward. *Shift.* His boots caught the stone of the opposite wall, and he pushed back and up, twisting in the air in time to push off from the west wall again. It took him matter of seconds, but it felt like an eternity of pushing and twisting, of *shifting*, until finally he caught the edge of the walkway and pulled himself up.

He sat on the roof catching his breath, and sought out the scent of his pursuer. The man had gone several hundred paces away from the alley. His scent had changed from determination to desperation. Within moments the scent vanished into the confusion of rain.

Aleksei sighed deeply, resting his head against the low wall at the edge of the roof. His headache had come to a rolling boil.

The fire crackled in the hearth, casting uneven shadows across the room. Jonas sat in his armchair, staring blankly into the flames.

Beside him swayed a stack of heavy volumes, a pen and inkwell atop them. On the floor before him were several pieces of parchment, containing the notes he'd made during his research. The information on those sheets had long since been absorbed. Now it was simply a matter of interpreting it all.

"There's got to be more to this." he muttered to himself, chewing at his lip in frustration. There were a great many pieces missing from the puzzle arrayed before him, yet it seemed beyond his abilities to divine what those pieces could *be*.

A knock came from the door behind him, and Jonas turned irritably, "Come in."

Aya entered, treading softly across the intricate carpets, before taking a seat across from the Prince.

"I'm sorry to bother you so late, Jonas. It's just...I've had a vision."

Jonas arched an eyebrow, "Another one? And what did *this* one include?"

Aya looked up at him with a knowing look in her eyes, "I can't tell you the contents of the vision."

Jonas felt the hair on the back of his neck stand out straight. He understood the implication of her words. Prophets were only allowed to disclose the subject matter of their visions if the person receiving the information was unaffected by it. Her silence meant that Jonas had been in her vision.

"Is this the only vision you've had recently?" he asked after a long moment of silence.

"Yes. It's the first one since I saw the battle in Drava. Why?"

Jonas shrugged, "I don't know, I thought that you might have seen something else. I've been doing research on something I discovered in Drava, and it has me deeply worried. I was hoping you might have seen something in the Archanium relating to it."

Aya shook her head, "I've seen nothing else. Why, what have you discovered?"

Jonas took a deep breath, "When I encountered Emelian Krasik and Bael at the edge of the Relvyn Wood, Bael referred to Krasik as the 'Zra-Uul'. I remembered reading about it *some*where, but I couldn't place it. When I returned from Relvyn, I searched the Vault for the name."

Aya leaned forward, "What did you find?"

Jonas regarded her gravely, "The Zra-Uul is a host for a very specific type of magic. *Kholod* magic." Aya's green-gold eyes widened, but Jonas continued, "I'm still unclear on a great many things, but it seems the *magic* of the Zra-Uul works through some sort of vibration. When the Zra-Uul directs his power into another person, he can see their thoughts. Or, in the case of what I witnessed Krasik do to Bael, he can cause varying levels of pain in the person."

Aya frowned, "This sounds like a constructed magic, and an unusually complicated one at that. Why would the Kholodym *create* such a thing?"

"That's one of the pieces I'm missing." Jonas admitted unhappily.

"Was there any mention of his powers being limited somehow? Any sort of weakness?"

"Not that I could find, no. And it seems that since he can see other people's thoughts, he also possesses the ability to control them. He can alter *perception* in the minds of his victims. I'm not sure exactly what use Emelian Krasik will make of such talents, but considering his history, I think it goes without saying that few people would be more dangerous with such power."

"But how could something like this perpetuate itself for one *thousand* years? I mean, why wasn't the Zra-Uul destroyed during the purge, after the Dominion Wars, along with all the other terrors they created?"

Jonas sighed, "I wish I knew. There were several allusions to the transference of this magic, but none of them made any sense to me. I'm afraid my formal education has been rather lacking in terms of theory."

"Is it possible that more thorough documentation might exist somewhere else?"

Jonas considered a moment, "Not in Ilyar, certainly. The Voralla is by far the oldest structure. The Ri-Vhan are a possibility, I suppose. They have documents dated back to the Dominion Wars, detailing aspects of the Hunter's Mantle.

"But if not them, I would say the only other likely place would be the Basilica in Dalita. The angels keep scrupulous records and histories. If they encountered the Zra-Uul during the War, it would certainly be documented."

"I think we need to find out as much about this as we can." Aya said, "We don't want to assume *anything* about the nature of Krasik's abilities."

"I need to speak with Aleksei first. I don't want to make a move without consulting him." Jonas said, looking back to the other Magus.

Aya shrugged, "As you wish. Is he still in Mornj?"

Jonas nodded, "He hasn't moved in a few days now."

Aya frowned, "I wonder what he's doing down there."

Jonas smiled, "I'm going to find out tonight. I haven't contacted him through dreamspeak in quite a while, but I think it's necessary given the circumstances."

Aya seemed alarmed at the suggestion, "Jonas, do you remember how *difficult* that was for you before? There was a time or two when I wasn't sure you'd wake *up*."

Jonas waved aside her concerns, "I need to know what he's up to, what he's planning. Honestly, it's worth the risk involved. If he's discovered something in Mornj...."

Aya sighed, "But if you don't *survive* the encounter, it won't matter, will it?"

Jonas frowned, "Aya, that was a year ago. I'd like to think that I've managed a *bit* more control over the Archanium in the time since."

"Well, you'd probably better get to it, then. It's getting late, and if you haven't done this in awhile, it might take you longer than expected to find him."

Jonas stifled a yawn, "Very well. Get some sleep yourself, and I'll tell you what I discover in the morning."

She managed a smile, "Good night, Jonas. And tell Aleksei I wish him well."

Once she was gone, Jonas quenched the fire in the hearth, stepping into his bedchamber and pulling off his shirt and boots. He kicked his trousers into a pile in the corner and climbed into bed, waving his hand casually at the door. It shut and locked itself.

He laid down and closed his eyes, breathing deeply, concentrating on their bond. In his mind he saw it as a rope of burning gold disappearing over the horizon and to the south. Jonas took another deep breath and immersed himself in the Archanium.

The world faded away as he began to search for his Knight.

CHAPTER 30

A SOLDIER'S REDEMPTION

ALEKSEI LAY IN his bed, staring up at the ceiling. It had been a long day, and though exhausted, he didn't dare sleep just yet. His head pounded enough to make even the *thought* of sleep seem depressingly hopeless. There were enough tiny details running through his mind that he knew the headache wouldn't be leaving any time soon.

He had but to remember an order he'd given, or wonder about the execution of some such command, and the pain would flare up yet again, like he was putting a fan to a flame.

He was just beginning to wonder how long it would take for the kettles from the kitchens to be patched when a sudden wave of fatigue drowned out his thoughts, concerns, and even the blaring trumpet of the ache in his head. His vision swam, and the ceiling twisted at insane angles before he closed his eyes and succumbed to sleep.

The darkness lasted only moments, and then he was standing in a very familiar room. He looked to his immediate left and saw Jonas sitting in an armchair, his green eyes twinkling merrily.

"There you are." he said.

Aleksei smiled, but his eyes dulled quickly under the returning pain of his headache, "It's been a long time since you've used our bond like this."

Jonas sighed, "I know, and I apologize. I know how this can tire you, but I'm afraid it's rather urgent."

"I'd a feeling it would be."

The Magus frowned, "What's wrong?"

Aleksei waved a hand dismissively as he sank into the chair opposite the prince, "I just have a headache, that's all. I've got a lot going on down here."

"What do you mean?"

"I had to excuse the commanding officer of the garrison. It seems no one's paid much attention this far south in quite a while. The man was a bare step above a criminal. I've spent the last several days trying to regain some semblance of order."

"How's it coming?"

"Better than you might think. The men in Mornj are eager to follow orders and turn this place back into a respectable operation. It just takes time."

Jonas nodded his understanding, "Have you sent troops to Drava yet?"

"Yesterday. I haven't seen Ilyana or Marrik yet, and I'm hoping that they'll encounter the troops on their way here and turn around. At the pace my men were planning to set, I think lumber production should resume in the next two or three weeks."

"Did you figure out *why* your orders were being ignored?" Jonas asked.

Aleksei's face darkened, "As a matter of fact I did. It seems—"

He was in mid-sentence when Jonas' bedchamber melted away. His eyes snapped open, staring once again at the ceiling. The Mantle was writhing across his shoulders in agitation. Aleksei sat up.

There was someone else in the room.

His eyes adjusted rapidly to the darkness. He could make out the figure standing by the door. Whoever it was had obviously expected Aleksei to be asleep. The shadow stood there uncertainly for a moment, then began to creep forward.

"Who's there?" Aleksei demanded.

In response, a gout of flame rushed towards him.

Aleksei dove forward, tangling himself in his blankets as he did so. He felt the heat from the fire as it rushed above his head, setting his mattress ablaze.

He twisted savagely to free himself from the wool blanket, then leapt to his feet and saw the Magus turning towards him. He rolled to the side as a thunderbolt blasted the air where he'd been standing. Aleksei landed on his hands, then pushed himself back to his feet and ran towards the door. His sword was with his shirt on the other side of the room, and he doubted he could keep dodging the Magus long enough to get it.

Instead he threw himself out into the hall and raced towards the stairway leading down to the street. He could feel the Magus mere paces behind him. There was a rush of fire, but Aleksei managed to turn down another hall a moment before it reached him.

He realized as he ran that the men who had been standing guard were dead, lying limp in the hallway. Whoever was pursuing him had wasted no effort on stealth.

Aleksei burst through the main door of the garrison and out into the cool night air. He glanced from right to left, then sprinted up the hill and towards the market. If he could lose the Magus in the sprawl of the city, he might be able to hunt the man and take him by surprise. But first he had to escape.

He rounded a corner and darted into an alleyway. As he ran, he searched the air for the man's scent. It came to him heavy and strong. The Magus was very close.

He was so consumed with the proximity of the Magus that he didn't see the body until it was too late. Aleksei's foot caught on the corpse, and he was thrown to the street. The hard cobble of the alley split his right knee and he inhaled sharply. He rolled onto his back and started as he caught sight of the dead man he'd tripped over.

It was Colonel Balwick.

His throat had been cut savagely, and one eye was missing. Aleksei gritted his teeth. If he allowed himself the luxury of time right then, the Magus would have him.

He forced himself to his feet. His right leg refused to support his weight, but still he tried to lunge forward. He *had* to get away. If the Magus managed to kill him, he would kill Jonas in the same instant. Aleksei could *not* allow that to happen.

The Magus appeared in the alleyway, and Aleksei bit back a curse. Instead, he reached back to Balwick's corpse and groped at the man's belt. His hands found a knife and he pulled it free. The balance was poor, but Aleksei thought it would do the job.

"Enough running, Lord Captain." the Magus said coolly. "I'll try to make this quick. My apologies to the Prince."

Aleksei didn't respond, hefting the knife and praying to the gods that his aim would be true. He felt the hair on the back of his neck stand on end as the Magus summoned the Archanium around him.

Time slowed.

Aleksei brought his hand back to hurl the knife, even as the air began to spark with the power of conjured lightning.

And then everything *shifted*.

The light that was gathering around the Magus vanished. At the same moment the man lurched a pace off the ground. Aleksei watched it all through confused eyes, his exhausted mind not comprehending the events unfolding before him. The Magus flew to the right and struck the wall. His body crumpled to the ground.

A man was standing over the still form of the Magus. He stepped back, drawing a sword with him that glittered crimson in the lamplight from the street. In the dim light, Aleksei's eyes widened in surprise.

"Rysun?"

The Major swiftly wiped his sword on the body of the Magus, then rushed to Aleksei's side, "Lord Captain, are you alright?"

"I'm *alive*, Major. But my leg's a bloody mess."

Rysun slipped himself under Aleksei's right arm and lifted the Knight from the cobbles, "We need to get you to the infirmary so they can set that knee. You don't want that to heal wrong."

Aleksei tried to nod his agreement, but found himself

overwhelmed by his weariness. He tried to thank Rysun, but was unconscious before he had the chance.

Ilyana hurried through the halls of the garrison, Marrik a pace behind her.

They had arrived in Mornj only an hour before. Upon hearing that Aleksei was at the garrison, they'd made their way there as fast as possible, only to be informed that he was in his quarters recovering from an attack.

She stopped as a healer turned the corner and started at seeing a Magus and her Knight appear so unexpectedly. "Can I help you?" the woman asked.

"I'm looking for Lord Captain Drago." Ilyana said breathlessly.

"He's in his room, the one with the large iron-bound door on the right side of the hall. But please, if he's sleeping, *don't* wake him. He needs his strength."

Ilyana thanked the woman, moving down the hall with a touch more grace, knocking once on the door before pushing it open.

Aleksei sat in his bed, his legs covered by a quilt. Maps and papers were scattered across his lap. He looked up irritably when the door opened, but a smile overtook his scowl when he saw her.

"I was wondering when you'd arrive."

Ilyana smiled warmly, "We met your soldiers about halfway here, and they said they'd escort the villagers back to Drava. Their commander said you were still in Mornj getting things straightened out, so we thought we'd come lend a hand."

Aleksei nodded thoughtfully, "I can use the help, I assure you."

"What happened?"

Aleksei's face darkened, "I was attacked by a Magus. One steeped in the Nagavor. He nearly killed me, but Major Rysun managed to sneak up on him from behind. If he hadn't been there...." He let the silence hang. "When I was running, I tripped and split my knee. I can't walk very well at present, and I've been told to limit my movement as much as possible."

"Can you ride?"

He sighed, "Fortunately, I'm allowed to do *that* much. I was actually about to leave the garrison to Rysun and head back to

Kalinor. I'm just about finished here, but I didn't want to travel north alone. If you and Marrik aren't too tired from your journey here, we can leave tomorrow."

Ilyana glanced back to her Knight, who nodded his assent. She turned to Aleksei, "If we can get a meal and a good night's sleep, we can be ready at dawn."

Aleksei smiled, "Good. Why don't you go down to the barracks and let the corporal assign you your rooms. The healers gave me a sleeping draught, so I'm afraid I won't be very good company in a few moments."

Ilyana chuckled, "Alright, you get some sleep. We'll see you in the morning."

She turned to go and Marrik stepped forward, giving Aleksei a squeeze on the shoulder and a nod.

Aleksei smiled at his friend, "Get some rest, Marrik."

When they had gone, Aleksei rested his head back on the pillow and closed his eyes. He took a deep breath, and when he opened them, he found the early light of dawn filtering through his window.

His headache had abated a bit, though the sleeping potion left him feeling disoriented. Aleksei wondered if the potion had kept Jonas from contacting him through his dreams. It seemed odd that he wouldn't have heard from his Magus in the two days since their communication had been interrupted.

The doors of his chamber opened, and Ilyana looked in tentatively. "You're awake." she said, sounding somewhat surprised.

Aleksei nodded, leaning forward and pulling the sheet away. His right leg was splinted and bound. He pulled himself to the edge of the bed and reached for his shirt on the bedpost.

Ilyana collected his few personal possessions and pushed them into his canvas pack, hoisting it onto her shoulder before handing him the wooden crutch the healers insisted he use.

"Is there anything you need to do before we leave? Anyone you need to see?" Ilyana asked, helping him to his feet.

Aleksei shook his head, "I've prepared a letter for Major Rysun, along with instructions for the running of the garrison. Things should be alright here, at least for a while."

With Ilyana's help he made his way out into the hall and down to the stable yard. Marrik had to bodily lift him onto Dash's back, but once he was up, he had no trouble keeping his balance or controlling the horse.

Once again, he thanked the gods he was riding Dash, rather than Agriphon. The warhorse was impressive, but young and impulsive. It would have required his full range of mobility to ride the stallion, whereas Dash was more than used to his handling.

They were headed out of the stable yard when the doors burst open and Rysun hurried out into the morning light.

"Lord Captain Drago!" he called. "Lord Captain, where are you *going*?"

Aleksei pulled Dash to a halt and turned to address the Major, "I need to return to Kalinor, Major. There are some...issues there that require my immediate attention. I'm leaving you in command."

Rysun looked confused, "Lord Captain?"

Aleksei smiled at the man's bewilderment, "I can't be here to watch over things all the time, Major." He leaned forward and grasped the man's arm, "You're a good man, Fredrick. Do as you've been trained, and you'll have few troubles. You saved my life, and for that *alone* you have earned not only my confidence, but my thanks."

Rysun seemed surprised, but he nodded.

Aleksei straightened in his saddle, "Take care, *Colonel* Rysun."

Rysun tried to hide his glee under a smart salute. Aleksei returned the gesture, then turned Dash and rode out of the yard.

Upon reaching the street, Aleksei realized that Marrik had arranged for an escort to take them to the edge of town, so he wouldn't be too jostled trying to maneuver around carts and other riders. While he hated feeling helpless, Aleksei was thankful that their trip to the city walls was smooth and uneventful.

The day wearied on, the sky growing dark with clouds only five leagues outside of Mornj. They had gone but a few leagues more before the rain returned.

Ilyana rode up next to him, her face etched with concern, "Should we pull to the roadside till the rain clears?"

"Where were you planning to take shelter?" He swept his arm to indicate the land around them, "We're in the Southern Plain now.

There will be some live oak, perhaps, but nothing that you Northerners would call a proper 'tree'. In any event, we don't have *time* to stop. It might rain for one hour, or five. I have no interest in giving up so much distance on the basis of an inconvenience."

Ilyana's face darkened, "I am concerned for your *health*, Aleksei. It isn't good for someone in your condition to be exposed like this."

Aleksei raised the hood of his travel cloak, "If we stop now, here, by the end of this shower, the roads will be all but impassible. We'd have to cut cross-country. I know this land better than either of you, so I would be the one scouting the land to find a route for us. I hardly see how that's better than riding a few leagues in the rain."

The Magus tried to keep her sigh to herself. Surely, she thought, it wasn't surprising that Aleksei was just as stubborn as Jonas. The two men were as close as any Knight and Magus, and part of it must be that they shared certain similarities of character.

The small party rode on for several hours in silence. The rain lifted around mid-afternoon, but it remained overcast until the sky darkened into evening.

They made camp under a strand of live oak, finding the earth firmer there than in the surrounding countryside.

Ilyana used brushes of flame to dry and warm the ground, and they spread their bedrolls atop as many dry oak leaves as they could find. It was far from comfortable.

"I'll take first watch." Aleksei said after dinner was done with.

Marrik shared a dark look with his Magus, "Aleksei, you need your rest."

Aleksei returned the Knight's stern glare, "Which is exactly why I'll be taking first watch, so that I am neither woken too early, nor is my sleep interrupted."

The other two shared an unhappy look. It was not a tone of voice Aleksei often used, certainly not with his friends, but they recognized it for what it was. This was not their friend speaking, but their Lord Captain.

Aleksei watched them ready for bed, then waited patiently until they were asleep before climbing out of his bedroll. Using his crutch to gain his footing, he spared one glance towards his companions. When he was satisfied that they were sleeping soundly, he limped out of the camp.

He wasn't quite sure how far he'd have to go; that much wasn't clear to him. As he limped, he fought the urge to scratch at the Mantle. It was all he could do not to stop completely and indulge himself.

Aleksei had traveled perhaps a hundred paces when he heard a low, guttural growl.

He stopped and turned to face the cougar sitting behind him.

The itching flared until it was practically unbearable. Aleksei gritted his teeth as the cougar rose, and walked gracefully towards him.

The Knight dropped to his good knee and reached out his hand, feeling the Mantle swell with fire and anticipation.

The cat was but a pace from him when there was an explosion of flame between them. The cougar snarled and darted away into the darkness. Aleksei coughed with surprise as the burning itch of the Mantle flared to a brilliant crescendo, before settling back into inky oblivion.

Ilyana was at his side a minute later, "Aleksei! Are you alright? I woke and you were gone, but Marrik's the one who heard the cat. Did it attack you? Show me where you're hurt."

Aleksei came to his feet crossly, leaning heavily upon his crutch, "I'm *fine*, Ilyana. It didn't attack me. It was...." He stopped himself, taking a deep breath. How did he explain that the cat had been trying to *help* him?

He shook his head, hobbling back towards the camp, where Marrik was waiting with his bow drawn.

"It didn't attack me." he muttered.

Ilyana stared after the Hunter, utterly at a loss.

Chapter 31

Restorations

By the time Kalinor came into view two weeks later, Aleksei felt as though the skin across his back was on fire. It had supplanted even his grinding headache and the throb in his knee as the primary source of pain in his life, yet there was nothing he could do but grit his teeth and bear it, just like everything else.

The fire in his knee hardly seemed more than a tickle in comparison, and while he hadn't broached the matter with Ilyana, he doubted there was much she could have done for him in any event. The Mantle seemed to be little connected with the Archanium, if at all.

But stranger still were the thoughts that had plagued his dreams the last several nights. While he still waited for any communication from Jonas, other, darker thoughts pervaded his sleep. Images of blood-red eyes. The sound of a man's scream.

They seemed at once wholly incomprehensible and perfectly lucid. He hoped that Jonas would know what to make of it all.

They rode under Kalinor's great white walls, and Aleksei felt himself relax. He'd come to find something deeply comforting about being enclosed within those walls, a feeling of security he'd only known before in the upper branches of the Seil Wood.

The Palace Lawn was bustling with activity from the city. Aleksei rode with his friends only as a far as the Voralla before setting off towards the Palace stables. He had many things to take care of, and he didn't want to waste any more time with pleasantries than he had to.

Master Collins seemed pleased to see Aleksei return. "Lord Captain, I'm so relieved to see you back home." the man said, bowing deeply. "Your disappearance caused *quite* a stir around here, I must say."

Aleksei smiled warmly at the older man, ignoring the other's surprise as he gingerly dismounted onto his good leg and withdrew his crutch from behind his saddle. "I hope no one was too put out by my departure, Master Collins."

The man shook his head, "Not in the least, Lord Captain. We only hoped everything was well."

"Thank you for your concern, Master Collins. I hope to make it all the better momentarily."

He began to move towards the Palace, leaving the groom to scratch his head at the oddity of his reply.

As much as Aleksei had been able to put his anger out of his mind during his stay in Mornj and the subsequent journey north, seeing the Palace itself revitalized his ire with a vengeance.

He worked his way through the brightly lit corridors with a slow, methodical pace, keeping his objective at the forefront of his mind as he moved.

Servants passed him, regarding him quizzically as he hobbled by. A few offered aid, but he refused them. Some of the Guardsmen also offered their assistance, and Aleksei could see in their eyes that they were pained to see him like this. While he appreciated their sympathy, he had no need of their pity.

When he reached the door he sought, Aleksei was pleased to see light coming from under the door. Hugo Malak was home. Aleksei would have been greatly angered to find Lord Malak at his country estate after he'd come all this way north for the express purpose of dealing with the man.

Aleksei considered knocking, but decided against it. He did, however, pull his knife and cut away the splint from his leg. After a moment of consideration, he decided that this was as good as it was going to get.

And while he doubted it would be as impressive an entrance as it might have been were he in full command of his legs, Aleksei was quite sure that a lord of such importance and wealth as Hugo Malak would be most surprised to find *anyone*, even the Lord Captain, come into his rooms unannounced.

The door swung open, and Aleksei limped inside.

Malak sat at his desk, an unread document held in his hand as he stared at Aleksei's advancing figure. He was within five paces when Malak finally found his voice.

"Lord Captain Drago, what is the *meaning* of this?"

Aleksei reached the edge of the desk and used it to support himself, dropping the crutch off to the side.

"I've been hearing some *very* unpleasant things about you, Your Grace."

Malak was unimpressed, "I haven't any idea what you're talking about, Lord Captain." His lip curled in a sneer, "Perhaps you hit your *head* when you injured your leg."

Aleksei bit back his own mounting rage, "You've committed high treason, Malak. I have a confession from your underling, delivered to me directly. I have *seen* the results of your treachery with my own eyes.

"You are answerable to our Queen, to the people of the realm, for your actions."

Malak stood, "I will not allow for such wanton *slander*, Captain. Now if you'll excuse me, I have matters which require my attention." He stepped around his desk and walked swiftly towards the door. Aleksei turned and grasped the man's shoulder as he passed.

Malak froze.

Aleksei breathed deeply, golden eyes glittering. "You are answerable to *me*."

It happened too quickly for Aleksei to register.

The Mantle surged to life across his back and coursed down his arm, lightening as it extended until it pulsed a brilliant scarlet. The beseeching claws reached Aleksei's wrist and lifted away from his arm in thin, needle-like talons.

Malak opened his mouth to scream as the talons sank into his shoulder, filling the room with the odor of burning flesh. Malak gasped for breath, but each choking sob was weaker than the last. The tendrils pulsed and thickened as the moment dragged.

Aleksei felt life flow into him as the burning across his shoulders subsided, and his headache vanished. He glared at Malak. The Lord stared back in horror.

And then it was over.

Malak collapsed to the floor, lifeless.

Drained.

Aleksei stood above him, breathing deeply, feeling wholly restored.

It took him a moment to realize that his leg had mended. He glanced down at his hands, noting with some surprise that a scar he'd received as a boy was also gone.

He dropped into a crouch and touched his fingers to Malak's neck. The man was dead. Beyond dead, he was already *cold*.

A scream rent the air, and Aleksei regained his senses. He looked up just in time to catch sight of a fleeing servant girl. He ran his hands through his hair as reality washed across him.

He had just murdered one of the most important members of Parliament. A *traitorous* one, but one that had never been brought before any court. Worse yet, the kill had been witnessed.

"I've got to get out of here." he muttered, standing and glancing towards the door.

If he tried to leave that way, his own men would catch him. Or at least they would *try* to. In either event, Aleksei didn't want to force them to take any sort of decisive action. He certainly didn't want to hurt them.

Instead he ran to the window, preparing to pull it open. He wasn't yet so high that he couldn't either drop to the ground or perhaps find a way onto the roof. But as his hand found the latch, he caught sight of himself in the glass.

His heart staggered. The same vision from his dream, the same intense blood-red eyes, stared back at him.

Aleksei threw the window open and stepped out onto the ledge, trying to drive the image from his mind. Was he becoming a monster?

On some level, he knew he should feel remorse, or pity, *something* for Malak. He'd never meant to *kill* the man, certainly. But instead, he found only a cool sense that justice had been served.

His foot slipped on the ledge, and Aleksei focused upon the task at hand. There would be plenty of time for him to think about it once he got out of Kalinor. And for all that he'd wanted to reach the Palace from the moment he'd left Drava, he now found it to be the last place he wished to be.

Aleksei reached a drainage gutter and grasped it with his hands, lowering himself over the edge of the ledge and dangling several paces off the ground.

He took a deep breath and let go, falling out of time. He twisted as he fell, watching the hard ground rise swiftly to meet him. A pace above the ground his boots contacted the wall and he thrust outward, propelling himself into a dive roll.

The impact still knocked the wind from him, but Aleksei knew it wasn't half as bad as it could have been. He rolled to his feet and brushed the grass from his shirt.

After a cursory inspection of the West Lawn, Aleksei dropped into a lope towards the stables. If he was fast enough, the groom wouldn't have had a chance to send his things to his room.

He found the stable quiet, with only Master Collins and a few stable-boys brushing down the horses for the night. Master Collins gaped when he saw Aleksei running towards him, and the Knight reflected that it must be a disconcerting sight to see the same man hobble away on a crutch not half an hour ago, and return running easily.

"Master Collins, saddle Agriphon would you?"

The groom stared for a moment, then nodded, "As you command, Lord Captain. I've already had your things sent off. Would you like one of the boys to fetch them?"

Aleksei nodded, digging in his pocket and flipping a boy a silver mark, "Another one for you if you're back in five minutes."

The boy took off at a full sprint, and Aleksei followed Master Collins into the stable. "I have to leave again, this time for what might be quite a while." Aleksei confined his voice to a whisper as he spoke, "If anyone comes here and questions you, tell them the truth. I demanded my horse be saddled and said no more. I don't want any trouble for you."

Collins smiled kindly, "Thank you for your concern, Lord Captain, but my boys and I can take care of ourselves. Are there any messages you need delivered while you're absent?"

Aleksei considered, then nodded, "If the Queen comes by, tell her that I'm sorry. I would never do anything to put her in a difficult situation, but some things can't be helped. For anything more, she'll have to speak with the Prince."

Master Collins nodded, "As you say, Lord Captain. Ah, here is Geoff with your things."

Aleksei turned and took the saddlebags and bedroll from the boy, handing him a second silver in return. He turned and transferred the contents to the bags of Agriphon's handsome black saddle. A moment later he swung onto the stallion's back and reached down, shaking Master Collins' hand firmly.

"Your loyalty is appreciated more than I can say."

Master Collins nodded in silent response, and Aleksei booted his warhorse out of the stables and onto the road that led into the city. He was on High Street in a matter of minutes, and at the outer gate by the time the alarm bells began to ring.

"Better get a move-on, Lord Captain," muttered the guard at the gate. "They'll be making us shut down any moment. Wouldn't want you to be delayed any more than necessary."

Aleksei smiled, "Thank you, Worthing. Have a pleasant evening."

"And yourself, Lord Captain."

Aleksei rode at a brisk canter out onto the road, waiting until the gates had shut completely before he urged Agriphon into a full gallop. South, towards freedom.

And home.

Sammul glowered at the man standing before him. After a moment, he turned and walked over to the fire, warming his hands as he thought. Most perplexing indeed. And more than perplexing, it was highly *irritating*.

He hated mysteries.

"Surely there's a logical explanation." Perron was saying, dry-washing his hands and looking hopefully at the Magus.

Sammul sneered at the man, "Logical explanation?"

Perron nodded hopefully, "Murders of this sort just don't spring out of thin air, Sammul. They have to have motive, and more importantly, *means*. And at the moment, there *are* no means. In fact, there's nothing beyond the addled tale from a scullery maid you brought forth. *You* touch the Archanium, surely her description made some sense to you!"

The High Magus fought back an angry growl. The girl's bizarre story failed to induce any recognition in him. Everyone was looking to him and his Magi to solve a crime he couldn't even *fathom*.

No mark, no signs of struggle or force, and most importantly, no *blood*. Not only was there no blood to be found around Hugo Malak's body, there was no blood to be found *within* his body. It was as though he'd been drained dry. Yet no puncture wounds had been discovered, nor bruising of any kind.

Worse, there were no traces of the Archanium anywhere near the room. However Malak had been murdered, it had not been through any methods Sammul understood.

"My knowledge of the Archanium will do us no good here, Perron. The murderer did not use any form of magic I can divine."

Perron stared at him, "But surely that's impossible. Perhaps it's just a form you're not familiar with."

Sammul delivered the other man a dangerous look, "There is *no* form the Archanium may take that is beyond my sight. I can see its echoes in the voices of angels and in the incantations of warlocks. The nature of the user is of little consequence; the shadows of power leave traces all the same. But I tell you again, this crime was *not* performed with any aid of the Archanium."

Perron growled, "But if Drago did it, a death by use of the Archanium would naturally point to the Prince as an accomplice."

Sammul shook his head, "Which would be quite remarkable since the Prince departed for Dalita several days ago."

Perron shrugged, "It doesn't seem all *that* farfetched to me. Drago disappeared over a week ago, but there are reports of people having seen him in the Palace today, until shortly after Malak's death."

There was a knock at the door, and Sammul sighed in irritation, "Come."

A young errand boy stepped in and bowed to the two men, "Message for Chancellor Perron."

Perron accepted the parchment from the boy. As he skimmed the page a smile broke across his face.

"What is it?" Sammul asked, trying not to sound eager.

Perron glanced up, "It's a response to an inquiry I made at the South Gate of the city. The lieutenant in charge of the gate says that the Lord Captain exited through the South Gate just as the alarm was sounded.

"Now forgive me, Sammul, but it seems the means by which he murdered Malak are rather besides the point. How suspicious does it appear for the Lord Captain to appear seemingly out of thin air, stay only long enough for the murder, and then leave moments after?"

Sammul shook his head, "You may press all you wish, Perron, but the Queen would not accept his guilt were she to have witnessed the murder *herself*. Need I remind you that, above having a sterling record of service since his promotion, Lord Captain Drago is also the Prince's Bonded. That means that any action taken against the Lord Captain must in turn be taken against the Prince.

"Therefore, an execution is most obviously out of the question, as it would be the same as executing the Prince. And as much as you may wish for such a serendipitous event, it will not come to pass. Not while Andariana Belgi sits the throne, at least."

Perron smiled, "Then perhaps it's time we changed that."

Sammul arched an eyebrow, "Are you strong enough to make such a move?"

Perron shrugged, "We have strength enough. Malak ensured that the garrison in Mornj is not prepared to handle any effective uprising, and members of Parliament inclined to agree with our...grievances have been assembling militias, sending members of their personal armies to their provinces for months. We should have a sizable force assembled by now. Certainly large enough to overpower the Legionnaires in Mornj. After that, there really isn't another outpost until Keiv-Alon, and their garrison has a mere fifteen thousand. No, if nothing else, Hugo's death gives us the opportune moment to make our stand."

Sammul forced his face to become grave. It would not do to appear celebratory; he wasn't prepared to give Perron such insight into his own thoughts.

Before he could respond, another knock came at the door. "Come!" he barked.

It was another messenger.

"High Magus, the Queen demands your presence immediately."

Sammul sighed, "I'll be with her shortly."

The messenger saluted and hurried off.

Perron stepped forward and grasped Sammul's arm, "Now not a *word* of this to the Queen!"

Sammul regarded the man contemptuously, "You forget your place, Lord Perron. I'll try to make this brief." He stopped at the door and glanced back, "Try not to piss yourself from excitement."

He walked swiftly down the hall, becoming more and more aggravated with every step. The very *nerve* of sending for him. He was no lapdog. Then again, perhaps it was better she had not come herself. He would not have enjoyed explaining Lord Perron's presence in his office. No, for the moment he couldn't afford to be associated too closely with the man.

The doors to the Queen's chambers opened as he approached. Andariana did not get out of her armchair as he entered, she merely nodded at him in acknowledgement.

"Good evening, High Magus." She looked upset, though he sincerely doubted it had anything to do with Malak's death.

He bowed deeply, "Majesty."

"I would speak with you about Lord Malak."

"Indeed, Majesty. It is a great loss to the realm."

Andariana fixed him with a level glare, "While your words are most...*appropriate*, I have little interest in sentimentality at the moment. Rather, I am curious to know whether you have any light to shed on the subject."

"Majesty?"

She smiled, "Come now, Sammul, *surely* you know what I'm

asking you. I have had Legionnaires, physicians, and chemists paraded through here, and not a one of them can explain what occurred here this evening. It rather reminds me of Lord Bazin and Lord Captain Lenox's murders last year.

"I was hoping that someone of your position might be able to answer a few questions that seem to be rather mysterious in nature."

Sammul sighed. He didn't have to feign confusion on this particular subject, "I have inspected the area in question, as well as Lord Malak's body. There were no traces of the Archanium in either. I can honestly say, Majesty, that I don't have the faintest clue of what transpired between the Lord Captain and Lord Malak."

"I never *mentioned* the Lord Captain, Sammul."

Sammul cursed himself, "But surely you know, Majesty, that rumors are all over the Palace now. One must be suspicious at the nature of the Lord Captain's short visit."

"Indeed, High Magus, yet I'm sure you can understand my reluctance at accusing the commander of my armed forces of murder when we have yet to determine the actual cause of death. Is it not possible that Malak died of some common malady?"

Sammul arched an eyebrow, "His body was found drained of blood. And besides, Malak was not much past thirty summers, and not in bad physical condition. No, Majesty, I firmly believe that only murder could have transpired here tonight."

Andariana considered a moment. "You are, of course, aware of the implications in accusing Lord Captain Drago?"

Sammul nodded, "Some had occurred to me, Majesty."

"Then what would you propose we do?"

"Well, if nothing else, I believe the good Lord Captain should be present for any proceedings that follow. His sudden absence only appears the more suspicious."

"And if he went to join my nephew?" Andariana asked.

"The addition of the Prince's support could only help the Lord Captain, Majesty."

Andariana regarded him crossly, "Don't feign ignorance, Sammul. You know the Prince is presently in a *very* fragile situation. It may be that Drago's presence is required for the success of the Prince's journey."

Sammul bit back a laugh, "Majesty, the Prince is far more savvy than the *Lord Captain*. I doubt the addition of Drago's presence will make that much of a difference to anyone."

Andariana sighed, "Perhaps you're right. Jonas does seem to handle things admirably on his own. Very well, Sammul. Issue a summons for Lord Captain Drago. Have it sent to every major city in Ilyar, just in case he might be headed in a different direction than we first perceived."

"What of Dalita?" Sammul asked.

Andariana chortled, "Oh, *imagine* the day Kevara Avlon would allow me to send a military unit within a hundred leagues of the Dalitian border. *That's* a laugh.

"If Drago is guilty, I *hope* he's running north. The angels will harbor him against any indictment Parliament levels. I need hardly remind you, High Magus, of how little love was lost when my younger sister disappeared, rather than be brought to trial by the Angelus."

Sammul shook his head, feigning regret, "Joel's death was a greater evil than we could have imagined."

He watched Andariana, noting the way her face fell at the thought of her sister. She loved Rhiannon dearly, and had searched for her tirelessly during the first decade after her disappearance. But there came a time when one had to let go. And Andariana Belgi had mastered that art long ago.

"You are dismissed, High Magus." she said quietly.

CHAPTER 32

HOMECOMING

ALEKSEI FOUGHT TO keep his eyes open. He felt as though he'd been riding for an age, and while Agriphon was still full of energy from being stabled so long, his rider desired something in vigor.

The only thing that kept him in the saddle was the knowledge that the Guard would soon be after him. He had to gain as much distance between himself and Kalinor as possible before they began searching.

At first he had thought it best to go directly to Seil Wood. But while he had hoped the Wood might take him nearer to his father's farm by the same magical means She had employed to send him to Drava, it wasn't worth bringing the ire of Ilyar down on the Wood for his own selfish purposes.

He would never do that to the Wood, to Roux. He would *not* pull the Ri-Vhan into this. The knowledge that they would have aided him unconditionally was enough for him.

Instead, Aleksei made his way south, alone. After all, they would probably expect him to head north, where he could feel Jonas like the heat from a flickering candle, and where he might find sanctuary among the angels.

But no, there was only one place he could, in good conscience, seek aid. It also happened to be the *last* place anyone might think to look for him.

In the year he'd been in Kalinor, he'd not once had the opportunity to visit his father. They wrote each other, of course, and Aleksei sent money as often as he could. But in all honesty, he'd had little time for such a long trip.

It pained him greatly that the first time he could make it down was not as the Lord Captain of Her Majesty's Legion, but as a murderer and a fugitive.

As he rode, Aleksei recalled the last time he had traveled to his farm. It had been at the height of confusion for him, as he'd made it to Kalinor in only a few days, rather than weeks. He'd just rescued Tamara from an assassination attempt, and he remembered clearly the radiant pride on his father's face.

What would Henry say now? Aleksei needed to hide for a while, until he heard from Jonas, and he *knew* what was awaiting him back in Kalinor. Once Jonas was made aware of everything that had transpired, it would be easier to settle upon a more permanent course of action.

The farther south he traveled, the more his thoughts consumed him. He passed farming communities, fearful that his presence might bring danger to them. He avoided the villages, preferring to camp in the wilderness, rather than leave an obvious trail.

But when he reached the walls of Keiv-Alon, he realized that sooner or later he would have to venture back into civilization. His rations were running low, and this close to the edge of winter, it would be difficult to find food enough to live off the land.

He needed supplies, and this was likely the last decent market he would find before Voskrin, some two hundred leagues south.

Still, he thought, *better a large city to blend into than a small village. Less likely to be noticed.*

With that idea firmly fixed in his mind, Aleksei rode down the hill into the valley dominated by the great city.

At first he feared detection at the gates, but found that the guards were no more interested in a lone traveler on an expensive horse than they were in the cart of turnips in front of him. He rode through without incident, and considered dismounting to lead Agriphon through the street. But as he glanced about, Aleksei saw how many Legionnaires there were. If he was spotted, his best chance would be on horseback.

He rode cautiously towards Market Street, keeping a careful eye for anyone who might be looking for him. While he doubted the word of Malak's murder could have traveled so far so fast, much less word of who was responsible, Aleksei was taking no chances that he might be traced.

The market had most of the things he sought, and in the matter of an hour he was done.

His saddlebags heavy with provisions, Aleksei turned Agriphon towards the south gate. He passed out of Market Street, and was about to turn onto South Street when something caught his eye.

Aleksei pulled Agriphon towards the wall of a small grocery, his attention riveted to the poster that was nailed there.

Wanted for the foul Murder of
Lord Hugo Malak of Relvyn:
The Lord Captain Aleksei Drago
Sought Dead or Alive – Handsome Reward for
Apprehension or Whereabouts

Signed in the name of Her Majesty Andariana Belgi
and under the ultimate authority of the
High Chancellor Bertrand Perron

His blood ran cold. They knew. That much was not so surprising, he supposed. But that he was wanted *dead or alive?* Wasn't that a little premature? He was more than surprised that Andariana would have authorized such a proclamation, as his death would forfeit Jonas' life as well.

Unless she doesn't even know about it, he thought to himself.

He looked again at the signature, and his suspicions were confirmed. If this was a missive from Perron, it was hardly surprising that he was seeking Aleksei's head.

Aleksei knew Perron and Malak had been friends, certainly. And as eliminating him would also remove Jonas from the equation, it only further served Perron's agenda.

Fortunately there was no description of him, and unless he paraded himself about town as the Lord Captain, there was no reason for anyone to suspect him.

No one in Keiv-Alon knew what he looked like. Outside of Voskrin, Kalinor, or the Wood, he was a perfect stranger to every person who saw him.

He turned Agriphon back towards the south gate, waiting impatiently for the guards to clear him before booting his stallion into a full out gallop. Gods, the sooner he got to the farm, the better.

Two more days passed under the constant threat of rain, but on the third day the sky cleared and, for the first time in what felt like years, Aleksei felt his self-possession return. His mind finally lifted from his own situation long enough to wonder about Jonas.

Where *was* he? Aleksei could feel him to the north, but at such a distance it was impossible to be much more accurate. As his sense of desperation faded, he was suddenly keenly aware of the gnawing loneliness in the pit of his stomach. A loneliness only Jonas could satiate.

Aleksei wondered if Jonas was even in *Ilyar*. Even in the brief period he'd spent in Kalinor, Jonas had seemed to be hundreds of leagues to the north.

Aleksei frowned at that thought. He didn't like the idea of Jonas going into strange territory, even if it was a nation tied to Ilyar by truce. He *especially* didn't like the idea of Jonas venturing there *alone*. He knew his prince was more than competent, but there was always the threat that something might escape his notice.

Such thoughts clouded his mind for several days, until finally even worries for his Magus were driven from his head. He crested a hill and found himself staring down upon a depressingly familiar sight.

Voskrin.

He took a deep breath and rode down the main road, forcing a smile as he noted how the familiar houses of his friends hadn't changed in the least. He wondered if any of them had left the village since he'd been gone, though he doubted it. *No one left the village, unless they absolutely had to.*

As he rode into town, an older woman stumbled on the path and fell in front of Agriphon. Aleksei immediately pulled the horse up short and vaulted out of his saddle. He reached the woman in a heartbeat, helping her to her feet.

"I'm *terribly* sorry, ma'am. Are you alright?"

She looked up with a kindly smile, and Aleksei blinked in surprise.

"Why, Aleksei Drago." she said with a laugh, "Mokosh be praised. What *are* you doing back in Voskrin?"

"Mother Margareta?" he asked in disbelief. "I...I've come to see Da."

She nodded knowingly as he helped her to her feet, "Ah yes. Henry has spoken of little else than your letters, you know."

"Has he?" Aleksei asked with an unconscious smile. "Surely there's more to talk about down here than my ramblings from Kalinor."

Mother Margareta snorted, "Hardly. But where *are* my manners? Do come in. Come in and have some tea."

"It's most kind of you to offer, Mother, but I...."

She arched an eyebrow, then turned and started walking slowly towards her house, whistling a tuneless song as she went.

Aleksei sighed, unable to suppress the smile the old woman always brought out in him, and led Agriphon behind her. No matter how high he rose in the rest of the world, Aleksei supposed he would always have to mind the word of Mother Margareta.

And somehow, that comforted him greatly.

He tied his horse up outside, stepping into her cramped little home and taking a seat at her table. She bustled about her tiny kitchen, humming to herself as she put the kettle on.

"So tell me, Aleksei, what else brings you down south?"

He frowned, "I beg your pardon?"

She turned to him, hands on her hips, "Oh, *come* now, boy. You haven't returned in a year, and you expect me to believe that you rode over six *hundred* leagues on a horse worth more than Henry's farm for a friendly *'hello'*? Let's not patronize one another, sweetheart."

Aleksei found it was all he could do not to stare at her. Could this *possibly* be the same well-meaning priestess who brought them cider pie every Festival, and prattled on about her little dogs for hours when she walked over to the farm to bless their fields? He had never thought her particularly frank.

"You know, dear, I was made Town Elder at last year's Festival. Yes, yes old Viktor Blok finally kicked off, so as the oldest person in town, I guess that made me a shoe-in." She chuckled to herself. "*Age* doesn't always mean wisdom, I'm afraid, but I do my best."

Aleksei smiled, "I think you're a perfect choice, Mother."

"That's kind of you, dear. But please, *do* call me Margaret. You're hardly a boy anymore." She turned and rummaged about in a cabinet next to the stove. "Though I must say, I was distressed to receive *this*."

She tossed a rolled piece of parchment onto the table. Aleksei knew what it was without having to open it.

"I didn't realize they'd send one to Voskrin." he said quietly.

"Frankly, *I'm* surprised they had the eggs to do it. The very *idea* that a boy's own hometown would turn against him on the word of Northern cityfolk. *Preposterous*."

Aleksei frowned, "Has the town seen it?"

She laughed, "No, why should they? So this 'Lord' Perron fellow can sully your name with your friends and neighbors? I *hardly* think so."

With a snap the parchment burst into flame. Aleksei jumped back in his chair, but Mother Margareta simply chuckled and brushed away the soot. He stared at her in surprise. The woman was a *Magus*?

She took a seat and leaned forward, as though nothing had happened. "Aleksei, my boy, you are a *hero* to the people of this town. Generations of hopes and dreams are realized in what you do every day, *believe* me.

"You make the young people of this village think of a world outside their cabbage patches, and that can *only* be a good thing.

Now tell me, where's the good in spreading the words of evil men?"

"But it's *true*." Aleksei said, somewhat more forcefully than he meant. He was surprised to find himself fighting back tears. "I murdered Lord Malak."

"And I'm sure he deserved it, dear." she said offhandedly, pouring herself a cup of tea.

He couldn't believe what he was hearing. "He committed treason, but he didn't deserve to die like *that*." he managed.

Margareta fixed him with a stern look, her steely blue eyes seeming to piece him to the core. "Aleksei, I am a firm believer that good men commit actions for a reason. They're rarely prone to accidents. If this Lord Malak died at your hand, then I have to believe that he deserved it, because I've only ever known you to be a good man. Do you understand?"

He thought for a moment, then finally nodded. "Yes, ma'am."

Aleksei decided it was best to allow Mother Margareta her illusions. "Mother...*Margaret*, I have to say, I'm confused. I never realized you were a Magus."

She scoffed, "*Surely* you did. What did you think I was doing in your fields every winter? Making some inane prayer and jinxing your rabbits? I take my duties *very* seriously, boy. I wouldn't be much of a servant to the Goddess if I didn't. Now then, there are some official matters I need to bring to your attention."

Aleksei frowned, "What do you mean?"

Mother Margareta shrugged, "As the the Town Elder, I have some issues that I need *you* to see to. As the Lord Captain of Ilyar, I believe it is your duty to preserve justice and peace in the realm. Am I correct?"

Aleksei nodded, wondering why he even bothered to be startled by this woman. "What's the problem?"

For the first time since they'd met in the road, she looked a little unsure, "It's about Pyotr."

Aleksei frowned, "Pyotr Krovel?"

"Pyotr married Katherine Bondar last year."

Aleksei blinked, "Pyotr and Katherine are *married*?"

Mother Margareta chuckled, "I can understand your surprise. I said the same thing, believe me." She considered for a moment before adding, "I think she grew tired of waiting for you to come sweep her off her feet."

In spite of himself, Aleksei was surprised, "*Me?* But Margaret, surely she never thought we were...."

She shrugged, "Girls can make some mighty big leaps in their heads when it suits them. Anyhow, they've been married for a few months now. I never thought too much of the match, I have to admit, but I did think better of Pyotr than *this*."

Aleksei sat up straighter, "What has he done?"

She sighed, "He's *gone*, Aleksei."

Aleksei's confusion deepened, "*Gone?* I'm not sure I understand...."

"Let me clarify for you. Pyotr has left Voskrin. He has abandoned his wife, without more than a word, to join the militia."

Aleksei felt a chill sweep through him, "And what militia would that be?"

Her face grew darker, "The one that Bertrand Perron has been amassing during the last two months. I sent a message to you, but I suppose you've not been in Kalinor of late."

Aleksei shook his head. Perron was raising a militia in the South? What could the man possibly mean by it?

And then it all clicked in his head. Every sign was there, staring him in the face. And he'd been too naïve to see it.

Malak was not the only one to commit treason, it seemed. And yet even as this thought occurred to him, the even more shocking realization that he could do nothing to alter this course of events struck him. He was a *murderer*. Why would the Queen listen to him? Why would *anyone* listen to him?

"Thank you for telling me this." he said finally, coming to his feet. "I think I'll call on Katherine, if you don't think it's too late in the day."

She smiled warmly, "I think she'd appreciate a friendly face at the moment. She's been lonelier than she cares to admit, especially with her brothers spending all their time on your father's farm."

He nodded, then rose and stepped out into the cool evening air. He left Agriphon at the post for the moment, walking purposefully across the village square, towards Pyotr Krovel's house.

There was a light on in the kitchen, but the rest of the house was completely dark. He knocked gently and stepped back onto the stoop.

"Is that you, Mother?" Katherine's voice came from the other side. It sounded weak and broken.

"Katherine?"

The door swung open and there stood Katherine Bondar, looking just as he remembered her but for the puffiness around her tear-swollen eyes. At present she looked like she was staring at a ghost.

"Great *gods*." she whispered. "What...what are *you* doing here?"

"Mother Margareta told me about Pyotr." Aleksei said gently. "I wanted to see how you were."

Katherine wiped her eyes self-consciously, "I'm...*well*, I suppose. As well as can be expected given the circumstances."

"May I come in?"

Katherine stiffened, "I'd prefer you didn't, actually. Everything's just a mess right now and, to be honest, I'm not too interested in having company."

Aleksei nodded his understanding, though he was a little surprised at her behavior towards him. This was no longer the rebellious sprite of a girl who had goaded him into hunting excursions against the will of her father.

And this was no love-sick slip of a girl. Before him stood a woman. Part of him, though, mourned his friend.

"Well, if you'd like to talk, I'll be at my Da's for a little bit. I'd be happy to lend an ear."

She managed a smile, "Thank you for your concern, Aleksei, but I've survived without you so far."

Aleksei bowed his head slightly. He understood the dismissal for what it was. "Good night, Katherine."

"Good night, Lord Captain."

And then she closed the door.

Aleksei walked slowly away from the house, thoughts and memories warring in his head and his heart. It hurt to be treated like a stranger by someone who had once been so close, and yet could he blame her? It was hardly as though he'd been the best friend since his departure the previous year.

Upon reaching his warhorse, he found that Agriphon was

anxious to get back on the road, which was surprising given how hard they'd ridden the last several days. Then again, Agriphon was young and full of fire. Aleksei knew that if he ever had to ride a horse into battle, it would *have* to be this one.

The moon bathed the road in a ghostly radiance, allowing Aleksei to ride the remaining leagues to the farm at a good pace. He reached it feeling tired, yet somewhat hopeful.

Upon first inspection, the farm looked just as it had when he'd left. The barn had a new roof, but beyond that not much had changed. He rode Agriphon into the barn and stabled him next to the Bondar boys' horses.

"Try to enjoy your rest." he muttered, patting the stallion's flank as he walked out of the barn.

As he approached the farmhouse, Aleksei was glad to hear the sounds of laughter from within. It was good to know that Henry was getting on well without him.

Aleksei considered knocking, but thought better of it and simply opened the door. The laughter stopped as the three men inside turned to regard the newcomer.

Their shocked silence lasted only a heartbeat, and then Aleksei was surrounded by such a cacophony of warm, jubilant voices that it left him stunned.

He was home.

⁂

Sweat rolled down the hard angles of Aleksei's face as he hurled the last forkfuls of hay into the loft. He grabbed the short length of gray toweling hanging from his belt and wiped his face, stepping out of the barn and back into the brilliance of the late Harvest sun.

A year of training had left him stronger than he'd ever been, and he was amazed by how much easier chores on the farm had become. For their part, the Bondar brothers couldn't but help stare at the bizarre, writhing black of the Mantle displayed so prominently across his broad, tanned shoulders.

Neither of them had summoned the courage to ask about it, but he could hear them whispering to one another when they thought he wasn't listening. There was little doubt in anyone's mind that the Aleksei Drago who'd left one year ago was a very different man from the one who had returned.

Henry, for his part, seemed so overjoyed to see his son that he hardly took note of either the Mantle or the changes that had taken place in his son. The most distressing change to Henry was the loss of Aleksei's Plains accent, but even that returned within two days' time.

"Boys!" Henry called from the house, "Supper's on."

Aleksei smiled as he pulled his shirt off the hook in the barn door and made his way back towards the house. After a year in Kalinor, it was an enormous relief to return to simple farm work.

He met Kiriel and Ruslan on their way in from the field. While the brothers were cordial and pleasant, Aleksei knew he made them apprehensive.

It was odd that *he* should be the one intimidating *them*, as his whole life they'd been the biggest men he'd known. They'd even roughed him up on rare occasions.

He recalled thinking that men like Kiriel and Ruslan had nothing to fear. Never in a hundred years would he have thought himself capable of inspiring the same feelings in *them*.

They mostly passed their time with him by asking questions about Kalinor. And was it really true that he was bonded to the Prince? And was the Princess really as beautiful as they'd heard? And had the Queen herself been the one to knight him?

And while Aleksei was only too happy to oblige them with the truth, and his answers to their questions about Jonas had brought color to both men's cheeks to say the least, he couldn't help but feel that his responses only served to distance himself from these people.

Only his father seemed completely unimpressed by what Aleksei had spent the last year doing. He was proud, of that he left little doubt, but it never changed the fact that this was his farm. And on his farm, everyone followed his orders, whether you were the son of a cooper or the Lord Captain himself.

The day before, Henry had scolded Aleksei for tying the hay up incorrectly. Kiriel and Ruslan had watched in horror, not believing that anyone would scold the Lord Captain of Her Majesty's Legions.

Their horror became surprise when Aleksei merely apologized and set about retying the bales. What they didn't understand was that for the first time in a very long while, *he* wasn't the one giving the orders. His father had given him the greatest possible gift in allowing him to relinquish command, if only for a few days.

That night, while Kiriel and Ruslan were cleaning and closing up the barn, Henry handed Aleksei a glass of warm apple brandy and sat with him before the fire.

"So, do you mind if I ask you about it?" his father said quietly.

Aleksei frowned, "Da?"

Henry nodded at Aleksei's shoulders, "Those...marks. I assume there's a story behind them?"

"I don't know that I'd call it a *story*. The Wood called me to Her, and sent me on a proper Hunt. A great fire-breathing serpent, just a hatchling, something called a Salamander?

"Thank the gods I couldn't see a thing, or I doubt I'd have even held my ground, much less manage the kill the blasted thing." Aleksei chuckled at that last bit, but noticed that his father was looking increasingly confused. He forged ahead rather than risk an explanation, "As a reward, the Wood gifted me with *this*. She called it the Hunter's Mantle."

"She *gifted* this to you?" Henry asked, perplexed.

"I'm still not entirely sure what it *does*." Aleksei allowed. "I've only tapped into its abilities once. I killed a man, and it restored me."

Henry considered a moment before responding, "Then it is powerful magic indeed. Wood magic is legendary for its abilities to grant life, but to drain it *away*...I never heard of such a thing in all my time with the Ri-Vhan." He considered a moment, "What does Jonas make of it?"

"I'm not sure yet. We've had a hard time finding anything about it at all, and even what we *have* found is so old it might not even matter anymore. He doesn't even know I killed Lord Malak yet."

"Are they going to come after you?" Henry asked after a long silence.

Aleksei sighed, "I can't say. Probably, but I didn't tell anyone where I was headed. My greatest fear is that they seek out *Jonas* to get to *me*.

"I've been listening to our bond, and he hasn't been happy, but he hasn't been in danger either. This is the *worst* possible time to be so far from one another."

Aleksei took a breath as the depth of his predicament fell across him, "How do I...*handle* the idea that I'd enter the Aftershadow, and pull him along, without him knowing it was even *happening*?"

Henry studied his son's face for a long moment, studied the tears brimming in the corners of his son's coyote-gold eyes.

"You love him, don't you?"

Aleksei inhaled, then nodded firmly, "More than *anything*, Da. And he loves me. Our bond makes our connection incredibly intimate as it is, but this, *this* is unlike anything either of us has ever felt."

Henry set his brandy down and stood. Aleksei abashedly rose and Henry stepped forward, wrapping his arms around his son, "Love is a curious thing, Son." he whispered after pressing a kiss into the boy's golden hair.

"I've *always* believed you were destined to accomplish greater things in your life. Your mother felt the same way. We never imagined you'd be the *Lord Captain*, but we always hoped you'd be this *happy*. Jonas is a good man.

"The first time I saw him, standing in my doorway, I could tell how nervous he was. He was so relieved to see the Princess, and yet it was *you* who had him on pins and needles. The gods only know what the boy would have done if you'd refused him. I've never seen a man so desperate, or so relieved, so *elated*, when you said 'yes'."

Aleksei looked away from his father, trying to keep the tears back. This was the *last* conversation he'd expected. At the very least, Henry wasn't quizzing him on the particulars about what happened in his bedchamber.

The same couldn't be said for the Bondar brothers, who were more than a little curious about how a farm boy from Voskrin had found his way into the Prince's sheets. There were details Aleksei refused to provide, of course, but he had hinted at enough to set both men's faces aflame, if nothing else than to make them uncomfortable enough to cease with their endless queries.

Aleksei wasn't used to men he'd known since boyhood asking questions about his life or his relationships period, much less on such an intimate level. But bedding the Prince was a different matter entirely, especially when the Prince's bedmate was the bloody Lord

Captain. And a Ri-Vhan *Hunter*. And a man the Bondar brothers had beaten bloody little more than a year before behind Redman's Pub, for making their sister cry.

Yet now he was bound to the bloody Prince of bloody Ilyar? And the *Lord Captain* to boot, not to mention the Prince's Archanium Knight? Aleksei had been amused at the awed expressions on their faces when he'd provided even the simplest of details. Awe, and from Kiriel's scent, more than a little jealousy.

"Well," Henry said, releasing Aleksei from his tight embrace, "I'm glad you decided to come here instead of somewhere else. If you can't be safe at home, then–"

A shout sounded from outside and Aleksei reached for his sword, only to realize that he'd left it on his bed upstairs. Running as fast as he could, he took the steps two at a time, not even bothering to buckle his belt on as he ran back downstairs and drew the blade.

"Stay here, Da. Bolt the door." he whispered as he rushed out into the night.

The moment the night air hit him, Aleksei could feel them. *Men.* He sacrificed seconds to test the air for another unmistakable smell. *Steel.* Weapons had been drawn. He felt their edges cutting into the air.

Assassins.

He heard sounds of a fight from the barn, but as much as he wanted to help Kiriel and Ruslan, it was the band of five hiding behind the farmhouse that gave him the greatest concern. Their heartbeats pounded in his ears like a galloping thunder.

He darted around the house, careful not to make a sound. Around the corner he saw them, just as he'd imagined. There were five, but their heads were all aimed at the barn. Obviously they hadn't been expecting too much of a fight, because they weren't paying very close attention.

Aleksei slid up behind the nearest one, cutting his throat savagely and covering his mouth so that the only sound to escape was the light splash as the body landed in a pool of its own blood.

His follow-up swing decapitated the next man. The sound of his head striking the ground alerted the others, but by then it was too late.

Time slowed as Aleksei darted into the middle of them and wove his deadly tapestry, pulling a knife from one assassin hurling it into the eye of another. The remaining two drew short swords.

Aleksei rolled to the side, coming up with a hard side-swipe that relieved one man of his arm. He gripped the armless man and ran him into the second man's blade. As the first man dropped, Aleksei rammed his knife into the second man's heart.

He bent and retrieved his sword, then ran for the barn.

The sounds of fighting had mostly ceased by the time he reached the barn door. Inside he found Kiriel and Ruslan, one holding a sickle, the other a pitchfork. Around them lay three dead men. The two remaining were holding knives, though they looked worse for wear.

Aleksei walked in purposefully, cutting the first of two men down instantly. The second turned just in time for Aleksei to slide his sword into the man's throat. He held the sword in place as the assassin fell to his knees. Then he slowly withdrew the blade. The man died with a gurgle.

"Are you alright?" he asked, looking up at the two brothers.

They looked pale, and he supposed they were probably in shock, but they appeared uninjured.

"Let's get back to the farmhouse. If there are any more of them, it's best to keep together."

They followed him out of the barn and back towards the farmhouse. As they approached, Aleksei saw that the door had been kicked in and his heart quickened. Oh gods, *why* had he left his father alone?

He burst into the house, shouting his father's name, only to find Henry leaning against the wall, unharmed but exhausted. On the kitchen table lay a man, wheezing his last breaths. Aleksei had but to look at the bloody kitchen knife on the floor to understand why.

"*You....*" the man on the table gasped, and Aleksei walked to his side.

"*Who* sent you?" he demanded.

"We...we didn't...expect...*you* here. He said it...it would only be... be *three*." The last words were breathed out haltingly as the man died.

Aleksei stared at the corpse incredulously. He gripped the dead man's arm, searching for a pulse, even a faint throb to suggest the man still clung to life. Nothing.

He cursed violently and grabbed the body, pulling the corpse off the table and out into the yard. They weren't *expecting* him? If they weren't expecting him to be there, that meant they hadn't been after him. And the only other person they could have targeted was....

"Oh *gods*." he grunted as he unceremoniously dropped the man's corpse to the ground.

"Aleksei?" his father said from the doorway.

Aleksei turned, his mind racing, "Get your things, Da. We have to leave."

Henry frowned, "Leave? What are you...."

Aleksei pointed at the man's body, "They were here for *you*, not me. Someone is after *you*."

"That's madness. Aleksei. Why would anyone want to kill *me*?" Henry demanded.

Aleksei fixed his father with a steady gaze, "Because they can't kill *me*. I have no family to speak of, besides you. They couldn't deal with the Ri-Vhan. But *you*, you're an easy target out here, all on your own."

Henry looked lost, "But...but surely...."

"*No.*" Aleksei said forcefully, "We're leaving. Right now. Kiriel and Ruslan will accompany us only as far as Voskrin. We'll spend the night with Mother Margareta. No one will know to look for you there, and she's a Magus besides. We'll be safe there. And then in the morning, we leave."

"For where?"

Aleksei answered with the safest, closest place he could think of, "Mornj."

"But *Aleksei*," Kiriel began.

"Do as I command." the Lord Captain barked. "If we stay here, *you* die. This farm isn't worth your lives. And as much as I love it, I'm not willing to give it mine, either. We leave, and we leave *now*."

The other three men glanced at each other, then turned back into the house and began collecting their things.

There was no longer any question who was giving the orders.

CHAPTER 33

OLD WOUNDS ASUNDER

THE STREETS OF Kuuran shone in the midday sun, rose-colored sandstone blossoming from the soft green plains into undulating rows of civilization. Through the center of the great city flowed the mighty Ylik Water, a ribbon of soft azure and turquoise amidst the cherry glow of the city.

Jonas regarded it all from far above, watching the Dalitian citizens and angels make their way about before he set his sights upon the golden prominence of the Basilica.

The Basilica: seat of Angelic Rule and crown of vanity.

Still, he supposed, there was something to be said for time and tradition. The Basilica was one of the oldest structures in Dalita, possibly in the known world. The only one he *knew* to be older was the Voralla. But then the Archanium Magi of old had always been more organized than the angels.

Jonas flitted down into an alley, waiting until he was sure no one was paying attention. With a thought, he shifted into his human form, stepping out into the sunlight and High Street traffic.

He had dressed as he thought the Angelus might expect to

receive him. After all, this was not Ilyar. The humor of the nobles at home would not excuse his preference for casual dress here.

No, *here* the archangels stood on high ceremony for afternoon tea, and those born into higher stations were expected to look the part. And while he did not cherish his emerald silk coat or his fine black trousers, he wore them well; the angels would find nothing lacking in his performance.

He reached the arching entryway of the Basilica and sighed, but there was nothing for it. The information that might be within was worth far more to Jonas than a day or two of discomfort. He stepped inside.

If the ornate decorations that covered the outer walls of the Basilica hurt his eyes, the interior left him blind. The walls were covered in bright tapestries from Ilyar, the floors set in golden marble from Fanj. Priceless chandeliers hung from the ceiling, their crystal forged from the finest sands of Zirvah. It was the pinnacle of wealth in Dalita, the home of the Angelus, and the spiritual and political capital of the nation.

He was less than ten paces within the structure when a low-ranking angel approached him, "Greetings. I am Zerdon. What is your business in the Basilica today?"

Jonas smiled warmly, "I'm here to see the Angelus."

Zerdon's eyes widened, "Truly? Have you an appointment?"

Jonas shook his head, "Alas, there was no time. But the Angelus *will* see me."

Zerdon offered no obstruction, he merely nodded his head, finally taking in Jonas' physiology. The angel stiffened, almost seeming offended by Jonas' presence. By his prodigious chest, and complete lack of wings.

A man built for flight, but lacking the means.

"As you say, milord. If you would be so kind as to visit the Offices of Audience, I'm sure they can take care of you there."

Jonas nodded his appreciation, "Excellent, thank you."

He walked past the angel and in the opposite direction of the aforementioned offices, heading instead through a large marble archway and into an expansive, overly elaborate corridor. As he walked, he ignored the curious glances from passing angels. He doubted there were very many humans who used these passages, but then again, he wasn't just *anyone*.

A point that would be made all too clear in a very short while.

After navigating several bends in the corridor, Jonas realized he'd become completely turned around. A very pretty young angel was walking past him, and he stopped her.

"I beg your pardon, Angelica, but I'm afraid I've become lost. Which way is the Office of the Angelus?"

The angel looked him up and down skeptically. If she noted his peculiar construction, she didn't let it show on her face, or in her voice. "I'm afraid I don't recognize you."

Jonas nodded, "Understandable. I've just arrived from Ilyar, you see. I have an appointment with the Angelus."

"Regarding?"

"The use of some of the Basilica's more...sensitive facilities." Jonas said, never dropping his smile.

He understood the purpose of the interrogation, certainly. He would have been very suspicious had he encountered anyone in Kalinor searching for the Queen.

The angel watched him for a few moments before nodding, "Very well, good sir, I will take you to the Fount myself. I am the Angel Leigha."

Jonas arched an eyebrow, "Ah, the first-born Cherub. I'm flattered."

Leigha's finely-crafted features registered surprise. She seemed most interested to know how a man from Ilyar was so well versed in Dalitian royalty, especially obscure royalty. But rather than quiz him any further, she lead the way down the hall.

"Do you have a name, sir?" she asked as they walked.

"I do, though you'll forgive me if I don't hand it out just at the moment. No offense is meant, I assure you, but the nature of my visit is sensitive."

Leigha nodded, "As you wish."

They walked in silence for what seemed hours, though Jonas knew it only amounted to a few minutes. When Leigha brought them to a halt, it was before a sharp drop-off in the corridor.

Before them spanned a massive pool of brilliantly clear water. In the center of the pool, perhaps a hundred paces from the nearest shore, stood a small palace. The sheer scope of the Fount reminded Jonas of the Basilica's incredible scale.

"Here you are, milord. The Office of the Angelus. Though if you were planning to swim, I would recommend you carry your boots as I'd imagine they would weigh you down."

Jonas smiled at her. He was amused to see that, while she had fulfilled her promise to take him here, she had in no way truly aided him. Were he some foolish assassin, he would pose no greater threat to the Angelus than an infant.

"My most sincere thanks. Your assistance has been invaluable."

Jonas winked at her, then shifted into his sparrow form and flitted across the Fount. When he returned to his shape on the other side, he spared a satisfying glance behind him at the astonished angel, then stepped into the palace.

The interior of the palace was far more comfortable than ostentatious, a distinct reversal after the gilt and glamour of the Basilica. Someone actually *lived* here, an observation made clearer from the pleasant and unassuming layout of the place.

He was only a pace inside when a very alarmed archangel appeared in front of him, great silver wings billowing out behind him.

"*Explain* yourself, human." the angel bellowed, his voice echoing in the small confines of the room.

Jonas frowned and touched the Archanium. The angel's voice vanished from the room, leaving him surprised and enraged. Jonas beckoned him forward and whispered in his ear.

The archangel stepped back incredulously, then gave a resigned nod.

"*Thank* you." Jonas said politely, releasing the Archanium.

The angel grunted his grudging acceptance.

Jonas passed by the archangel, ascending a broad flight of stairs and walking to the massive wooden door at the end of the hallway. He took a deep breath, composed himself as best he could, and stepped inside.

The room itself was warmly lit, decorated in velvets and satins in greens, oranges, and a striking shade of peach. Behind a large, carved desk sat a small woman, her petite golden wings languishing behind her as she wrote.

"Well, you got past Malachai. That's impressive in itself, I suppose. What do you want?"

She looked up and froze.

The quill slipped from her tiny hand and splattered ink across her parchment, splashing a few drops across the front of her fine white gown. She didn't notice.

Kevara Avlon had lived a long and full life, though she was nowhere near its end. Jonas wondered if, in such a life, she had ever found herself so disoriented.

"Upon my word," she whispered, "but how you favor your father."

Jonas smiled, though there was little warmth in it, "Hello, Grandmother."

"I...I didn't realize it had been so long."

Jonas walked forward and stopped at the edge of his grandmother's desk, watching her casually. "In a palace full of mirrors, I hardly believe that you have missed the passage of time."

She looked up at him with her great, luminous blue eyes, "You inherited your mother's cruelty."

"And my father's sense of justice. Which do you fear *more*?"

She opened her mouth to speak, but Jonas held up a hand.

"It's been twenty-three years since the death of your son, Kevara. Twenty-three years since you *took* my wings. Twenty since I was orphaned, and as many years since you abandoned me to the fate of a war-torn nation."

"Jonas, there are no words for what I have done to you. I know that."

Jonas leaned forward across the desk, "Perhaps, but do you *feel* it? Do you have any *idea* what it means to me, Kevara? You might have thought you were aiding justice by playing my mother's accuser, but you *cannot* know what it is to grow up with only shadows and memories to comfort you at night."

She averted her eyes, "Why have you come here? Certainly you did not travel all the way from Ilyar to accuse me of making you an orphan. God *knows* I live with that every day as it is."

"No," Jonas said softly, "I have not come to remind, but for payment."

Her eyes widened, "Payment?"

"You owe me a *very* great debt indeed, *Grandmother*." He spat the word. "And I would satisfy part of that debt today."

She spread her hands wide, "I have little to offer, I'm afraid, but what I possess is at your disposal. What do you require?"

"Information."

Kevara Avlon sat straighter, "Go on."

"I want access to your records. Not the Basilica Library, but the personal library of the Angelus. I don't want the texts you feed the masses. I want the *truth*."

She nodded, "I see. Well, I cannot promise you'll find what you seek, but you are at the utmost freedom to look."

Jonas bowed his head slightly, "Many thanks."

Without waiting for another word, Jonas turned on his heel and stepped out of the room. He ignored the slightly puzzled, half-reverent look on the face of the archangel outside. As humiliating as he knew it was for Malachai to be bested, it had to sting all the more being delivered at the hands of Jonas Belgi.

He stopped a moment and addressed his grandmother's consort, "The library?"

Malachai regarded Jonas blankly for a moment, then nodded, "Follow me."

He led Jonas down a series of halls, and finally to yet another wooden door, this one as unadorned as the last. "The library." he said simply.

Jonas pushed the door open, and for a moment felt a thread of despair slide through his heart. Shelves upon shelves towered above him, bearing more volumes than he could ever hope to read in a hundred lifetimes. He turned to the archangel.

"Who knows these books?"

Malachai frowned, "What do you mean?"

"Who knows how these books are arranged? Surely there is a rhyme and reason to their organization. Who would know such a thing?"

Malachai considered before answering, "The Angel Leigha

would probably have the most useful knowledge for your purpose."

Jonas nodded, "Send for her, would you?"

Malachai opened his mouth angrily, but Jonas stopped him with a glare. "Don't pretend to be blameless in this sordid family tale. You are as much to blame for what transpired as *she* is."

Jonas had been in the library for half an hour when he heard that silvery voice behind him.

"Hello, Cousin."

He turned with a smile, "Mine's the pleasure, I assure you."

Leigha crossed her arms and arched an eyebrow, "I must admit to being surprised at your departure earlier today. I had not thought humans capable of such...creativity."

Jonas chuckled, "I know very few who are."

She regarded him for a moment, then dropped her arms to her sides and closed the door behind her. "So what is it you need, exactly?"

"Two things. First, I need to see your texts on the Demonic Presence."

⚜

Leigha felt a chill run through her. He *knew*. Jonas had read the signs correctly, just as the Angelus predicted. And now he was *here*.

"And the second subject of inquiry?" she asked, her curiosity piqued.

"I need texts from the Dominion Wars." Jonas said matter-of-factly. "And more specifically, I need texts pertaining to the Kholodym."

Leigha frowned, "*Why?*"

Jonas' face grew grave, "Because not *all* their magic was purged from the land."

Leigha shook her head, deciding not to ask any more questions for the moment. "The books in the front of the library are the most recent. If you'll follow me, Prince Belgi."

He followed his cousin, noting that the light became dimmer the deeper into the library they traveled. After a few minutes, Jonas began to get a true sense of what comprised most of the space in the tiny palace.

They finally entered a narrow room, the dust covering the

tabletops providing some idea of how frequently these rooms were used.

"Here," she said, waving her arm along a wall, "are all the books dating back to the Dominion Wars. The ones referencing the Kholodym Dominion specifically are at the back, those on the Presence are in this front cabinet. Is there anything else you require?"

"Yes," Jonas said quickly, "I require that *you* stay here and help me."

She looked surprised, "Really? I thought you'd rather be alone."

Jonas shook his head, "I don't know these books. It would take me *ages* to find what I'm searching for. I'd appreciate any help you could lend."

Leigha shrugged, "As you wish. Malachai said I was to help you however I could."

She walked past him and began to pull volumes from the cabinet, "Any particular aspect of the Presence?"

"Yes," Jonas said, trying to read the titles of the books she pulled, "anything that references the Cherubric Parchment."

Leigha laughed and handed him a thick red text. "Here you are. The Cherubric Parchment, in full."

Jonas' eyes widened, "I didn't know a copy of this still existed."

Leigha smirked, "*That's* not a copy. As far as the rest of the world knows, it was destroyed in the last Age. And we'd prefer to keep it that way."

Jonas sighed and nodded.

The angels had their secrets, and they guarded them zealously. This was a core component of the Angelic Faith, but as such it was also incredibly dangerous.

The angels had spent millennia guarding the raw contents of the document, disseminating the pieces they deemed fit for mass consumption, while guarding some of its more controversial passages for only the most enlightened and educated of the fold.

The book wasn't even supposed to exist, much less leave the sacred protection of the tiny island.

But he was a prince among angels, just as he was amongst the Ilyari, and in return for his discretion and silence, certain protocols could be circumvented.

The gravity of the moment was not lost on him.

Leigha watched him for a long moment, finally seeming satisfied that they understood one another. She returned to the shelves, moving farther back into the room, "What aspect of Kholodym Dominion is of particular interest?"

"I'm looking for information about something called the Zra-Uul."

A cloud of dust fluttered up from where Leigha had dropped one of the ancient texts. She quickly snatched it up, dusted it off, and slid it back into its place. She looked at him curiously, then nodded.

"Very well. Come with me."

CHAPTER 34

THE COLORS OF BETRAYAL

THE DOOR BANGED open and Andariana stormed in, ignoring Sammul's rising protest. She pulled back the curtains from his bed and gripped the front of his nightshirt.

"Where *are* they?" she demanded.

Sammul wiped the sleep from his eyes, startled at having the wards placed around his doors so unexpectedly shattered. "*Whom,* your Majesty?" he asked blearily.

She pushed him back onto the bed, "Don't pretend ignorance. I don't have time to play games. I want to know *where* they went, and I want to know *now!*"

"Majesty, if you'll just be reasonable,"

"*Reasonable?*" she roared, "When half of Parliament vanishes in the middle of the night with nothing save a letter from the Chancellor citing 'Unacceptable Doctrines of State' as *justification?* Don't you *dare* lie to me, Sammul. You were seen meeting with Perron yesterday. Don't you *dare* pretend ignorance of this."

Sammul had sufficiently woken now, and he fought to hide his bemusement at the situation. "Majesty, I will admit that Chancellor Perron came to me for counsel yesterday. But I urged him to bring his grievances to Your Majesty in as diplomatic a means as he was capable. I never dreamed he would simply *vacate* the Palace!"

"And go *where*, Sammul? *Where* would he flee? To his lands? The man controls half the *Southern Plain*. His home is not fifty leagues from *Igraan*! Surely he would not be so *stupid* as to run such a short distance from my winter estate! Unless, of course, he means to press a civil war, at which point he wouldn't much *care*, now would he?"

"*Majesty*," Sammul said, sounding scandalized, "surely you do not believe that members of Parliament would press a civil war over something so trifling."

"*Trifling*, Sammul? The suspicious death of one of the most powerful landed nobility, in combination with my unwillingness to press the point beyond summoning the Lord Captain, is *exactly* the sort of thing Perron would seize upon. If he has been planning this, which I daresay he *has*, what better moment than the present to make his move?"

"But Majesty," Sammul said patiently, "Lord Perron isn't a member of the royal family. Even if he wanted to take your throne, the people of the realm would never stand behind him. He doesn't have a drop of Belgi blood in him."

"I know that," Andariana snapped. "*That's* what has me worried. If Perron is willing to take a risk like this, it means he's either more foolish than I ever believed possible, or he's found someone he thinks he can control. I don't have to chase at phantoms to hazard a guess, either."

"I'm afraid I'm at a loss, Majesty."

She scowled. "Emelian Krasik was never *executed*, Sammul. And a madman may be unpredictable, but I daresay Perron is stupid enough to put one on the throne."

Sammul stared at the Queen. How had such a thought even entered her *head*? Was it possible she was far more astute than he had ever believed?

"I want a statement issued to all the towns and cities where you sent the summons for Lord Captain Drago *immediately*. I need him more urgently than ever, but in his capacity as my Lord Captain, not as my prisoner."

"Majesty?" Sammul asked, growing more alarmed.

"If Malak was in on all this, which I imagine he *was*, then he died a traitor's death. Good riddance to bad rubbish. Lord Captain Drago, if he *was* responsible, has done us a great service by executing the late Lord of Relvyn, wouldn't you *agree*?"

"Why...yes, of course."

She breathed deeply for a moment, then nodded, "Thank you, Sammul. I...I apologize for the *abrupt* nature of my entrance, but I was rather taken with the shock of the moment."

Sammul did his best to smile, "Quite understandable, Majesty."

"Well, good evening, High Magus."

She swept from the room.

Sammul lay back against his pillow, vacillating between joy and despair. On the one hand, all their plans were falling beautifully into place. On the other, the Queen was far more intuitive than he had given her credit for.

It was only by lucky chance that Jonas was not also present, or Sammul would fear losing the scheme altogether.

Still, there was the chance that some enterprising fellow would deal with Drago for him. He could only begin to fathom his glee upon hearing that the Prince had dropped dead with his Knight. What a *tragedy* that would be!

Sammul smiled to himself. With any luck, Aleksei Drago would not set foot in Kalinor again for a long while. And by the time he made his way back, it would be too late.

⁂

Wherever Jonas had expected Leigha to take him, *this* wasn't it. Rather than entering yet another dusty, time-forsaken storage room, the angel took him out of the library entirely. She walked up the stairs, back down the hall, and into the office of the Angelus.

Jonas followed her, noting the surprised expression on Kevara Avlon's face as her granddaughter reached into her bookshelves and withdrew a slender volume bound in pale blue leather. The front of the volume was marked with a curious emblem Jonas had never seen before.

"I believe this should prove sufficiently instructive."

Jonas glanced down at the silver leaf on the front. He could hardly believe what he read.

The Properties and Constructions of Parasitic Energies. Jonas studied the curious mark that dominated the book's front. At first glance, he'd assumed that the symbol had been tooled into the leather along with the lettering, but on closer inspection he realized that it had actually been *tattooed* onto into the flesh before the book had been bound.

"This...." he began softly.

"The binding is human." Leigha confirmed, ignoring her grandmother's scowl.

Jonas glanced up at his cousin, "I was actually going to say that this is *Kholod.* This symbol...." He had seen it only once before, in an ancient illustration kept in the depths of the Voralla, though it might as well have been burned into his mind's eye.

It appeared to be a simple pictogram, an eight-pointed star rendered in red, bordered by a black circle. However, as Jonas examined the image more closely, he realized that the symbol was actually composed of two separate four-pointed stars. One was long and thin, it's black, needle-narrow points flaring to the four cardinal directions, puncturing the circle and dividing into four distinct arcs, each arc interrupted halfway by a black spike.

Each spike echoed the ordinal points of the second, smaller star, half the size of the first, but thicker, its center containing the core of its larger counterpart, while its points remained completely enclosed within the circle.

The symbol was remarkable for a variety of reasons, the most obvious being its base simplicity. Of all the symbols and diagrams Jonas had encountered during his studies, this single symbol remained the clearest, the most primitive in construction.

No symbol used to represent the Archanium, to teach Magus or angel, Ul'Brek or warlock, was comprised of so *few* elements. He had spent long nights in conversation with Ilyana and Aya about their own interpretations, but one common similarity had always been painfully present. This symbol existed wholly *outside* the

Archanium.

Whatever it was, whatever it meant, there seemed no question that it was born purely from the occult practices of the Kholodym Dominion.

This was *it*. If the words on the page could be interpreted any number of ways, this symbol could not. Jonas knew that in his hands, he held the answers he sought.

He smiled at his cousin, "*Thank* you for this. Could you please have this sent to my rooms with the Parchment?"

Leigha glanced uncertainly at her grandmother, who studied him for a long, tense moment before finally nodding.

"I'll see to it." she said simply, tucking both volumes under her arm as she left.

"Well, Jonas, are you *satisfied*?" Kevara Avlon asked, sitting back in her chair.

Jonas considered, "I can't tell you. I'll let you know when I'm finished."

She sighed, "As you wish." And then she paused as she considered her grandson. "I see you've been paying attention."

Jonas nodded gravely, "I'm pleased to see that I'm not the only one. I trust you're taking the proper precautions?"

Kevara Avlon shrugged, "What can one do beyond a certain point? I've sent guards to watch the Cathedral. But enough books speak to the inevitability of our situation."

Jonas' face darkened, "What are you *talking* about? Just because two gates have been opened in *no* way means that the Prime Gate will fail."

The Angelus waved her withered hand at the shelves on either side of her. "There are prophecies in these books more ancient than you can imagine, and *all* point in the same direction. The Demonic Presence will be freed one day or another, it's just a matter of *when*."

Jonas could barely contain his horror, "Are you telling me that you're *resigned* to the fact that this...this *Pilgrim* will succeed? That you're going to *allow* him to free the Presence?"

Kevara Avlon scowled, "Don't be obtuse. The Prime Gate still retains its seal. But don't trust so deeply that the One-God won't allow such a thing to come to pass, either. I sincerely doubt the entire

Host could stop a Magus who's managed to open the first two gates, *especially* if he has the Prime Key. Such a man has not come along in one thousand years, but if the One-God sees fit to permit such a thing now, so be it."

"You understand," Jonas growled, "that such blind faith only weakens you. As I recall, you've trusted such things in the past, and they have *consistently* failed you. But this time, your dogma goes beyond mere *idiocy*."

The Angelus rose angrily from her chair, but Jonas fixed her with a glare so malicious that it gagged the words forming in her throat.

"I sincerely hope the rest of the world doesn't pay the price for your complacence."

He turned and walked from the room, finally coming to a halt at the edge of the Fount itself.

"Your words hurt her more than you know." Malachai said from behind.

Jonas clenched his jaw, and turned to regard his grandmother's consort, "You'll forgive me if my sympathy is limited."

"She's only doing what she thinks is right. It's *all* she's ever done."

Jonas narrowed his emerald eyes, "Good intentions won't rescue her when the Demon comes for her soul, nor will they stir my compassion."

With that he shifted and flew across the Fount in a burst of wingbeats, returning to his human form the moment his feet touched solid ground.

Jonas turned and favored the older angel with a parting nod.

He sighed, pulling his mind from petty insults and anger too old to hurt any longer. If these books contained what he hoped, they would go a *very* long way in aiding his understanding of what Ilyar now faced. What the *world* faced.

Jonas turned on his heel, deciding it might be best to discover where his rooms were. He'd had as much of this sordid family reunion as he could safely tolerate.

While he'd first thought to find lodging in the city, the amenities of the Basilica had beckoned all too soon. After all, as the third-born Cherub himself, he apparently commanded quite auspicious quarters.

In short order he found the Offices of Residence. Upon presenting his name, Jonas was immediately led to a large suite overlooking the river. Two unassuming angels guarded the doorway, but neither acknowledged Jonas as he moved to open the door. He thanked his guide, then stepped inside and bolted the door behind him. No sense wasting time.

The books he had selected were already lying on a small marble table, set beside a divan near the large picture window, giving him the impression that his cousin saw a similar urgency in their situation.

The small hours of the morning crept up on him before he even realized the sun had set. He was both hungry and exhausted, but he knew there was something more important that he needed dealt with.

It seemed an eternity since he'd last spoken with Aleksei, and now he desperately needed his Knight's advice. More than that, he *missed* the man. He wondered where he was, and how he was getting on.

Jonas laid down on the divan and closed his eyes. And then he began to search.

While distance did not exist within the Archanium, he still had to deal with the massive expanse of physical space that separated him from his Knight. At the moment, all he knew was that Aleksei was somewhere very far to the south.

Hours slipped by, but Jonas was resolute. He had done this many times before, though never from so far away. But while the distance seemed enough to cripple him, their bond was stronger than most.

What at first seemed like the glow of a candle began to burn brighter. The closer he got, the easier it became, until he was practically flying towards his Knight's sleeping mind.

"*Aleksei.*" he whispered.

A world opened up around him. Massive expanses of empty space fluttered out from under his feet and enveloped him in colorless mist.

Jonas concentrated.

Were he closer, it would have taken a mere thought to shift his environment from Kalinor Palace to Aleksei's farm, to anywhere he could imagine. But strained as he was, Jonas decided it was best to use the room he currently occupied. Its image was freshest in his mind, and it required the least of his energies to replicate.

"*Aleksei.*" he whispered again. "*Aleksei, I have need of you.*"

He hated having to use the age-old phrase, the one he'd first used to lure the man to Kalinor. It felt so long ago that he had sought out a stranger. A stranger who had turned out to be the most important person in his life. A stranger he now loved deeply.

He had been different then, impatient and selfish. Jonas had spent the last year trying to atone for the force with which he'd pulled Aleksei away from his home, from his father, from everything that he knew.

But hate it as he may, it was still one of the only means he possessed that he knew would catch the Knight's attention in a dream.

His means were justified a moment later, when Aleksei's dreamform materialized before him.

"*Jonas?*" his Knight asked, rubbing his eyes.

Before Jonas had a chance to respond, he was caught in Aleksei's heartfelt embrace. Aleksei kissed him hard, and there was a desperation there that surprised Jonas.

Finally the prince stepped back, glad he didn't have to actually stand in dreamspeak. "Now honestly, I haven't been gone for *that* long."

Aleksei chuckled, but Jonas caught the man's nervous air. "*You,* of all people, oughta know that a great deal can happen in a small amount of time." He looked at the Magus meaningfully, "Especially to *me.*"

Jonas frowned, "What are you talking about?"

Rather than answer, Aleksei pulled his shirt over his head. Jonas watched in confusion as the other man extended his arm. The Mantle rippled down his arm and, upon reaching his wrist, lifted away in angry red talons.

Jonas' eyes widened.

"I killed Hugo Malak." Aleksei said flatly.

"With *this?*" Jonas asked, indicating the Mantle. He reached forward and the tendrils swirled towards him. Aleksei tensed, but the Mantle twirled around Jonas' wrist, stroking his exposed skin and sending warm prickles down his spine.

Aleksei frowned in confusion and dropped his arm, allowing the Mantle to contract. "I...*drained* him. At the time, I was crippled, but by the time the Mantle was finished with him, I was...restored, I suppose."

Jonas could hardly credit his hearing. It was *exactly* as he'd read. He hadn't even realized it at the time, but Aleksei was in possession of a *very* dangerous constructed magic. Though the question remained, dangerous to *whom?*

"Why didn't it attack you?" Aleksei asked after a long moment, staring at his wrist, at the writhing blood-red tattoo, almost as though betrayed.

"Probably because it *can't.*" Jonas said softly, recalling what he'd read about parasitic magics. "You and I are intertwined. It would no sooner hurt me than you. I think it sees us as the same person. And it would never destroy its *host.*"

Aleksei shivered at the word. "You make it sound like it's alive."

Jonas shrugged, "On some level, I think it is. I don't think this is something the Wood *did* to you; I think it's something she *placed* on you. Like a leech, but apparently this leech works in reverse."

Aleksei shook his head. "I don't have time to try and understand this. Jonas, Perron issued a proclamation for my capture. *Dead or alive.*"

Jonas' attention whipped back to Aleksei, "*What?* He doesn't have the authority for something like that."

"I didn't think so either, but it's all over southern Ilyar."

Jonas cursed to himself, "The sheer *audacity!* That's akin to signing a writ of execution. For *me. No* one in Ilyar has the right to order such a thing. Where are you now?"

Aleksei sighed, "In a field, northeast of the farm."

Jonas frowned, "The *farm?*" And then he understood. Aleksei wasn't stupid enough to have remained in Kalinor after Malak's death. He wondered how long ago all of this had happened, if Aleksei had already had time to get that far south.

"Someone sent assassins, Jonas."

"*Who?*" he could feel the heat of his anger, the magic burning and swirling around his fingertips, should he choose to invoke it. He pushed the urge away, and the Archanium whorls dissipated in a burst of color and crackling.

"I don't know. But they weren't after me. They didn't even know I'd *be* there."

"*Henry?*" Jonas whispered.

Aleksei nodded.

"Where are you headed now?"

"Mornj. It's the safest place I know of, within a ready distance."

Jonas sighed, "Alright. Go to Mornj. I'll try to get there as fast as possible. If you have to leave for some reason...." He stopped and thought a moment, "If you have to leave, I'll *find* you. I'll stop in Kalinor, and tell Andariana what you've told me. We'll get this straightened out, Aleksei."

The Knight's broad shoulders slumped in obvious relief, "Thank you."

Jonas offered a half-smile, "I've found some *very* valuable information here, but I don't want to take the time now to explain. You're going to need your energy for traveling. I'll try to come to you again, in three days time."

Aleksei sighed, "Alright. Be careful."

"You too. I love you."

Aleksei smiled. That handsome smile that always melted Jonas' heart. The smile that at once conveyed love, and a constant, unspoken apology that Jonas never completely understood.

The world melted away around Jonas. He felt himself flowing back into his room in the Basilica. His eyes snapped open, and he stood.

Jonas walked to the door the led onto the balcony, stepping out into the cold night air. This far north, Harvest had already surrendered to winter.

The Ylik Water shimmered in the moonlight. He spared a moment to take in its simple beauty. There had been a period in his life when he'd found more time to enjoy such small pleasures.

But now that time had passed. *Now* he lived with the weight of concern engendered from friendship. From love. And right then he was more concerned for Aleksei than he'd been in a long time.

Jonas stepped onto the railing of the balcony, controlling his thoughts and banishing his doubts. He needed to get to his Knight as fast as possible, and he didn't have time to spare.

With a grim determination, Jonas dove off the balcony, rising a moment later on the wings of a great falcon. He resisted the urge to throw out a cry to the night, as the exultant freedom of flight overcame him. The sensation was intoxicating.

He spiraled higher and higher into the night-black, finally settling on a strong current. The ground rushed beneath him as he raced south, towards Ilyar.

Towards *Aleksei.*

⟡

Andariana sat in her chamber, considering the options before her. It was easy enough to assemble her available forces, but there was no target to strike. What she *truly* needed was her Lord Captain.

And while she commanded a far superior Lord Captain of the Legion than his predecessor, he did her little good if he couldn't be reached.

But *surely* Sammul had summoned him! She'd commanded it ages ago. What, she wondered, could be keeping him? In the past, Aleksei had been extremely punctual, and as a result she could only imagine some great catastrophe forcing his uncharacteristic delay.

A sudden tap at her window startled her from her reverie. After a moment, the tapping returned, this time more insistent.

Andariana groaned irritably and stood, gliding to the window and throwing it open.

A tiny bird flitted in, perching on her bed.

Andariana studied the bird curiously. At first, she presumed it to be either unusually trusting, or simply stupid. But upon further inspection, she found the tiny sparrow to possess the most extraordinary green eyes.

"Hello, Aunt." Jonas said as he shifted back into his human form.

She yelped at seeing the bird shift so quickly, "*Jonas!*" she said breathlessly, "This is *indeed* a surprise." She studied him suspiciously, "Where did you learn to do that?"

Jonas grunted as he stretched his shoulders, "Not from Sammul, I can assure you. But you may be satisfied that I've done my own bit of study in the field."

She shook her head, desperately suppressing her wonder, "You take more risks than you should."

"As do you, dear Aunt." Jonas countered. "I understand the Southern Lords have departed."

Andariana nodded, "It would seem so, though I still don't know exactly *why*. I can't *imagine* they would rally around a madman like Krasik."

Jonas sighed, "Who else could they possibly choose?"

Andariana turned her face away. She couldn't bear anyone catching sight of her fear just then, "I felt the same might be true, I'll admit. But to be faced with it is another matter entirely."

"I'm sorry to be the one to inform you, but it's worse than you fear."

She looked at him sharply, "What do you mean?"

"Krasik has grown stronger since you last dealt with him."

Andariana frowned, "His military will swell with Perron's added muscle, but I doubt he is a tactician to match our Lord Captain...."

"Before I departed for Dalita, I mentioned that Emelian Krasik had been referred to as the 'Zra-Uul'. While with the Angelus," Jonas shared a meaningful glance with his aunt, "I was able to read a good deal on the subject."

Andariana sat down, "And what have you to report?"

Jonas sighed, "We are in a great deal of trouble."

CHAPTER 35

AN UNCERTAIN SNOW

THE INN WAS small, though by no means shabby. Henry observed it with the same critical eye he'd reserved days before for a bushel of wheat. It had obvious flaws, certainly, but the exterior was satisfactory on the whole. Bad advice for evaluating any bushel of produce, but Aleksei seemed capable handling any internal rot in the inn, should the need arise.

Aleksei turned to his father, "This'll do."

Henry glanced back at the tavern and nodded. It had been almost two decades since he had traveled, much less lodged, away from home. He readily bowed to his son's own newly-gained expertise.

Aleksei nodded towards the stable, "I'll get the horses settled. Would you grab us a room?"

Henry handed his son the reins and walked inside, hopeful not only for a room, but a pint. Perhaps even two. It had been a hard day's ride from the farm, and while he understood the severity of the situation, and the necessity of the pace his son was setting, he also recognized the opportunity to unwind from such stresses.

After all, Aleksei had been dealing with this sort of intensity for a good while now. Henry had spent the last twenty years of his life in the calm complacence of a farmer on the Southern Plain. That experience hardly lent itself to harsh rides across the Plain, or brief stops at rough inns.

He approached the counter with a ready smile.

"Begging your pardon, ma'am," he said with a small bow to the proprietress, "I am in need of a room."

"One silver crown." she said, eyeing him up and down.

Henry's eyes widened, "A piece of *silver*? For a *night*? That's madness! Surely you charge a more reasonable fee than *that*!"

"It's a silver crown or get out." the woman spat.

"Fifteen coppers." came Aleksei's forceful voice over Henry's shoulder.

Henry turned in surprise to see his son standing there, looking for everything to be a lord or a knight. *Well*, Henry supposed, Aleksei *was* the Lord Captain, and an Archanium Knight besides. More than either of those, his son was consort to the bloody *Prince*. By all rights, that made him far more than any petty lord.

"Fifteen coppers and not a penny more. Unless, of course, you'd like to extort messengers of the Lord Captain?"

The woman's eyes narrowed, "*Aye*, sir. Fifteen coppers it is. A favor, sir, for the *good* Lord Captain."

Aleksei smiled charmingly, "And tell me, ma'am, what would you be thanking the Lord Captain for?"

She shrugged, "I've heard the rumors, sir. He's done away with Lord Malak, hasn't he?"

Aleksei chuckled dryly, "That's the word. If it's to be believed."

She rested her hands on her hips, "Well I say it is, and *I* say it's a crying shame they're after him for it. Did us a favor, if you ask me. Malak did nothing but tax us into the ground so he could go on getting fat in Kalinor, with all the other leeches. Serves him right."

Aleksei said nothing to that. He merely threw down the coppers and bowed his head, "Good evening to you, ma'am. What room are we taking?"

"Third on the left, upstairs." she said after a bit of consideration.

"Much appreciated, ma'am."

Aleksei took Henry gently by the arm, and led him to the room the woman had indicated. After bolting the door securely, he turned to find his father staring at him in surprise.

"You *lied* to that woman." Henry said matter-of-factly.

Aleksei paused, "In a way, I suppose. What would you have me do? Announce my presence for every pickpocket and cutthroat in the room to salivate over? I have no interest in killing anyone tonight. Do *you?*"

Henry looked away, but shook his head. Aleksei sighed. It had never occurred to him that it might be difficult to explain the necessity of deception his career sometimes required. Certainly not to his father.

"Jonas is coming to meet us in Mornj, Da. I mean to meet him there as quickly as possible. You've seen the work I have to do sometimes. You helped me burn the bodies. So why are you surprised by one small deception?"

Henry shrugged his shoulders, "I don't know, Son. I know that you kill people to keep your own life. And Jonas', of course. I understand that. It's basic survival. But I can't help but feel we robbed that woman."

Aleksei arched an eyebrow, "Why? Because we paid less than she demanded? No, Da, she wasn't cheated. But *you* would have been, if you'd handed over that silver crown. The world isn't black and white, Da. Not like that.

"The innkeeper thought she could get a few more coppers out of you, because she knew you weren't from 'round here. I had the same thing pulled on me when I visited Keiv-Alon for the first time. But even *then* I knew it was wrong, even if I wasn't sure how."

"You've always had a good eye for justice." Henry muttered.

Aleksei fought back the groan building in his throat. "The point is, you're not on the farm anymore, Da. You're not in Voskrin anymore. These people won't respect you for being honest or hardworking. They don't care about that.

"All they care about is how much money you have, and how easy it'll be to get it away from you. They won't breathe down our necks *too* hard, because they think we have important friends. But if we were just commoners, there would be no concern for our wellbeing, only for the profit we represent."

Henry refused to meet Aleksei's eyes, "I didn't realize life in the city turned you into such a cynic."

"I'm *not* a cynic, Da. But I also understand people better than I used to. I could live each day a happy man if I believed everyone in Ilyar was helping each other out, and serving the common good, rather than their own interests. But it's just not so.

"Even the angels in Dalita are driven by power and gold to some extent. The men and women who claim to be so pious in service of their gods or goddesses have *some* self-interest. *That's* what living in the city has taught me."

Henry nodded, but said nothing. Aleksei gave up trying to justify himself to his father. If Henry didn't want to believe his son, no amount of argument would change that.

Aleksei just didn't want his father to have to learn the hard way, as he had. There would be no mystical bond to a powerful Magus to save Henry, were he to make a mistake.

"I'm going to the stable." Aleksei said finally. "I want to make sure they brushed Agriphon down properly. Will you be alright up here alone?"

"I managed quite well in your absence before." Henry grumbled, with but a trace of bitterness. "I believe I can manage again."

Aleksei sighed to himself and stepped out of the room, shutting the door firmly behind him.

He hated this. What had *changed*? When he'd first left the farm, it had been all he could do to keep from running back. But now...now there was this tense civility between himself and his father.

The man seemed more a stranger than the kind, gentle man Aleksei remembered. While they'd been on the farm, everything had seemed much as it used to be. But ever since they'd been on the road, Henry had been different.

He's probably just adjusting to the change. A familiar voice echoed in his mind.

Aleksei froze, his hand on the door that led out into the stable yard. Then, with a mixture of joy and disbelief, he flung the door open and rushed outside.

A light snow was falling, the first snow of the season. It had already dusted the corral and the yard, but there was no mistaking the green-eyed sparrow perched puffed-up on the gate. Aleksei grinned, coming a few paces short of the gate and standing still.

"You said you'd meet me in Mornj." he said softly.

The air currents were stronger than I'd expected this time of year. Jonas responded with a hint of amusement.

After a long moment, Aleksei realized that the Magus didn't intend to shift back into his human form.

"What's wrong?" he asked.

We need to talk. Jonas thought gravely.

Aleksei's smile faded. Matters, it seemed, were far more serious than he'd first believed.

Jonas flitted onto his shoulder as Aleksei walked into the stable, questioning his Magus while he located and checked his horse.

"Did you find what you were looking for?" Aleksei asked gently.

Something to that effect, yes. We believe the Prime Gate remains sealed for the time being. But the Angelus seems blithely unconcerned about the Presence being unleashed.

Aleksei frowned, "Does that seem out of character?"

Not particularly, which is cause enough for alarm. But even if the seal is unbound today, the Gate won't open until the next full moon.

Aleksei nodded, "Well, seeing we just had one a few days ago, it'll be a few weeks before the next one."

Precisely. When I can find the time, I'd like to fly to the Cathedral of Dazhbog, just to make sure everything is being properly looked after. But for the moment, I'm afraid we'll have to trust my grandmother at her word. Things are of more pressing importance here.

Aleksei looked at the little bird sharply, "What do you mean?"

Half of Parliament has disappeared. Including Chancellor Perron. All the Lords involved are landed in the southern half of Ilyar.

"And let me guess," Aleksei muttered, "they're rallying around Krasik?"

I read some things in Dalita that are far from encouraging. When I spoke with Andariana, she corroborated a great deal of it. Krasik's magic is much more fearsome than I'd first imagined.

As Aleksei listened to Jonas' description, his eyes widened in surprise, "But then why has Krasik waited to make his presence known? Why not press sooner?"

Because he wasn't strong enough. From what I understand, surviving the power of the Zra-Uul is no small feat. This is Kholod magic. I have no idea how it ended up bound to a human host, but I think the experience nearly killed him. I'm guessing he's spent the past twenty years regaining strength, and learning.

He was never a stupid man, and he's the sort to know what manner of power he commands before making his move. His sudden readiness must signal that he has a considerable grasp of his abilities.

"That would certainly support the interchange you witnessed between Krasik and Bael." Aleksei muttered.

The only question, Jonas continued, *is what they're planning to do* now.

Aleksei sighed heavily, "And that's going to be the real trick, isn't it? They have to make the next move before we can get a solid idea of their intentions."

Jonas chirped irritably, *I'm pretty sure I can guess at their intent, Aleksei.*

"It's not that simple." The Knight growled. "Realizing that Emelian Krasik will stop at nothing to get Andariana off the throne is hardly enough information to prepare a defense. We have to know what they're planning before we can begin to generate our response.

"They might attack Mornj to secure a military base of operations. It's what *I'd* do if I were pressing this war. Or they might take all their available troops and drive hard for Kalinor, while they think our guard is down.

"I'm not sure what kind of tactician Krasik is, or if he's even actually in command. These are things we *have* to know before we can start to arrange our troops."

Aleksei could tell Jonas was angry, but he knew the anger to be more directed at the situation than at him. Still, he knew his Magus didn't like being corrected, even if Aleksei was right.

So, we wait *for them?* Jonas asked after a long moment.

Aleksei paused, "Well, not necessarily. When you found Krasik in Relvyn, did you catch sight of the Drakleyn?"

Jonas shook his head, *I was on my way there, but he was on the mountain path. I didn't get far enough into the pass to see anything.*

"But there's the possibility that *some* part of the structure still exists?"

Jonas shuddered and stretched his wings, *I suppose so. Why?*

"Because," Aleksei said, golden eyes glimmering in the firelight, "I think we might have found our renegade nobles."

⁂

Colonel Fredrick Rysun stood at the window, a missive from Her Majesty gripped tightly in one gloved fist. A week ago, he'd fancied himself a blessed man. He'd been granted a second chance, and he intended to prove himself worthy of the Lord Captain's faith.

But it seemed the gods were fickle in their benedictions.

He'd received the news of Lord Perron's disappearance not an hour before men started disappearing from the garrison. At first, everyone assumed they were simply out on watch duties. He should have realized the danger of desertions from the beginning.

But he'd been too trusting. He'd even sent out search parties for the missing men, thinking they'd been caught out in one of the heavy Harvest rains Mornj was suffering lately. But then the search parties had vanished as well.

Finally, the reality of the situation sank in. And now *this*.

While the Queen wasn't asking for his head, he wondered how safe he could truly be after he'd allowed so many men to vanish without a trace.

And then there was the matter of the garrison. His force had been cut in half already, and there was no telling how many more would try to desert before all was said and done.

With so few men, it would become very difficult to hold the garrison, should the city come under attack. And Rysun had to believe that, if so many soldiers were deserting, there was a chance they were all headed in the same direction.

His mind was awash with the logistics of holding Mornj, when a knock sounded at the door.

The Colonel turned, at once hoping for and dreading another communication from the Queen. "Enter." he said, projecting all the bravado he could muster into his voice.

The doors swung open, and Rysun's eyes widened in surprise.

"L...Lord Captain!" he stammered, falling to a knee.

Aleksei swept into the room, followed by two men Rysun didn't recognize. "Get up, Fredrick."

Rysun stood immediately, eyes still averted at the floor, "Lord Captain, let me start by apologizing for my shameful care of this garrison, and the men you placed under my command. It seems I am cursed to fail you."

There was a pregnant pause, and he finally glanced up as the silence grew unbearable.

The Lord Captain stood stock still, his thick arms folded across his chest, "Colonel, I'd like to discuss some matters of grave importance. For starters, how long will it take to strip this garrison?"

Rysun blinked, "Lord Captain?"

"We don't have much time, Colonel. This garrison must be stripped of its weapons and supplies, and those men who still remain loyal must be made ready to march immediately. I have no intention of handing over the most fortified structure in the South without so much as a whimper."

Rysun tried to sort out all his questions and understand what Aleksei was telling him to do at the same time. It was not an easy task. "Begging your pardon, Lord Captain, but *who* is going to take the garrison from us?"

Aleksei's golden eyes glittered, "The enemy, Colonel. All those men who have vanished in the night. Every man who flocks to join Emelian Krasik's banner.

"The first of them will have already arrived in Krasik's stronghold by now, and his ranks will be swelling. We need to render this garrison as defenseless as we can before they return."

"Sir? You don't plan to hold Mornj? To even *try*?"

Aleksei scowled, "Do you honestly believe we *could* hold this garrison? This *city*? We're already outnumbered five to one, and that's a rough estimate at best. Colonel, I am not in the habit of throwing away the lives of good men.

"Garrisons can be repaired, cities rebuilt. But the lives of your men cannot be returned once they are taken. No, you will strip this garrison of everything of value. I also want the gate ropes cut, the wells salted, the latrines filled in, and every door bolted as tightly as possible. I want this place in such shoddy condition that they won't *want* it."

Rysun nodded, "As you command, Lord Captain."

If it had taken him a moment to catch up, the moment had passed.

Chapter 36

Baiting the Trap

Aleksei sighed, "Thank you, Colonel." He gestured to the younger of the two men behind him, "Prince Belgi will help you with some of my more...*unusual* orders. Put his talents to good use, Colonel. We won't get another chance like this to prepare for the enemy's arrival; we *have* to make the most of it."

Jonas stepped forward and smiled at Rysun, who seemed to be at a loss for words when faced with his prince. "Colonel, perhaps we could step out into the hall? I have some thoughts that I'd like to discuss with you before we begin."

Rysun nodded dumbly and followed Jonas out of the room. When the door shut, Aleksei turned to his father, "I need to ask a favor, Da."

"What could you possibly need from *me*?"

"I need your cooperation. And *so* far that hasn't exactly been guaranteed."

Henry grunted, "I will aid you in whatever way I can, Son. You know that."

Aleksei took a deep breath, "*Good.* Because I need you to

accompany Colonel Rysun and his men into the Sulaq Hills."

"*What?*" Henry demanded, flushing with anger.

"I'm sending them into the wilderness, Da. They don't know the territory; they don't know how to survive out there. They'll have supplies to last them for a few weeks, but right now it's impossible to say how long they might have to wait for me to call them.

"In the meantime, I need you to teach them how to survive in the brush. You know that land, Da. You know how to live off it, and you can show Rysun's men."

"Are you *asking* me?" Henry said softly, "Or *ordering* me?"

Aleksei's face hardened, "Whichever is required."

Henry said nothing for a long moment, but he finally nodded, "Very well, Son. And what will *you* be doing while we're out in the brush digging up roots and boiling river water?"

"Defending Kalinor."

Henry stared at his son, suddenly speechless. It seemed no matter how many times he was reminded of Aleksei's position, it never quite sank in. The thought of his son in command of all the military forces in Ilyar was simply beyond any thought Henry Drago had ever entertained.

"Yes, that's right." Henry said finally. "I...suppose I'd forgotten."

It was a weak answer to such a statement, he knew. But perhaps, Henry mused, the reason he couldn't accept Aleksei's powers of command was because he didn't *want* to.

Henry loved his son dearly, and to think that he was going to be standing on the gates of the capital while an army marched towards him, an army led by a madman possessed by a strange power that even *Jonas* couldn't completely comprehend...it was almost more than he could bear.

And what would *he* be doing? Teaching soldiers to dig for grubs and fish in the wilds. For *what? Why?* So Aleksei could send them word if he *survived?* Henry could not have been more dismayed by the situation. He'd just given voice to it when Jonas spoke from behind him, "Fortunately, your approval is not necessary, only your obedience."

Henry turned, "Then you are fortunate, Highness, for that is all I can give you."

Jonas smiled sadly and bowed his head, "And I appreciate it, Henry Drago. More than you could ever know."

"Are you *dead?*"

Bael looked up at his sister, blood streaming from his eyes.

"No, Sister, I am more alive now than ever before."

Darielle rolled her eyes. "*Yes*, little brother, but your body has most certainly died. You heart no longer beats in your chest, lest I am mistaken."

Bael laughed, "Does it *matter?*"

Darielle shrugged, "It would to some. I trust you are satisfied now?" He glared at her, but it only seemed to amuse her all the more. "Ah, I see."

"It's impossible to describe, really." he whispered, looking away. "The power, the *hunger.*"

"Everything you've dreamed of, I'm *sure.*" she drawled.

"And more. *So* much more. Now I am more than a match for even *you*, Sister."

Darielle let out a surprisingly powerful laugh. "Don't let your mind run away with you, dear. You may have allowed the Demonic Presence into your soul, but it is still weak. Time in this world will make it stronger, but for the moment, I wouldn't go about announcing myself."

"Oh?" Bael growled, suddenly furious at her mockery, "And why should I listen to *you?*"

Darielle sighed, "Just some sisterly advice, I suppose."

Before Bael could respond, she vanished.

He looked around the vast cavern, but she was gone.

"No matter." he muttered. "We have much to do before we deal with *her.*"

Yes, the Other voice thrummed, much *to do.*

The door opened, and Rysun bowed to Jonas, "Highness, I've sent the orders you requested."

Jonas nodded, "Thank you, Colonel." He turned to Aleksei, "I'm going to go take care of a few things. When will you be ready to leave?"

Aleksei paused for a moment and considered. They couldn't afford to stay in Mornj much longer. If he was going to get to Kalinor in time to mount an adequate defense....

"Within the next half hour." Aleksei said finally.

Rysun's face registered his surprise, but Jonas nodded, "I'd second that." He turned to the Colonel, "Will that give you enough time to get the information you need from me and the Lord Captain?"

Rysun winced, but managed a nod. "I believe so, yes, Highness."

Jonas smiled, "Excellent. Well, if you'll excuse me, gentlemen, I have some urgent matters to attend to."

Rysun turned to Aleksei, "Half an *hour*, Sir?"

"I have to get back to Kalinor as soon as possible. It's only a matter of time before Krasik launches his attack, and I intend to be ready for him when he does."

"And what of us, Sir?" Rysun inquired softly.

Aleksei smiled in a way he hoped was reassuring, "I need you and your men to disappear for a while, Fredrick. I need Perron to think you've all deserted or joined him."

"You want to make twenty-five thousand men *disappear?*"

"Twenty-*six*." Aleksei corrected, "And I'm sending my father with you. He will take you into the Sulaq Hills, where you will camp, and await word from me. I'll send orders when I have a clearer picture of what we're dealing with. Until then, I need you to stay out of sight."

Rysun frowned, "And you believe we'll be able to survive in the wilds, Sir?"

Aleksei nodded firmly, "I do. You will have all the provisions of this garrison to sustain you for a time. And as I said, my father will accompany you. He knows the land. He will train your men, show them how to hunt, how to track. Combined with the supplies you'll be taking from the garrison, I believe you should be able to live from the land for a few weeks, until I can send word to you.

"If absolutely necessary, start a supply chain from Keiv-Alon, but be careful not to betray your actual position *or* your allegiances, if possible. Until one side or the other makes the first move, it'll take weeks, perhaps *months* before half the realm knows which end is up.

Keiv-Alon is central enough to be divided in its allegiances at best, and nowhere near as well-guarded as Mornj.

"If winter hits too hard in the Hills, there's always the chance we might have to take the city, to weather the men through Solstice. But it's impossible to predict too much of the future until we know Krasik's plan."

Rysun bowed his head, "As you say, Lord Captain. When do you want the men ready to march?"

Aleksei sighed, "You'll leave in the morning, Colonel. You'll start south, then swing up to the west through the Southern Plain and into the Hills. I don't want to make it too easy on anyone who might be following you."

Rysun nodded, knowing that there was no sense in arguing with the Lord Captain. Aleksei knew what he was doing, and Rysun knew the time to ask questions had passed.

"As you command, Lord Captain."

Aleksei spent his remaining time in the garrison briefing Rysun on what he and Jonas had learned about Krasik, in addition to his best guesses as to Krasik and Perron's movements in the coming weeks.

"It's difficult to speculate on the strategies of a madman, but if someone more rational is in charge of troop movements, they're going to have to start moving before the snows set in. Otherwise, they could end up trapped in any number of places between Relvyn and Kalinor. In all likelihood, Krasik will attempt a siege of Kalinor for the winter, hoping to starve us into submission."

Rysun was staring at the map laid out before him, his mind racing just to keep up with Aleksei's pronouncements. He was still a young man, and had only fought minor skirmishes against raiders along the Yrini border. But he had enough experience to appreciate his Lord Captain's foresight. And more impressive still, Rysun saw where Aleksei was going with it.

"You want to keep us in the brush until there's a siege," he thought aloud, "so that by the time Krasik's force gets comfortable holding Kalinor, we can disrupt their supply line from behind and cut them apart piece by piece. We'll know the land by then; we'll be hardened and battle-ready. And they'll have grown lazy, sitting around waiting for the siege to end."

Aleksei's eyes glittered with pride, "Very good, Colonel. From your position in the Sulaq Hills, you should be in perfect proximity to any supply lines Perron and Krasik establish between Relvyn, the Southern Plain, and northern Ilyar. Furthermore, you'll be far enough south that it will take weeks for news to reach Krasik. Those weeks will wear on his army.

"By the time you and your men arrive, Krasik's men will be half-starved and frozen. All that will be left for you is a simple clean-up operation, which I will be able to aid from within the Palace."

"It's perfect." Rysun breathed. "Assuming that Kalinor is actually the target."

"Hardly perfect, Colonel, but it *will* work, assuming that Krasik falls into the trap I'm setting. If he does something unexpected, all *this*," he gestured to the map before them, "will be nothing more than worthless conjecture.

"But I have confidence they'll commit the majority of their forces straight for the capital, splitting off a smaller force to solidify training facilities and supply lines along the southern border; advancing north as their numbers grow.

"That would give them this garrison as a fortified base of operations, feeding into their supply chains while we're trapped in Kalinor. Many of these men aren't warriors. They aren't prepared for a long war. They need to make their coup quick and surgical, or else the whole thing will fall apart."

Rysun was opening his mouth to agree when the door opened and Jonas stepped into the room, looking enormously satisfied with himself.

"We need to get on the road." he said softly.

The Knight sighed and nodded to his Magus. He folded his field map as Jonas turned his attention to Rysun.

"Colonel, I have infused the walls of this fortress with a particular sort of magic. A surprise for Perron, if he arrives to take the city. But one of the triggers is extremely time-sensitive. Therefore, I *must* ask that you and your men be gone from the garrison no later than noon tomorrow. After the sun reaches its apex, this garrison will become a *very* dangerous place."

"I understand, Highness." Rysun said emphatically.

"I hope that you do, Colonel. For *all* our sakes."

The Prince stepped back into the hall, leaving Rysun with a very unsettled feeling in the pit of his stomach. Gods, what sort of magic was Jonas referring to? He glanced at Aleksei, but if the Lord Captain had any clue as to what Jonas was talking about, his face betrayed none of it.

Aleksei finished packing his map into its hard leather case and smiled reassuringly at Rysun, "I have the utmost faith in you, Colonel. I look forward to hearing of your arrival in the wild."

"Where shall I send my reports, Sir?" Rysun asked as Aleksei reached the door.

"Kalinor." Aleksei said automatically.

Rysun frowned, "But it will take you *weeks* to reach the capital."

Aleksei smiled secretively, "No, Colonel. Not if things go according to plan. I'll look forward to hearing from you."

And then the door shut, leaving Rysun with his new orders in one hand, and what seemed to be the weight of the world slowly collapsing onto his shoulders.

CHAPTER 37

WOMAN BY THE WATER

THE ROAD LEAVING Mornj was characteristically crowded with the carts of farmers and traders, sprinkled occasionally with a peddler's wagon or a lone rider. Rysun had been all too happy to give Jonas a horse after both the Prince and Aleksei repeatedly refused Rysun's initial offer of a carriage.

Staring ahead at the slow-moving traffic, Aleksei knew they had been right to take the horse. A carriage wasn't nearly as maneuverable or adaptable as the roan mare Jonas was riding, and it would have made travel cross-country impossible.

While Aleksei was determined to avoid taking to the hills and woods that ran parallel to the road, he nevertheless wanted it to remain an option.

As the afternoon dragged on, the traffic began to break up. Soon they had the road to themselves, as the other occupants drifted away to nearby farms, or to one of the small villages that dotted the countryside.

"How long do you think it will take to reach the Wood?" Jonas asked, when he was certain they were alone.

Aleksei shrugged, "Depends on the weather. If it stays clear, we can be there in a week. If not, longer. Impossible to say at the moment, though."

Jonas nodded, settling back into the comfortable silence that saturated their journey.

The farther east they traveled, the more uneven the land became. At first it was barely perceptible, but after another several leagues, small hillocks began to pop up here and there. On the horizon, Jonas could see the beginnings of the Relvyn foothills, gently announcing the approaching mountains. Conversely, the wooded spans became less and less frequent. By the time evening approached, there were no trees in sight.

Jonas recognized the pattern well. It was very similar to the land surrounding the Seil Wood. He knew from personal experience that there were other, less tangible links between the Seil and Relvyn Woods.

A few leagues more, and they were met by a tributary of the Ylik Water, running alongside the road.

"We should probably stop for the night." Aleksei said, jolting Jonas from his thoughts.

Jonas looked up at the sky and saw the leaden cloak of darkness approaching. He nodded his agreement and followed Aleksei off the road.

As they rode north into the hilly pastureland, Jonas scanned the earth before him for badger holes. Aleksei had long ago explained the danger that animals of the wood and field posed to horses, and Jonas had been an apt pupil. After all, as much as he might want to ride at a breakneck gallop towards his destination, nothing would serve to slow him down more than a lame horse.

Aleksei brought them to a bend in the tributary, here little more than a creek, and dismounted. "I'm going to find us some food before it gets too dark. Can you start the fire?"

Jonas nodded and climbed off his mare. He removed a spike from his saddlebags so he could tie the mare's reins, but Aleksei shook his head, "Let her graze for a while. Agriphon knows not to wander too far, and she'll follow his lead."

The Prince shrugged and returned the spike, withdrawing instead flint and steel from another bag, and setting about for some kindling. It would be easy enough to light a fire with magic, but this close to the Relvyn Mountains he wanted to be *very* careful about touching the Archanium. He couldn't be sure who was watching.

Aleksei waited around just long enough to make sure everything was in order before he slung his bow over one shoulder with his quiver, and headed into the hills. He knew what he was looking for, though not how far it was. The earth seemed to speak to him, guiding his feet over the hills, pulling him north.

As he walked, thoughts raced through his head. He ran through the plans he and Jonas had already discussed, searching for any cracks in their reasoning. No matter how many times he convinced himself of their soundness, it seemed unlikely that he would ever be truly satisfied with his tactics until they were executed.

That was the only true measure of a strategy. All the double-checking and logic in the world wouldn't make a lick of difference if the enemy decided to move irrationally. It was that imperfect human element that was so often the downfall of even the most carefully crafted strategy, the most seasoned commander.

He crested another hill and stopped. Below lay his destination, a small watering hole where the local wildlife came to drink.

A woman stood by the water's edge.

At first, Aleksei took her to be a local farmer's wife or daughter, come to collect the next day's water supply. But as he drew closer, he realized that her gauzy gown was much too fine for an ordinary farm girl. No, he now recognized the gaze she leveled at him for what it was.

She was waiting for him.

"Evening," he said briskly, pulling his bow from his shoulder and gripping it in a relaxed, but vaguely threatening manner. He had seen too many things in his life to be lulled by the woman's slight stature. Physical size was no measure of one's strength, or lethality.

She smiled coolly, "Lord Captain Drago."

Aleksei set about waxing his bowstring, pretending to ignore the woman as he prepared to hunt. Gods, who *was* she; how did she know *him?*

"My presence doesn't perplex you?" she said after a moment of silence.

"Should it?" Aleksei grunted, still directing his attention to his bow.

She shrugged, "Perhaps not. We are both children of time, if not quite the same."

Aleksei offered no response. Instead he drew an arrow and began to check its fletching. He could sense the woman's growing impatience. This was obviously not what she had expected from this encounter, and that suited him just fine.

Finally she spoke, "Perhaps I have overestimated you, Lord Captain Drago. I took you to be determined, driven to survive. Your display of apathy towards my presence is most unexpected."

He spared her a brief glance.

"Tell me something, Lord Captain. You are in possession of a *very* dangerous skill. You have been gifted with the power to drain life on a whim, and in the process restore yourself. *Why* then do you still put your trust in the crude weapon you now hold?"

Aleksei didn't even pause to consider his response, "The Mantle on my shoulders is no less a tool than the bow in my hands. I do, however, find the bow a more merciful means of taking life. I have no desire to inflict suffering upon innocent creatures."

Her smile faded, "Compassion. It will aid and hinder you in the days to come."

For some inexplicable reason, Aleksei felt his skin prickle at her words. He was suddenly aware that the woman's words rang of absolute *truth.*

He realized where he'd heard such a tone before.

"You're a prophet." he said flatly.

"I've been called such before."

Aleksei scanned the horizon for signs of animals coming towards the spring. He sensed none, but that might well change once the woman was gone. Her presence grated on him.

"I have no interest in your penny prophecies." he grunted.

"You *might,* if you knew what awaited you. And the truth they contain." she said seductively.

"I don't doubt their truth. But I have no desire to have my future *dictated* to me. I'll make my own decisions, and if they coincide with your visions, so be it. If they don't, I'll be no worse off for it." Aleksei said resolutely.

"I wouldn't be *quite* so confident about that, if I were you." she said, now sounding infuriatingly amused. When Aleksei refused to press her onwards, she continued, "I did not come here to offer specters of your impending death, or dire warnings of battles yet to fight, Aleksei Drago. The gods know there will be plenty of *those* in the time to come.

"But for now, I merely require you to understand your own part in this great game as it unfolds. And that you appreciate your present...limitations."

Aleksei groaned. Perhaps if he heard her out, she would leave him to hunt in peace. "Very well, ma'am. What do you have to say?"

Jonas was heading back to camp, arms loaded with small sticks and a few actual pieces of wood. He was proud of his collection, considering how far they were from the Relvyn Wood. He was in the midst of wondering whether some of the less natural looking pieces could have come from old wagons, or perhaps furniture abandoned by the roadside, when he felt it.

The wood fell to the grass with a chaotic clatter as Jonas took off running, moving as fast as his legs would carry him. Panic rose in his heart as he sent his thoughts ahead of him, searching for the source of the bizarre disturbance.

It was as though someone was touching the Archanium, but instead of merely immersing themselves in it, as Magi did, this being was somehow *twisting* it.

Danger was very near.

Worse still, the strange vibrations were radiating from a place in immediate proximity to Aleksei. Jonas knew that when he found his Knight, he would find the source of the disturbance.

At the moment, he wasn't sure if that was better or worse.

The closer he came to Aleksei, the stronger the bond became. He now knew that Aleksei was less than a league away. Unfortunately, that could end up being very far indeed, especially on foot.

Jonas wished to the gods he could turn into a bird and fly to his Knight, but he knew better than to risk that. Touching the Archanium from this distance could spell disaster. No, he needed to remain unannounced for as long as possible.

His lungs burned from lack of oxygen. Jonas gulped air, pressing himself even harder than before, until his bond alerted him that he was mere paces from Aleksei.

Jonas caught sight of a small hill, and realized that Aleksei had to be on the other side of it, or else he would be visible.

The Magus rushed up to the top of the hill, unleashing his restraint on the Archanium as he reached his destination.

An enormous sheet of flame burst into the air behind him, poised to flow down onto whomever might be threatening his Knight.

What greeted his eyes was nothing near what Jonas had anticipated.

Aleksei stood at the edge of a small pond. A few paces in front of him stood a woman wearing a gauzy dress. She was saying something to Aleksei, but the Knight did not appear threatened, or even anxious.

Jonas let the flames fitfully die.

"Welcome, Jonas Belgi." the woman called calmly.

"Who are you?" he demanded, walking slowly down the hill, the Archanium blazing around him.

Aleksei may or may not know what she was, but now that Jonas was close enough, he had no doubts.

"You may call me Darielle." she said softly.

The woman was a prophet, and not in the way that Aya might catch a glimpse of things to come. Rather, this woman was tied intricately to one of the most confusing and dangerous regions of the Great Sphere.

To one of the Forbidden Realms.

She existed *around* the Archanium, rather than *within* it. Her power was a total enigma to Jonas, an absolute magical anomaly, yet he knew enough to both fear and respect her power.

"What do you want?"

She smiled sweetly, "I have completed my business with the Lord

Captain. And I have none with you." The prophet looked back to Aleksei, "We will undoubtedly see one another soon, Lord Captain. Good day."

And then she was gone.

Jonas relaxed as he felt the peculiar twisting of the Archanium ease. He dropped down to the ground, gasping for breath as the adrenaline faded from him.

Aleksei was by his side a moment later, "Are you okay?"

Jonas took a few more gulps of air before responding, "That woman. What did she *want* with you?"

Aleksei looked away, "She said she was a prophet. She said she'd come to tell me about my part in 'the great game'."

Jonas stared at Aleksei for a long moment before nodding.

Aleksei frowned, "Does that make sense to you?"

"A little." Jonas admitted. "Aya has referred to the future as 'the great game' before. This woman, this...*Darielle* obviously thinks you're rather special. Prophets usually don't seek people out to tell them their parts. It's considered taboo unless the person in question is particularly important. Knowing your role can change your reactions."

Aleksei nodded his understanding, though Jonas could tell his thoughts were elsewhere.

"Why don't we head back to camp." the Prince said after a long period of silence.

Aleksei looked up, as though he hadn't heard a word of what Jonas had said, but then he smiled, "Camp. Alright." It was the most forced smile Jonas had ever seen on the man.

They walked back in silence, Jonas pausing only to collect his scattered bundle of sticks.

The horses were waiting patiently for their return, Agriphon pawing the ground in greeting as Aleksei approached.

The Knight walked over to his horse and stayed there for a better part of an hour, grooming, checking tackle, and generally doing anything else he could to occupy himself.

Jonas left Aleksei to his thoughts. It was apparent enough that his Knight was processing something profoundly unsettling.

As Jonas laid out the fire, he recalled that there were rules for not sharing prophecy with those it mentioned. After all, you might hear something you didn't understand, or couldn't accept. What if Aleksei had been told that Jonas would die, but that he would somehow survive?

He was confidant such a thing was impossible, but he had also studied a great deal of prophecy in the Voralla. If time had taught him anything, it was that people regarded something as impossible only because no one had managed it before. That did not mean that it *couldn't* be done, only that it *hadn't*.

He sat down before his pile of sticks and began set them alight, trying to push his natural paranoia away. Now that he had used the Archanium in an impressive but completely useless display on the hilltop, any Magus within a hundred leagues would know exactly where they were, so there wasn't really any point in trying to maintain their stealthy approach.

Still, Jonas decided he needed to learn to survive outdoors without relying so strongly on the Archanium. Who knew when he'd have to do just that in the future? If there was one thing Jonas hated, it was being unprepared.

They were in afterglow by the time he actually managed to get the grass to catch light, and even then a gust of wind struck and blew it out. Jonas growled in irritation, tossing his flint and steel aside and willing the sticks to burst into a merry flame.

He sat back with a contented smile on his face as a wicked yellow inferno ravaged his tiny sticks.

As afterglow faded into night, and Jonas looked up to search for Aleksei. It had been well over two hours since they'd returned from the pond, and now he found the Knight missing entirely.

There was a thump behind him, and Jonas nearly jumped out of his skin. He turned to find Aleksei standing there, two thin, measly rabbits lying dead at his feet.

"I'm afraid this is the best we're going to do this late into Harvest." Aleksei said softly.

Jonas looked helplessly at the rabbits, then back to his Knight. Aleksei actually gave him a genuine smile for the first time since the pond, and crouched down to fetch the rabbits.

He sat next to Jonas, and began the repulsive task of skinning and gutting the animals. Jonas watched in horrified fascination, disgusted but simultaneously intrigued by the way the lagomorphic anatomy was constructed. He had never taken on the shape of a rabbit, but suddenly he found it an interesting challenge.

Aleksei picked up the two longest sticks from Jonas' makeshift woodpile, spitting the rabbits and laying them side by side over the fire.

Jonas hoped that Aleksei would open up to him, perhaps give him some idea of what Darielle had said, but the Knight seemed content to sit in silence and stare into the fire as the rabbits sizzled on their spits. Jonas sighed in irritation and closed his eyes, casting himself into the Archanium.

In his opinion, the Magi in the Voralla often mistook the Archanium for a mere tool, rather than the constantly changing, infinitely powerful force that Jonas understood it to be. He had never learned more about its workings than he had from simply drifting on the rainbow chaos of its waves, sensing the different regions that divided it, and receiving a deeper appreciation for the way everything was woven together.

Jonas lost track of time just drifting, and suddenly realized that he was getting very hungry. He pulled himself out of his trance and opened his eyes.

It was dark, only the brilliance of the stars and the low burning red of his little fire providing illumination. At first he wasn't even entirely sure where he was, but then he felt the warmth from the dying embers.

Jonas sat up, and only then realized he had been lying down. He looked down at the bedroll wrapped around him, and found that while he had been suspended in the Archanium, Aleksei had put him to bed.

Now the Knight sat a pace away, his eyes alert in the dark night.

"Aleksei?" Jonas asked softly, wincing at the brittleness of his voice.

"Yes?"

"I don't suppose there's any of that rabbit left, is there?"

Aleksei chuckled, shifting from where he sat on his bedroll. Then he leaned over to Jonas and offered him small, shadowy object. Jonas realized a moment before his hand closed around the bottom of it that it was one of the spits.

"Thank you." he murmured, before tearing into the cold rabbit.

It was practically flavorless, of course, but Jonas hardly cared. He ate every scrap he could find in the darkness before tossing the remains onto the pile of coals just a pace away.

"Better?" Aleksei asked.

"Much."

"Good, now get some sleep."

Jonas frowned as he lay back down. There was something in Aleksei's voice that worried him. *Gods*, how he wondered what Darielle had told the Knight to make him so pensive.

True sleep took him the moment his head touched the bedroll.

The next few days passed without much change. Aleksei remained just as reserved, though no less alert. Jonas began to feel edgy as they neared the Relvyn Wood. The days passed to completion, and yet they encountered no one, which was not to say there were no signs of life. As traffic on the eastern road had dwindled, Aleksei had picked up on something far more intriguing.

The road was far more heavily travelled, primarily from men on foot, than warranted any proper explanation this late into Harvest, especially this close to the Wood. Aleksei spent a great deal of time scouting the road and the surrounding woodland, confirming his suspicions.

In the past several weeks, a great many men, many wearing Legion-issued boots, had used this road, each and every one of them seeming to have the same destination in mind.

But by noon of the seventh day, the Relvyn Wood finally came into view. And with it, a very perplexing sight.

"Is that..." Jonas began.

Aleksei nodded, answering before Jonas had finished, "Drava."

Jonas could hardly believe his eyes. What he had left behind as a battle-ravaged village of foresters and herdsmen had been completely transformed in the weeks since their departure. A stout wall of spiked wooden posts now protected the village, a sturdy gate opening periodically to admit a shepherd and his flock, or a villager off on some errand or another.

They approached the gates by mid-afternoon. A sentry looked down at them from the guard tower, "Who are you? State your business."

"Lord Captain Aleksei Drago. I'm here to address the people of your village."

"About *what*?" the sentry demanded.

Aleksei's eyes narrowed, "The nature of your defenses. Now open the gate."

"I must apologize, Lord Captain," the man said the title as though it was an alien sound on his tongue, "but we *cannot* open our gate to you without the approval of the village council."

"And why not?" Aleksei asked, now frowning in confusion. "What are you watching for?"

The sentry looked unsure, "*Spies*."

"Spies, soldier?" Aleksei spoke the honorific contemptuously.

"Aye, spies." the sentry said, sounding more and more uncertain with each passing moment. "From the North?"

If Aleksei had been confused before, he was now calm as death itself. Jonas decided it was better if he simply didn't say anything at all.

Aleksei looked meaningfully at his Magus. Jonas heard the command as though Aleksei had shouted, even though the Knight hadn't uttered a word.

He sighed.

Something was *definitely* wrong with Aleksei. He was generally much more lenient with words. Actions were always a last resort.

Nevertheless, Jonas knew what he wanted.

He reached into the Archanium and touched a particularly nasty region of the Great Sphere, deep within the chaotic rage of the Nagavor, channeling his intent towards the gate.

There was a brilliant flash. The gate was outlined in purple light for a split second, and then it was gone, leaving only a wisp of ash and smoke.

Aleksei gave the gaping sentry a cursory glance, "Thank you."

And then he rode Agriphon into the middle of the village green, waiting patiently for Jonas, for the people of Drava, to join him.

Jonas sat atop his horse, listening to the reactions of the people around him. It seemed that while a few recognized Aleksei, the vast majority were confused as to who this man was, and just how he'd demolished their gate.

"Now just a minute!" a young man cried, pushing past people gathered on the green and marching up to Aleksei, his eyes narrowed. "Just *who* do you think you are, marching into our village like this?"

Aleksei glowered down at the man, "I'm the Lord Captain of Her Majesty's Legion. *You* are?"

"I...I'm the mayor." the man stammered.

"And tell me, why have you surrounded your town with a wall? Who are you defending Drava *from*?"

The mayor looked as though he were about to cry, "F...From the invaders, from the North."

"By '*invaders*' I take it you mean the Legions of Ilyar." Aleksei said coolly.

"That...that's right." the mayor squeaked.

Aleksei glared at the man. He looked to be just over twenty summers. The Knight studied the mayor for a long moment, then looked up to the crowd of people gathered before him.

"People of Drava," he bellowed, "this will be your *only* warning. If you stand in opposition to the Crown, you *will* be defeated. Your rebellion is gross ingratitude for the protection provided to you by the Crown, and by *me*.

"I take this act of rebellion as an affront against all that I have fought for. I have risked my *life* for you, and you repay me with *treason*?"

"What will do you, then?" shouted a man from the crowd, "Cut us all down right now?"

The crowd started to laugh, but the terrible anger in Aleksei's eyes silenced them, "No, I won't cut you down. You've proven yourselves unworthy of my blade. I'll instead deliver you a harsher fate. I will leave you to suffer the due consequences of your actions.

"Those who want a life beyond this village should leave *now*. By the end of this 'rebellion', *one* of us will be proven right, the other wrong. But know this, people of Drava. If you *should* survive this war, and I am proven the victor, I will *not* be merciful."

With that, Aleksei turned Agriphon around and spurred him into a gallop. Jonas followed, his face as impassive as Aleksei's. The same absolute rage that burned in Aleksei's heart now surged in his own.

He was at once surprised and pleased that Aleksei had recognized Drava's fortifications for what they were. Jonas had merely grasped that Drava was preparing for the coming war. But Aleksei had always understood common people better than he had.

They were out of Drava in seconds. After half a league, Aleksei slowed Agriphon, redirecting him towards the Wood. Jonas followed, hoping that when they reached the forest, Aleksei would slow down and give his Magus some indication of what was going through his head.

A moment after they'd reached the tree line, Aleksei slowed Agriphon to a trot. Jonas caught up to him and glanced at his Knight. Anger was still etched into the man's face, but Jonas could sense it softening across the bond.

"What will happen to them?" Jonas asked after a long while.

Aleksei did not divert his eyes from the path, "I gave them fair warning. If they listen, they'll leave. The rest will stay. And then Relvyn will swallow them. They will wake one morning to find their houses gone, their precious wall reclaimed. And then they will wander through the forest, searching for food and water, yet finding neither, until they too are consumed by the Wood."

"Do you think that's fair?" Jonas asked carefully.

"It's *just*." Aleksei responded.

Jonas nodded to himself, understanding that right now it was best not to argue with his Knight. After all, Aleksei was not only operating in his capacity as the Lord Captain, but also as the Hunter of the Wood. Aleksei had told him of the Relvyn Wood's strange connection to the Seil, and how the Seil had beseeched him to protect Relvyn.

"How deep *is* this Wood?" Aleksei asked suddenly.

Jonas frowned, "I'm not exactly sure. I flew over most of it the last time I was here, but I would guess somewhere around fifty leagues?"

Aleksei brought Agriphon to a halt. Jonas did likewise, then looked questioningly at his Knight.

"At this rate, it will take us days to travel fifty leagues." Aleksei said calmly. "We need to get there faster. I'm not sure we *have* days at this point."

Jonas nodded, not bothering to ask how Aleksei planned to get them there "faster". In this Wood, Aleksei was in his element. All Jonas could do was follow diligently, and hope not to get lost in the process.

Aleksei looked around for a moment, seeming to take in the trees, the underbrush, the sounds and smells of the Relvyn Wood. And then he spoke.

"Father Wood, we are in haste. Take us to your eastern border so that we might fulfill our mission and return to our home."

Jonas listened carefully, waiting for something to happen, but Relvyn remained motionless.

He realized Aleksei was watching him, and he smiled, "Shall we proceed?"

Aleksei opened his mouth as though to speak, but then seemed to think better of it. Jonas sighed and rode next to his Knight, ever deeper into the Wood.

They rode for several minutes in absolute silence, during which Jonas looked about, trying to discern their location. If the Wood had responded to Aleksei's request, they would soon find themselves at the edge of the mountains. If, however, this forest was not quite as attuned to Aleksei's voice as the Seil Wood, then they were in for a *very* long ride.

No sooner had the thought crossed his mind when a bend in the path brought them in view of the forest's edge.

Aleksei smiled to himself, whispering a thanks to the Wood as they approached the rugged chalk path that lead to the ruins of the Drakleyn.

"We'll leave the horses here." Aleksei said, dismounting and tying off Agriphon's reins so they wouldn't get tangled in his absence.

The Prince dismounted and did the same, though he was less than pleased at the prospect of hiking several miles of mountain terrain.

Aleksei fixed him with an arresting golden glare, "Jonas, it might be better for you to assume another form. It will be much easier to explain a lone man going in and out of camp. Two might be a bit trickier."

Jonas chuckled to himself, ignoring Aleksei's dour demeanor. "Any suggestions?"

"Something *useful*."

The Magus blinked at the response, then closed his eyes. He considered the shape of a coyote for a moment, but then decided that he would be too easily recognized if he ran into Bael or Krasik.

Then he had an idea.

Reaching into the Archanium, Jonas fixed the image in his mind, then envisioned himself melting into the new form. He clutched at the Archanium, pulling it around himself, willing his body to change.

Nothing.

Again, Jonas gripped the spellform and forced the image in his mind to conform to his desire. After a few aborted attempts, Jonas finally managed to transform thought into action.

When he opened his eyes, Aleksei was staring at the small mountain pony that was his Magus in staggered surprise. Jonas smiled, shivering at the odd feeling that prickled across his flesh. Aleksei actually laughed for the first time in days.

"Well, it won't be the *first* time I've ridden you."

Jonas shrugged, which translated as violently shaking his enormous head. Aleksei turned to Agriphon, removing a few supplies from his saddlebags. Then, still looking greatly amused, he climbed onto Jonas' back.

"Still," the Knight said into his ear, "better not let anyone get too close to us. I'm not sure I could explain a pony with green eyes."

Jonas chuckled, then glanced at the two horses. Agriphon was regarding him contemptuously, as though his very presence was an insult to the beautiful warhorse.

He resisted the urge to nip at the stallion as he trotted past and out onto the trail. The day was wearing on, but Jonas knew it would be a long time before either of them was allowed to rest again.

CHAPTER 38

THE DRAKLEYN

AS THE ROAD wound up through the pass, the air grew cooler. Aleksei found himself wishing he'd brought something heavier than his light leather coat.

Jonas plodded along steadily, keeping his thoughts to himself, which suited Aleksei just fine. For his part, Aleksei had quite enough to think about without having to balance his thoughts against conversation.

His encounter with the Prophet Darielle a week before had left him shaken. Her dark portents haunted him, and it was all he could do to focus on the task at hand.

Aleksei had been around prophets before. Aya had delivered prophecy in his presence, and he had been none the worse for it. But his experience with Darielle had been very different indeed. When she spoke the words, Aleksei saw images in his head. He would have shared her visions with Jonas, if he thought it would do any good.

But he knew better.

No, the fewer people who saw Darielle's visions, the better.

Aleksei wasn't even sure *he* believed most of them. After all, he had heard similar predictions from doomsayers in city squares. It didn't take much talent to predict a gloom-ridden future for a realm on the verge of civil war.

But Aleksei had the sneaking suspicion that her words rang true. Why else would she seek him out so specifically? Why not tell Jonas? Why *him*?

As they ascended higher into the mountains, the air became thinner, and *colder*. His doubts receded with the vegetation. Snow began to fall after an hour of climbing, and Aleksei began to worry for his Magus.

"Are you warm enough?" he asked, speaking into Jonas' ear.

"If I get any warmer I might catch fire. I know you might be catching a chill up there, but I'm climbing a mountain and carrying a husky farm boy." the pony responded crossly.

Aleksei sat back, trying to restrain his laughter.

The silence returned, and his mirth faded. Aleksei found himself suddenly thirsty. The comforts of palace life had caused him to forget how dry the air was in the biting cold.

He drank from one of the waterskins, then dropped back sullenly into his thoughts.

"Your Mantle is fierce indeed. Such a shame you don't truly wield it. The Demon's fires will rage all around you, but you won't put out one fire by igniting another. It will take your very last breath to finally drown it all in an ocean of blood. But when it crashes down upon you, promise me Aleksei Drago, promise me you will swim. Promise me you will run."

He winced as the images accompanying the words crashed through his mind unbidden. The screams of men filled his ears. They pleaded with him, but the Mantle drank them in anyways. He could smell men burning as he ran from the encroaching flames of the Demon's wrath. It was almost more than he could bear, but he forced himself onwards.

Aleksei shook his head violently as the visions vanished in their completion. *No!* No, there *had* to be a way to prevent that. Aleksei knew the visions for what they represented. It was the fall of Kalinor. It was the slaughter of his men at the hands of Bael, and all his dark magics. And it was proof of his own cowardice in the face of danger.

He closed his eyes against the fading afterimages, but he couldn't rid his mind of the screaming, or the stench. It was as though Darielle had etched it into his mind so that he could never forget, as long as he lived.

"Aleksei?"

Jonas' voice brought Aleksei back to the present with a jolt, and he opened his eyes. For a moment, he was confused as he stared out into the horizon. The Relvyn Mountains soared into the distance for leagues before finally succumbing to the Autumn Sea. Then he realized that Jonas' head was directed not ahead, but *below* them.

Aleksei craned his neck over the edge of the path, and almost fell off Jonas' back. Before them, the mountain sloped down into a gentle valley. Rising against the opposite cliff were the shattered remains of the most threatening structure Aleksei had ever seen.

The Drakleyn.

But worse by far was the sight of what awaited them beneath the Drakleyn's imposing edifice. Rows upon rows of white triangular tents, pitched in perfect Legionnaire form. *Thousands* of them.

"How many do you think there are?" Jonas asked in choked disbelief.

Aleksei thought of all the reports he'd heard of Legionnaires abandoning their posts to rally around Krasik's banner. He had hoped that a majority of those were men returning to their homes, to defend against the inevitable fight. Now he knew just how mistaken he'd been.

"I...I don't know. If they're following standard Legion practice, there are four men to each tent. So I would estimate their force at around seventy or eighty thousand."

"And how many troops do *you* command?"

Aleksei realized that he didn't actually know. He hadn't returned to Kalinor since the desertions began. The only force whose size he was even remotely certain of any more was Rysun's.

"At present, only thirty-one thousand I can count on. Twenty-six with Rysun, and five in Kalinor."

"I'm sure there are more than that who retain their loyalties." Jonas said, but the doubt in his voice was heavy.

Aleksei nodded dumbly, his eyes still fixated on the rows upon rows of pointed white tents. The last report he'd received estimated the total size of the Ilyari Legion to be around one hundred thousand men strong. Looking down into the encampment, it wasn't difficult to guess who held the upper hand, if only in sheer weight of arms.

"We're going to have to change our strategy." he muttered.

"So what are you planning?" Jonas asked after a long silence.

Aleksei started, emerging from a stream of statistics and numbers that had suddenly taken on a vital level of importance. "We need to get to the Drakleyn." he heard himself say.

"That was my thought as well. If we can get a sense of what they're planning, we can mount an appropriate defense."

"We'll have to go through the camp." Aleksei said flatly.

"Is that really wise? What if you're recognized?"

Aleksei bit his lip, running various scenarios through his head. Yet ultimately, there was no way around it. A few hundred paces into the camp, the cliffs became so sheer as to be impassable.

"It's the only way." he said finally. "I can talk my way past the tents. It's just a matter of what happens when we reach the Drakleyn."

Jonas looked out into the encampment, "I think I have an idea. You just get us past the soldiers."

Aleksei shrugged, "If you say so."

Jonas backed up slowly from the cliff's edge, then turned and descended into the valley. Aleksei found himself suddenly very thankful that he wasn't wearing anything that would indicate his rank.

It was going to be dangerous enough walking through a sea of deserter Legionnaires who may have seen him in the past year. Being the Lord Captain was about as low profile as being the Prince's Archanium Knight.

It was near sunset by the time they reached the valley floor.

The snow was falling harder now, and Aleksei noticed that it already reached Jonas' ankles. If it kept up like this, they were going to have a difficult time getting back through the pass.

As they approached the first row of tents, Aleksei saw a sentry running towards him.

"State your name and region." the man huffed.

"Ilia Bondar," Aleksei said without pause, "from the village of Voskrin."

"That on the Southern Plain?"

Aleksei nodded, "Yep."

The sentry pulled out a small ledger and made a note with a charcoal stylus, then tucked it back into the pocket of his coat.

"All the boys from the Plain are camped at the northeast corner of the valley. Just ride straight ahead towards the command center. You can't miss it."

Aleksei bowed his head in thanks, then urged Jonas forward.

While the deserter camp appeared to be a dream of Legionnaire efficiency, closer inspection proved such a vision to be false. Among the rows of pristine white tents was an entire city of carts, stalls, campfires, and sleeping rolls that suggested that the army was much more hodgepodge than Aleksei had first presumed.

He wasn't overly surprised. This army was not privy to the supply lines that had long ago been established to ensure that the Legions were fed and clothed properly.

As a result, they had to take what they could get. If that meant buying meat pies from a few enterprising fellows from Drava or one of the other small lumber villages bordering the Relvyn Wood, then so be it.

Aleksei also noted that few of the men wore Legion-issue coats. Here and there he would see a deserter wearing the scarlet and sapphire of the House Belgi, but for the most part their clothes were patched and worn.

There were obviously no inspections taking place to ensure that everything was taken care of, and as a result he could see signs of wear in the men's equipment. Some had even left their boots outside to rot in the snow.

But just as Aleksei was feeling an overwhelming disgust for these men, he also understood what an enormous boon this could be. He may have a fraction of their numbers, but his men were disciplined, well-trained, and well-armed.

Their swords were sharp, their armor was kept in good repair, their clothes were mended and clean. Such things not only made for more efficient soldiers, but also helped keep the men healthy and free of disease. And disease could lay waste to an army just as effectively as swords or spellcraft.

After riding through what seemed like leagues of white tents, Aleksei finally caught sight of the end. He rode up to the last tent before the valley wall, and looked to his right. There, rising into the darkening sky, stood the remains of the Drakleyn.

"Alright, what's your plan?" he whispered.

"Look straight ahead. Do you see that outcropping of rocks?"

Aleksei looked up and saw a small collection of boulders huddled next to the Drakleyn's outer wall. "I do."

"You'll dismount there so I can shift. And then we'll need to do a little reconnaissance."

"You'll go inside?"

"If I can find out where Krasik meets with his generals...."

Aleksei appraised the structure of the ruins. "I can circulate among the men." he announced as Jonas stopped behind one of the great boulders, "See what they've heard."

Jonas came to halt, and Aleksei slid off the mountain pony, which rapidly transformed into a sleek golden coyote.

Try to find a grapple and rope while you're there. I have a sneaking suspicion we'll have to scale that wall before the night is through. Jonas thought, a moment before he disappeared from view.

Aleksei nodded and sighed heavily to himself, pulling up the collar of his coat and stepping back into view of the camp. No one paid him any mind as he wound his way through the rows of white tents, keeping his ears tuned for any conversation that might be useful.

From just a cursory examination, Aleksei knew that his first suspicions had been correct. Order was lax. It would be easy for disease to spread, for men to freeze to death, or even *starve* without anyone noticing. Every good officer woke up in a cold sweat with such concerns, especially with so large a command.

"Just making my job easier." he muttered.

"...arrived tonight, I heard."

"Perron too? Or just that other one...*Declan.*"

Aleksei turned in the direction of the voices, and walked casually by. Four men were standing inside a tent around a small fire. The top of the tent had been opened up to let the smoke out, but despite this effort, the air in the small space was practically opaque.

He stepped into the tent and slipped next to a fellow who looked like he wouldn't notice if a Salamander sat on him.

"Perron too, I heard. That means they're *all* here now."

"So what're they gonna to do, then? Surely we can't be set to march 'til the *snow* melts."

"That's what *I* thought. But I heard from Bert that there's talk of marching in a few *days*."

"*Days?* That's *madness!*"

"Still, it's got to be a fair sight better than sitting 'round here." the man next to Aleksei coughed.

"When're they gonna talk formal?" Aleksei asked gruffly into the smoke.

"Formal? Ah, there's a big council planned tonight. Bert up in the castle, *he* says Perron was in a right state about it. I bet the old boy'd like a pull off the bottle and a pretty girl 'bout now, but no sir! He's gonna to be sittin' with Krasik and the Dark Man himself!"

Aleksei nodded to himself. Krasik and Bael. So Perron was less than thrilled by the prospect of a war council?

An idea began to hatch in Aleksei's head. He needed to get back to the boulder field. Gods, he hoped Jonas had discovered where the men were going to meet.

If they could find that out, they might actually be able to listen in. It was a long shot, but worth the risk if they could learn *anything* about what was coming.

"Come on." Aleksei said, taking the coughing man next to him and steering him out of the smoky tent. "Let's get you some fresh air."

"Thank you kindly, Captain."

Aleksei tensed before realizing that the man hadn't recognized him. He patted the man's shoulder, wincing as a coughing fit overcame the soldier. Aleksei would wager his command that whatever illness this man had would be spread throughout the troops come spring. And soldiers couldn't fight if they couldn't breathe.

He suddenly recalled Jonas' request. "Say now, you wouldn't know where a good bit of rope and a grapple could be found, would you?” Aleksei asked after they'd walked several paces from the tent.

“Sure thing, Captain.” the man coughed. “My tent's just here on the left. I've got one you can borrow.”

“Thanks, friend.” Aleksei said, following the man into his tent.

“What do you want with it anyhow?” the sick man asked as he rummaged around in a pile of equipment.

“Me and some of the boys want to tie up this horse we found wandering around, but every rope we try breaks. Can't get the blighter to stay put.”

It was the weakest excuse Aleksei had ever managed to fabricate, but the sick soldier just laughed, “Oh yeah, them horses can be a handful. 'Specially in *this* weather.”

Moments later, Aleksei was threading his way back towards the boulders. He exited the camp without incident, sidestepping the sentries, and was soon standing behind one of the giant rocks.

Aleksei stood with his back against the boulder, keeping his ears tuned for the crunch of approaching footsteps. Unfortunately, the snow buried all but the most pungent smells emanating from the camp, so he was unable to track by the wind.

The sky was black as pitch by the time Jonas returned. As a coyote, his pale gold coat blended in so well with the snow that when he shifted back into a man, Aleksei nearly jumped out of his skin.

“You wouldn't *believe* the state of that place.” the Magus muttered.

“I don't know, it couldn't be worse than the camp.”

Jonas gave Aleksei a look that said he begged to differ. Finally the Magus asked, “Did you hear anything worthwhile?”

“As a matter of fact I did. Perron arrived this morning with several of the Southern lords in support, including Declan. The men I was listening to seemed to think there was going to be an important tactical summit tonight.”

Jonas nodded, “That matches what I heard in the Drakleyn.”

“Any idea where this meeting will be taking place?”

“Perron kept moaning about having to go all the way to the north tower.”

Aleksei arched an eyebrow, “You *saw* Perron?”

“No one notices one extra mouse when the whole place is

crawling with rats." Jonas chuckled.

"So which one would you call the north tower?" Aleksei asked, looking up at the bluff prominence of the fortress, and the small forest of towers that dominated its skyline.

"The north tower was the command center when the Drakleyn was a weapon." Jonas pointed towards the tower in question. "From the embrasures, you can see the entire valley. As you can imagine, it makes for a highly defensible position."

Aleksei's eyes traced a trail of walls and ledges back from the north tower, towards their position on the western side of the wall.

"We can get there from here." Aleksei declared, tying the rope to the grapple and looking to Jonas for confirmation that he agreed.

Jonas breathed a deep sigh, then looked up at the wall towering above them. "Are you ready, then?"

Aleksei nodded. "Can you tell where Bael is?"

Jonas embraced the Archanium and searched for the Magus. After a moment to searching, however, Jonas realized that there were too many of Bael's Magi in the valley to single the man out.

"There're too many. I can't–"

All at once, the hundreds of Magi filling his head vanished. In their place, Jonas could only feel Bael. Or at least the walking abomination that Bael had *become*.

"Jonas?" Aleksei asked, stepping forward and gripping the Magus' arm as he swayed.

His eyes snapped open, "I think I've found him."

Aleksei searched the bond, and felt a river of revulsion flowing through the prince.

"Are you alright?"

Jonas steadied himself against the wall. "I just...I didn't expect him to be this *strong*. It's like nothing I've ever felt before." He turned and pointed to the base of the tower, "He's still down there. Has been for a few hours, but I have a feeling he'll be present for any tactical decisions. His abilities will tip the scales in a very different way than we've dealt with before."

"So as long as he stays put, we've got time. If we can get into the war room before they do, we might have a chance of listening in."

"Of course," Jonas said thoughtfully, "if we're too late, there's also the chance that he'll sniff us out and hunt us down."

Aleksei growled. "Let's try to keep our minds positive for the moment."

"Very well then," the Prince said, gesturing towards the wall, "you may climb when ready, Lord Captain."

A moment later, Jonas scurried up Aleksei's trouser leg and climbed into his shirt pocket. Aleksei looked down at the tiny brown wood mouse peeking out at him, and chuckled in spite of himself. There was wonderful irony in the idea of Jonas Belgi turning into a mouse that never failed to amuse him.

Stepping up to the wall, Aleksei let out several lengths of rope and spun the hook. He waited until it was whistling, then released. The rusted iron shot into the air, sailing clean over the wall. Aleksei gave it a few measured pulls, finally catching it among the jagged stones.

Gripping the rope in both hands, he planted one boot against the stone of the wall and pulled himself up, hand over hand. In a matter of moments, he reached the top and lifted himself onto the edge of the wall. It took a second to unhook the grapple, and then he was jogging across the narrow, snow-covered pathway.

He reached the joint where the wall connected with the body of the fortress, and looked down into the courtyard. From this height, Aleksei estimated there to be at least a score of sentries below him. If all went according to plan, none of them would ever be the wiser to his presence.

Aleksei found his way along a short ledge that protruded from the main structure. It was broken in places, but nothing he couldn't jump. His main concern was to avoid kicking snow on the sentries beneath him.

If they saw him now, he was dead.

Fortunately, none of the men seemed to pay much attention to anything above their eye level. They seemed more concerned about an uprising from the lower ranks than the lone man hugging the walls twenty paces above them.

He reached the far side of the ledge and found himself standing just beneath a guard tower.

Aleksei took a deep breath, knowing that there was no other way to reach his target. He was going to have to climb the tower, and silence whomever was up there before an alarm was raised.

For a long moment, Aleksei breathed in the frigid winter air and concentrated on what he was about to do. He couldn't afford a misstep.

Then he stretched upwards and gripped the snowy edge of the battlement. Marshaling all his strength, he heaved himself up and over the short wall.

One guard stood with his back to Aleksei. From the looks of it, the guard was more interested in the goings on down in the courtyard than with keeping a good watch.

Aleksei slipped his sword from its sheath and stepped quietly behind the man, preparing to run him through.

At the last second, the man leapt out of the way and pulled his knife, lunging towards Aleksei. The Knight altered the course of his blade and swung it at chest height, hacking almost completely through the man in one clean sweep.

And then he realized he was staring into the shocked eyes of Pyotr Krovel.

Aleksei lost his grip on his sword and stumbled back, staring at his childhood friend as the man dropped to his knees and coughed a stream of blood.

And then he died.

Aleksei sat down in the snow, his breathing matched only by the hammering of his heart. Tears leapt into his eyes even as he searched for a way to understand what had just happened.

Aleksei? Jonas asked. *Aleksei, are you alright?*

The Knight nodded, but there was no energy, no conviction left in him. He felt drained, as though he'd just been struck by lighting. The world was spinning, and he could hardly begin to keep his balance.

Aleksei leaned to the side and violently retched into the snow. His stomach was on fire, and the smell of blood and viscera didn't help matters.

Jonas climbed down Aleksei's coat and into the snow before shifting into a man. He walked over and looked down at Pyotr Thatcher's cold, glassy eyes, then back at Aleksei.

"Who was he?"

"His...his name was Pyotr." Aleksei said brokenly. "We grew up together. When I went back to the farm, I was told he'd left his wife for Perron's militia. At the time, I didn't really understand the weight of what was happening, so I didn't think much more of it. But I *never* thought...." His words broke off as quiet sobs overtook him.

Jonas wrapped his arms around Aleksei's shoulders. He could feel the conflict taking place within the Knight. Aleksei whimpered into Jonas' shoulder, and Jonas hugged his Knight tighter. It was difficult for him to see Aleksei so upset, and yet at the same time he realized that Aleksei was going to have to deal with his grief by himself.

Of course, it certainly didn't help that not a handful of days before, Aleksei had been delivered a prophecy containing the gods only knew what, or that he had this very day *condemned* a village he'd risked his life to save.

Aleksei finally broke away from his Magus and stared in disbelief at the empty husk of his former friend. Bitter tears stung his eyes, as emotions he couldn't hope to name crested and crashed through him.

And then Jonas was shaking him gently, "Aleksei, you *have* to get up."

The Knight looked up at him. It broke Jonas' heart to rush the man, but they had no choice.

"Bael's heading for the tower." he whispered. "We *have* to get there before he does."

The Archanium Knight shook off his despair and came silently to his feet. The hilt of his sword had grown icy, but he gripped it grimly and twisted it out of Pyotr's chest, taking only a moment to wipe it off in the snow.

Jonas heard Aleksei mutter a prayer to Volos as he climbed back into the Knight's pocket. Aleksei made sure Jonas was secure before he hurried to the other end of the guard tower, doing his best to still the hurricane of confusion whirling within him.

The north tower soared above them.

Aleksei clenched his jaw and reached towards one of the jagged stones that jutted from the tower wall. Kholodym architecture possessed none of the simple lines or smooth purity of Ilyari masonry, so it was the work of a moment for Aleksei to find adequate hand and footholds.

The difficulty came in the form of *time*.

Every other moment, Jonas' voice would report Bael's progress in his mind. And so Aleksei pulled himself up recklessly, ignoring the danger that increased with every pace as he rose above the valley floor.

He reached the apex of the tower and hauled himself onto the edge. It took him a moment to grasp the complex layout of the fist-sized roof tiles, but once he understood the pattern, Aleksei reached forward and lifted one of the slate shingles away.

Jonas scurried from his pocket and peered over the small edge created by the tile's absence. And then he scrambled out of Aleksei's sight, onto one of the thick rafter beams that supported the roof.

Aleksei watched him disappear into the darkness of the chamber before sliding the tile back into place. He didn't like leaving Jonas to go it alone, but at present it wasn't possible for him to follow. He just had to hope no one had the presence of mind to look *up*.

Inside, Jonas glanced over the edge of the beam, breathing a sigh of relief when he saw that he was the only one in the room. He ran carefully across the beam, positioning himself over the center of the large round table that dominated the chamber.

The door opened beneath him. Jonas looked down to see Bael sweep into the room and take his seat by an imposing fireplace set into the far wall.

Even from his position in the rafters, Jonas could feel the intense change that had come over the other man.

He felt sick. This was no longer a mere Magus. Beneath him sat something indescribably evil, something wholly and completely *Other*.

The door had hardly shut before it banged open again. Men filed into the room, and Jonas tried to register each face, but it was much more difficult than he had first imagined. His mouse-eyes were ill-suited for this sort of thing. He slowed his breathing and concentrated on listening to their voices, relying on his superior hearing to fill in the blanks.

"Gentlemen," Emelian Krasik began softly, "I am pleased that you all made it here safely. What with this weather we're having, it was a concern. The troops have to eat, and you *know* how winter can be."

The nobles around the table glanced at one another uncertainly. Jonas shivered at the memory of his last encounter with Krasik, the way he was perfectly lucid one moment, violently mad the next.

"*Now* then," Krasik said, "tell me your plans for my war."

A man Jonas recognized as an exhausted and filthy Bertrand Perron cleared his throat, "According to the documents we managed to discover, Her Majesty's Legions stand at a crossroads. As you know, the Legions are made up of men sent from each nobleman's province.

"The largest of these estates are located in the South. As the noblemen gathered here this evening, myself included, have thrown our lots in with you, so too have the allegiances of our men shifted. And as we contribute the majority of men to the Legion, you now control the majority of the troops in Ilyar by proxy."

Krasik looked bored, "You have told me nothing of *interest*, Lord Perron. Pray, *when* will these troops be prepared to march on Kalinor?"

Perron choked. "*Kalinor*, Sire? Is that not a touch rash? I was thinking perhaps Mornj would be an excellent starting point."

He gave a piercing cry and clutched at his head. Blood gushed from his nose and ears, drooling down the front of his tattered coat, and spreading in a crimson umbra across the fine silk.

Krasik sighed, "Perron, I have explained this *before*. I don't *want* to wait. I don't *want* to patiently work my way up the spine of Ilyar until we're all so exhausted that the forces of Kalinor break us like rotten reeds. Need I remind you that I have attempted this once before, and I found such methods...*most* inadvisable."

Perron finally allowed himself to sit back in his chair and gulp in air as he fought to keep back tears. "Yes, Your Grace. Of *course*, Your Grace."

Krasik leaned forward, "I have *studied* the actions of Andariana's Lord Captain. Drago could be a formidable tactician. *Therefore,* I believe that any campaign waged against him will, *despite* our superior number, result in our defeat.

"So rather than launch such a traditional campaign, where we would almost *certainly* be outdone in a series of short and decisive battles, I propose a swift, strong stroke at the heart of the realm. *If* we can overwhelm their defenses before reinforcements arrive, we may be able to take the capital before anyone realizes there's a war in progress. And *if* any of you have studied your history, you will know that with the capital falls the kingdom."

"With *all* due respect, Zra-Uul," a man Jonas recognized as General Barnes ventured, "the Lord Captain is just a boy. *You* have the greatest generals of Ilyar behind you. Why would you fear a man so untested?"

Krasik shrugged, "His defeat of Bael's little toys in Drava was sufficient proof for me, General."

"But Zra-Uul," Perron said softly, "*if* we assault Kalinor, how will we break through her gates? The walls of Kalinor are reinforced with the magic of the Archanium. The stones of the city gates will repel any magical attack thrown at it."

"Kalinor *will* fall, Perron. This is no longer a topic worthy of discussion."

"Even if Kalinor *does* fall," Perron pressed, "the men will have to be fed throughout the winter, which leads me to my next question."

"The men will eat well in Kalinor." Krasik said simply.

"I have no doubt of that, Zra-Uul, but what of the time between then and now?"

Krasik smiled, "We have *plenty* of food to last us a month or two on the road. That should be sufficient to take the city, don't you think?"

Perron looked dumbfounded, "L...Lord Krasik, winter has only just begun, and the pass is already snowed in! It will be *months* before we are able to move our army from this valley. Our only solace as of now is that no one knows where we *are*. I can guarantee you that if Drago knew we were here, come spring he'd have an army waiting at the edge of the Wood to tear us to pieces the moment we showed our faces."

"Lord Perron," Krasik said, now very angry, "I will *not* be thwarted by something as inconsequential as *snow*. It will be dealt with in time to begin our march tomorrow."

Jonas had heard enough. He knew where the conversation would head from here. Perron would argue for a while longer, but in the end Krasik would get what he wanted. Jonas would learn nothing more here tonight.

No, now they needed to get out of the Drakleyn as fast as possible.

Jonas hurried back along the beam and pushed mightily against the tile he had used as an entrance. Aleksei lifted it out of his way, and Jonas scurried out. A moment later, Aleksei was racing down the wall of the tower.

The clock was ticking.

CHAPTER 39

STRENGTH IN DESPERATION

JONAS PLODDED THROUGH the snow, now nearly up to his chest. Aleksei clung to his back, shivering from the extreme depth of cold. Night had brought a drop in the temperature unlike any Aleksei had experienced, and while Jonas was protected by his thick fur, Aleksei had never been so vulnerable.

It had been relatively simple to escape the Drakleyn much the same way they'd entered, though one of the sentries had tried to stop Aleksei as he rode for the hills. Aleksei had made something up about getting a message to a rebel officer in Mornj, and had finally persuaded the man to let him pass.

The gods only knew why he hadn't simply unleashed the Mantle. Who would have noticed a frozen corpse in the snow with all the other chaos of the camp?

Jonas had galloped up the trail, but soon found himself mired in powder. It had taken hours to struggle through to the pass. And as the night crept inexorably forward, the temperature plummeted lower still.

Now they rode through the pass itself, and Jonas was growing nervous. Not only was his Knight frozen to the bone, but Jonas was also navigating between two enormous snowdrifts. He was keenly aware that one wrong step could trigger an avalanche that would instantly bury both of them under a thousand tons of snow and stone.

Still, he kept putting one hoof in front of the other. Twice he stumbled, but managed to regain his footing at the last second. As long as it had taken to reach the pass, it was nearing dawn by the time Jonas struggled through to the other side.

He suddenly burst out of the pass' rocky confines, and had to restrain himself from galloping as hard as he could for the Relvyn Wood. If he broke into a gallop now, he could still set off the snow in the pass.

"The *pass*." Aleksei breathed in his ear.

"What?"

"Collapse the *pass*."

Jonas frowned, but then he understood. An avalanche, if properly executed, could work mightily to their advantage. He turned to face the pass and reached for the Archanium.

Even as a small boy, Jonas had heard the heroic tale of the Magus Elise, the woman who had single-handedly managed to send a mountain crashing down on the Drakleyn. Her cunning, and the Magi's subsequent victory, were legendary. But the part that was so often left out of the saga was the *way* she had achieved it.

Jonas attempted to apply a similar principal now, though he was unsure he fully understood its finer points. He felt his way around the Archanium, searching the swirling confusion for anything that felt *right*. He directed his intent, inhaling sharply when the spellform suddenly blanketed his vision.

Choosing four points at random throughout the snowdrifts, Jonas focused his will into the Archanium, pouring his need into the spell with every fiber of his being.

There was a sharp *crack*, and the mountain rumbled violently.

He turned and, feeling Aleksei grip his neck tighter, galloped down the mountain as fast as his legs would carry him. The snow crested behind him after a hundred paces, but he kept running until he reached the point where the snow gave way to the rocks and shrubs, announcing the presence of the Relvyn Wood. He turned to survey the damage.

The deep cleft of the pass had vanished amidst the mass of white that now blanketed the entire mountain. Here and there, boulders protruded from the snowy wall. If it continued to snow at the same pace, morning would find the entire army effectively sealed within the valley. It might even give them enough time to mount a proper defense.

Jonas hurried down the remainder of the trail, only slowing to a trot when he reached the tree-line.

Their horses were waiting patiently, although Agriphon still looked irritable. Jonas supposed that returning with Aleksei in his present condition wasn't going to make the warhorse any more disposed to like him.

He shifted back into a man very carefully, crouching down onto the path, and setting Aleksei down slowly. The Knight had fallen unconscious at some point during the ride down the mountain, and now his breath came in ragged, shallow gasps.

Jonas slid his arms under Aleksei's back and knees, picking the man up with every ounce of strength he possessed, and carrying him over to Agriphon. "I need to ride you so I can keep him from falling off." he managed, lifting Aleksei's powerful frame onto the horse's back.

Thankfully, Agriphon didn't give Jonas any trouble. He was able to hold Aleksei up in the saddle and turn Agriphon deeper into the Wood, with the mare trotting contentedly behind.

As he rode, Jonas realized that in Aleksei's current state, there was no real way to get back to Kalinor. He had been relying on Aleksei's bond with Relvyn to take them to the Seil Wood. Without it, he would simply be riding through the Wood like any other man.

Unless....

"Father Wood," he called out, feeling a touch foolish, "I *need* Your help. Your Hunter is ill. He *has* to get back to the Seil Wood so that he can be healed. I beseech You, will you open Your paths to me?"

Jonas wasn't sure if he should expect an answer, or if the Wood could even *hear* him. This was an older magic than he'd ever experienced, something far more primal than the refined feather-brush of the Archanium.

So he simply kept riding deeper into the Wood, his arms wrapped around Aleksei's thick chest to keep the man from falling out of the saddle, his thighs burning from gripping Agriphon's flanks to steady himself. Hours passed. Jonas' arms grew heavy and numb as time slipped by, but he gritted his teeth and held on tighter.

And then the air around him suddenly changed. He stared as the trees melted into one another. Jonas wondered if his exhaustion was causing him to hallucinate, but a moment later the Wood reformed around him.

This was no longer the Relvyn Wood.

No sooner had he made this observation than there was a flash across the Archanium.

"*Jonas?*"

The prince looked up to see the most comforting sight he could have possibly conjured in that moment: golden eyes, glowing in the darkness of the Wood.

He managed a weak smile, "Hello, Roux."

⚜

Aleksei smiled, feeling the familiar warmth of healing infuse his aching muscles. He opened his eyes and found Jonas standing over him, his handsome face contorted in frustration. The Magus' hand was pressed against Aleksei's chest, and he could see the light of the Archanium passing into him.

"How did we do?" he grumbled, surprised at how raspy his voice sounded.

Jonas jumped at hearing his voice before forcing a bright smile. Aleksei knew from their bond that it was less than genuine. "Well, I collapsed the pass. But there are a few *other* things that I'm less pleased with."

"Such as?"

Jonas sighed, "I think Bael's already opened the Prime Gate."

The Knight nodded, "I'm not surprised. Darielle said something to me that backs that up."

"She didn't tell you how to *fix* it, did she?" Jonas asked lightly,

484

clinging to his fake smile.

Aleksei chuckled, his chest burning like a bonfire. "Good gods," he gasped, "what *happened* to me?"

Jonas' smile faded, and Aleksei suddenly saw how tired the man truly was. "You ended up with some severe patches of frostbite, not to mention a *very* unpleasant lung sickness."

Aleksei groaned, "There were a lot of sick men in the camp."

"Hardly surprising, given the state they're living in." Jonas muttered. "I've been healing one thing at a time since Roux brought us up to the village."

It suddenly occurred to Aleksei to take notice of his surroundings. He was lying in the middle of the warm, circular room that acted as a hub for the Ri-Hnon's household. Several questions came tumbling off his tongue, but he hadn't finished the second word when a bout of explosively painful coughing overtook him.

Jonas shook his head, returning his hand to Aleksei's chest. The warmth flooded back through him, and Aleksei breathed easier.

"Slow down," Jonas said gently, "and try not to inhale too quickly. I still haven't purged everything from your lungs, and you're breathing much faster than you should."

Aleksei tried to slow his breathing, "I can't get any air." he admitted after a moment. "I feel like I'm *suffocating*." He concentrated, and attempted measured breaths. "Jonas, how did we *get* here?"

"Honestly, I don't know. Only that we *did*. If we hadn't, you'd be in a very sorry state right now."

Aleksei attempted agree, but was instead taken over by another coughing fit. When the coughing finally subsided, it was all he could do to catch his breath.

Jonas looked into Aleksei's eyes, then concentrated harder on healing. He didn't want to jump to conclusions, but this was beyond worrisome.

While it was true that he'd been healing Aleksei for just over five hours now, only the first few moments had been spent repairing the damage done by frostbite. As a superficial malady, the Archanium had little difficulty infusing the tissue with life, and reconnecting it to the nerve fibers and blood vessels that surrounded it. But this infection, this was something altogether different.

Try as he might to burn it away with the Archanium's light, the infection grew back in an instant.

Roux entered the room, concern written across his face. He had spent the night listening to Aleksei cough, and to hear it continue unabated had to be alarming.

Jonas looked into the Ri-Hnon's eyes, and saw his own deep-seated fear reflected.

You look like you just got beat up. Aleksei whispered through the bond.

Jonas looked back at Aleksei. He tried to smile, but failed. "It's just...I don't know how to *fix* this."

Aleksei's confusion became an expression of sympathy, "Jonas—"

The Magus held up his hand, "This is something I'm simply incapable of, that's all. I've gotten so used to being able to solve *everything*, just as long as I tried hard enough. But *this*...I'm out of ideas, Aleksei." His voice broke. "I'm *afraid*." He even laughed at that, but there was no humor in the sound. Aleksei detected tears in the corners of Jonas' eyes.

"But the Healers will be able to fix it." Aleksei said, looking up at Jonas and performing a fair approximation of hope.

"Aleksei, they've already *come*. Gaitan said they did everything in their power, but...."

And in that moment, Aleksei understood. Jonas wasn't afraid. He was *terrified*. For the first time in his life, he was at a loss.

Jonas looked to Aleksei, and found his eyes closed, his breathing quickened.

"I'll be fine." Aleksei panted, "I just have to be careful for a little while, that's all."

Jonas nodded uncertainly, "Well, as soon as we get back to Kalinor, I'm going to order you to a week's bedrest."

Aleksei laughed, "I'm not sure circumstances will allow for that."

"I'm not *joking*, Aleksei." Jonas snapped. The smile faded from the Hunter's face. "I'm not sure you appreciate how *serious* this is. This is something I can't *heal*. The Archanium won't *touch* it. If this gets worse, if you can't *fight* this, there's a good chance you'll die." He paused for a moment before brokenly breathing, "*We'll* die."

"What do you want me to do?" Aleksei demanded. "I can take to my bed like an invalid and hope it doesn't get worse. And you can sit in your library, and watch as Emelian Krasik and his men pour across the Lawn, and we can *all* die very swiftly by one of the eighty thousand swords that will be rushing towards us. Or I can take the chance that I'm worth more up and about and ill than I am asleep, in bed, and probably just as soon for the axe.

"I think you'll agree that it's better to die fighting for something you love, some*one* you love, rather than being cut down in your bed."

Jonas stared at his love in silence, finally looking away. He had no response. Intellectually, he knew what Aleksei said was true, and yet he couldn't make his heart understand that the same thing that could save Kalinor would also force him to sacrifice the man he loved more than anything else in this world, or those beyond.

And to sacrifice *himself* in the process.

Jonas let loose an exasperated sigh, "Why can't you just go down to the forest floor and find some willing sacrifice to restore yourself? What's the bloody point of having the Mantle if you can't use it when it matters the most?"

Aleksei looked away from his Magus, the fire and the fight within him evaporating. "I...I can't. I don't know how to explain it, but ever since I killed Lord Malak, I've hardly been able to so much as sense it, much less *summon* it. Not *properly*."

"That's preposterous." Jonas snapped. "You showed it to me only days after Malak's death."

"In a *dream*, Jonas. But so far, that's the closest I've come to actually calling it forth. I don't know how I did it the first time. I tried my damndest when I was talking our way past that sentry, but no matter what I try, it doesn't respond. Like it's forsaken me."

"Aleksei," Jonas said softly, "I won't be in Kalinor to watch over you. I won't be there if something happens. You will be *alone*."

Aleksei's hackles rose, "What are you talking about?"

Jonas lifted something from the floor. Aleksei squinted in the dim light, and realized he was looking at a rough, tattered book. It was bound in heavy slabs of bark, the paper pressed from a variety of leaves.

"This is a Ri-Vhan document from the Dominion Wars. It details the accounts of the first Hunter, of *Richter,* and his dealings with the Demonic Presence.

"Aleksei, this book predates even the oldest manuscripts in the Voralla. Only the angels have a comparable document, yet this is by far more valuable. This is written from the perspective of the Magi at the time, and as such it is far more comprehensible to me."

"And what does it say?" Aleksei asked weakly.

"It says that we're all going to die." Jonas answered despondently, casting his green-eyed gaze away. "Aleksei, I *have* to go to Dalita. I have to go to the Cathedral of Dazhbog. If the Prime Gate is open, then I need to see it for myself. We *cannot* continue to guess and jump at phantoms. The longer we do, the less time we're preparing for the reality of our situation."

"And you can't send a messenger bird? You have to go *personally?*"

"The Cathedral is supposed to be a *myth,* remember? No bird knows its location. There are few enough *people,* and of them I'm the only one who could reach it quickly."

"But why the sudden urgency? We have until the next moon."

Jonas placed his face in his hands. Aleksei could feel the depth of the Magus' exhaustion and despair through the bond.

"What is it?" Aleksei demanded, sitting up. Dread rose within him. "What aren't you telling me?"

"You said yourself that the full moon was a few days ago. But did you *see* it?"

"It's been overcast on the Southern Plain for weeks, but the calendar doesn't *lie,* Jonas. It's not exactly difficult to determine when the full moon rose last."

"I'm not disagreeing with you. But Roux has told me that the sky here has been clear for weeks."

Aleksei frowned.

"The books all agree on *one* thing. The Prime Gate only opens upon the full moon, after the key is used. But on such a night, even the moon cowers for fear of what it might behold."

"That's ridiculous. How can the moon *hide?*"

"It's meant to serve as a warning." Jonas snapped. "When the moon fails to rise, it signals that the Cathedral of Dazhbog has been defiled.

"Aleksei, I *have* to be certain. I *have* to know what we're dealing with."

The Knight rested his head back on the pillow, realizing how agitated he'd become. His heart hammered in his chest, its incessant *thump* matched only by his own short, painful gasps for air.

He had no knowledge to lend, no magical forest to carry them there. Jonas was leaving, going somewhere impossibly dangerous, and for the first time, Aleksei simply couldn't follow, no matter how he wanted to.

"Don't leave me." he whispered, feeling panic well up from deep within.

Jonas wasn't able to hold his tears back any longer, "I *have* to. I'm sorry. You *know* how much I want to stay with you, but we have to know what's coming for us. And I'm the only one who can get there fast enough."

Aleksei felt a frightened sob bubble to the surface. "I know."

It was the best he could muster before turning away.

No matter how he much loved him, Aleksei couldn't bear for Jonas to see him crying just then. He couldn't allow his prince to see him give up hope.

⁂

"Begging your pardon, Lord Captain, but I'm not *entirely* sure I heard you properly."

Aleksei cleared his throat, and tried not to look as helpless as he felt, "You undoubtedly did, Majesty. There are eighty thousand men camped in the valley beneath the Drakleyn. For the moment, they are trapped within the valley, but once the pass clears they *will* march on Kalinor."

"How long do we have to prepare?"

"Before they march?" He shook his head gravely, "A week? Two? Much longer than that and they'll be able to *dig* themselves out."

"And what is the state of our defenses?"

Aleksei winced, "At present we have five thousand men in the Guard, and three hundred and twenty-eight Magi, with an almost equal number of Knights, Majesty."

She waited for a moment, perhaps hoping that more figures were about to be announced, "Is that *all?*"

"In Kalinor, yes. To the south, there are twenty-six thousand in the Sulaq Hills with Colonel Rysun, and fifty-seven hundred in Keiv-Alon under Major Rixon.

"To the north, there are three thousand in Keldoan under Colonel Walsh, but both Major Rixon and Colonel Walsh are presently defending their cities against possible attack. As a fair number of Kalinori citizens made the journey to Keldoan with the remaining Lords of Parliament, it seems ill-advised to remove their only defense.

"Meager as our numbers are, I had thought they might be enough to defend against a smaller force. But eighty *thousand*...Majesty, we need every available solider we can get inside Kalinor as quickly as possible. As it stands, I hardly have enough to operate the anti-siege equipment we'll require, much less *fight.*"

"And how long will it take to move the men from the Hills to Kalinor?"

"An army of that size can only move a certain number of leagues a day, Majesty. I would estimate them to arrive within a month, perhaps faster if they push themselves to exhaustion."

A month.

It seemed an eternity with this threat hanging over them, and even when the men *did* arrive, there was no certainty that their numbers would be enough to make a difference.

"Send Colonel Rysun the order to march for Kalinor with all the haste he can muster." she said finally. Thirty thousand against eighty. "Now then, what is the state of the city?"

"The farmers have all been ordered to bring as much of their produce into the city as can be carried or carted. As it is winter, there is little to harvest at present, but all grain stores in the area are being relocated inside the city gates. I have ordered the carpenters' guild to cease civilian orders and begin constructing anti-siege armaments. Catapults, ballistae and the like. And the foundry has been instructed to step up production on projectiles, as well as repair all Legion equipment brought before them as a priority."

"So you think they'll put us under siege?"

Aleksei blinked in surprise at the question, "Majesty, a siege is our only *chance*. Open warfare against eighty thousand men would be suicide.

"As long as we can hold Kalinor, we can send out raiding parties to steal supplies, and whittle away at their men. Our walls are our primary defense at this point. But short of guerrilla warfare, we don't stand much of a chance in the field."

Andariana regarded him with surprise, "Are the Legionnaires *trained* in guerrilla warfare?"

Aleksei allowed himself a small smile, "No, Majesty, but the men of the Guard are *now*, as are the Knights in the Voralla. If necessary, I can arrange to have members of the Ri-Vhan come and instruct the Legionnaires from Mornj in the same tactics. It wouldn't be the first time I've made the request.

"But given enough time, we might be able to cut the enemy down to a more manageable size." He paused to cough for a moment, pressing his plain white kerchief against his mouth and leaning against the side of her heavy chestnut desk as the fit overtook him. When he regained what was left of his composure, he rose again. The white cloth came away from his mouth a deep and vibrant scarlet.

The Queen looked away, "I am gravely concerned for your health, Lord Captain."

"Me too." Aleksei grunted stolidly, "But at the moment, I've got no choice but to persevere. There's simply too much at stake. Jonas is doing what he can in the north, and I'll carry on here. If it makes you feel any better, many of the men marching towards us are likely consumed with the same sickness."

Andariana sighed heavily, dropping into her armchair by the fire, "I don't care for this type of warfare, or for striking down our own people, for that matter."

"Neither do I, Majesty, but the truth is that they share no such misgivings. As far as these men are concerned, they're *patriots*. They are fighting for a cause they believe to be just. They believe the gods are on their side. And this makes them *extremely* dangerous, Majesty."

"And our own men?"

Aleksei quirked a sad smile, "Well, Majesty, of course our men feel much the same, though with one crucial difference. *We* have been backed into a corner. And as such, we will fight with all the strength of desperation."

Andariana seemed suddenly tired. She stared into the fire, "How has it come to *this*. I've spent my entire life trying to avoid Marra's mistakes, but it seems that despite my best efforts, I find myself once again staring into the face of a civil war that could rend our realm to tatters.

"Gods, the House of Belgi will be remembered not for the decades of peace and prosperity, but rather for the specters of war and death that have repeatedly ravaged the realm."

Aleksei watched her carefully, taken aback at her sudden frankness.

"Very well, Drago, you are dismissed." she muttered after a pregnant pause. "I know you have a great number of orders to dispatch."

Aleksei bowed pointedly, "Majesty."

He stepped out into the hall, catching sight of Sammul and heading in the opposite direction. The *last* thing he wanted was to waste time justifying his actions to an idiotic fop.

"*Lord* Captain, a word."

Aleksei stopped in his tracks, resisting the urge to pretend as though he'd never heard the High Magus call after him. Instead, he turned and regarded the man with his closest approximation of a smile.

"I'm *very* busy. What do you want?"

Sammul sidestepped the insult, "I was merely curious, Lord Captain, whether you'd spoken to the Prince of late. I've not seen him stir from his rooms recently."

Aleksei allowed his face to betray no sign of emotion, "Prince Belgi is concerned about the coming war, High Magus. I think he's been searching for answers in the Archanium. And I know that he's prepared to meet any threat posed to this city and its people. Might I recommend that you advise your Magi to be equally prepared?"

Sammul looked shocked, "Lord Captain Drago, surely you are not suggesting that I ask the men and women of the Voralla to train for *war*!"

"That is *exactly* what I am suggesting." Aleksei snarled. "As I have said in many reports up to this point, I have firsthand knowledge of Magi in Lord Perron's camp. Magi who follow the farthest meridians of the Nagavor. If the Magi of the Voralla are not prepared to meet such a threat, then they will die. We will *all* die."

"But surely you can't believe Chancellor Perron will *use* such magic—"

"A commander doesn't always use every weapon in his arsenal, High Magus. He chooses the one that will do the most damage, and then builds his force around it. Lord Perron has lived in Kalinor for many years. He was one of the men pressing the case against Ilyana when she was charged with using the Archanium as a weapon. He *knows* the limits of your Magi.

"*Believe* me when I say that Perron will not hesitate to kill every man, woman, and child in this city with the Archanium. *Our* job, and more specifically *your* job, is to make sure that our forces can provide at least something of a counter to his Magi. If you cannot, we will die."

"But Lord *Captain—*"

"*Oh,* and since we've been doing your job *for* you recently, the actual threat is a Magus named Bael. He has unleashed something called the Demonic Presence. I suggest you look it up. And Emelian Krasik is running this whole operation. He calls himself the Zra-Uul, which is apparently some sort of Kholodym construct, so you might keep that in mind as well while you're training your useless disciples."

The glint of loathing was hard to miss in Aleksei's glimmering golden gaze. "Good *day,* High Magus."

Aleksei stalked away from Sammul without another word. He managed to contain his frustration until he reached his office in the upper east wing.

When a young aide entered, alarmed at the violent pounding emanating from the Lord Captain's office, he found Aleksei red-faced at his desk. There was a conspicuous hole in the plaster behind him.

"Ah, Master Richmond." Aleksei said pleasantly, "Would you go fetch one of the messengers? I have an errand of utmost importance."

Richmond nodded uncertainly, glancing at the shattered remains of a field chair in the corner. "Right away, Lord Captain. City or country?"

"What?"

"Your message, milord. Is it meant for the city, or will the messenger need to go out into the countryside?"

"Countryside."

"Thank you, milord. I'll fetch him presently."

Aleksei reached into his desk and removed a small stack of paper. He dipped his horn pen into the inkwell and began scratching out a missive to Rysun. After a few moments, he sanded and blotted the freshly written orders, sealing them with golden wax. Rysun would recognize the urgency of the papers within.

"*Gods*," he muttered, "if my father could see me now."

There was a knock at the door, and Aleksei looked up in surprise. Richmond must have run all the way there and back with the messenger to return that quickly.

"Enter." he said, sitting back in his chair.

A young man hurried in, red in the face and panting, "Messenger Jonathan Tanner to see you, Lord Captain."

"At ease, Master Tanner. I need you to take this," he said, lifting the sealed packet of orders, "to Colonel Rysun in the Sulaq Hills. I'm afraid I don't have an *exact* location for you, but they'll be along one of the tributaries of the Ylik Water, and several leagues off the road. These are documents of *tremendous* importance. Take two horses and change them out if necessary, just *get there* as soon as possible."

"As you command, Lord Captain."

ᪧ

Tanner stepped forward and took the sealed packet from the Lord Captain. He saluted one more time, then raced from the room. The doors banged closed behind him as he dashed through the east wing.

He had reached the doors to the Lawn when a voice sounded behind him.

"Tanner! We got a request for Keiv-Alon. Can you field it?"

He bit his lip. The Lord Captain had stressed speed at any cost, but he could just as easily swing up through Keiv-Alon on his way back to Kalinor.

"Who's it for?" he asked.

"Some noble in town. Looks like he pays quite well, too."

"Alright, give me the address. And *quickly*!"

Gods, if the Lord Captain knew he was doing this...but he wasn't losing *that* much time. It would just be a quick pickup. He wouldn't get paid until he returned with the response.

A few minutes later, he was riding his horse at a breakneck pace down Tailor Street and onto Swallow Avenue. He leapt from his horse's back and ran to the door, banging on it frantically. Gods, but he had to *hurry*!

The door swung open, and a well-dressed man greeted him, "Ah, you'd be the messenger."

He nodded, "Where's the package?"

"Upstairs. If you'd be so good as to follow me."

Tanner followed the man up a long stairway and into an empty room. There was a fire in the hearth, but otherwise it looked as though this house had been cleaned out in a hurry.

He felt the hand on the back of his head, but before he could even open his mouth, he collapsed to the floor.

Sammul stood over him, shaking his head at the sight. Poor boy. He wondered whether this child had woken up with any premonition that this day would be his last.

Sammul rooted through the messenger's bag until he found the Lord Captain's orders. He pulled them from the case and tore them open, reading them over.

And then he tossed them contemptuously into the hungry fireplace, smiling as all those golden seals, all those shimmering wheat stalks the Lord Captain was so fond of, blackened and melted away in the inferno.

CHAPTER 40

DEMON'S DIRGE

THE LAST OF the mountains vanished beneath Jonas as he shot towards his target. Beneath him, the tiny cliffside town of Krilya punctured the cliffs an instant before Dalita crumbled into the Grey Sea.

He dove towards the village, recklessly gaining speed as he neared the earth. Mere moments before he struck the rocky soil, Jonas pulled himself up and flared his wings, sharply breaking his descent.

His boots struck the ground and he straightened, looking around to see if anyone had seen him.

There were a few vaguely curious glances from children, but for the most part he was ignored. Remote as Krilya was, its inhabitants were not selected by accident.

Here and there he noted an angel, but the town's populace were primarily humans from Ilyar. Or more accurately, *priests* from Ilyar.

"You have come to worship?" a dry voice asked hopefully from behind.

Jonas turned to regard an ancient man. He was stooped over a cane, and wore a tattered shroud of ocher cloth. Jonas recognized him immediately as the High Priest of Dazhbog.

"Your Eminence," Jonas said quickly, "I need to go to the Cathedral at once. I fear the sanctuary is in danger."

The High Priest nodded his head gravely, "And well you *should* fear, young Magus. But I'm afraid you are a touch late."

Jonas stopped, taking a moment simply to breathe. His grandmother had been correct. And whether it was due to her negligence, or to the intricacies of prophecy no longer mattered. The Presence had been released into the realm of life once again.

"How long has it been?" he asked weakly, allowing the days of harsh travel and over-taxing to finally catch up with him.

"I suppose it was two weeks ago. A small group came to the cliffs, but they did not stay in the village. They were gone by morning."

Jonas nodded his resigned understanding. The full moon. "I understand. I wonder, Eminence, if I might go down to the Cathedral itself. Though it has been defiled, a bit of guidance would *almost* be worth the journey at this point."

The High Priest bowed his head, and Jonas caught the unmistakable glint of tears shining in his eyes. "I have little doubt my Master would be most appreciative of your prayers."

Jonas rested a hand on the man's shoulder, then turned and made his way towards the edge of the village. As he neared the drop-off, a skeletal stairway became visible, leading down the face of the rock, and towards the churning sea beneath.

He took a deep breath before stepping onto the mist-slick stone, delicately taking the steps one at a time while concentrating painfully on his footwork. While he might have time to shift before he struck the water, he would prefer not to test his own strength after having flown so far, and for so long. As it was, his body was exhausted from spending so much time in the Archanium.

His feet only betrayed him once, slipping on the penultimate step. Jonas managed a leaping fall that landed him on the stone platform. He straightened and gazed up at the carved prominence that was the Cathedral's façade.

His eyes immediately went to where the Third Gate should be standing, encased in eons of wards and shields.

He was greeted instead by soot and splinters.

The Prince stepped into the Third Transept, noting the painful detail with which the space was rendered. The murals that covered the walls depicted the legend of the Magus Cassian in a series of elaborate scenes.

A great deal of love and devotion had been put into this place, and yet now it appeared to be all for naught. The structure had failed in its purpose, its guardians in their duties.

The Second Gate was also absent, though it seemed less violence had been necessary to force it open. Instead of ash and rent bits of blackened timber, there remained a simple stone archway leading into the next Transept.

This space was less intricate, the stone polished but unadorned, reflecting a more natural beauty. But what caught Jonas' attention were the traces of constructed magic that had, until so recently, resided at the center of the space. A pace from where he stood, Jonas felt the remnants of what he now recognized as the Revenant Spell.

"It was a *construct*." he whispered.

Jonas had originally assumed that the revenants in Drava had been the result of a specific spell that had been read rather, than constructed. The magic that still clung to this room told a different story.

The Magus Stephen must have come into the room and claimed the construct before his master had the chance. Or perhaps the construct had been drawn to the first through the door. Either way, once the spell had selected a master, no amount of skill in the either hemisphere of the Archanium would have allowed Bael to extract it for himself.

Constructs were ancient forms of magic, and so misunderstood by Jonas' peers that to be in the presence of even this echo was humbling. Jonas only knew enough to recognize it, but not to craft one. Such knowledge had been lost since the Dominion Wars.

And then Jonas remembered where he was, and realized that he was looking through the Prime Gate. Into the rough, cave-like hollow that, until mere days ago, had trapped the volcanic evil of the Demonic Presence. Even now he could feel its echoes, lingering in the stone. A profound *Other* had once been caged here.

The air split violently. Jonas cried out as the whip of conjured lightning struck him. He fell to his knees, clutching at his splintered shoulder.

"*Well*, it would appear that Master Bael was correct. He *said* someone was sniffing around in his wake. He never said it was *you*."

Jonas managed to turn his head enough to catch sight of a sandy-haired man, his fine clothes belying the ugliness of the power that surrounded him.

"Sammul." Jonas coughed.

The High Magus sneered, "This truly is a delightful moment, isn't it, Highness? I'm actually rather pleased my first spell failed to kill you. What a pity, if you were struck down without truly *understanding*. And what a waste of so many *years*."

As Sammul approached, his heavy boot strikes echoed through the transepts.

"*Although*," Sammul considered as he came to a halt before Jonas' kneeling form, "I *must* say I am displeased. The good Lord Captain will simply drop dead. Everyone will assume it was his malady that finished him off. And *you*, of course. I'll only have this memory to comfort me. But I suppose it will have to suffice."

Jonas could hardly focus his vision for the agony coursing through him. The pain, combined with his exhaustion, was threatening to overwhelm him. It was all he could do to retain consciousness.

"And *now*, Highness," Sammul said softly, "I fear we must part ways for the last time."

A red nimbus flickered around him, growing in strength, and deepening until it radiated the color of old blood.

Jonas knew he had only heartbeats before it was over. He hurled himself desperately into the waves of the Archanium, lashing out with the first thing his mind touched.

A shield of air snapped into existence just as Sammul's thunderbolt arched towards him. The shield shattered, deflecting the damage into the walls of the Cathedral.

Jonas drew himself to one knee and clasped another spellform. This one he chose with a bit more thought.

A gale bellowed from within the mountain, hurling both men

through the transepts and out towards the sea.

As he slid through the Third Transept, Jonas reached out with his functional arm, catching one of the intricately carved pillars and clinging to it. He held onto the spell with a newfound desperation, pouring his entire being into it, feeding the tempest. He *heard* more than saw Sammul tumble past him with a shriek.

Eventually, the wind died down. Jonas was only vaguely aware of it, *that* and the fact that he was still alive. He caught a glimpse of the High Priest's face before passing beyond the gates of exhaustion into what he could only guess were the cool, unrelenting arms of death.

Bael stood at the end of the trail, staring into the endless expanse of white before him. Behind the Demon, the armies of the Zra-Uul stood ready to march.

He opened his pallid mouth, tasting the frozen air for the Lord Captain's fear. The man would be petrified to discover that eighty thousand men were marching towards Kalinor in the dead of winter.

Through the Demonic Presence, Bael could feel the reverberations of Aleksei Drago's pain and desperation. Through the Archanium, he could sense the echoes of Jonas Belgi's handiwork throughout the pass. He could even grasp the type of spell the prince had used.

We can taste *it*. The collective thrum of the Presence slithered through his mind, sending a cascade of pinpricks across his skin. The voices still startled him at times, but even when it invaded his thoughts unbidden, it was a welcome change from the perpetual emptiness that had gnawed away at his being for so many years.

"Genius." he muttered to himself as the Archanium echoes flared up through the snow, painting a picture, telling the story as vividly as any illumination.

The echoes were hauntingly familiar in their construction, almost as though he'd cast them himself, though they lacked any of his own of brutality and force. It was as though Jonas Belgi had whispered across the meridians of the Archanium, and the mountain answered with thunder and destruction ten-thousand fold.

As much as he hated Jonas Belgi, Bael was not above acknowledging greatness when he saw it. The prince had conjured magic very similar to the spells the Magus Elise would have summoned one thousand years before, so perfectly apt for this particular obstruction. It was actually poetic in its simplicity, and it showed the casual use of an intellect Bael had underestimated in the past.

Watch that one. The Presence hissed in his ear. *Could be troublesome. Meddlesome. Stinks of Hunter and Wood. Stinks of* angel.

Bael frowned. For a moment, he had detected *fear* amidst the violent vibrations that filled his head. The Demonic Presence of legend had been a force that the Magus Cassian had *commanded,* though Bael had quickly learned that such tales were gross simplifications.

He no more commanded the Presence than *it* commanded him. But he needed it to survive in this world, and it relied on his tie to this earthly realm, to the Archanium, for sustenance. Without him, the Presence would fade from this world, forever locked away in the desolate plain that fool Cassian had stumbled into a thousand years before.

Though it had spent the better part of the last era sealed in the heart of a mountain, the Presence had grown comfortable in the soft, wet world Cassian had borne it into. It was loathe to leave it. A thousand years had sharpened its hunger, though without a human host, its strength had dwindled, a flicker once a conflagration.

We need time, Child. Time to feel, to learn, to feed. Feed Us, and We will grow strong in you. You will have what you desire. But only with time. You would be wise to fear, for now. Stinks of angel. Seraphima. *Dangerous. Deadly.*

Do not be baited. *Do not be* trapped. *Beware Cassian's Pride.*

A tremor rippled through Bael, nearly forcing him to his knees.

It was not the first time the Presence had recalled Cassian's Pride. Bael had asked questions, had tried to divine what it was about the words that disquieted the Presence so deeply. What did they *mean?* But every time the words entered his mind, they were immediately suppressed by a titanic wail, the single sound he'd heard from the Presence that deviated from the angry drone of its collective voice.

For all the bile the Presence held for its ancient host, Bael was beginning to suspect that it still possessed a shadow of the long-dead Magus. There had been moments in the dark when an image had flashed unbidden across his mind's eye, something from a world he didn't recognize, a face he'd never beheld.

A man's face, gold of hair and eye, a single, vivid white scar scrawled from his right eye to the hard edge of his jaw, as though tracing the track of a tear.

The moment he tried to concentrate on the image, it vanished like so much ephemera, and yet he found himself increasingly haunted by the obvious emotion locked in those sad, golden eyes; love unlike anything Bael had ever seen. He had recognized the shade of the feeling, had felt it pass through a heart not his own, and had discerned its nature only due to its omnipresent absence within him.

This had been something *primal,* and so alien, so unlike anything that had ever been directed at *him,* he scarcely believed it could be real. Such things existed in stories and songs, not in the cold reality of life. Life offered many things, but each carried an inescapable counter. Hope ending in despair, love ending in betrayal, life ending in death.

That was the world Bael recognized. *That* was a world Bael *understood.*

That love betrayed *Us. He* betrayed *Us. We stopped his heart. We thought he was Our puppet, Our vessel. We stopped his heart, but We could not kill it. You are better. You are* stronger. *No nasty Hunter, no Wood, no* angels *to save you.*

We are your salvation. We are your freedom. We want to feed. *Feed on the Hunter. Feed on the Wood. Grow strong. Stronger than* him. *Stronger than his* pride. *Than* love. *You* have *no love, Child, only Us. We will give you what you want. You will feed Our* hunger, *and We will make you strong.*

That one, the Presence spat its name for Jonas, *the* angel, *the one who stinks of Hunter and Wood,* that *one did* this.

Bael realized that the Presence had been growing angrier, that the longer it read the echoes of Jonas' spells, the longer it had to stew on someone of Angelic blood impeding its progress once again.

Its violent vibrations built into an aching crescendo that throbbed through Bael's core, until he thought his very being might shatter. It was the first true taste of the Presence's fury he'd felt since it had been released back into the realm of the living, but this time it had a target, an *enemy*.

His enemy.

You will take Us back there. *Where We were* born. *Where We were* caged. *Where We will suckle, and grow, and* consume.

Bael felt the Presence like a powerful hand on the back of his head, forcing him underwater, drowning him. He released his will, and his desperate need for control. He plunged into the violent torrent of the Archanium, the guiding hand of the Presence scattering the worst of the maelstrom.

The fragmented spell-structure of the Nagavor lifted from his vision like a veil, revealing a seething nether of burning, malignant green, yellow, and black. Spellforms billowed like smoke and shattered like crystal into a thousand jagged incarnations of malice and decay, before coalescing into great writhing serpents of crackling yellow-green energy surging through rivers of liquid darkness.

He was speechless, relieved that his body no longer required breath in the airless void that enveloped him. He stood in awe of the extraordinary storm that was the Demonic Presence, until time lost all meaning, his body frozen stiff on a distant mountain, while his mind witnessed a vision of power so staggering that he was only the second man to behold it in the history of Creation.

Our greatest mysteries may be well beyond you, Child, but consider this a promise. Protect Us, nurture Us, feed Us, and you will rise a god fit to break this pitiful world to dust, and reforge it into something worthy. *With Us. Together.*

Always *together.*

An ink-black spellform roiled and tumbled towards him, gathering a piercing wail that drowned out even the storm's chaotic rage. Bael clawed outwards with his mind, clawing at the ink-black even as it drooled through his fingers, even as it crashed into his chest, burning, *searing* his flesh and bone.

He could smell his skin blacken and burn, as his bones cracked and pierced the carrion his body had become. Through it all, he refused to scream, to beg for release. Bael opened his mouth, and exhaled into the frigid air.

The world exploded in Demonic fire.

A beam of pure malevolence erupted from him, boring into the wall of snow and stone, sending it up in a howling column of steam. The howl became a roar as the beam bore through the pass.

He heard another sound, and realized it was the men behind him. They were cheering him on, eighty thousand voices raised in worshipful praise. They thirsted for blood, just like him. They *hated*, just like him.

Bael fed their hatred into the fire, and it burned with new intensity. The mountain shrieked as the column of white billowed towards the heavens.

And then he burst through.

The dark fire flared out over the mountains, splashing across a cliff face half a league away, tainting the rock with slick black soot.

Bael withdrew himself from the Presence, from the Archanium, resisting the urge to collapse into the snow. The cheering of the men intensified to deafening levels.

Bael allowed himself a smile of triumph.

"Good Prince Belgi," he snarled to the skies, "we're coming for you."

⁂

Jonas was floating. All around him, ephemeral light-shapes squirmed and shook, swimming this way and that in a sea of blue luminescence. Thoughts and sounds echoed in his mind, but he was unable to assign significance. Time seemed frozen in place. And then, from the depths of this ocean of light, he *understood* something.

He was cold.

Jonas shook, trying to sit up. He needed to get his bearings, but he was frozen.

He reached for the Archanium, but found only silence. Silence so terrifying, it brought tears to his eyes instantaneously.

They froze before they could fall.

Gods, but he was cold!

And then, cutting through the strange nimbus sea, he heard a voice. It was the most beautiful sound Jonas had heard in his entire life, yet there was something strangely familiar about it.

With a startled gasp, Jonas sat up, panting for breath in the sudden vacuum. The air retained the same chill, but color had replaced the soulless blue-white of the light world. He was sitting in a bed, but he couldn't remember where in the heavens such a bed could *be*.

A hand pressed against his naked chest, and Jonas found himself gently pushed back into the pillows.

"You haven't completely recovered. You need sleep before the last of the effects wear off completely."

Jonas stared up into the luminous brown eyes of the Angel Leigha.

"Do you know your name?" she asked calmly.

He frowned, "Jonas?"

She nodded encouragingly, "Good. And the rest of it?"

Jonas arched a chestnut eyebrow, "What?"

Leigha sighed, and put a hand to his head. The fight came back to him in a thunderclap of memory. His hand went immediately to his shoulder, but his fingers found only whole flesh and bone.

"You've been healed, Jonas." Leigha said softly. "You're extremely lucky Autricus found you when he did, but even the magic of the High Priest is limited compared to the power of the Seraphima. He did everything he could to keep you alive until I could get here."

"Why *are* you here?" Jonas asked instead, willing his brain to regain some sense of what had happened since he'd lost consciousness.

"You're *welcome*." Leigha laughed. "I received the High Priest's summons a few days ago."

"Gods, how long have I been asleep?" Jonas asked, looking out the room's sole window for some sign as to the time of day.

"About a week. Autricus decided that waking you would prove too much of a strain on your body, so he kept you in an extended state of suspension until a healer arrived."

Jonas frowned, "And it just so happened that the healer they sent was the first-born *Cherub*?"

Leigha shrugged, "Grandmother figured only *you* would get yourself into such a situation at the Cathedral. She was going to send someone else, but I insisted. She was understandably reticent about letting me go, after what happened to the guards she sent last month."

Jonas nodded his understanding. It wasn't hard to guess what she meant.

"Now, I've kept you long enough. You need your sleep. I'll come check on you tomorrow, and we'll see how you're mending. Sleep well, Cousin."

Jonas smiled for the first time in what felt like years. "*Thank* you, Leigha."

She bowed her head slightly, then shut the door.

Jonas waited until she'd been gone for several minutes before closing his eyes. He had to be sure she wouldn't come back any time soon, or else there was no point in even attempting it.

A few moments later, he was floating on the tranquil waves of the Archanium, casting his mind to the south.

"*Aleksei?*"

And then he dissolved into dream.

⚬

Aleksei gave an exasperated growl of irritation, burying his face in his hands. The small roll of paper bearing the most recent intelligence from his spies in Relvyn drifted about his desk, before settling a few inches from his left elbow.

Emelian Krasik had crossed the mountains. *Somehow*, he'd managed to move a thousand tons of snow and rock out of his way, and was even now pressing north for Kalinor.

Thoughts and preparations raced through Aleksei's mind.

He hadn't slept in three days.

There hadn't been *time*. He'd been rounding up the citizens of Kalinor who were willing, ready for the journey to Keldoan, though more by far refused to be moved from their homes. He'd inspected the anti-siege equipment progress, and ensuring the foundry was producing enough arrowheads...the list went on and on.

And now this.

Aleksei was approaching his wits' end. Rysun's communiqués had been vague at best, cryptic at their worst. He still had no concrete idea of how far his men were from reaching the city. If they didn't arrive soon, it would be too late. For *any* of them.

"A force of eighty thousand men is marching towards me." he grunted. "I've got five thousand men, and a three hundred Magi who can't *quite* manage to conjure fire."

It was enough to thrust him into the waiting embrace of madness.

Aleksei reached under his desk and picked up a bottle of Dalitian firebrandy. He took a long pull before replacing the cork, returning it to its resting place next to his right boot. It wouldn't do for his men to see him drinking, but the pain the firebrandy manifested in his throat was the only thing keeping him awake any longer.

He reached into his coat and removed a fine, crumpled crimson scarf. The same scarf Jonas had worn the day they'd first met. He pressed the dark red fabric to his face, inhaling Jonas' scent.

His mind cleared, if just for a moment.

Aleksei?

A wave of fatigue crested over him and Aleksei coughed, shaking his head, trying to keep his eyes open. A second wave crashed across his consciousness, and his head struck a pile of reports.

He opened his eyes to find himself still at his desk. A weary, shirtless Jonas Belgi sat across from him. Though the room remained unchanged, Aleksei recognized the now-familiar sensation of Dreamspeak.

"You have *got* to get some sleep, Aleksei."

The Lord Captain smiled wearily at his Magus, "Sleep's a bit impractical at the moment."

"Aleksei," Jonas said, leaning forward across his massive desk, "you're not doing anyone any favors by torturing yourself."

"I don't have the *time*." Aleksei insisted, picking up the message from Relvyn and tossing it in front of the Prince.

Jonas picked it up and scanned it briefly, then let it fall back to the desk. "Good gods." he whispered.

"For all the good *They're* doing me." Aleksei growled sardonically. "And I still haven't gotten a clear answer from Rysun. All I know is that he's somewhere west of Kalinor, and that he's theoretically moving his men towards us as fast as he can."

"What do you think the problem is?"

Aleksei sat back in his chair, "I couldn't begin to guess. For all I know, he's picked up the bottle again."

Jonas scowled, "I hardly believe Henry would stand for that."

Aleksei conceded that Jonas had a point. He had a hard time

imagining Henry Drago sitting idly by while a man drowned his sorrows in drink. He knew quite well how little patience Henry had for such abject displays of misery.

"I just wish there was some way I could talk to him. I have a feeling I could get all this straightened out if I just saw him face to face."

Jonas suddenly looked hopeful, "Well, it's true *you* can't go talk to him. But I can."

"*You?*"

"I'm in Dalita now, but I can fly pretty fast. And a force of twenty-six thousand men...that wouldn't be difficult to find from the air. I imagine I could get to their position in a few days. And it would only take me a few more to get from there back to Kalinor."

Aleksei considered the idea for a long moment. On one hand, it was true that Jonas could be there just as fast as any of his apparently ineffective orders. But could he afford to lose Jonas for that long?

Suppose Bael decided to show up and cause trouble? Could anyone in the Voralla *truly* defend against such an attack? He'd already done without his Magus for a shocking amount of time, especially given his present condition.

In the end, it all came down to risk. Was it worth risking an attack from Bael, or one of his followers, just to get a message to Rysun? But then again, could he afford *not* to? After all, it was very difficult to create a battle plan when you were uncertain where the majority of your force was located.

"Alright." he said finally. "Get to him as fast as you can, and tell him that I don't care if men are dropping dead from exhaustion, just as long as he gets here *before* Krasik."

"Anything else?"

"No. *Yes.* Tell my father I love him."

The prince smiled and gripped Aleksei's arm comfortingly, "They'll get here in time. You'll see. After all, you sent Rysun the order to advance weeks ago. I can't imagine he's more than a few dozen leagues from the city."

Aleksei tried to smile, but had a difficult time adopting Jonas' optimism. The vision of his men burning swept across his mind, their screams filling his ears. He knew what awaited them if help didn't arrive in time.

"Any luck on *your* end?" Aleksei asked, deciding a change of subject was most definitely in order.

Jonas' face took on a new level of anger. Even from across the desk, Aleksei could feel the man's burning rage. "The Cathedral has been defiled. What's more, I was *attacked*."

Aleksei sat straighter, "*Attacked?* Are you alright? Who was it?"

"I'm alright. But Aleksei, we've *got* to do something. I was attacked by *Sammul*."

Aleksei felt his breath catch in his throat. "*Sammul?* I didn't think he *had* that sort of power."

Jonas shook his head, "I've been a horrible fool. I should have seen this ages ago, but I didn't want to believe it. Sammul was our second enemy Magus. He's been helping Bael this entire time. For all I know, he helped plan the rebellion. He probably *handed* Bael the Prime Key.

"You've got to tell Aya. Tell her she has to guard the Apsis, before anyone else can get there. And they'll have do something about his acolytes. Besides those we know, no one in the Voralla can be trusted. I don't know if Sammul is still alive, but if he *is*, he can't be allowed anywhere near the Voralla."

Aleksei nodded, his head spinning with the possible implications. "I'll see to it at once."

"Aleksei."

He paused, realizing that he had been rising from his chair.

"Take care of yourself, Aleksei. *Please*. For me?"

The dream office melted away, and Aleksei sat up, fighting off the clinging threads of sleep deprivation. He did his best to suppress another coughing fit. They were coming on stronger and stronger lately.

"Gods," Aleksei muttered to himself, rising to his feet, "and here I thought it couldn't get any worse."

He stepped out of his office, stumbling down the hall towards the Voralla. Every step seemed to pull him down towards the floor, and yet determination kept him moving. Aya had to be warned. The *Voralla* had to be warned.

Halfway down the corridor, he began to cough again.

Aleksei suddenly realized he was on his hands and knees. His vision swam, and he could smell the stink of blood on the carpet beneath him. He tried to struggle to his feet, but only succeeded in falling flat on his face.

He hardly registered the black as it consumed him.

CHAPTER 41

AN ANCIENT HUNGER

COLONEL CHARLES ANDER stared blearily into the yawning darkness, fighting desperately to stay awake. He had been summoned from his bed mere moments ago by a very excited sergeant, but as he stared into the mournful indigo of early morning, he could see nothing to engender such urgency.

"They'll be in view any moment, Sir." the sergeant promised earnestly.

All around Ander drooped equally-exhausted men, some going so far as to lean against the battlements of the city walls, others pacing in an effort to stay alert.

It had been a little over a week since he'd found the Lord Captain collapsed in the corridor, and yet he felt sure that any moment, an aide would appear to inform him of the Lord Captain's unfortunate but, sadly unsurprising demise. Despite the best efforts of the Ri-Vhan Healers and Magi to keep him alive, Ander knew without question that without Aleksei, their fantasies of victory would die.

"Colonel!" a voice rang out in his ear. He jumped, startled at the explosion of sound amidst the quiet.

"Yes, Sergeant, what is it?"

"Colonel, men approach."

Ander frowned and aimed his spyglass into the gloom. After a few moments, he realized he could make out shapes emerging. Columns of soldiers were marching towards them, thousands of men.

They wore the crimson and blue of House Belgi.

"Rysun." Ander breathed in relief.

"Do you really think so, Sir?"

"I doubt Krasik would permit his men to wear the Queen's colors. But we'll wait until they call us formally, see what they have to say for themselves."

The men along the wall began to rouse themselves, some whispering excitedly to one another and pointing down at the advancing columns. It seemed they were to be delivered at last.

"Hail Kalinor!" a voice rang out from below.

"Hail, soldier. Speak your piece." Ander called.

"Sir, the armies of Lord Perron are close behind us! Hurry, Sir, the gates!"

Ander opened his mouth to question the man further, but suddenly thought better of it. He turned to his sergeant and nodded, "Tell the gate house to open up. And *quickly!*"

The sergeant darted away towards the gatehouse, leaving Ander to stare down into the ranks of men. Aleksei had told him how long they had been in the wilderness, yet Ander noted how crisp their uniforms seemed.

Remarkable, he thought, that they had been able to maintain such a high level of personal discipline so far out in the brush.

The gates slowly ground open.

Ander watched impatiently, noting the restlessness of the men below.

A sound to his left caught his attention. Ander turned and almost tripped over himself at what he saw.

And then the world went mad.

❧

Aleksei sat up, coughing violently and staring around in

confusion.

He was in his own bed, staring at the richly paneled wall at the other end of his chamber. He was naked, the sheets drenched in cold sweat.

His heart hammered in his chest and in his ears. His chest felt like it was on fire. The fire licked up and down his body before escaping out his throat in short, barking coughs, and some part of him keenly understood one thing with absolute certainty: his sickness would shortly kill him.

He managed to roll onto the floor and pick himself up. Every step seemed another league before him, yet he managed to reach his small wardrobe and pull out a pair of breeches. Aleksei wasn't even sure how he managed to pull them on. One moment he was struggling with them, and the next he was lying on the soft carpets that covered the cold marble floor, breeches on and the coppery taste of blood in his mouth.

He had passed out. The gods only knew how long he'd been lying there.

Aleksei pulled himself back up and stamped his feet into his boots. As he stumbled for the door, he grabbed his sword belt from the wall and pulled his leather coat over his bare shoulders. Aleksei knew he was incapable of managing the buttons of his uniform in his present condition.

And then he ran.

At least, he *tried* to run.

In the end, he managed a sort of galloping fall that moved him jerkily down the corridor. Every few moments he would pause to cough, to spit up blood and phlegm.

"Gods," he gasped as another coughing fit finally abated, "I can't *take* much more."

Time lost all meaning, yet somehow he found himself standing before the doors leading out onto the Lawn.

As he stumbled across the grass, one of the Guardsmen saw him and rushed over, "Lord Captain! Lord Captain, what are you *doing* out here?"

"I need a horse." Aleksei choked, pointing to the mount the man was leading. "I have to get to the outer walls."

"*Sir?*" the man asked, not understanding.

"*They...can't...open...the gates!*" he coughed.

"I'll go straight away and tell them, Sir." the man promised.

"No!" Aleksei gasped. "No, *you* close the Palace gates. Sound the alarm. It may already be too late."

The man seemed confused. He could tell Aleksei was feverish. What if he didn't listen?

"What are you *waiting* for?" Aleksei barked.

"Here." the young man said, handing Aleksei the reins to the roan gelding. "I'll help you into the saddle, Sir."

Aleksei found himself clutching the horn of the saddle desperately as he fought to steady himself. The Guardsman had already run to the Palace wall to sound the alarm. Aleksei managed a feeble kick, but the roan sprang forward as though he were wearing spurs.

"Take me to the walls." he whispered, praying to the Gods that this horse could understand at least something of what he said.

He galloped through the city, down the central avenue and towards the South Gate. Everything was moving so fast, and it was impossible for Aleksei to make sense of it all. The only thing he was truly aware of was that they were heading south. The danger was south.

He had a chance.

Had it not been for the chaotic thunder of eighty thousand heartbeats roaring in his ears, Aleksei imagined he would still be unconscious in his bedroom.

But his Hunter senses told him very clearly what waited on the other side of that wall.

Aleksei lost time again during the ride, but when he swam back into awareness, he was being pulled off the horse by two Legionnaires.

"Lord Captain? Are you alright, Sir?"

"The *wall!*" he coughed. "I have to get to the gatehouse!"

The two men didn't ask any questions. They each wedged a shoulder under one of his arms, lifting him quickly up the towering series of stairs that led to the top of the wall.

"Colonel Ander!" one of the men shouted as they moved him

across the top of the wall, "Colonel, it's the Lord Captain!"

As they moved, Aleksei could hear the gates begin to open.

"Ander!" he barked fiercely, knowing there was no time to berate the Legionnaires for not taking him directly to the gatehouse. "Ander, don't open the gate!"

Ander was in front of him a moment later. "Lord Captain? What are you talking about?"

It was too late.

He could hear the massive grinding of the gates. He broke away from the two Legionnaires and lunged to the edge of the wall. The other three men followed, terrified he was going to tumble over the edge.

As a result, they were there when it happened.

Aleksei stared out into the sea of soldiers that poured into the city. For a moment, they all wore Belgi crimson and blue. And then the air above them shimmered, as though a great amount of heat had suddenly been released.

The orderly ranks of men in Belgi colors vanished. In their place surged a ragged mob of soldiers Aleksei recognized all too well.

The armies of the Zra-Uul had reached Kalinor.

"That's *impossible!*" Ander cried.

"Order an immediate retreat to the Palace." Aleksei commanded. "Get *everyone* back to the Palace as fast as you can. It's the *only* way we'll make it."

Ander dashed off in the direction of the guard station, towards one of the great alarm bells.

Aleksei turned to see Krasik's men swarming up onto the wall. The Kalinori guards were putting up a good fight, but there were simply too many rebel soldiers. The smooth, polished fighting of the Legionnaires was rapidly overrun by the sheer weight of bodies pressing against them.

One of the Legionnaires in front of Aleksei went down, leaving only one man to stand between himself and the sea of death raging towards him.

And then an enormous man was towering over him, a bloodied axe glittering in the torchlight. Aleksei knew he couldn't draw his weapon in time. The axe began its terrible descent towards him. He could smell the stink of blood and viscera on the weapon's rusted edge.

Shift.

Aleksei breathed in and out, wishing to the gods his head would clear. But it was too much to hope. His sight grew foggy with tears of pain as another coughing fit threatened to overtake him.

In a move of pure desperation, Aleksei reached up and clutched the man's meaty wrist, shoving with all his might against the weight of the swing.

Cruel black tendrils exploded from across his back with the suddenness of breaking glass. Thin strips of leather rained down as though falling through cool honey. The man actually managed to scream. Black became red as the Mantle feasted on the soldier's brutal life force.

And then Aleksei was standing over a dead man, his eyes glittering with rage.

Another soldier began to run towards him, but Aleksei raised his hand and directed his anger. The Mantle burst away from his wrist and struck like a viper, ripping away the man's life and feeding it into Aleksei's veins.

Aleksei paused and drew his first pure, clear breath in weeks. He felt as healthy as ever before. The air was cool against his face.

He was *restored.*

And then time pulled him back into its rapid flow. Aleksei wrenched his sword from its sheath, fighting his way through the river of men that poured around him.

Blades bit into him from each side, but before they could inflict serious damage, Aleksei managed to dart to one side or another and cut their wielders down. He fought on, yet could see no end to the mass of soldiers sweeping towards him.

Aleksei quickly understood that if things continued this way, he wouldn't last long.

The rebel to his immediate right screamed and collapsed. Aleksei frowned, until he noticed the tendril of smoke rising from the man's nostril. A moment later two men to his left went down. And then Aleksei realized that he could *see* the force killing these men.

It was the Archanium.

The wall around him erupted into a web of thunder and light. Aleksei threw himself to the ground as arcs of silver lightning laced their way through the men of Krasik's army. A moment later he found himself alone on the wall.

Aleksei came to his feet, looking around in bewilderment.

And then he saw the falcon diving towards him. A heartbeat before the bird crashed into him, it shifted. Aleksei stepped forward and caught the Magus as he fell onto the wall. Jonas kissed him hard for a long moment before breaking away.

"Go. He's *coming*."

Aleksei frowned as he followed his Magus down the crowded steps of the wall, ignoring the charred bodies that fell before him, "What are you talking about? *Who's* coming?"

But Jonas had come to a halt, staring straight ahead at the bottom of the steps.

Aleksei followed his gaze. His breath caught in his throat.

A figure was waiting for him. His features were indistinguishable, but the ebony nimbus wreathing his form identified him well enough.

Bael.

"Run."

Aleksei stared at Jonas, but the Magus didn't dare look back at him.

"Aleksei, *run!*"

The Knight looked over Jonas' shoulder to where Bael stood. The Demon smiled at him.

"Yes, why don't you *run*, Aleksei?"

Aleksei reached forward and gripped Jonas' shoulder. It was a touch that said he was sorry.

A touch that said good-bye.

And then Aleksei ran. He ignored Bael. He ignored everything around him. His feet pounded the stairs as he rushed towards the Demon. He could see Bael focusing the Archanium. He knew where the Magus' spell would land.

The bolt of black fire splashed across the white stone, narrowly missing Aleksei's boot as he ran forward and *up*. Time slowed as his boots pounded against the side of the wall. He ran over Bael's head, sliding to a halt as he cleared the Magus and dropping down behind him, sword extended.

Bael cried out as Aleksei's blade raked down his back. But the cut hadn't possessed the necessary power behind it, and failed to slice through the bone.

Aleksei's boots struck the pavement a heartbeat later, and he rolled out of the way just as Bael leveled a hammer of thunder against the stone.

And then Jonas was on the Demon, raking bolts of fire and thunder through the air as he struck the man's face with desperately balled-up fists. Bael managed to deflect the spells, but was unable to defend against Jonas' darting hands.

Bael stumbled back against the wall and ducked as Jonas leveled another punch at his face. The prince grunted in pain as his knuckles struck the wall. And then Bael was gone.

Jonas spun, searching the Archanium for his enemy's presence.

He felt Bael a moment before the man materialized. Jonas had only enough time to dive forward and tackle Aleksei to the street before the air above them erupted in fury and flame.

Hot fragments of stone clattered around them as Aleksei jumped to his feet. He darted forward, changing direction at the last second, sliding towards Bael on his knees.

The rough stones slashed through his breeches and frayed his knees, but Aleksei kept his eyes on the target. As he slid to a halt he reached out and gripped Bael's ankle. The Mantle exploded forward, sinking into the Dark Man.

For one exultant moment, Aleksei thought he'd won. And then the Mantle whipped away from the Demon. Pain such as Aleksei had never known coursed through him as he fell onto his side, convulsing while Mantle flailed wildly on the cobbles around him, trying to gather itself.

"*Idiot!*" Bael bellowed, kicking Aleksei soundly in the side. "You were a fool to reject me."

Jonas slammed into Bael an instant later, ramming his shoulder into the man's gut, knocking the wind from his lungs.

Bael flew back and struck the street, coughing up black blood as he came to a stuttering halt. Thunder rained down around him, bursting the cobbles and sending splinters of red-hot rock into the air.

The Demon cried out as the heat seared his face, but he managed to avoid the worst of the damage. Jonas was a hairsbreadth from unleashing his next spell when a bolt of dark fire erupted from Bael's hand, striking the prince squarely in the chest.

Jonas dropped to his knees, convulsing and desperately trying to breathe. His body seized up in agony. Bael stalked towards him triumphantly, and he could see the spirals of black flame once again spring up around the man.

Jonas knew he was about to die.

Bael cried out and collapsed to the cobbles.

Jonas stared in confounded confusion for a long moment, until he noticed the dark scarlet stain billowing from the center of the Magus' back.

Aleksei stood over the Demon, golden eyes glittering with bloodlust.

The Knight reached down for Jonas' hand. The Magus gripped Aleksei's wrist, but found himself unable to speak. It was all he could do to *breathe.*

I don't know what he did to me. he sent his Knight across the bond.

"It doesn't matter." Aleksei said softly.

Before Jonas could signal his confusion, the talons of the Mantle clawed down Aleksei's arm and spilled over his hand. Jonas gasped as it crawled into his skin, snaking its way up his sleeve and wrapping around his chest.

His body relaxed. He could feel his heartbeat return to normal. The fires that burned within him cooled in an instant.

Jonas gave a gulping cry of surprise as the Mantle fled from him, leaving him renewed.

His eyes turned to Bael's still body. "Is he dead?"

Aleksei nodded, "The knife struck his heart. He's got no pulse."

Jonas breathed a heavy sigh of relief. "We have to get back to the Palace."

Aleksei looked around at the bodies of men, Kalinori and rebel alike littering the streets. "The Guard will have been roused by now. If we're lucky, we can still reach the Palace Gate before it's sealed."

Jonas closed his eyes and breathed in deeply. When he opened his eyes, they were electric with the light of the Archanium.

"Follow me."

Colonel Ander shoved another rebel soldier off the tip of his blade and looked up from the fray, taking stock of the situation.

By some miracle of the gods, his men had held the southern Palace Gate. The other three were already sealed and holding. Atop the Palace walls, Legionnaires rained arrows into the massing ranks of the Zra-Uul's army. Yet for all their efforts, Ander knew his men were barely a ripple in the ocean of swords and spears crashing ceaselessly forward.

The only reason the gate held at all was due to the narrow confines of the avenues, preventing the overwhelming force from surrounding them.

"Colonel!"

He turned and saw the Archanium Knight Marrik striding towards him. He noticed the Knight's sword drooling blood into the street as the man approached.

"Colonel, we can't hold this gate much longer. What are you *waiting* for?"

Ander looked away from the Knight and into the sea of enemy soldiers. "I last saw the Lord Captain on the outer walls of the city. Since then I've had no word from him. But I *have* to hold out hope that he'll return safely."

Marrik grunted, "Sir, Aleksei was at death's door last I saw. I sincerely doubt he could have made it from the walls of the city in his condition. I can't even believe he *got* there. Whether or not he has fallen, he would *not* want you to hold the gate on his account."

"Nevertheless, I will hold the gate as long as possible. We have both seen the Lord Captain manage miracles in the past. Let us hope he can provide us with one more."

Marrik nodded curtly, "As you say, Colonel."

Ander sighed heavily as the Knight turned and reentered the fray. Was he holding out for an impossibility? Perhaps. But if Aleksei had fallen in battle, then the Prince was also lost to them. Without those two, Ander knew there was very little chance of victory.

There was a cry from the left, and Ander turned to see the line breaking up. The enemy surged forward aggressively.

"Hold the line!" he cried, rushing into the midst of the rebels and hacking away savagely.

The men rallied around him, pushing the throbbing horde back a few paces.

Ander pulled back again, realizing that he was bleeding from his shoulder in places where a spear managed to sneak past his light armor. Gods, but he hoped Aleksei would appear soon.

No sooner had the thought entered his mind than there was a terrific explosion from behind the invading ranks. A moment later, a burst of light erupted in the midst of the enemy line, hurling the charred bodies of men into the maelstrom. As the eruptions came closer, Ander began to wonder what could possibly be wreaking so much havoc.

Standing mere paces from the enemy line, he caught sight of the answer several seconds before anyone else.

Jonas Belgi stormed through the enemy like some divine vision of wrath, the air around him crackling. Every now and then he would point his hand towards a group of soldiers. A heartbeat later, the earth would lance upwards in a spike of light and thunder. And then the men were gone.

Behind the Prince stalked Aleksei Drago. The Knight looked impossibly healthy, even as he wove a tapestry of death with his glistening blade. Any who managed to avoid Jonas' spellcraft were cut down by the Lord Captain's sword.

A few moments later, the men caught sight of them. A collective cheer rang out from the lines, and the Legionnaires redoubled their efforts. The line actually advanced into the avenue before the gate. It swung open long enough to swallow Aleksei and Jonas before crashing back down upon the surprised rebels.

Jonas passed into relative safety, then stopped. Ander frowned as the Magus turned and raised a fist above his head. There was a thunderclap, and the enemy soldiers were flattened against the stones.

"*Retreat!*" he roared.

But rather than turn towards the Palace, Jonas remained facing the horde. Ander noticed the enemy stirring from their prone positions. Not twenty paces back, a man was on his feet. A nimbus of red light surrounded him.

Ander recognized the man as an enemy Magus only moments before bolts of fire began searing through the lines of his Legionnaires.

Jonas summoned the Archanium, and the air erupted in a brilliant blue flash. When Ander's vision cleared, the enemy Magus was gone.

"Close the gate!" Jonas cried, stumbling backwards towards the Lawn.

He was now the only man outside the gate. The enemy had regained their feet and were racing towards him, but Ander could tell he was too slow to make it in time. He was a heartbeat from rushing towards the prince himself, when Aleksei darted out in an impossible blur of speed and swept the Magus into his arms.

A moment later they were both inside the relative safety of the walls.

The Palace gate closed with a gut-wrenching *crack*. Ander allowed himself to relax as a wild cry was raised from the defenders of Kalinor.

He stood there, looking over the men who had survived. Of the five thousand who had been roused from their beds, it looked as though a scant fifteen hundred remained. Heavy losses had been taken, yet it was remarkable that any had survived at *all*.

"Lord Captain Drago." he called as he caught sight of Aleksei mere paces away. Ander dropped to a knee, "My Lord Captain. I understand the repercussions of my actions, of course. If you feel I am no longer worthy of serving under you, I will surrender my position. But I do beg the privilege of continuing to serve, even if it means fighting as a foot soldier."

He looked up, unsure how his commanding officer would respond.

Aleksei hardly seemed to have heard anything Ander said. Instead, he was intently watching the face of his unconscious Magus. After pressing his ear carefully to Jonas' chest, Aleksei carried him to an abandoned cart and gently laid him in the straw. Upon catching sight of his colonel, Aleksei turned.

"Get up, Charles."

Ander rose, but kept his eyes focused on the ground.

"I don't have *time* for this." Aleksei growled. "*All* of us have failed in some way, myself most of all. But neither of us has time to wallow in our mistakes."

"As you say, Lord Captain."

"Why don't you go around to the men, get volunteers for watch. Allow the rest to return to their beds. And see what you can do about getting some food in their bellies? At sunup, I will expect you in my office with your senior staff, whatever's left of them."

"As you command, Lord Captain."

And then Ander was off, leading his horse through the ranks of wounded, battered, unusually hopeful men.

Aleksei sighed and rubbed a hand across his face. *Gods*, but they had been lucky. But such luck couldn't last.

New plans would have to be drawn up. He would have to reassess their options. He'd spent weeks on battle plans that had been shattered beyond all hope within seconds.

He knew the mark of a good tactician was the ability to *adapt*.

Those who couldn't adapt ended up dead.

But before anything else, Aleksei had to take care of something far more important. He turned back to Jonas.

"How long have you been planning *that*?"

"What?" the Magus asked weakly, looking around in confusion.

"That stunt at the gate."

"Ten seconds?" Jonas laughed. "I was doubtful it would even work. If that Magus had shown up any sooner, it *wouldn't* have."

Aleksei nodded, gently lifting the prince and helping him make his way towards the Palace. He could feel the weight of exhaustion pressing down upon his Magus.

Jonas had joined the battle only after racing towards Kalinor in the form of a bird. He was using up precious reserves of energy just by keeping his eyes open.

"Out of sheer curiosity," Aleksei yawned, "where was Rysun last time you saw him?"

"Aleksei, he hadn't moved a league. Your messages were never delivered. For whatever reason, Rysun had no knowledge of the coming attack. When I reached him, he was horrified to learn what was happening."

Aleksei's face darkened, "Not *one* of my messages?"

Jonas shook his head.

Aleksei stared blankly into the space behind Jonas. His mind searched furiously for a possible explanation.

"Come on," Jonas said, wrapping his arm around Aleksei's waist, "you need rest as much anyone else."

Aleksei tried to resist, but soon found himself buried under a mountain of quilts, a warm fire heating his chamber. Jonas lay against him, his eyes fixed on Aleksei's face until they both succumbed to sleep.

CHAPTER 42

AND ALL THE POWERS OF HELL

"Now then," Aleksei said, glancing around the table, "assuming all branches are accounted for in some capacity or another, we'll begin. Sergeant Ballard, what's the status of our volunteer corps?"

A short, muscular man with close-cropped red hair stood and saluted. "Lord Captain, due to the suddenness of the attack, the volunteers were never called to action. They are currently following their standing orders to remain inconspicuous, and do as the rebels instruct them."

"Well, I suppose we can thank the gods for *that* much luck."

There was a murmur of confusion from some of the other officers, and one young man stood, "Lord Captain, how can the impotence of our volunteers be a *good* thing? Don't we desperately need their numbers?"

"To accomplish *what*, exactly, Corporal?"

The junior corporal looked suddenly nervous, "To fight the enemy, Sir?"

"Aye, they *could* be put into motion right now, to 'fight the enemy'. And they would be slaughtered. At present, those men and women would stand about as much chance as a straw house in a stiff wind."

The corporal blinked at the comparison.

"Sergeant Ballard," Aleksei said, turning away from the corporal, "I want you to find some civilian clothes. When this Palace is taken by Krasik's men, you will stand a far greater chance of survival if you aren't in uniform." He glanced at the rest of the assemblage, "That goes for the rest of you, too. They'll be looking for officers. If you can pass as stable hands and servants, you'll have a much better chance of living through the attack."

"But Sir," the corporal said, "is there *no* way to keep the enemy from taking the Palace? You seem to have conceded victory already."

"Corporal, I would like nothing better than to tell you that we have a chance of driving the enemy from our city, but such a view is impractical at this point. Better that we find ways to live through what's coming than to die, resisting the inevitable. We're all worth more alive.

"We *need* to get out of the city and regroup, and we'll have a better chance of that dressed as civilians. Hopefully they won't kill as many civilians, and some of us can reach the safety of the countryside."

"Do you wish me to remain in the city, Lord Captain?" Sergeant Ballard asked softly.

Aleksei nodded, "I need you to be here, to keep the men's spirits up. Occupation will not be kind to the people of Kalinor, and it will be easy to lose heart. I also need you here so that when we *do* return, our men will be ready."

Ballard saluted and returned to his seat.

"Where will we go once in the countryside?" Colonel Ander asked from across the table.

"Keldoan. After Kalinor, it's the most defensible city in Ilyar."

"But Sir," another officer asked, "what of Mornj? The garrison there is highly defensible. Wouldn't it be invaluable for staging operations in the South?"

"The garrison in Mornj has been dealt with in a very particular manner, Lieutenant. Prince Belgi and I have made a concerted effort to make it as unserviceable to the enemy as possible. *Trust* me when I say that we do not want to use it for anything besides a *very* unpleasant trap."

After the passage of another hour, Aleksei brought the council to its conclusion. There was little left to say, and they could only accomplish so much, given their circumstances.

"You have your orders, gentlemen. Any further questions should be referred to your commanding officers. You're dismissed."

Aleksei watched the last of his officers trail out of the room. He stifled a yawn, and glanced around his office before deciding he had better make an inspection of their fortifications, if nothing else than to keep morale up among the Guard.

Crystal clear dawn had tumbled into a poor excuse for morning, leaving a shattered sky of pale clouds and white light in its wake. Aleksei sighed, wishing the sky was laden with snow clouds instead. At least *then* Krasik's men would have to take shelter.

As he approached, the men on watch snapped to crisp attention. Aleksei returned their salutes casually.

"At ease, gentlemen." he said, glancing over the wall and into the heart of the city. In the pale midmorning light, Kalinor's streets glistened aubergine beneath a crust of old blood. "Has there been any activity?"

The nearest Guardsman shook his head, "Not so much as a *peep*, Sir. They've been lying low since the sun come up. A few lads showed up about an hour ago and fired a few arrows at us, but they were either too low or landed somewhere in the garden. No injuries to report or nothin'."

Aleksei nodded, "I've a feeling we'll *know* when they're ready to make their next move."

"Yes, Sir."

"Send me a messenger if there's any more activity. Even if it's just a few archers."

The Guardsman saluted. "Sir."

Aleksei patted him on the shoulder, "Keep up the good work, soldier."

He spent another half an hour circulating among the men, making idle chatter, and doing his best to keep their spirits up. But his own attempt at levity was punctured by the omnipresent memory of Darielle's prophecy.

Try as he may, Aleksei couldn't escape the sinking feeling that the worst of her predictions was yet to come.

As he moved among his men, laughing at their jokes, observing them amongst their friends, he couldn't help but wonder if these were the same faces he would see contorted in agony, as Demonic fire consumed everything around him.

Finally, he couldn't take it anymore. He extracted himself from the camaraderie, making his way back towards his office. There were a great number of tasks that required his attention before the day was through. And besides, the gods only knew when the enemy would make their move.

Aleksei shut the door of his office and sank into his chair with a sigh. The five hours of sleep he had managed were proving fitfully inadequate.

He drove thoughts of rest from his mind, pulling a stack of documents from his desk and fanning them out before him. They were divided into neat stacks, some white, others gold. Among them were orders for troop movements, statistics for all the major urban centers of Ilyar, allocations of resources, and endless requisitions from outposts and strongholds throughout the realm.

And each one was completely and utterly fabricated.

Aleksei had spent the hours since waking adding numbers together, and then changing them bit by bit until the information was beyond useless. It was like casting hayseeds in a wheat field.

He affixed his seal to each document in gold wax, signing them in emerald ink for good measure.

He held no illusions that the Palace would fall, it was merely a matter of time. On some level, he had known as much since his encounter with Darielle. But there was nothing in those visions that said he couldn't even the game a little before they were routed.

As soon as the wax was dry, Aleksei pulled the papers back into a neat stack, and slid them into the only drawer in his desk equipped with a lock. There, let some enterprising young rebel break in and find a cache of information beyond his wildest dreams. Aleksei knew the false figures almost as well as the real ones.

It would be entertaining to see how much credence Krasik gave his little hayseeds.

⋙⊛⋘

Jonas cried out, sitting up and patting himself down. No burns. Nothing. He relaxed against the pillows behind him and tried to fall back asleep, but it soon proved impossible.

The prince pulled himself out of bed, dressing in the dark. It was well into dusk, and he knew the enemy had regrouped by now. Despite the Palace walls surrounding them, Aleksei felt leagues away, his mind a thunderhead of frustration. Jonas pushed the other man's tumult aside.

He had his own storms to ride.

Jonas stepped out of his room and walked towards the east wing. As he passed Andariana's chambers, he stopped. The door languished open.

Jonas poked his head inside, and found the Queen in an odd state. Bottles were strewn about the room. His aunt was draped inelegantly over an armchair near the fire.

On the floor beside her lay a small piece of parchment.

Jonas stepped into the room and knelt, lifting the paper gently. His eyes scanned the faded words. The page fell from his hand.

"Jonas?" Andariana slurred. "I...Is that you?"

Jonas scooped up the parchment. "It is." he said, standing.

She looked at him, squinting, "What do you have there?"

"Your letter."

A pall fell across her face.

"*This* is why he hates you so much, isn't it?" he whispered.

Andariana nodded slowly.

Jonas looked down at the letter in his hand. At the name on the page.

Seryn.

The youngest of Emelian Krasik's sons. The boy Krasik had murdered with his bare hands.

Jonas sighed, "Does Tamara know?"

Andariana shook her head, "She still thinks her father was the High Duke of Jaenar."

Jonas nodded. The House of Jaenar. A convincing enough lie.

Andariana had been betrothed to the High Duke before the civil war broke out, though only on paper.

The House had been eradicated early in the war, and the High Duke along with it, but the betrothal lent legitimacy to Tamara's claim.

Given the circumstances of the time, it would be impossible to dispute Tamara's parentage, and he doubted anyone had thought twice about it. The secrecy of the marriage was a little suspicious, but under the circumstances, forgivable.

"What *happened*, Jonas?" Andariana mumbled, "How could *we*... I thought it was all *planned*...."

"We were missing a few pieces of vital information." Jonas responded wearily. "As a result, it was impossible for us to effectively hold the city."

"What?"

"I trusted Sammul far too long, for one," Jonas allowed, perhaps more for his edification than hers, "and his betrayal alone might have sealed our fate."

"What does *Sammul* have to do with this?" she demanded, staring at him with glassy eyes.

"Sammul tried to *kill* me in Dalita." Jonas snapped. "He's working with the *enemy*, Andariana. He has been playing us all for fools. The gods only know where he is, or if he's even still alive, but he's as much a threat to us as any enemy Magus."

"He's defending the Apsis." she whispered, her luminous green eyes suddenly frightened.

"*What?* What do you mean? Have you *seen* him?"

She nodded thickly, "Sammul came to me when the alarm bells started ringing. He told me that the enemy would be seeking the Apsis, and that he would guard it with his life. At the time, I hadn't *heard* of any betrayal."

"The Apsis." Jonas groaned, the agony of realization pulsing through him.

The Apsis. The one point where the Great Sphere of the Archanium touched their world. The Voralla had been built *around* it, to serve it, to protect it, an enchanted fortress designed to guard the most precious treasure in all of Ilyar.

And after the angels had defeated the Demon Cassian, the Magi had sealed the Apsis away behind shields of staggering strength. No one had touched the Apsis in a thousand years. In truth, no one had ever dared *try*.

Tears suddenly welled in her eyes. "Jonas, what can be *done*? Can he be stopped?"

But when she looked up for her nephew, he was gone.

Several hundred paces distant, Jonas powered himself across the Lawn on tiny, rapid wing bursts. But even as swiftly as he was moving, it took him far too long to reach the Voralla.

"Jonas!" Ilyana shouted as he headed for entrance. "What are you—"

"*Where is he?*" Jonas roared, tumbling into the ragged shape of a man on the Voralla steps.

"Who?"

"*Sammul.*"

"You *know* where he is, Jonas." she said softly, guiding him to his feet. "He's been guarding the Apsis since the city was breached. Before I could ask him what was happening, he marched into Vault.

"Jonas, he's triggered the breach protocol."

Jonas cursed violently. The ancient white marble steps of the Voralla splintered in a wave around him, echoing his anger.

"Which means he's sealed in." he growled finally, sinking. Defeated before the battle had even been fought.

The breach protocol, the ultimate fail-safe left behind to ensnare anyone who attempted to break the shields protecting the Apsis.

Once the first spell of the protocol was ignited, the rest followed in a cascade, neutralizing any possible threat. And Sammul had apparently been confident enough, or at least *stupid* enough, to trigger the chain. Jonas wondered if the High Magus was even still alive.

"He didn't even *warn* us, Jonas." Ilyana continued. Jonas would have forgotten she was even there, but for the racket she was making. "He just *did* it. No one even knew he'd returned. If Aleksei hadn't ordered the Voralla evacuated when he did—"

Jonas froze, "Aleksei ordered *what*?"

Ilyana frowned, apparently surprised that Jonas was finally responding to her, "Haven't you heard a single thing I've said? Aleksei sent orders to have every Magus and Knight keep out of the Voralla itself, to keep our senses trained on the enemy Magi. Not to engage them, but to report any strange use of the Archanium directly to him, or you, if we found you first.

"Of course, Sammul's acolytes ignored the Lord Captain's orders, so a few of us decided to keep an eye on them."

"Good thinking." Jonas barked automatically, keeping his anger in check with the greatest effort. How could he have been so *stupid?* Everything made such pristine sense, and yet he'd been blind to it the entire time.

And now it was too late.

"Aleksei knew this was coming." he whispered to himself. "He knew Sammul would seize control. He was trying to keep you safe."

Even as Ilyana opened her mouth to beg a question, Jonas was staring her down intently, "Round up fifty Magi and send them over to the west wing. The Queen *must* be protected. Get the everyone else *back* into the Voralla and defend it with your lives. The enemy will be here soon, and when they arrive you *have* to be ready."

"He's coming for the Apsis, isn't he? The Demon?"

Jonas nodded, "Aleksei was trying to protect you, but what he doesn't understand is that *you're* the last line of defense. The Demonic Presence is free, Ilyana. The Apsis is the point where the Presence first entered our world, and I think Bael's coming for it. Why else would the Demon care about something as trivial as Krasik's war?"

"Great gods," she whispered, "and he might even be able to break through the shields. Can you imagine such a creature having access to that much raw *power?*"

"I don't even want to contemplate it. Which is why you *have* to defend the Voralla. They might be stronger, but you, *all* of you, you're smarter. Your Magi know the halls better than anyone else; you'll have to use that to your advantage if we're to have any hope."

Her blue eyes shimmered with determination. "We won't fail you."

He pulled her into a quick embrace, "If you do, I doubt any of us will live long enough to know."

She pressed a quick kiss against his cheek, breathing, "Have a little faith."

And then she was gone, shouting before she was even a pace away.

Jonas turned and shifted into a falcon. He was atop the wall in seconds, searching wildly for his Knight before his feet had fully formed beneath him.

"Highness!"

He turned to find Colonel Ander rushing towards him. "Where is he?"

"His office, last I knew."

"Gods!" Jonas cursed. "Colonel, round up as many Guardsmen as you can and get into the Palace. There is about to be an invasion, and you *must* be ready to defend the Palace. Do you understand?"

Ander was off before Jonas had a chance to dismiss him.

The prince hazarded a glance over the wall, to where the enemy had regrouped behind a barricade of crates and wagons. Somewhere in that sea of bodies, Jonas could sense Bael's Magi. They had remained mostly dormant since the invasion began, but now they were preparing for something. He could feel it.

He could feel the Demon, like a malignant tumor somewhere amid the cacophony of chaotic energies. The aberrant nature of such power was almost enough to make him retch.

How Bael was alive was a mystery, and not one he had the luxury of solving.

Jonas found himself staring down into the camp, wishing there was a way to be ready for the thrust when it came. As it was, he felt tied for the sacrifice.

The clock tower chimed the last hour of dusk.

Night was coming.

⋘◉⋙

The air stinks of Hunter. Of Wood.

Bael sat in his meager tent, his eyes pressed closed as a physician threaded his dead flesh back together with cat gut.

We are closer. We can taste it.

Bael bit back his immediate response. The thrum of angry

hornets now filled his mind night and day without respite. While the Presence had been a welcome intrusion into his solitude at first, it now grated on his every nerve, leaving him on the constant edge of sanity, as the chasm of madness yawned wider by the day, a serpent unhinging its jaw to swallow the fattest sow on offer.

"We're near enough." Bael barked into the silence of his tent. The physician slipped with his needle and immediately began to apologize. Bael listened to man go on for several minutes before he understood that this simpleton was begging for his life.

"Finish your job."

As the man returned to his work, Bael was surprised to find that he felt some small level of compassion for the man. He was doing his duty, terrified that even the simplest slip could be his last.

Bael had spent his life in the shadow of fear, yet now he was beyond its grasp. He had no desire to punish those beneath him for the crime of their existence. He was not a *cruel* man, not given to anger without just cause.

This man is nothing to you. When he has finished his task, feed him to Us. We want to taste his desperation.

Bael felt the gentle prick of the needle as it slipped through his skin, felt the taut gut pull his desiccated flesh back together where Aleksei Drago's blade had sundered it.

No. he responded.

Pain seared through his core, but Bael ignored it, just as his father had trained him. He felt the throb of the Presence batter his bones, but Bael remained firm, even as the physician finished his last shaking stitches. The man knotted the gut and severed the line.

"Thank you." Bael said simply, offering the man a smile.

The man bowed deeply, "I am at your command, Lord Bael." He turned to make a hasty retreat, but paused at the tent flap. "Lord Bael," he said nervously, keeping his be-speckled eyes trained on the tent's carpeted floor, "while I have leant my services to our one true King, His Majesty Emelian Krasik, long may he reign, I am a mortician by trade."

"And?" Bael asked, allowing the silence to fester.

"*And*, Lord Bael, I am most skilled at joining dead flesh without leaving obvious scars. If you believe you'll require such...*services* in the future, I am at your disposal."

Bael was startled by the man's words. Looking back, he supposed that such a man would have seen his share of flesh, living and dead. But more than that, he was impressed by the man's gumption.

"I like you." he said finally. "What's you name?"

"Master Chappa, Your Grace."

Bael smiled, "Master Chappa, I have no doubt that the Zra-Uul has more medics and physicians than can be good for any proper monarch, but you know that *I* am something quite different. I would gladly ask for your continued assistance with my physical upkeep. *If* you believe yourself worthy of the position."

Master Chappa bowed deeply, "It would be my greatest honor, Lord Bael. Your circumstance presents the greatest challenge, and requires the greatest discretion. I will do my utmost to please you."

Bael snorted, but he noticed that the man was trembling like a dead leaf in a winter gale. He stood and rested a hand on the man's shoulder. "I have no doubt of that, Master Chappa. And if you can keep me intact, I'll ensure you a place at the highest table when the world is broken, and forged anew."

When Master Chappa looked up, Bael pressed his palm against the man's flesh.

He felt the hand of Presence overtake him, felt the veil of the Archanium slip away as an eddy of burning yellow flared through the muscles of his arm, crawling across his fingers and searing a rune into Master Chappa's forehead.

While he had never seen the symbol before, he found its meaning impossible to miss. *Property. Mine.*

The tent was filled with the acrid odor of burning flesh, and though Bael felt Master Chappa's body stiffen, the man didn't make a sound.

"You are marked. You are *mine*. Serve me well, and you will have everything you desire. *Fail* me, and you will spend an eternity screaming for a release that will never come. Do you understand?"

Master Chappa shuddered as Bael removed his hand. The rune flashed a vibrant yellow before seeping into the man's forehead. "As you command, Lord Bael. Direct me, that I may do your bidding."

Bael offered the man a smile, "See, that was simple enough,

wasn't it? When you leave this tent, ask for a Magus called Ethan. He will know what to do with you."

Master Chappa left, still bowing and praising Bael until he was out of sight. Bael let out a weary sigh.

You were kind. *You could have* fed.

Bael clucked his tongue. "It's not all about feeding. This body has to *survive* while you take your precious time. Our union has hardly gone unnoticed, and you demand caution, but also compel me with a thirst for the Apsis, in the heart of the serpent's lair.

"I'm a capable vessel, but I can't grant you access if I've been hacked to bits. When I need your fire, I will make my needs known. But you were cast from this world for a *thousand* years. Let me be your guide, but understand that emotion is not defeat.

"Cassian didn't choose you, you corrupted *him*. It's time you remembered that Cassian is dead and gone. *I* am your future, if you have one, and while you are weak, you will bow when *I* tell you to. To defy me now is to invite oblivion. You have already killed my physical form, but this vessel *must* be maintained. This hunger you speak of, this endless need to *feed*, has brought ruin upon you once before.

"And believe me when I tell you that I did *not* release you back into this world on a whim. I have gambled *everything*, and you will respect that, or our union is at an end."

For the first time in weeks, there was no harsh vibration, not violent thrum in agitated response.

When it came, it was the rumble of a distant storm, still far from sight. *The air stinks of Hunter. Of Wood. No* angel, *no* Seraphima. *We are* closer. *We can* taste *it. Take Us to it, and We will give you what you want.*

⚶

"Lord Captain!"

Aleksei sat up in his chair, looking around in bewilderment. "*What?* Who's there?"

"Lord Captain!" the voice called, now much closer, "it's the enemy, Sir. They're preparing some sort of offensive."

Aleksei blinked, and realized that a young Guardsman was standing right before his desk. He muttered a curse to himself as he realized he'd fallen asleep.

He jumped out of his chair and snatched his coat off a hook by the door. The aide who'd woken him was already waiting out in the hall. He took a moment to wipe the sleep from his eyes before joining the other man.

As they walked towards the double doors that led from the east wing onto the wall, Aleksei quizzed the man about their situation.

"What are their formations?"

"I don't know, Sir."

"Does it look like a full offensive? How many men are we talking?"

"I don't know, Sir." the boy repeated.

Aleksei felt suddenly cross, "Damn it, man, what *do* you know?"

"Sir, it's the Magi. The Magi of the enemy, Sir."

Aleksei broke into a mad dash, out the heavy doors leading onto the wall, racing the distance before finally skidding to a halt just paces from the southern Palace gate.

Below in the street, Aleksei could see thirteen Magi standing in a circle. A violent red nimbus enveloped each form, all save one. Save the man in the middle...Aleksei felt his heart constrict in his chest.

It was Bael.

Aleksei stared in disbelief.

Bael was *dead*. Aleksei's blade had punctured the Magus' *heart*.

An image suddenly flashed through his mind. He remembered the pain of the Mantle as it recoiled. At the time, he hadn't spared a second thought for the oddity, too embroiled in the consequences.

But now it seemed to make a strange sort of sense. The knife *had* punctured the other man's heart. Aleksei's Hunter instincts allowed him that much intelligence. And then he listened. He listened, and he *understood*.

Then, just as now, there was no heartbeat.

The man was dead. Yet as Aleksei stood there, staring at the Magus, Bael seemed very much alive.

Alive, and wrapped in black fire.

"Sergeant," Aleksei barked, turning to the commander of the archers standing not ten paces away, "bring me a bow."

The man hurried to Aleksei, handing him his own bow and quiver. Aleksei notched an arrow.

He took aim, commanding his every instinct. His blood surged as the thrill of the hunt pounded in time with his pulse. He released the shaft into the fading daylight.

It evaporated a pace from its target.

Aleksei cursed.

From the street, Bael looked up at him and smiled.

Aleksei's blood ran cold.

And then he knew where he was. *This* was the moment Darielle had foretold. *This* was the decision he had to make.

The air exploded in a storm of Demonic flame. Aleksei heard men cry out as the fire washed over the walls and crashed across them, broiling them within their armor, melting flesh to steel.

Time slowed, and Aleksei *ran*.

Chapter 43

A Broken Crown

Aleksei sprinted across the wall, dark fire soaring up behind him. As he ran, a thousand different horrors seared their way through his mind. The sight of his men burning in liquid fire, the storm of their screams. The pleading looks in their eyes as he abandoned them to the roiling dark, the breathless heat that inhaled their fragile lives like dry grass swept up in a conflagration.

Hatred boiled in his blood. Hatred for Perron, for Krasik, for *Bael,* for summoning such atrocities. And hatred for himself, for being powerless to stop it.

Tears stung his eyes as he ran. It was all he could do to keep moving, not to turn and pull their helpless bodies from the black flames, even as anguished faces vanished in whorls of char and spark. But any delay would only ensnare him in Bael's trap.

So he kept running, loathing himself more with every footfall. His men had promised to follow him to their deaths, but what of *his* oaths? What of *his* promises to lead them to victory, to guard them from the terrors that even now blackened their living flesh and bone?

His every step betrayed them, and he felt it as keenly as though it was branded into his flesh.

As Aleksei reached the heavy ironbound doors leading into the Palace, he kicked out fiercely, tearing one of the doors off its hinges.

Even as the Demon's flames ravaged his men on the wall, he could feel the flood of heartbeats pouring into the Palace from below, as Perron's men overran his barricades. Any moment now, the Palace was going to become a *very* dangerous place. But before that happened, he had duties to carry out.

The Lord Captain charged through empty hallways, turning here and there as he adjusted his position through the east wing of the Palace. It suddenly seemed as though place was built like a maze.

He stumbled into the eastern atrium, even as Krasik's soldiers were swarming up the grand staircase. Aleksei drew his sword. He could feel the Mantle pulse across his shoulders, itching to consume the lives of the men rushing towards him, burning with hunger.

A Fist of men spotted him, and moved to intercept. Aleksei charged straight at them. There would be no more running this day. He wanted *retribution* for the horrors Bael had unleashed upon his people. And he would trade Bael life for life if he had to.

The moment passed with a startling brilliance, built from the glimmer of his blade, his enemies' surprised screams, and a great deal of brilliant crimson.

And then he was through, leaving a trail of agony and gore in his wake as he burst into the relative sanctuary of the west wing.

Even as he turned the corner, Aleksei knew he was too late. The corridor leading to the royal apartments was swarming with soldiers and Magi. Aleksei leapt out of the way, as a bolt of fire scorched the space he'd occupied a breath before.

He rolled across the floor, ending up in a small parlor. Coming to his feet, Aleksei quickly barricaded the door with a divan, searching the room for an exit. The door rocked violently in its frame, reminding him that the enemy was in hot pursuit.

He caught sight of the window. It was the only other way out of the chamber, his one chance to survive. And he was going to have to improvise.

Aleksei kicked out the casement and ducked his head outside.

The door behind him would give way any moment. He had a handful of heartbeats before the enemy came pouring through the doorway.

In a moment of desperation, Aleksei ripped the curtain ties away from the wall and knotted the lengths of silk cord together. He drew his belt knife and tied one end of the cord around the hilt.

Aleksei leaned out the splintered window frame and looked up towards the roof of the Palace. Four paces from the windowsill, he saw a gargoyle scowling at the chaos below.

He took a deep breath, spinning the cord into a fury before letting it fly.

By some extraordinary grace of the gods, the knife blade latched in the gargoyle's mouth, catching amidst the ferocious panoply of stone teeth.

Aleksei breathed in, and leapt out the window.

Shift.

His boots struck hard stone and he ran, ignoring the ridiculous angle of the world as he darted across the wall of the Palace. A moment later, his boot made contact with the surface of a window and he crashed into the room, tumbling haphazardly across the floor and landing on his back.

A startled shriek greeted his arrival, and for a moment he found himself disoriented, gasping for breath. The world righted itself, and he realized where he was.

"Aleksei?"

He pulled himself to his feet, ignoring the way the room lurched and heaved. "Highness?"

Tamara was at his side a moment later, trying to hold him steady with her delicate hands. "Gods, are you *alright?*"

It took him a moment to register the question, and even longer to produce an answer.

"Fine." he managed, running a hand across his face and staring at the door that led out into the hall.

"They're at Mother's door!" Tamara hissed. "I can hear them from here."

He looked at her sharply, "Do they know you're in here?"

She shook her head, "Mother had one of the Magi trick them into thinking we're both in her room. There's a party of Magi with her now, keeping Krasik's men at bay."

"Not for long," Aleksei grumbled. "Come on, I've got to get you out of here."

She looked haggard, "I believe you'll find the doorway a little *crowded* at present."

Aleksei ignored her flippancy, looking back to the shattered window, "The door isn't our only option. Do you have any clothes better for climbing than that?"

The princess looked down at her satin gown, then back to Aleksei. He could see the distress in her face, and took it as a resounding negative.

"You're going to have to do some running, so you'll have to leave your shoes behind."

Tamara still seemed uncertain, but Aleksei caught a glint of determination in her eyes. She was terrified, but she had trusted him before, and he'd yet to lead her astray.

He leaned out the window and caught the edge of the silk cord he had used to engineer his entry. He leaned back into the safety of the bedchamber and ripped away two more curtain ties, securing them to his silk rope.

"Tamara," he said calmly, "I need you to do *exactly* as I say."

She nodded stoically, though he could see tears welling up in her eyes.

"I'm going to extinguish the lamps. We won't be able to climb to the roof if they can spot us against the window frame. I'm going to start up first. I need you to hold on to me as I climb up. Are you ready?"

Tamara nodded again, apparently reassured by his confidence. Aleksei snuffed the lamps, plunging the chamber into darkness.

They heard the door to the anteroom splinter.

"Hold onto my waist with all the strength you've got." Aleksei commanded, gripping the silk cord and stepping onto the edge of the window frame.

She threw her arms around him as he slowly pulled himself up the cord. Her added weight made the ascent difficult, but Aleksei kept his mind focused on the horrors that awaited them if he failed.

He kept climbing.

Hand over hand, he pulled both of them up until he reached the gargoyle. Taking a deep breath, he let go of the rope with one hand and grasped the edge of the Palace roof. Another breath, and he caught the roof in his other hand.

⚜

"Tamara, I need you to hold onto the cord." Aleksei said tightly.

"What if I fall?" she whimpered.

"You won't fall. You just have to hold it for a few seconds. I can't pull both of us onto the roof at the same time. I need you to let go of me. I need you to *trust* me. Just like on the Southern Plain, Tamara. Just like that."

The princess looked down at the fifty-pace gap between her and green Lawn below.

"Tamara!" Aleksei barked, reminding her of the immediacy of the situation.

She clenched her jaw and let go of his waist, grabbing desperately for the rope. Her weight pulled her down the length of silk, the friction burning her hands even as she held fast. Her soft feet hit the wall, and she pressed against the stone to stabilize herself.

Aleksei pulled himself onto the roof and reached down to the gargoyle's mouth. He gripped the cord in his hand, then leaned as much of his weight back against the roof as he could.

With all his strength, Aleksei heaved the rope hand over hand. After several pulls, the rope became slick with his blood, but he only gripped harder.

A few moments later, the Princess clambered onto the roof in an undignified stumble.

"Are you alright?" he whispered, pressing his bleeding hands against his trousers.

She nodded, her eyes shifting to the trails of crimson slowly spreading from his hidden palms.

"I'm fine." she insisted. "What do we do now? Aren't we trapped?"

Aleksei smiled, leaning perilously over the edge of the roof to disengage his knife from the gargoyle's mouth. It seemed amazing that the blade hadn't broken, but she kept her amazement to herself.

"There are roads through Kalinor beyond the ones you know." he admonished gently.

She didn't question him.

Aleksei took two steps towards the apex of the roof before realizing that his boots could not possibly give him the purchase he required. With an anguished sigh, he dropped back into a crouch and pulled them off.

"What are you *doing?*" Tamara hissed, glancing towards the edge nervously, as though any moment Bael's minions would come swarming over.

"I can't walk on the roof tiles in these boots." Aleksei muttered, pulling his left boot off and dropping it next to his right. "Looks like we're both going to have to be tender with our footing."

Tamara unleashed a string of curses that brought a blush to Aleksei's cheeks. "My entire life has been so bloody *sheltered. I hate* feeling helpless."

"I'll do my best to shield you from the worst of it, Princess. As much as I can."

"And I believe that, Lord Captain. I *have* to." Her steely Belgi gaze was enough to push him forward.

Aleksei moved, and she followed him across the smooth roof tiles of the Palace, trying to be as quiet as possible. Tamara wasn't quite sure *how* one was supposed to be quiet while walking over roof tiles, since every one she stepped on clattered and clanked. But Aleksei somehow managed it, so she decided she might as well do her best.

After what seemed like hours of treading lightly on the pale golden planks, Aleksei raised a hand. She came to an unsteady halt, and he pointed at the sharp drop-off not three paces before them. He pressed a finger to his lips, then crept forward.

Tamara remained where she was, uncertain whether he wanted her to wait or follow.

Aleksei crawled to the end of the roof and glanced off the edge, pulling back sharply a second later. Tamara crawled over to him, breathing in her own gasp in when she caught sight of a sentry. A man stood on the battlements not five paces below them. He was dressed in black, with a wickedly curved knife gripped in one hand. Its black blade dripped with the blood of a fallen Guardsman lying not far off.

The Archanium Knight turned to her, pressing his finger to his lips again for emphasis, then drew his knife.

Tamara's eyes widened as she watched him heft the short length of icy steel. The knife flashed from his hand. She hadn't even seen him move, but her ears heard the sudden gurgling from below. She leaned over just in time to see the man in black collapse into a nerveless heap on the battlements, Aleksei's knife handle sprouting up from the back of his neck.

"Serves him right." she grunted.

Aleksei gripped the edge of the roof, and slipped over the side. She wanted to warn him about the drop, but before she could muster the words he was gone.

Tamara looked over the side in horror. She had once seen a Guardsman fall half as far and break his leg. Yet when she caught sight of Aleksei, he was decidedly uninjured. He swiftly moved over to the corpse of the man in black and withdrew his own knife with a twist, wiping it on the dead man's clothes before returning the blade to its scabbard.

"Jump!"

Her eyes widened and she shook her head, unable to fight back her fear.

He grunted irritably, "Tamara, *jump*! I'll catch you!"

Again she shook her head.

"*Trust* me." he demanded.

She thought back to the last time he'd said that, mere minutes before. To the first time he'd begged it of her, more than a year before. She had trusted him then. He had always held his end of the bargain, and for all that he'd pushed her, he'd always kept her safe.

Stifling a sob, Tamara gently lowered herself off the edge as he had, then let go. A heartbeat later, she dropped into Aleksei's arms.

The force of impact drove the wind from her lungs, and she spent the better part of a minute regaining her breath. When her breathing finally steadied, Aleksei set her on her feet.

"That was a very brave thing you just did." he whispered into her ear.

Tamara felt a flush of pleasure at having made Aleksei Drago proud. She looked up to realize that he'd already moved to the battlements, where he was examining a length of coarse rope.

"What is it?" she whispered, joining him at the edge of the wall.

"It looks like our friend here climbed up the wall with this." he said, hefting a heavy iron grappling hook in one hand. "And it should be easier to go down than climb up."

"Go *down?*" she asked weakly, looking over the edge at the fifty-pace drop.

He fixed her with a cool golden-eyed gaze, "You're going to have to climb down yourself this time. I can't take us *both* down."

Her heart seemed to leap into her throat as his words sank in.

"But where are *you* going?" she whimpered as he swung his leg over the edge of the wall.

His voice came back, reassuring, "I'll go down in front of you. I'll show you how to climb down, but you *have* to follow my example."

She nodded, pretending her heart wasn't trying to burst from her chest. Her breath came in short gasps as she watched the Knight climb over the battlement and slowly lower himself.

"Grab the rope." he commanded.

Tamara took the rope in her hands and reoriented herself as he had.

"Lean back, holding tight to the rope." he instructed from below.

She did as he commanded, finding it far easier to slowly walk her way down the wall. Though the rope bit sorely into her hands, Tamara kept her whimpers to herself. She'd never endured this sort of physical difficulty.

Even when he'd saved her from the assassins on the Southern Plain, *he'd* done all the riding and hunting.

Still, there was no turning back now, and Tamara would not allow herself to give in to feelings of discomfort or fear when her entire bloody realm was falling to ashes around her.

Yet no amount of determination could make up for basic physical strength, and the farther she climbed, the weaker her hands became. Finally she stopped, trying desperately to catch her breath as she looked down to check her progress.

"Don't look down!" came Aleksei's sharp snap, an instant too late.

The street was spinning beneath her. It seemed to rise and fall before her eyes. And then she was hurtling towards the ground at a breathtaking pace. Tamara closed her eyes tight, opening her mouth to scream as the cobbles rushed up to greet her.

But even as she braced herself for impact, she was jerked roughly short. She opened her eyes experimentally, wondering when the end would come, and found herself floating over an expanse of cityscape. After a moment, she realized that something warm was trickling down her back.

She looked up, and nearly screamed at the sight of Aleksei's strained face.

One hand was clasping her left arm. Blood ran freely from his grip and down her arm, disappearing beneath the satin of her sleeve. His other hand held the rope tightly, but she could see a dark, slick trail vanishing up the rope and into the night.

Tamara reached feebly for the rope dangling in front of her and, failing that, reached upwards and caught Aleksei's wrist.

He made no attempt to pull her upwards, instead sliding farther down the rope. The glistening stain trailed after him, and Tamara realized that his hand would be nerveless gristle and bone by the time they reached the street far below.

Minutes passed, time punctured only by the grating rasp of raw hemp gnawing into Aleksei's hand, and the dripping of his blood down the back of her neck. She didn't hear him so much as whimper the entirety of their descent.

Tamara's feet touched the cold stone of the street, and a moment later Aleksei dropped to the cobbles, clutching his right hand close to his chest. Blood drooled freely from his left hand as stabilized himself against the Palace wall.

Tamara looked away from the crimson smear left on the whitestone wall. She glanced at Aleksei's face, but his expression betrayed no hint of pain.

"We've got to get out of the open." he grunted.

She nodded, knowing that enemy soldiers could show up at any moment.

"Where can we go? Krasik's men will be everywhere." Tamara whispered, suddenly feeling more frightened than she had all night. Despite how far they'd come, they were still as far from deliverance as they'd ever been.

Aleksei said nothing for a long moment, but rather seemed focused on remaining conscious. Finally, he stiffened, blinking away pain she could only imagine.

"Follow me."

⁂

Emelian Krasik kicked aside the remains of a richly upholstered armchair and stepped into the room. It still stank of blood and smoke, and here and there the fine carpets were marred with sprays of viscera.

His Magi had not been kind in their victory.

Krasik smiled as he came to the center of the room. Before him knelt the thin form of a woman, streaks of white running through her chestnut locks. Her emerald eyes burned with rage and determination, admirable in a woman of her maturity, and revolting.

"Isn't this an *auspicious* meeting, Majesty?" he asked softly. "I must wonder if you saw this coming, all those years ago? Or perhaps you thought your insult would go unpunished?"

Andariana gave him no response, save the single tear that slowly wound its way down her soot-stained cheek.

"Zra-Uul," a uniformed man interrupted, stepping into the room and bowing low, "your presence is requested in the chambers of the Princess Tamara."

Krasik's smile brightened, "Ah yes, the Princess. Tell me, is my granddaughter well?"

He watched Andariana as he asked, gauging the levels of her fear, her *hatred*.

"I...I'm not *sure*, Zra-Uul."

Something about the way the man floundered forced Krasik to turn, "You're not *sure*? Either she's breathing and she's alive, or she isn't and she's dead. Which is it, Commander?"

"N...Neither, Zra-Uul? She's...gone, Your Grace."

Emelian turned, glaring down at Andariana. The whore's face lit up in triumph. He reached down and rapped the back of her head, sparing a light brush of his power. The queen collapsed into a nerveless heap on the floor.

"Take her to one of the storerooms." he barked at the commander. "I don't want her taking her *own* life before I've taken my satisfaction from her."

The commander darted forward and swung the unconscious monarch over his shoulder. He hurried from the room.

"*Perron!*" Krasik roared.

There was the sound of low conversation from the corridor, and then Lord Perron took a dignified step into the chamber.

"Your Grace." he said with an infinitesimal bow.

"Tell me, Lord Perron, *how* it is that the Princess Tamara is not in her chambers? As of your last report, I believe she was hiding in there from our Magi."

"Indeed she was, Zra-Uul. But it seems that a rescue attempt was mounted between the time I received that report and the moment our Magi broke into her bedchamber."

"And I don't suppose you know where she is *now?*" Krasik asked, his voice soft and measured.

Perron sighed, "We found one man dead on the north wall of the Palace, and blood on the grappling line he used to scale the wall. We believe her rescuer took her out of the Palace by such means."

"Which means they're in the city."

"Yes, Your Grace. The sentries are all under strict instructions to open the Palace gates for no one."

"And what about the walls surrounding the *city?* The *sewers?* Are *they* being guarded as well?"

Perron cleared his throat, "With all due respect, Your Grace, it is impossible to monitor the entire sewer system *and* the city walls with our invasion of the city and the Palace in the state that it is. There is a standard night watch on patrol of the city. Any unusual activity will surely be dealt with by them."

Krasik arched a snowy eyebrow, "Lord Perron, there are certain residents of this Palace who are still unaccounted for. Residents who could be responsible for spiriting the Princess Tamara from her room and, in due time, from this city. *Despite* the diligence of your night watch."

Perron blinked in surprise.

Krasik heard the confused rumble of the man's thoughts as though Perron were blurting them aloud.

"The information *you* receive, Lord Perron, is at *my* disposal whether or not you choose to divulge it to me." Krasik groaned.

He hoped he sounded bored. Gods, he *was* bored. So much conquest, so much blood to whet his whistle, and what to show for it?

Perron stiffened.

Krasik read each thought before it trickled out of Perron's ear. The Chancellor was a silly man in the best of times, but this was a triumph! This was the culmination of his first invasion, and he was already fielding excuses like a first-day kitchen scull?

"In my experience, Lord Perron," Krasik intoned, "men of your station often think themselves to be in some way remarkable. This supports a belief that, while you may deceive others, you cannot yourselves be deceived. This is, I believe, the doom of your kind."

Perron tried to smile, "As you say, Your Grace."

"Now then, would you mind telling me the latest word on the whereabouts of Jonas Belgi or Lord Captain Drago? Or shall I dig for *that* as well?"

"The Prince has not been in his chambers since just before sundown, when he exited the west wing of the Palace. He has yet to return. The Lord Captain was stationed at the Palace gate, where we amassed our attack earlier this evening. He would have been in the blast zone of Bael's most...unusual assault."

"You do not honestly believe him *dead*, Perron."

"It seems unlikely." Perron admitted.

"Who among Sammul's useless Magi is missing?"

"The Magus Aya has not been seen, Your Grace. She is the only Magus in the Voralla that Sammul considered dangerous. All other surviving Magi have been rounded up as Lord Bael instructed, and placed under guarded arrest."

"Where?"

"In the Cathedral of Mokosh, Zra-Uul. It was the only secured structure that could contain their numbers."

"I trust they are under sufficient guard?"

"Of course, Your Grace." Perron responded quickly. "By our best Magi. Though it seems that even our weakest Magi are more than a match."

Krasik smiled, "Indeed. Sammul has done his job well. We'll have to find some suitable reward for him, if he survives."

"Yes, Your Grace." said Perron, his eyes fixed on the floor.

"Excellent. I am going to get some sleep. Contact Bael and let him know that I am returning to the camp."

Perron frowned, "You're not going to sleep in your *palace*, Your Grace?"

Krasik laughed harshly, "It is not *my* palace yet, Perron. And until it *is*, I have no intention of entrusting these walls with my life. I shall see you on the morrow. Perhaps dawn will bring news of victory. Remember, they cannot hide here forever. Either they will escape, or we will sniff them out."

"As you say, Zra-Uul."

Krasik nodded, then left the broken chamber.

Perron allowed himself a sigh of relief. He had survived yet another encounter with the man. To say that he'd gotten far more than he'd ever bargained for in the form of Emelian Krasik was an understatement of spectacular proportions.

What had begun as an efficient coup d'état was rapidly spinning out of Perron's control. And now he was charged with tracking down the two people who had made his life a misery for the past year.

Krasik might as well have commanded him to shoot down the sun and put the moon in a bag, for all the likelihood Perron had of catching *either* Jonas Belgi or Lord Captain Drago. And even if he *did* get his hands on either one of them, what was he to do? He supposed it would be easiest to have them killed on sight.

He might even get lucky. After all, only one had to make a mistake for him to be the victor.

He chuckled lightly to himself, not foolish enough to gain confidence, yet not quite as dejected as he'd been a moment before. Circumstances, he thought, were not necessarily as dire as he had supposed.

On a rafter far above, a tiny brown wood-mouse blinked its beady emerald eyes. When Jonas was sure that nothing new would be revealed, he scurried away through a crack in the wall, unnoticed, unseen.

Aleksei led Tamara through a winding series of alleys. From the stench of the rubbish bins surrounding them, they were near the butcher's markets. This was confirmed a moment later, when the alley abruptly emptied onto Butcher's Square.

Aleksei glanced at the garishly painted sign proclaiming their location and sighed, "I suppose it's as fitting as a place as any."

"Fitting for what?" she muttered.

He held up a ruined hand, "Wait here." His golden eyes narrowed, "And don't make a sound. If they discover your presence, we forfeit our escape."

Tamara nodded emphatically. Aleksei breathed a sigh and stole away from the alley entrance, hugging the shadows as he crept around the edge of the Square.

He sniffed at the air as he moved, making slight corrections in his position as their scents grew stronger.

While Perron's soldiers might be working to overthrow Belgi authority, most had been trained under the same regimens as any other Legionnaire in the past twenty years. A shift of allegiances shouldn't be able to tamper with that training too much.

Excepting, of course, that they broke their oaths to their queen. he thought bitterly.

As difficult as it was for Aleksei to cut down men who only months ago had been under his command, a deeper determination consistently won out. These men were here to dethrone the Queen, and all those loyal to her House. They had come to destroy the House of Belgi.

Jonas was not exempt from their planned retribution, and for that alone Aleksei refused to display even the meanest form of mercy. He felt their malevolence for the Crown as keenly as though it were leveled at him, but he cared less for that than the malice they held for his prince.

Long shadows suddenly spread across the Square. In the lamplight, Aleksei could make out three figures. Three figures to match three heartbeats.

A standard night's watch.

Aleksei watched the men walk the length of the Square. As they turned back towards the Market district, he struck.

"Guards!" he cried out.

They all immediately looked in his direction, but he was already gone. The moment the words left his lips, Aleksei was moving. He stopped a dozen paces from the nearest man, and cried out again.

The guard turned towards him. In the depths of the shadows, Aleksei prepared himself.

If this was going to work, he would have to take them one at a time.

When the man was within a pace, Aleksei lunged forward, clapping his hands on either side of the guard's head. The man opened his mouth to cry out, but no sound escaped.

Even in the darkness of the shadows, Aleksei could see the black tendrils of the Mantle burning crimson as they dipped into the man. Tiny talons of black shot across his eyes, red tendrils snaking out of his open mouth, licking at the air.

And then it was over.

The Mantle receded, flowing up Aleksei's arms and leaving the man cold and colorless.

Aleksei removed his hands from the man's head, leaving two streaks of crusted blood. He looked down at his palms, perfect once again, smooth and whole.

"Great gods!" a voice rang out.

Aleksei looked up and realized the remaining men had spotted him. One had already drawn his sword and was rushing towards Aleksei, the other not far behind.

Instead of drawing his own sword, Aleksei dropped down next to the corpse of his victim and drew the man's belt knife.

He waited until the first guard was within range, then flicked the knife underhand. For a moment it seemed to hang in midair, tumbling end over end. And then it stopped, only the hilt visible around the rivers of blood that gushed from the man's left eye.

Aleksei didn't wait for the last man to reach him. He came to his feet and stepped out into the moonlight. The man had his sword drawn, but Aleksei ignored it. He waited until the guard committed to his swing and sidestepped the attack. His hand closed on the man's throat and it was over.

The guard's body collapsed in a slack heap on the cobbles, as colorless and cold as the first man. A pang of sympathy tried to struggle up within him, but withered as it reached the surface. He didn't have time or patience for emotion at the moment.

"Tamara?" he whispered softly into the night.

She appeared after a long moment. She looked pale, as though she were about to faint. He could tell she'd been crying.

"Are you alright?" he asked gently.

She nodded, blinking away her tears, "It's just...I wasn't expecting...."

Aleksei said nothing. He knew that look in her eyes. It was fear. Fear of *him*. He had seen it before, in the eyes of the Bondar brothers at his father's farm.

Rather than respond, Aleksei turned back to the largest guard and began to strip him.

"What are you doing?" Tamara demanded, startled even in the midst of his small massacre.

⚬

Aleksei didn't look back at her, but instead stripped off his tattered leather coat. "I didn't have time to get properly dressed before Bael attacked the Palace. If we're going to get out of the city, I have to look the part. They'll never believe I'm one of them if I'm walking around barefoot in the middle of winter."

His mention of the cold reminded her how chill the air was, and how much her soft feet were suffering on the icy cobbles. She stepped on the hem of her gown, hoping that it might put some barrier of warmth between her frozen toes and the street.

As Aleksei pulled the dead man's uniform off of his limp body, Tamara found herself staring at the black undulations of the Mantle. If the night air was cool, those strange, writhing pitch paws across his muscular shoulders and arms made her feel as though she stood on sheets of ice.

They looked like they were grasping at him, clawing away at his flesh.

And yet they were *part* of Aleksei Drago, one of the kindest, most courteous men she'd ever encountered. The man had become a decided paradox since she'd first met him.

Aleksei pulled the dead man's shirt over his head, hiding the writhing talons and tendrils from her. He swiftly buttoned up the front, then pulled on the officer's wool coat. Finally, he pulled off the man's boots and stamped his feet into them.

"Where to now?" Tamara whispered.

"Well, we still have to find a way out of the city gates. Any chance you can fit into one of those uniforms?"

Tamara glanced down at the two men. An idea leapt out at her. "I have a thought."

Aleksei watched her for a long moment before shrugging. "Let's hear it."

"There are several access points in the city to the sewer system below. What with the invasion, I doubt there's been time yet to place guards there. The system drains both to the east and west of the city, beyond the gates."

Aleksei's face lit up at the suggestion. "That's *brilliant*. How do you know this?"

"I've been instructed in city affairs since childhood. One would hope it might prove useful at some point, no?"

Aleksei's offered her a proud smile. After a moment of consideration, he looked at the two other corpses and began pulling off the smaller one's boots.

"What are those for?" she whispered.

He finished yanking off the left boot, "I've asked some pretty harsh things of you tonight. But even *I'm* not going to make a princess walk barefoot through leagues of sewage, Highness."

"And you have my thanks for that." she breathed as she took the boots from the Knight, slipping her delicate feet into their cool, hard confines. It felt like she was standing in a pair of large leather buckets.

"Can you walk in them?"

She took a few steps and nearly tripped over her skirts. Aleksei caught her shoulders and steadied her.

"Well?" he asked.

She sighed, "I could manage it. But can I take them off for now?"

"Just carry them until you need them."

Aleksei turned and neatly stacked the bodies of the guardsmen behind a pile of broken crates.

He wiped his hands on his trousers. "Are you ready to get out of here?"

She nodded, realizing that her feet would soon be in the boots of a dead man. A man who lay with his confederates not five paces distant. She glanced over her shoulder as they walked away, and shivered.

Gods, she thought to herself, *Jonas is* bonded *to this man?*

But the more she thought on that, the less it surprised her. In fact, she found it *comforting.* There had always been something unspoken about Jonas, as though it was impossible to be shocked by him, because there wasn't a thing in the world he *wouldn't* do. After all, this was a man who had arrived on her windowsill as a *bird.*

The idea of his Archanium Knight being the same gentle giant who had pulled her from the path of an assassin's arrow a year before, the same towering farm boy who now wore deadly magic as a second skin, only served to match the same sort of sensibilities Jonas had always delighted since he was a boy.

Aleksei stopped in the middle of the street, sniffing at the air. Tamara watched him as he turned his head this way and that, testing the air with his nose like an animal.

She recalled the first time she had seen him. The confused, determined farm boy she had met then had undergone such a transformation since his arrival in Kalinor. And while there were moments that Tamara wished the farm boy would return, it was becoming powerfully clear to her just how important, and how *vital,* his transformation was.

Aleksei shifted direction, leading her east towards the industrial districts. The farther they went, the more nervous she became. This district would be under much heavier guard. No invading army would want the defenders to retake the smithy or the mills, with their grain silos.

"Here it is." Aleksei whispered, crouching in front of what Tamara finally recognized as a sewer cover.

"Impressive." she whispered as crouched next to him. While she had known that there were such entrances, the gods only knew how long it would have taken her to actually *locate* one.

He smiled and lifted the cover away. The smell that wafted up nearly knocked Tamara back. She began to think this hadn't been such a brilliant plan.

"Perhaps we should reconsider the gates." she muttered, slipping on the boots, and lowering herself gently through the entrance.

Aleksei bit back a chuckle, glanced around once more to make sure they hadn't been followed, and jumped down himself.

"This is disgusting!" Tamara gagged, standing a few paces away from him, up to her ankles in the Kalinor's waste.

Aleksei saw that her gown was dragging in the dross and drew his knife.

"Aleksei?" she whispered quizzically, as he took hold of her skirt and began to slash it.

"Your dress is already ruined, and the last thing I want is for you to trip."

She could hardly argue with that.

"So where do we go now?" she asked, holding her hand over her nose.

"This tunnel heads east," he said softly, tossing the rags of her gown to the side. "towards the Seil Wood. If we can get there, we'll be safe."

She nodded, resigned to spending the next hour trudging through raw sewage in a ruined gown, with the Hunter's blood in her hair and crusting down her back.

"Well then," she said with as much enthusiasm as she could muster, "lead the way."

CHAPTER 44

THE NATURE OF DEFIANCE

THE DOOR SHUDDERED. Tiny avalanches of dust showered down around Ilyana, but she hardly noticed. Not three paces away, Toma was screaming hysterically. Her Knight looked as confused and upset as she did.

"Quiet!" Ilyana shouted over the rumbling attacks sounding from the other side of the door.

Toma either didn't hear her or didn't care. Ilyana looked away from the hysterical Magus. "Tamrix, either *you* do something or I *will*."

Toma's Knight caught the murderous glint in Ilyana's eye, and moved swiftly to Toma's side. He placed his thick arms protectively around her, speaking in a soft tone that Ilyana couldn't make out.

Whatever he said had the desired effect, because a moment later the woman was merely sobbing into his shirt, rather than shrieking her lungs out.

Marrik was pressed tight against the door, shoulder to shoulder with Aya's Raefan. At present, no one was exactly sure where Aya was.

"This won't hold much longer." Marrik shouted.

Ilyana nodded, thinking furiously.

Only moments ago, the Voralla had been a vision of peace and tranquility. And then the Demon's Magi had appeared.

The enemy had hounded them though the halls of the Voralla, Ilyana and her Magi constantly falling back against the assault. This, she now knew, was what the Lords of Parliament had so feared when they had imprisoned her. Not a force of Archanium Magi who could fight, but one that could *defend*.

From the moment Demon's Magi swarmed through the Voralla, Sammul's acolytes had turned on Ilyana's small band of defenders, hammering at their shields with spells from the Nagavor unlike anything she'd ever beheld.

She had watched her friends cut down with spells of destruction so foreign to her that she could hardly believe they were being conjured by the same men and women she had known for *years*. Magi she had believed to be peaceful, loving students of the Akhrana.

Magi she had even looked *down* upon, for their weakness in the Archanium. Only now did it make sense. She knew the weakness of her own powers within the violence of the Nagavor well enough; she had just been shown their own inadequacies reflected back at her.

It had only been by the grace of the gods that she and a few others had locked themselves in a room with shielded doors. But even in the Voralla, such defenses could only hold for so long.

"Gods, what is Sammul *doing*? Why isn't he *defending* us?" Toma moaned from her corner.

Ilyana ignored the question.

"We have to find a way into the Great Hall." she shouted.

"I don't know if that's going to work." Raefan called.

"It's our only chance." she insisted. "It's the most defensible position in the Voralla. Sammul's locked in the Vault. The Great Hall is our only choice."

Marrik looked at Raefan and nodded his agreement. The other Knight sighed.

"How do you plan on dealing with our *friends* out there?" he demanded, wincing as another bone-crushing blow slammed into the door, cracking the wood.

Ilyana bit her lip. She had never done anything like this before. She didn't even know if it would work. But she had to *try*.

"Marrik, you're going to have to carry me. When I tell you to, open the door and *run*."

She turned and regarded Toma with a mixture of pity and disgust, "You might want to let Tamrix carry you, if you're unsure of your footing. We can't afford any mistakes."

Toma had been quietly sobbing the last few moments, but she nodded her understanding.

"Whatever you're going to do, do it *fast*." Marrik shouted.

The wail of the Nagavor outside intensified. The enemy Magi had apparently grown tired of her little game.

Time to change the rules.

Ilyana plunged into the Archanium, swimming through the miasma of spells for growth, healing, and middling shields. She passed the whorl for fire and kept moving. While she walked a lower meridian of the Akhrana, the spell she sought was still well within her abilities. More importantly, those amassed outside would never see it coming.

Ilyana swam forward and wrapped a length of blinding brilliance around herself. From outside she could hear the cries of Magi and soldiers alike as her light spell exploded into existence.

"*Now!*" she heard herself cry.

And then she was being hoisted up. She could feel Marrik's sinewy shoulder against her cheek. She weighed nothing to her Knight, even as he sprinted down the hallway, leaving blinded men and Magi behind him.

She sensed others ahead, though whether they were ordinary soldiers or enemy Magi was impossible to say. Ilyana unleashed her spell again mere heartbeats before Marrik rounded the corner, sparing him the eye-burning white by only the fraction of a moment.

Marrik did not stop, which she hoped meant they had bought themselves another handful of seconds.

"Marrik!"

Ilyana heard the shout a second before her body hit the floor. She cried out in surprise and pain, losing her grip on the Archanium and opening her eyes to stare into the glare of an angry soldier.

She rolled to the side as his axe clanked harmlessly off the Voralla floor. A moment later he collapsed to the ground, convulsing and gagging on his own blood.

Marrik pulled his sword from the man as she came to her feet. It was only then that Ilyana understood their position.

They were surrounded.

Raefan was pinned against one wall with three swords pointed at his throat. Marrik stood over her, panting and staring down four crossbows.

"Well *done*, Lady Magus."

She turned her head to see a man she knew by description, by *feel*, if not by sight: the Demon.

"I'm impressed with your ingenuity. I doubt a tenth of your idiot friends could have done so well." he said, an insolent grin plastered across his face.

Her life was forfeit. Her eyes shifted to the soldier closest to her. His attention was fixed on the Demon; the threat neutralized.

Marrik had taught her the basics of self-defense, and while far from being adept, she was decent with a knife. If she could move fast enough, Ilyana thought she could get a hold of the soldier's belt knife. She might have a chance to get to the Demon before he gripped the Archanium.

She could think of no other option.

Ilyana reached towards the solider. A wave of pain dropped her screaming to the floor before she'd so much as opened her hand.

"You'd like me to kill you, wouldn't you?" Bael said, shaking his head in disappointment. "I'm afraid I've already taken care of that technicality *for* you, milady."

He glanced at the men surrounding them, "Lock them up with the others. We'll have our fun with them soon enough. And send some men to those poor wretches she blinded. Heal them if you can, or just cut their throats. I don't really care." He turned and grinned at her, "Farewell, little Magus. I'll have this pleasure again *very* soon."

Ilyana hardly felt the strike against her head. She kept her eyes focused on the Demon, even as she sank into unconsciousness. Her hate blackened with her vision.

⚜

The path was impossible to see. Every now and then, Tamara would stub her toe on a protruding stone in the darkness. But even the sharp flash of pain was a relief after trekking through two leagues of refuse and excrement.

Still, she could think of a great many places she would rather be than walking blistered and barefoot through a shadowed Wood. Even the fact that Aleksei was leading her by the hand and knew his way through dark did little to alleviate her trepidation.

At least it isn't so bloody cold. she thought.

The farther they walked, the warmer it grew. If it would get just a bit brighter, she would dare to believe that things were taking a definite improvement to the sewer.

She had also noticed a sound growing steadily stronger for the last several minutes, but until now it hadn't filtered past her mind's litany of complaints, wishes, curses, and prayers.

"Are we near a stream?"

"Yes." came Aleksei's voice.

She realized a half-second later that he had stopped. Stepping back from the Knight, Tamara listened in the darkness for some sense of where the water was. She didn't want to slip, and add being soaking wet to her list of discomforts.

"I'm going to let go of your hand for a moment." Aleksei said gently. "There's something I have to fetch from the water. Don't move, alright?"

"I won't."

She heard his boots squelching through mud. A fibrous ripping cut across the babble of the stream, and Tamara's throat constricted with fear. Gods, but some sounds were disquieting in the darkness.

There were a few more thumps, and then something was coming towards her. This realization was punctuated only by the understanding that she could *see* something. It was faint, but it was glowing brighter as it grew closer.

"Alright." Aleksei's voice came from only a few inches away, eliciting a yelp of surprise from the princess. "It's alright. We need to wait a moment for the light to get bright enough. There's nothing around that you need to fear."

"I'm sorry, you startled me, that's all." she grumbled irritably. The joy of their escape had quickly eroded under her growing exhaustion and extreme discomfort.

After a few more moments of uncomfortable silence, Tamara realized that the space she had been staring into was more visible. She jumped at seeing Aleksei there, his dark golden eyes watching her, glittering in the ghostlight.

When he noticed that she could see him, he looked away. She followed his gaze to the bizarre object he held in his hand.

It appeared to be the stump of a massive mushroom, and it was glowing a brilliant blue.

"What *is* that?" she asked.

"It's called a rella fungus. The Ri-Vhan use them to see at night."

"What makes it glow like that?"

Aleksei shrugged, "This forest is home to all sorts of plants and animals. Some can be useful. The rella fungus is simply one of many examples I could name."

"So where do we go now?" she asked, looking around for the first time and appreciating how massive the Seil Wood was, how the trees towered hundreds of paces above them. From their place on the path, Tamara couldn't even make out the branches that made up the canopy.

"Now we find the Hunter's Horn." Aleksei muttered to himself, swinging the rella mushroom back and forth.

The pale luminescence splashed across the water of the brook, the trunks of the colossal trees that surrounded them, and finally settled on the path.

"It's a little farther down that way." he said, pointing with his strange torch.

"Did the Wood tell you that?" she asked as he began to walk.

"No," he responded absently, "I can smell it."

Tamara sniffed at the air experimentally, but all that came to her was the omnipresent fog of moldering underbrush.

It felt like another solid hour had passed when they walked around an enormous oak, and found a stunted willow tree bathed in moonlight.

Tamara was relieved the darkness hid her amazement. His senses were uncanny. He had led her unerringly through the labyrinth that was the Kalinori sewer system, then through a pitch-black forest, down paths with twists and abrupt turns, some seemingly hidden entirely save for a break in the foliage where an animal had passed through earlier. The more time she had to study him, the more she became convinced that Aleksei Drago was somehow...*joined* with nature.

"Hold this." he said, passing the rella mushroom to her.

She took the glowing stalk tentatively, fearing it might be hot, but found it surprisingly cool to the touch.

Aleksei knelt in front of the little tree and bit the end of a long, twisted branch. He pulled away from the tree, and Tamara realized that the branch's end was shaped like the mouthpiece of a clarion.

"Someone should be along shortly." he muttered, taking the rella mushroom from her and tossing it casually to the side.

"Won't we need that?" she asked softly, not yet willing to abandon their only source of light in the cavernous Wood.

"We shouldn't."

"Shouldn't *what*?" A new voice asked.

Aleksei turned, unperturbed by the sudden presence of another.

"Gaël, thanks for responding so quickly."

The man, a tall blond with the bluest eyes Tamara had ever seen, smiled warmly, "No thanks are necessary, Hunter." He glanced over at Tamara, and his eyes flicked to Aleksei quizzically.

"Gaël, may I present the Princess Tamara? Highness, Gaël of the Ri-Vhan."

Tamara nodded her head slightly, thanking the gods that she wasn't in the presence of anyone whose rank required her to curtsy. Under the present circumstances, she didn't think she was capable of it.

The man bowed deeply, then straightened and looked around the Wood curiously. "Is she the only one you brought?"

"For the moment, but there will undoubtedly be more. I need to speak with Roux immediately."

"I'm sure the Ri-Hnon will be most eager to aid in any way he can." Gaël said as he reached out for their hands. Aleksei took his right and, after a moment's hesitation, Tamara took his left.

The world lurched violently. She closed her eyes against the sudden barrage of white and pale gray shapes flashing past her. Everything was moving too fast and too slow at the same time. And then, just as quickly as it had begun, the sensation vanished. She found herself standing in the middle of a vast wooden platform.

Small huts surrounded her, their walls constructed of heavy vines growing up and around their supports, until the circular walls took shape. Their roofs were thatched in ferns and river reeds.

She was speechless.

Of course, she had *heard* of this place, but only in the context of legend. The hidden Ri-Vhan city of Arbre-Saule.

After a few moments, she realized that Aleksei and Gaël were staring at her. She shook herself out of her reverie and smiled warmly, "Master Gaël, your city is a marvel. I have dreamed of Arbre-Saule, but I never imagined I'd see it myself."

Gaël looked puzzled, then smiled, "Ah, you know it by a much older name. We now simply refer to it as the village. I hope you aren't disappointed by what you find here. But thank you for your kindness, in any event."

Tamara looked around in wonder as they walked toward the far end of the village, "Right now, this is the most wonderful place in the world."

She walked next to Aleksei for several minutes in silence, listening to the conversation he'd struck up with the other man. They were discussing hunting ,from the sound of it. She had never felt so keenly out of her element.

They passed another grouping of huts, finally stopping before what Tamara assumed was the equivalent to a manor house in this strange floating city. It was grown from the center of one of the mammoth oak trees that supported the various platforms and stairways of the village.

The roof was formed from the great, leafy branches of the tree that supported it, the walls an infinitely complex maze of bark and flowering vines. The door, if it could be called such a thing, was a plain sheet of reeds.

The door swung open, revealing the most exotically beautiful man Tamara had ever seen.

His eyes were gold. Aleksei's eyes shone a plain brown in comparison. His hair was a mass of tangled curls. He was bare-chested, clothed only in a kilt of interwoven leaves and hide. Under his gaze, Tamara suddenly felt very different. Like prey.

Roux Devaan smiled and gave an all-but-imperceptible nod of his head, "Princess Tamara, I take it?"

She returned his smile, bowing her head a fraction more than he. "Greetings, Ri-Hnon." she said formally. "I've come to beg sanctuary of your house and hearth."

"The Ri-Vhan welcome you with open arms, Daughter of Ilyar." he responded, and she felt her face heat.

He looked away, and seemed to see Aleksei for the first time. A broad grin broke across his face, and he stepped forward to embrace his cousin.

As Aleksei stepped back, his face was grave, "We need to talk."

Roux nodded, stepping back into the doorway and inviting his guests to enter. He dismissed Gaël with a nod.

Inside, Aleksei quickly introduced Tamara to Roux's father. The old man bowed gallantly, then led Tamara from the room with promises of clean clothes and a comfortable bed.

⚹

Aleksei waited until both Theo and Tamara were out of earshot, then turned to his cousin, "Roux, I need get back to Kalinor immediately. Now that Tamara is safe, there's *so* much I have to deal with in the Palace."

Roux quirked a smile, "No worries, Cousin. I didn't think you'd arrived by accident. I'll grab my knife and we can go."

"Go...wait, Roux you're *not* coming with me."

The Ri-Hnon arched an eyebrow, "You must be mistaken. I most certainly *am*."

Aleksei opened his mouth to protest, but Roux forestalled him, "Aleksei Drago, like it or not, you *are* Ri-Vhan. You may be our Hunter, but *I* am your Ri-Hnon, and I'll be damned if you keep me from fulfilling my obligation to you. To refuse would not only be an abandonment of familial duty, but a betrayal of my people. *Your* people.

"Now then, if you have no further objections, I'll fetch my knife."

And then he was gone. Aleksei sighed, but couldn't help feel a little more confident. It would be a nice change to have someone fighting alongside him, and honestly someone of Roux's particular talents would come in handy. In any event, Aleksei was in a sorry position to refuse aid.

Roux returned moments later, his appearance altered only by the leather bands strapped across his chest. A small, curved knife was sheathed where the bands crossed over his heart. Its handle was carved from the horn from an animal Aleksei didn't recognize.

"Ready?" Roux asked, sounding almost cheerful.

Aleksei nodded.

Roux stepped closer to the Knight and held out his hand. Aleksei was taken aback until he realized that there was no reason for them to walk all the way out into the middle of the village, only to Dart down to the ground. It was just as easy to do it from where they stood. He took Roux's hand and the world lurched, flickering into white and gray before resolving into the organized chaos of the forest floor.

Aleksei took a moment to reorient himself, then turned to Roux. "Last chance. I won't think any less of you if you turn back."

Roux pointed to the path a few paces away, "That will take us to the Wood's western edge."

Aleksei cleared his sword in its scabbard, making sure it would come easily, should he need it. Then he stepped onto the path beside Roux.

It was going to be a very long night.

Jonas padded lightly down the hall, his eyes taking in both the deeply familiar corridors he had spent his life navigating, and the endless roiling storm of the Archanium.

Each of Bael's Magi burned like a tiny flame across the Great Sphere, and it took little effort on Jonas' part to spot them in the relative confines of the Palace.

He rounded a corner, gripping a spell he'd chosen only a moment before, as an enemy Magus came into view.

Jonas focused the full weight of his intent upon the man; on his connection to the Archanium.

It was like snuffing a candle.

There was a sound, like the splintering of a barrel, and the man dropped lifeless to the floor.

A solider came into view as the Magus fell. A second later, Jonas' thunderbolt cut cleanly through his torso, dropping him to the priceless carpet in steaming sections.

Yet for every man or Magus he struck down, there were three Kalinori corpses to match. Worse, this close to his own apartments, the faces were all familiar. While he was unpracticed at using the Archanium in such a brutal fashion, the cold satisfaction he felt for every life taken still served to temper his rage.

Somewhat.

Jonas reached the end of the corridor and paused, surveying the horror he'd wrought. No matter how many men and women he brought down, Jonas knew it would never be enough to make a true difference.

He had killed perhaps half a dozen Magi, all in the same manner, all without resorting to fireballs or thunderbolts. But the crushing trick he'd discovered only worked against Magi decidedly weaker in the Archanium than he. A more talented Magus wouldn't be so easily defeated, and the gods only knew how such a battle would end.

Jonas glanced out one of the shattered windows and saw that the moon was almost directly over Kalinor, casting an unearthly glow upon the multitude of white structures on Lawn. The beauty of it made his heart sick.

This place, his home, would soon belong to the enemy. No matter how many men and Magi he killed this night, that was not going to change. But *some* things still remained within his power to control.

Jonas shifted into a sparrow and flitted out the window, into the cool of the night.

He had told Aya where to meet him, should the Demon get through the gates. He only hoped she hadn't already been captured. Or killed.

The Lawn was remarkably still, considering the turmoil taking place within the Palace. It seemed everyone was either battling for control of the Voralla or the Palace. He knew that Colonel Ander was holed up in the bottom of the east wing with what remained of the Palace Guard, so it seemed likely that the heaviest concentration of Krasik's forces would be leveled there.

Jonas landed lightly on the grass and hopped into the shadows of one of the smaller chapels. He shifted from a bird into a coyote and stalked quietly along the edge of the building, using his now-superior eyesight to search for the prophet.

"Jonas."

He stopped at the sound. Before him was something he'd taken to either be a sack of grain, or more likely a corpse.

It was Aya.

"Are you alright?" he asked, swiftly shifting to his human form.

She nodded, coming to her feet. As she did, Jonas studied the curious garment she wore.

It was a peasant's frock, slashed and stained with a copious amount of blood. The blood had dried into a thick brown crust across the front of the bodice, making it stiff and gritty.

She hugged him, then actually allowed herself to smile, "You didn't think they could take me down *that* easily, did you?"

He returned her smile, "Not for a moment. Did you find what you were looking for?"

"They have her in the south wing, in one of the storerooms." Her eyes began to water, "Jonas, they have two Fists of men guarding her. If we don't get her out tonight...."

He pressed a finger to his lips, "Shh. We'll get her out."

"When will Aleksei return?"

"I'm not sure. I think he's on his way now, but it's hard to tell. All I know is that he's somewhere east of us."

"But he got Tamara to safety?" she pressed.

Jonas nodded, "I just came from the west wing. While I was there, I overhead a conversation between Krasik and Perron. They seem to believe that Aleksei somehow spirited her out of the city before they could even break down the door."

Aya chuckled, though tears were slipping down her cheeks.

Jonas allowed himself a small smile of pride. He wasn't sure *how* Aleksei had managed it, but if he had learned one thing in his experience with the man, it was that his Knight was *never* to be underestimated.

"So what now?" Aya asked.

He knew how she felt. Now that Tamara was safe, and they knew where Andariana was, it was hard to wait for Aleksei's return before making their next move. It could take him hours to navigate his way back into the Palace.

"I need you to go to her." Jonas said softly. "If nothing else, she needs to know that she hasn't been forgotten. Stay with her, just in case things take a turn for the worse."

"And how are you planning on getting me into the store room?"

Jonas smiled, his emerald eyes mischievous, "You *know* this Palace has an overabundance of mice."

The color drained from Aya's face, "No. Jonas...I...*no!*"

The prince folded his arms across his chest, "Aya, you are the only other Magus I know who can shift. Give me one good reason why you *won't*, especially when the stakes are this high."

"I *hate* it." she insisted. "It feels so *unnatural.*"

"That's because it is. But sometimes we have to make sacrifices for the good of the realm. And right now, we need to get to Andariana. The only way to do that, unless you've rediscovered the art of Fading in the past two hours, is to crawl under the door."

"I *hate* being so small." Aya insisted. "What if someone steps on me?"

Jonas rolled his eyes, "No one will step on you, Aya. No one will *see* you. But the longer we argue about this, the longer Andariana is going continue losing what's left of her mind, and convincing herself she's been abandoned."

Aya sighed deeply, then nodded. "Alright, *fine.* But this is the last time."

"Whatever you say." Jonas said with a shrug.

⁂

Aya resisted the urge to throttle the prince. It was all well and good for *him* to suggest shapeshifting. He made it seem as easy as breathing. But Aya had never been completely confident in her own abilities. It took a great deal of concentration to make herself so small, and even more to maintain her shape.

The entire practice was a gross affront to the natural order of things. People were not made to take up so little space, and the longer she spent in a different shape, the more keenly she felt that abhorrence. The last time she'd attempted it, she'd only managed to maintain the shape for three minutes. She'd been bedridden for a week afterward.

They waited a few minutes to ensure the Lawn was as vacant as it seemed. Then they took turns hurrying from the shadows of one building to another, pausing each time to make sure they hadn't been spotted, that no one new had come outside when they weren't watching.

When they reached the main doors to the south wing, Jonas turned to Aya, "Are you ready?"

"*Now?*" she hissed.

"If you walk in there like this, you'll be spotted in moments. Then you'll have to fight your way out, which I doubt you'd enjoy. Krasik has nearly a hundred Magi with him. Even *I* can't handle more than one at a time."

Aya sighed, "Very well."

She glanced at Jonas, glowering as she reached into the glittering swells of the Archanium. It was a relatively easy spellform to locate, as it shared no resemblance to any other spell she'd ever seen.

But bringing it to fruition was another matter entirely.

Aya felt herself shrink. She focused on the image in her mind, one that she had studied for hours upon hours for this very reason. Her shape would be determined by the image in her mind. If that picture was changed in even the subtlest way, it would be reflected in her form.

Finally there was no more space to shrink, no more fur to grow. She opened her eyes, and found herself a fraction of what she had been. Not far away, she saw the now-enormous shape of Jonas' left boot.

"I told you it wouldn't be hard." Jonas muttered. "I have complete faith in you. Just use your head and follow the wall. You'll be fine."

Aya drew as big a breath as she could, and gave an angry flick of her tail as she scurried off towards the main doorway.

CHAPTER 45

DARTING IN THE DARK

THE WHITE PALACE walls glimmered in the moonlight. Aleksei stared up at their snowy prominence, clenching his jaw.

Since crashing through Tamara's window, he had been swept up in his primary duty: getting her to safety.

But now that the princess was secure and he had returned to Kalinor, the magnitude of what had happened was sinking in.

These people had invaded his home without cause or justification, and he would do everything in his power to protect himself and those he loved. Kalinor had become a sanctuary for him, but as he gazed up at the great walls of the city that had harbored him, he felt no welcome. Only a cold expanse of stone, separating him from what he loved most.

Roux walked up and placed his hand against the smooth white stone, closing his eyes. Aleksei understood little of the Magi's Archanium, and less still about the way Treedarters touched it to leap from place to place. But from what little he *did* understand, he was asking something difficult of his cousin. Difficult, but not impossible.

"Do you know how thick these walls are?" Roux asked after a long pause.

"Seven paces. There are gardens lining the other side, with flowerbeds three paces wide. Make it eleven just to be safe."

Roux closed his eyes, focusing on the space beyond the wall. And then they were standing alone in the Palace garden.

Aleksei grinned, clapping his cousin on the back, "Perfect. Very impressive."

Roux allowed himself a small chuckle, "Well, you *would* say that, now that we've survived. I've a feeling you'd be singing a different tune if we'd appeared inside a wall somewhere."

"Hello boys."

Roux practically leapt out his skin at the sound of Jonas' voice behind them. Aleksei turned and embraced his prince. Roux studied the flower beds with an unusual intensity at the passionate kiss the two men shared. It had been brief, but hardly lacking in ardor.

"It's about time you showed up." Aleksei breathed.

"Sorry about that." Jonas grumbled, "I've had my hands full. Some problems arose that were altogether unavoidable."

Aleksei nodded, "How are we doing?"

"Andariana is in a storeroom under the south wing. Aya is with her, but she has a heavy guard, so some creativity might be necessary. We would have freed her ourselves, but Bael's Magi will be watching the area for any violent displays of the Archanium. The rest of our Magi have been rounded up and locked in the Cathedral of Mokosh."

A large grin broke across Aleksei's face.

Jonas smiled his shared understanding, "We can get them out through the crypt, if we're careful."

"The same way Bael escaped with the Prime Key." Aleksei chuckled. "What about the Guard?"

"Colonel Ander has regrouped whoever's left, and they're holed up in the lower east wing. Last I checked, they were under heavy attack but holding their position."

Aleksei took a moment to think, then looked back at his prince. "Any ideas how to go about it?"

"A few," Jonas admitted, "but nothing set in stone."

Aleksei nodded, "Alright. Roux, you'll follow me to the Cathedral. I'm going to need you to Dart one last time. I'll explain the particulars when we get there.

"Once inside, tell the Magus Ilyana who you are. She'll help you get the others' attention. Below the Cathedral is a crypt. At the back of the crypt is a tunnel that leads into the sewer system. Take the Magi back to the Wood. I'll meet you at the end of the sewer line."

"What if they won't listen to me?"

"As I said, find Ilyana. She'll help you."

Aleksei turned to Jonas, "While I'm getting Andariana out, I need you to go to the east wing. There *has* to be a way to get Ander and his men out of there. Look for a sewer line. If you can't find one, *make* one. There's another line that empties to the west of the city. Take the men west, and they *should* meet up with Rysun as he swings up from the Sulaq Hills."

Jonas sighed, "As you say. I suppose there isn't much more for me to do here at the moment."

Aleksei glanced out onto the Lawn, then met Jonas' green eyes. "I love you. We're going to get through this alive, alright? I *need* you to believe that."

Jonas quirked a smile. And then he shifted into a sparrow, flitting away into the darkness.

Aleksei heaved a sigh, then turned back to Roux, "Ready?"

The Ri-Hnon nodded, though Aleksei suspected he was a touch apprehensive about what awaited them in the dark.

Roux followed Aleksei through the maze of white buildings that were scattered across the Lawn. Ranging from chapels to small palaces, the structures provided excellent cover as they made their way towards the destination Aleksei had in mind.

Roux's nose told him where Aleksei was headed a moment before they reached it.

The stables.

"I'm going to go in and get a rough count." Aleksei murmured. "When you hear me draw my sword, come in and shut the stable doors. Got it?"

Roux nodded, his nerves seeming to evaporate as the thrill of the Hunt descended.

Aleksei took a deep breath, preparing himself for the violence he was about to unleash. Then he stepped around the corner, and walked confidently into the stable.

A Fist of men sat at the entrance, playing cards by lantern light. As he approached, they looked up, more in curiosity than alarm.

"What do you want?" asked one in the back of the group.

Aleksei nodded towards the back of the stables, "My horse."

There was a moment of confusion, as the men argued whether they'd been given the authorization to remove any of the horses. Finally, the man in the back turned to Aleksei, "Son, who sent you?"

Aleksei's face darkened, "No one *sent* me. I've merely come to retrieve my horse. And if that's not a problem, I'll be on my way."

Realization slowly dawned.

"You wandered into the wrong place, son." the man at the back growled.

Aleksei smiled pleasantly, "Really?"

"He's with the Queen!" another man roared, ripping his sword free of its scabbard.

A moment later, his head rolled across the floor.

The stable doors swung shut as Aleksei turned to the next man, who was struggling to pull his own sword out. Aleksei stepped forward and raked his blade across the rebel's stomach, following up with a quick cut across his throat, to keep the man from screaming. He left the man clutching helplessly at his guts.

The remaining three rebels had finally managed to pull their weapons. He silently cursed himself for not being faster. Three men at once could be a challenge.

He was about to engage them when a flash of motion caught his attention. He blinked at the space right behind one of the men, as Roux appeared out of nothing, tore his knife across the man's throat, and vanished just as suddenly. Aleksei's head snapped over to the left as Roux popped into existence, cut, then Darted away again.

As the first two bodies struck the floor, the third man backed away.

Aleksei was about to take advantage of the situation when Roux appeared behind the man, not even bothering with his knife this time.

One moment the man was standing there, looking for all the

world like he was about to piss himself, and the next he was simply *gone.*

As the man vanished, there was a muffled *crash* to Aleksei's left.

The Knight turned sharply to see a section of the stable wall bulging out, dust drifting towards them, and something sticking out of the whitewashed plaster.

Was that an *arm?*

Roux stepped out of the shadows on the far side of the room and approached cheerily, stopping by one of the corpses to clean his knife, before returning it to the sheath strapped across his chest.

"Not bad, Cousin." he noted as he stepped over the last corpse and surveyed the damage. "Though at first, I was afraid you were going to *talk* them to death."

Aleksei ignored him. Roux had a different perspective towards killing Ilyari soldiers. He didn't consider them his countrymen. These men were no different than animals to the Ri-Hnon.

"Where do you want to stash the bodies?" Roux asked, turning one over with a light kick.

"I have a plan for them, actually." Aleksei said, glancing around the stable for the materials he needed.

Roux looked perplexed, but didn't press any further questions.

He followed Aleksei into one of the supply enclosures, watching the Hunter sort through a variety of tackle and equipment before finally settling on a small cart.

Roux's curiosity got the better of him, "What's *that* for?"

"For the bodies." Aleksei grunted tersely. "Now come help me, I can't pull this on my own."

Roux joined his cousin, taking one of the hafts and pulling the cart into the center of the stable.

Aleksei stepped back into the enclosure and retrieved a harness built for two horses. He dropped it in front of the cart.

"Help me load the bodies. When I come back, I'm not going to have time."

They lifted the still-bleeding corpses, dumping them unceremoniously into the cart. When the corpses were loaded, the two men stepped back to inspect their work.

"Well," Roux said, noting that some of the men's eyes were still open, "the darkest field in the Aftershadow *is* reserved for rapists and traitors."

"With good reason." Aleksei spat, turning and walking deeper into the stables.

"Where are you going *now*?" Roux called.

"I have to check on a few things. I'll only be a minute." Aleksei responded, before vanishing from sight.

Aleksei hurried past the stalls until he reached the one he had been searching for.

Agriphon stood alert and ready. At the sight of his master, the great black warhorse stepped forward and grunted mightily.

Aleksei grinned, and ran his hand along the stallion's nose, "You didn't think I'd leave without you?"

He climbed into the stall and took down Agriphon's tackle, saddling the horse swiftly. As he tightened the last strap, the horse danced in excitement. But Aleksei placed a calming hand on the stallion's flank. "Not yet, boy. There's a bit more to be done."

The horse snuffled in irritation.

The Knight smiled and patted the stallion, then vaulted back over the stall.

He journeyed deeper into the stable, finally coming to the stall of the oldest horse.

"Dash." he whispered, "Dash, it's me."

Upon seeing Aleksei, Dash perked up and trotted forward.

"Dash," Aleksei said, "we've got a lot of work to do tonight. I'm going to need you to do something very important."

The horse shook his head, and Aleksei grinned. He climbed over the stall and saddled the draft horse, then patted Dash's golden nose, "I'll be back soon, boy."

The Knight slipped back over the stall, winked at his horse, and hurried back to the front of the stable.

Roux was waiting for him, leaning against the stable wall, twirling his knife across his knuckles. Aleksei fought back a laugh as the Ri-Hnon regarded him with almost the exact same expression he'd just received from his horses.

"I suppose we can go now?"

"We can. The Cathedral isn't far from here."

They slipped out into the night, hugging the shadows of each building they passed, until Aleksei brought Roux to the edge of the South Lawn.

"There it is." he whispered, pointing into the expanse of the South Lawn, to the only structure it contained. The Cathedral of Mokosh.

Roux glanced from the edifice of the cathedral to the steady stream of soldiers, both fresh and wounded, moving in and out of the Palace.

"We'll never get there without being seen." Roux grumbled.

Aleksei stared at his cousin for a moment before whispering, "Which is why *you're* going to Dart from here into the shadows. You'll be against the northern wall. About ten paces inside is the altar. It's about a pace and a half off the ground. If you can Dart above it, you won't have to worry about running into anyone."

Darting into occupied space was every Treedarter's greatest fear, and with good reason. The best result of any miscalculation was an immediate and extraordinarily unpleasant death.

Roux nodded, sweat beading on his forehead. "Here's to hoping I don't end up like that chap in the barn.... Wish me well, Cousin."

❧

The Ri-Hnon closed his eyes, focusing entirely on the Archanium. He ignored the myriad distractions surrounding him. Aleksei's steady breathing a pace away, the oddity of having the earth firm and flat beneath his feet, the moans of the wounded being transported back to the enemy camp; everything evaporated in the fires of his concentration.

He directed his intent forward, into the shadows of the great cathedral. And then he willed himself through the space between.

Roux opened his eyes a hair's breadth from the cathedral wall. He turned in time to see Aleksei melt into the shadows of the West Lawn.

The Ri-Hnon stared out into the darkness after his cousin for a long moment, then turned back to the task at hand. He was on his own in a strange land, and he needed to do exactly as instructed, before things took a rapidly dangerous turn for the worse.

Walking to what he guessed was the center of the cathedral,

Roux measured a pace and a half off the ground. He stepped back and set his eyes on the spot on the wall. It would probably be safer to Dart a pace higher, just in case there was something Aleksei had forgotten to mention about the layout of the cathedral.

Roux took a deep breath and cleared his thoughts. And then he Darted into the unknown space of a room he had never seen. Before the danger of it could even truly sink in, it was over. He appeared in the air over a heavy stone slab. In that instant, he could see several hundred people packed into the expanse of the cathedral. For a heartbeat, he went unnoticed. And then six hundred pairs of eyes found him.

Roux descended as gravity caught up with him. He landed in a crouch, dropping his hand to steady himself. And then six hundred voices roared towards him, along with about fifty bodies.

"Who are you?" an angry man demanded, pounding his fist on the altar.

Roux knew other questions were being shouted at him, but they were all lost in the cacophony.

For a moment, Roux felt the weight of panic sink into his stomach. He had made a terrible mistake. These people would never listen to *him*. What if someone attacked him before he had a chance to explain? Would he have to defend himself? He didn't want to have to hurt any of these people, but he knew that he would, if it came to that.

And then his years of leadership took over. He drew himself up. He had quieted more unruly mobs than this, and with less authority.

"*Quiet!*" he roared, stamping his bare foot angrily on the cold stone.

Six hundred shocked faces answered in silence.

"*Now* then," Roux growled, "I have been sent by Aleksei Drago—"

The shouting returned immediately. Some were outraged, others sounded hopeful, and a few were just sullen.

"He told you to be *quiet!*" a woman shouted.

Order immediately returned, a few people stepping away from the woman who had spoken.

Despite her size, she pushed her way through the crowd of Magi and Knights until she reached the altar, "Forgive them, Ri-Hnon. They're not used to listening to anyone but themselves."

Roux nodded, taken aback that she knew who he was.

"Would you happen to be Ilyana?" he asked hopefully.

"I am."

"Lord Captain Drago asked me to deliver you from your captivity."

Ilyana closed her eyes for a moment in a whispered prayer of thanks, then smiled up at the Ri-Hnon, "Thank you for coming. For our own part, we have been quite at a loss."

Roux stepped down from the altar, "We need to go down into the crypts. At the back lies a tunnel leading out into the countryside."

Ilyana frowned, "A tunnel?"

"It leads through the sewers."

The Magus' eyes lit up as the realization dawned on her. "Brilliant."

Roux looked up, addressing the larger group, "Once in the countryside, we will make for the Seil Wood. Lord Captain Drago has asked that the Ri-Vhan harbor you, until more appropriate arrangements can be made."

Small groups of Magi and Knights began to mutter about having to live in the trees.

"Idiots." Ilyana muttered. "Apologies, Ri-Hnon. I promise it's not normally the custom of these people to be so rude."

Roux shrugged, "They're only hurting themselves, Lady Ilyana. The more they argue, the longer they'll be waiting in this cathedral, at the mercy of enemy Magi who can and *will* kill them."

Although the comment was directed at Ilyana, Roux pitched his voice loud enough so that it carried in the cavernous church. Silence finally reigned supreme.

"Now then," Ilyana said crisply, "if you'll show us the way, we can get out of here."

⌘

Colonel Charles Ander was dead. He knew that as well as he knew his own name. Their weak barricade was already beginning to give, and he simply didn't have the men required for survival against such incredible odds.

No, there would be no victory. Even now he could imagine the tide that soon would crash through the dimly lit hall, sweeping steel across flesh and rendering the whole place scarlet.

"Colonel?"

Ander snapped out of his reverie, turning to the young sergeant standing before him. He could see that the man was about to collapse from exhaustion, which had become the standard throughout the men of the Guard since Bael's attack.

"Yes, Sergeant?"

"Sir, the men can't hold the barricade much longer. What happens when it breaks?"

Ander smiled weakly, "We fight, Sergeant. And we die honorably in defense of our queen and our realm."

The sergeant nodded. Apparently this wasn't that far from his own thoughts on the matter. "As you say, Sir."

Ander hated to be such a pessimist, but they were doomed. Emelian Krasik had too many men. Of the five thousand Guardsmen, only a scant fifteen hundred remained. And such a number was not nearly significant enough to defend the Palace against a force the size of Krasik's.

Screams rent the air and Ander closed his eyes. It was finally here. He took a deep breath and drew his sword. But when he surveyed the barricade, it was still holding. As he watched, one of his men stepped near the barricade, then stumbled backwards.

Ander hurried to the man, "What is it, soldier?"

"The barricade, Sir." the soldier stammered, "It's hot, Sir."

Ander frowned, "Hot?"

And then he felt it. Waves of rippling heat and the shrieks of men swept across them, and Ander gagged as the stench of burning flesh and hair clung to his nostrils. The screams abruptly stopped, leaving a horrible silence in their wake.

The men glanced at each other nervously, their eyes wide and alert, their swords gripped tightly. Whatever was going on out there, it would soon be coming for them. And when it did, they were prepared to go down fighting.

"Colonel Ander?" a voice called from the other side of the barricade.

Ander stepped forward. "Who's there?" he demanded.

"Colonel Ander, it's Jonas Belgi. Let me through."

Ander directed two of his men to remove the large chest-of-drawers that had served as their makeshift doorway before Krasik had brought the weight of his men down on them.

A tense silence followed as they waited to see if it was, as many of them suspected, a trick of the other side of catch them off guard. But if so, why the screaming? Why the heat?

And then the prince stepped through, looking exhausted and soot-stained but viciously determined.

The men dropped to their knees in a show of respect.

"On your feet, gentlemen. No one here has time for ceremony."

"Highness," Ander said uncertainly, "begging your pardon, but where are the men who were on the other side?"

"They're dead, Colonel. But more will follow. As I made my way here I encountered a large number of soldiers headed this way. They won't be far behind."

"But Highness, why have you come here? This corridor is a dead-end. It's a death trap."

Jonas nodded, "In its present form, yes. If you will allow me, I'd like to change that."

Ander hardly knew how to answer the prince. He finally managed a weak, "Yes, Highness."

Then he watched the prince with the same worshipful gaze that his fellow Guardsmen had already adopted.

Jonas walked past Ander and through the ranks of the Guardsmen, ignoring them as he walked towards the end of the hallway. Then he turned and addressed Ander, "Is there a latrine in this corridor?"

Ander nodded uncertainly, "Yes, Highness. In the room directly to your left."

Jonas turned and opened the door, appraising it for a long moment. The men turned and looked to Ander for explanation, but he shrugged his shoulders.

"Gentlemen," Jonas said from the door of the latrine, "I'd like for you to turn and stare directly at the barricade."

The men looked to Ander. He nodded hurriedly and turned as

Jonas requested.

There was a long period of silence, followed by a strange sort of humming. And then the entire hallway was bathed in an eerie white light. Ander heard a high-pitched squealing that reminded him of a blade being pressed against a whetstone, and then it was gone as suddenly as it had begun. Silence returned and Ander hazarded a glance over his shoulder.

Jonas was standing to the side of the corridor, arm braced against the wall. A plume of dust was slowly rising from the latrine and coating the walls in a thin sheen of pale gray. Gods, what had the man done?

"You may turn around now, gentlemen." Jonas said after a few moments.

The men all turned and stared. Jonas indicated the dusty latrine, "I believe our exit is finished."

And suddenly Ander understood. The sewer system. It ran under the entire city and emptied itself in two different places; the marsh in the west and the river to the east. If they followed it in either direction they could pass under the walls of both the Palace and city unmolested.

"Highness," Ander said, hurrying to where Jonas stood, "do you know the way through the sewers?"

Jonas nodded, "I do. We'll come out in the marshland west of here."

Ander could hardly believe it, "Then by all means, Highness, lead the way."

One by one the surviving men of the Palace Guard dropped eagerly into the bowels of Kalinor and made their way slowly west, towards freedom.

CHAPTER 46

SMOKE AND MIRROR

ALEKSEI SNIFFED LIGHTLY at the air, sifting through the spectrum of scents that were normally found in the storerooms beneath the kitchens, until he found the one he was looking for.

The scent of men.

There were ten of them, some filthier than others.

From his position, Aleksei could see they had built themselves a sort of breaker wall. It was constructed out of supply sacks, though a few crates had been pressed into service along the side of the barricade closest to him.

Aleksei hugged the wall, and kept to the shadows cast by the rebels' fire. He wasn't sure how the decision had been made to have *these* men guard Andariana, but he suspected that they were relying more on the secrecy of her location than on the aptitude of her guardians.

He reached the barricade, thankful for the crates that allowed him to remain hidden. No matter his speed or skill, if ten men came at him at once, he would likely lose. But as it stood, they didn't know he was there, and there was power in such stealth. In the fear of the unknown.

Aleksei dropped to a crouch and tested the air again. This close, the scents of the men were much clearer. He could hear their hearts beating. He knew where they were within their enclosure, and which of them had been dipping into the Palace's heady supply of wine.

One of the men was standing a mere pace from him, on the other side of the crates. Aleksei placed his hand against the cool stone floor, and let loose the one bit of magic he commanded. At first nothing happened, but he concentrated. Sweat beaded on his forehead as the minutes ticked by.

And then he felt it.

A thin black talon slithered out across his hand, and onto the stone. He focused his full attention on that single midnight dagger, forcing the rest of the Mantle back. If he relaxed his guard, it would simply swarm the nearest prey in sight, and he couldn't afford that.

The tendril slipped under the wall of crates and located the target, slithering up the leg of the man's trousers and sinking into his calf. From the barricade, Aleksei could hear the shouts of the other men, as their compatriot gasped and fell to the floor writhing.

Just as Aleksei predicted, none of them noticed the thread of reddening black trailing from their stricken companion, and snaking under the barricade. And then the man died, his life-force drained from his body. Their cries intensified.

"What *happened* to him?"

"Is there a pox down here?"

"Never heard of a pox that killed you *that* fast."

"What else could it be? He doesn't have a mark on him."

"What if it's one of them Magi? We've *seen* the sorts of things they can do."

"But they're not supposed to be able to do anything like *this*!"

"Did you *see* what Lord Bael did at the Palace Gate?"

"But he's fighting for *us*!"

"They lock up any Magi that try that stuff here."

Aleksei rapidly withdrew the Mantle. He was about to repeat the tactic again, when the men all let out renewed cries of terror.

"Great gods!" one roared, "Regg's turned *yellow*!"

"I'm feeling a chill, Sergeant! Is it the pox?"

Aleksei frowned, listening as their hysteria grew. The man had turned *yellow*? What in the world would have caused *that*?

He turned his attention back to the conversation. "Right, it's settled then. You two stay here, and sound the alarm if anything suspicious shows up. The rest of us will go for reinforcements. Surely there's a Magus they can send down to make sure all's to rights."

Aleksei slipped deeper into the shadows. He heard the two unfortunates who were to be left behind voice their fears, but their pleas fell on deaf ears.

Suddenly, seven men were stepping around the barricade.

Aleksei held his breath.

The men, however, were too frightened to do anything but scurry from the cellar as quickly as possible.

He waited until they were out of earshot. The remaining guards were trying to figure out what to do with their fallen comrade. The question of whether or not his body would give them the same disease was, however, never answered.

Aleksei took mere heartbeats to cut them down. The soldiers were so unprepared for the onslaught that neither of them even managed to draw a weapon.

He looked around, making sure he hadn't missed anyone else, before hurrying to the door of the storeroom and trying the door handle. It was locked. He glanced back at the corpses in the enclosure. While it was possible that there was a key on one of them, searching would cost him valuable time.

Instead he took a step back from the door, aimed above the small lock, and kicked out as hard as he could.

As he had hoped, the door burst inward revealing a large, poorly lit room, empty save for the two women slumped at the far end.

Aya stood and readied herself for a fight. Aleksei realized that, with the firelight at his back, she couldn't tell who he was. He could sense her gripping the Archanium, and realized that he had better identify himself.

"Aya, it's *me!*" he shouted, hurrying forward in case she had been planning to set him on fire just to be safe.

The Magus' connection to the Archanium faltered, then vanished. As he came into the light of their small lantern, Aya threw her arms around his neck.

"Thank the *gods*." she breathed. "Did my trick work?"

Aleksei smiled at her, "*You* turned the guard yellow?"

She nodded proudly.

He returned to the moment, moving past the triumphant Magus, and hurriedly crouching next to his queen, "Majesty?"

She opened her eyes weakly, staring at him for a long moment without speaking. He realized that she wasn't entirely aware.

"Majesty, I've come to take you out of here."

Andariana sat up and looked around in confusion, "But the *guards*...Aya told me there were half a score."

Aleksei offered a grim half-smile, "There *were*, Majesty. Three have been dealt with, but the rest have gone for reinforcements. We don't have much time before they get back. Now *hurry*, we have to get you out of the city."

"Out of the *city*." Andariana mumbled. She shook her head, "Drago, surely you know that there's no way we can get out of here alive. Certainly not *me*. They'll be looking for me."

Aleksei sighed and fixed her in his golden-eyed gaze, "Andariana, you're going to have to *trust* me. I can get you to safety, but we're going to have to move *now*."

Andariana watched him for a moment, then mirrored his half-hearted smile. "Very well, Aleksei. I place my life in your hands. Do what you will."

"Can you stand?"

Andariana frowned, "An excellent question. I don't guess I've given that a try since I was thrown in here."

With Aya's help, Aleksei gently pulled the queen to her feet. Andariana swayed unsteadily, but managed to find her balance.

"Krasik did...*something* to me when we were in my rooms. I'm not sure how quickly I can move."

Aleksei shrugged, "I'll carry you if I have to."

Even in her semiconscious state, Andariana seemed startled, "I don't think it will come to *that*."

Leaning lightly on Aya, Andariana followed Aleksei out of the storeroom and around the trio of bodies he'd left stiffening in the enclosure. Andariana paused only to casually spit on one of them before following him out of the warehouse and up the stairs to the South Lawn.

The Lawn was in chaos. It seemed that Roux had been successful in getting the Magi out, because the Cathedral doors had been cast open, and men and women were rushing in and out frantically. But their escape had also multiplied the number rebel forces on the South Lawn.

"This way." Aleksei growled, leading them along the edge of the south wing and up towards the West Lawn.

After an eternity of jumping from shadow to shadow, they came in sight of the stables.

"What are you planning?" Aya whispered uncertainly.

Aleksei hid his smile, "You'll see. I want the two of you to hug the darkness. I'll be right back."

⚜

Aleksei vanished.

Aya helped Andariana back into the shadowed recesses of the Palace, keeping Andariana's face from sight as best she could. Several soldiers ran past the two women, and her heart clenched in her chest, but they both remained motionless and the men passed them by.

And then Aleksei emerged from the stable. Aya blinked in surprise as Aleksei walked towards them, leading a small cart pulled by two horses. One of the horses was a fine black stallion that Aya recognized as Aleksei's warhorse, Agriphon. The other was an ancient draft horse that she had seen before, but hadn't realized was even still alive.

Both horses had been saddled.

He reached them and brought the horses to a halt. Rather than acknowledge either woman, Aleksei rushed to the back of the cart and began shifting something around. A corpse landed leadenly on the ground behind the cart. Then another.

Aleksei walked into the shadows where they stood and whispered, "Alright, get in the cart."

The two women stared at one another.

"I beg your pardon?" Andariana hissed.

He leveled the same look he'd used in the storeroom. "You *have* to trust me. I need you and Aya to climb into this cart and pretend to be dead. I'm going to place these corpses over you as camouflage, and then I'm going to drive us out of the city."

"Surely you don't think this will *work*." Aya whispered.

"We'll find out, won't we?" Aleksei snapped, his patience clearly thinning. "Now get in the cart."

Andariana glanced at the Magus, "You first."

Aya gave a heavy sigh and clambered onto the blood-blackened floorboards, coming face to face with a stinking corpse. His eyes were open and bulging. She laid on her stomach and closed her eyes, wishing she didn't have to breathe quite so often.

A moment later, she felt the queen flop unceremoniously next to her with an undignified grunt. She wondered whether Andariana had climbed in, or if Aleksei had finally lost his composure with the queen.

And then came the worst part. The two corpses that had been lying on the Lawn were laid across their backs, forcing them down into the gut-greased boards.

Aya swore she could feel something dripping on the back of her neck.

Aleksei walked around to the front of the cart and patted his horses, then gently led them towards the Palace Gate. Once he got out into the city, it would be the work of minutes to reach the East Gate. Getting *that* one open would be another matter entirely.

The horses plodded along steadily. Aleksei knew how fortunate he was that Agriphon was smart enough, and Dash old enough, to follow his lead.

As they approached the chaos of the Palace Gate, the guards began to direct their attention to Aleksei. He took a deep breath, then looked up at the men amassing before him. He kept a blank expression on his face until he came within a few paces of them.

"What do you want, soldier?" a lieutenant demanded.

Aleksei blinked a few times, as though trying to understand the question.

He summoned the most exaggerated Southern Plain accent he could recall, "Beggin' yer pardon, Lieutenant, Sir. I was told to take these here bodies out into the country. Magus Bael's orders, Lieutenant, Sir."

"I have received no such orders, soldier." the lieutenant snapped.

Aleksei ran a hand through his hair, its normal golden brilliance severely diminished by layers of dust and dried blood.

"Well, Sir, I admit I'ma bit *confused*. But me and a few other boys were rounded up by the Demon *himself*. He said these bodies were 'prime feed' for the Zra-Uul's magic army? Told us all to get carts from the stables, get these bodies out there '*post-haste*'."

At the mention of Bael's name the lieutenant flinched visibly. He glanced cursorily at the cart, then sighed, "Very well, soldier. Clark! Henderson!"

Two men rose and saluted, their eyes immediately trailing to Aleksei and his charge. "Sir?

"This boy has bodies for Bael. Take a Fist, each of you. Lord Perron's told us a hundred times not to let no magic out of sight. Follow him to the city gate, and see that nothing *weird* happens. Anything comes out of those carts, put a blade though this hayseed *first*, got it? You men are to burn *anything* out of the ordinary. Bael can find more corpses. And if he can't, we can always make more, starting with *this* nitwit."

The two men chuckled.

Aleksei offered the man a bright smile.

The lieutenant spat. "Get on with it."

"Thank ya, Lieutenant, Sir." Aleksei said with a nod. He patted Agriphon gently, and the horses started walking again, carrying the cart into the city, the guards practically stepping on his heels.

The farther they got from the Palace Gate, the easier Aleksei breathed. He realized, however, that getting out of the city would not be nearly so easy.

There were now twelve guards keeping a close eye on the cart, their orders fresh in their minds. And at any rate, the Palace Gate had been destroyed beyond all repair. All Aleksei had to do was walk through the soot-stained pavement where it had once stood, two idiots following behind him, another ten just behind them.

The East Gate out of the city, on the other hand, was massive, and under much heavier guard. Aleksei had been hoping to get deep into Kalinor proper, before helping Andariana and Aya into the sewers, just as he'd freed Tamara. The addition of twelve fresh men made that plan immediately untenable.

Worse still, it took a score of men to open even *one* of the gates, and rarely was that feat performed more than once a day. They would never get out into the countryside with such a story. The heavy guard only made Aleksei's every move that much more suspicious.

As he walked alongside his horses, Aleksei ran over a variety of scenarios in his mind. This was a case where force would serve only to hinder him. He needed his wits now.

A handful of minutes drifted by, and the East Gate came into view.

The men standing watch looked disinterested as he approached, nodding to the guards behind him.

"Evening, gentlemen. Or, golly, guess it's mornin' by now." Aleksei said, flashing the same vacant smile.

"What's with the guard?" one of the men standing outside the gatehouse demanded.

"Lieutenant's orders." Aleksei barked crisply. "Dangerous cargo and all that. I'd be mighty obliged if you'd open the gate for me. I mean, I wouldn't want these things to wake up while any of *us* was standing around."

The gatehouse guardsman frowned, "What's he *talking* about?"

One of the men commanding the guard spoke up. "Boy says Lord Bael *asked* for these bodies. Said something 'bout a 'magic army'?"

Aleksei's eyes widened, "Didn't anyone *tell* you?" When he was met with dead stares, Aleksei shook his head, backing away from the cart, "These bodies are 'chanted special by the Lord Bael *himself*. Great gods, any second they'll start moving about and wailing and *then....*"

The men finally managed to look alarmed. "I've heard stories about these things." one of the commanders muttered. "They eat *men,* just as you please."

The guard still wasn't convinced, "What're you going do once you get them out of the city?"

Aleksei started dry-washing his hands anxiously, "There's a Magus waiting for me, *us,* outside o'town. Bael said to take 'em, wants to corral them and get 'em ready to fight an' all. But if I can't get them there in *time,* they'll eat anything they *see.*"

No sooner had Aleksei said this than the bodies in the cart began to shake. The sound of nails scraping on wood and metal sent the men into a frenzy. An unearthly moaning sounded from the pile of dead flesh.

"*Gods!*" one of the soldiers cried, running inside the gatehouse and returning a moment later with a crowd of soldiers.

"Open the bloody *gates!*" another roared, pushing with all his might.

Aleksei started the cart forward, nodding his thanks to the men pushing the gate open, his face set in an expression of genuine worry. His guard remained firmly behind, leaving one lone simpleton to his fate.

And then they were out in the countryside, heading down the road and away from Kalinor. Aleksei swung himself into the driver's seat and allowed himself to breathe a touch easier the farther they got. Every now and then he would glance over his shoulder, searching the East Gate for signs that they had been discovered.

It didn't come until they were within a league of the Wood. The wind blew in from the west, granting Aleksei his warning. He could smell horses and sweat on the air.

Aleksei stopped the cart and quickly removed the harness from the horses, drawing both a safe distance from the cart. He hurried around to the back and pulled the bodies off of Andariana and Aya, helping the women out of the cart.

When both women were on their feet, he turned to Aya, "Set the cart on fire. I need it to be blazing."

Aya didn't ask him why, she simply turned and began torching the cart with waves of flame.

"We've got riders on our tail. I'll go engage them, you ride Dash into the Wood. One of the Ri-Vhan should find you, and take you to their village. Do you understand?"

Aya nodded, turning away from the cart.

She took Dash's reins and helped the queen into the saddle, before climbing on herself. Then the Magus booted her heels into the draft horse's side, and they shot off into the darkness.

Aleksei wasted no time watching them go. He glanced back at the cart, now blazing against the black sky of early morning.

Satisfied, Aleksei vaulted onto Agriphon's back. The warhorse surged beneath him, thundering like a malevolent shadow towards the oncoming riders.

He turned the stallion aside into the knee-high grass, reining him back far from the firelight, waiting until the riders passed him. The burning cart drew them like moths. He spurred Agriphon back onto the road and after the men.

Aleksei counted only five riders.

It made sense. After all, why would any more be sent to deal with one man driving a cart of possibly undead corpses? Aleksei knew that, in their panic to open the gate, no one had noticed the sort of horses he had pulling the cart of dead men.

He came galloping behind the riders, now stopped in front of the burning cart, shouting to one another. In the roar of the inferno, no one heard him coming.

In short order, he had cut down four men. The fifth managed to turn his horse around, but a heartbeat later Aleksei's knife ripped into his throat.

Aleksei rode up to him and pulled the knife free with a twist before the man had a chance to drop from his saddle. Then he wheeled Agriphon around toward the Wood.

Gods willing, he could still catch up.

Aya glanced over her shoulder, but all she could see in the distance was the brilliance of the burning cart. Still, she supposed it was having a similar effect on the riders heading for Aleksei.

She had confidence that the Hunter could handle the threat. She was less certain of her own abilities to navigate a place like the Seil Wood in the dead of predawn.

Dash seemed undaunted, however, so Aya guided him into the darkness of the Wood.

They rode in silence for several minutes before Andariana spoke, "Perhaps we should walk instead. If the horse steps in a hole, we'll all go down."

Aya nodded her agreement and helped the queen onto the path. They could hardly see in front of their noses.

"Aya, can you make it any brighter?" Andariana asked, fumbling in the dark.

Aya let out a regretful groan. They had all learned how to summon small globes of light, but it was not an easy trick to manage. If Aya held the lights, she would be able to do little else. But as it stood, they could barely see to put one foot in front of the other.

A moment later, several small lights flickered into existence above their heads.

The path began to take more twists and turns the deeper into the Wood they went, until Aya could have sworn they were walking in circles. She frowned, glancing around in confusion.

"What is it?" Andariana whispered, searching the darkness where Aya had been staring a moment before.

"I'm not sure. This place just feels...*familiar*. Like we've been here before."

Andariana looked about the Wood helplessly. Aya doubted she'd been paying any real attention to where they were heading. And in all fairness, Aya knew the queen's mind had been captured by countless other concerns.

From the moment they'd reached the Wood, Andariana had been filling Aya's ears with all the thoughts rushing through her mind. Her Palace, her throne, her *daughter*. The fact that the title of Lord Captain didn't seem nearly grand enough for the services that Aleksei Drago had provided her on this night alone.

Aya briefly tried to imagine Lord Captain Lenox out-smarting ten men, then packing her into a cart full of dead traitors and talking his way past two sets of guards. It was impossible to picture portly Captain Lenox being nearly so resourceful.

Something heavy flapped overhead, and Aya recoiled in fright. She looked up, but saw nothing past the brilliant glow of her little lights. She supposed there could be a million bats up there, and she would be none the wiser.

"Wait." Andariana hissed, turning to regard a particularly dense burst of undergrowth. "I think there's something back here."

Aya followed the queen into the underbrush, thinking all the while that they shouldn't leave the path, or they might never find it again.

Dash suddenly reared and turned away, ripping his reins from

Andariana's hand and galloping away into the night. Aya stared after the horse in frustration, then turned back to the queen.

But Andariana's attention was fixed dead ahead. Aya stepped next to the queen, gasping as the depth of night suddenly gave way to a large clearing.

Moonlight bathed the scene before them in brilliant, ghostly light. A field stretched out for well over three hundred paces. In the center of the field, a tall, spindly tower rose imperiously into the sky.

A heavy *thud* sounded behind her, and Aya turned to find the most massive creature she had ever seen staring down at her. Its head resembled a wolf's, but the two black wings rising from its back suggested something else entirely.

It snarled just as she opened her mouth to scream.

CHAPTER 47

CASSIAN'S PRIDE

ROUX STUMBLED OUT into the fresh, clean air of the Ilyari plain, gasping for breath. Gods, but it *stank* in that tunnel! He stepped away from the rivulets of waste that were trickling into a tributary and collapsed at the water's edge, ripping off the accursed boots he had stuffed his feet into before plunging into the river of sewage.

Some poor clergyman may wonder where he'd misplaced his finest pair, but Roux couldn't imagine *any*body wanting these particular specimens back.

He would never understand how his cousin was able to spend each and every day with those things trapping his feet so tightly. Then again, he had enjoyed the protection they gave him from the swirling sea of human waste.

Magi and their Knights were now filing out into the open air, some raising their arms exultantly to the heavens in thanks, others retching into the river.

Ilyana emerged and made her way over to him, her Knight Marrik a protective pace behind.

"We owe you a great debt, Ri-Hnon." she said, breathing in deep gasps of the clearing morning air.

"I'd hold your gratitude until I've brought you to safety, Lady Magus. We're not in the Wood yet. Aleksei warned me that patrols could be scouring the countryside by the time we emerged."

"For us?"

Roux rubbed his face in exhaustion, realizing that dawn was almost upon them.

"For you, for the Queen, for the Princess, for Jonas, for Aleksei. You name someone, Emelian Krasik's going to be searching for them."

Ilyana looked at Roux in disbelief, "You're telling me that Aleksei managed to get Tamara *and* Andariana out of the Palace?"

Roux threw up his hands, barely holding his exasperation in check, "I can't *promise* it, but assuming everything went according to plan, yes. He brought Princess Tamara to the Ri-Vhan village earlier last night, and I offered my assistance. When I left him to take the lot of you out, he was heading to the south wing to free the Queen."

Ilyana looked up to the star-littered sky, breathing a sigh of relief, "Gods be praised. If he managed that...."

Roux just shrugged his shoulders. It was not the first time he would be astounded by something Aleksei had managed. He thought it fitting that Jonas Belgi seemed to have garnered a similar reputation. The two men were a fine compliment to each other.

He suddenly realized that the reason she was talking to him was because the entirety of the Voralla had exited the tunnel. He jumped to his feet, ashamed that he had been so easily seduced by the softness of the grass and the cool of the water.

"Come on," he called, "we still have half a league before we reach the Wood."

With Ilyana's help, Roux got the Magi and Knights moving at a dogged pace for the tree line, all the while watching the western horizon for signs that they had been discovered.

When they were within a hundred paces of the Wood, people began to step out of the trees. Men and women dressed in simple, earth-colored clothing. Roux gave a great sigh of relief.

The Ri-Vhan had found them.

Two by two, his people began to take the Knights and Magi back to the village. In moments, the unruly crowd had become an organized few. And then they were gone.

"Roux!"

The Ri-Hnon turned to see Aleksei galloping towards him on his great black warhorse. He looked even more exhausted than Roux, but there was a fire in his eyes.

"Where are they? Have they already gone up?"

Roux frowned, "The Magi? Just now."

Aleksei shook his head, "No. The Queen and Magus Aya. They were supposed to meet up with you."

"We've only just arrived at the Wood's edge, Cousin. They could be enjoying a cup of tea by my fireside and I wouldn't know."

Aleksei grunted irritably, "Well then, I suppose we should go up and see. If they're not there yet, I'll need to start searching."

Roux quirked a smile, "If they're in the Wood, you can find them, Aleksei. Besides, how much trouble could they honestly find in the dark? They could hardly have made it a league into the Wood, even if they walked all night."

Aleksei arched a golden eyebrow.

"Come on then, we'll go up and you can see for yourself." Roux said.

He offered Aleksei his arm, but the Hunter shook his head. "I'd prefer to pull as little notice towards the Ri-Vhan as possible. Let's get a little deeper into the Wood."

Aleksei rode into the Wood for several minutes before finally pulling Agriphon to a halt. He dismounted and turned to the stallion. "Stay here. I'll be back as soon as I can."

Agriphon snorted indignantly, but seemed to understand the Hunter. Roux snapped into existence next to him.

"When you're ready."

Roux reached out and gripped Aleksei's arm. The world flashed into whites and grays, then back into the familiar surroundings of the village.

Aleksei searched the crowd of Magi, almost in a panic, until he found Ilyana.

"Have you seen Aya?"

She frowned, "I thought she was with you and the Queen."

"We got separated. I know they rode into the Wood, but I don't know where they went."

"Why don't you just ask the Wood?" Roux suggested from behind.

Aleksei winced.

"Mother Wood," he said aloud, oblivious to the curious glances he received from the Magi and Ri-Vhan alike, "I'm looking for the Ilyari Queen and a Magus accompanying her. Are they within your boundaries?"

They are. came the soft, sweet voice of the Wood.

"Where are they?" he asked quickly.

This time there was a much longer pause before the answer arrived. *They have passed beyond My sight. They have wandered away from the shelter of the trees.*

Aleksei turned to Roux and stared at him for a moment, clearly at a loss.

"She says they've passed beyond Her sight. Something about wandering away from the trees."

Roux frowned, shaking his head.

"What *is* it?"

"I *might* know where they are, Aleksei. But we can't go there. *No one can.*"

Aleksei blinked in dumbfounded silence, "I don't understand."

"I wish I could explain it better," Roux said earnestly, "but the truth is, we don't *know* much more than that. Just that we've received replies from the Wood in a similar manner before. She's tried to guide me to a place that I can't reach. It only happens when we try to locate people who've become lost."

"Lost? Like children who can't find their way back to the village?"

"Children, older Ri-Vhan whose minds have gone soft. Lost, as in they never return to us. They just *disappear.*"

Aleksei ran his hand through his hair before turning his face back to the black canopy. "Mother Wood." Aleksei pleaded, "Mother, have they been taken captive?"

All who venture into the darkness return changed, *Hunter. None return as they were made. None. They are changed forever. By* him.

Even in the dim village firelight, Aleksei paled, "*Him?* Who are you talking about?"

The one who lives in Darkness, Hunter.
The one called Azarael.

Bael stood near the chamber's center, his eyes fixed on the point hovering mere inches from his face. To the naked eye, there was nothing of significance to behold in the cavernous chamber, only stark white walls and a single doorway. That doorway had been sealed for an era, barring men and Magi from reaching Ilyar's greatest treasure.

The Apsis. The one place in all of known Creation where the Archanium laid against the realm of the living like a second skin.

The stone beneath his feet faintly hummed with the untapped energy that emanated from the chamber's center. Even without seeing through the Archanium, Bael could detect a subtle warping of the air surrounding the Apsis.

This was the place where Cassian had first reached across worlds. This was the exact point that the Demonic Presence had first been birthed into the realm of the living.

As though conjured from his thoughts alone, Bael found himself suddenly immersed in a memory of this room, a vision from a dead era. He'd caught glimpses of it before, but now he saw each heartbeat pass with painful precision.

He saw a figure standing in the chamber's center, the full might of the Apsis illuminating a golden man, infusing him with the full might of the Archanium.

An agonizing ballet played out, and Bael watched in startled surprise as the golden man lashed out with the same flurry of black tendrils that Aleksei Drago had leveled against *him*.

Whatever it was, it had the same effect then as now. He watched the man, who could only be the legendary Richter, crumple to his knees. He watched as Cassian's hand reached out and touched Richter's shoulder, infusing him with the poison of the Presence.

And then something very strange happened.

Bael *knew* what was coming. He could feel the sudden lance of the Seraphima as it shot through Cassian, could feel the Presence scream in agony at the alien magic's intrusion. But the attack had been too unfocused, too diffuse to incapacitate him. The Presence rallied, commanding Cassian to Fade to safety.

No.

The word crashed through the Presence, through *Bael*, nearly shattering his sanity with its force. With its indomitable *intent*. Bael had grown to believe that the Presence had leant Cassian the power that had very nearly consumed the world.

But that one moment of defiance planted a seed of doubt in Bael's stock-still heart. What if this union had been based on a lie? What sort of entity had he aligned himself *with*?

The Seraphima tore through Cassian a second time, stronger, swifter than before. Bael's vision swam as Cassian collapsed to the floor, his eyes now staring directly into Richter's.

The ancient Hunter was paralyzed with poison, but his eyes still shone with that same desperate love that confronted Bael every night in the darkness.

As the Seraphima's claws sank deeper into Cassian, into the Demonic Presence, the Presence tried to lash out, to escape, *anything* to free itself. And Cassian once again exerted his will. *No.* Keeping his connection to the Archanium, and *through* the Archanium, holding the magic of the Presence close so it could not flee.

And Bael suddenly understood Cassian's Pride.

He felt the Magus' determination, his *desperation* as he kept the Presence at bay, knowing that *this* would be the end of his existence. *Embracing* it. And for what? The Presence reviled Cassian because, even after a thousand years, it had never been able to comprehend *why* he had surrendered to the angels, to *Richter*, in the end.

Lying there, staring out through a dead man's eyes and into that golden gaze, Bael thought that some part of him understood. This had not been some sacrifice for the greater good, but one final act, made by a man for the sake of the one he loved. Richter would not survive their final encounter, but Cassian was determined that Richter's sacrifice would not be in vain.

Cassian had wanted it all to end, but more than that, he had desperately wanted his last moments to be with Richter. He had sacrificed the last fragment of his humanity, his *will*, for a chance to say goodbye.

Bael heard the Presence's death rattle, its hunger insatiable, even in defeat. He watched Richter succumb to the poison a heartbeat later, his face registering a sort of pain that Bael could scarcely believe.

A final flash of white cut the memory short.

He blinked, finding himself unmoved, a pace from the Apsis.

He could feel the Presence tremble within him. It was excited. It was *terrified*. This was the site of its greatest triumph, its delivery into his world, and its greatest defeat. Not at the hands of the angels, as legend claimed, but rather as a casualty of Cassian's Pride.

He was weak. *You will be* strong. *Claim what is yours, Child. Drink deep. Take your fill. Teach your foes to fear what you have become.*

Bael craved the power of the Apsis, but still he hesitated. There was something about that memory, that final moment between Cassian and Richter, that gnawed at him. He had stared into Richter's eyes, even as the life had bled from him, and he had seen something *pure*, unbreakable even in the thrall of death.

With a jolt, it came to him.

Those golden eyes, so full of love and sorrow, and yet so hauntingly familiar. Familiar because he had seen another pair of golden eyes mirror that expression. It was the look Aleksei Drago had shared with Jonas Belgi before their fight on the wall.

It was familiar because, then just as now, the Presence within him had served as the harbinger of destruction and decay, eternally bent on corrupting something so *sterling,* Bael hardly credited its reality.

Aleksei and Jonas hadn't given up, and despite Bael's superior power, he had been bested. He had underestimated both men, believing Aleksei to be very much the poor farm boy of yesteryear; Jonas to be inexperienced, and over-impressed with his talents.

Bael had never accepted the idea of the two men as one unit, each *complimenting* rather than *restricting* the other.

You have no Knight, Child, but you are the master *of* many. the Presence whispered, its powerful throb now little more than a subtle buzz. *You have no need of such a crutch. They draw strength from each* other. *We draw strength from you, as you draw from Us. You have no need of their kind.*

Bael straightened, stepping into the swirling distortion that was the Apsis. The deep vibration of the Presence was silenced in the sudden cascade of energy that rushed through him. His head snapped back and he opened his mouth to scream, but no sound escaped.

As suddenly as it had begun, the moment was over. Bael stood in the center of the Apsis, feeling the power of the Archanium thrum through him. The pulse of the world, every living being a beat that throbbed from the earth, bursting through him before exploding into the sky. Yet to the naked eye, he stood in an unfurnished room, alone.

His thoughts drifted back to the scene he had just shared with his predecessor. The love that had passed between Richter and Cassian. The way Cassian's love, Cassian's *Pride*, had ultimately doomed them both. *He* would be stronger. *He* would not fall victim to love, to emotion of *any* kind, if it separated him from what his heart truly desired.

What was more, his followers would never choose between duty and a Knight. Knights were liabilities. Their death spelled the death of their Magus.

Bael suddenly found the entire premise as absurd has his father had before him. He had no Knight, *would* have no Knight. He was of royal blood. He needed no outside aid. He had the Presence. He would be as a *god*. And his followers would do just that. *Follow*.

They would train themselves as ultimate weapons, without care for another, without the liability of love. They would be his soldiers, and without fear of love, they would only lust for *conquest*.

The memory of Jonas and Aleksei's farewell flashed across his vision once more, but this time Bael pushed it aside in revulsion.

That was not how a Magus, how a *prince*, ought to act. He suddenly felt that his cousin had done him a great service in prying Aleksei Drago from him. Better Jonas be burdened by that ignorant fool than Bael. Bael was a prince among men, never the *equal* of some poor hayseed.

We want you to taste *it,* the Presence panted, *taste it* now. *You touch it, it caresses you, it worships you. Find them.* Feed *them to Us. They smell* sweet. *Find them.* Feed *them to Us. All of them. Like little fish, dripping. Wriggling. Alive.*

Bael deliberated a moment before selecting a pale, nearly-transparent swirl from the hurricane of reds and blacks and golds. His mind was lit with a million pulsating pricks of light. One light for every life within the city's walls.

He had but to reach out to the light he sought, and snuff it.

"Jonas Belgi." he whispered, summoning the object of his hate, near ecstasy as the violence of the Archanium threatened to tear his wits to tatters.

Nothing.

The lights held constant. Bael felt a twinge of irritation, but it was quickly lost in the storms raging across his mind.

"Aleksei Drago."

Nothing.

Anger surged through him. Well, perhaps both men had managed to escape the city. The Demon within him roared.

That last look, that pained glance between Cassian and Richter, so swiftly shifting into a mirror between Jonas and Aleksei, dragged a horrible thought into the back of his head. He felt icy talons claw at his stomach.

"Andariana Belgi." he whispered, now slightly hoarse.

Nothing.

Bael ran through the names he had heard bandied about in the past few years. "The Magus Ilyana."

"The Princess Tamara."

"*Sammul!*"

Nothing.

Bael crumpled to his knees with an anguished cry, clutching his head. He had worked so *hard*, had sacrificed so much, and for *what?* A few buildings and a shoddily-trained military force. *Wasted.* Everything *wasted*!

His rage exploded outwards in a wail of Demonic fire. The flames burnt the white stone black, the pristine marble drooling down the wall like candle wax in the heat of Bael's torrential tantrum.

The walls of Kalinor shook with his fury.

Henry Drago sat astride his horse, watching smoke billow up from the Palace Gate. With his spyglass, he could see that the gates had ceased to burn, though he imagined they would smolder for days.

Sentries walked back and forth along the wall, but they wore either the gold and purple of House Perron, or the red and green of House Krasik. He searched the city, and then the Palace grounds for any signs of House Belgi's ruby and sapphire, but found nothing.

Colonel Frederick Rysun rode up next to him, "Anything?"

Henry shook his head, putting down the glass and restraining a heavy-hearted sigh. They had double marched for days, sleeping only a few hours at a time. Life in the wilderness had toughened the men in ways that training alone simply couldn't. But even their newfound reserves of stamina and determination had not been sufficient to move them three hundred leagues in the time they'd been allowed.

Kalinor belonged to the enemy. A new flag flew atop the Palace, the Krasik crow perched atop the skull of what Henry could only guess was the Belgi ram.

"The city's been taken." Rysun said softly, "The southern Palace Gate is a cinder. I'm sorry, but I can't imagine very many survived the attack, Henry."

Henry nodded, though for some reason he didn't feel concerned for his son. Living with Rysun and his men for so long had given Henry an opportunity to see Aleksei through the eyes of his men. Never before had he realized how much they revered and idolized his son.

This appreciation had developed into a queer kind of confidence. Henry watched the men, saw their enormous faith in their Lord Captain, and after a while he couldn't help but succumb to the same devotion.

He looked away from their camp, down into the marshland that spread before them for a league, then slowly rolling into the plains that swept across most of northern Ilyar. He wondered if they could have reached the city in time, had they taken a different route. Or would they simply have run into the same crushing force that now dominated the Capitol?

A sudden movement caught his eye, and he squinted into the haze that shrouded the marsh. His eyesight wasn't what it had been when he was younger, but Henry swore he saw men emerging from one of the rocky outcroppings dotting the marshland.

"Colonel, look there." he said, pointing towards the marsh.

Rysun held up his spyglass glass without question, directing his gaze down amongst the rocks. Henry followed suit, stunned by what he saw.

Almost two hundred soldiers had spilled out into the marshland, and more kept trickling out of what appeared to be a tunnel leading into the rocky outcropping.

"Great gods!" Rysun bellowed, then turned to summon Sergeant Orman.

"Sergeant, take a squad of men and some fresh horses down to the marsh. We have men down there who need help."

The Sergeant saluted and hurried away. Within moments, a lone man was riding back up the hill.

"Colonel." the man called as he reined in his horse before them.

Rysun saluted, "Hail, soldier. Who am I addressing?"

The man smiled, "Colonel Charles Ander, of the Palace Guard. I must say, my men and I are beyond relieved to finally see some friendly faces."

Rysun nodded, "I imagine those have been in short supply of late."

Ander chuckled, "To say the least. I honestly thought we were done for before the Prince showed up."

Henry leaned forward eagerly, "Jonas? Is he here?"

Ander suddenly looked uncertain, "Well, we *thought* he was, but when we exited the tunnel he was no where to be found."

"But he *was* with you until then?" Henry pressed.

Ander nodded, "He was. And who are you, sir?"

"Henry Drago," the farmer said proudly, "I'm the Lord Captain's father."

Ander snapped into a smart salute, "A pleasure, Sir. Truly."

Henry tried not to smile too widely.

"Colonel Ander, how many men do you have?"

Ander's face fell, "A little more than eight hundred."

Henry blinked in surprise. That was less than a fifth of the size of the Guard. Then again, he supposed, casualties had to have been high when the gate burned, or when they sacked the city.

"Very well then," Rysun said finally, "bring them to our camp."

"Colonel?" Henry asked as Rysun turned to go.

"Yes?"

"Where are we headed now?"

Rysun bit his lip in an uncharacteristic show of doubt. "Keldoan. The Lord Captain told us to head to Gedon if we ran out of food, but Keldoan is far more defensible. And if he is indeed still alive, we're going to need every able man to fight for us. I'd rather be behind a wall than out in the open.

"Until we hear from him, or hear what *happened* to him, we can only await the day when he'll lead us back into Kalinor. But we can't fight the horde they've built as we are."

Henry nodded solemnly, then followed the Colonel back to camp, his thoughts finally wandering to his son. Was Aleksei safe? Was he *alive*?

"Good gods, Henry," he muttered to himself, "*you* told him to go north. If anything has happened to that boy, it'll haunt you for the rest of your days. This day, and every dawn to come."

EPILOGUE

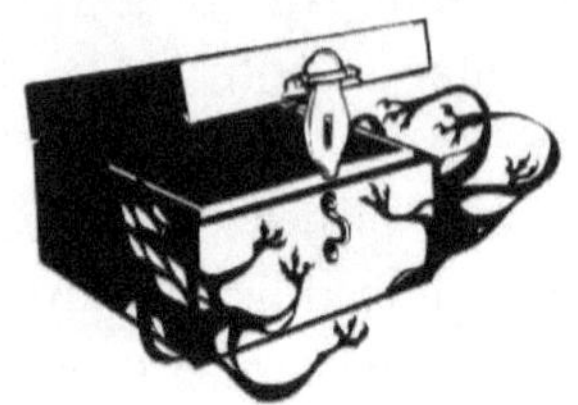

A PYRE FOR THE UNREPENTANT

LORD SIMON DECLAN pulled his gelding to a halt, surveying his men as they marched past. His heart fluttered with a strange mixture of hope and terror. Much remained to be accomplished, yet with the fall of Kalinor, so much more became possible.

He and his men had ridden hard from Relvyn to reach Mornj in time, and it seemed their efforts were not in vain. With the Lord Captain missing, and a substantial number of troops unaccounted for, it was only a matter of time before an army appeared prepared to defy Krasik's forces.

They could *not* afford to lose Mornj to Drago.

Krasik's Magi had brought word only hours before of their victory in the North. And while part of him regretted leaving the comfort and security of Kalinor behind, his fate had long ago been decided by men far more powerful than he.

It had been hard at first, and he was still uneasy about regarding the Queen as his enemy, but Emelian Krasik had other plans for him.

There were but trifling matters to be cleared up from the aftermath of the invasion, and Krasik and Perron were more than capable of dealing with those personally. Thus, the secondary force was directed to secure the southern fortresses. A plum like Mornj could hardly be allowed to spoil.

A clarion blast sounded, announcing their arrival in the garrison. Declan snapped out of his reverie, and focused on the task at hand.

Ahead of him, the garrison of Mornj glistened in the morning sun, kept from their control for so long by Krasik's mad lust for Belgi blood.

He smiled as his men wound slowly up the road and into the fortress. This would prove a boon, and one managed without bloodshed. Mornj boasted the most defensible fortress in the South, and now it was *his*, without a single casualty.

The discovery of the Lord Captain's secret documents in Kalinor had been an incomparable treasure for the cause. With those safely in his possession, Perron had seen immediately that Drago was putting all his weight into Mornj, and had been for quite some time. One did not accumulate such a wealth of supplies by accident.

And so with the Magi had come new orders, committing the entirety of their secondary force to the garrison. Still, whatever Perron's intelligence might contain, this victory still belonged to Declan, if in name only.

"*Let* them call me useless." he muttered smugly.

In truth, these supplies were desperately needed. Krasik was a poor judge of the sheer weight of materials required to maintain an army of such magnitude, especially in winter, and they had yet to establish supply lines to feed and clothe the troops. If nothing else, Declan was pleased that the men would at last have proper equipment and, should the gods be merciful, full bellies for once.

Beautiful morning is it not, milord?

Declan turned to regard the man who had spoken, but found no one behind him.

One can always smell victory in the air, milord. It is the scent of high spirits and hope. And blood, of course.

Declan was staring directly at the source of the voice, yet he could discern no one. It was enormously confusing.

"Where *are* you?" he demanded, trying not to sound frightened. "Show yourself!"

You don't need to see me, Simon. You know who I am. the voice insisted, sounding increasingly familiar. *Is your mind so clouded by the might of your prize that you don't recognize my voice?*

Declan's eyes widened in what he refused to call fear. That voice...no.

"Who are you?" Declan snarled, his fear finally betraying him.

He ignored the startled glances of the men passing by, of the townsfolk going about their business, and looked around wildly.

But something in the back of his mind told him he knew the answer to that question.

It was a mistake to cross me, Simon. You used to respect me. Respect would have served you better.

And suddenly Declan knew the voice. It came rushing back to him in a thousand moments of admiration, fear, humiliation, and reverence.

"Show yourself!" he barked. "Where are you, Jonas!"

This is a mere warning, Simon Declan. Jonas' voice echoed, *You should never have betrayed your queen. And you should never have defied me.*

Declan had barely registered the words when the entire city was rocked by a volcanic explosion.

His head snapped around toward the garrison, just in time to see the magnificent fortress consumed in a ball of brilliant light and flame. And then the screams of burning men reached his ears, etching the horrific sounds permanently into his brain. But the shrieks of the burning were not nearly so heavy as the silence of the dead.

You have entered into a war, Simon Declan. Let it be known that, as you fight by rules of your own making, so shall I. My mercy for you and your kind dies with the flames of Mornj.

Declan sat on his horse, staring at the destruction before him. In his heart, he knew that the battles were over. The board was set, the pieces in motion.

The war had just begun.

Following is a preview

of

Book 2 in the

Archanium Codex,

A WICKED WIND,

Coming in Autumn of

2020

THE ANGEL ADAM drifted on the wind, staring down into the smoldering remains of Kalinor Palace's southern gate. Smoke billowed from the site, and amidst the char and sulfur, Adam detected the distinct odor of burnt flesh.

Were he a mere man, Adam might have wondered at the source of destruction. As it was, the stink of the Demonic Presence was practically overwhelming. He watched the rebel troops meandering through Kalinor's thoroughfares; from this height they looked barely larger than ants.

His chest tightened as he reached into his coat, withdrawing a slim strip of parchment. The Angelus would *not* be pleased if he returned empty-handed.

He studied the series of notes inscribed on the parchment, notes that made up the musical name of his quarry. He closed his azure eyes and took a deep breath, summoning the Song.

And then he began to weave the notes through the Archanium, opening himself to the gray morass of swirling shadows. A single, brilliant whorl of crimson and turquoise arose, wrapping itself around him and singing a counter-melody into his mind.

His eyes snapped open and he twisted in the air to face north. There, at the edge of the horizon, he could hear an echo of his Song.

Adam breathed a heavy sigh of relief. His target was alive. He hadn't failed the Angelus. He might even be *redeemed*.

"I'm coming for you, Jonas Belgi."

Jonas Belgi collapsed roughly onto his face, panting savagely as he tried and failed to struggle to his feet. The high grass whipped wildly in the gale that surrounded him.

He tried to stand again, and managed to stumble into a crouch.

The sky was black with storm clouds, and the air was rapidly growing colder. His pursuer was close.

It had been the matter of an instant. One moment he had been in hot pursuit of Sammul. The man had staggered from the Voralla in the small hours of the morning, and Jonas had been waiting.

But no sooner had Sammul shown his face when he'd Faded out of sight.

It was not welcome news to Jonas that his suspicions were

correct. Somehow, Bael and his followers had rediscovered the lost art of teleportation. It was an incredibly difficult skill to master, and it gave the other side yet another advantage that Jonas could hardly stomach.

He had followed, though shapeshifting remained a terribly painful procedure and took considerably longer than he would have liked, despite being many times faster than horseback. But Jonas had only managed to make it a dozen leagues north of Kalinor before he ran into the windstorm.

Since landing, the wind had risen to a howl. It was all he could do to keep his feet on the ground anymore.

A light shot into the air a few hundred paces away, and Jonas felt his heart skip a beat. He knew the source of that harsh yellow-green light.

The Demon had found him.

Jonas reached into the Archanium and the air around him stilled, allowing him to stand. If Bael was this close, there was no point in hiding any longer. He had no choice now but to fight.

The nimbus of light was moving closer. Jonas could make out the shadow of Bael's form as he neared.

The Prince pulled the Archanium tighter to himself, reaching into the Nagavor as deeply as he dared and lashing out.

The air split as a bolt of pure white shot down from the sky.

The spell splashed across the nimbus, but only halted Bael for a moment. Jonas cursed and reached out again, this time into a very unfamiliar region of the Archanium.

He dropped to his knees as the spell erupted.

The earth rose up in huge, jagged chunks, yawning open under Bael's feet and cracking to Jonas' knees.

The Magus gasped for air, staggering to his feet to view the incredible devastation he had caused. The crack in the earth yawned six paces across. At the bottom of the crevasse lay Bael's unmoving form, still wrapped in light.

Jonas lashed out again, clapping his hands together as he forced the earth back together in a thunderous crush.

The aftershocks threw him the ground, knocking the wind from him. His vision swam as he stared at the black sky.

Even as he tried to right himself, Jonas found that his limbs were numb, and unable to support his weight. He was shaking violently. He had nothing left.

He closed his eyes and breathed in short, shallow bursts, trying to find the necessary energy to lift his head.

There was a deep rumbling, and Jonas managed to roll to the side as something exploded from the earth, showering him with soil and stones. He coughed violently in the dust, staring into the enraged face of the Demon.

"Pity." Bael snarled, extending a hand throbbing with yellow light.

Jonas screamed as his vision was overtaken by a burst of deadly sun.

※

Adam plummeted towards the earth. It was dangerous to allow himself to fall such an incredible distance, but judging from the ripples he'd felt in the Archanium, he had very little time.

A figure appeared beneath him, wrapped in yellow-green light and ebony fire.

Adam wasted no time, plunging past the veil of the Archanium and deep into the Angelic magic that was the Seraphima.

Blue light enveloped him, filling him with the cold, crystal purity, the unrivaled beauty of the Host's combined Song.

With an ease born of years of practice, Adam set the Demon in his sights, unleashing a heaven-flare.

The Demon vanished a heartbeat before the flare struck the earth, filling the air with an earsplitting crack, and sending up a spray of burning grit and ash.

Adam's wings spread rapidly to his sides, and the angel felt the powerful muscles in his chest and wings strain and tear as he struck the ground. He reached out with the Seraphima, searching for the Demon.

It was gone.

Adam came carefully to his feet, checking over his wings for damaged feathers. While he had managed to slow himself considerably, he hadn't avoided injury completely.

He flexed his ivory wings experimentally, finding them sore but functional. The earth he had landed on was unexpectedly soft, as though it had been recently turned. A quick glimpse into the Archanium explained everything he needed to know.

As his head cleared, Adam began to search for any signs of the Prince. His Song had located Jonas moments before the Archanium had exploded into the battle he had just interrupted. Adam was still unsure whether the man had survived.

He closed his eyes, and listened to the still morning around him. He picked out a flock of kite birds twittering in the high grass, and something else. A faint scratching emanating from the east.

Adam hurried in the direction of the sound, finally locating a prone form. It was a young man, probably in his twentieth summer, or near enough.

He was wearing fine enough clothes, though not nearly so magnificent as would befit a prince. His face was contorted in an expression that Adam had never beheld. But by far the most striking feature were his wide, unblinking eyes.

His unblinking yellow-green eyes.

Adam knelt over the Magus and pressed his hand to Jonas' heart. He quickly summoned a song of healing, steeping himself in the Seraphima. The man's face calmed, and Adam breathed a sigh of relief. The prince was clearly submerged within the Presence, though hopefully not too deep.

Adam silently breathed a curse to the One-God. It was one thing to locate a man, provided he was given a proper musical signature. But it was quite another thing to pry someone from the claws of the Demonic Presence.

Of the entire Host, Adam knew of only one angel he could trust with his quarry's life.

He slipped his arms under the Prince's frame and flapped his wings experimentally. He was indeed sore, but he had no other option. With a few mighty wing bursts he was airborne, the Prince of Ilyar cradled against his chest.

"Just see me to Shangri-Uun." he whispered, glancing to the heavens above him. "*Please.*"

<h1 style="text-align:center;"><u>Acknowledgements</u></h1>

This novel and the saga that follows it first began germinating in my mind when I was 16 years old. In the nearly 20 years that followed, the characters and plot lines have developed, deepened and matured, as have I. While the first proper draft of this novel was completed in 2003, time, education, and experience have each helped shape a world that I believe is worthy of its characters, and worthy of the readers who find their way to it. Innumerable people have entered my life and, in some cases both sad and necessary, exited it. To acknowledge them all would be impossible, and thus I will only make brief mention of some individuals without whom I truly could not have grown this idea into the novel it is today.

First, to Bradley Collins, thank you for being a refuge of sanity in an otherwise mad world. You keep me grounded in the best way possible, yet you never try to hold me back. I am forever indebted to you for the unconditional love you provide every day. This novel wouldn't be where it is today without your support, encouragement, and dogged belief in me.

To Dr. Thomas J. Garza, thank you for consistently challenging me, presenting me with new and exciting ideas, and bringing your unique brand of joy to the classroom and to my life in particular. Thank you for always providing a safe space for me to test out new ideas without fear of judgment or reprisal. I was honored to be your student, and feel even more privileged to be your friend. You were a second father when I needed one most, and for that alone I will always be in your debt.

To Dr. Elizabeth Richmond-Garza, thank you for changing

the way I think. I could never put a price on the education I received from you, nor should I want to. You were instrumental in shaping me as a person when I was quite malleable, and there isn't enough gratitude in the world to properly thank you. Being your student has been one of the greatest joys of my life, and I am honored to call you my friend.

To Charles Boyd, I don't know where I'd have been without your friendship and your creativity, but I know I wouldn't be here. Working with you, creating in our little vacuum from grade school through college and beyond has been one of the greatest pleasures of my life.

To Joshua Torres: There are no words that could possibly express my love and my gratitude for everything. So instead, I will simply say thank you, from the bottom of my heart.

An enormous thank you to my editors and beta readers. This book would not be where it is without Roshan Price and Rob Hendricks reading early drafts back in 2006 and providing wonderful feedback. Thank you to Michael Sherrod and Dr. Melissa Sherrod for reading multiple drafts, and for the time you spent editing the text. Thank you, Elise Barrett, for contributing truly insightful commentary and encouragement. Yours is an opinion I value highly, and it gave me much-needed confidence when I was doubting myself. To Amanda Johnson, thank you for your editorial wisdom. Your commentary truly helped me avoid some traps I didn't know had been set.

To my family and friends, thank you for decades of support, encouragement, and thoughtful-but-honest critiques. I've been told to only show your work to family and friends if you want meaningless praise, and you certainly proved that, in my case, that's absolute rubbish. Those of you who read this offered insightful critiques and honest reactions that might have crushed a lesser man, but ultimately made me stronger. I'm so excited for you all to finally get a true sense of what I've been working towards all these years.

Finally, to everyone reading this, thank you for allowing this world and these characters into your lives. I hope they have as profound an impact on you as they have on me.

About the Author

Photo Courtesy of Jeremy Minnerick

Nicholas McIntire has been telling stories since he was old enough to form words. This is the first novel he has published properly, though the dozens of previous projects he has created will doubtfully ever see the light of day (at least in their current forms).

He lives in Fort Worth and Fort Davis, Texas.

Follow Nicholas on Twitter at twitter.com/NickMcIntire

Follow Nicholas on Facebook at facebook.com/NGMcIntire

Keep up-to-date with Nicholas and the Archanium Codex at his website NicholasMcIntire.com

If you enjoyed The Hunter's Gambit, please consider posting a review on Amazon and Goodreads. It would mean the world to me.

~NM